# THE SECRETS OF
# JIN-SHEI

Alma Alexander was born in Yugoslavia, grew up in Africa and now lives in the USA with her husband. She is currently working on her next novel.

D0974668

# ALMA ALEXANDER

## *The Secrets of Jin-Shei*

HarperCollins*Publishers*

HarperCollins*Publishers*
77–85 Fullham Palace Road,
Hammersmith, London W6 8JB

www.**harpercollins**.com

Published by HarperCollins*Publishers* 2004
I

This novel is entirely a work of fiction. The names,
characters and incidents portrayed in it are the work of the
author's imagination. Any resemblance to actual persons,
living or dead, events or localities is entirely coincidental.

A catalogue record for this book
is available from the British Library

ISBN 0 00 716374 6

Typeset in Sabon by
Palimpsest Book Production Limited,
Polmont, Stirlingshire

Printed and bound in Great Britain by
Clays Ltd, St Ives plc

# Acknowledgements

I suppose I could go back a long way to trace the provenance of the thanks I owe for this book. The editors who worked with me on the manuscript – Renee Sedliar in the United States and Susan Watt in the United Kingdom – were absolutely wonderful, and I was overwhelmed by the sheer enthusiasm that this book generated with the people who were in charge of preparing it for publication. But they would probably never have seen this book if my remarkable agent, Jill Grinberg, hadn't loved it first. And she would probably never have seen it but for the advice of another sterling agent, Anthea Morton Saner, who, astonishingly, still remembered my name nearly a decade of silence after our first contact. And Anthea would never have heard of me if it hadn't been for the fact that I learned her name through reading one of my favourite authors in the world, Guy Gavriel Kay, who continues to inspire me every time I pick up one of his works . . . and so it goes. No book is ever born in isolation, and this one is no exception – and the names of the people who fed this one with faith and passion and inspiration would make a list almost as long as the book itself. To all those named in this paragraph, and many, many more – my thanks.

Special thanks are due to some special people who had nothing to do with the publication process, but everything to do with the way the book grew up. To the 'beta readers', who were the first to encounter this story as it was being shaped – Mark and Sharyn in Australia, the Monday Nighters in Florida, and especially Toni for asking a single significant question. To Carol Schmidt, who was instrumental in providing me with the fundamental building block of my story by introducing me to *nushu*, the women's language of China. And, always, to my husband Deck – my first-line editor and an unequalled comprehensive one-man support system, without whom it would all have been so much harder.

to the women who shaped my life

my grandmother
for her unconditional love

my mother
for her sometimes deeply bewildered pride

and to my own jin-shei circle
(you know who you are)
for everything

# THE SECRETS OF
# JIN-SHEI

When I was a girl and the world broke, I thought I would always divide my life by that night in the mountains – the day before, the day after. Nothing would ever be the same. I remember the noise like thunder when the earthquake came, and the smell of blood and ashes in the air, and the way my skin felt gritty with the dust of the shattered Palace, and the taste of fear and loss metallic on my tongue. I remember the surprise I felt to see the sun rise that morning. But the sun rose, as it always did, as it always would. And I lived, and the world I knew died.

I grew up in this new world, and I thought that nothing would ever hurt me again.

I was so young – so very, very young.

But I learned quickly there are so many places for pain to hide in this earthly life we are given to live, outside of the blessed realm of Cahan, the Three Heavens where the Immortals dwell. I was loved by those who were born to love me – my mother, my children – and by those who chose to love me – my husband, and the sisters of my heart. And I lost or outlived them all, and now I am an old woman waiting in the starlight until the sun rises, once again, on a brand-new day – waiting for the day that the sun will rise and I will see the dawn on the shores of that river which I must cross before I am together once more with the ones I have loved.

I have lived in three Imperial reigns. Mine was the time of love and fire, of pain, of loss, of joy, of grief, of laughter, of greed and arrogance and dreams and betrayals. Mine was the world of family, and of ancestors, and of the bond of jin-shei, the sisterhood of women which shaped the society I had been born into. I belonged in my world, and it belonged to me – and yet it was but one tiny corner of Empire in which I too played my small part.

All women in Syai are given the gift of the secret vow, the promise that is everlasting, the bond that does not break. I shared my own life with a healer, an alchemist, a sage, a soldier, a gypsy, a rebel leader, a loving ghost and an Empress who dreamed of immortality and nearly destroyed us all. The years of sisterhood. The jin-shei years.

Kito-Tai
Year 28 of the Star Emperor

'We dream in Atu until we are called again
to the tears and toil of the life
and are born, and learn to walk again
in Liu.'

Qiu-Lin, Year 3 of the Cloud Emperor

# One

It had been the hottest summer in living memory. The letters that came to the Summer Palace from those left behind to swelter in the Imperial Court in Linh-an were full of complaints about the heavy, sultry heat that wrapped and stifled them until they gasped for breath, the clouds that built up huge and purple every day against the bleached white sky but never brought anything except dry lightning and a distant threatening rumble of thunder. And it was barely the middle of the month of Chanain. Summer had only just begun.

But there were few left in Linh-an. At the Summer Palace in the mountains, although it was still hot enough for servants with enormous peacock feather fans to take up posts beside the royal women's beds until they fell asleep at night, one could raise one's eyes to the distant white-capped peaks and be comforted with the dream of coolness. There was always a breeze in the gardens, too, whispering in the leaves of the dwarf mountain magnolia trees planted around the inner courtyard. It was pleasant to linger there in the early morning, when the bird chorus was just starting up, or in the late afternoon with its long shadows and golden light. The voices of wild crickets mingled with captive ones in tiny wicker houses which hung concealed in the trees. There were cool ponds and fountains where water played over the smooth mottled grey stone brought here from a great distance by a long-dead Empress to grace her gardens. There were white flowers and red ones, some with a golden cast, and some with heavy purple petals making their heads nod in the breeze. And there were the butterflies.

It was the butterflies that brought Tai there. She was not of the Court, not even of the Court's retinue; by rights she should have had no real access to the Imperial gardens at all. Imperial life was complicated. Down in Linh-an, the great capital city, the lives of the women of the Imperial Court were governed by endless rounds of etiquette and protocol. There were people to see, petitioners to receive; the higher-ranked princesses and concubines held their own courts, and were expected to grace public ceremonies with their presence and attend to the day-to-day business of their own households. All of this required strict rules about attire and adornment. Summer was the only time when a woman of the Imperial Court of Syai was permitted to appear outside her bedroom without the mandatory hours of preparation and perfection. Here, in the Summer Palace, the Court was on holiday; the women were allowed to wear their hair down, to emerge from the seclusion of their rooms without the heavy ceremonial outer robes, to go barefoot in the gardens.

And summer was the only time that the ladies had the time to devote to the preparation of the necessary ceremonial garb for the Autumn Court at which they were all to appear to mark their return to Linh-an from their summer frolics. Everyone required a brand-new formal suit of robes for that occasion, and the Summer Palace was always a happy muddle of bolts of sumptuous silks, bright velvets, furs for lining hoods and tippets, and a thousand embroidery hoops with half-finished flowers and hummingbirds.

Tai's mother, Rimshi, was always part of the entourage which the Imperial ladies took to the Summer Palace. Rimshi was a sorceress with the needle. She could transform silk and velvet and brocade into lavish robes, and her services were much in demand. Ever since she had been widowed, three years ago now, Rimshi had taken Tai with her to the Summer Palace. Tai had been just six when she had first come here clinging to her mother's skirts, and had been fussed over and petted and spoiled with sweets and the royal cast-offs from princesses unlikely to be seen in public twice wearing the same suit of Court garb. Tai had a closet full of luxurious robes which her mother carefully re-cut and re-shaped into clothes suitable for her to wear. She was nine now, but she had become so much a part of the Summer Palace gardens by this time that nobody even thought about questioning her presence there.

She would find an unobtrusive perch in some out-of-the-way courtyard and dream her way through lazy summer mornings listening to the cricket chorus and watching the bright butterflies flutter from flowerhead to flowerhead, contrasting white and blue and violet and vivid orange against the blooms and foliage. One of the gifts that had percolated to her that particular summer, from a bored royal concubine who could not master the art of using them, was a set of coloured chalks and a sheaf of thick creamy rag paper. Tai had loved the idea of drawing the somnolent summer gardens. She was only just beginning to have an idea of how the chalks worked, and her first few efforts were crude and garish, in an attempt to overcompensate from what she was used to, brushes and inks and the cheap thin paper she could get back home in Linh-an. But she was learning, and these dazzling summer butterflies were her favourite subject.

She was smudging the finishing touches to a surprisingly delicate rendition on a hot, slow afternoon, sitting in the mottled shade of an ancient twisted chestnut with her feet tucked tidily away under her robe and oblivious to everything else around her, when she was startled to hear a voice from behind her.

'That is actually very good,' the voice observed, a young woman's voice, sounding at once lofty and warmly approving.

Tai, who had paused in her work and had been sitting with her eyes tightly closed and her head lifted in a pose of furious concentration, dropped her paper and scrambled gracelessly to her feet. The voice was patrician, aristocratic, and in any event anybody in this garden had to be part of the Imperial Court and it was not etiquette for Tai to be seated in the presence of a woman from the Court.

The owner of the voice was perhaps only a few years older than Tai, but even in the permissive *déshabillé* of the Summer Palace there was no mistaking her rank. She wore a light summer robe that left her arms indelicately bare, and they had taken on a golden glow from the sun, but her hair was gleaming and plaited with pearls where it coiled in thick black braids under a wide-brimmed hat which shaded her fair complexion. She was leaning on the trunk of the chestnut tree with one hand, and it was placed with the long-fingered elegance of one trained to grace in every movement. Her eyes were dark, slanted up at the corners, touched up with kohl –

languid, friendly, but with a definite glint of imperiousness lurking in the corners together with a hint of irrepressible laughter.

Tai dropped to one knee, lowering her eyes.

'Oh, don't,' the Princess said, waving her up. 'It's summer. It's too hot for protocol. You draw well. What is your name?'

'Tai, Highness.'

'Rimshi's girl? I think you were presented to me once. A year ago, maybe two. You've grown.'

Tai searched her memory frantically. She had been presented to several Imperial ladies, but one so young? This young Princess could not have been more than maybe fourteen or fifteen herself; that would have made her . . . what . . . perhaps thirteen when Rimshi had presented her little daughter to her. There couldn't have been many.

There weren't many. There was only one. Antian, First Princess, Little Empress, the heiress to Syai's throne.

Tai, who had started to rise at the Princess's behest, dropped down into the courtesy again.

'Your Imperial Highness,' she squawked.

'I said, rise,' said Antian. 'I recognize your tools. Hsui never could apply the chalk properly. I'm glad she had the sense to give them to someone who would make better use of them. Do you usually draw with your eyes closed?'

The question was unexpected. Tai blinked. 'Princess?'

'That's what made me come here to you,' Antian explained patiently. 'I saw you from across the court, and you were alternately concentrating on your art and sitting there with your eyes tightly shut . . . and sometimes your hands were moving on the paper even when your eyes were shut. This intrigues me.'

Tai smiled. 'I close my eyes so that I can see,' she said.

It was Antian's turn to look surprised. 'You close your eyes to *see*?'

'I cannot draw from life,' Tai said. 'I can see the butterflies on the flowers, but before I can draw them with my hand I have to close my eyes and draw them in my mind.'

'Ah,' said Antian softly. 'I would like to take a closer look at this drawing.'

Tai's first instinct was to hide the paper behind her back, a childish gesture as natural as it was futile. 'Princess . . . it is not very good . . . yet . . .'

10

Antian held out her hand. Obedience and deference, things Tai had been painstakingly taught and bred to, won out over diffidence; she brought the paper out and gave it up reluctantly. Antian studied the sketch, tapping her lower lip with the fingertips of her free hand.

'Yet?' she queried at last. 'This is fairly accomplished, if indeed you are a beginner.'

'I have drawn in ink, Princess, just patterns, and then in silk.'

'Silk?'

'Embroidery. My mother has made sure that I practise needle art.'

'You embroider?' Antian said, raising an eyebrow. 'How good are you?'

'You are wearing some of my work, Princess,' Tai said, unable to quite hide a smile.

Antian glanced down at the hem of her robe, where a swirling pattern of stylized birds was embroidered in scarlet thread. 'Yours?' she asked, lifting the hem of her skirt to observe it better, sounding impressed.

'Pattern and needlework,' Tai said.

Antian dropped the robe, straightened, handed back the drawing with a small imperious motion of her hand. 'You interest me,' she said, and gave Tai a small smile. 'We will talk again.'

Tai dropped into obeisance again. 'Princess.'

But she was gone, a small gesture bringing her entourage of four attendants to fall in line beside her. Tai, raising her head, saw the straw hat bend as the Princess said something to one of the four ladies who had waited for her on the path while she had stopped to talk to Tai; the sound of soft laughter drifted back to where she stood with her chalk drawing still in her hand.

The light had changed, and the sun was almost dipping behind the mountains to the west. The Palace was built clinging to a mountainside; its gardens were tiered, its courtyards enclosed in the safety of high walls and the pavilions of the cloistered women, but there was a series of open terraces on the various levels of the gardens which hung almost suspended from the face of the mountain, separated from the sheer drop only by a carved stone balustrade, and from which the steep valley opened up towards the west in a breathtaking view. At sunset the narrow ribbon of the river, a long, long way below in the valley, turned into a thin skein of gold thread – only for a few minutes, when the angle of the sun

11

was just right, a river of gold flowing off into the mysterious west. Tai could not believe that she was the first to discover this moment of beauty, but either everyone else was already weary of it or perhaps the open balconies made visitors nervous, because she inevitably had the place to herself when she came on her sunset pilgrimages.

On this day, distracted by the encounter with Antian, she was late – almost too late. The glow was already starting to fade when she got to her perch. Usually she left with the sun, coming to this place only to salute its setting, but this time she stayed, watching the sky darken into amethyst, then violet, then deep blue-black. She watched the stars come out above the sharp black silhouettes of the mountain peaks, and had the oddest feeling of transience, as though all of this was just a glimpse, as though the world would turn away in the next moment and she would never see the twilight in the mountains again.

She stayed on the terrace, curled up deep in thought and dream, until the sun-warmed stone against which she leaned had turned cool to her back, and then made her way back through lantern-lighted courts to the outer apartments where she and her mother were housed.

'You are late,' Rimshi said as she entered the room they shared.

'I met the Little Empress,' Tai said, perhaps by way of explanation.

'Oh?' Rimshi said. 'Your dinner is on the table. Eat, and tell me about it.'

'She wore a dress which I embroidered,' Tai said.

'And . . . ?' Rimshi prompted when Tai appeared not to wish to go beyond this simple statement.

But that was all that Tai had to tell about the encounter at this time. The rest, she was still thinking on. *We will talk again*, the Princess had said. Whatever had she meant? Her life and Tai's touched rarely – would not have touched at all had Tai not sneaked into the Imperial gardens to draw butterflies.

Rimshi did not push it; she and her daughter had a good close relationship, and it would come when Tai was ready to talk about it. 'It's late,' she said when Tai had done with her food, clearing the dishes away and setting a pile of scarlet silk and a tangle of bright embroidery thread on the matting next to the oil lamp where she would be finishing off the day's work. 'The yearwood, and then bed.'

The yearwood box was at the foot of Tai's bed, as always. The small carved chest which had been given to her at birth contained the record of her years – the small neat bags containing the bead strings for the years past, marked by bold numbers brushed in ink, and the delicate split wand of the yearwood itself with its beaded strings of the current year. Siantain and Taian hung completed from their pegs, forty beads on each string, a record of another spring of her life having passed, another spring of the reign of the Ivory Emperor. The current string, Chanain, the first month of summer, had only ten beads on it – the first week, with a knot below it. It was the end of another week this night, and Tai obediently extracted ten ivory beads from the box and strung them carefully onto the Chanain string with the help of the bone needle attached to the end of the string. Another week; Chanain half-gone now, a knot tied with small neat hands at the end of the ten beads. Tai worked with focused attention; this was almost an act of weekly devotion for her, this counting of her days. Her task completed, she glanced to her mother for approval and received a nod and a smile.

The duty done, Tai turned to a less demanding task but one that she had always enjoyed a great deal. She fetched her inkwell and brush and the cheap journal book she had been given on New Year's Day, its thin paper already curling as she opened the cowhide binding. There was a lot to write this day, and nothing at all; for a while she sat nibbling on the already well-chewed end of her wooden brush, and then wrote with quick, neat strokes, forming the *jin-ashu* letters of the secret language which her mother had been teaching her since she was six years old:

> *Met Princess. She liked my drawing. She wore my embroidery. I was proud of both, even though I don't think I am very good with the chalk yet. Saw sunset from balconies, and the golden river flowing west, as always. Saw stars come out. Today something has changed.*

13

# Two

Tai stayed away from the inner gardens for several days after her meeting with the Little Empress. She could not have said why – she had felt both exhilarated and frightened by her encounter with Antian, and something in her preferred to avoid a repetition until she could sort it all out in her head.

She made herself useful to her mother instead. She had been trained well, by a renowned artist, and despite her tender age she was already an accomplished seamstress and needleworker, with a gift for design and a meticulous transformation from sketch or a mere mind-picture to magnificent Court garb embroidery. The hem on Antian's gown had been simple, an early attempt. By this time Rimshi was trusting her daughter with gold embroidery, with designs including pearls and little pieces of coloured glass, with complicated swirls representing dragons and water-serpents. Tai had been working on one particular design, using the stylized symbol for the Female Earth symbol of the Buffalo – her own birth sign – for some time, her small, neat stitching covering the hem and the edges of a heavy formal outer robe made of stiff brocaded golden silk; she used her days of self-imposed exile from the gardens to devote herself to finishing this complex task. When she handed the completed robe to Rimshi for inspection, her mother smiled at her, covering her mouth with one hand as was her habit to hide a missing tooth.

'This one is for your friend,' Rimshi said.

Tai would not have claimed the friendship, but knew immediately to whom Rimshi was referring. Her cheeks flushed scarlet. 'For the Princess? This is for the Little Empress?'

'Herself. You cannot avoid what is there for you,' Rimshi said, rather cryptically. She was given to being oracular sometimes.

Tai went back to the garden the next morning, early, while the quick-drying summer dew was still on the flowers. Some were still closed, sleepily waiting for the sun to clear the high walls and pour

14

its golden light into the courtyard, and others were open, eager, breathing in the morning air. It was already warm.

She had brought her drawing stuff but the garden was still drowsy with morning and only just stirring into life. She rarely went out onto the balconies in the morning, because their treasure lay in the sunset hour, but she decided to go out and sit looking at the mountains until the butterflies returned to the inner courts.

She had thought she would be alone out here, but drew a startled breath as she padded out onto the smooth paving stone of the terrace, paper and chalk under her arm, and saw that someone was already there.

Someone with her hair dressed in two long, simple, unadorned black braids which reached almost to the backs of her knees, dressed in the sleeveless robe whose hem Tai recognized. Someone who turned at her approach, and smiled, motioning her forward.

'I looked for you in the garden,' Antian said, with only the faintest tone of command in her voice.

'I was working on a robe,' Tai said. And then, because she couldn't help it, smiled. 'Yours, Princess. The one with the buffalo border. I share the sign.'

'I have not seen it yet,' Antian said, returning the smile. 'I look forward to it, knowing the hand that worked it. Have you been drawing?'

'Not in the last few days, Princess.'

'Call me Antian,' said the other, with a wave of her hand. 'We are alone, and there is no need for protocol here, in this place, halfway between heaven and earth.'

'I come here in the evenings,' Tai said carefully.

'And I, in the mornings,' said the Princess, with a little laugh. 'And nobody else I know comes here at all.'

'Why?' Tai asked, looking at the valley and the river below them. The light was different, bright, molten-white summer morning sunshine; it almost blotted out the looming mountains with its sheer intensity. 'Why the morning? You can't see anything.'

'My time is less my own in the evenings,' Antian said. 'Tell me about what you come here to see.'

So Tai described, haltingly at first, then with increasing confidence, the golden river flowing into the sunset – and then the new thing she had absorbed for the first time only the other day, the

15

stars coming out in the summer sky. Antian listened, not interrupting, until Tai came to a halt and drew a deep breath, her eyes still shining with her vision. She realized that the Princess was watching her with a small smile of admiration lighting the slanted dark eyes.

'You have a gift,' she said. 'You have the sight and the tongue of a poet. Not only through your hands but through your heart and your mind and what you see and you hear.' She tossed her head impatiently. 'So few around me have that ability,' she said, 'to paint me a picture – with chalk, or with thread, or with words. I have to come here at sunset one day and see these things of which you have spoken. Would you like to join my household?'

The last was unexpected, a question that rounded the corner of the rest of Antian's words and ambushed Tai with the force of a blow in the stomach. Her eyes were wide with consternation, but what came out was something that was surprised out of her, something that, had she had the remotest chance of thinking about, she could never have said at all.

'No, Princess.'

They stared at each other in mutual shock – one because she was not used to being refused, the other because she could not believe that she had just uttered the words of refusal to the face of an Imperial Princess.

But Tai knew why she had said what she had said. Driven to explain, to take back that blurted *no* that had come tumbling out of her, she raised the hand which still clutched her chalks and her paper.

'Princess . . . Antian . . . I . . . I am honoured. But my mother has told me . . .'

'Don't look like that. You are not a slave, and I won't go out and buy you with gold,' Antian said, her voice startlingly sad. 'I like the way you make me see things. That's all.'

'My mother has told me something of the Imperial Court,' Tai said. 'Of the way things are done, they have to be done, the way everyone's life is planned and controlled, the way you have to make sure your hair is in place and your hands are in position and you are not allowed to smile or to talk or to look where you are not supposed to look.'

'Yes,' said Antian, 'I know.'

'I would have to be like that, too. And that would mean . . . I couldn't watch the butterflies.'

'I know,' said Antian again, this time with a sigh. 'You are right. It is a life that binds. You made the buffalo robe with vision but I will wear it with ceremony. I was just wishing . . . for someone to let me see the things that ceremony makes me blind to.' She looked up at the battlements behind them, rising tier upon tier, and straightened. 'I should probably go in now,' she said, suddenly reverting to a curious formality. 'I will look forward to seeing you in the gardens again soon, Painter of Butterflies.'

'Wait,' said Tai impulsively as the Princess turned to leave. Antian turned her head, watched as Tai fumbled within her sheaf of papers, extracted the drawing she had been working on the day Antian had first seen her in the gardens. She held it out, suddenly shy. 'I'd like you . . . to have this . . . if you want to.'

Antian took the somewhat smudged drawing with a small smile. 'Thank you,' she said. There was the slightest of hesitations, as though she had meant to say something else and caught herself, and then she merely inclined her head in a tiny regal motion and turned away.

Tai stayed on the balcony for a long time, alone, staring out into the valley.

'The Little Empress liked her gown,' Rimshi said to Tai when she returned to their room later that day after an afternoon fitting session with the princesses. 'I told her it was mostly your work, and she was pleased to give me something for you.'

Tai looked up, wary. 'For me?'

'So she said.' Rimshi raised her hand to cover her smile. 'I have brought it to you, here. She said, "Tell your daughter that this is for the butterflies and for the golden river."'

Tai took the small square package wrapped in an oddment of scarlet silk and unfolded the material to reveal a small book, a journal with a hundred pages gleaming white and blank and waiting to be filled with thoughts and visions, bound in soft, bright red leather with leather ties to hold it closed. Tai's hands caressed the smooth binding, opened and closed the book several times. Tears which she could not explain stung her eyes. This, after she had told Antian *no*?

'This is a precious thing,' Rimshi said, observing her daughter's reaction. 'She thinks highly of you, it seems.'

'She likes what I see,' Tai murmured.

'Ah,' said Rimshi, still smiling. 'Use it well, then, to share that vision.'

'Look,' Tai said suddenly, lifting a piece of very fine paper which had been laid between the last page and the back cover. 'There is something else here. Look!'

'It looks like a letter,' Rimshi said.

Tai looked up in consternation. 'I cannot read letters!'

'This one you can, I think,' Rimshi said. 'She would have written in the women's tongue.'

'*Jin-ashu*? The princesses know *jin-ashu*, too?'

'All women know *jin-ashu*,' murmured Rimshi. 'It is our language, the language of *jin-shei* – passed from mother to daughter from the dawn of time, letting us speak freely of the thoughts and dreams and desires hidden deep in a woman's heart. Of things men do not understand and do not need to know.'

Tai opened the folded piece of paper with reverence. 'There is only one thing here,' she said.

'What does it say?' Rimshi asked, although she knew, and her heart leapt at what her daughter had just been given.

Tai lifted shining eyes. '*Jin-shei*,' she whispered.

*So young . . .*

Rimshi had been twelve years old when she had exchanged her first *jin-shei* vow – with Meilin, the daughter and heir of a family which owned a thriving silk business in Linh-an. It was in their workshop that the young Rimshi had first seen silk thread, had first touched silk cloth, had embroidered her first clumsy sampler in silk – all when she was younger still, much younger than twelve years old. And then the friendship with Meilin had deepened into something else, and they had said the words to each other – *jin-shei*. After that Meilin, the elder by a handful of years and therefore more accomplished, saw to it that Rimshi's talents were noticed, and she had been given training and instruction in the silk embroidery.

*Jin-shei* had shaped Rimshi's life – it was *jin-shei* that gave her the gift of her trade, and it was *jin-shei*, with another *jin-shei-bao* who had gone on to be an Emperor's concubine, that had given her the place to practise it. Rimshi had told Tai about the second story and Tai knew all about the romance of it, the glory of the poor but beautiful girl being taken into the Imperial Palace to be a princess.

Tai knew only the light of *jin-shei*, its joys; Rimshi had thought she would still have time to teach her daughter about its duties and its responsibilities. And now it was here, offered by a girl who would be Empress one day.

It could be refused, simply by making no response to the offer, by not accepting *jin-shei* by responding with the same words. But Rimshi looked at Tai's face and the bright wide eyes and could think of no reason for her to refuse this great gift that she had been offered. There would be time still, Cahan willing, to teach Tai about the true meaning of the sisterhood – time enough for everything.

But right now it was a star, a bright and glorious thing that lit up Tai and made her whole being glow with the joy of it.

'*Jin-shei*,' Tai repeated, almost with awe. 'The Little Empress wants me to be her friend.'

Rimshi slipped an arm around her daughter's thin shoulders and hugged her into her side, tightly. 'The Little Empress,' she said, 'wants you to be her sister, my Tai.'

# Three

Summer wrapped Linh-an, the capital city of Syai, like a shroud. The walls of the city shimmered with it well before the bells of noon from the Great Temple. But summer or winter, the Imperial Guard compound had its routine. The trainees traditionally found something to whine about in every season of the year. Come late autumn they would complain about being expected to do their drills in the cold rain; in winter they would carp about chilblains and frostbite; now, with summer just beginning to settle in, they did their manoeuvres in the cobbled practice yard, the heat reflecting off the grey compound walls, the straw-covered cobbles warm through the thin soles of their practice boots in which their feet slid and sweated. The orderly hierarchies were observed here as everywhere in Linh-an – the élite cohorts practised in the cool of the early morning, or in the early evening when the evening breezes would start to cool their bare arms, sheened with sweat. They made it all look so easy – the choreographed fights with single blade, double blades, iron-tipped staves, unarmed wrestling in the corner of the yard where the ground was left unpaved to lessen risk of injury. They wore black pants, tucked into their boots, and black sleeveless practice singlets, men and women alike; a bandanna tied low on their forehead mopped up the sweat dripping into their eyes. These were the old pros, the survivors, their arms tattooed with the insignia of several Emperors. The oldest of them wore up to three or even four – the tusk for the Ivory Emperor, currently on Syai's throne, then the sigils that had belonged to the Sapphire Emperor, the Serpent Emperor. Two even wore the sign of the Lapis Emperor, the oldest of the Guard, the best.

The current cadre, Guardsmen and Guardswomen with a single tattoo or maybe two, trained straight after the élite forces while the mornings were still as cool as they were going to be in that molten summer, or just before them, in the shimmering heat which pooled in the courtyards in the late afternoon. That left the practice yard free for the rest of the day for the young ones, the children raised by the Guard to fill their ranks.

Often these were the sons and daughters of the Guard, but these children were not forced into their parents' profession, and there were always gaps to be filled. With the unwanted, the orphaned, the abandoned – the ones adopted, clothed and fed by the Guard, the ones who owed their life to the Guard. It wasn't indenture, quite, but in some ways it was worse. Although there was always a theoretical way out for a child like this, they were never allowed to forget their debt to the Guard, and by the time they were old enough to choose for themselves they could not choose other than the only life they had ever known. Sometimes barely weaned babies, still in their swaddling clothes, were found abandoned on the doorstep of the Guard compound – orphans or children from families too poor to raise them. That had been Xaforn's lineage.

The only thing Xaforn knew about herself was that she belonged to the Guard. There had been nothing left with her when she was found – no amulet, no word, not even a name. All of what she was, all of who she was, she owed to the Guard. She had started watching the élite forces at their daily drills when she was barely five years old, and by the time she was seven and her own cadre of youngsters had been started out on the basic falls, rolls and gymnastics training she had been practising a few things on her own and shone out like a diamond. She was tough and wiry, long-legged, with promise of height; hard daily physical exercise kept her lean and limber. Within six months of starting training she had been plucked from the novices who were still stumbling around getting no more than bruises out of their early training and started as the youngest trainee in the cadre two levels above raw beginners. She was two, even three years younger than everyone else in her 'class', and the fact that she was better than many of them earned her few friends in the cadre. She preferred it that way. She was one of the few to take whatever the season threw at her without a word, without a whimper – summer sweats or winter chills, she was Guard, and she trained with a focus and a silent concentration which sometimes scared even her teachers.

'That one will kill early, or be killed,' they'd tell each other, watching Xaforn go through her exercises.

'Be killed in training,' they'd add, as they watched her challenge much more advanced opponents to practice fights, and lose, and challenge again with her strategy and her movements changed from one fight to the next, learning from every defeat, every mistake.

'She scares me,' one of the three-tattoo élites had murmured once, watching Xaforn trying to perfect a particularly difficult kick, doing it again and again, losing her balance, refusing to accept defeat. 'Give her a few more years in the practice yard, and I'd send Xaforn to guard the Palace alone against an invasion of barbarians from the plains. They'd be dead of exhaustion before any of them got close enough to wound her.'

Xaforn didn't know about that remark, but she trained as though she was trying to live up to it. She trained as though she was preparing for some imminent war that only she could see coming.

Her only vanity was her hair. Most of the women in the Guard cut theirs short; it fit better under helmets and took less care. Xaforn's was in a long braid which she usually wore wrapped tightly around her small head; but sometimes, when practising alone, it was left to hang down her back and it whipped as she whirled and kicked and rolled her way through the fight exercises. For some reason this made her look even more dangerous. She was due to turn ten at the end of this long, hot summer, and already they were talking about promoting her up to yet another level in the coming autumn. She would be training with the fifteen- and sixteen-year-olds, the class only a year away from full induction into the Guard.

She fully intended to join the Guard at the first opportunity offered to her. When she was fourteen, maybe; thirteen, even. There could be uses for someone as young and light on her feet as Xaforn was.

But, for now, she was still young, she was still a trainee, she was still fair game for chores and message-running if someone more senior managed to collar her before she gave them the slip. Leaving the practice yard, braid swinging, mopping the sweat glistening in the hollow of her throat, an equally sweaty and flushed Guardsman stopped her at the entrance to the compound.

'Ah. Good. You can run the errand for me, and I can get back to my business,' he said pleasantly. 'Captain Aric is needed at the Palace. See that the message reaches him.'

'Where is he?' Xaforn shouted at the Guardsman's retreating back.

'How should I know? That's why I'm sending you,' he retorted, trotting away back to the group fencing with sword and dagger out in the yard.

Muttering imprecations under her breath, Xaforn broke into a jog and made for the inner compound where the living quarters were. She didn't like that part of the compound – perhaps it reminded her too much of all that she had never known. Foundlings and orphans, the children left to the Guard to raise, were housed separately in their own dormitories; the closest they came to experiencing actual family life was observing the family compound, watching children sired or borne by individual Guards tumbling around the inner courts while the women of the household squabbled and cooked and chased toddlers intent on finding trouble. There was a part of Xaforn that fiercely desired the closeness, the sense of belonging, that seemed to cling to these walls – and another part of her despised it for its weakness, its vulnerability, for being the soft underbelly of the Imperial Guard. For Xaforn, family meant only the cadre – the group of warriors that she had been raised to become a part of. She had never known a mother or a sibling; her life had been lived under discipline, not affection. She was incorruptible, unbribable, there was nobody whose welfare mattered to her enough to tempt her into betraying her calling – and she could see a Guardsman father hesitating at the threat of a knife held to the throat of one of these cherished children.

At a cursory glance the courtyard appeared to be full of only the vulnerable ones, just the women, the children, the families. But then she noticed Aric's daughter, Qiaan of the long face – few people could lay claim to ever having seen that girl smile – and veered off to intercept her.

'I've been sent to look for Captain Aric,' Xaforn said without preamble. 'Do you know where he is to be found?'

'He was here earlier,' Qiaan said, with studied unhelpfulness. Her eyes were hooded, her expression carefully blank. As a child of an Imperial Guard captain, she was steeped in Guard traditions – but Xaforn, the foundling, belonged to the Guard far more comprehensively than Qiaan, its daughter, had ever done. Qiaan could not, had never been able to, understand the devotion to duty, to being a honed weapon. She didn't know what she was, but she knew what she wasn't – and she wasn't Xaforn's kind of animal at all.

Xaforn would have been tearing the eyes out of anyone who would attempt to make the grave error of turning her into a lady who wore silks and reclined gracefully in Palace luxury; Qiaan had likewise snarled at the merest suggestion that she might consider the Guard as her path in life. All the children were asked; only a few of them accepted, but even those who did not were still Guard enough to admire or at least appreciate the Guard and the lineage it gave them.

Qiaan, however, was different.

Qiaan's father was a high-ranking Guard captain, and his duties frequently kept him away from his family, but at least he was affectionate to his daughter when he was with her. But her mother, Rochanaa, veered between a kind of despairing affection and an inexplicable coolness; sometimes it seemed that it was all she could bear to just look on Qiaan's face. Bounced between these reactions, the child had never known what reception her overtures to her mother would receive, and had, in the end, stopped making any. By the time Qiaan turned eleven her relationship with her mother had soured and solidified into something scrupulously correct and curiously formal. With her father all too often physically absent, and her mother abdicating emotional closeness, Qiaan was adrift, detached from her own immediate kin and incapable of belonging to the often insular 'family' of the Imperial Guard. If anyone had asked her, she would have dismissed the idea of ever having wanted to achieve this distance from the Guard and all that the Guard meant – but she was reminded of her failures, her possible inadequacies, when she met up with someone who truly belonged, like Xaforn.

The two of them reacted to each other like two explosively opposite chemicals in an alchemist's alembic, aching to absorb the best they saw the other as possessing. They were still too young to understand the reasons why.

Face to face in the courtyard, Xaforn, the younger by fully a year, managed to draw herself up and give every impression of looking down on Qiaan as someone clearly younger or inferior. 'The captain is wanted at the Palace,' she said, 'and I will go in search of him myself. But you ought to have enough respect for his position and his duty to make sure the message reaches him as soon as possible, if I do not find him.'

'Oh, I know all about *duty*,' said Qiaan, a little acidly. 'Good hunting, Xaforn.'

'Soft,' hissed Xaforn, just before she swept out of earshot.

'Besotted,' Qiaan returned, making sure she had the last word. She was rather good at that.

Both girls departed, pursuing their own errands, equally stung. It was the summer, it was the heat. Tempers were frayed everywhere.

But this was the summer of trial for both of them.

Xaforn was intent on *becoming*. All her life she had been a chrysalis, and this was the last summer she would have to wait for her metamorphosis. If she was good, if she stayed ahead of the pack, autumn would bring promotion, and the next year would, maybe, bring more than that. Xaforn knew, knew with a passion born of yearning, that once she was a full-fledged Guard she would always have a place to belong, she would know who she was, she would have a home.

Qiaan was equally focused on *being*. She was cast in a role, but one which she found it difficult to interpret. She was young, but she was not unobservant – and there was a coolness between her parents, a coolness which she could sense deepen when she entered the presence of both of them at the same time, a coolness which her mother then passed on to her when her father departed once again to take up his duties at the compound and the Palace. Qiaan was an unwitting pawn in some adult game – but that was just an instinct, not a knowledge, and she had no idea how to act in order to lessen the impact of the situation on her own life. She tried to be a dutiful daughter, to the best of her ability. When her mother, a transplanted Southerner who was sometimes fiercely homesick for her own people, thawed far enough to share some aspect of her childhood or her culture with Qiaan, the child tried to listen, to learn – but those times were rare, and it was more common by far to be rebuffed by a cool word or a refusal of a touch. Rochanaa did her duty and passed on to Qiaan all that a mother should teach a daughter – but no more than that.

They were both, Guard foundling and Guard daughter, fiercely lonely.

In the third week of Chanain, with summer coming to a boil and the skies bleached white with the heat within city walls, Xaforn turned a corner in the Guard compound and discovered four boys surrounding a hissing and bedraggled cat. They appeared to be passing something from one to another, laughing, keeping it from the cat which was trying to get at whatever it was, ears flat, fangs bared, howling.

The boys were all three or four years older than Xaforn, and at least two of them were Guard family. Ordinarily she would have left them to their hijinks – what business was it of hers what they were doing to the cat? But then she distinctly heard the thing being tossed from hand to hand whimper softly, and caught a glimpse of a spread-eagled kitten tied to a pair of crossed sticks.

The Guards were just, fair, honourable. This was part of the training, the foundation of Xaforn's 'family'. Wanton cruelty had no place here. Besides – although that had nothing to do with it, of course – she rather liked cats.

'Put it down.'

The timbre of her voice took even her by surprise. It was low, level, dangerous.

One of the boys turned – not one of the Guard ones – and obviously failed to recognize her. He saw a girl, long braid swinging forward over her shoulder, dressed in wide trousers and summer over-tunic, bare feet thrust into a pair of rope-soled sandals.

'Sure,' he said. 'You want to play? *Ow!*' Distracted, he'd allowed the mother cat a free swipe, and she had caught him squarely across the shin. He kicked, hard, swearing first at the cat and then, turning, at the girl who had been the indirect cause of his wound – and who had not moved.

'Put it down,' Xaforn repeated, taking on the kitten's cause. One of the other boys did recognize her, and tugged at the scratched one's sleeve.

'Dump it,' he advised his friend, eyes flickering over Xaforn. 'Not that one.'

'You afraid of a *girl*!'

'That girl, yes. She's a Guard.'

The other boy snickered. 'A trainee Guard kid. I got me a trainee Guard kid. Let's see what they teach them in classes.'

Both the Guard boys were now hanging on the arms of the young show-off, but advising caution merely seemed to inflame his desire to make trouble. It had been he who had been holding the spread-eagled and weakly meowing kitten in his hands; now he tossed it to his fourth companion, who stood looking indecisive as to whether to listen to his gang leader or the two insiders who seemed to have information that the leader lacked.

Xaforn was a head shorter and much lighter than her opponent, and all the boy saw was a thin girl who had challenged his authority. One good blow, and it would be over – she'd be across the courtyard, in a heap in the corner, and there would be good blue bruises all over her face the next morning – or at least that was the plan. He swung, and he never knew what hit him. Xaforn ducked under his arm, pivoted on the ball of her foot, came up behind him and landed a blow on the small of his back and across the kidneys which felled him to his knees, and then drove the edge of her hand into his solar plexus as he tried to rise. He swayed for a moment, his eyes crossed and focused on the tip of his nose, and then fell face first into the cobbles.

The rest, throwing down the kitten, fled.

It had taken a fraction of a second. Xaforn was left in possession of the field, triumphant, a little guilty.

'You aren't supposed to beat up the general population,' a voice said, apparently giving tongue to her guilt.

Xaforn looked down. On her knees on the dusty courtyard cobbles, heedless of a pretty silk robe, Qiaan was extracting the kitten from its torture apparatus.

The mother cat had retreated a few steps and now stood growling softly deep in its throat, but making no sudden movements.

'What are you doing here?' Xaforn said waspishly.

'Just passing through, same as you,' Qiaan said. The kitten fell into her hands, freed at last, barely breathing. Its eyes were still closed. 'I don't even know if it's old enough to be weaned yet.'

'Will she take it back?' Xaforn said, coming down on one knee beside Qiaan to have a closer look at their prize. Both girls were completely ignoring the erstwhile bully, who was still on the ground, groaning.

'Even if she did,' Qiaan said, 'it might die. It's so tiny. I wonder where those bullies found it.'

'They probably killed the rest.'

The mother cat snarled, but when they looked up at the sound she was gone, melted away into the shimmer of heat. Xaforn sighed.

'Well, that's that.'

'Do you want it?'

'What would I do with it?' Xaforn snapped. She'd been caught in a moment of softness and it rankled – especially because it had been Qiaan, of all people, who had been the one to see her succumb to it.

'Then why did you save it?'

'Because they were Guard,' said Xaforn. As though that made all the necessary sense in the world. In her world, it did.

Qiaan could even understand it. But her understanding didn't change matters. 'It's dead anyway, then,' she shrugged. But she tied her sleeve into a makeshift sling and cradled the weakly mewling kitten into it. It quested with its tiny nose until it found her finger, and then it started sucking on the fingertip, hard, making tiny complaining noises when it refused to yield any sustenance.

'What are you doing?'

'I'll take it home,' Qiaan said. 'See if I can't find something. Milk going to waste. Something.'

'Sappy.'

'Mad,' countered Qiaan.

They got to their feet, spun apart. Behind them, the poleaxed young bully was only just beginning to sit up and shake his head in confusion. The girls stalked off in opposite directions, and then Qiaan turned to look at Xaforn's stiff, retreating back.

'You can come see her if you like,' she called softly.

Xaforn paused, half turned her head. 'Why would I want to do that?'

Qiaan shrugged. 'To see if she survives the Guard.'

Xaforn's braid snapped like a whip as she turned. 'It wasn't Guard did that to it!'

'To *her*,' Qiaan said. 'And if they hadn't you would never have interfered. I'll be seeing you.'

'Witch,' muttered Xaforn.

'Bruiser,' came floating back, just as Qiaan passed out of sight.

Xaforn turned away. She tried to scowl, but however hard she schooled her features her mouth kept on coming up into a twisted little grin instead. Of all the people . . .

But she had an awful feeling that she could not resist going to see the cat. *She*. That pathetic little bundle of ragged fur, bloodied and weak and barely flickering with life. How did Qiaan know it was a female?

# *Four*

Xaforn shared a dormitory room with three other Guard foundlings. She had a utilitarian relationship with her room-mates – she did not have anything much in common with any of them. She had both given and received bruises from sparring sessions with all of them, but they shared the space amicably even if Xaforn didn't join in with the giggles and the compound gossip the other three girls were prone to. The single Guard members were given to transient and shifting flings with others in their cadre, and Xaforn's room-mates always seemed to know who was attached to whom any given week. Xaforn did not particularly care to know, and had developed a habit of generally tuning out specific conversations, those spiced with heavy doses of titters and whispers. But gossip was also a mine of information about the general day-to-day lives in the compound and Xaforn did not dismiss everything that found its way into her room through her chatty bunkmates.

She was sitting on her bed fixing a broken sandal barely a week after the incident with the kitten when a comment involving 'cats' found its way past her defences, and she lifted her head fractionally, starting to listen without giving the least impression that her attention was suddenly on things other than the half-completed repair job in her lap.

'. . . *adorable*,' one of the girls was saying. 'It must be only a few weeks old, and it must have suffered something terrible, there are still marks on it where it had been tortured.'

'Where did Qiaan get hold of it?' asked another.

'She won't say, she says nothing of where she found it or how she got it,' the first one said. 'But I think it's going to make it. She still feeds it four, five times a day; it suckles on her finger like a baby, An told me.'

So. The kitten lived. Xaforn bent over her sandal, obscurely pleased at the news. She made a mental note to keep an ear open for news of it – of *her* – her lips quirked again, remembering Qiaan's quiet insistence on that point. She toyed briefly, as she had done a number of times already in the past week, with the idea of visiting the cat – the *cat*, not Qiaan – and then dismissed it, as she always did, staunchly resisting the impulse. There was nothing for her in the inner compound, with its teeming children, its squabbling women, its *families*, its cats.

She muttered a soft curse under her breath. The kitten's tiny, vulnerable face, the delicate suckling on Qiaan's finger, the scrabbling little wounded paws . . . Xaforn jabbed a repair hook too deeply into the rope sole of her broken sandal, annoyed at the kitten's insistent hold on her mind's eye. She had interfered because two of the torturers had been *Guard*, damn it all, not because she was a bleeding heart for waifs and strays. She didn't care what happened to it, after. She didn't. She could swear she didn't. She was glad the little thing had clung to life, but she'd tried to dismiss the creature from her orbit and she had every intention of forgetting about it. Especially now that she knew it had survived.

But the cat incident seemed intent on coming back to haunt her. The day after she had overheard the conversation about the kitten's well-being, Xaforn was summoned into her cadre leader's presence.

'Is it true?' JeuJeu, the scarred veteran in charge of training for Xaforn's group, demanded without preamble as soon as Xaforn came into her cubicle.

Somehow Xaforn didn't need to ask what she was talking about. She clenched her teeth. Qiaan – Qiaan probably told them everything.

'It was Guards who were torturing it,' Xaforn said, with a touch of defiance.

'Guards,' JeuJeu repeated blankly.

'There were four of them, and two were Guard trainees,' Xaforn said. 'This was not . . . honourable.'

JeuJeu was betrayed into a grim smile. 'You took on four older boys on behalf of a half-dead street cat because what they were doing was not *honourable*? For the love of Cahan, Xaforn. Did you know who the boys were?'

'Just the Guards,' Xaforn said.

'The others were far more important,' JeuJeu said. 'The one you landed in the House of Healing for five days was the son of a City Councillor. His father was not pleased.'

'The City Councillor's son is a bully and a fool,' Xaforn said trenchantly. 'He was told by the others –'

'Yes?' JeuJeu prompted when Xaforn came to a grinding halt. When Xaforn remained stubbornly silent, JeuJeu heaved a deep sigh and sat back in her chair, stretching her legs out before her and crossing them at the ankles. 'I'll tell you, then,' she said. 'The others told your target that he shouldn't mess with you. He didn't listen. He paid for it.'

'Am I in trouble?' Xaforn asked warily.

JeuJeu laughed, a sharp bark of a laugh, betraying amusement but not mirth. 'Oh, a great deal of it,' she said. 'You broke so many rules that it would probably take me less time to enumerate those you did *not* break. There are people out there exceedingly angry with you, who won't forget your name in a hurry. But you took on an adversary against the odds – they were bigger and there were more of them – and you did it on a matter of principle.' JeuJeu shook her head. 'Yes, I'd say you're in trouble. But I also dislike interference with Guard matters, and they were in the compound. So technically they were in our jurisdiction. And it was *our* cat.'

Xaforn, who had kept her eyes down, stole a look at JeuJeu's face at those words. The damn cat had become a symbol, somehow.

And it hadn't been Qiaan who had squealed. It had been that malicious bully with his flabby muscles and soft belly. Once he had recovered enough to whine, that is. Xaforn allowed herself a small smile at that thought.

JeuJeu caught it. 'Don't look so smug, you aren't getting off scot-free,' she said sharply. 'We're holding you back this autumn. You're ready to go up a level, but you obviously need to learn more about strategy and prudence. So your cat has cost you advancement, this round.' She saw Xaforn's stricken face, and allowed herself to smile. 'For what it's worth, it is my own considered opinion that it won't matter one whit, and that you *will* be the youngest Guard to be inducted into the Imperial Corps. But it will be a year later than you hoped. Xaforn, I don't want you to learn the wrong lesson from this. I am proud of you. *We* are proud of you. You understand honour; now you must start learning to weigh when and how it can best be defended. You could have come to me with this and I would have done something about it – I like torture no more than you do.'

'But the cat would have died,' Xaforn said softly.

'Maybe,' JeuJeu said. 'And maybe not. And maybe both it would have been alive and you would have had your promotion. And maybe you'd never have known what it was that you really believed in.' JeuJeu's smile turned a little wry. 'Truth? I don't know that I would have done any different. I'll see what I can do for you, for my part. You may go.'

Xaforn left, her thoughts churning. She found herself utterly ambivalent about the cat, the bully, her actions. Her gut told her she had done the right thing; her reason railed against her having risked anything at all that would have harmed her sole focus, her chance of *belonging*, of being Guard – full Guard, part of that family – as soon as she could make that happen.

That cat.

The damned cat had survived. The odds had been against the kitten, just as they had always been against Xaforn achieving impossible goals. Xaforn was not blind to the irony of this. She was suddenly curious to see how the cat was doing – but that would mean, of course, going into the family quarters again. Where Qiaan was.

'I might as well get it over with,' she muttered. 'I should probably never have meddled at all.'

Xaforn wore such a fierce scowl as she came through the archway and into the inner compound that perfectly innocent children instinctively sidled out of her way, avoiding the sense of being

31

somehow at fault which circled around Xaforn just waiting to find a target to land on. The scowl only deepened when she emerged from the passageway leading through into the inner garden surrounded by the mews where Captain Aric lived, and found Qiaan seated on the grass, a straw hat on her head, and another on the ground beside her which had been made into a nest of sorts where, now, a black kitten with white-edged paws curled up asleep. There were a dozen children there, some playing knucklebones, others acting out domestic dramas with rag dolls or attacking each other furiously with wooden swords, a few of them keeping an eye on the kitten and waiting for it to wake up and enchant them with its antics.

The damn cat had become a celebrity.

Xaforn's scowl deepened even more when a few of the noisier children lapsed into silence, watching her progress across the yard. A couple of the small faces registered alarm.

'Don't be scared,' said Qiaan, who hadn't turned to look but somehow knew that the children had become wary. She was supposedly addressing the children, but her voice had been pitched for the visitor. 'She's just come to see Ink.'

'*Ink*?' Xaforn repeated, blindsided by the fact that the cat had survived long enough to gain a name.

'One of the little ones said she looked like somebody had been holding her by the paws and dunked her into a pail of ink,' said Qiaan, with a straight face.

Coming closer, Xaforn noticed the paper smoothed over a wooden board in Qiaan's lap, and a small bottle of ink, the writing kind, beside her on the grass. 'What are you doing?'

'Drawing her,' Qiaan said, turning the board.

'It isn't very good,' Xaforn said tactlessly, studying the brush-and-ink rendition.

Qiaan shrugged. 'Doesn't matter,' she said. 'It's only for me.'

Xaforn, somehow always on the defensive with Qiaan's particular brand of passive resistance, sidestepped. 'I suppose it's better than I could do.'

The kitten chose this moment to stretch and yawn, revealing sharp, delicate and somehow impossibly feral needle-like teeth. It opened one eye, just a narrow slit gleaming green in the black fur of its face, and then both, giving Xaforn a guileless, wide-eyed stare.

Captivated, Xaforn reached over a finger.

'Careful,' said Qiaan, 'she . . .'

The kitten began purring softly, butting its head against Xaforn's fingertip.

'. . . scratches,' Qiaan finished, and then grinned. 'Well, look at that.'

The cat was a tangle of conspiracies. Xaforn flushed, snatching her hand back. 'I just wanted to make sure she was all right,' she said.

Qiaan smiled again at the 'she'. Xaforn and the cat continued looking at one another warily. Still smiling, Qiaan picked up the narrow brush lying by the inkwell, dipped it into the ink and sketched out a few letters of script beside the cat picture. She blew on the ink gently to dry it, and Xaforn's attention switched back to her.

'Here,' Qiaan said, picking up the paper and handing it to her visitor. 'You keep that.' Her eyes were veiled behind long dark lashes as she added, 'Although it isn't very good.'

Xaforn took the paper automatically as it was thrust at her, and her face settled back into its scowl.

'What's this?' she said, staring at the letters Qiaan had put onto the page.

Qiaan started to answer, and then stared at her. 'You don't know, do you? And how could you?'

Caught in an inadequacy, straight after having been pilloried for being far too good at what she did, Xaforn flushed darkly. 'Perhaps I didn't need to know.'

'*Jin-ashu*,' Qiaan said. 'The women's language.'

Taught from mother to daughter. Rochanaa had done her duty by this, at least – Qiaan knew the script of the women's language, the secret language. But who had there been to teach foundlings like Xaforn? Qiaan stared at the other girl, curious and oddly astonished by this discovery. Did none of them know it? Were all the female Guards who had come here as foundling babies illiterate in this secret that the women of Syai had cherished and passed down from generation to generation for a thousand years?

She could not believe that. So much of her world was built on its existence.

Or was it just Xaforn herself – did Xaforn slip through the cracks, so intent on belonging to the Guard that she never learned how to belong to herself and her heritage?

'It says "Ink",' Qiaan said, her voice completely free of sarcasm or mockery, the twin weapons with which she often faced the world. She picked up the brush again, dipped it into the ink, sketched out a new set of letters on a shred of paper which had been lying underneath the sketch she'd handed to Xaforn. She handed over this, too, without a word to the other girl. Xaforn took it, stared at it.

'So I can't read it,' she said. 'So?'

'It says *jin-shei*,' Qiaan said, suddenly a little unsure of herself, of the impulse that had made her offer this sacred trust to the one person in Linh-an who apparently had neither knowledge nor appreciation of it.

Xaforn may have been ignorant of the secret language; she could hardly have grown up female in Syai, foundling or not, and not be aware of the existence of the *jin-shei* sisterhood itself. But this was a female mystery, a women's secret, and it was something that Xaforn had dismissed as irrelevant to the life she chose to lead.

'What use do I have for that?' she said, raising as shield the brashness and the roughness of her warrior training – the male attributes thrown up to parry the insidious attack by the softness of the feminine in her, ruthlessly suppressed since she had taken up weapons and chosen to learn how to kill. 'And what's in it for *you?* You, of all people, and me?'

'Do you think there are no *jin-shei* sisters in the Guard?' Qiaan said. 'You are ignorant, then. This is every woman's heritage, be she princess or the lowest urchin in the beggar guild.'

'The beggar women know *jin-ashu*?' Xaforn said sceptically. 'I don't believe it.'

Qiaan shrugged. 'The beggars may be largely illiterate but their women will have enough *jin-ashu* to communicate with someone like me,' she said. 'You can believe it or not.'

'I'll think about it,' Xaforn said abruptly, coming to her feet.

'You can choose to accept it, or not,' said Qiaan. 'But *jin-shei* is not something that can be unsaid. You have the paper.' She glanced at the kitten, which was contemplating the twitching of its own tail with a hunter's deep concentration, and smiled. 'We share the cat. And someday – *jin-shei-bao* – there may be a better drawing of the cat. And you can write her name on that yourself.' She met Xaforn's eyes, squarely, without flinching. 'Or your own.'

'I'll think about it,' Xaforn repeated, backing away. Her eyes slid off Qiaan, lingered for a last moment on the kitten, and then she stalked out of the courtyard, her shoulders hunched.

'Temptress,' she muttered as she departed, clutching the drawing of the cat, trying not to let her eyes stray constantly to the mysterious symbols on the paper. Letters. Writing. Language. Sisterhood . . .

'Coward,' Qiaan responded.

Xaforn had to clench her teeth against the sudden urge to laugh out loud.

# *Five*

Nhia had started out thinking of the Great Temple of Linh-an as a deliciously confusing maze, a labyrinth, a box within a box.

To the child that she had been, the place was enormous, layered like a lotus flower, and full of mystery. Its outer walls were white-washed with lime, like some of the poorest houses in the city; its three massive gates, cut into this white expanse, were old and scarred wood and had no air of holiness or even magnificence except maybe for their immense size. But they always stood open – except for one single night of the year on the Festival of All Souls when the Temple was closed to be purified – and they were gateways to a constant stream of worshippers hurrying in and out.

Nhia, who had practically grown up on the Temple's doorstep, knew the outer rings of the Great Temple intimately.

The First Circle, running right around the inner perimeter of the whitewashed walls, was primarily taken up with Temple vendors and the stalls of diviners and soothsayers – and Nhia claimed the acquaintance of most of them, at least by sight. Some had been there for as long as she had been coming to the Temple – old Zhu, and his incense booth so meticulously devoted to one particular scent a day ('It only confuses the customers when you show off everything you've got,' he had confided to Nhia once, nodding sagely); the Rice Man, whose name she had never learned but whose family of eight children and their ailments and joys Nhia and her mother had known for years; So-Xan the yearwood bead-carver and his young son and apprentice, Kito.

Trestles within individual booths were neatly laid out with such merchandise as incense sticks suitable for individual deities or specific prayers, bowls in appropriate colour or pattern, flasks of rice wine or tea, grains of rice or of corn and powdered dyes. When Nhia was a curious toddler only just starting to lisp questions – before life had made her mother taciturn and edgy – she had demanded explanations for all of these mysterious offerings and paraphernalia.

'Why yellow bowls, Mother? Why only thirteen grains, Mother? Why tea and not rice wine, Mother?'

'Yellow bowls for Lord Sin, because he is Lord of the East and that's where the yellow sun rises. Thirteen grains because of the thirteen lessons of Ama-bai. Tea and not rice wine because the Sages are lower than the Emperors.'

Nhia was to remember those times with a pang of regret. It had been years since she had asked her mother a question like that. Years since she had expected a reply from her.

Other stalls in the outer cloister housed the makers of carved yearwood sticks, or sold funeral arrangements, preparation of the paper effigies of the things the deceased needed to take with them into the next world, amulets or talismans, marriage and betrothal tokens, or – slightly clandestinely, because the Temple officially frowned on these – low-level alchemical potions guaranteed to increase fertility, virility or long life. *Ganshu* diviners elbowed one another for space here, their clients waiting in patient queues for their turn inside the screened booth where the diviner performed his or her work.

An open corridor cut across this cloister from each of the three gates, and led through into the courtyard. Beyond a narrow strip of grass rose a clay wall with three arched openings in line with the three gates; it was painted a ghost-blue, a colour which was almost white except for the wash of blue that made it look like the sky of Linh-an in the full blaze of the summer sun. The wall surrounded a perimeter precisely one flagstone wide around the next level of the Temple, the Second Circle, a building painted the same colour as the wall around it, itself boasting an inner cloister surrounding an open court. But this cloister was clear of anything requiring an exchange of money. It was two storeys high, with an open balcony above the lower cloister. The entire inner wall of the building, on both floors, was a catacomb of wall alcoves and niches, with space for incense and offerings; each niche held an image or a figurine before which some devotee was praying with a fragrant incense stick smelling of cinnamon or flower essence or rain grass in one hand and a bowl with precisely counted rice grains in the other.

Many niches were empty, their own particular deity yet to appear. These were the Later Heaven deities and spirits, the lesser Gods, the spirits of Rain and Thunder and Wind and Fire, Tsu-ho the Kitchen Spirit of Plenty, Hsih-to the Messenger of the Gods, the Syai Emperors of old, and the Holy Sages. This was the place of propitiation, of honouring the Wise, of paying respect to the Great, of asking for advice. Nhia would sometimes drift past the niches with supplicants (sometimes more than one, companionably sharing a deity's time and attention and often the offering) and absorb the whispers going on around her – whispers asking for help, giving thanks, telling the Kitchen God of the success of a particular feast which was held in the midst of plenty and humbly giving him credit.

'Please, Rain Spirit, our fields are parched and drying, we humbly come to ask . . .'

'I offer rice and grain in humble gratitude, for my son has found a good bride . . .'

'O Holy Sage, who knows of these things, I come to ask for guidance, for the examinations are near and this problem is too great for me to understand . . .'

'Holy Hsih-to, Messenger of the Gods, please help me make my husband stop being angry at me – for I did not mean it when I said to him . . .'

'Help me, Hsih-to, for my mother-in-law is driving me distracted . . .'

These were the simple questions, but they were also the most fundamental ones, the ones lives were built on – and the shrines were open, and there were few secrets. This was the backbone of the Way, the little things that, left unattended, would grow into catastrophes – but which were still small enough, human-scaled enough, to belong to these lesser Gods and spirits and for which the greater deities were not to be disturbed.

For more, for greater miracles, the three arrow-straight corridors leading from the outer gates pierced this Circle full of incense and whispers. Within the inner courtyard of this Second Circle stood another building, this one painted a darker blue, the blue of an autumn sky. Its inner cloisters, also on two floors, were quieter, more sparsely populated. Here, in the Third Circle, there were fewer niches, and the Gods in them were the lower deities of Early Heaven – Cahan, the Spirit Paradise. Here resided Yu, the general of the Heavenly Armies; Ama-bai the Great Teacher; the Rulers of the Four Quarters – Kun, Lord of the North, Sin, Lord of the East, T'ain, Lady of the West and K'ain, Lady of the South. These were the weavers of human fates, the first deities in the tiers of the Heavens with real power over lives, dreams and destinies. Nhia's astrological antecedents had been complicated – she had been born between two Quarters, and her mother had made offerings to both Sin and K'ain, making sure that she left no stone unturned when she came to pray for Nhia – but it seemed that the in-between children were neither Ruler's responsibility and Nhia's mother's prayers had fallen in the cracks.

It was more expensive to come here than in the Second Circle, for the deities of the Third Circle had their own attendants who tended to the offerings and the lighting of candles and incense sticks so that all was harmonious and acceptable. There was no companionable sharing of Gods and altars here. People came to the Third Circle with a purpose.

Another level deeper in stood the Fourth Circle – not a round building like the others, but a three-sided, three-storey structure. Each of its three sections, all three floors of it, was devoted to one of the Three Pure Ones, the rulers of the Three Heavens of Cahan – the Shan, the I'Chi, the Taikua, the realms of Pure Spirit, Pure Energy, Pure Vitality. The building was painted a darker blue, inside and out, and inside its many candles and lanterns gleamed like stars. The place was full of silence and mystery, and Nhia loved to lose herself here sometimes, when she had hoarded enough coppers to buy an offering rich enough to allow her into this Circle. The inner garden, separating the Third from the Fourth Circles, had scented flowers, and meditation areas with golden sand raked smooth and granite rocks placed as focus for a supplicant's thoughts. The altars in the Fourth Circle were carved in smooth marble or covered with costly golden silks, tended by special attendants clad in blue and gold and sworn to each deity's service. There were secluded alcoves where those who came to honour these deities could withdraw after making their offering to the acolytes, and commune in private with the God they had come to revere.

The three straight corridors passed through this quiet, holy place too and finally entered the heart of the Temple – a midnight-blue tower standing in the middle of the inner court of the Fourth Circle, the home of the Lord of Heaven. The worshipper entered this place barefoot, leaving shoes outside the gates, for this was holy ground. Nine small altars ringed the centre of the Tower, three to each gate; these were followed by an inner ring of three larger ones, one per gate, where oil lamps always burned to signify the presence of the God. Beyond these, three steps on a marble platform, was the altar of the Lord of Heaven where the Emperor himself came to sacrifice for Syai's well-being on the eve of every New Year – an altar where a holy fire burned in a central bowl and cast a flickering light on the carefully arranged offerings tended by one of the three Tower priests. High above, reachable by a catwalk that clung to the walls of the Tower well away from the altar, hung the gigantic brass bell which was rung by the priests every day at noon.

A complex place for a complex faith, an orderly set of beliefs on which heaven and earth were made, a creed which assigned everything to its perfect, particular place.

Nhia had been brought there for the first time when she was a babe in arms, barely born, perhaps a week old – her mother had brought her in, purchased amulets, purchased potions, offered her child and her child's troubles to the deities of the Second Circle and begged for deliverance. But Nhia's twisted leg and withered foot did not go away. The child crawled a lot later than most children did, unable to put any weight on the crippled limb; she had not walked until she was almost four years old, and even then it was with a pronounced limp. By that time her mother had progressed to the Third Circle, entreating for salvation from higher authority – but no amount of incense or rice wine helped, and *ganshu* readings were inconclusive.

The Temple was a daily stop, and more often than not Nhia was required to accompany her mother the supplicant so that she could show the Gods just what they had to do for her. Any other five-year-old or six-year-old or seven-year-old, and as the years wore on

Nhia reached and passed all those milestones, would have started pulling the Temple apart stone by stone from sheer boredom. Nhia was different. Her physical disability focused her mind on things others might have missed, and even as a very young child she was an acute observer and an astute interpreter of the throngs of humanity she saw parading in and out of the Temple every day. By the time she was ten she had taken to coming to the Temple by herself. She would strike up conversations on the theology of the Way with some of the younger and more indulgent acolytes of the outer Circles, or some of the older ones willing to indulge an interested and precocious child. It was all couched, as much wisdom of the Way was, in ancient tales and fables. There were many, but there was one which most of Nhia's Temple friends always returned to in the end.

'When the evil spirits tricked Han-fei into raiding the Gardens of the Gods . . .'

'I know, I know,' Nhia would interrupt when this sentence was offered to her. 'He picked too many of the plums from the Tree of Wisdom, and could not carry them, and had to leave all of it behind when he was driven from the Garden by the angry Gods. I know, *sei*, I know. The plums of wisdom should be taken one by one and savoured. But I would still like to know . . .'

The Temple teachers would shake their heads and smile.

But Nhia was told much, and had seen more than any Linh-an child her age and twice as well born as she could lay claim to. She had even glimpsed the Tower altar by the time she was eleven.

By the time she had turned thirteen, Nhia could recite the correct offerings for any deity within the Great Temple – their composition and their timing – to a precise degree. Her mother, Li, had exhausted her avenues of help and appeal in the living world, the healers and the hedge-healers and every connection she had ever had, including her handful of *jin-shei* sisters. Nothing had helped, and Li had turned almost wholly to the Heavens now, praying daily for intervention in the circumstances concerning Nhia's withered foot. But for Nhia herself that foot had long since ceased to be of any importance. She would listen to her mother's entreaties to the Gods, which had started out as abasement and pleading for a miraculous cure and had then proliferated into all kinds of peripheral demands – *Send her a husband who will care for her*. But Nhia knew that it was unlikely that she would ever marry, or at least unlikely that she would marry well – she was the daughter of a washerwoman, with no inheritance or dowry to speak of, and the handicap effectively removed any possibility of entering some wealthy house as a concubine whose children, taken as such children always were to belong to the primary wife, might stand a chance of inheriting something of their own.

Nhia's life had been written for her by the Rulers of the Four Quarters long before she was born. This much she knew from her conversations with the acolytes of the Third Circle. There would probably be no marriage, no children for Nhia – but there might be something different, something else. She just wished she knew *what*. Her mother still regularly haunted the booths of the *ganshu* readers for answers concerning her crippled child, answers which had a more and more direct bearing on her own life and needs as the years slipped by, but Nhia herself had spent a few precious coppers on a couple of readings from the cheaper *ganshu* readers – those in the bazaars, not the ones allowed access to the Great Temple, she couldn't even think about spending that much money on a whim. The readings had been inconclusive and vague, or the readers had been less than adept. Either way, the path Nhia was to tread remained opaque to her.

## Six

If Nhia had any gift that set her apart from the rest, it was to make people trust her – not necessarily like her, because she was a bright and intelligent child who appeared to know far too much for her age, and didn't hesitate to tell what she knew. But people would tell her things, people who otherwise had no business telling her anything, and it was partly this that pushed her into the path of the Gods when she came stumbling into the Great Temple barely a week after her thirteenth birthday, in that hot summer which held all of Linh-an in its iron grip.

The Temple was blessedly cool after the steamy streets, and Nhia paused to catch her breath and rest her aching foot in its special sandal. Her mother always had a spare copper or two for the Temple if Nhia asked, and she had come armed with a handful of coins with which she hoped to buy enough in the way of offerings to get her into the Third Circle.

Thin strips of garden separated each Circle from the next, complete with a handful of carefully cultivated trees bearing plums or peaches, symbols of knowledge and immortality, or just blooming with great scented flowers in their season. But the inner garden of the Third Circle was particularly lush and pleasant. Scattered pools held golden fish, and tiny artificial waterfalls added the murmur of running water to the serene hush of the inner Circles. It was in these gardens that Nhia often found the acolytes who were willing to talk to her about the things that interested her. The Second Circle was full of a chattering and a muttering, and desperate attempts to hush whimpering or wailing children, and shuffling feet, and the occasional squeal or shout; it was hard to gather one's thoughts here, although Nhia sometimes came there to do just that as an exercise in concentration. But she preferred at the very least the quietness of the Third Circle or, if she had a choice, the hushed holiness of the Fourth.

She was out of luck with her offerings this time – her hoarded coins managed to suffice for barely enough incense to placate one of the Second Circle Sages. But her luck turned when she met up with one of the acolytes she had got to know better than most in the time she spent at the Temple, and was invited to come through with him into the Third Circle as his guest. Nhia accepted gladly, contemplating half an hour or so of pleasant conversation, but they had barely crossed into the inner court of the Third Circle when another acolyte hurried up to them and whispered something in Nhia's friend's ear with an air of agitation.

'I apologize,' said Nhia's acolyte courteously, 'but it seems I am urgently required elsewhere. We have one of the Nine Sages in the Fourth Circle today, and he has been . . . demanding. But please, walk in the garden. I will see if I can return when my duty is done.'

'Thank you,' Nhia said.

He bowed formally, and hurried away with his companion.

The Nine Sages were almost mythical beings to Nhia. They were learned men and women, great Sages, most of whom would gain niches in the Second Circle of the Temple at their passing and many of whose predecessors already inhabited their own niches there. They were adepts of great power and knowledge, Imperial advisers, the first and most honoured circle of the Imperial Council. One of them had crossed into the Later Heaven fairly recently; Nhia had been in the street crowd at his funeral parade, and had been deeply impressed at the cortège and at all the implements, meticulously recreated in folded and painted paper, which he required to take with him to the Afterworld. His successor – each Sage named his successor in the circle before he died – was a mystery; nobody had yet seen or heard of the new Sage, none of the common people anyway. All that was known about him was that he was male. He had already been the subject of much street gossip. Stories had it that he was no greybeard; he was not young, to be sure, because no youth could be a Sage – certainly everyone knew that much. That left a virile man, in the prime of his life, and everyone from the portly matrons making virtuous sacrifices in the highest Temple Circles to the painted bazaar strumpets was speculating on whether he had taken a wife or a concubine or whether he intended to do so. Nhia wondered briefly and with a spark of passing curiosity whether it was in fact the brand-new Sage who had sent the acolytes of the Great Temple into such a frenzy of activity, but it was unlikely that this would be something that she'd ever get close enough to find out.

Left alone in the gardens, Nhia sat for the better part of an hour contemplating the languid, overfed fish in one of the pools, happy to snatch a moment of perfect peace. It was as she was getting ready to leave that her disability returned to haunt her. She put her weight on her crippled foot in an awkward manner while stepping up onto the paved path leading to one of the gates, and the weak ankle gave way. Nhia crumpled to the path with a gasp of pain.

A hand extended in assistance swam into her field of vision, blurred by the sudden tears that had come into her eyes. Surprised, she took it, and was helped gently to her feet and supported until she gained a steady balance. Only then did she raise her eyes, blinking owlishly, to look at who had come to her aid.

The man's face was young, unlined, the hair long and lustrous and tied back in a plaited queue like the workers wore – but his hands were not worker's hands, and his eyes were not a young man's eyes. The hands were smooth and white, nails manicured, a sure mark of an aristocrat with servants at his beck and call, even if it wasn't for the telltale fall of expensive material of his gown that spilled in carefully arranged artless folds as he bent to help Nhia up. The eyes were opaque with ageless wisdom, dark and kind and utterly mysterious.

'I . . . thank you, I am fine now,' she said, knowing as surely as she knew her own name that she was addressing someone a thousand times removed from her in rank and stature and appalled at her temerity in saying anything at all to such a personage. By rights she should have stood quietly with her eyes downcast until addressed directly.

The man dropped one of his hands from her shoulders, and Nhia attempted to stand unsupported but made the mistake of supporting her weight on her weak foot again. She tried to hide the inadvertent wince, but obviously failed when a cultured voice with a Court inflexion and intonation said, 'I think not.'

He slipped an arm around her shoulders and helped her off the path, steering her to the nearest bench in the gardens, and letting her subside gently onto the seat.

'Thank you,' she said again, helplessly.

'Did you come here to pray about this?' the man inquired courteously, inclining his head the merest fraction to indicate her foot, not naming the affliction, as politeness demanded.

'No, *sei*. No, my Lord, that is my mother's reason for visiting the Temple.'

'Oh?' he said. 'And not yours?'

'I come here to understand, not to beg for petty miracles,' Nhia said, and then bit her lip to prevent a small gasp from escaping. She had offered a discourtesy, at the least, and he could take her remark as borderline blasphemous if he chose.

'How old are you?' asked her benefactor instead, unexpectedly, after a pause which might have indicated surprise.

'I turned thirteen only a few days ago, *sei*,' Nhia said, relieved to be back on safe ground.

'I have heard the name of a young girl who comes here to talk of the spirits with the Temple acolytes,' the man said thoughtfully. 'Would that be you? What is your name, child?'

'NhiNhi,' Nhia said, instinctively giving her child-name, the name her mother had called her by when she was a baby, and then flushed scarlet. 'I mean . . . Nhia, *sei*.'

44

'Nhia,' he repeated, with an air of committing it to memory. 'Well, Nhia, seeker of wisdom, perhaps we shall meet again.'

Nhia dared a quick, flickering look to his face. 'Yes, *sei*,' she said, aware that she sounded like she was indicating an agreement to that future meeting instead of a simple response that his words seemed to demand.

He straightened, gestured to someone out of Nhia's line of sight, and then bowed to her lightly – *bowed* to her! – and strode away in a whisper of expensive silk robes.

Nhia realized she was trembling.

When hurrying footsteps approached her a moment later, she lifted her eyes to meet the intensely curious gaze of her friend from the Third Circle. 'What did he say to you?' the acolyte demanded, sounding astonished. 'Do you realize who that *was*?'

Still thunderstruck, aware of a murmuring crowd gathered in the cloisters which had been a collective witness to this strange encounter, Nhia stared at the gate through which her young lord had disappeared. 'I think I do,' she whispered. *One of the Nine Sages is in the Fourth Circle today . . .*

'He is Lihui. That was Sage Lihui. He is the youngest of the Nine Sages, the one who came to honour us today. I saw you fall at his feet and I was afraid, but he . . .'

Nhia's eyes were wide as saucers. She had been right but . . . a Sage? A Court *Sage* had stopped to raise a crippled child, to ask her name . . .

*Perhaps we shall meet again*, he had said.

Perhaps the *ganshu* readers had never told Nhia about this encounter because it had never been meant to take place. The acolyte had trusted her with the information that a Sage was in the Temple; the collapse of her ankle might have been pure chance, but a part of her had known at whose feet she had been thrown, and had guided her tongue as she had spoken to him.

Nhia looked around at the flickering lights of candles and oil lamps of the Third Circle, at the haze of brightness surrounding the weavers of human fates, the Rulers of the Four Quarters, and smiled to herself. She had put herself in the paths of the Gods this day. Perhaps she had just taken her first fragile step beyond the veil which *ganshu* had drawn over her life and destiny.

# Seven

'For the love of all the Gods, Khailin, and for the last time – not today! The Chancellor . . .'

Khailin's face set in mutinous lines. 'The Chancellor! That means I won't see you until nightfall, and *that* means I don't get my lesson today.'

'Think of it as a day of rest,' said her father, with some impatience. Then he smoothed the frown off his forehead, and sighed. 'Khailin, knowing your *hacha* letters is not going to magically –'

'I know,' Khailin said. 'I know what it won't do for me. But there is so much out there that I want to know, and that I will never know if I can't . . .'

She faltered under her father's rather stern gaze. 'And you do remember, I trust, that these lessons are based on a proper attitude on your part. I will not have you interrupting me, Khailin. It shows disrespect to your parents.'

'Yes, Father,' Khailin said, resigned.

'Good. That's settled, then. We will resume our lessons when I return from the Palace. In the meantime, I suggest that you pursue your . . . other responsibilities. I will have to speak to your mother about that. Within a year or two you may well be married and will have no time for indulging such whims as books and studies.'

Khailin bowed to her father with the exact degree of respect that was required, keeping her eyes lowered so that he wouldn't see the rebellion in them. Cheleh, Court Chronicler, permitted himself one affectionate feather-like brush of his hand on his daughter's hair before bowing back to her with the proper degree of acknowledgement and leaving her alone in her chamber.

When the door safely closed behind him, Khailin picked up a tasselled cushion from her bed and threw it against the wall with a muted cry. She had just come to an interesting section of a text her father did not know she had purloined from his scroll library, and she had become thoroughly bogged down in it. She had hoped to wheedle some information from him that day, without letting on that she had the scroll, of course, and finish reading the text that evening. It was an old astronomical treatise, written by a Sage from a long-dead Emperor's court; Khailin could tell, even with her inability to completely understand, that much of it was already obsolete, but there had been several descriptions in there which matched something she had been able to observe herself in the night sky with the distance viewer her father had in his study. She had hoped that she would be able to extract enough information from this scroll to confirm her own observations, and perhaps find out where she could obtain more recent material on one particular celestial object which had caught her fancy, a red-gold sphere with an annulus around it.

She had started wheedling her father to teach her *hacha-ashu*, the script of the common tongue, when she first realized that *jin-ashu*, the script her mother had been dutifully teaching her since she had turned four years old, was not the language in which the really interesting things were written. *Jin-ashu* was a woman's language, and it was the heart of a woman's world. Its writings tended to be confined to poetry, legends, stories, the wisdom of hearth and home, letters between *jin-shei* sisters (whether separated by the length and breadth of Syai or three streets apart in the same city). *Jin-ashu* dealt with the everyday and the commonplace, the household chatter of wives and mothers, the pouring out of an unrequited love or the transports of delight of a new wife just initiated into the pleasures of marriage. Khailin had seen a few of the latter, although she was still to undergo her Xat-Wau coming of age ceremony and was considered far too young for what were sometimes frankly erotic letters between grown and sexually initiated women. But Khailin read what interested her, and if she could sneak an astronomy treatise out of her father's treasured library, her mother's stacks of *jin-ashu* letters were a considerably simpler problem to riffle until she found material that caught her eye. She knew considerably more than either of her parents suspected about what awaited her as a young woman who was rapidly approaching marriageable age.

In fact, she had already started keeping an eye out for likely prospects – young men sufficiently learned to have access to the things that she wanted to find out, or wealthy enough to buy such access, or both. Unfortunately most of the younger suitors she had considered – the ones her parents would consider suitable – were also dismissed early, on the grounds that they were simply too boring to be of any interest. Khailin wondered if she would be able to hold out for a husband who might be considerably older than her but whose age would be traded off for the fact that he could be more easily cajoled by a young wife to allow her to do the things that Khailin had every intention of continuing to do. Study. Read.

A diffident knock on her door interrupted her thoughts, and at her barked call of admittance a servant, hands together and bowing deeply to her young mistress, came in to announce that Khailin's presence was required by her mother, the lady Yulinh.

'Tell her I will attend her at once,' Khailin said, and the servant backed out, bowing again.

Khailin sighed. She suspected her father had stopped off in his wife's quarters to suggest that she take Khailin in hand today, and she knew what that meant.

She wasn't wrong.

Lady Yulinh was a great believer in the power of purification and meditation. She visited the ritual baths frequently, an activity that Khailin profoundly despised for the same reason that she found *hacha-ashu* more interesting than *jin-ashu* – she didn't do well when cooped up in the presence of undiluted femininity for long. She found most of the women at the baths tedious, gossipy and unspeakably dull. They found her far too direct, almost abrasive, certainly bordering on rude although she was careful not to directly antagonize any of the matrons whom she might find as a mother-in-law one day. But being on her best behaviour and flawlessly and icily polite for three to four hours at a stretch, which was how long her mother's purification bath rituals usually took, exhausted her and made her severely irritated. Even her mother had learned not to take her along to these occasions any more often than she could help, and to stay out of her way for a while on their return home until Khailin could work out her waspishness on some unsuspecting servant.

Visits to the Great Temple were another matter. Lady Yulinh was possessed of sufficient stature and financial backing to be regularly admitted into the Third and even the Fourth Circles of the Temple. She insisted that her daughters – for her younger daughter, Yan, had been required to attend these devotional trips since she was eight – perform the required rituals and protocols with her, but once the official part of the visit was over the girls were free to use their time at the Temple as they wished until Yulinh was ready to leave. For Yan, that meant a return to the more colourful and more interesting First and Second Circles; she had become an early addict to *ganshu* readings and to soothsayers of every stripe. Khailin chose to linger in the inner Circles of the Temple, the Third and Fourth Circles, the ones with fewer people and more power. She preferred her knowledge empirical and her data neatly proved and documented by experimental protocols – but knowledge was knowledge, and the more empirical chemical and alchemical branches of study all had roots in the Temple and the deities it housed. The rest would come.

At least it was the Temple that Yulinh proposed that day. She did not mention the baths, at least not directly. Khailin was grateful for that mercy, at least; she didn't think she could have handled the baths with any degree of grace that day. The Temple was at least a potentially worthy substitute for the missed reading lesson.

Yulinh and her daughters were deposited at one of the Temple gates in their sedan chair, followed by a couple of quiet servants who had followed close behind in a second chair. Yulinh sent one of the servants to purchase a particular kind of incense, the other to obtain a bottle of rice wine and the proper amount of rice and beans for the supplication ritual she had in mind. Then she swept past the teeming corridors of the First Circle, heading into the inner sanctums. Her two daughters, eyes piously downcast, trailed at her heels.

They had gone straight through to a shrine to I'Chi-sei, one of the Three Pure Ones. Yulinh had been suffering from a lethargy and a lack of energy lately, what with the oppressive heat of the summer. Khailin was privately of the opinion that her mother might have done better to have stayed in the Second Circle and asked succour of the Spirit of Rain instead of beseeching a God of the Early Heavens for the energy which the hot dry weather sapped from her, but she held her tongue. When her mother was immersed deeply enough in her devotions not to notice that Khailin was absent, she slipped away unobtrusively and went seeking her own enlightenment.

In the gardens of the Third Circle Khailin found an acolyte drawing a finely detailed sand painting mandala in an oiled wooden frame. He was seated in front of her favourite shrine, that of Sin, Lord of the East, the deity who was ascendant in her own birth sign and to whom she had a special devotion. Khailin stood watching him for a while, her hands tucked decorously into the wide sleeves of her red silk tunic. She knew better than to interrupt, but when he took a break, sitting back and reaching for a flask of rice wine left at hand, she knelt down next to him.

'What is it for?' she asked.

'It is for a lady wishing for a favour from the Lord Sin,' the acolyte said courteously. 'This will be placed in his alcove with a lamp filled with holy oil, until such time as the lady tells us that her wish has been granted, or that she has withdrawn the petition.'

'Do they work?' Khailin asked. She had seen them before, the sand paintings, placed in shrines beside more prosaic offerings, beautiful and cryptic and mysterious. She had never seen one being prepared at such close quarters before, and inspected it with some curiosity. 'What do you use to dye the sand?'

'Are you wishing to join the Temple some day, young *sai'an*?' the acolyte asked, smiling. 'These are Temple secrets. We do the Gods' work. As for whether these are successful, that is not something we are in charge of. We facilitate the contact. The wish and the granting of it are between the one who prays and the God who listens to the prayer.'

'I have heard the saying that the Gods help those who put themselves in their path,' Khailin said. 'But this sand painting . . . this is so passive. It's like there's too much *cha'ia* energy here, and not nearly enough *chao*.'

The acolyte raised an eyebrow. 'You are learned, young *sai'an*.'

'Is it not better,' Khailin said, 'to know the prayer and to make something that answers it? If a sickness, then an elixir, or a medicine. If a child, then a way of conceiving, or a way of adopting. If a lover –'

'That is too much for the Gods' acolytes to aspire to,' said the acolyte hastily, cutting her off. 'And much of that, people do get. But not from here.' He made his disapproval obvious, but did not explain it further.

Khailin, however, had already read enough to know of the dichotomy of alchemies in the Way of the Cha in which the Gods and spirits of the Great Temple were enshrined. That had been in one of the earliest scrolls she'd taken from her father's library. She had practically learned the thing by heart:

50

*Cha is the path of the spirit and energy and power. Cha is part of every thing and every creature in the world. Pure Cha is what the highest Heaven is made of, a perfect place where the male and the female, the* chao *and the* cha'ia, *meet and meld in flawless balance and equilibrium, where the Seeker loses the self but becomes the whole world . . .*

That was the ultimate goal of the internal alchemies of the Way of the Cha, anyway – seeking ways to meld the adept's spirit with the Unknowable, become one with the Gods. The internal alchemy, the *zhao-cha*, was all about ethereal realms which could only be gained by the incorporeal, the spiritual.

The external alchemy, *yang-cha*, was more concerned with understanding the here and now. The empirical science. The part of the Way which drew Khailin's deepest interest.

But the Great Temple denied the greatest achievements of those who chose the path of the external alchemy. Astronomers were misunderstood, their findings languishing in old scrolls for only other astronomers to read. As for the preparation of the elixirs, the powerful ones which brought strength, knowledge, even (if legend was to be believed) immortality – those were too secret for the scrolls in Khailin's father's collection, their existence only hinted at in darkly mysterious terms until Khailin was driven to distraction with all that was left unsaid.

'If you will excuse me,' the acolyte began, back to high courtesy, acolyte to supplicant. But he was interrupted by the sound of sandalled feet slapping against the stone flags of the Circle in some haste, and then the wearer of those sandals, another acolyte, came into view around the corner of the cloister. He was almost running, the expression on his face close to panic. At the same time two more acolytes came hurrying out of the Fourth Circle gate through which Khailin herself had emerged and, seeing the mandala-drawer seated before his unfinished masterpiece, made their way towards him. All three newcomers reached the seated acolyte at more or less the same time.

'You're wanted,' began the one who had come running around the corner.

But one of the others, maybe senior in rank or just more prudent than the rest, raised a calming hand, cutting the more impulsive speaker off before he could blurt out things it was not appropriate for a non-initiate to hear.

'Brother,' he said, addressing the seated acolyte, 'there has been a call from the Fourth Circle. I have been sent to gather the necessary assistance. If you will lay aside your task for a moment, please come with me.' He turned to Khailin. 'If you will excuse us, young *sai'an*, the Temple calls us to obey.'

Khailin, getting to her feet and keeping her face inscrutable enough to hide her curiosity, placed her hands palms together and bowed to them with the reverence due to their station. The one who had spoken bowed back. The mandala-maker had risen too, making obeisance to the Lord Sin in his alcove before stowing the half-finished mandala under the altar for further work when he returned. Then all four of them, with the one who had dismissed Khailin speaking to his companions in a low voice, departed for the gate to the Fourth Circle in some haste.

Left alone, Khailin considered hauling out the mandala for a closer inspection, but happened to glance up first and met the blind stone eyes of the scowling carved effigy of Lord Sin. A superstitious dread stirred in her, and she offered a hasty obeisance in appeasement, trying to scotch any such irreverent thoughts as she backed away. She might not believe in the power of the mandalas to do any practical good, but other people did, and that did invest them with some power. Khailin had already learned to respect power.

Respect it enough to crave it.

When she tried to return to the Fourth Circle to rejoin her mother and sister, Khailin was politely but very firmly refused admittance.

'But my mother, the lady Yulinh, is in there,' Khailin said. She was not above pulling rank if she could not get her way by any other means, and in this place it was Yulinh's rank that mattered to those in power.

'I think not, *sai'an*. The Fourth Circle has been cleared for a very special occasion. If your lady mother was indeed here with her devotions, she has no doubt already been escorted elsewhere to complete them.'

'But . . .'

'I am very sorry, *sai'an*.'

'Where would they have taken her?'

'Perhaps the shrine of Ama-bai,' suggested the guard.

Khailin turned away, frustrated. The Third Circle was a little more crowded than usual, with a low murmur of voices in the usually hushed garden, but her mother and sister were not at the shrine of Ama-bai. Khailin continued her circumnavigation of the Third Circle, hoping to run into them. She took her time. Something was going on here, she could smell it, and her curiosity was twitching at the undercurrents like a cat watching the mousehole for movement. Her first circumnavigation yielded no Yulinh and no Yan. Other people were standing around, their own devotions obviously interrupted, whispering softly to one another and looking faintly puzzled, and one serene-looking girl of about her own age sat on a bench in the gardens, contemplating the fish meditatively. But there were no answers.

Until, on her second circumnavigation, now prowling restlessly in search of clues rather than her family, Khailin happened to come in line with the girl on the bench again. The girl rose to her feet as Khailin watched, took a few awkward steps to reach a paved pathway of one of the corridors leading through the Circles, and then collapsed in an ungraceful heap as her leg appeared to give way beneath her – almost precisely as an honour guard of acolytes had passed by that particular spot in advance of a man clad in a rich robe and looking like he walked in power.

Every instinct in Khailin quivered at the sight of him. Here was the embodiment of the knowledge she was seeking. It clung to him like an invisible cloak.

How she knew this she did not know, but she watched hungrily as the man bent to raise the crippled girl – for her foot was crippled, Khailin was close enough to see this clearly – and then guide her gently to a seat in the garden, allowing her to subside onto it. They exchanged a few words, very low, too low for Khailin to make out – and then he bowed lightly to the girl and signalled to his escort of acolytes, who moved forward once again. Khailin manoeuvred herself closer, and was in earshot when a young acolyte came hurrying up to the girl in the garden.

*That was Lihui, the Sage Lihui.*

Khailin's family was part of the inner Court. She knew of the death of one of the Nine Sages, and of his successor. Nobody had yet seen Lihui in the Palace; it was rumoured that he was waiting for the Autumn Court, at which he would be formally presented to the Emperor, to mark his official entry into society.

And he had spoken to this plainly dressed, crippled child.

What had he said to her? Who was she? How was it that she had caught the eye of one of the most learned and most powerful men in Syai – just by choosing the precisely correct moment to collapse on the path at his feet?

Khailin did not know who this girl was, the one on whom fortune had smiled here in the Great Temple under the eyes of the Gods.

But she would find out. She would make it her business to find out.

In the meantime, she turned and left the Third Circle, rejoining the buzzing throng in the Second where the passing of the Sage was still being loudly and gleefully discussed. Yan had a particular favourite among the lesser spirits of the Second Circle, an ugly little figure made of mud and rushes; it was at this shrine that Khailin hoped to find her missing family. The provenance of this deity, and thus his power and his ability to accede to prayer, appeared to be a mystery to everyone Khailin knew, including her own mother – but the hideous little effigy of the unknown spirit obviously had more worshippers than just Yan because his altar was always overflowing with offerings. Nobody ever saw anyone actually place anything on that altar, or admitted to it, which had made Khailin say to Yan once, baiting her little sister deliberately, that it was a distinct possibility that the little spirit simply worshipped himself. But Yulinh had thought the idea sacrilegious and had made her displeasure at such remarks plain.

Now Khailin wore a small smile as she went in search of the mystery spirit's shrine. She thought she might have at last – finally – found a use for the ugly little thing. She'd light an incense stick in front of the mystery God, and ask him to help her solve a mystery.

Help her find the crippled girl.


# Eight


Nhia mulled over her encounter at the Temple as she limped home. It was something she hugged close. She might have told little Tai, the daughter of the widow seamstress who lived a block up from Nhia's compound, because Tai had a knack for listening and for both making something a big thing and for keeping it in its place at the same time. Tai was young enough to be impressed and old enough to know why she was impressed. But Tai and her mother were at the Summer Palace, helping primp the Imperial ladies for the coming Court, and Nhia was stuck in the sweltering city enduring the season as best she could. She found herself a little surprised to find what a dearth of choices she had for a confidante; with Tai absent, it had narrowed down to . . . to herself. Herself and the things that people who gave her their instinctive trust gave her. But that was different – that was her being talked to, instead of doing the talking.

On the way home through the streets that shimmered with heat and swirled with dust-devils in the alleys, she allowed herself a brief bitter moment of self-pity. Would it have been different if she had been able-bodied? Would the miraculous cure of her gimpy foot also bring her a friend or two she could share her dreams with?

The day was far advanced; Nhia had spent too long at the Temple, even by her mother's admittedly biased measure.

'You're late,' Li said. 'Did you find what you sought at the Temple?'

She always asked that. As though there could be a different answer than the one she always got. Her tone, however, was a little pointed this time, leaving unspoken the barbed implication that whatever Nhia had been looking for there could have taken considerably less time.

'Yes, Mother,' said Nhia, gritting her teeth, coming up with the customary reply to the usual question, choosing not to respond to the undercurrents. 'The Temple was fulfilling.'

There could have been a different answer this time, but Nhia, for all that she ached to talk about what had happened, shied from discussing it with her mother. There would be too many questions, too many conclusions being jumped to, too much extrapolation and speculation, possibly far too much unwarranted excitement. That was not what she wanted, not right now.

Li, not knowing that there was anything beneath Nhia's terse and colourless reply, appeared to be content with the response that she had expected, and delved no deeper. She handed Nhia a pile of mending to be done while she got on with folding the washed, starched and ironed linen ready to go back to clients before starting on ironing the next batch. There could have been nothing more calculated to dampen Nhia's enthusiasm and initial euphoria. This was what she was. This was what she would always be. Daughter to the woman who did the laundry and the mending for the wealthy and the well-to-do. The *crippled* daughter of the woman who did the laundry. Someone who could help stir the sheets in the vats, her eyes smarting from the sharp bleach her mother used, or mend small tears in fine tablecloths or women's underwear. It wasn't even a craft or a thing of beauty, the sort of thing the much younger Tai could already accomplish with her own needle and the silk embroidery thread. Nhia was neat but her hands were not as skilled, nor her mind that way inclined. For her, the needle was neither more nor less than simple drudgery.

Her mother's two heavy black irons were set to heat on the heating plate laid over raked embers, and Li had already started on the chore of fiercely flattening recalcitrant starched linen sheets which haughty servants would soon be tucking onto patrician beds draped with brocaded hangings. Li ironed with a fixed snarl on her face, as though punishing the sheets for the pleasure stains with which they had arrived in her establishment – for all the laughter, and the whispers, and the joy with which they mocked her own solitary existence. Li was not widowed – there would have been some sort of honour in that, at least, and she could have held her head high just as Tai's mother, Rimshi, had done for years. It was worse, far worse. After Nhia's arrival, Li's husband had hung around only long enough to realize what his life would be like from then on – the desperate piety, the offerings, the talismans, the *ganshu* readers, the endless pilgrimages to the Temple, the souring, unrewarded faith – and then he had quietly left one day, simply melting away, taking a change of clothes and his yearwood and nothing else at all. The most bitter blow had been when the rumours had reached Li and her abandoned daughter that her errant husband had established residence on the outskirts of Linh-an, and was openly living with another woman with whom he had started another family. With whom he had a chubby, angelic son who was almost three before Li found out about his existence. A *perfect* child. Already able to toddle. Nearly ready to run.

A living reproach to the woman who had borne the crippled daughter.

For some reason it was the ironing that brought all this out in her. Most of the time Li was ready to blame the cruel Gods and deities for her lot in life – but when she ironed, through a queer chain of associations, it was all Nhia's fault – Nhia's fault that she had been born, that her mother had lived for nearly twelve years now without a man to warm her own bed, without the need to wash her own sheets clean of one night's pleasures and starch them into crisp cleanliness breathlessly awaiting the next. Nhia knew the pattern, if not the actual details behind it; she knew the lines that crept onto her mother's face, and knew very well just when it was prudent to make herself scarce.

Nhia found it hard to walk for very long or very far, but somehow there was enough strength in the twisted foot to operate her mother's pedal-powered linen delivery cart, and so that had evolved into her particular chore. Rimshi, with her Court connections, had helped Li get a lot of commissions from households associated with the Court. There was no obligation there, no duty, no *jin-shei* tie even – but Rimshi had not needed the weight of a *jin-shei* pledge to offer what help she could. But while summer was Rimshi's busiest time, preparing the Imperial women for the Autumn Court, summers were always a lean time for Li – simply because the actual Court removed to the Summer Palace and that meant no copious quantities of carelessly soiled laundry from the women's quarters and no substantial commissions or generous gratuities from those rich enough to be able to afford them without qualms. But there were other households, on the fringes, and it was mostly those to which Nhia pedalled with her cartload on those summer days.

She preferred to do her rounds in the early mornings or in the late, late afternoons when the sun was not beating down with quite as much fury as during the molten, white-hot middle of the day – but the summer heat was infinitely preferable to Li's icy and unspoken reproach which inevitably returned to roost in the rafters of their hot little room when Li laid the black irons in the fire. Seeing the instruments laid ready, Nhia deferred the mending, pausing only long enough to grab a broad peaked hat which hung over her face and shoulders and tie it securely under her chin with coarse ribbons before scuttling out of the house.

Her deliveries were marked on each individual bundle, on a piece of recycled paper with names and addresses in *jin-ashu* script. Li, despite being constantly torn between her devoted love of her daughter and constant dutiful prayers to unheeding

Gods to heal the child and the bitterness which held that same child responsible for her lonely, abandoned existence, had held up her share of that particular bargain. *Jin-ashu* was her daughter's heritage, it belonged to her as much as it belonged to every woman in Syai, and Li made sure that this, at least, Nhia was not cheated of.

The delivery cart was equipped with a small bell, and at its summons a household servant usually emerged from a side door at any given household to pick up the clean laundry, deliver the next batch of dirty laundry, and hand over Li's fee, which Nhia slipped into a waist pouch which she wore underneath her tunic. There were only five deliveries to be made that afternoon but Nhia could feel the sun sucking the energy out of her as she pedalled through the dusty streets, could feel rivulets of sweat snaking down along her spine and beading her forehead. Her hair felt damp and plastered down; her straw hat's snug presence on her head felt like a vice around her temples before she had gone halfway along her route. She passed a sherbet seller who had grabbed a shady spot underneath a courtyard archway and was loudly hawking his cool drinks, but she had spent all her spare coins at the Temple that morning and it was more than her life was worth to hazard any of Li's hard-earned fee money on such indulgences. A sherbet paid for in the coin of Li's acid accusations of profligacy on Nhia's return home was entirely too expensive for Nhia to contemplate. So she just allowed her mind to cool itself on the thought of the sherbet and pedalled on, resigned, to fulfil her chores.

The household of Cheleh, the Court Chronicler, was the last stop on her list. The Chronicler lived in a brick pagoda house of two storeys with a bright red tile roof. It was surrounded by a low wall, with the *hacha-ashu* symbols for prosperity and happiness – common symbols even those unlearned in the script could recognize – painted on the pillars of the gateway which led through it into the Chronicler's leafy yard, shaded by a number of magnolia trees. The temperature dropped perceptibly as Nhia drove her cart through this archway and around to the back of the house, riding in the shade of the trees. There even seemed to be a breath of wind here. She paused for a moment, breathing deeply, taking the time to remove her hat and mop her forehead and temples with her sleeve, feeling reprieved enough to look up at the leafy canopy curled protectively around her, between her and the implacable sun, and smile.


Impatient at the sedan chair bearer's pace, hot and stifled in the curtained enclosure she shared with her mother and docile younger sister, Khailin's mood was dangerously volatile as the chair approached home. The Temple trip had been augmented by a brief and unscheduled stopover at the hated ritual baths, which had done little to improve Khailin's disposition, and the long, hot, stuffy trip home had only served to bring her temper from what had been a low simmer up to a definite readiness to boil explosively at the least provocation. Her skin felt greasy from the oils and balms from the bath, her pores clogged and unable to breathe, her clothes sliding unpleasantly on skin slick from sweat and ointment. Apparently unconcerned with such physical discomforts, Yulinh was dozing, reclined into the cushions in the back of the chair; Yan was sitting gracelessly with her legs crossed in an indecorous manner, playing with a couple of puppets in her lap. Yan was entirely too much like a puppet herself, Khailin thought with a savage little frown. She did what whoever was pulling her strings wanted done; she was the perfect child, obedient, respectful, and completely lacking in any initiative or curiosity.

Khailin had peered out of the sedan chair's curtains just as the bearers had started to turn into the courtyard, and caught a glimpse of the painted symbol on the left-hand pillar of the gate. *Happiness*. Indeed. Her current rather sour mood saw that sign only as a vague mockery today.

She caught a glimpse of a figure on a pedal cart moving slowly away under the trees at the back of the courtyard, and her eyes narrowed a little at the sight of the cart's occupant. For a moment it could have been anybody, any one of a thousand thin Linh-an waifs, clad in homespun, features shaded by a huge straw hat. But even as the sedan turned and started to bear Khailin out of sight of the cart and the figure on it, even as she clutched at the sedan chair's curtains and peered intently at the disappearing cart, the girl on it fumbled under her chin and lifted off her hat, raising her face to the trees, giving Khailin one brief but adequate glimpse of the features she had committed to memory earlier that day at the Temple.

Could it really be this easy?

The little ugly God in the Second Circle was going to have a good fat offering the next time Khailin found herself at the Temple, if indeed this was the same child who had spoken with the Sage Lihui. Khailin scrabbled out of the chair almost before the bearers set it down, drawing a lazy reproof from her somnolent mother.

'Khailin, when are you going to learn that a lady –'

'I'm sorry, Mother,' Khailin said in swift, automatic and thoroughly meaningless apology, and raced into the house.

The thick walls of the pagoda made the air inside soothingly cool after the hot streets, but Khailin didn't stop to enjoy the change. She skidded around the entrance hall and past the curved staircase leading up to the second floor, and through the door under the stairs, carefully painted to make it practically invisible in the wall, into the back hallway and the servants' quarters. A woman bearing a tray with delicate porcelain cups on it danced out of Khailin's way, whisking the tray aside before Khailin smashed into it. A half-closed door further along the corridor stood ajar, giving Khailin a glimpse of a noisy, crowded kitchen. She nearly ran down another servant, this one bearing a neat bundle of laundry in a white linen bag. At the end of the corridor, a lacquered red door led outside – the back door for deliveries and for the servants' quarters, the door which opened out into the back courtyard. Khailin flung it open, but emerged with a degree of calculated, stately slowness, not wanting to erupt outside looking like she was chasing demons. She was in time to see the back of the cart bouncing away around the corner of the house, with the girl, now wearing her hat again, bent over the steering bar. Seeing just the narrow childish back topped by that gigantic hat like some sort of exotic mushroom . . . it was hard to be certain . . . but a sure instinct of recognition made Khailin smile to herself.

It was a simple matter after that to find out who the girl was and what she was doing at Cheleh's house. Less than four hours had passed since Khailin had first set eyes on her in the Temple.

She made a mental note to find out just *who* the little ugly deity was.

# Nine

'We are here because of *jin-shei*,' Rimshi said to Tai as they sat up late, talking, on the night that Antian's gift and invitation had arrived from the Little Empress.

'I know,' Tai said, reaching with delight for one of her favourite fairy tales, the one that had been lived, had been real. 'You were *jin-shei-bao* to one of the concubines, and she made the rest of them come to you for their Court gowns . . .' Tai had heard the story many times before but never tired of hearing about it – the story of Xien, her mother's friend and *jin-shei* sister, the only child of a poverty-stricken family from the warrens of Linh-an whose bewitching dark green eyes and lotus-blossom skin Rimshi had been instrumental in bringing to the notice of the Imperial agents, and who had been raised to the Imperial Court to be the Emperor's own love. Xien had never borne the Emperor any children, but she had been a beloved companion for years before a wasting disease took her when she was far too young. The Emperor had mourned her, and the Court had missed her; but by the time she was gone Rimshi, the companion of Xien's childhood and her *jin-shei-bao*, was an essential without whose lavish and meticulous adornments on their garb the ladies of the Court felt incomplete and underdressed.

Now Tai had followed in her mother's footsteps and had gained a sister in the Imperial Court of Syai – but a sister of far higher lineage than Rimshi had ever aspired to.

Tai knew about *jin-shei*, the theory and the protocol of it, but now it had suddenly leaped off the pages written in neat rows of *jin-ashu*, had taken a real physical shape from the ethereal words of her mother's early stories. It was real now, it was hers. She had asked, in feverish excitement, what she had to do in response to the note the Little Empress had sent with her gift of the red leather journal, and Rimshi had instructed her to send a return message bearing the same words. It was Rimshi herself who took this reply back to the Palace, that same evening, and Antian had received it from her hand with a smile.

'Tell her that I will look for her in the gardens tomorrow,' she had said.

'I will, Little Empress,' Rimshi said, bowing.

It was sealed, thus. Tai had been too keyed up to even think about going to bed, so Rimshi had made them both some green tea and they sat up well past Tai's usual bedtime, talking about the magical day.

'How do I talk to her? What do I call her?' Tai had been in and out of this Court for years, tagging at Rimshi's heels – but it had always been as someone who was there as an adjunct to somebody else. Someone whom the Court found necessary. A child, who ought to be invisible, addressing nobody and making sure that she was not observed by anyone long enough to *be* addressed. Now, it would be different . . . or so Tai imagined. In all the tumult she had forgotten that she knew how to talk to this Princess, that she had done so already on the lost little balcony that morning.

'She will not wish you to be too formal with her, now that you are her *jin-shei*,' Rimshi said. 'She wanted a sister and a companion, not a servant or a slave. She has enough attendants; she wants a friend.'

'But I don't know . . .'

'Hush, Tai-*ban*. You have to sleep this night. It will come right in the morning. This is the beginning, that is all – the *liu-kala* of your first *jin-shei* bond. It is barely born, in its first age, it cannot be expected to do all and know all.'

'But it isn't *her* first, is it?' Tai asked.

'I do not know; this is something that you will find out. This is how the circle grows – if she has other sisters in *jin-shei* she will tell you about them. They then may become your own, through her, if you choose to pledge with them – or they will remain your *jin-shei-bao* by proxy, a sister of a sister. But that is something that lies between you and your *jin-shei-bao* and concerns nobody else at all. I know of this one, now, because I am your mother, and it is still my task to know – but once you are of age, and that is not too many years in the future, this is something that is yours and yours alone. I probably will not know who your *jin-shei* sisters are when you are eighteen or twenty. I may not even know how many there are in your circle. And that is the right and proper way.'

'Eighteen?' Tai said, settling back into her pillow, suddenly sleepy. 'That won't be for a long time.'

Rimshi stood over her, smiling, for a long time after she had fallen asleep, her dark hair spilled over the pillow. But her eyes were too bright, and the smile was a little sad; a whole tangle of emotions were filling Rimshi's mind and heart. She was proud that Tai had been chosen for a tie so deep while still so young – and by no less a personage than the Little Empress herself. But there was also a fear, the fear born of her own past. The story she had never told Tai, who had idolized her father and was still mourning his loss.

Rimshi had been sixteen when Tsexai had begun to court her; he had done it so subtly, so deftly, that she had not even realized that she was falling in love until it was done, and sealed, and irrevocable. And then Meilin had come to her, and Rimshi had known from the expression on her face that she had come with a hard thing to say. And it had been hard. It had almost been more than Rimshi could bear.

'Tsexai . . . his family owns a business like to our own,' Meilin had said. 'So do two other families, but none have heirs of marriageable age. Like me. Like him. My family is all set to approach his, to ask for his hand, for me. Rimshi, if this does not happen, my family is going to be ruined – we are the smallest of the silk mills, and we cannot survive – and it is up to me – and I have to do this, this marriage has to happen. I know he wants to wed you. Has he approached you yet?'

Rimshi had shaken her head mutely.

'Then if he does . . . when he does . . . will you refuse him? I know what I ask, but I ask it for my family, for my ancestors. I'm sorry, Rimshi, I'm sorry, but I am asking you, in the name of *jin-shei* – I have no choice.'

And neither had Rimshi.

Tsexai had asked; Rimshi had refused the marriage token; Tsexai had married Meilin. They were, as far as Rimshi knew, happy together – they had a large family, and the combined business of both families was thriving.

For a long time Rimshi had mourned, and when Gan had come for her she had accepted him, although he was much older than her and she was not in love with him. But he had been a good man, a caring husband, and a doting father for Tai, their only daughter.

When Gan had died, Rimshi had honestly mourned him – and it had taken Tai a year to smile again.

*What will* jin-shei *give you, my daughter? What will it ask of you?*

From Rimshi it had taken joy, but it had returned contentment, and a good life. And a daughter she loved fiercely. A daughter she would never have had with Tsexai. Oh, children, probably – but not Tai, not the Tai with whom the Gods in Cahan had graced Rimshi's life.

She gazed on that daughter now with a strange premonitory dread, a heavy, sure knowledge that Tai's fragile shoulders would have to bear the responsibilities of an Empire before this particular *jin-shei* binding was played out to its end. She had said to Tai that she was only just stepping out on this path, that the *jin-shei* was in its infancy, and this was true – she would only wake to its first morning on the next day. But where, oh where, was it taking her?

Tai woke early, fretful, on the next morning. Her mother was still asleep on her matting, mouth slightly open, revealing the gap in her teeth. It was far too early for breakfast, it was barely dawn outside, the sky still dark and glimmering with stars. But Tai knew that she would not sleep again – she was fully awake, and all that this day was still to bring was quivering in her already. She got dressed very quietly, trying not to disturb her mother, thrust her feet into her sandals and slipped out of the room. She had meant to go into the garden for a while, but found herself angling for the balcony instead, the one where she had met with Antian on another early morning. For the first time since she had started spending her summers here in the Summer Palace Tai saw the sun rise over the mountains, painting distant snowy peaks first pale pink and then gold as the orb of the sun rose higher and spilled down the steep mountainsides. She watched the stars going out over her head, one by one, smaller and more fragile spirits extinguished by the blaze of the royal sun in the heavens. It was a thing of beauty and sadness and immense expectation, like waiting for something to be born.

She had brought her journal along, the new red one that Antian had sent her, and sat down on the cold stone slabs of the terrace which the sun hadn't warmed yet, with the journal in her lap, her little inkpot beside her, her *jin-ashu* letters as tiny and neat and meticulous as her embroidery.

*Saw the sun rise. Mother talked about* liu-kala *last night, and she was right, I feel something new beginning all around me. But nothing begins except that something else has ended, and I wonder what has ended for me this day. Like one of the stars in the sky this morning, I am gone – gone, but there is something else now where that which I was used to be – something greater than I was. Just like the stars vanish into the morning, and the sun appears, and all is light.*

'I didn't think I'd find you here so early,' a soft voice interrupted her thoughts.

Tai's head came up. It was Antian, her hair in two plain long plaits again, looking much younger than her fourteen years, smiling.

'I came because you told me mornings were beautiful here too,' Tai said. 'And . . . I could not sleep.'

'I was eager for the day, too,' said Antian. She inclined her head a fraction at the red book Tai held, her smile broadening. 'I am glad to see it is useful.'

'It is beautiful,' Tai said, her fingers caressing the soft leather where they held the notebook. 'I have never owned anything so precious.'

'Then I will have to see that you get another just like it when you finish it,' said Antian, sounding genuinely delighted. 'And then another, every year, my gift. Perhaps you'll share some of its contents with me some time.'

'Thank you,' whispered Tai. It was not a specific thanks she was expressing, not just for the notebook or the promise of its eternal replenishment; she was thanking Antian for opening the world to her a little, for sharing a wider sphere than Tai could ever have aspired to on her own.

Antian understood, and reached out a hand. 'Walk with me,' she said.

Tai closed the journal notebook, folded the lid down firmly onto her inkpot, tucked everything into a pocket of her tunic, and reached out her own trembling fingers. Antian took her hand, tucked it under her arm, and led the way. Side by side like that, with the same dark hair braided in the same long plaits with Tai's only a little more untidy than Antian's, they really did look like sisters. Real sisters, sharing the same blood and kin.

*But this is better*, thought Tai, her heart beating very fast. *We are jin-shei. We are sisters of the heart.*

They left the balcony arm in arm and crossed over into the garden where the butterflies were waking, the flowers were beginning to open and the air was heady with scent. For the time being they did not talk; they exchanged a word here and there, when one of them would point to a hummingbird or a bumble-bee as if neither had seen them before and whisper, 'Look!' For the time being, that was enough. They had to learn to share time, to meld two different lives which had been running in two different streams until last night and had now merged into something bigger, deeper, stronger.

'Look,' said Tai, yet again, pointing to something that had caught her eye in the garden. But she was also pointing at the pillars of the shaded cloister where the garden merged into the first open pavilions of the Summer Palace, and as she pointed a thin, fox-faced girl maybe a year or so younger than Antian peeled her back off a pillar on which she had been leaning, gave the two walking girls in the garden a smouldering look, and turned away sharply as though she had been stung by the sight of them.

Tai snatched her arm back, embarrassed. The girl had been wearing turquoise silk, and her hair was dressed formally, with silk flowers and pearls.

'Who was that?' she asked, cowed. The look that had whipped her had not been friendly.

'That?' Antian said, smiling sadly. 'That was my sister. My angry sister. That is Liudan.'

But the look on Liudan's face had not been anger. It had been a recoil born of fear. And pain. And loss.

'From mother's arms to cradles
to cribs we grow, and rise
to our feet and walk; and when they
    lay the first milk tooth
of Lan into a silk cloth where a fond mother
keeps it always
we are no longer babes.'

Qiu-Lin, Year 5 of the Cloud Emperor

# One

*It is very quiet out there tonight.*

Tai paused, lifting her brush from the page of her journal, listening to the silence.

This was the first year that she had been in the Summer Palace without her mother – Rimshi had developed a debilitating cough and chest infection over the previous winter, and her physician, the healer Szewan who attended the women of the Imperial Court and who had been sent to take care of Rimshi by the Empress Yehonaia herself, had counselled against travel. But this was the second year of *jin-shei* between Tai and Antian, the Little Empress, and Tai had been invited along in her own right as a guest of the Court. She had not been given the quarters she and her mother usually occupied, out on the fringes of the Palace, in the outer courts. She had a room to herself this summer, close to Antian's own suite – a room with a window that looked out into the garden, a room full of billowing curtains and soft cushions. There was even a servant who left a beaker of iced tea in the room every morning, when the heat came, as she did in all the women's chambers.

Tai felt awkward accepting all this. She also felt isolated. That she was *jin-shei* to Antian was an open secret in the Court – but there were times that the hallowed precepts of *jin-shei* did clash with the more traditional strictures of status and class, and many of the inhabitants of the plush women's wing in the Palace did not much like it that a commoner was invited to live amongst them. Antian was of age now, however; Tai had been a guest at the Little Empress's Xat-Wau ceremony only that spring, and was witness to

69

Antian's grandmother, the old and fragile Dowager Empress, placing the red lacquered hairpin through Antian's lustrous piled-up black hair. Antian was an adult, according to Syai custom. She was also a senior member of the Imperial household, with her own personal court which was now her responsibility. She had asked Tai to the Summer Palace, and the other women had to at least be polite.

Or that was the theory of it. Tai had learned to tell the difference between three very specific kinds of women in the Court where she was concerned. There were those who were genuinely pleasant, and offered a smile or a kind word in passing even when Tai was not accompanied by Antian and they felt constrained to be polite in the presence of Tai's powerful friend and protector.

There were the ones who would pass Tai in silence if they came upon her alone, but smiled and fawned upon her when she was in Antian's company; Tai soon learned to recognize a smile that did not reach the eyes and the touch of cold, reluctant fingers.

And then there was Liudan.

In the two years of her *jin-shei* tie to Antian, Tai had completely failed to get anything but cold hostility from Antian's sister Liudan. It had started on the very first day of the *jin-shei*, when she and Antian had been walking in the very gardens that her room now gazed out into, when she had pointed at a flower and seen Liudan's recoil from her.

*That was my sister. My angry sister.*

Antian had explained about Liudan, later.

'I was only two when she was born,' Antian had said, 'but my mother was the Empress and everyone spoiled me. Every concubine's child is taken to belong to the Empress, of course, but when Liudan was born, Cai – that's her mother – did not wish to give her up to be raised by a wet-nurse and then the Court.'

'Which one is Cai? Have I met her?' Tai had asked.

'No,' Antian had said, shaking her head. 'Cai is dead. She was at the Court for only a few years, but she lived her life like a comet.'

'Where did she come from?'

'She was a daughter of a poor farmer, up in the miserable rocks and stones of the north country. He could not afford to keep her – she was the ninth child in the family, the sixth daughter – and so he took her and two more of his daughters and brought them to

Linh-an, and sold them into concubinage. Cai was the only one who made the Imperial Court.'

'What of her sisters?' Tai had asked, her eyes wide.

'Who knows? Cai never did, or at least never spoke of them after to anyone here in the Court.'

'So what happened?' Tai had asked, held rapt by the sorrow she could sense between the lines of this tale, by the tendrils with which this sorrow had snared Liudan herself.

'She might have been happy,' Antian had said. 'I don't know, I was only a child. Cai caught the Emperor's eye quickly enough, but rumour had it not for long. She did bear him a daughter, though. One of only three daughters, including me, that he sired on his women. And we were all more or less born at the same time, too – there is just over a year between me and the next daughter, and then another year between her and Liudan. She's the youngest of the female line. The rest, well, his line runs to boys. His sons, now, range from their twenties to babes in arms.'

Tai was old enough to do the numbers on this. Inheritance went through the female line in Syai; the Emperor might rule the land, being male and having that power vested in him, but he came into his power through the woman he had married and who had been his path to the throne, and his legacy rested in the daughters he had sired. So the Emperor had secured his succession, and then provided a couple of spare heirs to the Empire, two other daughters, in case anything happened to the Little Empress. The boys would be married off well, and were of no further importance.

But Liudan was the Second Spare, born of a mother who, once her duty was done, became a shadow in the Court, no longer noticed, no longer needed, supplanted by other women in the Emperor's retinue of concubines. The only thing of value Cai would have had would have been her child . . . but Tai had extrapolated from Antian's earlier words. Cai had not wished to let others raise her daughter – and perhaps, if she had borne a son, she would have been allowed to keep the child and rear him. But she had borne a potential heir – one twice removed from the throne, to be sure, but a potential heir nonetheless – and the child was taken away from her not long after it was born.

'She must have been very lonely,' Tai had said.

'She had two of us she grew up with,' Antian had said, misunderstanding and applying Tai's words to Liudan, of whom she had just been speaking.

'I meant Cai,' Tai had said. 'What happened to her after Liudan was born? When did she die?'

'I don't really know,' Antian had said thoughtfully. 'I do know they said that she was pregnant again less than a year after Liudan was born – but after that, I don't know. It may be that it was thus she died – in childbirth – her and the babe both because when she disappeared from the Court there was no child left in her wake that I know of, male or female. But then there were the rumours.'

'Of what?'

'She was in some sort of disgrace,' Antian had said. 'I don't recall what, but she had done something that reflected badly on her. And that meant on Liudan, too, on her child.'

And Tai had suddenly understood Liudan's recoil in the garden. 'She was the one left behind, wasn't she?' Tai had whispered. 'The child of the erring one. Without friends. Except you, Antian. Except you.'

Antian had looked at her with lustrous dark eyes. 'You see? You always understand. Yes, she grew up as the Third Princess, the youngest in protocol, the last in line, the not-quite-needed. And her mother had fallen from grace, and nobody wanted any part of her other than her continued existence.'

'And she was afraid, wasn't she? That morning in the garden, she was afraid that she would be the price of my coming into your life. She'd be abandoned if you chose another companion.'

'Oh, she was never a *companion* – not like that – she is my sister.'

'Is she mine, now, too?'

'No, the *jin-shei* bond doesn't mean you have to take Liudan on,' Antian had said with a smile. 'Not like that. She is my blood-sister, and that makes it different from the *jin-shei* bond. And she is wrong, in that I am not going to abandon her just because I have found a *jin-shei-bao* to share my heart with. But she has always felt the edge of the Court turned at her, and she has always been angry at the world. And she has grown up alone, for all that these halls are teeming with brothers, sisters, and women who had been her mother's companions.'

'She is very pretty,' Tai had said.

72

'So was Cai,' Antian had said. 'I don't remember her, not really – but there is a portrait that the Emperor had done, on ivory – the miniature stands in the Palace back in Linh-an. I'll show you some time. She was very beautiful.'

'It was a pity she was not loved,' Tai had said.

Antian had given her a strange look. 'Yes,' she had said slowly. 'It was a pity.'

It was the custom of the Court that one of the heirs always had to stay behind in Linh-an when the rest of the Court came away to the Summer Palace – just in case of some calamity. In the year that Tai and Antian entered into *jin-shei*, the third sister, Second Princess Oylian, had been the one to have remained in the sweltering capital city over that long hot summer. The year after that it had been Antian herself. This third summer it was Liudan's turn – and Tai, despite a guilty cast to her sense of relief, was not entirely unhappy that she did not have the angry Third Princess watching her and Antian together with smouldering, jealous eyes. Her feelings for Liudan ran the gamut from pity to deep resentment that she should be the focus of so much undeserved hatred for no better reason than that she was Antian's chosen companion.

Second Princess Oylian was a gentle, pliant, pleasant girl who drifted through life – she was a stream of water which flowed around obstacles rather than try and shift them.

'The worst thing that could ever happen to Oylian and to Syai,' Antian had said to Tai once in a low whisper one early morning out on their balcony on the side of the mountain, 'would be for her to ever become Empress. Whoever her Emperor proved to be, he could make her do whatever he said and she would do it to keep the peace. She was born to a family, not an Empire.'

But the Second Princess would smile at Tai, even if she didn't have much to say to her. Liudan would simply sweep past and ignore her whenever she could. Tai was the danger – Tai was, like Liudan's own mother had been, of common stock, only one step removed from Liudan's own now-high station, a reminder of what she could easily have been if she had not been born royal. The Third Princess was a complex mixture of insecurities – left adrift because she was the second spare heiress and therefore less urgently needed than Oylian, left alone because of her mother's fall from grace for reasons that even Liudan herself did not really understand, afraid of the thin veneer that separated her royalty from the land-grubbing poverty from which her mother's family had come. Liudan wanted the royalty, needed it as a shield against all kinds of terrors – and it was a thin shield, barely there. She was only Third Princess, after all.

But this summer, the summer that Antian had invited Tai up to the Summer Palace as her guest, Liudan was mercifully absent, back in Linh-an, suffering the summer heat in the Imperial Palace – and probably doing it with better grace than the other two would ever have done because at least it was a signifier of her status, an indication that she was important enough in the hierarchy to be preserved and sheltered against the potential of disaster. And her absence meant that Antian and Tai could laugh more freely, more often, without waiting for Liudan's brooding presence to cut the laughter short when they met her eyes.

In a way, though, Liudan's hostility was what made Tai aware of her own status in this Court – although Liudan's presence was uncomfortable, she and Tai were two points of the same star, both sisters to Antian after a fashion, balancing one another. Without the unconcealed hostility of that one amongst all the Imperial women, it was somehow harder for Tai to winnow the genuine from the sycophant in the rest of the Imperial royal women in the Summer Palace. It was as if, with Liudan there, Tai was on her guard against Liudan alone. With her gone, Tai was on her guard against everybody else.

But she was here, now, in the royal quarters, bent over her journal by candlelight even while the sky lightened in the east. She and Antian were to meet at their balcony that morning, later, but Tai had woken early, uncomfortable about something, not sure what had woken her – until she had picked up her inkwell and her brush and her journal and it had come into focus for her.

*It is very quiet out there tonight.*

She stared at the line she had written down, and became preternaturally aware of the stillness that had broken through the depths of sleep to wake her, the silence that surrounded her, the world holding its breath. She thought she heard, far away in a kennel somewhere, the despondent howl of a trapped dog, but even that was there and gone almost before she had had a chance to identify the sound. The silence was absolute.

And then the mountain shuddered, and crumbled.

# Two

In less time than it took to blink, silence was a memory. Masonry groaned; things skittered across the surface of the lacquered table, or fell to the ground, leaving the floor strewn with debris. Above it all there was an indescribable sound that was half heard and half absorbed directly through bone and muscle – the roar of wounded stone.

Instinct had taken over in the first moment of terror, and Tai had streaked out of her room and into the garden, out under an open sky. She felt the ground shake under the soles of her bare feet, staggered to keep her balance, lost the battle, fell sideways into a bed of swaying flowers still closed in the pearly pre-dawn grey darkness. Before Tai's horrified eyes the tiered Summer Palace folded into itself as though it had been made of sticks and leaves, walls falling inward, tiles falling in slow motion and tumbling end over end before shattering into dust, columns snapping in two or falling sideways and knocking out the next column in line, collapsing them in turn like dominoes. Graceful arched windows and doorways became piles of broken brick and crumbs of plaster; wooden window frames snapped like matchsticks. Glass was a precious thing and not often found outside the Imperial Palaces, and even there rare and used sparingly; now, with the wooden frames bending and breaking, the night was alive with the eerie sound of breaking glass, like fairy chimes.

A tree groaned and began to fall over, in slow motion, pulling its old roots out of the ground.

Lifting her eyes to the top of the mountain whose peak had always towered above the Summer Palace, Tai became aware with a shock that the peak had vanished. It was partly the huge rocks from the disintegrating mountainside that had helped wreak this havoc – smashing down on top of buildings, flattening structures in their path, rolling onward in destructive fury. One had levelled a fountain in the gardens, and the spilled water, still dark as the night it reflected, saturated the flowerbeds and flowed into the courtyards whose cobbles looked as though they had been ploughed.

Somewhere in the ruins of the Palace a spark started, then a fire. Then another. And another. Columns of smoke rose into the sky; the air tasted acrid with dust and ashes and fear.

When the noise of tumbling rocks and crashing buildings had subsided at last, leaving an echo ringing in Tai's ears, she began hearing another sound – human voices, groaning, screaming, weeping. She became aware that she was herself uttering small whimpering sounds. Curled up in the middle of a once-graceful flowerbed, now sodden and blighted out in the shattered gardens, she was barefoot, an almost translucent nightrobe all that she wore – but she was whole, and unharmed, and still clutching the red leather-bound journal that had been Antian's gift.

Those who had been deeper into the warren of the Palace and had no way to get out . . . those who had not woken to the silence before the wrath of the Gods . . . those who had tried to run but had not made it out fast enough . . .

They were all still in there.

In the wreck of the Summer Palace.

In the piles of still settling dust and rubble, under the weight of a mountain.

*Antian.*


The sky was lightening in the east, and dawn crept over the ruined Palace, brighter, faster now that the mountainside which had reared up against the eastern sky was gone.

Dawn. Early morning.

The balcony on the mountain.

Her rigid fingers wrapped tightly around the red book that had been Antian's gift, Tai scrambled to her feet and stood, indecisive, torn, in the shattered garden. Her nightrobe was streaked with mud, her feet and her face smeared with mud and with dust; she had an urgent need to go and do something – help those buried in the rubble, dig with bare hands until she found someone whom she could haul out of the wreckage – and knew that the only one she wanted to find was Antian, the Little Empress, lost somewhere in this chaos. And unable to move – because if she ran to the Palace Antian could be out on the balcony, and if she chose the balcony Antian might die buried under the weight of the broken Palace.

She saw someone running towards the buildings, a weeping servant, followed by another who clutched an awkwardly bent arm and had a face smeared with blood. It might have been this that decided Tai. There would be others coming to the Palace soon – not everything had collapsed, surely, and there had to be people who could move, who could help – but nobody else knew that Antian was going to the balcony that morning. If she was there, then nobody knew to go to her aid.

She turned, and ran.

Somehow the gate that led to the outer balcony was still intact – its capstone in place, the wall surrounding it deceptively innocent and peaceful in the early morning light. But taking a step through it, and looking up, Tai realized for the first time the extent of the catastrophe that had touched the Summer Palace that day.

The mountain above the Palace wore a different shape. Half of it was gone, vanished. The mountain peak had disintegrated, and a lot of it had fallen down into the buildings and the courtyards of the Palace. The rest of the mountainside had sheared off in a layer of stone and mud and simply slid down the slope, taking a large chunk of the Palace with it.

The lacy pattern of open balconies hanging over the river that flowed golden when the sun was setting was no more. The mountain's face was a gaping wound of broken balustrades, platforms teetering over nothing, piles of shattered stone a long way below, all the way down to the river. Some balconies had been ripped off completely, and gaping holes in the walls opened from the Palace courts directly out into the abyss. Others were hanging on by a narrow ledge only a single flagstone wide, or by part of a balustrade. Yet others were crazy, broken, multi-levelled wrecks with holes where flagstones had smashed or been ripped in half, looking as though they were being observed with a mirror put together from glass shards, each reflecting a different angle, different aspect.

Tai stood at the edge of this devastation, eyes wide with shock. If Antian had been out here . . .

She tried calling, but her voice seemed to have died in her throat, and all that came out was a soft wail. But the sound seemed to have triggered some response, for the broken stones sighed and whimpered and a familiar but very weak voice replied.

'Who is there?'

Tai's first reaction was a rush of relief, a fierce joy, the sheer euphoria of hearing that voice at all. And then that soft voice dropped, fading into almost a whisper. '*Help me.*'

*No!* screamed Tai's mind. But she stifled it, tried to cling to the happiness she had felt a bare moment before, batted at the sudden rush of tears with the back of her hand. Almost unwillingly, not wanting to see what lay beyond the ruined balcony, not wanting to know the inevitable, Tai crept carefully forward towards the edge, peering over.

Just out of arm's reach, on a ledge of broken flagstone caught on a rocky protrusion on the mountainside, lay Antian, the Little Empress. One of her long braids had curled on her breast in a long black rope, like a living thing that had come to comfort her; the other had slipped down her shoulder and now hung over the edge of her resting place, swinging out into the chasm below her. She held a hand – always graceful, still graceful! – to her side in a fragile kind of way, as though she was trying to staunch a wound with no strength left to do it with, and indeed there was a dark stain that was spreading into her robe underneath her fingers. Her hand was smeared with red; so was her face, with a gash on her forehead oozing a thin stream of blood into the corner of her eye and down her temple and another graze red and bleeding along the line of her jaw. One of her legs seemed bent at an unnatural angle.

But her eyes were lucid, and she tried to smile when Tai's face appeared over the edge of the ruin above her.

'Don't move,' Tai said, her voice catching a little. 'I'll go get help.'

'Wait . . .'

But Tai was already gone. There had been something about Antian that she could hardly bear to watch – a kind of brightness, an aura that was more than just the first fingers of the dawn's golden glow, an otherworldly light that told her that Antian had already taken that first irrevocable step into the world beyond, the world of the Immortals.

Tai skidded into the courtyards, panting, her eyes wild, her feet bleeding from scratches and gashes delivered by the broken cobblestones she had stumbled over in her haste. There were people in the courtyards now, but only a few of them were actually moving about or doing something constructive. Bodies were laid out in the garden, and a handful of bloodied survivors had been taken to a sheltered area where one or two servants, themselves bandaged and bleeding from scratches or hobbling on makeshift crutches, tried to tend to them. Someone was crying weakly for water. Somebody else was weeping, a curiously steady sound, as though she did not know how to stop.

A young woman in a white robe streaked with dust and blood was leaning over a woman's body, gently probing with long fingers, but even as Tai watched she straightened with a sigh, closing her eyes. Her expression told it all.

Her face was familiar, underneath its coating of grime, and Tai fought her own panic and fear to dredge the name from her memory – this was someone who could be useful – who was it – she *knew* her, it was precisely the person she had come looking for . . .

*Yuet*. The name swam into her mind, followed by another – Szewan – the healer woman who had tended Tai's mother that spring. Yuet had tagged at Szewan's heels. Yuet was the healer's apprentice.

Szewan was in Linh-an. Yuet was here. Yuet was the healer.

Tai ran to the older girl and snatched at the sleeve of her robe.

'Come! Oh, you must come! It's Antian – it's the Little Empress – she needs your help.'

The young healer turned her head, blinked in Tai's direction for a moment, the words not sinking in. Then, as she parsed the sentence, as she realized what had just been said, she sucked in her breath.

'Is she alive?'

'Yes. *Yes!* Hurry!'

Yuet drew a shaking hand across her forehead. 'The Gods be thanked for that, at least!' She showed no sign of having recognized Tai, although they had met several times during the spring, but right now Yuet would have been hard put to recognize her own mother. All she could see was the death all around her, the death written in the broken women they were scrambling to dig out of the ruins, the despair written in the faces of those who had come to the call for help, themselves bruised, cut, bleeding. The death written in the toppled mountain that had annihilated everything.

The Emperor and the Empress were both dead. The rescuers digging in the rubble of the Palace knew that much already. Oylian, the Second Princess, they had not found yet – and that could not be a good sign. And now, this . . .

'Take me to her,' Yuet said, turning away from the body at her feet and starting out towards the ruined Palace.

'This way!' Tai, who had not let go of her sleeve, tugged her away and across the gardens.

Yuet stopped, confused. 'Where is the Little Empress?'

'She was on one of the balconies . . . out on the mountain.'

What little colour was left in Yuet's cheeks drained away. 'What in the name of Cahan was she doing there? When this was all coming down?'

'We were supposed to meet at the balcony this morning.' Tai pulled at Yuet's arm. 'Hurry!'

Yuet followed, frowning, until her eyes suddenly lit briefly with recognition. 'You're from Linh-an, you're her *jin-shei-bao*.'

'Hurry.' Tai seemed to have forgotten every other word she ever knew. All that was beating in her heart, in her blood, in her mind, was *hurry*. The broken doll on the ledge below the balcony, that was just the shell of Antian – but if they didn't hurryhurry*hurry* the shell would melt and shred in the mountain winds like a cloud and disappear for ever . . . and this was Antian, the Princess who laughed, who cared, who loved, who would be Empress one day . . .

Yuet had the presence of mind to snag a relatively able-bodied male servant on their way to the balcony, surmising – rightly – that Antian would have to be extracted out of some unspeakable wreckage before she could be helped. But that hadn't prepared her for the devastation of the mountainside when the three of them finally emerged onto what was left of the little balcony. Yuet gasped, her hand going to her throat.

'She survived *this*?' Yuet said breathlessly.

Tai had run to the edge of the chasm. 'Antian? Antian, I'm here. I brought help.'

The manservant reached out and scooped the struggling Tai out of harm's way, and peered carefully over the edge himself.

'We would need rope, I think,' he said.

'There is no time for that now.' Yuet had approached and was

80

gauging the distance between herself and her patient. 'I think there is space enough. Lower me down, and then go fetch a rope and another pair of hands to help you. This will need doing gently. Dear sweet Cahan, she is still alive. Princess? I am coming down to you.'

Antian whispered something, very softly, and Tai thought she heard, *No, it is too dangerous*. But Yuet had already grasped the manservant's wrists with her hands, and he had wrapped his own fingers around her wrists and was trying to judge the most stable spot to lower her down on.

'I don't think there's a good place,' Yuet said at last. 'There's no time, there's no *time*! Lower me down there and go get help!'

'Yes, *sai'an*.' He grasped her wrists firmly and the corded muscles in his arms knotted as he lowered her slowly, gently, down to where Antian lay. Yuet felt her feet touch something solid, then it lurched beneath her heel. She gasped.

'Wait!'

'I won't let go, *sai'an*,' the servant said, his voice tight with the effort of holding her suspended above the tumbled chaos at her feet. 'Not until you tell me.'

Yuet felt with her foot, found a foothold that felt solid, tested it. It held. She brought the other foot closer, fitted her heel into the arch of the grounded foot like a ballerina, found her balance, stood. The manservant felt one of her long fingers tapping at his wrist.

'You can let go now. Go, get a rope. Get help. For the love of Cahan, run!'

'Yes, *sai'an*, I go!' He released her arms, turned, and ran back the way they had come. Tai could hear him calling out urgently as he ran, but then he was dismissed from her mind and she knelt on the edge of the ruined balcony and craned her neck down to see what Yuet was doing.

The healer shifted her weight very gradually, very carefully, aware that a single false move she made could send both her and the Little Empress tumbling all the way down to the bottom of the chasm below.

'I come, Princess. I am coming.'

'It's too late,' Antian whispered, her voice a breath.

Yuet bit her lip, looking at the broken body at her feet. The fingers of Antian's hand, lying over the spreading black stain on her robe, were slick with the blood that had seeped through. The cut on her forehead was starting to clot but was still seeping, and a thin stream of it had flowed past the corner of her eye and down her temple, soaking the glossy black hair. Yuet could read the signs, and the signs were all over the Little Empress – the pallor of her skin, the white shadow around her lips, the shallow breath that moved the thin ribcage beneath the blood-soaked robe. This was just one more face of the death that Yuet had found at every turn in the Palace that grim morning.

'Oh, no,' Yuet found herself whispering. 'No, no, no, *no*.'

'Do something,' Tai said desperately from the edge of the balcony, just above them.

Yuet took another careful step, which brought her right up to Antian's body, and went down gingerly on one knee. 'Let me see, Your Highness.'

Antian allowed her hand to be removed from her bloodied side, her eyes closing. Her lips were parted, and she breathed so shallowly that Tai, staring at her from her perch on the edge, could not swear that she breathed at all. The breath came a little more sharply as Yuet's gentle fingers probed the wound in Antian's side and came away bloody. Yuet kept her eyes lowered, looked down the line of Antian's hip and onto the unnaturally bent leg, allowed her fingers to linger there as well, drawing another sharp gasp of pain.

'That's just a broken leg, we can mend that,' Yuet said soothingly. 'I will make a splint, just as soon as we get you up.'

Antian's eyes opened, cloudy but alert. 'What . . . happened to . . .'

Yuet tried to look away but a sudden rush of tears she could not hold back betrayed everything, and Antian bit her lip.

'They are dead, aren't . . . they? All of them?'

'I . . . I don't know, Your Highness, but . . . we have not found Second Princess Oylian yet.'

'So she won't . . . be Empress,' Antian said, and glanced up to catch Tai's eye. It cost her something, because she could not help a soft moan as she tried to turn her head. 'And neither . . . will I.'

'It's just a broken leg,' said Yuet stubbornly.

'And this?' Antian whispered, only her eyes flickering down to her side. It seemed that her eyes were all that she had the strength to move.

'Where *is* that man with the rope?' Yuet snapped, fretting.

'I can help you,' Tai said suddenly. 'I can help you bring her up here.'

'You can't hold her weight,' said Yuet sceptically, glancing up at the slightly built eleven-year-old on the ledge above her.

'She is not heavy. And if you will hold her from below, I can catch her up here.'

'We should not move her at all!' Yuet said with an edge of despair in her voice. 'Let alone a push-me-pull-you method like that! Her ribs . . .'

Tai's breath caught on a sob as she turned around and scanned the gardens behind her for any sign of the returning manservant with the rope and the reinforcements. 'She'll die.'

*She is dying anyway. She will be dead by the time the man gets back here.* The thought was as clear in Yuet's mind as though Szewan, her mentor and the master-healer woman to whom she was apprenticed, had spoken them while standing right beside her.

She glanced up again, to where Tai had risen into a crouch, tense, weeping. Then down, at the fragile broken body at her feet. Then at the ledge where she stood, precarious, unstable. If she moved too fast, too carelessly, if she turned an ankle on a loose piece of rubble . . .

'All right,' she said abruptly. 'Wait there until I say.'

There was a long tear in Antian's robe; she must have caught it on something as she was pitched over the edge and fell. Yuet took hold of the fabric and ripped it all the way, leaving herself with a ragged strip of silk in her hands. She folded this up into a thick wad, tucked it underneath the robe over the wound in Antian's side, took off her own belt and tied the pad into place.

'Can you hold on to that, Princess? Just so that it doesn't move?' She lifted Antian's almost lifeless hand and placed it over the makeshift pressure pad. It was not going to help. Nothing was going to help, but she might as well try.

Antian's hand landed with her usual grace. 'I'll try,' she said weakly.

Yuet looked up.

Tai straightened. 'I'm here. What do I have to do?'

'I will try and lift her. Can you reach down for her shoulders? Oh, what are we doing?' Yuet said, aghast. 'We'll all be down there in pieces in a minute!'

'I can do it,' Tai said. 'I can *do* it!'

'We'll kill her,' Yuet whispered despairingly, looking down at the girl at her feet.

Antian's eyes opened again, and there was a shadow of a smile in them. 'You cannot do that,' she whispered. 'It is out of your hands.'

Yuet was seventeen years old. She had had her Xat-Wau ceremony nearly three years before; she had been first apprentice and now assistant to Court Healer Szewan since she was seven years old. She was good. She saved lives. And right now all she wanted to do was bury her face in her hands and weep for the pity of it.

All her choices were doomed here. Antian was right. Yuet could not kill her – because, except for these last few breaths of pain, she was already dead.

'Help me,' Yuet said to Tai, waiting on the ledge. She checked the tie on the pad, made sure it was as secure as it could be, lifted Antian's slender body as gently as she could. Antian let out a soft sob of pain and Yuet winced; she could feel the blood from Antian's side seep warm and wet into her own robe as she held Antian against her body; she cradled the Princess for a moment, shifting her grip, and then slid an arm along her back, laying Antian's spine against the long bones of her own forearm, straightening the Princess's body as much as she was able. 'Just keep your hand there, Princess,' she said, anything, just to keep talking, for Antian to hear voices. 'Stay with us. You . . . what *is* your name?'

'Tai. I'm Tai.'

'Tai – catch her under the shoulders – gently, gently – slowly. Have you got her?'

Antian's shoulders were on the edge of the broken balcony, her head lolling sideways. Tai had both hands under her shoulders, trying not to pull on the wounded side, using her arm and shoulder to keep Antian's head from lolling down onto the stone. 'I have her,' she gasped, straining. Antian was a small-boned girl with a fragile build, but she was a dead weight in their arms right now, her eyes tightly squeezed, her face a mask of pain, her breath coming in short sharp gasps.

For a ghastly moment Tai thought her grip was slipping, that Antian's silk-clad shoulders would slide from her fingers and that she'd have to watch her fall, all the way down, all the way into that river she had once watched flowing into the sunset and thought golden. But something gave her the strength and she managed to get Antian anchored on the edge of the solid remnant of the balcony. Then, miraculously, other hands arrived and somebody took up the slack, supported Antian's body where Tai could not reach, helped lift the Princess up and lay her gently down against the wall of the balcony. Someone reached over and helped Yuet scramble back up; Tai, all of whose attention was on Antian now, heard something break and go tumbling down, crashing and crumbling against the mountainside, and a part of her shuddered at the sound, but that was all in the background.

Antian's lips were white with pain; the pad against her side was soaked with her blood. Yuet herself looked like she had been stabbed in the heart, a dark red stain spreading across her robe, as she came to kneel on Antian's other side.

'They brought a stretcher, Highness, if we can just get you . . .'

'You have done,' Antian whispered, 'what can be . . . done. Tai . . .'

She tried to lift a hand, but it barely cleared her abdomen before falling back weakly. Tai reached for it, weeping openly.

'What is it, Antian?'

'Do . . . something for me . . . *jin-shei-bao.*'

'Anything,' Tai said. 'You know it.'

Antian's eyes closed. She squeezed Tai's hand, once.

'Take care of her,' Antian said, almost too softly for Tai to hear. 'Take care . . . of my sister.'


# Three


A rush of white noise roared in Tai's ears as Antian's lifeless head rested on the arm which she had slipped underneath the nape of Antian's neck as support. For a moment she could not move at all. She felt like the entire Palace was coming down in ruins all over again, only this time she was inside it, deep inside it, and it was all falling on her and around her and burying her with the pain. It took Yuet several tries before she could get a reaction from her, but Tai eventually became aware that the older girl had her by the shoulder and was speaking to her in a gentle voice.

'Tai. *Tai*. Listen to me. Look at me. *Look* at me. Good.' Tai had raised her eyes, her pupils dilated with shock, her face stark. 'I have to go back to . . . they will take care . . .' Yuet's voice faltered for a moment, and then she seemed to change her mind, come to a different decision. 'No. *You* go with them. Take the Little Empress back to the summer house in the garden. Make sure she is tended with honour.'

Tai stared at her, swallowed what tasted like bitter aloes. 'I will.'

'I will look for you, after. I have to go and take care of . . . of whoever is left up there. I will come for you. I am relying on you.'

'I will do it,' Tai said, getting to her feet.

Yuet could see that she was not entirely steady as she stood beside Antian's body, and did not feel happy at leaving her alone – her healer's instincts told her that what Tai needed right then was someone to cling to, a warm blanket, something hot to drink, all the things needed to stave off shock. But all this was the healing of the mind. She was not physically hurt, and there were others out there who would need Yuet, who might be pulled out of the rubble half-alive, whose lives Yuet could save.

Yuet looked up at the waiting servants. 'Take the Little Empress to the summer house.' She hesitated; all hands would be needed, but she could not just leave Tai alone. 'One of you,' she said, 'stay with her and with Tai. And somebody find Tai an outer robe.'

'Yes, *sai'an*.' The man who had gone for help bent down and gathered Antian's body into his arms, very gently, as though she was a precious porcelain doll, and waited for Tai to lead the way. Tai turned away from the edge of the ruined balcony without looking out to her river again. She walked past Yuet without a word, almost without any sign that she was aware that the healer stood there.

'I shouldn't leave her alone,' Yuet murmured to herself as the servant bearing Antian followed the younger girl into the garden.

But already she could hear the screams and wails, the pain and the terror that was waiting for her in the rubble of the Summer

Palace. The voices drew her; for a moment she forgot about Tai, she forgot about Antian whose life's blood she wore on her own robe. There were other lives.

The morning had fled quickly. They put out two of the smaller fires but the biggest one, the one that had started deepest in the ruins, quickly spread out of control. Thick columns of black smoke rose into the innocent blue of a flawless summer sky, and orange tongues of flame added to the day's gathering heat. There were survivors – but few, so few, and the lines of bodies covered with sackcloth grew.

Yuet was perched precariously on the edge of a hole she and a few other able-bodied survivors had been excavating into the rubble, chasing down an elusive sobbing cry they had thought might indicate someone alive down there, when the first aftershock hit the mountain. The pile of debris that Yuet had been standing on tilted, nearly throwing her into the hole, and then settled at a different angle, a different slope. When the panicked shouts had settled down, they could no longer hear the voice they had been following in their attempts at rescue, and Yuet had called her team of aides off.

'It's useless, look, it's all fallen in down there.' She looked up and out across the debris, wiping sweat and dust and drifting ashes out of her eyes, and straightened up as she met the eyes of Antian's little *jin-shei-bao*. 'You? What are you doing here? Are you all right?'

'I want to help,' Tai said, her voice trembling just a little. She wore a borrowed gown, at least two sizes too large for her, and looked pitifully small and young and fragile.

'Wait there a moment.' Yuet scrambled down from her pile of rubble and came to stand next to Tai, lifting her chin with one hand, peering into her eyes. 'You should be lying down somewhere and . . .'

'Please,' said Tai, 'I cannot. Let me help.'

Yuet hesitated. 'There is little that you can do.'

Someone shouted out, a shout that held gladness; Yuet looked up. A senior servant of the women's quarters, his tunic torn and his face and arms scratched and sooty, came scrambling over at a trot, carrying something in his arms.

'It's a miracle, but he is still alive,' the servant said, offering Yuet a bawling baby swaddled in a torn silk wrap. 'I don't think he is hurt, even; the crying is just fear and hunger.'

Tai intercepted the child, cradled him in her arms, and he stopped crying, blinking up at Tai's face with a puzzled expression and teardrops caught on his long dark lashes. 'Shhhh,' Tai said, rocking him gently against her. 'Shhh, it will be all right. It will be all right.'

The ground trembled again under their feet, and Tai could not suppress a cry, clutching at the child, who whimpered but did not resume his desperate wailing.

'Where did you find him? Are there . . . ?'

'No,' said the servant, dropping his eyes. 'Only that one. His mother is dead.'

'Are there other children?' Tai asked.

Yuet nodded. 'Maybe half a dozen or so. From swaddling babes like this one to six- or seven-year-olds. They're in the outer wing.'

'I know it,' Tai said. It was the wing where she and Rimshi had always stayed when they were at the Summer Palace. 'I will take care of the children.'

'You need . . .' Yuet began, but Tai lifted glittering dark eyes and Yuet stopped, biting back what she had been about to say.

'I need to do it,' Tai said, very softly. 'For *her*.'

'Go,' Yuet said, after a pause. 'Go, take care of the children.'

'You are still wearing . . .' Tai began, but then her eyes filled with unexpected tears again, and she turned away quickly, gathering the child to her, and was gone. Yuet glanced down at her robe, and smoothed down the part where Antian's bright blood had now dried into a stiff brownish stain. Yes, she was still wearing . . . she was still wearing Antian's own blood.

She almost forgot about Tai and the children in the next few hours, taken up with trying to cope with the aftermath of the disaster. She set broken limbs, tended burns, cuts, grazes, gashes and bruises. She cleaned and bandaged and gave out some sedative herbs to the worst-off. She took control of the servants, sent a clutch of them to set up a makeshift kitchen, brew copious quantities of soothing green tea, prepare a meal for the shocked survivors. In the Imperial Palace, decimated of its royalty, Yuet, the healer, reigned as queen for the day, and none questioned her or disobeyed her.

When she finally circled back to the children, they were no longer in the place where she had told Tai they would be, and after some searching she finally found the whole small group in the stables. There were more there than she realized; the survivors from the villages close to the shattered mountain had crept to the Palace in pitiful groups of two or three at a time, seeking help, and Tai had shunted all the children into her group. There were now maybe two dozen youngsters there. Tai had herself commandeered a single servant, and between them they had cleaned out several mangers and made them into makeshift cribs for the youngest babies. Some of them were wailing from hunger, but they were all clean and freshly swaddled and many of them were blissfully asleep. Tai had discovered a litter of eight-week-old puppies in the kennels, and had brought them out to the stable yard where the older children played with them happily, squealing with delight at puppy antics.

Yuet stopped dead, watching the scene; it was the first sight she had had all day of innocence and contentment. She felt the weariness fall from her shoulders, a little, at the sound of children's laughter.

She found Tai huddled inside the stables themselves, sitting on a bale of hay with her chin resting on the knees drawn up against her chest into the circle of her arms. White-faced, with dark circles under her eyes, she looked as though she had aged ten years in the space of the last few hours.

'You have wrought miracles,' Yuet said, coming up beside her.

Tai looked up, without releasing her legs from the circle of her arms. 'You have had the harder task.'

'May I?' Yuet said, indicating the bale, and Tai shifted sideways, giving Yuet space to subside beside her with a sigh. The healer knuckled her eyes, kneaded her temples with weary fingertips. Her head ached abominably. Her heart ached worse.

'I am glad you were here,' Tai said suddenly.

Yuet looked up, startled. 'What?'

'You care,' Tai said.

'I care about life,' Yuet said.

She could not remember a time that she hadn't had a calling to heal. Her very earliest patients had been the handful of animals on the tiny homestead where she had been fostered when she had been orphaned at barely four years of age. And then, aged only six, Yuet had stood beside her foster mother as she spoke to a passing dignitary, no less than a healer to the Imperial Court of Syai. Yuet's foster mother had made some respectful remark about the health of the royal women, and somehow it had come out that she herself was suffering from a blistering headache at the time.

'Willow bark,' the young Yuet had piped up before the royal healer had had a chance to respond. 'You should boil up some willow bark.'

'Hush, child!' Yuet's foster mother had said, embarrassed at the utter lack of decorum shown by the orphaned child whom she had charitably taken into her household less than two years before, mortified that her teachings had not instilled better manners in the girl.

But the healer had lifted her eyebrows and was gazing at Yuet with interest.

'And what would you do for a stomach ache?' she had asked, almost conversationally.

Yuet had told her. The information had been accurate, and delivered without an ounce of self-consciousness or shyness.

The healer had smiled, and it had gone no further at that time. But less than a year later the letter had come to the house, written in flowing *jin-ashu* script, asking if Yuet wished to be apprenticed to the Imperial healer in Linh-an.

Yuet had had a very clear sense of her future, and knew that she would probably have graduated quite naturally to becoming the healer and still-woman for her village's wounds and sicknesses, both animal and human. But even as a very young child she had always possessed a profoundly practical and realistic streak, and she had realized that she'd just been offered an extraordinary chance to pursue her calling in the far more exalted sphere of the Imperial Court when she had apprenticed to old Szewan. She had gone to the city the morning after Szewan's letter reached the homestead where she had spent her earliest childhood.

She could not have known then that this day would come, that disaster would be a price she would have to pay.

Before Tai had spoken, she had not even realized that she was afraid, but now she suddenly faced it – that small flicker of fear that had been part of what had driven her to the lengths to which she had gone. There was healing – and then there was the fact that this was the Imperial family, and that there might be questions raised about what she, Yuet, had done or had not done, whether any of the dead could have been saved with a more experienced healer at the helm, or someone who had simply made different decisions at critical moments. The numbers were already devastating – there had been fifty-eight people in the living quarters of the Summer Palace when the earthquake had struck; some were still unaccounted for, but the bodies of more than half of them were laid out in the gardens and four of those bodies had once belonged to the highest of the Imperial family of Syai.

Tai's words were balm, unexpected, healing to the healer – here was someone who was there with her, who had seen what had happened, who could vouch for the decisions that she had made.

But Tai was far away again – or as near as the shattered gardens, the ruined balcony, the dying Princess in the first golden light of the dawn.

'I wish . . .' she whispered, very softly, almost to herself.

'What do you wish?' Yuet asked after a beat.

'I wish I knew how to keep my promises.'

If Tai was Yuet's witness, Yuet was hers. She had been there when Antian had spoken her dying words. *Take care of my sister.*

'She wanted you to be there for the Third Princess. I mean, for Empress-Heir Liudan,' Yuet said slowly.

'Liudan hates me,' Tai said simply.

Yuet reached out a hand and laid it over Tai's fingers where they interlaced around her knees. 'She does not. She will not. She will need a friend.' She paused, suddenly unsure of what she was about to do, but it felt true, it felt *right*. 'And so will you. I know I am not the Little Empress, I know I cannot take her place, but if you wish it I will be *jin-shei-bao* to you, I will help you keep your promise.'

Tai had turned her head a little to look at her, a long, steady look, and then nodded imperceptibly. 'You are still wearing her own heart's blood,' Tai whispered. 'I think she would wish it. *Jin-shei.*'


They limped back to Linh-an, the survivors, with a slow, snaking line of horse carts bearing twenty-seven bodies in caskets draped in the white of mourning. The walls of the city – massive constructions of dressed stone, nearly sixty feet thick at the bottom and almost forty feet high – were almost hidden, from the north approach, by the white ribbon banners that had been hung from the top battlements. The broad ribbons shifted and eddied in the breeze, and from a distance it looked like the walls themselves had come alive and were trembling with sorrow.

The people of Linh-an met the procession in the streets, standing silently as it wound its way through the north gate and into the heart of the city, almost eight miles of twisting roads to the Great Temple which waited to receive the four most important bodies – the Ivory Emperor, his Empress, the Little Empress Antian his heir, and Second Princess Oylian. The houses the procession passed were hung with white ribbons, like the outer walls, or banners with inscriptions of blessing or farewell. The city was stunned. The country reeled.

The survivors grieved.

Tai had returned with the Court, back to Rimshi, her still ailing mother, and had clung to her for a long time in silence after the cortège left its dead in the Temple and those who returned from the Summer Palace had gone their separate ways. Tai would not speak of it at all for days, just sat white-faced and silent in a corner of the room or spent long hours at the Temple. There was little spare money to make all the offerings such a death demanded, but Rimshi set aside every copper that she could; Tai burned incense sticks, and offered up rice and saffron for the safe passage of Antian's soul into the Immortal Lands.

The Ivory Emperor, Antian's father, was given his traditional niche in the Hall of the Immortal Emperors, in the Second Circle of the Temple. The new shrine overflowed with the offerings of the people who came filing past to pay their respects or offer up their grief.

But Antian was not the Emperor, would never have a niche for herself where people would come and pray to her bright spirit. Tai would think of this, her eyes bright with tears she could not seem to shed, as she sat beside the Ivory Emperor's shrine and watched the cascades of white mourning candles fighting for space with incense holders for sticks saturated with frankincense or lilac essence, with piles of peaches symbolizing immortality, with mounds of rice and of tamarind seeds. The Ivory Emperor would become a lesser God. Antian would remain a fading memory.

But Tai could not cry. The loss was lodged too deep, like a dagger in her heart, and she nursed the pain fiercely – it was as though she believed that this alone would keep Antian alive for her. The funeral would not be for another twenty days, so that the Emperor's body and those of his family could lie in state for the proper period. The period of mourning for a dead Emperor was fixed at nine months for the nation, three years for his surviving family. For three years Liudan, now the Empress-Heir, would be allowed to wear only pale colours and no silk garments, in mourning for her family. But because of the way that the Emperor and his family had died, the unnatural and violent way in which they had been taken, it had been decreed that there would be a full year of mourning for the city, during which time all would wear white ribbons and pieces of sackcloth on their garments. But for Tai this marking of time was meaningless. She had seen too much on that morning in the mountains, she had lost something that had barely begun to bloom into a rich and treasured thing in her life, and her mourning was deep, and absolute, and she felt as though it would never end.

When the tears did come, it was not at the Ivory Emperor's shrine, or at the sight of his mourners there, or even as she lit her own candles on Third and Fourth Circle altars for Antian. It was an ordinary thing that set her off, not the memory of loss, but a reminder that life went on without pausing to grieve for what was lost, that each sunset was followed by a new dawn . . . that a new Emperor would follow this one.

She had been on her way to the gate, stepping out of the Second Circle into the chaos of the First, and had happened to pass close enough to the stall of So-Xan the yearwood bead-carver to notice the bin of carved bone beads out by the side of the trestle table, and Kito, So-Xan's son, patiently rasping at the carvings, smoothing the round beads into even, featureless globes which would be dipped into white lead paint and sold for the duration of the mourning year to be strung onto the yearwood sticks to mark the passage of the time.

It was this, finally, that reached out and drew the dagger from Tai's heart. She did not expect the pain, the rush of heart's blood that followed the simple realization that something was *over*, irrevocably over, that the reign of the Ivory Emperor was done . . . and that Antian would never choose the Emperor who would take his place.

Tai's breath caught; she staggered, catching herself on a nearby booth for support.

Kito happened to look up, took in the white face, the wide eyes dilated with shock, and dropped the bead he had been working on back into the bin he'd taken it from, leaping to his feet.

'Are you all right? You look ill.' He closed the distance between them in two long strides, cupping Tai's elbow, bending over her solicitously. 'Xao-jin!' he called, summoning the proprietor of a booth four or five trestles down. A round, moon-shaped face popped around a partition in response. 'Bring me a cup of green tea! Hurry!'

Something had snapped, and Tai suddenly found herself racked by great heaving sobs, shuddering convulsively as the tears came. Kito steered her into the inner recesses of the bead-carver's booth, installing her on a bench, leaving her side only long enough to step out and grab the bowl of steaming tea brought by the man he had summoned and murmur a brief word of thanks. Then he was back, dropping to one knee beside the bench on which Tai sat and wept as though her heart would break.

'Here,' he said, 'drink this. It will make you feel better.'

The very absurdity of this comment made Tai hiccough and gulp down some of the brew. Kito's concerned eyes never left her face, at least not until he was satisfied that some colour had returned to her cheeks and that, although she was still weeping soundlessly with an inconsolable grief, she was in no imminent danger of doing herself damage from it.

There was an awkward moment of silence in which Tai would not raise her swimming eyes to look at him and he sat back helplessly, at a loss as to what to do next.

'Are you all right now?' Kito inquired at last, as she cradled the nearly drained tea bowl between her hands. It would have been impolite to ask, they did not even know each other's names, but Kito had always had a high degree of empathy for people and some part of Tai's pain had reached out and touched his own spirit. He found himself wanting to do something to help, anything, but not knowing the cause of it could not do anything to alleviate it.

Tai understood his reluctance to ask, but felt that she owed him an explanation for bursting into tears upon catching sight of him at his work.

'It's . . .' she began, but her voice was still thick with the tears. She swallowed, hard, fighting back a new wave of weeping. 'The Ivory Emperor's beads. You were . . .'

Kito glanced back at his abandoned task. 'Yes,' he said, and his voice was oddly gentle. 'I am making the mourning beads. And after that I will have to make the regency beads. For the Empress-Heir is still too young to be raised to the throne, and we do not know yet what the next reign's bead is going to be.'

*Liudan*. In all the time since she had nursed her grief for her lost *jin-shei* sister, Tai had given little thought to the promise she had given as Antian lay dying. Take care of my sister, she had said. Liudan. The angry one.

The Empress-Heir. The Empress to be.

'But how can I do that?' she gasped, out loud, answering her own thoughts. How was she to fulfil her last vow to Antian? Liudan had never given Tai the time of day. She was three years older, proud, wounded by too many things Tai could not heal – and yet Tai had promised to take care of her.

'Pardon?' Kito said, startled.

Tai finally raised her eyes, and there was gratitude in them, and a warmth of what was almost affection. She got to her feet; Kito unfolded his long adolescent frame and rose also, accepting the tea bowl she handed back to him.

'Thank you,' she said, and even managed the shadow of a smile. 'You have helped.'

*She is beautiful*, Kito thought, irrationally, the thought having just swum into his mind from the Gods alone knew where. A part of him scoffed at it, because there was nothing of beauty in Tai's flushed cheeks and eyes that were red and swollen from first the unshed tears and then the ones that had come out in a torrent of released grief. But there was something in that half-smile that was luminous.

She bowed to him, formally, her palms together and her fingers laced, and stepped away, about to leave the booth.

'Wait,' Kito said suddenly, instinctively.

He reached into the bin of the carved beads he had been working on, took out a whole one as yet unmarred by his ministrations, and folded Tai's hand around it.

'They will not,' he said quietly, 'all be destroyed.'

The smile on her face lit up her eyes, just for a moment; her fingers closed tightly around the bead. Tai nodded her thanks, backed away, escaped through the outer gate into the streets of Linh-an, leaving Kito staring after her with an expression of astonishment.

# Four

Tai was not part of the funeral procession which wound its way through Linh-an's streets when the Emperor and his family were taken to their resting place. She could have been, if she had asked – for a *jin-shei-bao* had every right to follow a sister to her funeral. But this was too raw still, much too private and too deep a grief to expose it to the crowds in the streets. Tai had thought she could pay her respects her own way, just by being in the throngs on the pavements when the procession passed, but she had been resigned to being unable to see much of Antian's last journey from within the crowd which would gather in the streets. All of Linh-an would be there, the throng would undoubtedly be five or six deep on the pavements – she would have to bid farewell to the sister of her heart from behind a wall of humanity. But the Gods, who had given her so much and then capriciously took it all away again, seemed to have repented of their whim and now showered Tai with many small gifts as if to make amends.

One was an unexpected friendship begun in the bead-carver's booth. It had been Nhia, Tai's neighbour and friend, who had finally formally introduced the two – she had been acquainted with Kito and his father, amongst the many craftsmen and merchants in the Temple's First Circle, for most of her young life. Nhia had accompanied Tai on one of her Temple visits during the weeks prior to the Emperor's funeral, and Kito had chanced to notice them, and called out a greeting.

'We are kept busy,' he had said, in response to Nhia's polite inquiry as to his well-being. But his eyes had been smiling at Tai, and hers were downcast, although her mouth curved upwards a little at its corners. Nhia's eyebrow rose a fraction, and she said smoothly, as though she had noticed nothing at all, 'I do not know if you have met my friend. Tai, this is Kito, son of So-Xan, the bead-carver. Kito, this is Tai, daughter of Rimshi, the seamstress.'

They bowed to each other.

'Perhaps you will share another bowl of green tea with me some time,' Kito said. He had been addressing, in theory, both girls – but since Nhia, for all the length of her acquaintance with him, had never partaken of green tea in the bead-carver's booth she assumed there was a story behind this tea party which excluded her.

Tai had blushed. 'I would enjoy that,' she said, and once more Nhia was excluded.

Nhia passed over the mystery with studied innocent ignorance. 'Perhaps later,' she murmured, and was rewarded by both her companions throwing startled glances first at her and then, very briefly, at each other. They had made their farewells, and the girls had passed on into the Temple while Kito pretended to turn back to his work – although both Nhia and Tai were sharply aware of the weight of his eyes on their backs.

'He gave me the last Ivory Emperor bead,' Tai had said to Nhia by way of an explanation as they walked away. 'I saw him polishing the carvings smooth, making the mourning beads, and he gave me a whole one, one he had not yet marred. He gave me my memory back.'

'And a bowl of green tea,' Nhia murmured.

Tai blushed again, uncharacteristically. 'I was crying,' she said softly. 'That was . . . the first time I cried for her.'

Nhia knew that there had been some connection to the Court, over and above Rimshi's usual Summer Court duties, but she had not known what – and this sentence was cryptic, to say the least. But she was Nhia, and people trusted her – and Tai, after all, was her friend, perhaps her only friend. And now that Antian was gone, there was no secret any more. Tai raised her head and met Nhia's eyes.

'She and I were *jin-shei*,' Tai said. 'This was the third summer that I shared with my heart-sister. And there was so much in those three years, Nhia, so much! I have already lived a lifetime with her. And now she is gone.'

She had still not named a name, but since this was connected to the Imperial Family it had to be one of the two girls lying dead in the Temple at this very moment.

'*Jin-shei?*' Nhia echoed. 'With Second Princess Oylian?'

'With Antian,' Tai said. 'With the Little Empress.'

Nhia's step faltered a little. 'You were *jin-shei-bao* – to the Little Empress? How in Cahan did that happen?'

So Tai told the tale again, as they sat side by side on one of the benches by the pools of the Third Circle gardens. The tears ran free now, leaving trails on her cheeks as she spoke, and Nhia's eyes filled in sympathy. She hugged Tai at the end, unsure of what to say to lay balm on the hurt – but she was Nhia, and she was overflowing with the stories and the parables and the wisdom that she had picked up during her years within the Temple's walls, and now she pulled one from her memory.

'When Han-fei crossed the Great River and entered the realm of the Gods,' she began, smoothing away Tai's hair from her eyes with a motion as tender as a mother's, 'he walked far without meeting anyone, and keeping his eyes on the ground, so that he would not offend any being he met by looking at them without their permission. By and by he came upon a beach, and the beach opened onto a great lake, and the lake was dark and still, like a mirror, and beautiful. More beautiful still was the thing which he saw in the lake – glorious mountain peaks, rank upon rank of them, rising majestic and capped with snow, so high that the sky above them was eternally sprinkled with stars. "O, beautiful!" he said, and fell to his knees in worship of it. And a voice said to him, "This is the image, Han-fei, now look up and behold the truth." And Han-fei looked up, and the mountains were real and stood around the lake in all their majesty and were not offended that he looked upon them, and knew them, and loved them.' She paused. 'It may be,' she said gently, 'that the thing which you shared with the Little Empress is just a reflection of something greater and truer that will come to you, that she came to you to show you the way. That she was the image on which you must now build your truth.'

Tai suddenly turned and gave Nhia a fierce hug. 'You've always been my friend,' she said.

'Sometimes I think you've been my only friend,' Nhia said with a trace of bitterness.

Tai sat back and gave Nhia a long look. 'That's not true,' she said. 'Everybody likes you. People are always asking you what you think. People trust you.'

'People have never *liked* me, Tai,' Nhia said.

'But you've solved all sorts of problems back in SoChi Street.'

Nhia dismissed that accomplishment with a wave of her arm. 'That's not the same. People trust me, yes. Sometimes I think people tell me more than they think I ought to know. But that leads away from affection, not towards it! If they know I know all those things about them, yes, they trust me – but they will never like me. Folks never like those who know too much about them.'

'You're one of the wisest people I know,' Tai said sturdily, loyally.

Nhia smiled. 'That's because you haven't met many people yet.'

'I have,' Tai said rebelliously. 'In the Summer Palace . . .'

The words sank into a pool of silence that was sorrow. Nhia reached over and squeezed Tai's cold fingers.

'I know you have lost something wonderful,' she said. 'But you've always been a little sister to me, Tai. Sometimes you really were the only person I could talk to. Whatever else happens in either of our lives, I wanted you to know that. It doesn't make up for the Little Empress, but . . .'

'But I've had a real, live *jin-shei-bao* living next door to me all my life and I never knew it,' Tai said.

Nhia gave her a startled look. 'That's not what I meant,' she began, but Tai turned her hand and laced her fingers through the older girl's.

'But I mean it,' she said, 'if you wish it.'

For a moment, Nhia could not find the voice to speak at all, and then, when the words did come, they were raw with emotion.

'I can hardly take the place of the first heart's sister, of the one who would have been Empress,' she said, 'but I'll be your sister if you want me to be. I would be proud to have you call me that.'

That had been the second gift, another *jin-shei*, another place for the love that had been Antian's legacy to be bestowed.

The third gift of the Gods had been even more unexpected.

# Five

Although she'd been coming to the Temple since she was a babe in arms, it had been only in the last year or so that Nhia's presence had begun making a real impact there. She had barely turned fourteen when she and a young acolyte she had been in conversation with had been approached by a politely deferential older woman who posed the question – to the acolyte – as to which deity she should approach with her problem. 'Help me, blessed one, for I am not certain which of the Gods would be best to approach – I am not worthy of what is being asked of me, I need to know . . .'

It had been Nhia, aged only fourteen and not bound to the Temple hierarchy at all, who had responded to this plea, with a story of Han-fei, the hapless adventurer whose encounters with Gods and Immortals were such a fertile ground to harvest good advice from.

'When Han-fei met with an Immortal beyond the river Inderyn where the Heavens are,' Nhia had spoken into the expectant silence, while the Temple acolyte was still pondering the question, 'he threw himself at the feet of the Blessed Sage and would not raise his eyes from the hem of the robe that the Immortal Sage wore. "I am not worthy, O Blessed One, I am not worthy!" The Sage said, "What do you see when you look into the mirror, Han-fei?" And Han-fei said, "I see a man with no beauty in his face and no wisdom in his mind and no humility in his spirit." And the Sage bade Han-fei take a mirror from his hand and said, "Then look again, for what I see is a man with the beauty of face which is a reflection of the modesty of his soul, with the wisdom of mind to know what he does not know, and with the humility of spirit to spend his life in trying to learn and understand the things he is ignorant of. Rise, Han-fei, for you are worthy."'

The woman had taken Nhia's hand and kissed it, in silence, and backed away, bowing. The acolyte had stood and stared at Nhia for a long moment.

'Where did you learn that tale?' he had asked.

'I hear many of them, in these halls,' Nhia had said. 'I see the teaching monks with the children in the courtyards sometimes. I listen, and I remember them.'

'That is good,' the acolyte had said carefully, 'except that the one you just told has never been one of the teaching tales. For all I know, it has never been recorded as having happened to Han-fei.'

'I didn't just make it up!' Nhia had protested, her heart lurching into her heels. 'I must have heard it.'

'You invented it, Nhia, and it was perfect,' the acolyte had said.

Nhia's first reaction was a rising panic. 'Don't tell anyone,' she pleaded. 'I won't do it again. I just meant to . . .'

'But why ever not?' the acolyte had asked. 'You're a natural teacher. Perhaps one day you will even be a real part of this Temple; you already know more than some who have been pledged to it for years.'

Whether or not the acolyte told anyone about the incident, Nhia never found out – but only because events overtook her. Even if the acolyte had held his tongue, the woman to whom Nhia had told her Han-fei tale obviously had not.

Haggling over a fish at the marketplace, perhaps a week or so after the encounter at the Temple, Nhia turned to a gentle tugging on her sleeve and was surprised to recognize the seeker from the Temple. The woman was accompanied by a brace of small children, one of them only a few years younger than Nhia herself, all of whom stared at Nhia inscrutably. Nhia stared back, nonplussed.

'I wished to thank you, young *sai'an*,' the woman said in a low, deferential voice. 'You have helped me understand. My husband's mother is in need of your wise words, also, but she is bedridden and cannot go to Temple often. Perhaps if you would come?'

'But I am not one of the blessed ones of the Temple,' Nhia had said helplessly.

Just for a moment, the woman looked surprised, and then her expression settled into certainty again. 'Maybe you are not one of the ones wearing the robes, *sai'an*, but you have the wisdom of the Immortals in you. My mother-in-law would be grateful if you would come. If only for a few moments. We live in ZhuChao Street, in the yellow house on the corner. If you please, *sai'an*.'

Nhia had wanted nothing more than to bolt into the midst of the marketplace and to lose herself in the crowds – but she could not run. She could not ever run. Not from this; not from anything. The irony of this made a wry grin touch her lips. The woman interpreted this as acceptance, or dismissal – in any event she had backed away, bowing, accompanied by her brood.

Several other customers at the fishmonger's stall had been witness to this exchange, and the fishmonger himself, who had known Nhia from babyhood, stood with her intended purchase still in his hand.

'So you are a Sage, now, young NhiNhi,' the fishmonger had said. There was an attempt at levity there, but there was something else also – a curiosity, a careful interest. The marketplace lived by gossip and rumour, this was how the news was spread from one corner of the sprawling city that was Linh-an to the next. There was, maybe, a story here.

'I am no such thing,' Nhia had said, very firmly, and had brought the subject of the conversation back to the fish.

But another woman had stopped her in the street two days later, asking a very specific question. The question concerned the child whom she held by the hand and who stood staring at Nhia with the blank obsidian gaze which was very familiar to her. She had worn that mask herself. The child's other arm and hand, not the one held by her mother, were thin and withered, her fingers bent into a piti-ful claw which she held folded into her belly. This was another Nhia, a cripple whose mother was driven to ask for help where she thought she could find it.

Perhaps it was this that made Nhia speak to her. There had been a parable to fit. Then she had told another tale, directly to the child, another Han-fei story but one aimed at the old pain so familiar to herself, trying to ease the little one's burden. She had been rewarded with a softening of the eyes, a shy smile. The mother noticed, and her own eyes lit up. She took the incident away with her, cherished it, spoke of it.

After that, more came.

Somehow, before she reached her fifteenth birthday, Nhia had found herself sitting in an unoccupied booth in the First Circle one morning, telling teaching tales to a gaggle of children at her feet. At first it was an irregular thing, just every so often – when sufficient numbers of young disciples accumulated around her, Nhia would sit down somewhere, they would all subside on the ground around her, and the cry 'A story! A story!' would be raised. But it quickly grew into something more. Something that became striking enough to warrant the attention of the Temple priestly caste. Several times, in the middle of one of her tales, Nhia would look up and catch the glimpse of a discreet observer, an acolyte draped in Temple robes, who would stand with eyes downcast and hands folded into his sleeves and listen intently to what she was saying. When she caught their presence, Nhia tried to be careful and tell only the tales she *knew* she had heard before here in the Temple, told by the Temple Sages and teachers. But it was sometimes hard to remember which ones she was sure about. All of the stories she told sounded so old and familiar to her. Which ones were old and venerable teaching parables, and which ones had she just invented?

Li, Nhia's mother, had been wary of the whole thing, and afraid that the Temple would take exception to Nhia's activities – especially since she often told her stories in the Temple's own precincts.

'These are games,' Li had said, 'and they can be dangerous. You are setting yourself up above the people. You have had your Xat-Wau, and you are no longer a child, Nhia – think about what it is that you want to do with the rest of your life.'

'But perhaps I am already doing that,' Nhia had said slowly.

No marriage; no children; she had come to terms with that. But perhaps these could be her children, the ones who came to her and whose lives she knew she could touch, could sometimes heal. She had much to learn – but already, it seemed, she had much to teach, also. A part of her gloried in it. Her body could not run – but her spirit could fly.

But Li had not been entirely convinced of her daughter's calling. She had even gone so far as to approach one of the higher-ranked Temple priests, and ask for absolution if Nhia presumed.

'We considered chastisement,' the priest had told Li, 'but first we listened to what she had to say. She makes the children hear her. She has said nothing to which we have taken exception. We think that it has gone far enough that, if she did not do it here, she would do it elsewhere – out in the marketplace, or in the streets.'

'Not if you forbade it, *sei*.'

'But why would we forbid it? Those she touches come straight home to us. She does the Temple's work,' the priest had said. There had been something complacent in his smile, but the priests of the Temple had always been pragmatic about their religion. A Temple which had an entire thriving outer Circle devoted to the commerce of faith could not be other. 'But I understand your concern – we will make sure she is taught.'

So Nhia's life had started to turn around the Temple, more and more. She taught the young, and in her turn she learned the meditations and the mental purifications of the *zhao-cha*, reaching out to touch the edges of the luminous, following Han-fei into the gardens of the Gods in search of the Fruit of Wisdom.

Khailin, daughter of Cheleh the Chronicler, had made it her business to keep the crippled girl who had attracted the attention of Sage Lihui under observation. In the months following that encounter in the Temple, Khailin had found out that Nhia frequented the Temple Circles, and had many friends there. She also found out that she and Nhia had more in common than she had thought. Although their focus and their ultimate desires were different, coloured in part by their differing stations in life and their place in Linh-an society, they shared an interest in the Way and in the manner in which it functioned. Nhia's interest was more in the wisdom and the purity of the path – the *zhao-cha*, the internal alchemy of the mind and spirit, the calling of the sage, the seer, the wisewoman. Khailin was more attracted to the *yang-cha* – its rituals, its mathematical magic, its chemistry, its eminently practical nature. They had both been driven to learn, to understand. This was something which Khailin could build on. This could even be part of the reason the Sage Lihui had been interested in Nhia; perhaps he had been drawn to the fierce flame of curiosity, intelligence, yearning to learn. Perhaps, Khailin thought, she and Nhia could be useful to one another.

So she had started keeping an eye out for Nhia at the Temple. A part of Khailin marvelled at how Nhia had found a way of gaining access to all the disciplines of the Way. And she had done it all without reading a single *hacha-ashu* manuscript about forbidden things. Khailin was uncomfortably aware that her own time was running out.

She had already rejected several suitors whose representatives had come bearing the *so ji*, the carved jade marriage proposal token. All it had taken, as tradition had it, was her refusal to accept the small sculpture into her own hands from the formally attired elderly aunts and cousins who had been entrusted with its delivery. *As my beloved wishes*, the words had originally meant. If the bride or groom being courted accepted the token, the marriage proposal was deemed to have been accepted, and the betrothal was official from that moment. Khailin's suitors had not been to her liking – one had come from a large and tradition-hidebound family, which would have trammelled her like a wild bird in a cage; another had been a man quite a few years her senior, with whom she already had a passing acquaintance at Court and whom she could have accepted except for her utter inability to get past his constantly sweaty palms which, upon reflection, she decided she could not bear near her on a regular basis.

When two emissaries of a prince of Syai came calling just before her Xat-Wau ceremony was due to take place, Cheleh had made it clear to his wayward older daughter that another refusal would have been severely frowned upon. The Prince was young, positively callow, precisely the kind of vacuous young man Khailin had no wish to marry. She could see herself delivered into the soft life of the noble houses, being an obedient young wife, having to obey endless rules of protocol and decorum, having to endure the hated ritual baths with the rest of the pampered ladies – perhaps never again to have access to the kind of arcane information she craved or the opportunity to test her knowledge . . . but, on the other hand, she would be a princess, which was a kind of power in its own right. And the young husband-to-be might be sufficiently mouldable into the kind of husband Khailin could live with. The kind of husband who could, if necessary, be hoodwinked into closing his eyes to her study of the *yang-cha*.

Khailin had accepted the Prince's token, gritting her teeth. The wedding would take place the following summer, but in the meantime Khailin had done her best to make sure that her betrothal did not interfere unduly with the last year or so of freedom. It could turn out well – it might have been for the best – but sometimes she wished savagely that her body was crippled like Nhia's was – that a good marriage had been harder to arrange. That she had been given more *time*.

But perhaps Nhia herself would open a few doors.

So Khailin made sure that their paths crossed in the Temple, that Nhia learned to recognize her face, that they started nodding at one another in passing, that they finally exchanged a word of greeting, and then of conversation. Khailin the courtier had cultivated Nhia with all the precision and cunning of any seeker in quest of favours from a higher-ranked aristocrat or sage.

For once, the things that Nhia was being told were not because someone instinctively trusted her with the information, but rather because this was the information that somebody else wished her to know. Since she had never had to field such an approach before, she had not recognized it as artificial; she had accepted Khailin's overtures, after a startled wariness that such a one would seek her company, with pleasure. She had found a companion of her own age with whom she could discuss the things that interested her.

They spoke of many things, and Khailin, despite the initial venal motives with which she had approached this relationship, found herself growing to like Nhia. She was surprised by a stab of jealousy when Nhia inevitably spoke of Tai, her only close companion before Khailin herself had appeared on the scene.

'She is so small and delicate,' Nhia had said to Khailin as they walked in the Temple, less than a week before the Emperor's funeral procession was due to take to Linh-an's streets. 'She wanted so much to say goodbye, but she won't even see it, not if she is out in the street, behind the crowds.'

Nhia had not mentioned the exact nature of Tai's connection with the Imperial family, but Khailin's curiosity was aroused, and she was nothing if not practised at extracting the information she required.

'We will all mourn,' Khailin said. 'This summer has brought great loss to Syai.'

'No,' Nhia said, shaking her head, 'for Tai it is more.'

'She spent summers at the Palace?' Khailin asked. 'With her mother? You said her mother was the Court dressmaker?'

'Rimshi is the seamstress, yes – and she has taught Tai well, too.'

This was straying too far into minutiae. Khailin brought it back to the Palace. 'How old is she now – she is a few years younger than you?'

'Eleven,' Nhia said.

'A few summers at the Palace, and she is but a child. It's been a tapestry to her, a living dream. I can see why it would be hard to let go.' But then Khailin had suddenly trailed off, her eyes becoming thoughtful. Her family was part of the Court, and she and her sister, although they did not attend the social occasions at the Imperial Palace frequently, attended often enough for someone like Khailin to pick up on Court undercurrents. And one of those undercurrents, in the past year or so, had been a connection forged by Antian, the Little Empress. The Princess who had been killed in the summer's earthquake.

Tai had wanted to say goodbye.

For Tai, the mourning was more than that of the land for its anointed.

'But I can understand,' Khailin said, taking a chance. Putting two and two together and coming up with a conclusion that was tenuous but of which she was suddenly very certain, she made her voice sound compassionate and deceptively assured. 'It would be hard to come to terms with such a loss. Losing even just a friend to a calamity like this would be difficult. A sister . . .'

Nhia's head had come up sharply, but she said nothing for a moment, watching Khailin's face. Khailin allowed her features to soften into a small sad smile. 'There was talk in the Court. The Little Empress and a companion she had taken to spending time with. That *was* your Tai, was it not? I thought I heard mention of *jin-shei*.'

'Yes,' said Nhia after a pause, 'they were *jin-shei*.'

'But that should be enough to ensure that Tai is given a place of honour, if only she spoke up that she wished to be there.'

'You don't know her,' Nhia murmured. 'She was First Princess Antian's *jin-shei-bao*, but she would never take advantage of . . .'

She might have manipulated Nhia into offering up the confidences, but the sudden brightness that crept into Khailin's eyes was genuine. 'I have never had one,' she said. 'I have never had a sister who understood me, who knew me. Yan does what our lady mother tells her to do, without looking right or left – if she were told to walk off the edge of a cliff she would do it and never question why. She would go into the marriage they have planned for me, and be utterly content with it, as she would be content with everything.' She glanced at Nhia, and veiled her eyes, suddenly afraid of showing too much of her emotion. 'If I were to die,' she blurted, unable to keep the words under control as firmly as her features, 'there would be nobody to mourn me.'

'Your parents . . .' Nhia began, but Khailin cut her off with a sharp motion of her hand.

'Nobody,' she said with conviction.

'I would be sorry,' Nhia said after a pause.

'As you are my friend?'

'Yes, as I am that.'

'Would you be my sister if I asked you?'

'Are you asking for *jin-shei*?' Nhia said, suddenly sitting very still.

It had not been quite what Khailin had intended. Her emotions were still high, though, and even as they washed over her and made the blood rush into her cheeks she was also thinking, with a rational part of her mind, that this was what she had wanted, *exactly* what she had wanted, when she had set out to draw Nhia into her circle. For *jin-shei* sisters, it would be easy to twine lives and fortunes together – and Nhia could be the only thing left to Khailin, the only source of knowledge, of that power that she needed to keep within reach if she were to remain herself and whole. It would not be the first *jin-shei* bond which had been born out of a more prosaic need rather than of a purity of heart – but even those, according to Khailin's mother's stash of *jin-ashu* literature, were overcome by the power of the vow. However it began, it always ended as a powerful binding. Someone would care. Someone would *be required* to care.

'Yes,' she whispered.

Nhia reached out hesitantly and took her hand. 'If you wish it.'

Khailin felt a weight she had not known she was carrying slip off her heart, and she sat up a little straighter, leaving her hand in Nhia's for a moment.

'Tell Tai,' she said abruptly, 'that she is welcome to watch the procession from the balcony in my family's house. They will pass along our street.'

That had been the third gift.

Instead of trying to find a way to see past the shoulders and the elbows of the crowds in the street, Tai and Nhia had ascended the spiral staircase in Khailin's home and had stood on high, Linh-an's crowded, mourning streets below them, and the three of them had watched the Imperial funeral procession from Khailin's balcony.

First came the drummers, their instruments fluttering with white ribbons, beating a slow marching pace. They were followed by the carts piled high with the offerings for the dead. The first few carts carried the intricate copies manufactured in paper and papier-mâché of the items the dead would require in the afterlife – there were three life-size sedan chairs, draped in cloth-of-gold; an intricately painted and folded miniature paper carriage complete with figures of horses, intended to transport the spirits to Cahan; a number of full-sized human figures with folded hands and painted faces, servants to take care of their needs; cups, fans, musical instruments, writing tablets, a paper replica of the Imperial Diadem, all meticulously crafted, created, painted, ready to be set to the flame as the bodies of the dead were given to the fire, the ashes of all these necessities mixing with the ashes of the dead, taking form in Cahan where they would have need of them. These carts – and there were a number of them, each carefully compiled for each one of the four dead – were followed by others, bearing ingots of gold and silver, draped with white banners inscribed with prayers and blessings and others extolling the virtues of the departed, and then still more, glowing with shimmering white candles, bearing plates and bowls laden with stacks of ceremonial honey cakes, pomegranates and peaches, and flasks of rice wine.

It took a long time for this all to pass by, but finally a long sigh out in the crowded street heralded the arrival of the first of the four bodies in the procession.

Grief had set Tai's shoulders as she watched the four caskets pass by, each placed on a cart drawn by a single white horse and piled high with white flowers – some real, some artificial silken creations. The horses paced slowly, each led on a rein by an Imperial Guardsman cloaked in white, each cart surrounded by an honour guard – twelve Guardsmen for the Emperor and for the Empress, six for the Little Empress Antian, four for Second Princess Oylian. Behind the last cart, Oylian's, walked the remnants of the Imperial Court.

They were led by Empress-Heir Liudan, walking alone, her feet in simple rope-soled sandals, robed in a plain white cotton gown. Her hair was dressed in two long looped braids, and banded with white ribbons; she wore no make-up, her eyes untouched by kohl, staring fiercely in front of her as she paced behind her sister's cart. She looked neither right nor left, seeming to concentrate on just putting one foot in front of another, her head held high. She had never looked more regal.

'She always wore formal dress, even in the Summer Palace,' Tai murmured. 'She was always so – so *royal*. Now she looks . . .'

All three girls looked closely at Liudan as she walked in Linh-an's streets to lay her family to rest, and each of them saw a different thing.

Khailin saw the future Empress, the high royal pride of the small tilted chin, the nobility of carriage and posture. Nhia saw past all that, looking deeper, and saw flickers of fear beneath the haughtiness. Tai saw her through a beloved ghost, and saw the loneliness, and the pain, and that same sense of loss with which she had once looked at Tai herself when she had first believed that Antian was turning away from her.

And Liudan saw nothing, heard nothing, walked in white silence behind her dead, her spirit a fierce emptiness, an empty vessel waiting to be filled with her life's destiny.

# Six

Yuet, the healer's apprentice, had watched the procession of the dead from the window of her room, on the top floor of the home she shared with her mistress, the healer Szewan. Her view was not quite as good as Tai's but she too had been watching Liudan walk behind the biers, and she was remembering the conversation she had had with Tai in the stables of the shattered Summer Palace. *I will help you keep your promise.*

Liudan walked alone, isolated even in this tragic procession, her eyes bright and burning in her pale face. Watching the girl, Yuet was painfully aware how prescient Antian, the dead Little Empress, had been. Yuet's path had crossed with Liudan's several times in the halls of the women's quarters, on the occasions that Szewan the healer had had to visit the Third Princess or her sisters during some childhood complaint. Yuet and Liudan had never spoken directly; Yuet had always been in Liudan's presence as Szewan's assistant and helpmeet and had been expected to be at hand to help Szewan with whatever she required, with her head bowed and her eyes downcast. But even under those circumstances Yuet had formed a clear impression of the girl. Liudan had always had the knack of appearing to be proud and strong and self-sufficient, but she was still vulnerable and dependent on others, more so now, in fact, than she had ever been before. She was an Empress in waiting, but she was still a child.

Officially so, in fact. Many of Liudan's contemporaries had already had their Xat-Wau rites by the time they reached her age, but Yuet knew that Liudan herself had still not started her monthly cycles, and had therefore still not reached an age at which girls were ceremonially taken across the threshold from childhood to womanhood. Yuet herself had been fourteen years old when her own Xat-Wau ceremony had taken place, so it wasn't unheard of – but Yuet was unimportant, a healer's apprentice, and her passage into adulthood had not been something upon which the world had turned. In Liudan's case, her status as a minor child meant a formal regency until such time as the Empress-Heir could be properly taken through her Xat-Wau rites.

Yuet had not had time to watch Liudan in the procession for long before someone came knocking on the door of the healer's house with a screaming child who had fallen and fractured her wrist while perched on a high windowsill trying to see the carts and the mourners. It had been Yuet who had had to deal with the patient. Szewan was getting old, arthritic and half-blind. These days she preferred to act in an advisory capacity, and leave the actual work of administering treatment and medicines to her young apprentice. Many patients had stopped asking for Szewan altogether, and simply called for Yuet's services. Szewan had been talking for some time about officially retiring and passing her practice over to Yuet completely, but there were still some clients – the older people, who had spent their entire lives under Szewan's ministrations, and a large portion of the clannish Imperial Court families – who still insisted on at least having her present while Yuet swabbed, bandaged, and concocted poultices and draughts. By the time Yuet had set the child's broken wrist, immobilized it with a splint and sent the patient and her mother on their way, the procession was past and all that was there to be seen was over.

The crowds were thinning, some streaming to the place of the burning where all the paper offerings would be displayed on and around the four pyres before the whole thing was set alight; that spectacle would draw many witnesses. But for the city the show was over, and the mourning was about to begin.

Liudan and the rest of the Imperial Court would return to the Linh-an Palace in sedan chairs, via a less circuitous route, out of the crowd's eye, once the immolation ceremonies were over; and once they did so the business of governing Syai would become an issue that would occupy the high-ranking ones in the Palace for some time to come.

*I will help you keep your promise*, Yuet had told Tai. But, as she cleaned up after her patient, Yuet found herself wondering how she could have possibly made such a rash statement. Tai had been *jin-shei-bao* to the Little Empress – but that was where the connection to the Court began and ended, and Yuet was certainly in no position to further that connection. She herself was still officially a healer's apprentice – a journeyman, to be sure, and more and more independent, but nonetheless still coasting on Szewan's own reputation where the Court was concerned. She certainly had, and would have in the future unless things changed rather quickly, no intimate access to Liudan herself except in Szewan's presence, and certainly no means to procure such access to someone like Tai. Perhaps Tai could have used the *jin-shei* connection to gain entry into the Court itself, but Liudan would be very careful with her favours and allegiances right now, especially during the regency period, and the fulfilment of Tai's promise, a promise doubly binding because it had been asked by a dying woman and in the name of *jin-shei*, seemed bleakly improbable.

Szewan had come to the window briefly to peer at the procession but had not stayed long.

'My hands are hurting me terribly,' she said, rubbing her swollen, arthritic knuckles. 'I'll take a poppy draught and retire to bed for a few hours. You can handle anything that comes up.'

'I'll make the draught,' Yuet said.

Szewan grunted in assent, reaching out to draw the shutters closed, trying to keep the worst of the heat out of the room.

She had already divested herself of her outer robe and had slipped in under the thin sheets in her shift when Yuet came up with the cup of poppy. Her nose twitched at the draught as Yuet proffered the cup.

'It smells strong,' Szewan said.

'I made it strong,' Yuet said. 'If you are in enough pain to retire to bed in the middle of the day, you may as well try and sleep through the worst of it. As you say – I will handle anything that comes up.'

'One of these days,' Szewan said, taking a delicate sip of the sleeping draught, 'I will have to draw up the papers properly, and make you a partner. You are no longer an apprentice, Yuet-*mai*.'

Yuet blushed. 'I'll never know all you know,' she said.

'You already know more than you think you know,' said Szewan shrewdly, 'and, I think, more than *I* think you know. Sometimes I believe you keep secret notes on everything I say and don't say. When I am gone and you go through my papers, there is little that you will learn that you have not already found out.'

'I listen, Szewan-*lama*.'

'I know,' said Szewan. 'Sometimes you hear far too much.' She yawned, showing a mouth with many teeth either missing or yellow with age and decay, and handed the cup back to Yuet. 'I will sleep now. Leave me.'

Yuet bowed her head in acknowledgement and withdrew as Szewan closed her eyes and pillowed her withered cheek on her arm.

'I will sleep now,' she murmured again, as Yuet closed the door gently behind her.

There were no further emergencies that morning, and only one house-call she had to make on an ailing patient too ill to come to her, so Yuet spent the morning in her stillroom, making up the supplies of the herbal remedies she used to ease the more common aches and pains of Linh-an and checking up on the stocks of the more rare medicines whose existence was written down in secret books and only in *jin-ashu* script where a woman might read of them. She looked in on Szewan just before she left to see her patient, but the old healer still slept peacefully, snoring gently through her parted lips. Yuet's patient appeared to be on the mend – still weak but definitely improving, sitting up and taking solid food for the first time in many days – and Yuet returned home feeling pleased with herself.

She was met by first disaster, and then potentially deepening catastrophe.

The first person she saw as she stepped into the entrance hallway of the chambers she shared with Szewan was the woman who served the healer's household as cook and maid-of-all-work. She stood in the hall, wringing her hands, her expression equal parts panic, fear and grief. Yuet's heart stopped for a moment. She instinctively knew what must have happened – but stood frozen, her hand still on the door handle, staring at the servant in silence.

There was a dose of guilt in the servant's demeanour, too.

'I heard her breathing funny, mistress – I swear I didn't know what to do, and you weren't here, and I went in and I saw – she was breathing funny, mistress, and she was lying on her side with her face into the pillow so I came in to look and I just tried to turn her head, just a little, so that she could get air, and she just . . . she just . . .'

'Oh, dear Gods,' Yuet whispered.

'I'm sorry, mistress, I didn't know – I shouldn't have touched her – I should have waited – I should have sent for you – I should have . . .'

'Is she . . . is Szewan dead?'

The servant burst into tears. 'Yes, mistress, she is dead. I turned her head, just a little, so that she could breathe and she, she, she choked and started coughing and then choked again and it was as if she couldn't get enough air, and then . . .'

'Enough,' said Yuet, her eyes full of tears. 'It is not your doing.' She hunted for an activity, something to give the servant to do, something familiar to calm her nerves and soothe her panicked guilt. 'Go . . . go make some green tea. Bring it to the sitting room.'

The servant sniffed, wiping her eyes with the back of her hand. 'Yes, mistress.'

Yuet closed the door behind her, very slowly, kicked off the sandals she had worn to go outside and set down the leather bag she had carried to her patient's house. She made her way into Szewan's sleeping quarters, walking softly on the balls of her bare feet, as though a sharp noise could wake her mistress.

*I gave her a strong poppy draught. What if it was this . . . ? Should I have made it weaker? Oh, dear Gods.*

Szewan was lying half on her side, half on her back – the ministrations of the servant, no doubt. Yuet checked, but it had not been any physical obstruction that had blocked Szewan's airways – she had not choked on her tongue or anything like that, an event that Yuet had seen occur and had prevented more than once with patients who suffered from fits or seizures. On that, at least, she could reassure the poor cook, who probably thought that her very touch had made the old healer drop dead in her bed.

*Perhaps it was just age.*

Yuet arranged Szewan's body in a seemly manner on her bed, laying her on her back and crossing her arms on her thin ribcage. As though there had not been enough death in Linh-an in the month just past. There would be things to arrange with the Temple – there was no immediate family and it would be up to Yuet, the apprentice and the closest thing to a relative old Szewan had in this world, to perform the funerary rites required. But already she was thinking ahead. *She said I was no longer an apprentice*, Yuet thought to herself as she fussed with the bedclothes. *But the papers hadn't been drawn up yet. What if . . . ? What happens now?*

There was a tap on the door.

'Tea, mistress.'

Yuet crossed to the door. 'I am coming.'

The servant was still wringing her hands. 'It's so sudden, mistress, I never meant . . . I didn't mean to . . .'

'You have done nothing wrong. I have looked at her and there are no signs of anything but that you tried to help,' Yuet said again, soothingly, calming the woman down. 'There will still be work for you here.'

That was part of the servant's panic, the fear that she would be dismissed now that the household had changed. She seemed to relax a little at this reassurance, but Yuet found herself wondering if she was in fact in a position to give it. She stepped into the sitting room to pick up the bowl of steaming green tea which the cook had brought in on a lacquered tray, and then went into the tiny alcove that had served Szewan as an office, piled high with scrolls and papers and bound books of recipes for medicines, patient records, agreements, licences and other legal documentation. Somehow Szewan had never quite planned for dying. Yuet knew she would need to go through all this anyway, it was all her responsibility now, at least until she found out otherwise – but she was looking for practical things, for things relating to what would happen to the healer's practice now that she was gone, whether a journeyman like herself, who had not yet been quite promoted to full mastery, could take over now or if she would need to go looking for some other Linh-an healer with his or her master's papers and hand over all of Szewan's accumulated treasury of information to this . . . this usurper.

*I should have the papers drawn up*, Szewan had said. Barely a few hours ago. If only there had been a witness to that – to the utterance which to all intents and purposes graduated Yuet from journeyman to full-fledged healer.

There was. There might have been.

If the cook was led to believe that her having heard that, that her willingness to swear that she had heard that, may have a direct bearing on her livelihood in this household, then maybe a notary could be found . . .

Yuet set the bowl of tea aside, and it grew cold, forgotten, as she immersed herself in Szewan's papers. In rebuilding a future which, through sins of omission, looked as though it might disintegrate around her.

She owed it to Szewan, safeguarding her secrets. She owed it to Szewan's high-born patients, details of whose illnesses ought not to become bargaining chips for healers who had not earned the trust or the confidence of those patients.

She owed it to Tai, to her *jin-shei-bao*, to whom she had made a promise – which she might never be able to keep if she was dispossessed of her status and her position. She owed it to the dead of the Summer Palace earthquake, some of whom had passed in their caskets beneath her window that very morning.

She owed it to Liudan, the survivor.

She owed it to herself.


# Seven


Yuet spent a sleepless night amongst Szewan's chaotic records, trying to make sense of the world she had inherited. She had finally retired to her room in the last dark hours before dawn and fell into a fitful doze; she was not at her best when she was shaken awake only a few hours later by the servant.

'Mistress? I'm sorry, mistress, I would not disturb you, but there is a message from the Court, for Mistress Szewan. The man says he must have an answer.'

'Did you say anything to him about Szewan?' said Yuet, sitting up, shocked awake.

'No, Mistress Yuet. I said I would come and wake you.'

'Thank you. Please tell him I will be there at once.'

It was light outside, full day. Yuet drew on her outer robe in feverish haste, rebraided her tousled hair into a semblance of tidiness with swift, practised fingers, and paused to splash a handful of cold water onto her face, dabbing it dry with one of Szewan's fine linen towels. It would have to do. It was just a messenger, after all.

The man who had come with the message waited in the hallway, having refused the servant's invitation into the sitting room.

Yuet greeted him with a bow, and he returned it politely.

'How may I help you?' she asked.

'The healer Szewan is required at the Palace, immediately.'

'She is . . . unavailable,' said Yuet carefully. She most emphatically did not want the news of Szewan's death prematurely escaping from this house. She needed time, time to set up her world, her life. Time to organize her future. 'I am Yuet, her apprentice . . . her partner. Is someone ill? May I be of assistance?'

'If it please you, Mistress Yuet, I come from the Chancellor. *Sei* Zibo requests the presence of healer Szewan at a meeting of the Imperial Council this morning.'

Yuet's mind raced. Imperial Council? This had to do with the regency. Why did they want Szewan?

The answer was obvious. Liudan.

'When is Szewan's presence required?' Yuet asked.

'The meeting is in an hour's time, Mistress Yuet. I was sent to escort the healer to the Palace immediately.'

'If you will wait here,' Yuet instructed, 'I will need a few moments to make a few arrangements and then I will accompany you myself.'

'But it is the healer Szewan who . . .'

'She is, as I say, unavailable at this moment,' Yuet said with a veneer of serenity which hid a wildly beating heart. She was going to gamble on something here; it was a good thing that this was a simple

117

messenger, not a Guard with specific orders, not someone who would think things through and demand explanations. This man was of a lower tier, someone used to taking commands from somebody who knew how to give them, who would follow the last firm command that he was given. All she needed to do was remain firm. 'Wait here. I will be out as soon as I am ready.'

He was looking a little unhappy, but he bowed his acquiescence and took up a waiting stance at the door. Yuet went back to her room and summoned the servant, who came in so quickly that Yuet was sure she must have been lurking just outside the door, listening.

'Help me,' she said. 'I need assistance with dressing my hair. I will go to the Palace in Mistress Szewan's name. It is a good thing. At least I will be able to pass on the news without sending wild rumours out. The messenger is waiting to escort me there, we need to be quick.'

The servant nodded, taking up a comb even as Yuet unbraided her hair and shook the rippling dark mass of it out. It spilled, straight and thick and long, almost down to her knees. 'As simple as formality will allow,' she instructed, hunting for ornaments on the table in front of her, reaching for the white ribbons of mourning that had to be woven into her hair, sorting out silver clasps to hold the rest of it up. 'In the meantime,' she said, while the servant's deft fingers plaited and coiled, 'allow no one into the house until I return, and say that Szewan and I are both unavailable at the moment. Take down details of anyone who needs urgent help, and I will deal with that when I get back. But nobody waits here, and nobody gets past you into the house. Is that clear?'

'Yes, Mistress Yuet,' the servant said, her eyes wide.

'And when I return I will need to talk to you,' Yuet said, 'about Mistress Szewan.'

'Yes, mistress,' the woman said, her voice faltering a little.

Yuet left her with that small seed of disquiet. It would do her good to worry on it for a while.

She donned a fresh shift, laced an inner robe of pale silk at her throat, shrugged into a heavy brocade outer robe suitable for a Court appearance, ran a final check over her hair and her make-up, made sure she was wearing the white ribbon of mourning around her sleeve, and swept out of her chambers with a final warning to the servant to lock up after her and not allow anyone into the house.

The escort had a hired sedan cart waiting, obviously in deference to Szewan's age and infirmities, and since there had been no countermand issued he simply helped Yuet into it and gave the signal for the driver to depart. The streets were empty of people, still wrapped in mourning for the dead Emperor, normal commerce still operating in fits and starts; from within the chair Yuet could hear the intermittent calls of street vendors but the cart was given free passage, not jostled by other conveyances or forced to wait while one of higher rank swept by, and they were quickly at the gates of the Palace where they were admitted, after a brief hesitation, by one of a pair of Imperial Guards on duty. The chair was trotted into an inner courtyard; Yuet's escort handed her down from it courteously, she thanked him, and he left her with a bow.

Alone before the entrance to the Imperial Palace, Yuet drew a deep breath, aware that her hands were shaking. Szewan had meant to do this, she was sure – had meant to promote Yuet into a full partner, with every right to be here in her place – but she had not done it yet, *she had not done it yet*, and Yuet was already making plans to remedy that oversight.

*After* she had already made her presence here an accepted fact.

Another Imperial Guard, standing just within the door she pushed open, gave her a stiff formal bow, questioning without words.

'The healer, summoned by *Sei* Zibo, the Chancellor, for a meeting of the Council,' Yuet murmured, carefully avoiding names, praying the Guard would demand none.

He did not. He offered her another small bow, one of acknowledgement, and indicated that she should follow him. Yuet gathered her brocade robe about her and walked behind him with her head held high like a queen. The Guard delivered her into an empty room, its two high arched windows looking out into a green garden courtyard with a stone fountain, with a carved and painted dragon winding sinuously around the outer rim, in the centre.

'If you will wait,' the Guard said, bowing out, leaving her alone.

With a rustle of silk Yuet walked across to the windows and studied the graceful garden outside. Its paths were strewn with crushed stone and white sand, raked smooth, and there was a pair of peacocks right underneath the fountain, tails spilled over the path in a sweep of indigo and purple. It looked like a painting of Cahan's courts, peaceful, almost holy.

'I was expecting to see Healer Szewan,' a voice interrupted her reverie.

Yuet turned.

She had never met the High Chancellor of Syai, but she knew him by sight, as did most of the citizens of Linh-an, from his appearances in processions, at the Temple, in the street on holy days when he walked out to give alms to the poor. High Chancellor Zibo was dressed today in the full formal regalia of his office, including the inevitable white ribbons of mourning – the high stiff collar of his brocade tunic, seemingly propping up his several chins; the brilliant silk sash; the heavy gold chain of office. His greying but still glossy hair was twisted up in heavy rolls held with ebony sticks with silver tassels. A sense of presence and importance surrounded him like an aura.

Yuet sank into a deep obeisance.

'I bear grave news, *sei*. The healer Szewan passed into Cahan last night. I am her apprentice and her partner, Yuet. I come in her place if I may be of service.'

Zibo was frowning. 'This is unfortunate. This is very unfortunate. You will need to present your credentials to us, of course.'

'*Sei*, I was woken this morning by your messenger and I came at your summons as soon as possible. I did not have time to gather anything to bring with me this morning.'

'Yes, yes. But you are so young. I wonder if we shouldn't seek another, more experienced, healer to take over the care of the Court.'

Yuet raised her eyes briefly. '*Sei* – Healer Szewan was privy to many things in the Court, some of which were closely guarded secrets. I have locked her office so that none may have access to her records, save myself only who worked with her. I will give these records over to you if you wish – but I am already part of the confidentiality which she and the Imperial Court have established. She was trusted, *sei* Zibo, and she trusted me. I may be young, as you say, but I was trained by the woman whom this Court came to for every ailment for forty years, and I am at your service, and the service of the Imperial Court. If you would tell me how I may help?'

It had been almost impertinent. She had practically interrupted him. But if she'd given him a fraction of a second more he would have graciously thanked her, told her to go home and pack up

Szewan's records, and hand them over to . . . to whichever Linh-an healer he picked to take her place.

At least she had made him stop and think. When she stole another look at his corpulent face, he was frowning, tapping his chins with one pudgy finger.

'Yes, yes,' he said. There was a trace of impatience in his voice. 'You say you were her partner?'

'Yes, *sei*,' Yuet said, digging her nails into the palm of her hand where he couldn't see them behind the brocade sweep of her robe.

'You were the healer at the Summer Palace, were you not?' he asked suddenly, his eyes glittering.

Yuet forced herself to meet his gaze, although her heart suddenly skipped a beat. If he chose, he could find things in her actions on that dreadful day which would forever bar her from any access to the Court whatsoever. 'Yes, *sei* Zibo,' she said, controlling her voice. 'I was there. I was there when they found the body of the Emperor. I was with the Little Empress Antian when she died.'

Zibo stared at her for a long moment, his face inscrutable.

'We will honour Healer Szewan's judgement for now,' he said at last. 'You will have to present your credentials to us as soon as you have begun the formalities for her funeral ceremonies, of course. Your continued status will depend on those. For now, who knows but that a young healer might be exactly what we need. With the problem.'

'What,' said Yuet delicately, choosing to ignore the matter of the credentials for the moment, 'is the problem?'

'Liudan. The Empress-Heir.' Zibo heaved a deep sigh, which made his chins cascade over his collar in interesting ways. 'Well, I suppose there is nothing for it – she insists that a healer examine her, after all, and you're here. Follow me.'

'The Empress-Heir?' Yuet questioned as she fell into step two paces behind him, as protocol demanded. 'But your messenger said something about an Imperial Council.'

'There will be a Council meeting,' Zibo said. 'The Council awaits the results of your examination of the Empress-Heir.'

Mystified, but unable to ask any more questions to which Zibo obviously expected her to provide the answers, Yuet followed the Chancellor through sumptuously appointed corridors and chambers and up four flights of stairs until they finally arrived at a gilded set of gates guarded by a pair of female Imperial Guards.

'The healer,' Chancellor Zibo said, making a gesture in Yuet's direction. 'Take her to the Empress-Heir. And when she is done, have someone conduct her to the Council Chamber. We will await her there. Healer, take what time you will need. Be aware we wait upon you.'

'Excellency,' said Yuet, offering another deep bow as he nodded to her and swept away.

One of the Guards opened the gilded door and motioned with her hand. 'This way.'

Yuet followed her into a corridor whose costly glass windows, veiled with swathes of silk so fine that it was almost see-through, looked out onto yet another magnificent garden, this one a tapestry of willow and bamboo. The Guard led Yuet past half-open doors through which she could catch glimpses of richly appointed rooms, or hear murmurs of conversation or soft music, but they saw no other living human being until the Guard stopped at a firmly closed door twice the height of all the rest, gilded and carved with inter-twined dragons, and knocked on it twice.

'Your Highness, the healer.'

The door was opened by a young serving girl, dressed in white cotton leggings and a white robe which reached down to her mid-calves. Her feet were bare. She ducked her head at the Guard, in silence, and motioned Yuet inside. Yuet inclined her head at the Guard by way of thanks, and followed the summons.

The door opened into a small anteroom lit with candles, and the servant girl padded over to another door, twin to the first, in the far wall and pushed it open, motioning for Yuet to enter.

The many-panelled glass windows of the inner chamber opened like doors, out onto a wide balcony with a carved stone balustrade. Empress-Heir Liudan stood out on the balcony, her hair loose down her back, her feet thrust into thin slippers against the chill of the stone flags of the balcony, wrapped in a robe that tied around her waist with a broad sash. She had her back to the room, and her shoulders had a rigid set.

When she did turn to face Yuet, who stood waiting in silence to be acknowledged, it was in a swift savage whirl which set her hair swinging, and she was already speaking.

'I need your help, I need to ask you . . .' She faltered, her eyes narrowed. 'You? I was expecting the old healer.'

'She was unavailable, Highness,' said Yuet carefully, offering a deep bow as she spoke. 'My name is Yuet. May I be of assistance to you?'

Liudan chewed on her lip for a moment, thinking.

'Perhaps it is even better,' she said. 'You would understand.'

'Understand what, Highness?'

'I have told them I have started my cycles,' Liudan said abruptly.

*I should have known*, Yuet thought to herself. With hindsight, it was obvious – no cycles, no Xat-Wau, a regency until Liudan could prove herself to have reached physical adulthood. If she could convince the Council that she was, in fact, due her Xat-Wau ceremony immediately, there would be no regency.

'You told them you were bleeding, they wanted proof, you asked to be examined by a healer, hoping to convince the healer to go along with your story although it is not technically true?' Yuet said.

Liudan flashed her a look, somewhat startled. She had not expected it to be summed up so baldly, without even an honorific to soften it. 'They are just waiting,' Liudan said, 'to put me away again, somewhere safe, for Cahan alone knows how long. I've always been the Third, the spare, and now my own body is betraying me. It's not as though I would be lying, it's going to happen, isn't it? It happens to everybody, after all, and I'm already old enough for it to have happened to me over and over again, but . . .'

'I understand,' Yuet said. 'It never mattered, not with me, but I was your age, maybe only a few months off, when mine came.'

'So you'll help me?'

'Princess,' said Yuet, meeting Liudan's eyes squarely, 'my assistance to you, however willingly offered, may be short-lived.'

'How so?'

'You spoke of having expected "the old one" – Healer Szewan is dead. She spoke to me only hours before she died of drawing up papers elevating me to full partner. She died before she did so, to the best of my knowledge. I have told the Chancellor that I *was* her partner, which is the only reason I am here at all – otherwise you would have been seeing a very different face before you right now. But he spoke of credentials, and I am meant to produce those for him before tomorrow. If I do not, then my words carry little weight. I have a witness,' Yuet said carefully, 'who will swear of Szewan's intent. But I need to find a notary willing to draw up the papers, now, after Szewan's death.'

Liudan stared at her for a long moment. 'I think I can help you with that,' she said at length. 'If you do what I wish, I become Empress. If I become Empress, I can protect you. If I send you the notary before the day is out, will you tell the Chancellor that I am no longer the child that he believes me to be?'

'I will swear to it,' Yuet said calmly. 'I will even produce proof of it if he demands it. I will take such proof away with me now.'

'What?' Liudan was not one to waste words.

'These are women's quarters, someone here is into her cycles right now. If you can find me a woman who is bleeding, her rags will serve as your proof if necessary.'

Liudan considered this for a moment, and then strode across the room to pull a brocade ribbon that hung from the ceiling. It was a summons, and it quickly brought the servant girl from the ante-room. Liudan gave a series of swift signals with her hand, and the girl bowed and backed out again. Yuet watched with interest.

'Sign language?'

'She is deaf, and she cannot speak,' Liudan said. 'There are times I find that useful. She and I communicate very well by sign.'

'What did you tell her to do?'

'Get your proof,' Liudan said. 'It is something I had already considered, but they would not necessarily have taken my word for it, not when so much is at stake. I know that at least one of the Council princes was looking forward to a year or so of regency rule. I needed someone else's backing.' Her eyes were smouldering with a slow anger. 'They have always considered me someone they didn't have to reckon with. All of them. Not a single person in this Court has ever cared about me.'

'Not all, Princess,' murmured Yuet.

Liudan whipped her head around. 'What do you mean?'

'I was at the Summer Palace when they all died,' Yuet said, her voice very low. 'I was with your sister, the Little Empress, when she drew her last breath; I wore the rush of her heart's blood on my robe all that long awful day while we looked in the rubble for the bodies of the dead.'

'Antian,' Liudan said, with a sharp dismissive motion of her hand. But she had been an instant too late with the reaction, and Yuet could read a hurt there, the sense of abandonment.

'Her last words, if you did not know this, Princess, were about you,' Yuet said.

Liudan turned away, but not before Yuet had glimpsed the naked, raw need in her eyes. 'They were?'

She would not ask what Antian had said. There was a carapace of pride which she wore like armour, and she would not let anyone past that. Not yet.

'She asked her *jin-shei-bao* to love you, in her name,' Yuet said.

Liudan broke away, walked with swift angry steps to the open balcony doors and tugged them shut with a force that shivered the glass within them.

'She asked the one for whom she left me to *love* me?'

'Tai said you hated her.'

Liudan snorted inelegantly.

'Princess, she promised to do it. She has no idea how, but she promised. You will be doing her a kindness, and your royal sister honour, if you would meet with her.'

Liudan was watching her again, her eyes kindled. 'And what is your stake in this?'

Yuet met her gaze squarely. 'I watched Tai make a promise to a dying girl, and I watched her agonize over that promise afterwards. I watched her perform a small miracle in the chaos of the earth-quake's aftermath, all in your sister's name. If ever there was love between *jin-shei* sisters, it was there with these two. It made my heart ache to see her left alone, just as you have been.'

'I have not,' Liudan began haughtily, drawing herself up to her full height, her thin foxlike face sharpening into points and angles of outrage.

Yuet cut across the protest. 'I don't know if you have *jin-shei-bao*, Princess Liudan. Perhaps, if you do, you will begin to understand what it took to make such a promise. And I . . . I promised my own *jin-shei-bao* that I would try and help her keep that promise. It is partly because of this that I am ready to help you with your plan now.'

'Because of Tai?' Liudan asked. 'You are *jin-shei* to Tai, too?'

'We pledged after the earthquake, yes,' Yuet said.

'I suppose she wants *me* to pledge to her too,' Liudan said. 'She's had a taste of Court, and she . . .'

'No, Highness. Not Tai. I wish you would meet with her. I wish that you did have a *jin-shei-bao* of your own. It would make what you face here easier for you.'

'There isn't a woman in this Court . . .' Liudan's eyes lost focus for a moment. She had stepped back into her own mind, into her own memories. Of a time *before*, when she was young, and when whispers of her mother's fall from grace had wrapped Liudan in the shroud of Cai's sins. Of the way that the women around her would be flawlessly correct to her, but none would smile at her with a genuine warmth – except the Empress once or twice, distantly – and except *her*. Antian. The lost sister who might have been the only person at the Court to truly love Liudan.

But it was too late for that; that world had gone. What remained was only the protocol and the infinite politeness.

'There isn't a woman in this Court with whom I would want to tie my fortunes in this way,' Liudan said, finishing her thought with a sharp cutting motion of one graceful hand. 'I don't trust any of them not to betray me at the first opportunity.'

'But you trust me,' Yuet murmured.

Liudan smiled, a smile that was not entirely pleasant. 'But then you have just told me something that gives me a hold over you. I can destroy you if you betray me.'

'But it would have been nice to be able to trust without that safeguard, would it not?'

Liudan scowled. 'What do you want of me?'

The servant girl returned, scuttling into the room, bearing something wrapped in scraps of material. Liudan motioned for the package to be handed over to Yuet, and the servant did so, bowed to Liudan, and departed once again.

'Will that do?' Liudan asked as Yuet lifted a corner of the wrapping and inspected the contents of the package.

'I think it will, yes,' Yuet said, letting the wrapping drop again. 'I go to the Council now. They will no doubt return their verdict to you in good time. If I may take my leave?'

'Go,' said Liudan.

Yuet made a deep obeisance, and retreated. At the door, she turned and looked back; Liudan had not moved, standing stiffly in the centre of her empty, opulent room. 'I would have a few more of these on hand,' Yuet said softly, indicating the package she held. 'Just in case. And if you retire to bed for a while and plead feeling unwell – offer an explanation, if you are pressed, that it is cramping – it will probably go further to prove your status.'

She bowed again and was about to depart when she heard Liudan say her name. She turned her head. Liudan's shoulders had relaxed a little, and her face had softened into something resembling gratitude.

'Thank you,' she said. 'I will not forget this.'

'Empress,' acknowledged Yuet with a small smile.

Liudan actually managed to offer a thin smile in return. 'Your Tai . . . I will think on it.'

Yuet inclined her head, dropped her eyes, bowed deeply, and went out of the room closing the door after her. The Guard who had brought her here waited outside in the corridor when the little servant girl had let her out.

'Take me to the Council chamber,' Yuet said serenely.


# Eight

There had been hostility in the Council chamber. Regencies meant revenues, and, as Liudan had observed, at least one of the Council princes had scowled rather too openly when Yuet informed the Council that, instead of planning a regency government, they should all start concerning themselves with preparing Liudan's Xat-Wau ceremonies. They would have their troubles with that, given the tradition that a girl's grandmother traditionally placed the red pin of Xat-Wau into her hair – Liudan's grandmother, the Dowager Empress, had not been at the Summer Palace and had thus survived the earthquake but she had been in Linh-an for the simple reason that she was bedridden, practically crippled and nine-tenths senile. Getting her involved in any kind of ritual would be impractical if not impossible, but all Liudan's other senior female relatives were dead or missing in the earthquake. Thankfully, Yuet thought as she had left the sulky Council, that was not her problem.

Her problem was Szewan, and whether Liudan would keep her word.

She spent another few hours, after her return home, in Szewan's office, sorting things out, re-filing documents according to her own system, making sure that she was indispensable for making sense of the treasure trove that was Szewan's store of records. Yuet did discover a deed to the house, which Szewan *did* get around to annotating properly before she died, and discovered that she had been made the sole heiress of Szewan's home and her possessions. There really *was* no other family, it seemed. Yuet felt a pang of pity for the old woman who had taught her her trade, who had apparently outlived everyone she knew, but a part of her simply smiled and filed away the document in a safe place. It would help with her claim to full partnership. Szewan had already, in a technical sense, designated Yuet her heir.

Liudan did keep her word.

Yuet had cleared the decks in preparation for the notary's visit. She had asked the cook, couching the question in terms which implied that any answer other than yes could harm the servant's own prospects as the household in which she worked disintegrated around her, if she had overheard Szewan's words about making Yuet a full partner. The cook's memory was suddenly full of instances where she had heard Szewan say just that.

A notary from the Imperial Court had presented himself at Yuet's door that evening, with full instructions. The healer's cook and servant had been summoned and her statement that she had witnessed Szewan's intent to raise Yuet into partnership taken down and sealed by the notary, who then drew up two copies of the articles of partnership. The task took him most of the night, and Yuet herself stayed up with him until he was done. The document was written up in formal *hacha-ashu*, which neither of the women could read but which both signed in fine *jin-ashu* hand and which was then countersigned by the notary himself as formal witness and as an agent of the government. In the morning, having given the cook a small bag of silver and a promise of perpetual employment in her household for as long as Yuet was head of it, Yuet presented herself and her 'credentials', the ink barely dry on them, to the office of the High Chancellor of Syai.

She was still a few months shy of her eighteenth birthday, but Yuet was officially the Healer of the Imperial Court of Syai. She had done it.

The formalities involved with laying Szewan's body to rest occupied Yuet's next few days to the exclusion of everything else. She arranged for the appropriate prayers and offerings in the Temple, for the cremation of the body, for the disposal of the ashes. Her patients – Szewan's patients – had to be informed, and those not in need of urgent attention stayed away in deference to these arrangements, sending in messages of condolence and offerings of ceremonial honey cakes or white banners with inscriptions extolling Szewan's virtues which Yuet hung from the windows of the house of mourning.

She did take on the emergencies, though, especially ones associated with the Imperial circles. When an Imperial Guard came to her house at a late hour one afternoon to summon her to the Guard compound to look at an injury, Yuet gathered up her things and followed him back to the practice yard.

At first Yuet took the figure slumped against the far wall of the practice yard as some child who had snuck in to watch and had fallen asleep against the wall. A closer look revealed that the 'child' wore the sparring garb of a trainee Guard, and that the arm lying across her ribcage was not laid there in a casual way but rather as a support enabling the hurt girl to breathe without too much pain. Yuet dropped into a crouch beside the patient.

'What did you do to yourself?' she asked. 'Let me look.'

'I didn't . . . do anything . . . to myself,' she was informed roundly, if breathlessly, by her patient, whose obsidian dark eyes glittered with both pain and annoyance. '*He* did it to me.'

Another Guard trainee, head and shoulders taller than the young patient and maybe three or four years older, shrugged sheepishly. 'I really didn't mean it,' he said. 'She was too damned good, and I first lost my temper and then forgot who I was fighting and fought as if I had one of my own classmates as a partner. I should have given her some leeway, she has hardly begun with the quarterstaff, and she doesn't have the strength yet. But she's too good, I say.'

'Flattery . . . will not get you . . . off,' panted his erstwhile partner. 'I'll . . . get you . . . back . . . *aaaah!*'

The last was a yowl of pain as Yuet's fingers probed the girl's side.

'Not for a while, you won't,' Yuet said. 'I think he's cracked a couple of ribs. I need to bind you up, pretty tight, and there will be no sudden movements for at least a month.' The flat rebellion in those dark eyes as they flashed up and met Yuet's made her mouth quirk in a smile. 'Well, I could say a few days, and you would go out and do things, and then you would come to me in three weeks and complain that you couldn't lift up a kitten with that arm, and you'd be right. You want it to heal clean, don't you? What's your name, firecracker?'

'Xaforn,' said the firecracker in question. 'I'll be out of commission for . . . a *month*?'

'At least,' Yuet said.

Xaforn shot her sparring partner a black look. 'You wait,' she panted, 'until I am . . . myself again . . . and don't you dare tell me . . . you won't fight me again.'

'You'd better not,' Yuet said, amused, addressing the older Guard. 'Or I have a feeling that she'd crack your staff over your head.'

'Rematch later, then,' said the older boy, laughing. 'I should have known better than to take you on, Xaforn. You don't give *up*!'

'Damn right I don't.'

He saluted, still laughing, and withdrew. Yuet helped Xaforn hobble back to her quarters, and taped up her bruised ribs as she sat on the edge of her bed.

'Xaforn,' Yuet said as she worked. 'I have heard of you. You're the fierce one.'

Xaforn shrugged her shoulders, winced.

'Don't do that,' Yuet instructed. 'In fact, don't do that for a while. Find some other way of letting people know how tough you are.'

'Are you sure about the month?' Xaforn said, scowling.

'Why? Do you plan on giving me a hiding too when you can move again?' Yuet asked, laughing.

After a moment, Xaforn laughed along with her. 'I have no idea what to do with myself all that time,' she said.

'Learn a craft,' suggested Yuet.

'Will you teach me healing?'

'You need to sit still,' Yuet said, startled but amused. 'Not run around taking care of patients. Besides, you're already taught field medicine as a Guard, aren't you?'

'Some,' said Xaforn. 'I wasn't . . . serious.'

'I know,' Yuet said. 'Is there anyone who can spend some time with you? A companion?'

Xaforn hesitated for a moment. 'I suppose I could always visit the cat.'

'Pardon?'

'I rescued a cat,' Xaforn said cryptically. 'And now Qiaan wants to teach me *jin-ashu*.'

Yuet regarded her, a little startled. 'You don't know *jin-ashu*?'

'I was foundling,' Xaforn said. 'Guard raised me.'

'Ah.' There had been no mother to teach this little wildcat the niceties of her heritage. 'And who's Qiaan?'

'She wants to be *jin-shei*,' Xaforn said. 'I still haven't told her yes or no.'

'Well,' said Yuet gently, 'now would be as good a time as any to learn *jin-ashu*. And a *jin-shei-bao* is a good thing to have when you are hurting and need help. I would accept your Qiaan's pledge.'

'Have you got one?' Xaforn asked bluntly.

'Yes,' Yuet said.

'What do you *do*?' Xaforn asked, perplexed. The concept was both familiar and alien to her – she knew about the basic principles of *jin-shei*, but she had never quite got down to the bottom of this mystery. It all sounded very emotional and impractical, and she wasn't convinced that any of it was useful to her in the life she had chosen.

Yuet found herself telling the story of the Little Empress, for the second time in a handful of days, and in considerably more detail. Xaforn was listening intently.

'I don't think Qiaan has had one before, either,' Xaforn said, when Yuet had finished her story. 'I wonder if she even knows what she has asked. You know a lot about it.'

'No,' Yuet said, 'only what I have seen, and experienced. That is not much.'

'You have just one?'

'I had another,' said Yuet, 'a long time ago, but she died from the pox when she was fifteen and I was fourteen. After that, no, I didn't have any more – until recently.'

'Would you be mine?' Xaforn said.

The question was so thoroughly unexpected that Yuet was momentarily left speechless in the face of the request. Xaforn saw her expression, and misinterpreted it. Her face started closing.

'I only thought . . .' she began, but Yuet raised a hand to stop her.

'I am sorry. You startled me. If you think Qiaan is not quite sure what she is offering you, do you know what *you* are doing?'

Xaforn nodded mulishly. She wasn't going to speak again.

Yuet blinked a few times, still astonished. 'I have no idea why you wish it,' she said, 'but I guess a Guard would find a healer *jin-shei-bao* useful, at that. So, little sister, if you really wish this . . .'

Xaforn nodded again. 'I do. You can teach me things, and then Qiaan won't think I am stupid.'

Yuet laughed. 'So you have decided to accept Qiaan too?'

'Yes, I think so. There's the cat.'

'You'll have to tell me about this cat some day,' Yuet said, entertained. 'I'll look in on you tomorrow. No fighting. I'll know, remember? Send for the cat, if you have to, but stay *still*. Understood?'

'Yes. Thank you.'

When she left, Yuet was still smiling, shaking her head in amusement. Xaforn was left lying on her bunk, flat on her back, her head turned towards the doorway through which Yuet had left, the expression on her own face inscrutable.

# Nine

When another summons came from the Palace, less than two weeks after her initial encounter with Liudan, Yuet was a little startled. Her initial surprise, however, quickly spiralled into outright astonishment.

In a brocaded parcel tied with silk tasselled cord, addressed to her in elegant *jin-ashu* script, Yuet found three separate messages. The first message was a formal invitation to the Empress-Heir Liudan's Xat-Wau ceremonies, to take place the following day at sunset. Yuet had almost expected that one – after her statement to the Council it was a matter of time, and she was sure that Liudan would have pressed for the ceremony to take place as soon as it could be arranged.

The second message, a letter in Liudan's own hand, took Yuet's breath away.

*They tell me* jin-shei *should be based on any number of things, but that guarding one's back is not one of them – and they are probably right. But you were right in that I find it hard to trust anybody at all. They took my mother away from me when I was a child and replaced her with nothing; and then I was left to atone for her fall from grace. I still don't even know what it is that she was accused of, although I hear rumours all the time. I have few friends in this Court. I hated your Tai for walking in without effort and taking the only affection that was ever freely shown me – Antian's. But that* jin-shei *had been begun for all the right reasons, I understand. So because of that and because of what I cannot help but be, I tell you three things. One is that I will see your Tai, Antian's Tai, once this ritual is over and I am my own mistress again. I make no promises further than this, but I will see her, and I will speak with her of Antian. The second is that I have no senior female relatives left alive in the Palace aside from my ancient honourable grandmother, the Dowager Empress, whose health has deteriorated badly in the last few months and cannot even make it to the ceremony unless we hold it in her sick-room, as you will be aware. I require someone, an adult female close to me, to put the red pin in my hair tomorrow night. There is precedent for* jin-shei *sisters to do this for an orphaned or otherwise isolated* jin-shei-bao, *so the third thing is this: I want you to put the red pin in my hair.*

The third message was a slip of fine silk paper tucked into the fold of this letter. It bore just the two words: *jin-shei.*

A little Guard girl, and the Empress of Syai, all in the same week. And Yuet had thought that becoming *jin-shei-bao* to Tai, who had once been the Little Empress Antian's, was reaching high.

Liudan's letter touched off a quivering strand of guilt as well as an ironic recognition in Yuet – guarding her back, although not the primary nor the only reason that she had offered *jin-shei* to Tai, had certainly been part of her own reasoning back in the mountains at the conclusion of that bitter, shattered day that the world had fallen apart around them all. Now she had been offered the same thing, on much the same terms; the difference was that Tai had not known the terms, not completely, and Yuet understood Liudan's motives far more precisely.

Still. *Jin-shei*. To an Empress.

Her message to Liudan had been short, and to the point.

*Jin-shei. I will be there.*

The Xat-Wau ceremony was a small one, with a small circle of invitees, mostly only the barest minimum necessary for official purposes. Part of the reason for this was that the Court was still in mourning – and would be for a long time – so that lavish celebrations could not be put on in good conscience, but part of it was the simple haste with which Liudan had pushed this through once approval had been given. The attendees, apart from Liudan herself, included a handful of the women from the Imperial Court who were there as attendants for Liudan, the High Chancellor and two other Council members, Temple priests, Yuet and Tai.

Tai had had to be practically bullied into going by Yuet.

'She hasn't asked me, I don't belong there,' she kept repeating stubbornly when Yuet had first broached the subject.

'She said she wanted to talk to you,' Yuet pointed out. 'Isn't that what you wished to accomplish?'

'Yes, but she said later, when it's all over, when she's Empress.'

'Tai, she *will* be Empress in days. And as for "later", she might as well have meant after the ceremony.'

'You don't know that.'

'Yes, I do. Now come on, and work with me on this. I said I'd try and help you keep your promise to Antian, and I've got you this far. Now you've got to follow me.' She paused, startled by the sudden glint of tears on Tai's eyelashes. 'Now what?'

'I wonder . . .' Tai began, and Yuet suddenly realized what the obstacle was. It would be Liudan who would get the sanction of adulthood, Liudan whose path to Empire would be smoothed.

Not Antian.

Yuet sighed, and reached to smooth Tai's hair. 'Who knows,' she murmured, 'but that they were both born for this, Tai. And that you had some part to play in it all.'

'What?' Tai said, wiping her face with the back of her hand with the swift smearing motion of a child. 'Antian was a miracle to me, and Liudan is a promise.'

'Exactly. The promise.'

So Tai had capitulated in the end and had accompanied Yuet to the Palace as the sun dipped to the west on the following day, and they were admitted to the room where the Xat-Wau ceremony was to take place.

All the other guests were there and waiting when Liudan was finally conducted into the room by two of her women, precisely as the last light died and the day dipped into twilight. She had been given special dispensation to wear a sumptuous silk gown in flaming scarlet for the occasion, although she still wore white bands around her arms in recognition of her mourning. Her hair was down, combed into a smooth waterfall of black silk, held only by a pair of ivory combs. The attendants escorted her to a carved mahogany chair placed beside a small, silk-draped table which bore a profusion of hair-dressing pins and clasps such as crowded the dressing table of every woman in Syai. On a special cushion by itself lay one large straight hairpin, richly carved and polished to a satin-smooth sheen, dyed red.

Two of the priests set up a soft background chanting as the hair-pin, on its cushion, was brought by one of the women to the third priest, the highest-ranking amongst them. The priest placed his hands on the pin and laid a blessing of the ancestors on it, and the goodwill of the Immortals on the woman who would wear it into her adult life. Then he turned and held the pin out to Yuet.

She had been holding Tai's hand throughout the ceremony. Now, aware of everyone's eyes on her – not all of them friendly – Yuet let go of Tai's clinging fingers and stepped up to the priest. The pin was heavy; it was heavier than she had thought it would be. It was heavier, surely, than her own had been.

It was heavy enough to bear the weight of an Empire.

Yuet turned to where Liudan sat on her throne-like chair, straight-backed, gazing straight at her.

*I'm crowning her*, Yuet thought for a moment. This was what this moment unofficially was – neither more nor less than a crowning ceremony, without which the young Empress could not lay her hand on the helm of her land. And she, Yuet, had wrought this. If she had balked at Liudan's plan, Liudan might still have managed it, but not without casualties. As it was, she and Yuet had staged a minor coup, decapitating a regency in its infancy, channelling all the power into Liudan's hands.

Yuet nodded at the two attendants standing next to Liudan's chair, and they bowed to the Empress, took up combs and clasps, and expertly started coiling up the shining mass of her black hair into the complex loops and coils of a Court lady's coiffure, pinning it up with hidden pins and clips and then decorating it with the lacquered combs and jewelled hairpins, until Liudan glittered like a gem in the candlelight. When they were finished, the two women dropped to their knees beside the chair.

Tai, in the audience, shivered as she watched. This was the image she had always carried of Liudan – glittering, royal, proud. Even at the Summer Palace, where women relaxed the rules of Court protocol, Liudan had worn her hair dressed formally with ornaments of flowers and butterflies and dragon combs and jewelled pins. It was as though she had always needed to remind everyone of her status, of the fact that she was royal. Antian had never needed that – Antian had had the innate grace of the highborn, could talk to people from every walk of life, from the highest to the lowest, and make all feel at home. She had still had that even when she had been running around the gardens with bare arms and her hair in a hoyden's pair of long braids. Liudan's royalty, on the other hand, was somehow far more fragile, and therefore treasured, and on display. If she had ever succumbed to Antian's careless disregard of her own royal status, Liudan, the spare heir, could have simply been left on the sidelines, disregarded. She had been taught everything that an Empress would have needed to know but she had never been expected to have occasion to use that knowledge, not from where she stood in the succession. So she had always made sure that everyone knew that the knowledge, the royalty, was there.

The hair was done.

Everyone in the room – they had all been standing, Liudan was already technically Empress and nobody of lesser rank had permission to sit in her presence unless she bade them – went down onto one knee as Yuet, the only one still on her feet, raised the red pin of Xat-Wau and slid it smoothly into the crown of hair, her eyes holding Liudan's.

'Long life, and fair reign,' Yuet said, very softly, subsiding to one knee in deep obeisance at Liudan's feet.

She could see, in the candlelight, Liudan's eyes shining with unexpected tears.

Tai, shivering violently, could almost see the gently smiling ghost of Antian standing behind Liudan's glittering form. Liudan's own expression was inscrutable, and Tai wondered for one brief and infinitely painful moment if Liudan herself had spared any thought for Antian on this night.

The others had departed, afterwards, and Liudan retired to her chambers. It was there that the young deaf servant conducted Tai and Yuet within the hour. By the time they arrived Liudan had changed from her Court scarlet robe into a simple wraparound gown, and her feet were in silk slippers, a small but telling rebellion against the strict mourning rules. Her hair was still dressed in the Xat-Wau style, the red pin still in place, but her eyes glittered more brilliantly than any of the jewels she wore tucked into her dark crown of hair.

'So, tell me,' Liudan said, her voice touched with a hint of out-right malice. 'Tell me about her.'

'I never meant to come between Antian and those she loved,' Tai said in a low voice. 'I don't know why you believed that.'

'Because she spent little time with me back in the Summer Palace after you came into her life. She had been kind to me, one of the few that were, the only one of those four whom I wear *this* for that I actually missed.' She plucked at a white ribbon in her hair. 'Sometimes I feel like such a fraud. I do not mourn the man who was my father, because I hardly knew him. I saw him in private, in any kind of informal encounter, maybe twenty times in my entire life. And the woman to whom my mother's concubine status made sure I belonged never wanted me, and was content to have me rattling around in the bottom of the royal basket as a back-up heir in case anything happened to the Little Empress or Oylian.' She turned away suddenly, with a savage little toss of her head. 'Everyone doted on her, you know,' she said.

'Antian? You were *jealous* of her?' Tai said. 'Why? You were both born to the Empire.'

'*She* was. I should probably, if they had thought about it, never have been born at all. Even now, when I cried for her, every time I balked at something it was *The Little Empress would have* this or *The Little Empress wouldn't have* that. It was hard enough living up to her when she was alive, but now it's impossible.'

'You aren't her,' Tai said. 'You must pursue your own happiness.'

Liudan blinked at her, startled. 'Don't presume to tell me what I must do.'

'Tai,' Yuet said warningly.

'But I must,' Tai said. 'She said you were angry. Perhaps you have reason to be. But please don't be angry at me for being happy that she chose me, or at her for loving me. Because I don't think there will be another human being who will mean to me what she meant to me. And because of her . . . because of her . . . I made her a promise and I don't have any real way of keeping it but at the very least I had to see you and tell you that if there was anything I could do, in any way, for her sake, I would, I know that I cannot do much and that you are thinking I am crazy with the grief of it to even speak this way. But – if the time should come – I had to say that. I had to see you and tell you that.'

Both the older girls were staring at Tai with astonishment, but she had had her say and now she dropped into a deep obeisance to Liudan. 'Thank you,' she said, her voice almost inaudible but very steady, 'for speaking with me.'

Liudan suddenly laughed, and Yuet, who hadn't been aware that she had been holding her breath, let it out with a sigh.

'I begin to see why she liked you,' Liudan said. 'Very well. You have my word that if there is ever anything you can do for me you will have your chance, little *jin-shei-bao*.'

Tai looked up sharply. 'But she said . . .'

'She said what?'

'She said . . .' What Antian had actually said was that being *jin-shei* with her didn't mean that Tai had to take Liudan on. But at the last moment Tai caught herself before repeating the sentiment in such undiplomatic terms, and rephrased. 'I didn't know it carried over,' she said.

'It doesn't,' Liudan said. 'It pleases me to claim it, since you offer it.'

'I did?'

'Of course. You made her a promise. You were hardly promising to protect me against the High Council – you can't – just against the rest of the world when it gets to be too much. And for that, you're *jin-shei*.' Liudan laughed again. 'So we're all sisters here, then. What a strange circle for an Empress to take her first steps into the world with – but with a devoted friend and a healer by my side it looks like it might be an interesting journey.'

138

Later, after they had taken their leave of the young Empress still drunk on her first taste of power and Yuet had delivered Tai back to her mother's house, Tai had sought out her journal again. She had meant to write an account of the Xat-Wau and of the way she had seen Liudan's eyes glitter in the candlelight, and of all that Liudan had said to her that night. Instead, she found herself writing a poem.

> *She steps on the dais of power, and her crown*
> *is her pride, and her wound*
> *is her fear.*
> *The world will come to her, asking,*
> *and I will be there to listen*
> *when she makes reply.*

Tai brooded over the words on the page, feeling oddly prophetic in that moment, and then lifted her head and listened as the night-noises of her neighbourhood spilled into her room through the open window and wrapped her in their comforting, familiar cocoon – the yowl of a prowling cat, a distant echo of human laughter, the clicking sound that the shod hooves of the refuse-collector's mule made on the cobblestones as he made his rounds with his cart in the darkness of Linh-an's night streets.

'Ah, what a commotion is made here!
The young girl's grandmother fastens her hair
with her first ivory comb, and how changed,
    changed utterly
her eyes look in her face . . .
and even the boy who grows up to be Emperor
wakes up in excitement
on the morning of Xat-Wau, the ceremony
that says "I am a man today."'

Qiu-Lin, Year 8 of the Cloud Emperor

# *One*

Autumn Court was understandably subdued the year of the earthquake. There were few large gatherings, and when Liudan appeared at those she was distant, withdrawn and drab in her mourning garb. Rimshi's artistry was little in evidence that year, although it pleased Liudan to wear an embroidered jacket in public – a jacket made from cream-coloured linen and worked with dyed cotton, breaking no mourning attire rules by introducing so much as a silk embroidery thread but still sumptuous enough to cause whispering in the shadows of the Court. That had been Tai's work, and partly Yuet's – it had been Yuet who had procured the jacket, and Tai had worked her magic on it, and they had given it to Liudan on the occasion of her birthday. She was a Fire Cusp, born close to midnight on the last day of Kannaian, sharing the qualities of the Lion and the Dragon. Tai had worked both into the embroidery, lazily stretching tawny lions twined with long sinuous red-gold dragons with small red glass beads for their eyes, the only nod to the mourning rules an intricate pattern in white thread which wound its way about the sleeves. Liudan, accepting the gift, had actually been betrayed into a genuine smile.

'Whatever gave you the idea?' Tai had murmured to Yuet, at the Court occasion where the jacket made its first appearance. They had been watching some of the women as the jacket passed, the widening of eyes, the trail of whispers behind cupped hands.

Yuet shrugged. 'You heard her yourself. She is nothing if not forthright, and total deep mourning for Liudan is nothing if not hypocritical. It would have been tough on her to survive this Court without at least a little defiance.'

'You understand her,' Tai said.

'I was orphaned at age four,' Yuet said. 'My "official" mourning lasted well into my seventh year, and I was too young to even remember my parents properly. I remember resenting that, somehow. With her, it's all magnified by the Imperial drama. If I showed defiance, I was chastised as unfilial; if Liudan does, she is both unfilial and unspeakably shocking. The whole country is staring at her right now. It can't be comfortable.'

'So the jacket . . . ?'

'. . . is an escape,' Yuet said, grinning. 'Look at her.'

Liudan was wearing the jacket as if it were dripping with gold and pearls, and once the initial shock had passed she had received a restrained compliment or two – at which it had pleased her to mention that the embroidery was a gift made by Tai. Before the end of the Court session Tai had been approached by two other Court women with veiled inquiries about the possibility of obtaining something similar. What the Empress wore was an immediate Court trend. Tai, letting her eyes slide past these potential customers for a moment, caught Liudan's bright and sharply amused gaze. She had taken the opportunity to put a squirming Tai into the spotlight as part of the gift of the jacket.

Apart from the small scandal that the jacket had caused, it had been a slow and quiet Court, a mourning Court. The attire was muted by the mourning white; the galleries were empty of musicians; people spoke in even lower whispers than usual in the formal corridors of the Imperial Audience Chambers.

Khailin, bored, hoarding her last summer of freedom like a miser does his gold, seeking to make every moment count for something, coaxed a highly reluctant Nhia to attend Court with her – for no other reason except that she wanted to inject a bit of liveliness and controversy into the stuffy Court circles. Nhia had thrown increasingly desperate excuses at Khailin's feet, but Khailin, with that inimitable and fairly frightening single-minded focus which sometimes drove her so hard, had managed to counter them all, either providing a solution Nhia could not counter or dismissing the 'problem' out of hand. 'I have nothing suitable to wear' had been met with one of Khailin's own dresses; 'I don't know how to talk to anybody' had been roundly dismissed as Khailin pointed out that a great many people who had met Nhia at the Great Temple would disagree with that statement. Nhia's corollary that the Temple was hardly the Imperial Court had been met with an acerbic demand for Nhia to provide her with the exact differences which made the Temple any more approachable than the Palace.

'I cannot walk so far, nor stand so long,' Nhia protested weakly in the end, throwing her physical infirmities into the fray.

'I'll get you a cane,' Khailin said. 'Consider it a belated birthday present. And you need something that fits your new stature anyway.'

'What new stature?'

'You're a near-Sage in the Temple,' Khailin said, and there was a thin edge of something so like envy in her voice that Nhia stared at her in confusion. Khailin, envious of *her*? Of the poor washer-woman's crippled child? In Cahan's name, why would she be?

But Khailin had dismissed that, too. Within a few improbable days she had procured a finely carved mahogany cane with a heron's head for a handle, the right size and weight, and presented it to Nhia without taking the least account of Nhia's protests. Equipped with the cane, a silk dress which needed only a little bit of alteration (and Tai had gleefully obliged Nhia with that) and the addition of a white mourning ribbon to be presentable in Court, her hair piled up in an elaborate Court style arranged by Khailin's own personal maid, Nhia found herself at an afternoon audience of the Autumn Court without quite knowing how she had got there. She hid her bewilderment well, but was betrayed every now and then into a double take over something she had never encountered before.

'Who was that?' she hissed at Khailin as a man dressed in bright brocades only nominally hemmed with a white ribbon swept past them on some urgent errand.

'Chehao, eunuch of the women's quarters, Chief Eunuch Abahai's right hand,' Khailin reported.

Nhia stared. 'A real eunuch? I don't think I've ever met one before.'

'Yes, a real one,' Khailin said, amused. 'There are a number of them around here. The Imperial women needed a layer of guardians who were incapable of tasting the royal honey if they wanted to, hence the eunuchs. That's also the reason for the female cadres of the Imperial Guard – their primary duty is guarding the women. From themselves, maybe.'

Nhia glared at her. 'You're going to be one of the Imperial women yourself in a few months,' she retorted.

Khailin's smile disappeared. 'I know.'

'And that? Who's that?' Nhia said into the brooding silence, trying to distract Khailin from the gloomy prospects of her marital future.

'One of the Sages,' said Khailin, immediately diverted, as usual, by the appearance of real power. 'Two of them, actually. Look.'

'How in Cahan can you tell?' Nhia said, staring at the two grey-haired men who had entered the audience hall and stood talking quietly to each other in an unobtrusive corner, managing to give the impression that they were blissfully unaware of the attention they generated.

'They're ancient,' Khailin retorted. 'You won't find many old men in this Court. They're on the Council or they are Sages . . . or they are eunuchs, but the eunuchs who reach that age, and they are rare, are gloriously fat and unable to move without a cart and horse.'

'Inside the Palace?' Nhia said, diverted once again.

Khailin snorted. 'You will find that there are more asses inside the Palace than out. There are always enough to pull a cart.' She peered at the two Sages without giving the appearance that she was staring at them, a Court skill she had learned when very young. 'Those are the Lion Sage and the Eagle Sage,' she said after she completed the scrutiny.

'How do you know?' Nhia asked, interested.

'Their robes. The pattern of the embroidery on the cuffs of their sleeves. And the rings.'

'What rings?'

'Each Sage wears the ring of his sign.' Khailin turned around in some perplexity. 'You ought to know these things, Nhia! Rumour has it you're practically a Sage yourself!'

'Hardly,' Nhia murmured. 'I tell teaching stories at the Temple.'

'And your own teachers say you are a marvel.'

'How do you know that?' Nhia asked.

Khailin flushed. 'I listen at doors.'

Nhia opened her mouth to say something but Khailin's hand closed around her wrist in an almost painful grip. 'Look who's here.'

Nhia turned her head, and gasped.

She hadn't laid eyes on the man in two years, and on this day, and for this occasion, he was dressed in far more sumptuous style than he had been that day at the Temple – but there was no mistaking Lihui, the Ninth Sage, the youngest Sage, the great lord who had once reached down to help a crippled child up in a Temple garden. His gaze had swept the room as he had entered, and did not linger on the two girls – but Nhia would have known those eyes anywhere. She still sometimes dreamed of them.

'Which is he?' Nhia asked.

'What?'

'Which Sage is he? If the other two are Lion and Eagle . . .'

Khailin tore her eyes from the three Sages with difficulty and faced Nhia. 'There are nine Sages in the circle, and eight of them bear the rings of the creatures of their Element – Lion, Pike, Boar, Eagle, Hummingbird, Buffalo, Swan, Dragon. The Ninth Sage belongs to all the elements and to none of them. He is the highest of them, he rules them all . . . but you *know* all this.'

'I know of the Sages, Khailin,' Nhia said gently. 'What you speak of is arcana. It's like telling you that you know all about the Temple because you know which Gods and spirits live in which Circle. No, I don't know it. I don't even know how *you* know so much of it.'

Khailin stared at her. 'I always thought that you knew more about the Way,' she said slowly. 'I thought that was the reason he had stopped to speak with you that day in the Temple. Because you knew things. Because he wanted to . . .'

'*Who* spoke to me in the Temple?' Nhia said, confused.

'*Him*,' Khailin said, indicating Lihui with her chin.

'You were there?'

'I saw it happen.'

Nhia found herself recalling the meeting with Lihui in precise detail, the way her blood had surged when he had raised her up, the way she had almost stopped breathing when he had actually bowed to her in that garden in the Temple, the way she hoarded the experience, sharing it only with Tai, not even with her mother, how she had analysed it and poked it and prodded it and finally tried to forget it as fluke, as chance, as an accident of fate.

Khailin had been there.

Khailin had watched it, and analysed it in her own way, it seemed. And made of it something quite other than what it had been.

'But it meant nothing at all! That brief encounter was all it ever was.' Nhia paused, her heart thumping painfully as something sharp and hard-edged sliced into her. 'Is that the first time you knew I existed?' she asked. 'Is that why you wanted to get to know me?'

Khailin pressed her lips together until they were a thin white line, squaring her jaw. 'At first,' she admitted.

Nhia had looked away, but not before Khailin saw her eyes sparkle with sudden tears.

'Please don't,' she said, genuinely upset, more upset than she had believed she could be. 'I said, at first. After a while, I liked you – I really liked you. If it hadn't been for that wretched Sage, I never would have known you existed, we never would have even met!'

'My foot hurts,' Nhia whispered, staggering backwards a step to lean against a convenient wall.

She misjudged her angle, found her back slipping sideways on the smooth stone pillar, and only kept her balance through sheer force of will and by clinging to Khailin's cane with a hand which showed white on the knuckles. *I am not, I am not going to make a spectacle of myself here*, she thought furiously as she struggled to stay on her feet.

A strong hand unobtrusively slipped behind her shoulder blade, straightening her up, and was instantly gone – so fast that Nhia was almost unable to swear that it had been there. But it had been – and it was the same hand that had been there once before. The Sage Lihui stepped up from behind and to the side of her, and offered both girls a delicate courtly bow.

'I seem to remember,' the Sage murmured, 'another girl whom I helped to her feet once. *Nhia*, is it, as I recall?'

'Yes, *sei*,' Nhia gasped, astonished that he remembered her at all, stunned that he remembered her name.

He smiled. 'I have been hearing that name,' he said. 'The Temple Circles are humming with it. Do not blush, my dear; all I have heard has been a credit to you.' He turned his head marginally in Khailin's direction, and she dropped into a deep obeisance. 'And who is your companion?' Lihui inquired, his obsidian eyes serene.

Khailin looked up. 'I am Khailin, daughter of Cheleh, Court Chronicler,' she said boldly.

'Ah,' said Lihui. 'Yes.'

His simple reply seemed to imply that this, too, was a name he

148

knew, but that the things he had heard about Khailin were not quite as bright and good as Nhia's reputation.

'Well,' said Lihui pleasantly to both girls although his gaze lingered for a moment longer on Khailin, 'it has been an unexpected pleasure meeting with you again, young Nhia. I have been keeping my eye on you for a while. Lady Khailin, I am delighted to make your acquaintance. Now, if you will excuse me, I have an appointment I am already late for.' He gave them another slight bow, turned with a graceful courtier's motion and was gone.

'You're blushing,' Nhia said, looking at Khailin.

'Am I?' Khailin's hands flew up to cover her face.

Nhia's expression had passed from hurt to curious. 'What is it that you thought you could gain, Khailin? I have no connections and no friends in high places, and I could never . . .'

'You do now,' Khailin said with a passion. 'I'm sorry I made such a mess of things, but I'm not sorry that I made you my friend, my *jin-shei-bao*. There is always that, now, you know. That doesn't dissolve.'

'I know,' Nhia said.

'I really did need you, Nhia,' Khailin said. 'I still do.'

'I understand, I think. I really do.'

Khailin's eyes now filled with unexpected tears, and Nhia sighed.

'Oh, don't,' she said. 'Please don't. Find me a place to sit, instead.'

Khailin threw a swift glance around the room. 'There is a bench over there on the far side by the pillar and I think we could . . . ah, Cahan, not now.'

'What is it?'

'The Empress,' Khailin said, sinking into another obeisance and urging Nhia to do the same by the pressure of her hand. 'Nobody will sit now, and we cannot withdraw unless she gives us leave.'

Nhia glanced up through lowered eyelashes, trying to catch a glimpse of Liudan as she swept past. Tai's circle, that one. Tai was the one who had somehow fallen in with the women of the Empire. *What if*, thought Nhia suddenly, the pale wraith of the recent betrayal swaying before her eyes, *Tai's jin-shei had never meant anything other than a need, a want . . . not a sharing . . . and she had put so much of her heart into that bond with Antian, and now she is stuck with it, with its legacy, and what could Liudan possibly want with her?*

'What are you muttering?' Khailin hissed. 'Are you in pain? I could try to . . .'

'Nothing,' Nhia said hastily. 'Who's that with the Sage over there?'

'Where?' Khailin's eyes whipped around seeking Lihui, but it was one of the other Sages that Nhia had noticed, one of the older ones, who was now accompanied by an ethereal old woman dressed in pale silk, her thin white hair braided into a coronet above her brow and shining through her elaborate Court head-dress like living silver.

'That's the Lion Sage,' Khailin whispered. 'And that is his Lady.'

'What are you planning now?' asked Nhia after a moment. She had learned to recognize Khailin's sudden silences as sparks of inspiration which Khailin would cogitate on when they struck her – some sort of nefarious plan, some mischief, something that she ought not to have had the opportunity, the knowledge or the where-withal to achieve but which, once she had gone through all the ramifications in her head, she managed to do anyway.

'Nothing,' Khailin said slowly, her eyes following the Lion Sage and his Lady as they made their slow, careful way across the hall, watching them receive bows and deep courtesies, and then the Empress's own attention for a few moments, while a bevy of richly caparisoned Imperial princes stood laughing ineffectually among themselves, largely ignored by the rest of the Court, in another alcove, nursing large flagons of rice wine.

## Two

Khailin was not the only one troubled by thoughts of marriage.

Liudan had thought that pushing through her Xat-Wau ceremony would give her more power over her own destiny, but she was only partially right. The Council had accepted the loss of the regency, if not with joy then at least with good grace. But Liudan was young, and the Council's chance at political power was not limited to questions of whether or not she had attained her majority. There was also the question, as important if not more so than the first, of ensuring the dynasty's survival. Of marriage. Of heirs.

'You want to know the most ironic thing about this whole situation?' Liudan had said to Yuet and Tai in a tight, furious voice. The two of them had been summoned to attend Liudan one cold, rain-swept late autumn evening. They had been allowed to shed their soaked cloaks and were given mulled wine in fine porcelain cups to wrap their cold hands around as they sat by the fireside, but that was the extent of the hospitality – they were there to listen, and they did, dutifully. 'After all that, after the risk I took in faking it all! Do you remember, Yuet, that you told me to take to my bed and pretend I was cramping because they would believe me more if I displayed certain symptoms? Well, I woke up the next morning, Yuet. And I was. Just like you said – cramps – and before the Xat-Wau was fully set in motion I had qualified for it in truth as well as in your writ. And the moment that was out of the way, they are all over me again. I thought it was over, and now . . .'

'And now you find that it is all only just beginning?' Yuet said. 'It shouldn't surprise you. There are plenty of people who are waiting for the smallest chance to find a place of power.'

'What do they want?' Tai said.

'You are such an innocent, *jin-shei-bao*,' Liudan laughed.

Yuet turned her head, looking at Tai. 'They want her to marry, of course. They want her to choose the Emperor.'

Liudan, pacing the floors of her chambers like a caged lioness, grimaced.

'But there is the mourning,' Tai said.

'Yes, and thank Cahan for that – it has some uses. I cannot, under law, contemplate marriage or any such ceremony before my period of mourning is up – or, in any case, that would be the case if I were some peasant's child mourning for my parents – if I were my *mother* before she came here.' Liudan laughed, a little grimly. 'Sometimes it's a blessing not to be royal, little sister. But they could not even let *her* rest in her ashes for a month before they threw *her* suitors at me.'

'Whose suitors?' Tai said, honestly confused.

It was Yuet who put it all together again. 'They want you to choose an Emperor from among Antian's suitors?'

'Even there,' Liudan said savagely, 'it's no more than a question of what Antian would have done. They want me to choose the way she would have chosen.'

'That's not fair,' Tai protested.

'No,' said Liudan, pausing in her pacing to stare at her. 'So what would you have me do?'

'Me? I can hardly advise you.'

'You can when I ask you for it. You have to when I ask for it.' Liudan grinned. 'You took that on with *jin-shei*, Tai. That's what a *jin-shei-bao* is for – wise advice.'

'Then you should not ask me,' Tai said. 'I am not as wise as Nhia is, and she is your *jin-shei* too, if you will pledge with her.'

'Nhia? Who is this Nhia?'

'They speak of her highly,' Yuet said. 'She has wisdom and grace, for all that she is so young. She even teaches at the Great Temple, and she is not yet sixteen years old.'

Liudan settled on some cushions by the fire, gesturing imperially for a goblet of wine to be brought to her. The little deaf servant girl, who was still Liudan's primary attendant despite the jockeying of a number of Court ladies to become intimates of her chamber, hurried over with a goblet, and then withdrew again into the shadows. 'Tell me about her.'

'You know that case that was brought before the Court at the open audience just the other day?' Yuet said. 'The land dispute over the peach orchard?'

'Yes, I remember,' Liudan said. 'The two men who both claimed it as theirs. One of them, as I recall, said that the other unlawfully harvested the peaches from the trees before they were fully ripe and sold them in the markets for his own profit, although the grove belonged to the one who had spoken. And the second man swore that the land was his, and that the peach trees were planted on stolen property by the other man's father. I remember. What of it?'

'I was there,' Yuet said, 'and I told Tai of it, and she spoke of it to Nhia. And Nhia came up with the perfect solution to the problem.'

'What was it that she proposed to do?' Liudan asked, and Tai reported on what Nhia had had to say on the vexing case. By the time she was done Liudan's eyes were sparkling with interest. 'Indeed. Why did you not come and tell me of this at once? So young, and so wise. How is it that I did not know of this jewel in my city before?'

'She has been moving freely in the city and the Temple,' Yuet said. 'But she has a way of keeping herself unobtrusive. She is crippled, and she does not like the limelight.'

'Crippled how?'

'Her foot has been withered and clubbed since birth,' Tai said. 'She walks with a cane, and cannot stand for long.'

Liudan tapped her teeth with her fingernail, thinking. 'There was someone . . . I noticed someone in an audience, not that long ago.' She gestured again and the servant girl approached. Liudan signed something at her in their own secret sign language, and after a pause the girl signed back, ducked her head, and disappeared out of the chamber.

'She will find out,' Liudan said. 'What are you smiling at?'

'You didn't need to send the poor thing away from the fire,' Tai said. 'If you want to know who she would have come to the Court with, I can probably tell you that – it must have been Khailin, Chronicler Cheleh's daughter.'

'And how do *they* know one another?' Liudan asked, sitting up a little straighter.

'They are both interested in the Way,' Tai said. 'Nhia tells me they talk a lot about that. They are also . . .'

Liudan shook her head, laughing. 'More sisters I did not know about? I am inclined to give her judgment. In public court. Tomorrow. Make sure she is there.'

'You weren't meant to tell *Liudan* what I said!' Nhia cried when Tai presented her with this Imperial ultimatum.

'Why not? It was a good solution!'

'Yes, but she has the Council and the Sages for all that, and if she now trots me out they will all be *looking* at me.'

'Yes,' Tai said, gazing at her with the fond, proud gaze of a true sister, 'they will. And they will be seeing a beautiful spirit. Nhia, forget about what you once were. You are a new person, and you are wise, and you are my beloved friend and sister whom I will send in there looking like a queen of Cahan. Trust me. Now come, we must go to Khailin.'

'Khailin? Is that necessary?' Nhia said, so oddly that Tai turned to stare at her sharply as she spoke.

'What's the matter? Have you two had a falling out?'

'No. Well, not exactly,' Nhia said. 'It's just that I have a few things to think about where Khailin is concerned.'

'Fine,' Tai said. 'I was going to ask for the loan of another dress. You two are of a size and it would be so much easier if I could only tuck and pin a few seams rather than do the whole thing from scratch, but I guess it's time you had your own finery, at that. Come here.'

'What are you up to? Tai, you cannot make me an entire Court gown in one night!'

'Oh, yes I can.' Tai flung open a closet in her room and rummaged at the back where a stack of robes lay folded neatly with silkpaper layering in between fabric folds. 'I have a lot of those. Many of them Mother has never had a chance to rearrange for me, and I will certainly never need them. So you might as well have one. Try this one on. I think it will fit you.'

'Whose was this?' Nhia gasped, the fine silk of the undertunic flowing through her hands as she shrugged into it, running her fingers over the stiff embroidery on the outside robe.

'Antian's,' Tai said abruptly, keeping her eyes downcast and dropping down to one knee to inspect the hemline of the robe.

'Antian's?' Nhia said. 'But won't Liudan recognize this? Won't there be an insult if I wear . . .'

'They often wear the Court robes only once before they are discarded,' Tai said quietly. 'It would take a prodigious memory to recall the details of all these gowns. Nobody will know.'

'But Tai,' Nhia's eyes were bright and soft as they rested on Tai, 'I cannot take this. It was Antian's, it is something that you need to . . .'

'She was your *jin-shei* too,' Tai said. 'And I cannot think of a better use for it. Stand still, would you? And hand me those pins on the table? It's a good fit, if I can only get the hem taken up a little. And I can add a white ribbon or two on the sleeves. The Court is tomorrow noon. You'll be all set.'

'I cannot stand for six hours!' Nhia wailed.

But she was there with Tai and Yuet the next morning, as Liudan had wished. Yuet had a phial of mild poppy juice in her pocket, in case Nhia's foot became a problem and needed immediate attention.

In the gown that had been Antian's, her hair swept up with a set of Yuet's ivory combs and a tiny pair of jewelled pins that Antian had once given Tai, Nhia looked remarkably poised and grown-up; Tai, at her side with her hair dressed very simply and her own gown cut with the plainness of a robe that a child might wear to a grand occasion, suddenly looking very young.

Liudan swept into the audience chamber late, keeping everyone waiting at least half an hour. Even in deepest mourning she managed to remain spectacular, her hair glossy and adorned with strings of tiny crystal beads which (in deference to mourning) were not jewels but which so trembled and shivered in the light that they may as well have been. Her face, bare of make-up, was graced only by her brilliant dark eyes, and that was more than enough.

The three by the Imperial dais sank into obeisance as she came up.

'Empress,' Tai said, formal here in the audience chamber before the people, 'may I present Nhia of Linh-an, one who is both teacher and student at the Great Temple.'

Liudan extended a hand. Nhia took it, and Liudan's grip tightened slightly as she helped Nhia rise from her obeisance with some semblance of grace. 'Your reputation precedes you,' she said. 'I am pleased that you came to my Court. I know of your . . . infirmity, and I do not wish to make this occasion a trial for you. I therefore give you permission to sit.' She clapped her hands and a servant came hurrying over with a small carved chair and set it below and to the side of the throne. Liudan mounted the dais, settled herself on her own seat, and gestured at the chair. 'Please,' she said courteously, 'be seated.'

Crimson, aware of every eye in the room upon her as the only one singled out to sit in the Empress's presence, Nhia sensed waves of hostility, curiosity, even fear, coming from the gathered throng of people. She dared not look up.

'Thank you, Highness,' she said, her voice very low. Tai helped her get settled on the chair. Liudan was smiling.

'The Court is now open!' a herald declared. 'My Empress, the first petitioner is Second Prince Wei-Hun.'

The procession of people coming up to present their credentials, state a case or ask a boon seemed to go on for hours. Tai was beginning to think that Liudan had forgotten all about the case of the peach orchard, or that Nhia's presence had been merely a whim on Liudan's part – but she should have known better, she told herself when the herald announced the last case to be presented at the audience.

'We call the two litigants who presented their case to Her Imperial Highness in recent days concerning the ownership of a peach tree orchard. Come forth and receive judgement!'

The two men stepped forward, falling to their knees at the foot of the dais. Liudan stared at them with an implacability that made them both squirm.

'I have thought upon your problem,' she said, 'and taken advice from one who may be the youngest sage in my Empire.' She turned that smile back on Nhia for a moment, and Nhia, in this moment, found the strength to raise her head and meet the Empress's eyes squarely. Liudan's gaze sharpened a little, and her smile quirked at the corners; courage she had always appreciated. She inclined her head graciously at Nhia in acknowledgement of what the gesture had cost her, and then turned those fierce eyes back on the two combatants. 'I therefore give judgment. I find you quarrelsome and selfish. Let it be done thus: let the grove be cut down to the last tree, let the land be ploughed with salt, and let it remain between you as a warning ever more.'

One of the men glanced at the other. 'If that is your command, my Empress, so let it be done.'

'No . . .' said the other weakly.

'No?' Liudan said, her voice silky and dangerous. 'You refuse the judgment you came here to find?'

'No, my Empress. I do not. If that is your will, then let it be done. But if I may turn your hand, then I will beg for the life of those trees. My father planted them, and I have tended them, and they bear no guilt in this that they should pay the price of my pride in them. If it be a choice I would rather hand them over to my neighbour myself and never more lay claim to them except that I may watch them grow old in their bounty.'

Liudan sat very still, and the other man had turned to stare at his companion in utter stupefaction. Then Liudan rose to her feet. Behind her, Nhia also rose; it was her gaze that the one who had

156

resigned his claim to the grove managed to meet, and what he found there made him stare back at her, his mouth open.

'The man who would save the grove,' Liudan said, 'has greater claim to it than the man who would destroy it in order to claim a hollow victory. You have won yourself your father's trees. And you, O destroyer, will there need to be a fence made between you and the trees high enough so that you cannot get over it to harm them? Or will you give your word here, now,' Liudan turned, grasped Nhia's hand and pulled her forward firmly, 'to the woman whose wisdom made the judgment here today?'

'I . . . I give my word,' the man stammered. 'The trees will not be harmed by me or mine so long as the grove stands.'

'Let it be so,' Liudan said. Still holding Nhia's hand, she started down the steps of the podium. 'Ladies,' Liudan said over her shoulder, to Yuet and Tai who were standing rooted to the spot with surprise, 'attend me in my chambers.'

She said nothing more until the four of them were safely ensconced behind the closed doors of her inner chambers. Then she let out a whoop of pure delight.

'That was one court they will not forget in a hurry,' Liudan said, delighted. 'Well. I have decided what I will do about my other problem. They wish me to choose the Emperor? Very well. I shall. But at the very least they will have to provide me with a different set of suitors than those tailored to my predecessor. It stands to reason that the stars and the compatibilities will need to be worked out anew, doesn't it?' She laughed again, a laugh of release, of a joyous spirit. 'And when they do I will go into retreat and think on it. And I want you to come with me.'

'Who, Princess?' Yuet said, caught by surprise.

'All of you. I will take you and an attendant or two and nobody else. I will seek wisdom and advice in the highest places that I can – I go to ask my heart's sisters and the beloved spirits of my ancestors for counsel. Be ready; we may leave at a moment's notice.'

'Where are we going?' Tai asked, suddenly breathless with an oppressive foreboding.

Liudan looked at her with an almost playful malice, like a kitten playing with a grasshopper unaware of its ultimate fate. 'To the place of all Imperial retreats, of course,' she said. 'To the mountains.'

# Three

The Imperial astrologers took longer than Liudan might have liked for their deliberations, and it was almost mid-Tannuan before they were finished, full into winter. It was a wretched winter, too, racked with storms and early snow flurries even as far south as Linh-an itself. Yuet, mindful of Tai's painful associations with the mountains where the Summer Palace had once stood and not entirely certain that she herself could handle a return to that place so soon, suggested to Liudan that a winter retreat might be rescheduled for warmer climes – a long sail down the river, to Sei-lin or even as far down to Chirinaa and the sea – but Liudan did not seem very happy with the idea. The retreat into the mountains was merely postponed until such time as more clement weather allowed for the trip to take place.

The young Empress waited out the winter in the Linh-an Palace with ill-concealed impatience. On the last day of Sinan she announced to her *jin-shei* companions that the small caravan would be leaving for the mountain retreat on the next day.

Yuet looked pointedly at the window, lashed by a cold and persistent rain. 'It's still winter, Empress.'

'Tomorrow,' said Liudan obstinately, 'it is spring. I want this done.'

'I can make this trip,' Yuet said. 'But neither Nhia nor Tai are wealthy. They do not have the furs and the warm cloaks. We will freeze up in the mountains, Liudan.'

Liudan laughed. 'Cloaks, I can give them.'

And she produced two for Yuet to take with her when she left the Palace and convey to their intended recipients.

Yuet found Tai sitting alone in the outer room of her chambers, bent over her journal. So intent was she that she had obviously not heard Yuet's knock on the door and started violently at the sound of her name being spoken. Her brush smudged a neat letter as her hand jerked. She scowled at it.

158

'Now I've made a mess,' she said, reaching for the blotting sand.

'Never mind that now,' Yuet said. 'You have to pack.'

'What?'

'She's finally decided on a date,' Yuet said.

Tai blanched. 'Why does she want me up there with her, Yuet? I never wanted to see that place again.'

'I know. Neither did I. Not this soon, anyway.'

'The weather . . .'

'I know,' Yuet said again. She shook out one of the cloaks she'd brought in draped over her arm, held it out to Tai. 'I tried to bring that up. Her response is that you will at least be dressed for it. She sends you this, and another for Nhia. I have to go home and pack; we leave tomorrow. Will you go get Nhia? Both of you, come to my house with your luggage tonight. We will leave from there in the morning.'

'Why is she so stubborn?' Tai said, taking the cloak with unwilling hands.

'She is a Dragon,' Yuet said philosophically. 'The Dragon-born are the most bull-headed, obstinate, downright intractable people of all. And this Dragon is Empress. She has waited in the shadow of others for too long, doing their bidding – and now that she can, she does what she wants. I'll see you tonight.'

Yuet departed, leaving the other cloak folded across the back of a chair. Tai stared at the two cloaks for a moment, and then turned back to the red journal. It was the same one that she had clutched while the Summer Palace had crumbled around her, the same one in which she once wrote of the stillness of a summer night just before the world was shattered.

Now she was going back. Tai picked up her brush again, and sketched a neat line of new *jin-ashu* characters on a new page.

*Oh, Antian, my heart's sister. It seems I go on a pilgrimage – keeping my promise to you, in a way, and taking it back to lay at the feet of your ghost. They say that the bones of the earth remember the feet that walk upon them, if those feet belong to a great spirit – I know that the northern mountains recall your quiet step on their marbled stone, and still sing of it in the early mornings, in*

159

*the time you loved to spend alone on the mountainside. I*
*know that I will hear your footsteps there. I miss you.*
*I still miss you so.*

She paused, her brush poised over the page, aware that her eyes
were stinging with tears, and then dipped the point of the brush
into the ink again. Often these days her thoughts came out in
poetry.

> *I go to see again*
> *the spirit that I loved in the summer*
> *as a winter ghost*
> *and to lay my sorrows*
> *at her feet.*

Tai contemplated the verse for a moment, sighed, blotted the latest writings and closed the book carefully so as not to smudge the
pages. Leaving the smaller of the two cloaks Yuet had brought in an
untidy pile on the chair on which she had been sitting, she took up
the other one and went in search of Nhia.

Nhia wasn't at home, and Tai, who could not afford to let the
Imperial edict languish in a message which might get delivered
too late, left the gift cloak at Nhia's rooms to await her return
there and bent her steps towards the Great Temple. The day was
perfectly miserable; she arrived at the Temple soaked, her hair
wet and clinging to her face in long damp tendrils, the bones of
her shoulder blades outlined precisely beneath a cloak wringing
wet and adhering to every line of her body. She dashed into the
shelter of the Temple's gate and paused to shake herself off like a
damp puppy. A massive sneeze took her entirely by surprise,
closely followed by a second; her eyes watered, and she sniffed
experimentally.

'Oh, wonderful,' she muttered. 'All I need is a cold.'

'Tai?' said a familiar voice.

She looked up and saw Kito the bead-carver's son, his mouth
twisted into a rueful grin. Tai sniffed again, rubbing at the tickle in
her nose with the back of her hand.

'You always seem to be around when I'm at my worst,' she said,
but she was smiling.

'Tea?' he suggested. 'It might serve to ward off pneumonia.'

She nodded, distracted from her Nhia search, and he escorted her back to the booth where, now, an elderly man with a flowing white beard sat carving a *so ji* sculpture.

'Father,' Kito said respectfully, 'I bring you Tai, my friend, in need of sustenance. I have invited her to accept a bowl of green tea. May I be excused for a few minutes?'

The old carver looked up, his eyes glittering dark coals. When he smiled, his entire face disappeared into a sea of wrinkles, and the eyes glimmered from the depths like twin bright sea creatures.

'Indeed,' he said, and his voice was kind. 'It is pleasant to make your acquaintance at last, young Tai. I have been hearing about you.'

'Sir,' Tai said, bending over the old man's hand in a gesture of respect. She felt another sneeze rising to tickle her throat, and held her breath to try and stifle it. A sideways glance showed her that Kito had turned a fine shade of pink, but he said nothing, merely bowed to his father in thanks before he escorted her out of the booth.

The sneeze took her with an explosive force just a couple of steps away, so violent that a couple of people in nearby booths looked up, startled, to see what had just blown up.

'You're going to catch your death of cold,' Kito said. 'What was so important that you had to come rushing here today of all days? Look around you, the place is practically deserted – people know better than to . . .'

But his words had been ill-advised, if concerned, because they suddenly brought to mind her errand. She stopped dead, sneezed again, and looked up at him in consternation.

'Nhia! I have to find Nhia! The Empress wants us to leave tomorrow and I have to get her to . . . to. . .' Her eyes watered as she fought another sneeze.

Kito's eyes were wide with incomprehension, but his expression was firm. 'You will do no good to yourself, to Nhia or to the Empress's commands if you fall sick. Hot tea. Over here. And I will send a boy to look for Nhia for you.'

'Thank you,' Tai got out before exploding again.

The bowl of hot tea Kito thrust into her hands was a welcome warmth, for she had started shivering violently. Kito had removed her outer mantle and replaced it with his own dry one. It was three

161

sizes too large for Tai and all-enveloping, but blessedly warm. After he had collared a passing boy, thrust a copper into his hand and given him instructions, Kito came back to Tai's side.

She looked up, smiling. 'The Young Teacher?' she said quizzically, having overheard his command to the boy.

'That's what they call her around here,' Kito said. 'She was "The Little Teacher", but that was before the Empress laid her hand upon her. Now they are more respectful.'

'You know about that?'

'Who doesn't?' Kito said. 'That judgement made the marketplace almost as soon as it was uttered in court. It was a teaching tale, all by itself. When you are done with that, let us return to my father's booth – that is where I told the boy to tell Nhia to look for you.'

So-Xan, the bead-carver, was not in his seat when they returned, but his tools had not been put away, only laid aside neatly on the bench indicating that the master craftsman would return very shortly. The carving he had been working with was not in evidence.

'Whose *so ji* was he working on?' Tai asked, curious.

'The daughter of the Fourth Prince,' Kito said. 'Her kin are planning on offering it to a merchant's family here in Linh-an later this spring. I am told that the match is a done deal already, that this is just a tradition which needs to be followed in order that the Gods may smile upon them.'

'It was beautiful,' Tai said. 'Have you ever done a *so ji* yourself?'

'Twice,' said Kito proudly. 'In fact, I am carving one now, for a young woman on XoSau Street. Do you wish to see it?'

'Please,' Tai said.

He ducked into the booth and unlocked an inlaid wooden chest at the back, extracting something carefully wrapped in several layers of rough silk. 'It is not the pale jade, not the expensive kind,' he said, peeling the wrappings away, 'but I love the deeper colour of this stone, it's almost blue in places. See?'

Kito held the carving out for Tai's inspection, and she instinctively reached for it, and for a moment both sets of hands were wrapped around it as they bent over the small, exquisite stone. And then they suddenly realized what they were doing, at almost the precise moment that the realization was articulated by Nhia's voice just outside the booth.

'Are you two plight-trothed?'

Tai snatched her hand back, and Kito flung a corner of the silk back over the carving. Tai's cheeks were a flushed pink when she emerged from the carver's booth.

'We have to go back and pack,' she said to Nhia in a low voice, choosing to ignore her comment completely, giving Kito a chance to compose himself and put the carving away. 'Yuet came to me only a few hours ago. We leave with the Empress tomorrow, for the retreat.'

'*Now?*' Nhia said. 'But I've a session started with . . .'

Tai sneezed. Nhia glared at her. 'And you got soaked running after me over here, didn't you?' she said. 'And you're going to go and shiver up in the mountains tomorrow, at a time when most sane people are still going south to escape the snows. You don't even have the . . .'

'If you're going to tell me I haven't anything warm to wear, you're wrong,' Tai said. 'Liudan sent us both warm winter cloaks. Your session will have to wait on the Empress's pleasure.'

Nhia's eyes softened. 'She has not been gone long,' Nhia said, and she was not speaking of Liudan. 'And you haven't seen that place since you left it to bring her body back to Linh-an, have you? Liudan has a cruel streak.'

Tai dropped her eyes. 'Perhaps I *need* to go,' she whispered. 'To lay her ghost. To make my peace.'

Kito had composed himself sufficiently to emerge from the shadows of the booth, all adolescent dignity. Tai turned to him, still faintly pink-cheeked, and shrugged out of his cloak, handing it back to him with a bow. 'My thanks,' she said.

'My pleasure,' he said. 'I do not know what the Empress has commanded, but I hope it goes well, for her, and for you. And I hope to see you again when you return to the city.'

'So,' said Nhia as the two girls hesitated in the gate of the Great Temple, watching the still-driving rain in the streets outside and steeling themselves to throw their shivering bodies out into it, '*are* you?'

'Am I what?' Tai said, with coolly deliberate incomprehension.

'Plight-trothed,' Nhia said wickedly. 'I *saw* it, you know. Witnessed, it's a concluded thing, done, all that it needs is a formal contract. When's the wedding?'

'I haven't even had my Xat-Wau yet,' Tai retorted, blushing furiously again. 'He was showing me his work, there was nothing . . .' She paused, held her breath, and then sneezed again with a force that threw her back against the doorway.

'That's it,' said Nhia, dropping the teasing for the time being and instinctively lowering her voice. 'Whatever it costs, we need a sedan chair to get us back. Wait here; I will arrange it. If we *have* to follow Liudan on this little ruse of hers, at least let us leave the city healthy enough to face the mountain winter.'

'Ruse?' Tai said, turning to follow Nhia with her eyes as the older girl turned back into the Temple.

Nhia paused, throwing a startled glance back at Tai. 'Liudan was right, you are an innocent sometimes,' she said. 'Of course it's a ruse. She's buying herself time.'

'Time for what?'

'Time to choose a man of her own desire, and not one the Court thrusts upon her,' Nhia said. 'I'm afraid our Empress is unlikely to be ruled by anyone other than herself.'

'Antian would not have been so obstinate,' Tai whispered.

'Antian was more subtle,' Nhia said. 'From what I know, from what you told me of her, the Little Empress would have done what she needed to do, but from within the cover of dignity and decorum and tradition. With Liudan, it is anyone's guess.'

'I do miss her,' Tai said.

'I think we will all miss her before long. Miss what she was, what she could have been. Liudan is a wild thing, and wild things are unpredictable and dangerous, and not held by a word of command or of restraint. Liudan has the eyes of a lion. Wait there, I'll be right back with the chair.' She paused, casting around a wary glance. The gate and the corridor nearby were deserted except for the two of them at that moment, but Nhia was suddenly and uncomfortably aware that they had been discussing the Empress of Syai in very frank and familiar terms while out in public. It was, to say the least, a breach of protocol. 'We'd better talk about this later,' she said. 'We'd better get back home and get ready.' *Ready to follow the lioness into her mountain lair*, she thought to herself. But that was not a thought she would have uttered out loud on the doorstep of the Great Temple. Not even to Tai.

# Four

They did not, after all, stay at the Summer Palace.

They could not have done. The place was a shattered wreck, and it was still shrouded in drifts of snow at this time of year. It was full of wind-whispers, and the winter-bare branches of the trees creaked and groaned eerily in the empty gardens, but other than this Tai found it remarkably free of ghosts when she walked up to the ruins, alone, on the day after they arrived at their nearby lodgings. There was nothing of Antian here any more, not even a memory. Antian belonged to the summer – bright flowers nodding in the warm sunlight, butterflies, summer stars hanging in the heavens in the long, lazy dusk of hot days. Tai had found it hard going to force her way up the winding road into what was left of the Palace courtyards. No carts had gone that way for a long time, and the snow was set hard and deep on the path – but there had been tracks in the fresh powder on the top of the old packed snow, as if someone else had been there recently. As though someone else went there often.

Tai had not expected to see the one who had made the tracks – the footprints were of booted feet, but small, a child's or a young woman's, perhaps – and had been considerably startled to catch a glimpse of a darting and oddly furtive form scuttling into concealment as she made her way into the gardens. She could not see much, and when she called nobody answered, but the one thing that she did notice, when the creature's wrap had slipped down over her shoulders as she ran, was that the other visitor was a girl whose hair was an improbable and unusual shade of golden chestnut which hung in wild, burnished red-gold curls around a pale, narrow face.

She looked like no one Tai had ever seen before, a spirit of the mountains, maybe – slight, lithe, moving with an athlete's grace and a fawn's light-footed speed. Tai tried looking for her, peering into the shadows of the ruined Palace into which it looked like she had vanished, but there was no sign of her. Not even tracks showed where she had disappeared to, as though she really had been an immortal sprite out of Cahan, out to play with a mortal seeker's eyes.

Whoever she was, it had not been Antian, not even an echo of her spirit.

Tai didn't spend long at the ruins. They were empty for her.

When she returned to the mountain inn where they were staying, Liudan, sitting by the fire in a simple plaited willow chair which her presence managed to make into a throne, stopped her as she walked past the open door to the inn's common room.

'So. Did you find her?'

Tai paused. 'I do not have to seek her here, Liudan. She is always with me.'

'But the first thing you did was go back,' Liudan said. 'To *her*. To the ghost.'

'She is gone. You are here,' Tai said.

Liudan's eyes sparked with something – a touch of jealousy, annoyance, regret, maybe even understanding – but she did not speak.

She would never have admitted it, not even to her own *jin-shei-bao* or perhaps particularly not to her, but Liudan's own first instinct had been to return to the ruins of the old Palace. Tai had had no more than a brace of magical summers there, but Liudan had grown up with the beauty of the Summer Palace gardens, with its wicker cricket cages and the brightness of its flowers . . . and with the presence of the vanished Princess who was at once a bond and a sundering between the two *jin-shei-bao* who survived her. Liudan could remember the times that she spent playing knucklebones in the garden with Antian when she was very little, or Antian reading to her from a slim volume of old legends penned in elegant *jin-ashu* script by some long-gone Imperial ancestress. The Summer Palace gardens held the echo of the only laughter Liudan had shared in her lonely and isolated existence in the Imperial household. And she could also remember, vividly, the stab of jealous rage which had accompanied her first glimpse of Antian and Tai walking together among the fountains of the Inner Court.

'But I have not abandoned you, my sister,' Antian had told her, later, sitting beside her on her bed just before they had all retired that night.

Liudan had been mutinously silent, her head turned away so that she would not be betrayed by the glint of a too-bright eye, and Antian had finally sighed and leaned over and kissed her on the brow and had said quietly, 'It is your own silence that keeps you alone. You know, I think, that I will always be there for you.'

For a moment, there in the sitting room of the mountain inn, Antian's presence had been very real, her face almost shaped by the air that shimmered between Liudan and Tai. But Liudan had said nothing in response to Tai's words, and finally Tai, respecting that silence, made her obeisance to the Empress and retreated into the room that she shared with Nhia.

Nhia was there, leaning over Yuet's shoulder as she pored over an old leather-bound volume thickly and neatly inscribed with *jin-ashu* script. The book looked damaged, its edges eaten by what looked like charring, some of the script partly obliterated by damp which had smeared the ink across the pages.

'Look at this,' Nhia said. 'They showed it to Yuet this morning; apparently someone lugged it all the way down from the wreck of the Palace during the summer.'

'When the scavengers were there,' Tai said, sniffling, trying to stifle one of her explosive sneezes. She had brought those with her from the city, legacy of that mad dash to the Temple to retrieve Nhia for the mountain retreat. 'What is it?'

'I'm not sure,' Yuet said. 'I'm still trying to decipher it, but it looks like Szewan's hand to me, nobody else could do *jin-ashu* in a manner quite this small and crabbed – until her hands gave out, that is, and I started keeping the books. But this looks like it's ten, maybe twenty years old; she was still writing up her own cases then. So far it's pretty ordinary, but it looks remarkably like a copy of the Blackmail Book.'

'The *what*?' Tai said, astonished.

Yuet laughed. 'That's what I always called it. Her secret patients. The ones that were exotic, or unusual, or suffered from diseases or conditions too embarrassing, delicate or dangerous to keep open records of.'

'There is such a book? Did she really use it to blackmail people?' Tai asked.

'Hardly,' said Yuet, but after a small pause. She could see where arcane knowledge, judiciously applied, could be useful . . . but this was not something she would discuss with her two non-healer companions. She had handled Szewan's book even while the old healer had still been alive, and had riffled through it after her death while she had been going through the rest of her papers. But she had not, in fact, had time yet to go through the Blackmail Book properly. She had every intention of doing so soon.

She had known nothing about the existence of a second volume.

'Why would she keep a copy of such a book?' Tai asked slowly. 'And somewhere out of her direct control, too. She wasn't even at the Summer Palace that last summer.'

'Did you ever see the healer's quarters in the Summer Palace?' Yuet said. 'They were mine that last summer. And if I had not known exactly where to look, not even I would have been able to find this book. I'm sure that there were things that Szewan wanted to remember, and it was safer to leave them hidden in a place where nobody would know where to find them than to carry notes back and forth across the continent in her backpack.'

'But nobody counted on the earthquake,' Nhia said. 'The book must have been thrown from its hiding place when the Palace crumbled.'

'Do you think someone has read it?' asked Tai, her eyes quite round.

Yuet dismissed the possibility with a wave of her hand. 'The Traveller women have *jin-ashu*, but they don't practise it nearly as much as we do,' she said. 'It was probably found by someone from the village when they were picking over the ruins for spoils, and then tucked away as a memento. Nobody would read Szewan's hand for pleasure.'

Yuet hoped so, at least. She was already making a mental note to have only a single copy of any such book that she herself might start to keep, but she had already come to the conclusion that the safest place for any really dangerous secrets was a healer's memory.

'She was a shaman as well as a healer,' Nhia said. 'Look, she kept a notation of the phases of the moon. Is that relevant in healing? I didn't know.'

'It might be, when you're gathering certain herbs or fruits,' Yuet said, closing the book and laying a protective hand on its cover. She trusted her sisters but some of the things referred to in this volume would be better off being seen by as few eyes as possible.

'But that's alchemy,' Nhia said.

'All life is,' Yuet retorted. 'They at the Temple apply it differently than we do in the Healers' Guild – I concoct medicines and poultices where they concoct elixirs and potions. The difference is that the healer's ones are used to heal and the magical ones are sometimes used to kill.'

Nhia roused in defence of her beloved Way, her hackles up. 'That isn't true, Yuet, not like you mean it! The healers have their own poisons!'

'Yes,' Yuet said, suddenly haunted by the image of herself handing the poppy draught to Szewan on her last morning. 'I'm sorry. I didn't mean to imply anything.'

A servant knocked on the door of the room. 'If it please you, ladies, the Empress wishes you to attend her for supper.'

'How long are we going to stay here?' Tai asked Yuet in a low voice as the three obeyed this summons and started down the stairs to where Liudan waited.

'As long as she says,' Yuet said. 'I hope it isn't too long, but I don't know, and I have no idea what she expects us to do.'

At least part of what Liudan expected them to do, apparently, was simply keep her company – at least one of the three had to be in attendance to the Empress at all times during the day.

The ghost of Antian may not have been present in the winter ruins of the Summer Palace, but she made her gentle presence known after all.

'I'm told you write poetry,' Liudan said to Tai on the third day, as they sat by the fire in the common room.

Tai looked up with some consternation. 'I . . . yes, I do.'

'I would like to hear it,' Liudan said, her soft words nevertheless a command.

'It is hardly good enough to be read in public,' Tai protested.

'Reading them to me is hardly reading them to the public,' Liudan said. So Tai brought down her red journal and read some of her verses, the ones she could bear to lay open to scrutiny. Liudan heard them with the ear of an unexpected connoisseur.

'Those are good,' she said when Tai's voice faded away at the end of a stanza. 'You remind me of Qiu-Lin.'

'The Cloud Emperor's Empress?' Tai said, flushing.

'She was also one of our greatest poets,' Liudan said. 'All

169

Emperors need advisers, wise men, generals, soldiers, courtiers, people who flatter them and obey them and tell them what they want to hear. But sometimes there are things they *need* to hear, and for that every Emperor needs a poet. They see the things that other people close their eyes to, and tell about it.'

'And live in fear,' Tai said.

Liudan raised an eyebrow. 'What are you afraid of?'

'Laughter,' said Tai softly.

'I am not laughing,' said Liudan. 'Some day, perhaps you'll be *my* poet. As Qiu-Lin was the Cloud Emperor's, and defined his reign and his time through her words.'

'I don't write in *hacha-ashu*,' Tai said. 'I don't know how.'

'Neither did she,' Liudan said shortly. 'I will see to it that it is transcribed.'

Somehow it had jumped from the general to the specific. 'I am not good enough yet,' Tai said, her eyes lowered, tracing the edge of her journal with a trembling finger.

'I know,' said Liudan, and Tai's eyes flew up – but the Empress was not mocking. 'However, I think that one day you will be. You have an eye, a way of seeing things.'

'That,' said Tai, 'is what Antian used to say to me.'

'Well,' said Liudan after a diamond-edged silence. 'Perhaps she knew it, too.'

Released from their shift with Liudan, later that day, Tai and Yuet walked into the village. Tai watched the people scurrying in the street with interest. Fair-skinned and blond, in the manner of the mountain tribes, they were exotic and beautiful to Tai. She had had few real chances to observe them before; she knew that they used to travel the plains frequently, but their kind was rarely seen near Linh-an now.

'The last time I remember seeing them, I was very young, I was only a baby, really,' Tai said, turning with interest after yet another blonde girl, bareheaded in the pale winter sunshine. 'These people *are* the Travellers, aren't they?'

'Some of them, yes,' Yuet said. 'They are nomads by nature; villages like this one are rare. I think this one has the kind of permanence that it had simply because it was so close to the Palace, and there was work to be had there.'

'I remember, there used to be a fair in Linh-an in the summer. There were acrobats, and trained animals, and people who juggled flaming brands. Once Mother bought me a bright set of ribbons from the Travellers. But the fair hasn't been to the city for a while. It's been years.'

'You're right,' Yuet said. 'There used to be a show every year, two, one for the city, one for the Emperor. They really were that good. But then they started coming more and more rarely, and it's been, oh, five years or more now since I've seen any Traveller caravans in the city. And there's certainly been no shows at the Palace for a while. They just vanished.'

Tai looked up. 'Like the spirit. Up at the Summer Palace ruins.'

'The spirit? Whatever do you mean?'

Tai had not told Yuet of her climb up to the Palace on the day after they had arrived in the village; she did so now, describing the girl she had glimpsed, the shadow in the snow.

'She had the most astonishing hair,' Tai said. 'A reddish gold, like a coppery lion's mane. Like . . . like *that* girl.'

A female form had just crossed the village street ahead of them, muffled in a shawl but with enough bright hair showing for Tai's eye to be drawn.

'That's her, Yuet,' she said now, with an edge of excitement, pausing to turn and stare after the hurrying girl.

'Are you sure?' Yuet said sceptically. 'In the depths of that shawl, she could be somebody's grandmother.'

'Not with that hair,' Tai said. 'And the way she moves. I'd know her anywhere after that first time I saw her. The snow dancer. She moved like her feet never touched the snow. She hardly left any tracks at all. Let's follow her!'

'For the love of Cahan, why?' Yuet asked, perplexed, turning to stare at the younger girl.

'Well, for one thing, I've never seen hair that colour in my life,' Tai said, laughing, and then succumbed to a sneezing fit that left her eyes watering and her ears ringing.

Yuet was shaking her head. 'You are strange, little *jin-shei-bao*. We cannot just follow a free woman to her house like she was an escaped bondservant. Besides, I'm getting cold, and as for you I should probably never have let you talk me into this walk in the first place. You should be tucked up in bed, by rights, with a hot cup of tea. Let's go back to the inn. I've had my exercise for the day, and Nhia will need rescuing.'

'I suppose,' said Tai after a pause, sounding vaguely mutinous and wholly unconvinced. But when Yuet turned back towards the inn, she followed, trying to sniffle quietly enough for Yuet not to hear.

They found Nhia in suspiciously little need of rescuing. Autumn Court was traditionally a time when the people – from the city and from far afield in the countryside – could present their petitions for judgment at the Emperor's hands. Nhia and Liudan had been discussing some of the more vexing cases which had been presented at that year's Autumn Court, and the judgments that had been given as advised by the Council and the Nine Sages. Liudan looked up as Yuet and Tai entered the room, divesting themselves of scarves and outer cloaks, and her eyes were sparkling with fierce amusement and admiration.

'I should have appointed Nhia as overseer of the Nine Sages as soon as I had anything to say on the matter,' Liudan said. 'She *understands* things the others merely know.'

Nhia flushed at the praise, and changed the subject. 'Where have you two been?'

'Walking,' Yuet said. 'Thinking. Why is it, do you think, that the Travellers have abandoned the city? I remember them coming every year; even Tai remembers them coming often enough to have made an impression on her. But I cannot remember seeing any of them in Linh-an in the last six or seven years. Maybe longer.'

'Perhaps they didn't like the company,' Liudan said.

Yuet raised an eyebrow. 'In Linh-an?'

'In the Palace,' Liudan said. 'The bored princelings have always liked Traveller women. There are plenty of old grievances which are still brought out in women's quarrels – I never paid much attention to them when I was very little, but when I was old enough to start understanding the things that were being said around me, I recall hearing one Princess Consort screeching at another that at least her husband had properly established concubines in his household and didn't need to lower himself to a Traveller slut.'

'At least the Traveller woman would be gone in a few weeks,' Nhia murmured. 'Would your shrieking Princess prefer to have a rival safely and permanently ensconced in some house in the city?'

172

'A few do,' Liudan said complacently. 'Ones they don't know about.'

'How in the name of Cahan do you know that?' Nhia said, startled.

'My little deaf servant girl learns much that she is never meant to know, because people assume that if she cannot speak, she cannot think,' Liudan said. 'She may not be able to hear but I sometimes think she can read lips even without watching someone's face, and she has a great knack for discovering secret and revealing little scribbles which are thoughtlessly thrown away. I find that useful.'

'Marriage is so complicated,' Tai said.

'But you have your sweetheart already contracted,' Nhia said, grinning.

Yuet, who had been frowning at this exchange as if it reminded her of something that was buried just deeply enough in her memory to be maddeningly out of reach, looked up at this. 'Oh?' she said, with a sudden answering grin of her own.

'Who?' Liudan asked.

Tai blushed and scowled blackly at Nhia. 'Nobody. I mean, he is just a friend. He has always been kind to me.'

'Right,' said Liudan promptly, 'I'll have them start preparing the banns as soon as we get back to Linh-an.'

Tai's eyes were wide with panic, and even Nhia sat up, startled, at that announcement – Liudan was Empress, and what she said she would do could easily be done. But Yuet could see the usual playful malice shimmering beneath Liudan's straight-faced Court mask, and moved in to deflect the barb.

'Have you given any further thought to your own, Liudan?' Yuet said.

The liquid amusement dimmed a little in Liudan's face. 'Mine?' she asked silkily.

'That's ostensibly why you are here, to pick an Emperor,' Yuet said. 'They'll want something from you when we get back.'

'Well, we aren't going back just yet,' Liudan said. 'And I have a surprise for you tonight.'

'What?' Tai said, willing and eager to be diverted.

'You'll see. At dinner. It's odd that you should mention Travellers today, though.'

'You've got a juggler?' Tai asked, her eyes sparking.

'The ones that juggle fire? Hardly, that's not a safe pursuit for indoors, especially not in these small rooms in wooden houses,' Liudan said. 'You'll just have to wait and see.'

The subject of marriage seemed to be closed.


The surprise turned out to be quite a different one than Tai had been anticipating.

After the evening meal was done, a large part of the inn's common room was cleared of benches and trestle tables and the floorboards swept clean. The glow of the fire and dozens of candles bathed the room in a rich golden light as a trio of Traveller men came in and took up position in the far corner. One of them carried a flute, one a stringed instrument similar to a southern guitarra, and the third a small drum with an animal hide stretched tight across a tubby wooden barrel. Their faces were carefully expressionless, but they gave the distinct impression that they would rather have been wrestling bears in the wilderness than sitting in the Empress's makeshift drawing room this evening. Liudan seemed oblivious of it. One of the men glanced up, caught her eye, received a regal nod from her, and said something in a low voice to his companions.

The flute player started alone, drawing out a wistful, thin tune that suddenly reminded Tai of the lost balcony on the ruined mountainside of the Summer Palace. But the first phrase was quickly overlaid by first a countermelody by the guitarra, and then by a heartbeat rhythm by the drum.

Three other men, wearing the kilted dress of the mountain tribesmen and ankle-high deerskin boots, entered as the music began speeding up and flowing into an infectious and driving beat. They launched into a vigorous dance, full of tightly leashed male power, holding their shoulders and backs straight and stiff while their feet wove a complicated pattern of beats on the bare wooden floorboards.

When they were done, Yuet let her admiring eyes follow them out of the room. 'If their women look like that too, no wonder the princes cast covetous glances at them,' she whispered to Liudan. 'Are you sure that no *princess* ever tried to keep one?'

Liudan grinned.

One of the dancers, walking with an almost feline grace, returned to the room bearing a long sword. Nhia sensed a tensing in the Guards standing at attention behind the four girls, but the dancer with the blade paid them absolutely no attention whatsoever. He laid his weapon on the floor, balancing it edge upwards. The music swelled again and the dancer wove a pattern of precision and danger as he pirouetted around the naked sword, his deerskin-booted feet touching the floor lightly a hair's-breadth away from the blade.

Liudan was smiling. 'They are good,' she murmured.

'They are reputed to be as good with it in their hands as at their feet,' Yuet said.

'I know,' said Liudan. 'I've seen them dance both kinds of dance. They're as good as any of my Guardsmen. Better, perhaps.'

'Not Xaforn,' Yuet said, with a small smile, remembering her feisty little *jin-shei-bao* in the Guard compound.

Liudan turned her head slightly. 'Who is Xaforn?'

'One of your Guard,' Yuet said. 'One with a reputation. She beats up other trainees regularly, and sometimes, when she's in particularly fine fettle, she even takes on full Guards in the training court. She's a fierce little thing who doesn't quit. And she'll be all of thirteen years old this coming year.'

'Someone to keep an eye on?' Liudan said, with a raised eyebrow.

'It might prove useful,' Yuet said. 'She has spirit and a quick intelligence.'

'That is a solid character reference. How did you come to know her well enough to know this? Was she a patient?'

'Of a sort. She got a couple of ribs cracked by a senior trainee with greater strength and a greater reach, and I patched her up. She was not happy to be ordered to bed for a month after that accident – and the first thing she did when I allowed her to start training again was get back into good enough shape to call out the same opponent who had put her out of action in the first place and make him beg for mercy!'

'You will have to tell me more about this child later,' Liudan said. 'Here comes another dance.'

This time it was four women, dressed in the brightly dyed ankle-length skirts and gathered peasant blouses of their tribe.

They were all between their mid-teens and mid-twenties, bare-foot, long-limbed and graceful, their long fair hair spilling loose over their shoulders. The youngest girl's mane reached almost down to the backs of her knees, and curled riotously around her face.

'Ai,' sighed Nhia, who had quite unconsciously reached out to touch her own withered leg, a silent regret that she herself would never know what it felt like to move with grace, to dance, 'she looks like the Morning Star if it chose to take human shape.'

Tai reached out and squeezed Nhia's hand.

The music was different for the women dancers, with softer edges, but without losing the heart of spirit and passion that the men's dances had been woven around. The women whirled in complicated patterns, their skirts swirling up and revealing flashing glimpses of shapely ankles and muscled calves. Two of them wore thin chains of some pale metal around their ankles, and the fine links sparkled like silver in the light.

Tai started clapping in rhythm with the dance, in pure delight, and Nhia laughed and joined her; soon Yuet was doing likewise, with only Liudan sitting up with her hands folded with royal dignity in her lap. The dancers had plainly not expected that; they had entered the room wearing a uniform expression of a tense wariness and, perhaps, a glimpse of a concentrated focus on the dance they had been about to perform. When the clapping started in their audience, the youngest girl had been betrayed into a smile after catching Tai's eye.

All but the eldest were smiling by the time they concluded the dance, and bobbed their heads to the enthusiastic audience. And then Tai gasped inadvertently as another girl slipped into the room, bearing a handful of bright scarves.

The girl with the bright chestnut hair who had been up at the Summer Palace. The spirit girl. The snow dancer.

Their eyes met, very briefly – and the other girl's were dark under her pale brows, as dark as Tai's own. Then she dropped her gaze, handed the scarves to the oldest dancer in the room, and ducked out again. There had been mutiny in her face, and there was a corresponding frown on the face of the dancer who had received the scarves; the bright-haired girl's presence in the room had clearly not been sanctioned. Tai turned, caught Yuet's eye, opened her mouth to speak . . .

Yuet, with an instinct she did not understand but obeyed implicitly, gave a quick unobtrusive shake of her head. *Say nothing.*

Tai subsided, confused.

She saw very little of the scarf dance, and the one after that, where the men came back in and rejoined the women and all the dancers did a joyous circle dance as the conclusion of their performance that evening. She bid a distracted good night to Liudan and the others, after the musicians and the dancers had packed up and left, and retired to her bed. She had wanted time to try and puzzle things out, but sleep took her unexpectedly, and with it, a vivid dream the like of which she had not had before.

She walked a Summer Palace which was both whole and shattered, in her dream; if she looked directly at a pile of rubble she saw what was but if she was looking elsewhere with that same pile on the edges of her vision the wall which used to be there stood whole again. In the same manner, when she came to the gateway leading up to Antian's balcony, the terraces beyond looked like they had always done, with the mountain rearing above them, but they were at the same time only ghostly echoes of themselves, the mountainside riven beneath them.

On the incorporeal surface of this beloved balcony, Antian stood on what was alternately solid flagstone and thin air. She was smiling at Tai; and as Tai ran forward to greet her, she changed, flowing into the chestnut-haired girl from the Traveller village – and then into Liudan – and then back into her own gently smiling self.

*Take care of my sister*, the spirit said, smiling. She reached out a hand. *Promise me that. Take care of her.*

*I promise*, Tai said in her dream. Her own trembling fingers sought Antian's and just as they would have touched Tai woke with a start and sat up in bed. Nhia snored gently in the other bed in the small room, in the far corner, but otherwise she was alone. Her heart was beating like the drum of the Traveller musicians, as though she had just danced the full measure of the sword dance.

'Who?' she whispered, to herself and to the spirit which had visited her in the night. 'Who is she?'

# Five

It was closer to three weeks, rather than the more traditional single week of retreat as practised by all her Imperial ancestors, that Liudan decreed a return to Linh-an. None of her companions were any the wiser as to what her decision was in terms of choosing her Emperor, which was ostensibly the reason for the whole journey up to the mountains.

Liudan was perfectly happy to discuss any subject under the heavens with her three *jin-shei* sisters. Her mood was even downright playful at times. She shared of herself as much as she was capable of sharing – she discussed statecraft and the intricacies of the Way with Nhia, and with Yuet, the oldest and most sophisticated of them all, the fascinating topics of people and the way they functioned. She had long, serious discussions on art and poetry with Tai; her remarks about the potential of Tai's poetry had been no Imperial whim, lightly said and quickly forgotten. But what was to have been the purpose of her withdrawal into the mountains – the choosing of the next Emperor of Syai – seemed to have been conveniently buried out of sight, and Liudan showed no sign of wanting to resurrect it.

There had also been no discussion of the Traveller girl who had haunted Tai's dream.

'Say nothing, yet,' Yuet had told Tai. 'There is something here that I think I ought to have known about, but right now all I have is an inkling. I know nothing for sure, and I will not until I get back to the city and to my records, to Szewan's records. Until then, say nothing to anyone. Leave her the life that she has – don't draw attention to her at all. I will look into it, and let you know if I find anything.'

But Tai had been frustrated and curious, and the day before they left the village to return to Linh-an she had gone back to the Summer Palace – again by herself, this time closer to her own favourite time of the day, when the sun was hanging low and golden above the mountains.

She did not know what she had expected to find, but it was not what met her when she climbed up the still snow-covered slopes and through the hushed, empty gardens. In a sunlit corner of a ruined courtyard, like a scrap of tapestry come to life, she saw the girl of her dream dancing, alone.

Her eyes were closed and her arms, bare despite the still-wintry nip in the air, were raised above her head, her wrists bent in graceful arcs, like the wings of a white bird. Her bright hair was loose and streamed in riotous curls, catching the late afternoon sun and glinting red and gold as she whirled to music she alone heard echoing in her mind. She was very fair, her skin like fine porcelain, veins showing blue at her wrists, and her mouth was full and parted as she danced. It was hard to guess at her age because her movements were a woman's movements, her body a woman's body with curves at breast and hip, but her face, and the shape of her mouth, and the curious abandon to her pleasure, were all a child's.

The awareness of not being alone any longer, something that caught her in mid-movement and shivered the shape of her dance into fragments like a falling mirror, was that of a wild thing – neither woman nor child but an unwary mountain beast trapped against a cliff by a hunter. Her eyes flew open and she grabbed at her shawl, draped untidily over a bare tree branch, wrapping herself back into anonymity and turning to flee into the lengthening shadows at her back.

'Wait!' Tai called out, flinging out an arm to stop her. 'I mean you no harm! Don't run! What's your name?'

'I do not talk to the Court people,' came the unexpected reply, in a soft, oddly accented voice – it was dark and low, and older than Tai expected. 'Go home! Leave us alone!'

And then she was gone again.

Tai did not tell Yuet of this encounter, preferring to wait until Yuet came up with some answers of her own. But the strange mountain child was much on her mind as the Linh-an women, the 'Court people', made their way back to the city after Liudan's three weeks of grace.

The Council demanded the results of her meditations on the day after her return to the Palace.

'I will make an announcement,' Liudan said, 'on my birthday. Not before.'

179

She would still be only fifteen years old on her next birthday, in the summer. Still young enough – in theory – to be reined in, bound by tradition, controlled. The Council, advised by the Sages, allowed her the further grace. But speculation did not stop running riot, and the city's betting shops did a brisk trade on which of the suitors Liudan would take as her Emperor at the end of that summer. This Autumn Court would be very different from that of the previous year.

Tai came home determined not to allow Yuet to let the matter of the identity of the Traveller girl slip from her consciousness, but she was soon sidetracked by other events.

The first was the arrival of a very important milestone. Her cycles began two days before she turned twelve, and her Xat-Wau ceremony was scheduled for the fourth day of the third week of Taian, the day that had been the Little Empress's birthday. Tai was no Empress, and her ceremony was far simpler than Liudan's had been – in fact, there was no Temple priest present at all, and it was Nhia, her friend and *jin-shei* sister, who spoke the words of the coming-of-age blessing over her. The only other people present had been Yuet, a smiling brace of neighbours who had been invited in for the celebration, and Rimshi, now seriously ailing and seated throughout the ceremony in a deep cushioned chair and a rug, despite the summer temperatures outside, laid over her knees. Her hands trembled these days, and the Xat-Wau ceremony seemed also to seal the inescapable fact that it was Tai and not her mother who did more and more of the fine embroidery work for the Imperial Court these days.

Nhia had wanted to invite Kito, but Tai, at the last minute, had balked. This occasion would be recorded at the Records Office, right there beside the Temple, and there would be the offerings to be made to the proper spirits, and it had been Nhia who had purchased Tai's special Xat-Wau bead for her yearwood at So-Xan's stall so that it might have been Kito himself who had carved it – but she had suddenly been furiously shy at his being present at the rites which promoted her from child into adult woman. She had been practically in tears over it before Nhia realized that it was not just a reaction to teasing but something far deeper than that, and had wisely abandoned the issue.

Frail and delicate as she was, Rimshi had insisted on being part of the ceremony. It was she who placed Tai's Xat-Wau red pin

180

through the upswept crown of her hair. But it seemed that waiting for her daughter to reach this stepping stone to adulthood was the only thing that was keeping Rimshi alive. Shortly after the ceremony, at which she had still been able to move around the house and had been bright-eyed and proud and happily accepting the congratulations of her guests and the messages of those who did not come – even Liudan had sent a special gift for the occasion, which impressed the neighbours immensely – Rimshi took permanently to her bed, and, despite all Yuet's ministrations, did not look likely to leave it again. It was this looming problem and not the mysterious Traveller girl they had left behind in the mountain village that occupied Yuet's mind.

When Rimshi passed into Cahan, Tai would be orphaned. This child – well, she was no longer a child, legally, now, but Yuet always thought of sweet, quiet, small-boned Tai in those terms – was her *jin-shei* sister, and therefore her responsibility. Rimshi had left Tai with both the skills and the clientele to pursue a career as a seamstress and sought-after needlewoman – if not one that would gain her riches, then certainly one that would more than adequately support her – how was she to live on her own when Rimshi was gone? And under whose protection?

She broached the subject with Tai herself one evening, towards the end of Kannaian, with Tai bent over the sumptuous folds of a Second Princess Consort's new Autumn Court robe and Rimshi, whose job it would have been to finish such commissions until only a few short months ago, asleep in the next room.

'Do not bury her just yet. I am not ready to give her to Cahan,' Tai said in a low voice, her eyes on her work, her hands busy with bright silken thread and fine steel needle. 'She is still with me. She has much to teach me.'

'I know,' Yuet said gently. 'But when Szewan died I was left alone and it took me utterly by surprise. And I was quite a few years older than you are. I worry about you.'

Tai looked up with an affectionate smile. 'I know, *jin-shei-bao*. But things will fall into place as the Way unfolds. Nhia always says that Cahan knows what it is doing.'

'Nhia is often at the Court these days,' Yuet said thoughtfully. 'Between the pull of Empress and Temple, do you see anything of her these days?'

'Less than I would like,' Tai said, reaching for a pair of embroidery shears to snip off a thread. 'She drops in every few days, but often it's a brief visit and she's on her way somewhere else.'

'Is she still teaching?'

'Mm-hmm,' Tai said, her mouth full of embroidery silk as she wet the end of the skein in order to thread a new needle. 'And learning. She studies with one of the senior priests in the Temple now. She says he is an interesting character. Apparently he says that meditation alone is capable of making him invisible. Nhia hasn't seen him pull that trick yet, but she says that there are times she wishes *she* knew how to do it.'

Yuet grinned. Liudan had taken a great fancy to Nhia, and kept her close. Yuet had an idea why Nhia would want to be invisible sometimes. 'Out of sight, out of mind, is it?'

Tai grinned back, an echo of unspoken understanding. 'Something like that. Speaking of out of mind, have you found anything out yet? About her, the girl in the mountains?'

'Actually . . .' Yuet had been at the Blackmail Books over the subject, but had found herself thoroughly distracted by the rich mine of esoteric information they contained. She could see the value of such a document, and had already earmarked a special journal for her own volume. Szewan, however, had been collecting material for decades, and it was hard not to follow beguiling red herrings in her search for the Traveller girl's identity. But Yuet was not about to admit this to Tai. 'I'm looking, I just haven't found my evidence yet.'

Tai had turned serious. 'You still won't tell me anything? Not even this suspicion that you have?'

'Give me a few more days,' Yuet had said.

She had gone back to her home that evening and hauled out the Blackmail Book that Szewan had kept in the city and its battered mate that had turned up in the wreckage of the Summer Palace, intent on just another cursory glance through them in the hope that her eye might snag on the thing she *knew* was in there but could not locate – but she had not reckoned on its usual power of distraction. With a couple of candles providing illumination, and a cooling flask of green tea beside her, she wound up reading late into the night.

Szewan was not linear. The records meandered, twisted, wound in tangled coils within themselves and with one another. The two books seemed to have been used as back-up copies of one another, but frequently one would contain information the other would not. It should have been easy to find the thread Yuet wanted, searching for the code word 'Traveller' in the heavily annotated and footnoted records – but Szewan seemed to have had inordinately much to do with Travellers when they had been frequenting Linh-an in previous years. This in itself was interesting, and something that Yuet marked for future investigation – just how did an Imperial healer of some repute find herself so closely connected to the Traveller clans?

From what she had observed, Yuet judged the mountain girl to be between maybe thirteen and seventeen years of age, not older. But in the space of the four relevant years which those estimates bracketed, any number of Traveller men and women seemed to have crossed Szewan's path. Some she even spoke of in intimate terms in her journal, as though they were close friends, or even kin. On the particular subject which she was pursuing, though, Yuet found herself tracking at least two women patients who had led her to dead ends – both had come to Szewan pregnant, but one of them had delivered a stillborn child and the other's baby, according to Szewan's notations, had died aged three from some childhood pox. There could have been no confusion over this because apparently the Travellers had been back in Linh-an at the time of the child's death, and Szewan herself had closed the child's eyes.

Yuet finally quit for the night, blowing out the candles and locking the books away again, away from other prying eyes, until she could return to them. Her dreams, when she retired to her bed, were nagging ones, as though she had seen something that was relevant to her search but had failed to give it the proper attention – both glimpsed that night, in her research, and seen a long time ago, sufficiently startling to have given her that sense of familiarity, of awareness, the recognition of the child in the mountains as being in some way significant and dangerous. There had been a name, a woman's name, Jocasta or Jovanna or something. It wove its way into her subconscious as she fell asleep, producing first a vivid sequence of a wild and unlikely flight of dream-fancy and then something very different – something specific, a memory not detailed but nevertheless precise. She *had* seen the entry in the Blackmail Books before. When she woke, she could remember a sense of shock, and a woman's name – an impulse strong enough to take her back to the Blackmail Books before breakfast.

This time, as though she knew exactly what she was looking for, she went straight to it.

*Jokhara*. The name was Jokhara. And Szewan was brutally explicit when she had described what had happened to the woman named Jokhara in a Linh-an winter night.

> *Jokhara was small-boned, fair, no older than sixteen or seventeen years of age. When I was summoned to the Emperor's quarters, she was almost unconscious, her naked body on the Emperor's bed. There was blood smeared on her thighs. The Emperor was afraid she was dying; I was able to reassure him on that score, but it was no thanks to his ministrations. The Emperor seemed uncertain as to whether she belonged to his household or not, but if she was a new concubine nobody had heard of her when I inquired at the women's quarters. Thus I made arrangements to take her to my own house, where I allowed her to come to naturally and had a woman of her Traveller clan present when she woke. She remembered very little of what had happened to her, but I told her Traveller companion that I believed she had been raped, and brutally so – she had resisted, and had been beaten into submission, and had been penetrated with what seemed to have been a large foreign object as well as a male member (because there were traces of male seed on her legs). It was too early to tell if any pregnancy had resulted. She was removed to the Traveller camp after several days in my care. Footnote: Injuries included bruising, sometimes severe on arms, legs, breasts and torso, and also on her temple, and also around her neck where it looked like she had been held in what was almost a stranglehold. Also in her private parts which I examined later.*

Armed with an actual name, Yuet could search with more focus for the first time, trying to follow the trail of the case. There had been little in the original account to connect the girl named Jokhara with the child in the mountains, but the time frame was correct, and there *had* been the gradual cessation of Traveller presence in Linh-an not long after this event – not hard evidence, perhaps, but suggestive in itself.

Jokhara's name came up twice more in the Blackmail Books. Once in the city book – barely a month after her initial rape she had been brought in to Szewan by a female Traveller companion, had been discovered to be pregnant, and had been issued with a dosage of herbs which would terminate the pregnancy.

Once more, in the mountain book, eight months after that, describing Jokhara's being brought to childbed.

Szewan had been present at the birth of the child, a girl they had named Tammary, according to the records in the book. A child whose birth was the culmination of an impotent rage by Jokhara, who had refused to take the herbs that Szewan had provided, who had wanted to bear the child of her shame so that she could teach it enough of its heritage to somehow shame the man who had begot it upon her. But Jokhara had never had the chance to teach her daughter anything. She was dead of milk fever before her daughter was a week old.

Tammary remained up in the mountains, to be raised by her Traveller kin.

That was the last time either of them had been mentioned in the books. But Yuet knew, knew deep in her bones, that Tammary was Tai's snow-dancer child.

Her mother's status had been moot, and there was no proof that Tammary's mother had ever been part of the Emperor's household, but Tammary was the Emperor's child, and all his children by a concubine were considered as belonging to his Empress. The eldest of his daughters was by tradition the heir to the Imperial throne.

And by the time Liudan, Syai's Empress, was born, the child that the Emperor had begotten on the Traveller woman was already four months old.

And now that Yuet knew of Tammary's dangerous paternity, she was also aware of how easily it could make Liudan lash out to protect her own position. Liudan seemed to be in control, but Yuet, of all people, knew all the insecurities that still clung to the young Empress even after she had apparently achieved her goals. Liudan had been no more than a figurehead for so long, had been powerless and dismissed as merely the back-up heir to a back-up heir, and a tainted one at that. Now that Liudan had reached the level where she was mistress of both her own fate and the fate of an Empire, Yuet knew that she was capable of almost anything to ensure her position. Yuet didn't want to believe it of Liudan, her own *jin-shei* sister and someone whom she had started to think of as friend, but she was desperately afraid that Liudan could destroy the child of her father's arrogant passions without a second thought if she feared Tammary could come between her and her legacy. With Liudan, of all people, the stark choice between *jin-shei* and Empire would be an almost impossible one to make.

# Six

The last week of Kannaian, like a final sting in the tail of summer, was hot and sultry. The sky was often full of angry clouds promising the relief of a storm, but somehow the storm never came. Each heavy day that passed only served to build up the weight of oppressive heat further on the city.

Yuet was given no time to ponder long on what she had discovered in Szewan's Blackmail Books. She had barely closed them after finishing her research on the Traveller girl named Jokhara and her daughter before a runner arrived to summon her urgently to the Guard compound. There was a problem.

The inner court, where the families lived, was a wretched place that morning. Yuet could sense it as she approached, a healer's instinct, even before the tragic and inconsolable wails of sick children began to penetrate her consciousness. These children cried with a helpless, hopeless intensity which implied that there was no comfort; their mothers and fathers were not leaping up to soothe them, to ease their misery. The crying hung above the courtyard like a shroud. It seemed to be coming from everywhere.

'What happened here?' Yuet snapped at her guide.

'It's been miserable, Healer Yuet,' the guide, a Guard trainee maybe a year or so older than Xaforn, said. 'There's been no fever, but everyone's been throwing up all night, or running for the privies. The children are particularly bad.'

'How long has it been going on? Why didn't someone call me sooner?'

'There were sick people here and there over the past week, but it was nothing like this,' the trainee said. 'Yesterday it was suddenly everywhere. Last night was unbearable.'

'What has been done so far?'

The trainee shrugged. 'I don't really know. I was sent to fetch you. They thought, yesterday, it might have been tainted fruit, or something like that. But then more people started falling ill, and some of them were small babies, and they had eaten no fruit, and . . .'

'Thank you,' Yuet said, cutting off the incipient speculations, which were of no value to her. 'Is it confined to the court or is it all over the compound?'

'So far as I know, nobody in the outer compound has been ill yet,' the trainee said.

'Let's keep it that way, then. You'd better not wander in and out of there at will, and pass the word that nobody else is to, either, until I clear it.' Yuet had been running the symptoms that had been described to her through her mental records, and was not happy with the numbers that came up. 'I don't like the speed of this, and I emphatically do not want the entire Imperial Guard coming down with acute ricewater bowel flux on my watch.'

A sour smell of vomit hung about the doorways of most houses Yuet passed. But she could not go into every house and interrogate some poor soul who happened to be a little less sick than the rest. She needed a central source of information. Someone who knew the inner workings here.

Xaforn had spoken of a girl . . . what was her name?

Qiaan. Daughter of a Guard captain.

It was a start.

Yuet peered into the nearest dwelling, letting her eyes adjust to the shuttered gloom inside. The place was empty except for one dozing woman sprawled on a low pallet by the far wall. Yuet noted a basin with a film of foul-smelling vomit still clinging to it on the floor beside the woman.

'Is anyone taking care of you?' Yuet asked, stepping inside.

The woman's eyes fluttered open. 'My husband was, but it took him too – he left for the privy.'

Yuet touched the inside of the woman's wrist with light fingers. There was no fever, but her pulse was only a faint, thready beat. Her

187

eyes looked enormous, circles of dark shadow underneath them. 'How long have you been ill?'

'I took sick last night,' the woman whispered.

A sound at the door made Yuet look up; a man, his skin sallow and his eyes bloodshot, was leaning against the doorjamb – presumably the husband.

'I will return,' Yuet said, straightening up. 'In the meantime, for the love of Cahan, drink plenty of fluid, both of you. Your lives may depend on that. Can you tell me where I can find a young woman by the name of Qiaan?'

The woman didn't answer, eyelids drooping again, but the man at the door still seemed to have enough wits about him to reply.

'That would be Captain Aric's daughter,' he said. 'She'll be at the officers' quarters, at the top of the court.'

The officers' quarters seemed a little quieter than the rest. A child who appeared perfectly fit and well was playing by herself out in the gardens, and pointed out Captain Aric's quarters to Yuet with a dimpled grin. The door was shut, but it opened to Yuet's touch when nobody answered her hail.

'Hello?' she called, standing on the threshold, her hand on the handle.

A low groan answered her, and, healer's privilege, she stepped in, leaving the door ajar behind her. In an adjoining room, a bed-chamber, a woman lay on a thin straw-tick mattress in a slatted wooden bed, the sheets twisted about her legs. She appeared to be in a fitful sleep. Yuet wasn't sure if it had been she who had made the noise or not. But as she hesitated she was addressed from behind by a youthful voice.

'Hello. Are you the healer?'

Yuet turned, and suppressed a gasp of surprise.

The girl that stood before her may have been a little shorter than Empress Liudan of Syai, and her body was still the coltish shape of childhood, without the sweet curves that Liudan was beginning to show – but in all other respects she resembled Liudan strongly enough to be her twin.

'I am Qiaan,' this Imperial double said. The voice was different, slightly higher pitched than Liudan's.

Yuet blinked, mentally shaking herself. *Just because I dug around in the Blackmail Book and came up with Liudan's half-sister, now I see them everywhere*, she chided herself sharply. 'Yes, I am the healer. And I've been looking for you.'

'Yes, Min said someone had asked after me.' Qiaan stood looking at Yuet with a quizzical tilt to her head. 'Is there some way I can be of assistance?'

'Are you sick with this disease?'

'No,' Qiaan said, 'but my mother and my aunt both are, and I've been taking care of a dozen children in the compound who are ill themselves and whose mothers have been sick enough not to be able to cope with it.'

'An organizer,' Yuet said, with a quick grin. 'You are most emphatically what I need right now. Xaforn told me your name,' she added, when a look of confusion started to creep into Qiaan's eyes.

Qiaan's mouth quirked. 'You are Yuet, aren't you? The one who fixed her ribs, and made her sit out the training for a month? She has spoken to me of you, too.' Her tone left no doubt that Xaforn may have done so in trenchant terms.

The woman on the bed groaned in her sleep. Yuet crossed over to the bed, and laid a hand on her temple. 'No fever, but she looks exhausted,' Yuet said in a low voice.

'This is the first sleep she's had in almost forty-eight hours,' Qiaan said. 'She was among the first who got sick. And she was not well before, even. It's taken a lot out of her.'

'Right,' Yuet said. 'We can talk outside.'

They left the bedside, closing the door of the sickroom behind them. 'Your mother?' Yuet said, indicating the room they had just left.

'Yes. My aunt is in the second room. She's been sick too but she hasn't been as bad.'

'Tell me when all this started.'

Qiaan gave a succinct and cogent summary of the previous few days, describing how the debilitating disease had taken hold in the inner compound. 'I don't know,' she said, 'but it might have something to do with the wells – one of the wells started to smell bad right after the first people started coming down with this flux. Once it did, people stopped using that well for drinking water – but by that time . . .'

'Qiaan!' A feeble voice that still managed to sound peremptory came from a back bedroom, its door pulled nearly to but not quite closed. 'I want water!' the querulous voice demanded. 'Where have you been? And who are you talking to?'

'My Aunt Selvaa,' Qiaan said, her voice resigned.

'Has she been drinking this tainted water you speak of?' Yuet said.

'I tried not to bring that water here after I had my suspicions about it,' Qiaan said. 'But the kitchen might have it. Things could have been cooked in it or washed in it.'

'Qiaan!'

'Coming, Aunt!' Qiaan started towards the second sickroom, grimacing at Yuet.

The healer followed a few paces behind. Qiaan was pouring water from a pottery jar into a shallow cup and offering it to the hatchet-faced woman lying on the pallet in this back room. The patient's eyes, raised to the girl with the water cup and full in the sight of Yuet as she approached the open door, were snapping with active dislike.

'You just abandon us here, we could die, and you go off.'

'Actually, there *have* been a few that died, Aunt,' Qiaan said with an edge of irritation. 'And I am not ill, and others could do with some help. There are children who . . .'

'You should care more about the woman who took you in,' Selvaa spat out. She was weak from dehydration, her voice was soft, but it carried, and the disease had stripped off whatever sheath of tact had been covering her dislike of Qiaan until now. 'My sister helped *you*. Cahan knew what would have happened if she had not forgiven . . .'

Qiaan stared at her in incomprehension, then reached out for her aunt's fingers. 'The others do not have fever, but you sound . . .'

Selvaa snatched her hand away. 'Water. Give me water. You owe me that, owe *us* that. We took care of you.'

'Let me,' Yuet interceded, stepping between the two. 'Your name is Selvaa? I am the healer, Yuet. How long have you been ill?'

'A week,' Selvaa said weakly.

'She took ill yesterday,' Qiaan said quietly.

Selvaa shot her a poisonous look. Yuet ignored both of them for the time being, turning Selvaa over on her back and palpating her abdomen. 'Does it hurt when I . . .'

Selvaa grimaced. 'Yes. No. I am not sure. I need water.'

'Yes,' Yuet agreed. She looked up and caught Qiaan's eye. 'And sleep. I will make you a herbal to help you get some rest. Qiaan, show me where I may make an infusion.'

They went back to the front room to pick up Yuet's satchel and Qiaan led the way to the empty kitchen area. Yuet sniffed at the water in a barrel that stood by the door, and Qiaan said, 'That one came from the clean well.'

'You will have to show me this other well,' Yuet said. 'In the meantime, put a pannikin of this on to heat for me.' She rummaged in her satchel and came up with a twist of silk, secured with a ribbon tie. Unfolding this on a clean section of the kitchen table, she measured out a quantity of the pungent ground herb it had contained and poured it into the container Qiaan had swung out over the hearth. They waited until the water with the powder in it boiled, releasing a rich green aroma in the kitchen, and then Yuet set the brewed potion aside to cool a little.

'When it's cool enough to drink, but still warm, give her a cupful of it – and to your mother as well, when she wakes. I will leave the rest of this packet with you; boil it all up, no more than a pinch or two per pan, and let the children have it – it will help them sleep, and help prevent the dehydration. I need to go back to my workroom and get some more of this, and I will be back with that. In the meantime, if you will find me at least one person who is strong enough to wield tools, we will seal this tainted well before it spreads any more contagion,' Yuet said.

'Is it the water?'

'Probably. I've seen this before, it's sparked by tainted food or water, and then it spreads fast,' Yuet said. 'Are there any others who are not ill? We may need a few people to nurse the worst-off through this. And we must make sure that there is clean water enough for washing. Wash your hands after you clean up after someone who is afflicted, and before you allow yourself to go near food or drink. The outer compound draws water from a different well, doesn't it?'

'Yes, several.'

'I will have to check those too. And I'll pass the word to other healers, lest this jump the water somewhere and spread into the city. It's hot, and people will drink tainted water if they aren't aware that it carries disease. And, Qiaan . . .'

191

Qiaan jumped, as though the sound of her name had interrupted some internal train of thought. 'Yes?'

'Through Xaforn, who is *jin-shei* to us both, we too are *jin-shei-bao* of a second circle,' Yuet said, smiling. 'You've done well here.'

Qiaan flushed. 'I am not sick,' she said. 'I did what I could.' She hesitated. 'My mother . . . should I have called someone . . . she is so weak. I don't know what else to do.'

'Make sure she has some of this when she wakes, too,' Yuet said, laying the back of her hand against the cup holding the herbal infusion to test the temperature. 'I'll be back with more presently.' She paused, looking at the faint scowl that had etched itself into Qiaan's forehead. 'Don't let your aunt upset you,' Yuet said gently. 'She is ill. People say strange things when they are not themselves.'

'You said yourself she had no fever,' Qiaan said. 'She is hardly delirious.'

'No, but she is suffering, and hurting, and full of self-pity – and you are what is there to pour it all out on. It means nothing.' Yuet reached out and squeezed the other girl's shoulder reassuringly. 'Don't worry. If we can isolate the taint, we can prevent it from spreading – and if we can stop those who are already sick from getting too dehydrated, we have a good chance of stopping this. Luckily it's isolated and contained here, and it isn't in the city. And it's going to get cooler soon, so the heat will not help spread it. Go, take in the infusion. I will be back as soon as I can.'

Qiaan lowered her eyes, took up the potion and went back to her querulous aunt.

Yuet, departing the inner court, went straight to her stillroom by way of a short visit to the Guard Commander on duty in the main compound to request a full short-term quarantine for the patients in the family quarters and immediate attention to the delivery of clean drinking water until the problem of the tainted well could be dealt with. She washed her hands with lye soap to make sure they were free of whatever agent was causing the infection in the inner court and raided her stocks of dried herbs, grinding a mixture of roots and leaves into quantities of fine powder and pouring it into stoppered earthenware flasks. She stowed each batch of the preparation in her satchel as she finished it, to take back to the compound.

As she worked, she heard a diffident knock on the thick oaken door of the stillroom, and left her mortar and pestle, wiping her hands on her stillroom smock as she did so, to answer it.

'I beg your pardon, mistress,' said the servant, 'I would not disturb you at your work, but there is a messenger from the Palace, and I thought . . .'

'Ask him to wait,' said Yuet. 'I will be right up, as soon as I've finished this particular batch. I will only be a few moments.'

'Yes, mistress.' The servant bobbed her head and turned to go back up the winding stone stairs leading down from the main house.

The messenger who was waiting in the anteroom wore the colours of Third Prince Zhu, Liudan's older half-brother. Yuet, distracted by too many things on her mind, cast about for a reason why that name should have been so meaningful to her right at that time, but could find nothing to attach it to and simply offered the messenger a professionally detached smile instead.

'Is there a problem in the Prince's household?' she asked politely.

The messenger bowed. 'The Royal Prince Aya-Zhu asks that you attend his bride at your convenience,' he said. 'She is somewhat indisposed after their return from their travels.'

Yuet's eyebrows rose a fraction. 'Prince *Aya*-Zhu? When was His Highness wed?'

'In the third week of Siantain, in the spring,' the messenger said.

'Ah. I was away from Linh-an then.' Yuet paused, as something suddenly struck her. The reason the name was familiar was because . . . because the Prince had been betrothed to . . .

She frowned.

Nhia had said something to her, back before they had left for Liudan's retreat. About the betrothal of Khailin, Chronicler Cheleh's daughter.

To Third Prince Zhu.

According to ancient custom, the bride and groom twinned their names at their wedding, the partner's name coming first in the new, hyphenated version. If Prince Zhu had married the woman to whom he had been betrothed, he should have been Khailin-Zhu, and his wife would have become Zhu-Khailin. Sometimes longer names were abbreviated, for the sake of ease of pronunciation, but 'Aya' did not sound like something that could easily have been extracted from a name like Khailin. If anything, Yuet would have expected a Khai-Zhu, or even a Lin-Zhu – but Aya?

'The Prince,' she said carefully, 'I thought he was betrothed to another lady, Khailin, daughter of the Court Chronicler Cheleh?'

'Third Princess Consort Zhu-Aya was of the house of the merchant An-Nhuy before her marriage,' said the messenger, and Yuet saw his lips purse in disapproval. But he was not saying any more, and Yuet, frowning slightly, turned back to professional mode.

'Is the Princess's indisposition of a serious nature?' she asked. 'I will come at once, if so – but if not, I would beg leave to make a detour first in order to deliver some urgently needed medicine.'

'The Princess is not in immediate danger,' the messenger said grudgingly after a moment.

Yuet nodded. 'I will be at Prince Zhu's quarters within the hour, then.'

She was a healer. She had responsibilities. The mysteries that were piling up around her had to wait their turn.


After delivering the first batch of medicine to the inner court and leaving instructions with Qiaan and the batch of able-bodied 'nurses' she had rounded up from amongst the stricken quarter, now quarantined against casual visitors, Yuet washed her hands with lye once again to make sure she was not carrying the infection out of the area and paid a visit to Princess Zhu-Aya. The Princess turned out to be suffering from nothing more serious than the first pangs of morning sickness. She was a plain little thing, sallow-skinned and so small-boned that Yuet, casting a glance on the narrow bony hips of the pregnant woman, had a twinge of misgiving as to how she was ever going to deliver a healthy child without succumbing to it. But she had no time to worry about that now. She had a far more immediate problem on her hands.

'I need an apprentice,' she muttered to herself when she left the Palace. It was barely noon, and she was already exhausted.

She stopped off at her house for just long enough to pick up another batch of her herbs, and leave word that she would be away for the rest of the day, suggesting alternative healers for those patients who came in with emergencies. Then she returned to the beleaguered inner court, where Qiaan was gamely holding the fort, and rolled up her sleeves.

She did not leave the inner court again for over a week, except to go back for more medicine.

Yuet had never balked at the messier aspects of the healer's craft. She had cleaned up blood, pus and excreta before. But there were very few helping hands here, and so many who needed help. With Qiaan's assistance they had moved the worst-off patients – which included Qiaan's own mother, who had lapsed into semi-consciousness despite everything that could be done for her – into a single space, a large communal hall where the populace usually gathered to hold dances or watch the occasional theatre troupe which came touring into Linh-an. Yuet had organized a number of low sickbed pallets, and the patients were lined up in rows, the smallest children separated in their own section where someone was on constant supervisory duty. Supplies of water and food were carefully vetted by Yuet herself, and, as she trained their eye and judgement for what they were looking for, by a number of understudies including Qiaan herself. A constant bubble of broth and herbal teas was kept going on the kitchen hearths by a number of other volunteers.

The sickness appeared to be contained; it did not spread outside the compound, and several of the city's other healers came in to offer their aid after word of the outbreak reached them. When the first of these arrived, Yuet finally allowed herself to go home and take a shift off, scrubbing herself clean and then falling into bed to catch up on a week's lost sleep. She stayed home for a day, letting her cook cluck and coo over her, feeling grateful for the luxury of being cared *for* instead of propping weak women up to take a mouthful of nourishment or making fractious, seriously dehydrated children drink foul-tasting herbals which would make them better.

There were several messages from her regular patients regarding chronic complaints, a number of them from the pregnant Princess who was not having a good first trimester – but Yuet contented herself with sending messages of instruction to all of them as to how to proceed in the interim period, and as soon as she felt rested enough to think straight again she took herself straight back to where the battle was being fought for children's lives.

They buried a number of those children, the smallest ones, the weakest ones, the ones who had no strength to endure the racking vomiting and acute diarrhoea that accompanied the sickness. In the deep night, by candlelight, there would be women and girls – healers or volunteers who had not fallen ill or had recovered enough to lend a hand – passing by the pallets of the fitfully sleeping patients, checking on their breathing, supporting children as they retched painfully over basins. It was a constant vigil, and it was made worse by the knowledge that outside the perimeter of this closed circle were the mothers and fathers of some of the children in this compound, Guards who had been out of the family area and were now banned from it until the sickness could be contained, who watched and waited helplessly while the healers and their helpers tried to snatch as many as they could back from the brink.

There were no new cases of the disease after the end of that first week, after Yuet had sealed the tainted well and all the drinking water was being fetched from other, clean sources until a new well could be dug for the compound. By the end of the second week those who would recover were out of danger – utterly broken, weak as newborn kittens, having lost a lot of weight, but alive and on the road to recovery.

Only then did Yuet order a massive cleaning of the compound, scrubbing floors with strong-smelling bleach and lye solutions, throwing new whitewash over walls. They burned the sickroom pallets as they became vacated.

The new-look compound, aside from its crop of recovering convalescents with straggling, unwashed hair and hollow cheeks, looked spruced up and almost brand new by the time they were done. When the quarantine was lifted, a little over two and a half weeks after Yuet had imposed it, the epidemic had been averted. There was mourning in the Guard circles for their losses, especially amongst the young and the elderly – but there was also great joy as the sundered families were allowed to come together once again.

One of the casualties had been Rochanaa, Qiaan's mother, who had slipped away very quietly one night. Qiaan had been with her, and it was in the circle of her daughter's arms that she had passed to Cahan, but she never knew it – at the very end she had lapsed into deep unconsciousness and had simply never woken up again. Qiaan had sat there for some time, her dead mother's head on her lap, quiet tears on her cheeks. But then she had arranged Rochanaa's limbs in a seemly position, kissed her on the forehead one last time, and appeared to wish to drown her mourning in the hard work of caring for other patients who needed her.

Selvaa had recovered, but had not offered her help as a volunteer – had, in fact, tried twice to leave the compound despite explicit instructions to the contrary. It had been Qiaan who had stopped her the second time; Yuet had seen the confrontation, but from a distance, and had not known what it was that Selvaa had said but she had seen Qiaan recoil from her as though she had been slapped. Then she had firmly gripped her struggling and protesting aunt's arm and marched her back to her quarters. Her face had been one thunderous scowl when she had returned to the makeshift hospital hall.

'I threatened that I would lock her in if I had to,' she muttered to Yuet.

'What did she say to you?' Yuet asked.

'What?'

'Just now, when you brought her back. I saw it. She said something to you again, something hurtful.'

'She said that I didn't have to feel guilty for having my mother die in my arms,' Qiaan said after a painful moment, 'because she wasn't my mother. Because . . . I was . . . adopted.'

Yuet shot her a startled look. 'Some people,' she said, 'make hurting a pleasure.'

'She may be right,' Qiaan said in a strange voice. 'I never really thought about it, not so as to try and figure out why or anything like that, but my mother always found it curiously difficult to like me.'

Yuet laid a comforting hand on the younger girl's arm. 'Whatever else is true, this is: she was your mother, she brought you up, and nothing Selvaa tells you is enough to deprive you of the chance to mourn her properly.'

Qiaan lifted her dark eyes, Liudan's eyes, to Yuet in a grateful look. 'You have been a miracle to us,' she said.

'I am a healer,' Yuet said, smiling a little sadly. 'I try to snatch the sick from the jaws of Cahan every day of my life.'

Qiaan suddenly reached out and hugged Yuet, hard, with tears

197

standing in her eyes. 'Cahan cannot have everything it desires,' she whispered fiercely. 'Thank you. For everything you have done here.'

'Any time you want a job, I'll take you on as an apprentice,' Yuet said. She was joking, trying to turn the emotional moment, but she found, to her surprise, that she was more than half serious. Qiaan had the patience, the understanding and, most important of all, a good dose of that gently bullying quality so essential in every good healer.

But she smiled and shook her head. 'I am not sure what I want to do with my life as yet,' she said, 'but I could not do what you do.'

'You did it here,' Yuet pointed out.

'Yes, but these were my people,' Qiaan said. 'People I knew, and cared about.'

'When you are a healer,' Yuet said, 'all people are your people.'

But she had not pressed it.

She went back home feeling as though she had just herself weathered a bad bout of the disease she had spent a fortnight nursing others through, and dealt with only the most pressing of emergencies before taking a few days off to recuperate.

Tai came in to see her with a batch of nut biscuits she had baked herself and a bunch of late-blooming chrysanthemums which she arranged in one of Yuet's vases. To Yuet, whose life in the past couple of weeks had been confined to the bare essentials, the biscuits were a touch of pure luxury. She munched on them, watching Tai fuss with the flowers, and pronounced them delicious.

'And how has the rest of the world been while I was out of it?' she asked, when the first hunger had been sated.

'Well, Prince Aya-Zhu and his unexpected bride were the sensation of the Autumn Court,' Tai said. 'Nhia is particularly upset – she has been so much part of the Court recently, and she had no inkling. She and Khailin had some sort of silly quarrel the last time they really saw each other and then Khailin disappeared from sight – and Nhia has no idea where Khailin is or what she is doing. Her mother would only tell Nhia that Khailin no longer lives there, and hinted that she is, in point of fact, married – but obviously not to her Prince, and the family apparently will not say to whom.'

'I'll get to the bottom of that,' Yuet said. 'The Princess is a patient. Pregnant and miserable. I'll find out what happened. Miserable patients will tell a lot as a sign of gratitude to a healer who eases their discomforts.'

Tai giggled. 'You *are* terrible.'

'What about you? How is your mother? I haven't had a chance to look in on her.'

'She sleeps a lot, but she is holding her own,' Tai said. 'The neighbours look in on her regularly if I am not there, so she is not alone.'

Yuet, about to say something, blinked suddenly as a thought occurred to her. 'Autumn Court,' she said. 'That is begun. Liudan's birthday was a week ago. She said that she would make an announcement then, choose an Emperor. I completely forgot about it, I was so immersed in the whole situation in the Guard compound. What happened, Tai?'

'She postponed it, to the end of the Autumn Court,' Tai said, keeping her face inscrutable.

'*Postponed* it? Again? And they let her?'

'They had little choice. One of the suitors on her list just wed someone else – just like Prince Zhu. It must be something in the water!' Tai stopped at Yuet's wince. 'Sorry. Liudan declared she wanted to give it further thought. They demanded, but she stood firm, and High Chancellor Zibo backed down but said that they would have a decision at the end of Autumn Court, or else.'

'Or else what?'

'He didn't specify, but according to Liudan the expression on his face indicated that it would be something long and painful,' Tai said.

'So she has . . . what?'

'Another week.'

Yuet was shaking her head. 'Stubborn and stubborn and stubborn. She will make a wrong step yet she cannot back out of. What did she make of the epidemic?'

'She sent food, and asked about you,' Tai said.

Yuet felt oddly disappointed. 'I would have thought . . .' she began.

'You didn't expect her to pay that much more attention to it, did you?' Tai said. 'With this Autumn Court hanging over her head like a blade, and scandals rocking the royal house, and Cheleh walking around like he had swallowed a sour pickle?'

'Did anyone ask *him*?' Yuet said.

'Nobody's *talked* to him for a month without getting either silence or snaps,' Tai said. 'One person who got a snap says that it's because he doesn't himself know where his older daughter is.'

'I need a holiday,' Yuet said suddenly.

'Yes,' Tai said, casting her a startled look, 'I think you quite legitimately do.'

'Your friend,' Yuet said suddenly. 'The mountain girl.'

'Yes?' Tai said, her attention suddenly sharpened.

'I think she is Liudan's half-sister. That the Emperor fathered that child on a Traveller girl, shortly before the Travellers stopped coming to Linh-an.'

Tai nodded slowly. *I don't talk to Court people.* That would fit.

'But you said that there would be danger?'

'If Liudan found out. She could be a rival for her. She has the blood.'

'But it goes through the female line,' Tai said, confused. 'How could that girl ever claim anything on Liudan?'

'Tammary. Her name is Tammary. And she is senior to Liudan – not much older, but enough. And she does not have to claim a thing – all that would be needed is for someone to claim it in her name. I don't know if she is married or promised yet – they have different customs up in the mountains – but she and her partner, and their issue, could be used to undermine Liudan – and although it scares me to think so, I believe that Liudan might be quite capable of leaping to the conclusion that they *will* be so used. What's the matter now?'

Tai had gone white. 'The dream.'

'What dream?'

'I dreamt of Antian in the mountains. She *changed*, in the dream, and turned into Liudan, and then into . . . into . . . what did you say her name was? Tammary? Into Tammary. And she said to me in the dream, *Take care of my sister.* And I said I would, again, just like that first time she had asked it of me. But which sister? Yuet, what am I supposed to do?'

Yuet was staring at her. 'Perhaps,' she said, 'we need to go back and pay another visit to the village. Just you and me this time. There are things here I think we need to know.'

# *Seven*

Nhia was a fractious and unsatisfactory student at the Temple in the weeks that Yuet vanished into the Guard compound to hold the epidemic at bay, and Khailin persisted in her mysterious absence. Tai was her usual sweet self, and always available to supply a willing ear to Nhia's self-reproachful discourses on how she should have dealt with the Khailin situation better, or provide a cup of calming tea and a soft cushion for the aching foot when Nhia came back from some Court occasion and needed to vent her frustration. But even that had not been quite enough. Nhia had wanted to go into the compound and offer Yuet her own assistance as nurse, chief potion brewer, teller of tales to sick children – whatever it would take to ease Yuet's burdens and to drown her own keyed-up energies.

Instead, she got a new teacher at the Temple.

The new priest who was assigned to supervise her studies was a boulder in the stream of Nhia's impotent furies. He allowed it all to flow around him, but was not moved an inch by it, and by his very stillness and immobility he forced Nhia to focus on her inner meditations.

'You are not focusing your mind,' her teacher would remonstrate, gently but inexorably. 'Focus. The light of your spirit should be a fine and a sharp one, not diffuse and distracted and floating about like a butterfly. You have to focus your wandering.'

'I *am* focusing, Xsixu-*lama*,' Nhia said.

The priest called Xsixu shook his head. 'There are two kinds of wandering, my child. The first is easy, and may be done by any spirit advanced enough to be sent out. It involves simply seeing, skimming over beauty, watching lakes and mountains and cities, admiring the architecture of great temples, following rolling rivers to the ocean, or just visiting distant relatives or friends. But when you do this your mind is lost, and possessed by the things it sees and touches. It is empty. You can travel all over the world, see all its wonders, exhaust your body and your spirit, and you have achieved nothing, nothing at all. You weaken your own vital energy without having achieved a thing.'

'But I am not . . .'

'Hush, child. You are. You are at the Palace, with the Court. You are at the Guard compound, with your friend. You are everywhere but here.'

'You said there were two kinds of wandering.'

'The second,' said the priest, 'is the pilgrimage you must make deep, deep into yourself – into the deepest and darkest mysteries of your very soul. It is the search for the Perfect Truth, the search for the word which will illuminate your path into the Way like a torch. It is the cloud-like wandering, and it is the key to entry into Shan, the Realm of Pure Spirit, the highest of the Three Heavens of Cahan. It awakens you, and makes of you the perfect illumination, a light unto others. You become an Immortal, and you guide others to follow in your footsteps.'

'Ah, Xsixu-*lama*,' Nhia sighed, 'I will never be . . .'

'You could be, child,' came the unexpected response. 'Leave the worldly things behind you and come with me now. Let us go where our spirits take us and drink from the Fountains of Cahan today. Your breathing. Control your breathing. Close your eyes, empty your mind, forget about the world, *forget*.'

For a moment, just before she obeyed him and closed her eyes, allowing herself to drift into the white light of the meditative state which she had learned to call up at will, Nhia thought she glimpsed the features of Xsixu change subtly, flow into something else, something naggingly familiar. His eyes had deepened, become more compelling, glittering dark orbs which were almost hypnotic in their power and which were so familiar, so *familiar*, if only she could stop and think for long enough to place them . . . but then she was into the light of the spirit, and his was a companion light, ethereal, disembodied, with no haunting eyes to distract her.

Xsixu insisted that Nhia spend at least two hours in meditation every day. He did not demand that they be spent under his direct supervision, but he would ask pointed questions if she had meditated outside his immediate presence in order to make sure that she was working towards the goals which he was pointing her towards. He was a hard taskmaster, harder by far than the gentle elderly priest she had been assigned as her teacher before Xsixu had taken over, and under his strict daily tutelage she found herself reaching and passing milestones that she had never believed herself capable of achieving.

He would send her away with teachings that she would write down in a special notebook in spidery *jin-ashu* script, to think on and puzzle over for hours afterwards. It would keep her awake at night, tossing and turning in her bed, worrying at his words for hidden meanings. She would get distracted every so often, remembering the maddening but elusive familiarity of those compelling eyes, and then remind herself sternly about his words on cloud-like wandering and resolutely shy away from thinking on anything that specific.

'Cultivate the inner self,' Xsixu would tell her. 'Focus on what you are. Do not let your mind and your spirit run wild – you will lose your nature, and your destiny, in the myriad distractions that the world offers you. Concentrate. Taste the waters of the Fountains of Cahan.'

Or, again, 'You have two minds. One is like dark, deep waters, mysterious, subtle, pure, quiet, containing no wild or distracted thought. It is not distracted by external glitter, or internal feelings like anger or frustration. It reflects, and when you dip things beneath its surface it absorbs and understands. The other is like the wind. It is in contact with external forms and shapes, and is pulled into whatever shape those things desire, pushed into forever seeking beginnings, and ends, and reasons, and never bringing anything to a conclusion because it is so stirred up by everything around it, restless and directionless. You must live in your water mind, not your wind mind. Look, look where your spirit lives and endures.'

And, on a third occasion, 'The true way to meditate is to have your mind as firm as the mountains, as impossible to move as the mountains, as focused as you can be – at all times of the day, whatever you are doing, walking, eating, lying down. Let nothing enter through your senses – your eyes, your nose, your ears, your mouth – that will distract you from your goal. Your mind must be focused. You must not be thinking about your mind being focused, because if you are thinking this, then it is an external thought and your mind is no longer focused on the primary idea. Cheating is easy, but pointless. Free your spirit, and you can travel among the stars.'

'Nhia,' Tai said when Nhia tried to convey some of these ideas to her over cups of green tea, 'you are starting to sound like you've gone straight from childhood into the ranks of the Immortals. Your teacher scares me.'

'He scares me too,' Nhia admitted. 'Never before has anyone asked me to be so wholly myself, without giving in to anything that comes from outside of me. I don't know if I can abandon the world to the extent that he wishes me to do it.'

'He sounds like he wants you to forsake everything that is not him and of his world,' Tai said. 'Your friends, your work, your daily life and living – nothing must be there but a sense of Cahan. Nhia, he scares me. He is asking you to *die*.'

'Of course he isn't, Tai,' Nhia said, laughing. 'Dying isn't what this is all about.'

'But he wants you to forget all about everything else . . . all about Liudan, about Yuet, about me . . . to be not Nhia, but a spirit-of-Nhia, alive and not alive, beyond our reach.'

'You don't understand,' Nhia said airily.

She was dismissing Tai's unease, trying to diminish it by making it sound unimportant. This belittling of genuine concerns, casting them into oblivion by declaring them irrelevant, was not the kind of mistake Nhia had made before. She had made a point of always treating people's problems as though they were real, as though they mattered, even when they had been trifles and easily solved. That care was part of what had made her a teacher, made her wise. Tai said nothing, but felt a flutter of disquiet touch her heart.

While Yuet battled with the demons of death and disease and Liudan juggled her Court to gain another week of grace, Nhia sank into the Temple, allowing Xsixu's words to echo in her mind in his presence and out of it, teaching herself the inner calm that he demanded. She was weak and frail – she knew this because she could not achieve the perfect peace, could glimpse the mountains of the Immortals of which she had so often told in her teaching tales but always dimly, their shapes blurred and distorted, as though she was looking at them from under water.

The first time she made her breakthrough into pure clarity of spirit, she exploded through veils of cloud like a winged spirit. She, Nhia, of the clubbed foot – the clumsy one, the one who would never have grace, would never skip, would never dance – she flew through the skies like an eagle, fell and swooped through air so clear that her cry of joy caught into a sob that was almost pain. She was so thoroughly terrified by the sharpness of the experience that she fell out of her meditative trance, gasping for breath, and found herself being supported gently by Xsixu while she fought for breath. His one hand was at her shoulder, keeping her seated in an upright position, and the other was gentle but firm against her back, between her shoulder blades. Just like once, another hand . . .

Nhia gasped for breath again, but this time it had nothing to do with her revelation or her achievement.

She knew.

She knew the eyes that had been taunting her from the edge of her consciousness for days. They belonged to the same man who had supported her before, on other occasions where her frail body had betrayed her, in just such a manner as he was doing right now. She knew the eyes; she knew the long-fingered, steady, aristocratic hands.

She blinked to clear her watering eyes, and turned her head to stare at the man whom she had known as Xsixu – the man who looked nothing like Ninth Sage Lihui of the Imperial Court.

Until this moment.

Xsixu's face seemed to shift in her mind, and flow, and the eyes that had haunted her days glittered suddenly in the features that she remembered. His black hair was still tied back in a workmanlike queue, his skin still smooth and with no trace of wrinkles, but just for an instant Nhia got an impression of looking down a vortex of uncounted years, of an immeasurable age, an ancientness of spirit that almost terrified her.

'*You?*' she whispered. 'How long has it been you?'

'All the time, dear child,' Lihui said. 'Since almost the very beginning. I persuaded the Temple to let you teach. When you came here to study you had a Temple teacher only for the barest beginning, just enough to start you off and make you interesting. Since then, all the teachers you have had have been me.'

'Why the disguises?' Nhia gasped.

'Are you all right now?' Lihui inquired solicitously, and when she nodded he sat back, releasing her. 'Why the disguises? My dear child, if I had stepped in as your teacher – as myself – right from the start, you would have believed that nothing you achieved had come from yourself. You had to learn to trust *yourself*, not the teacher you thought had all the answers.'

'But I am nothing . . .'

'Sweet girl. Whatever you will yourself to be, you can be. Have you understood nothing? Tell me, what did you see, just now, when you fell out of your sky?'

'You know?' Nhia gasped.

'What you felt, I felt. I am your teacher. I know your nature.'

Nhia found she was crying now, really crying, and could not seem to make herself stop. 'Wings. I had wings.'

'I know,' Lihui said, his voice gentle. 'I knew from the first moment I crossed your path. You were just promise, then – an empty cup. All I did was make sure that you were filled.'

'With *what*?'

'Your destiny,' Lihui said. 'You are an Empress's companion now, and the Temple's treasure. You do not need Xsixu any more.'

Nhia looked up, her face streaked with tears. 'But I have only just begun to understand. I still do not even know what I am.'

'Oh, I know what you are,' Lihui said. 'But when I said you no longer need Xsixu, I did not mean you should give up your studies. Indeed, not. You are at a critical juncture now, and you need the guidance of a mentor and teacher more than ever. All I meant was, Xsixu has taught you everything that Xsixu had to teach. From now on, you learn from me.'

Nhia could only stare at him, speechless.

'You need no book learning,' Lihui said. 'You know now that what you need for true understanding lies not within words imprisoned on a page. You must search for meaning, and for the principles behind meaning – and once you have comprehended the principle, discard it, and take the true meaning into your heart. Once you have grasped that, the mind will leave the external distractions, and you will know the Three Heavens of Cahan. I, Lihui, Ninth Sage of the Circle, promise you this.'

'What do I need to do?' Nhia said.

'Tomorrow you come to my house. The Temple has done what it can for you. Tomorrow you become my disciple.'

'I do not know where you live, Lihui-*lama*,' Nhia said after a heartbeat of silence.

'Do you not?' Lihui said with an odd note of challenge. 'I think you will find that you do. I do not want to tax you, you have had a breakthrough today. I suggest you take the rest of the day and meditate on your experience – but do not try to transcend again, not alone, not yet. That will come, in time. Tomorrow.'

He rose to his feet with the grace of a dancer, bowed to her, and left her.

It was an hour later, maybe more, that Nhia left the Temple teaching precinct, walking as though in a dream. Lihui. Lihui had been her teacher all along. A part of her wanted to go to somebody with this, to Tai and her gentle understanding, and a part of her shied from revealing it to anyone at all, not now, not yet. She lit a taper at the little altar in her room, and prayed to the Lords of the Four Quarters, the guardians of human destiny, for guidance. She received none. All she got back was a sense of danger, and also an exhilaration so vast that she could hear its wings beating, like those of the eagle she had briefly been.

She did not go to Tai. She did not sleep. She sat up at her window staring at the sky above Linh-an, watching the stars come into the sky, and then fade into morning.

When the sun was fully up Nhia dressed with care, in a silk inner gown and a Court brocade outer robe, and stepped outside into the street. She stood for a moment, emptied of externals, as Lihui had told her she must be, waiting to be filled with the knowledge of where to go to find him. With a sense of wonder she realized that he was right – that a path shaped itself in her mind, like a map, and she set her feet on it and walked, almost blind, into Linh-an's busy streets. People saw the rapt expression on her face and made way for her, as though she were royal; there was something around her that glowed, the inner light that was of Cahan.

Then someone jostled her, and it shattered, the whole illusion, falling into pieces around her feet like glass shards. Nhia looked around, bewildered, lost; she was in a part of Linh-an she did not know well. A woman with no legs, pulling herself along on an ingenious cart, stopped by her side.

'Alms, *sai'an*? Alms for the cripple?'

Nhia stopped, bringing her clubbed foot up into a comfortable position, and managed a smile. 'Alas, my good woman, you are asking another cripple, but I have a few coppers for you, here. Tell me, what street is this?'

The beggar woman stared at her. 'You look too Court for this street,' she said frankly. 'What brings you here, and walking? This is the Street of the Nightwalkers, and beyond, there, is the heartland of the Beggars' Guild . . . with your foot . . . but you wouldn't be seeking them, you are dressed too richly. What *are* you doing here, *sai'an*?'

'I don't know,' Nhia said, suddenly afraid. 'Can I get a sedan chair here?'

'Wait there,' the beggar woman said. She put two fingers into her mouth and gave a sharp whistle. Two urchins, perhaps only a few years younger than Nhia, tumbled out of the side alleys as if they had been waiting for just such a signal. 'Make sure no cutpurse gets her,' the crippled woman said. 'I'll go and see Brother Number One.'

Nhia backed up against a wall, and the urchins took position in front of her, making a defensive circle. Her senses preternaturally sharp, Nhia saw seemingly ordinary men and women turn in her direction, catch an invisible signal from the two guardians, and veer off again after giving her a scrutiny through eyes veiled by lowered lashes. One of the young guardians turned to grin at her, and revealed a mouth which was only sparsely populated with teeth.

'Don't worry, your ladyship, old Mara will do right by you.'

'Where *did* you come from, though?' The other urchin stared at her, and then turned to his companion. 'She couldn't have walked all the way from the Middle City. You saw her limping. I didn't see her coming until she tripped over Mara's cart. As if she stepped right out of that wall there.'

They headed off another opportunist, and then someone else approached, a man dressed in clothes that were threadbare but not ragged, strolling right up to the trio by the wall. The two urchins doffed the ragged round caps they wore.

'Brother,' one of the urchins said deferentially.

'I'll take it from here,' said the man pleasantly. The urchins ducked their heads, smiled their gap-toothed smiles, and melted away into the alleys again. Nhia's new companion offered her a small bow. 'I am Brother Number Two of the Beggars' Guild,' he said pleasantly. 'If you will follow me, I will take you to Brother Number One.'

'I do not wish to be . . .' Nhia began earnestly.

Her companion offered her a small bow, interrupting politely but firmly. 'This way.'

She was ushered down a narrower alley opening from the main street, and then into a doorway hung with a heavy leather curtain. The room inside was dim, lit only by candles and a flickering fire in a sooty fireplace. A number of people were inside, but Nhia immediately focused on a huge figure sitting in a throne-like chair by the open hearth. His hair was long and grey, and worn loose over his shoulders, held back by a filet; his face, criss-crossed with scars on the weathered, leathery skin, was possessed of an odd nobility of cast. His eyes, however, showed white with cataracts. He was, to all intents and purposes, totally blind.

'Come closer,' the blind man said, 'and do not be alarmed. What I do, I do in order to "see" you in my way.'

She approached as she was bidden, and he reached out a hand, tracing his fingers across her brow, her closed eyelids, her mouth, her chin, and up over her piled hair with its pins and combs.

'You are a strange catch for the Street of the Nightwalkers,' said the beggar king.

'I know who that is,' one of the other people in the room gasped suddenly, stepping forward. 'Brother, this is the one they call the Young Teacher in the Temple.'

Brother Number One cocked his head. 'What do our people say?'

'The reports are good,' said the one who had recognized Nhia.

'What do you seek here, *sai'an*?' the beggar king said, addressing Nhia.

'I do not even know where "here" is,' Nhia said. 'All my life I have lived in this city, and I know only a few streets of it well. How I came to be here, I . . . I couldn't tell you. It will sound strange to you, who are not of the Way, but I set out this morning from my house in search of my teacher, seeking a place the road to which I did not know. He told me I would know it when the time came. I let the knowledge fill me, and followed it. When next I knew myself, I was here. In your street.'

'You walked across town in that finery and you don't remember doing it? Who is it that you seek?'

Nhia hesitated, but the Beggars' Guild were not ignorant savages.

They kept themselves informed, sometimes better than anyone in the Palace. They would know of Lihui.

'The Ninth Sage Lihui,' she said after a pause.

She saw a swift exchange of glances between several of the people in the room, but could not interpret it.

'Lihui is your teacher?' the beggar king asked, and his tone had hardened a little. 'How is it that a man like that is the counsellor to one like the Young Teacher in the Temple? It is like a dragon teaching a swan. They both fly, but one spews fire and destroys and the other nurtures and protects.'

'What?' Nhia's eyes widened in shock. If she had expected the beggars to be aware of Lihui's identity, she had certainly not expected them to sit in judgment upon him.

'You will not find him anywhere near here,' the beggar king said, his voice cold. 'We know him, and we are wise to his disguises. Does he now send you to lull us into dropping our guard?'

'I do not understand,' Nhia said. 'I don't know of what you speak.'

'When he needs bodies for his work, he comes to the streets,' the beggar king said. 'He takes these people, the street people. My people. It matters little to him that there is a living human soul in the twisted bodies he rips apart.'

'Lihui is a Sage of the Imperial Court!' Nhia gasped. 'He does not do this abomination!'

'Your teacher is a dark alchemist,' one of the other men said. He stepped forward, into the candlelight, and Nhia saw his own eyes were gone, two white scars in their place. 'He did this to me, before I escaped his house. Others were not so lucky. What is he teaching you, Young Teacher?'

'He teaches me the Way,' Nhia said. 'He has been my guide to the Fountains of Cahan, to wisdom, to knowledge.' She swallowed hard, remembering her last encounter with Lihui. 'He gave me wings, even. In meditation I am whole, I can fly across all of heaven and not be weary.'

'This is much, for one like you,' the beggar king said after a pause, and his voice was full of understanding. 'They tell me you are lame.'

'I was born that way,' whispered Nhia.

'Your mother should have sent you to us,' said the beggar king. 'We would have trained you.'

'But I *am* training . . .'

'I have heard speech of the judgements you give for the Empress, for the ordinary people who come to her courts,' said the beggar king. 'We will send you home. But for the safety of your own immortal spirit, I advise you to stay away from the alchemist. He will pour poison into your fountains before you will drink of them. Xi, Lam, get a sedan and make sure she gets back to the Middle City safely.'

'Yes, Brother. Come, *sai'an.*'

Nhia, dazed, accepted the dismissal and the guiding hands of the two who were detailed to escort her. They were courteous, respectful, and quite firm; somehow, before she knew it, she found herself ensconced in a hired sedan chair, being carried back to the Temple. It seemed to take a very long time to get there. Nhia remembered how quickly she had got to the beggars' streets from her own threshold that morning, and found herself afraid.

They deposited her at the Temple, and she spent the next few hours sitting by herself in the gardens of the Third Circle, seeking some of the peace of mind that those gardens had always brought to her – but it was in those Circles that she and Lihui had first crossed paths, and that kept coming back to haunt her. She remembered his hands, lifting her that first time, right here in the Temple; supporting her in the Palace; holding her while she swam back into earthly consciousness in the teaching rooms. Gentle hands. The wise words that had accompanied them – the words she had committed to her study journal, just as he had said them, to think on and to seek wisdom and understanding.

A dark alchemist.

How was it possible?

Here in the Temple, far from the presence of the blind beggar king, some of the power of what he had said was stripped from it. His words rang strange, hollow; here in the Temple it was Lihui's word that held sway.

Somewhere in the back of her mind, as clearly as if she had heard them spoken beside her, she heard Lihui's voice shaping words: *I waited for you, Nhia. Where were you?*

Sleep came fitfully that night, and was full of both of them, Lihui and the beggar king. One said, *Come to me.* The other raised a hand to stop her, his blind eyes staring straight through her, *Do not go to him.*

211

She woke, wild-eyed, and it was Lihui's voice that had been the last echo in her mind. She dressed carefully again, as she had done the day before, and stepped out into the street outside her house. And this time nobody touched her, nobody jostled her, nobody stood in her way. Somehow, not quite knowing how, she found herself standing before a pair of wooden gates set into a high wall, all painted a dark red. The gates opened at her touch, and a silent servant waited inside, bowing to her, to conduct her into a pagoda house, and down a flight of stairs into a windowless room lit with braziers and two brightly leaping fires from two fireplaces set at opposite ends of the room. Painted panels with *hacha-ashu* writing screened parts of the room from her gaze as she swept her eyes across it. Dressed in a loose robe of crimson silk, Lihui turned from a table against the far wall, a half-full wine goblet in his hand. For the first time since Nhia had met him she saw him with his usually tightly braided hair loose over his shoulders, and it flowed well down past the middle of his back, rich and black, framing his face in a way she had not seen before and bringing the black glowing coals of his eyes into prominence.

'You are here,' he said, his voice light, almost conversational. 'Good. There is much to do; let us begin. Some wine?'

'I do not . . .' Nhia began, but he had already poured some into a second goblet, topping off his own in the process, and had crossed the room to her, handing her the glass.

'Over here,' he invited, stepping aside and handing her into the room as he closed the door behind her. 'Have a seat by the fire, and we will start. You are tardy, my student. I expected you here yesterday as I commanded.'

'I . . .' Nhia usually shied away from wine or any strong drink, but she had taken several small sips from the goblet she held in her hands, through the polite instinct of drinking from a glass handed to her by a host, or maybe through the sheer forceful energy of Lihui's presence – he had handed her the drink, therefore she must obey and drink it. But even those few small swallows seemed to have started her head swimming. Perhaps it was just that she was unused to it, but she snatched a lucid moment to realize that Lihui had set his own goblet on the table before them and was watching her very closely.

*Do not go to him*, the beggar king's voice echoed in her mind, urgent, a warning. A warning she should have heeded.

The tongues of flame from the hearth fire suddenly grew hotter and brighter, and the air in the room solidified into spiced honey in Nhia's throat. Her fingers opened, nerveless, slack; she never heard the glass shatter on the stone hearth when it tumbled out of her hand, her vision tunnelling into licking red flames and then into black. She reached out blindly, groping for support. The last coherent thing she remembered was Lihui's arm slipping around her waist as she spiralled into oblivion.

## Eight

*What a strange dream I had.*

Nhia, eyes still closed, was dimly aware of lying on a soft surface, a bed, but when she tried to turn and stretch and burrow back into sleep she found herself unable to move. Her arms were stretched loosely above her head, but when she tried to bring them down to pillow her face she realized that her wrists were tied together with something soft but strong which also anchored her arms to a solid and unyielding point behind and above her.

This was no dream.

Nhia's eyes flew open as memory flooded in. She was in Lihui's room, but this was a very different place to the one she had entered . . . how long was it . . . minutes, hours, days ago? Most of the concealing screens had been removed. A cluttered L-shaped desk and laboratory bench took up one whole corner next to one of the fireplaces. Half of it bore an eclectic mixture of laboratory equipment, distillation apparatus, alembics, assorted glassware with strangely coloured liquids inside, a mortar and pestle, and a small crucible with an open flame above which, as Nhia watched, something in a long-necked glass flask bubbled quietly. The other half was piled with books and manuscripts, an inkwell, a quiver full of writing quills and brushes, a roll of parchment prepared for writing and held down by several paperweights which looked like human skulls. Another skull, fitted with an iron band which hinged at the jaw, sat on a small three-legged stool beside the table, set upside down on its crown in a carved ebony base, its jaw 'lid' open.

The Sage Lihui, dressed in a dark draped robe fastened with a clasp on one shoulder, turned from his workbench as Nhia watched, bearing a pewter bowl in his hands. He glanced over at her, realized she was awake, gave her a half-smile and a courtly bow, and then crossed to the skull and carefully poured the contents of his bowl inside, closing the jaw on top of it as he did so. Then he picked up the skull in both hands, swirled it slightly to mix whatever was in it, and crossed the room to the bed on which Nhia was tied.

'Awake, my dear?' Lihui said. 'Good. Then we can finally begin.'

Nhia opened her mouth to speak but no sound came out, not even a whisper. Lihui saw the shock of that wash over her features, and smiled, setting the skull down on a delicately lacquered chest of drawers that served as bedside table.

'Don't try to talk, Nhia,' he said gently. 'You can't. I took your voice, for now. You will not need it for a while. All you need to do is listen to me, and to do what I need you to do. There is nothing wrong with your senses, in fact they are stronger than they have ever been, and we will sharpen even that.' He reached out, lifted her head and pillowed it on his arm, reached for the skull vessel with his other hand. 'Drink, Nhia. This will bring you to the edge of flight. This is a draught of immortality, waters from the Fountains of Cahan.'

The words were lancing – she had thought he had spoken in metaphors before, when he had mentioned the Fountains, but now she had a clear sense that he spoke of a thing that was as real and solid as his gentle but inexorable touch.

'Drink,' he said firmly, lifting the edge of the skull against her lips.

She felt liquid lap against her mouth, tried turning her head away in feeble defiance, but Lihui let her head fall back, just a little, tightening the muscles in her neck. Nhia gasped; her lips parted, the liquid from the skull vessel flooded her mouth, she swallowed convulsively. Lihui set her down, very gently.

'Good. It will take a few minutes. Just relax.'

Colours swirled in her vision as she lay back against the pillow, and then she rose above them, through them, every edge in the room

214

suddenly diamond-etched, sharp enough to cut. She heard rustles of small living creatures in distant dark corners of the room, saw the warp and weft of the weave in the canopy of silk stretched above the bed she lay in, felt the smoothness of silk caress her body – she was aware, suddenly, that she was not wearing her own clothes but a pale robe, twin to the one Lihui was garbed in, fastened at the shoulder with a metal clasp. The taste in her mouth was metallic, an unholy mixture of terror, raw panic, and the chemical soup that had been in the skull potion. The very air sang in her ears, every nerve ending in her body quivering with sensation.

Lihui glanced at her, seemed satisfied with what he saw, nodded. Nhia heard him start murmuring something, in a voice she hardly recognized, in a language she did not know, his back to her now, his arms raised as if in invocation, his long dark hair lifting and quivering at the ends as though in response to some unfelt breeze. His voice rose in a crescendo of power; Nhia heard herself screaming, but knew that she made no sound in the firelit room. Lihui touched the clasp that held his robe; it fell open and he discarded it, leaving it in a crumpled heap of silk on the floor, as he turned and strode back towards the bed. He was nude, his lithe, muscular body painted by light and shadows from the fire, his hair caressing his naked shoulders, his eyes a glow of triumph.

'It was good,' he said conversationally, in his normal voice, 'that you were physically marked. A beauty of flesh coupled with that beauty of spirit, and you would have been any man's prize. But with this . . .' His hand came down lightly on Nhia's withered leg, his fingers caressing the length of it until they reached the twisted foot. 'It took a Sage and a sorceror to see the inner beauty. And you have remained pure for me.'

Nhia whimpered, soundlessly, closing her eyes.

'You will feel,' Lihui said, leaning over to whisper into her ear. 'You will give. You will give . . . *everything*.'

She felt him touch the clasp on her own robe and the fabric slipped free; Lihui swept it from her in a single motion, leaving her lying naked and exposed on the silken sheets. Then his hands came to rest on her shoulders, still gentle, still frighteningly kind.

'And you are a beauty, after all,' he breathed, his thumbs slipping from her collarbone to sweep over her breasts. His touch was fire; Nhia writhed, turning her head away. 'Ah, more to come,' Lihui said. 'Don't use it all up now. I want it all. You have known no man before me, I think. Good. Good. The essence is made stronger. The first time, then, for the body; the rest, for the spirit. Feel it, Nhia. *Feel* it all.'

His hands slipped further down, caressing her breast, her waist, coming to rest on her hips. She felt the bed shudder, then her legs being pushed apart by his knees as his hands came down, further down, fingertips a featherlight touch on her thighs as far down as her knees and then back up on the inside of her thigh, gently, so gently . . .

'It may hurt, a little,' he said, almost apologetically, as his hands came together and brushed up and down between her legs. Nhia's body arched, twisted, but there was no escape from his touch, from his gentle voice, from his presence. She would not open her eyes, keeping them tightly closed, squeezing out hot tears between eyelids pressed together – she would not look, she would not, she would not give him even that much. But he was right in that he was taking everything, and her traitor's body with its preternaturally aroused senses writhed in both anguish and vivid shocks of pleasure that were hateful to her but which she could not barricade her mind against as he opened her with his long fingers and then, his hipbones hard against her own, he entered her with a grinding thrust and groan of his own pleasure. Nhia's hands were clenched into tight fists, her arms straining from her shoulders, her breath catching in painful sobs as a rending pain jack-knifed her body under Lihui's on the bed . . . and then it was over. He was lying on top of her, supported on his elbows, a hand pushing Nhia's hair away from her face, his voice a miracle of softness and wonder, whispering beside her ear.

'And now,' he said, impossibly, the meaning of his words a searing agony that made Nhia's eyes fly open in yet more anguish, only to meet the quiet triumph in his eyes, 'we begin.'

He pulled out of her and sat up, murmuring more invocations.

*What more do you want?* Nhia screamed at him, in her mind, still only in her mind.

Incredibly, he answered her there. *Your body is only a gateway to your soul, my dear. For the rest, we will have to go back to that place where you fly free. But never forget that I hold the power to bring you down. You die at my word, Nhia. Do not forget that.*

She felt him inside her then, not inside her body, a greater violation still, inside the heart and mind and spirit of her; he laid his gentle hand on it all, and it was the touch of iron.

*Fly*, he commanded.

And oh, she did – she was back in the sky that had terrified and exalted her so that first time she had experienced it, and this time it was even greater and bluer and more wonderful than she remembered, and beyond the blue there were stars, she could see them glittering, count them in their multitudes, her eagle's wings spreading to catch the wind as she climbed up towards them.

*Yes*, she heard in her mind, an exultant shout, not her own. *Yes!*

She opened her eyes then, at last, and looked. She saw a creature of fire rearing over her, his eyes glowing embers of burning red coals, his hair flames about his face. She saw a spirit that had been old when the world was young, its centuries heavy on it, needing sustenance to survive, to endure. She saw the thing that bound her to this monster, a thread of light, streaming into his open mouth; he was drinking her, all of her, taking the essence of a pure spirit and filling up the fiery vessel that was himself, glowing ever brighter as he drained her, sucked her dry.

Even as it came the vision blurred and faded. Nhia's eagle self became a ghostly echo, and slowly faded from the sky full of stars, or they faded from around her, growing distant and pale and insubstantial. In the earthly anchor of her body, she saw Lihui poised over her, his head thrown back, his eyes closed, his hands on her shoulders, and then even that vanished, slowly, from the outer edges in, as the potion in the skull seemed to lose effect and the cutting edges of things blurred back into just distant, fuzzy outlines and then dimmed into a uniform greyness which deepened into black. And then she knew no more.


When Nhia swam back to consciousness, she appeared to be alone in the alchemist's room. The fire on one of the two hearths had gone out completely, and the other was just a glow of embers; only the weak light from a couple of guttering candles pierced the gloom. She had been unbound, though, and lay curled up on her side, like a child, covered lightly with a sheet. A strand of her loose hair fell across a naked shoulder showing from under the sheet, and Nhia, bringing her bleary eyes to focus on it, saw that there was white in it, a white streak that snaked through the black tresses. She ached all over, as though she had been beaten senseless. A groan escaped her, and she wondered, vaguely, why the sound should have significance to her, before dredging from her memory the spell of silence that Lihui had cast upon her the night before.

And that brought back everything.

The groan turned into a soft whimper, and she curled herself around her middle, wrapping her arms around her shoulders and burying her face in the crook of her elbow.

'There's no time for crying,' another voice said, right beside her. A familiar voice.

Nhia lifted her eyes, bewildered beyond measure, to meet those of the woman who stood beside the bed – dressed in fine embroidered silk, the rings of marriage on both her thumbs, her hair coiled into a married woman's complicated formal coiffure, her eyes older by far than those which Nhia remembered – but still, without a doubt, Khailin, missing without trace for so long.

'He is at Court,' Khailin said. 'There is a little time before he returns. I cleaned you up, but I have no idea what he did with your clothes. It will have to be my dress. Hurry.' Her eyes softened a little as she read the hurt and puzzlement on Nhia's face, brightened with tears. 'So help me, Nhia, I did not know. The first inkling I gathered of his intentions was when he sent out the path for you to follow the day before yesterday. I tried to stop him, but I don't think I succeeded very well, and then yesterday, when he called you again and you came, there was nothing I could do, once he had you down here. I cannot stand against him, not yet. Not when he is in his full power. And he stretched out every ounce of it to get you here.'

'What . . . where . . . ?'

'No time,' Khailin said. She held out a gown. 'I think this one should fit well enough. Hurry. If you want to live, you have to be gone by the time he returns.'

Nhia took the gown with an instinctive gesture, sitting up, staring wide-eyed at Khailin. They were of an age, with only five months between them, but Khailin looked like she had aged ten years in the short time she had been gone. There were even fine lines around her eyes, or at least the illusion of them. She looked tired, but she was still Khailin, defiant, undefeated. Now she met Nhia's eyes steadily for a long moment, and then reached behind her to gather up a porcelain cup with faintly steaming liquid in it.

'When you're dressed, drink that. Don't worry,' she said with a brittle laugh as Nhia shied away from the cup, 'it is none of his poisons. It's just green tea. I wish I could give you something to eat, too, but there is no time, no time, and I don't want anyone in the kitchens thinking you're awake yet. Hurry. I must get you out of this house. On you, I think, he has laid no ban.'

'Ban?' Nhia repeated. She was feeling very stupid and fuzzy this morning, it seemed.

'There are no locks and keys in this place,' Khailin said bitterly, 'but he does not need them. I cannot step outside this house, he has made sure of that, and no message of mine can get past his spells either. Until he is sure of me. Until he knows that I will say nothing that will endanger him. Which means I'll probably live out the rest of my days here if I can't find a way to reverse the fiat. But not you. I will not let him have you. For the love of Cahan, Nhia, hurry.'

Nhia swung her legs out of bed, wincing as every small movement brought waves of pain and nausea washing over her. A dry retch shook her shoulders, as if she were trying to throw up some old poison, but there was nothing there – she was empty, drained, not even the dregs of spirit left in her. She dressed in numb silence and then limped over to the workbench where Khailin had gone. Nhia arrived just as Khailin finished sealing a tiny glass vial; the glass was thick and green, the contents of the vial only dimly glimpsed through it, and the seal had a loop through which a cord or fine chain could be threaded. Khailin thrust the amulet into Nhia's hand.

'His essence,' Khailin said. 'A few threads of cloth soaked with his sweat, a cherry pit he spat out, coated with his saliva, a drop of his semen, a scrap of parchment smeared with a trace of his blood. I would have added tears too, the five fluids, it would have made it much more powerful, but I have never seen that man cry. It will do as it is. Keep that with you always, it should work as an antidote to his sorceries. And it will let you know him again, if he comes in a different guise.'

'Khailin, I don't understand,' Nhia wailed at last. 'Where is this place? How did I get here? *What did he do to me?*' And then, staring at the way her friend and *jin-shei* sister had been changed, 'And what did he do to *you*? What are you doing here?'

'Where this place is, I don't know either,' Khailin said. 'I'm pretty sure it isn't in the Linh-an you and I live in. How you got here, I don't know, other than *he* brought you, and all I can do to reverse that is take your mind back to where it was before he caught you. What he did to you, however, may make that difficult.' She stared at Nhia, and there was pity in her gaze, and sorrow, and even guilt. 'I'm sorry I ever thought of you and him in the same breath,' she whispered. 'I don't know if you can ever get back what he took from you – what he needed to make him strong and young again. But I will not let him destroy you like he did others. Go, and live, and seek yourself again. As for what he did to me, he did nothing I did not invite him to do.' She laughed again, a mirthless, bitter laugh, lifting her hands and holding them out for Nhia's inspection, her rings glinting in the candlelight. 'I married him.'

# Nine

The final day of the Autumn Court dawned with a chrysanthemum-yellow sun in a perfect, clear blue sky. The early morning air was flavoured very faintly with a breath of the chill to come, but the day warmed up quickly. Yuet woke with a sense of danger and anticipation. This was the morning of the Closing Court. Liudan was out of time, out of all options. There would be a wedding this winter, and a new Emperor crowned in the spring when the New Year came. A new reign. A new dynasty.

Liudan was not scheduled to make her appearance until mid-morning, but Yuet, rising early and dressing into her most sumptous Court garb, decided to pay the Empress a private visit before her grand entrance. She gave her name to the Guards at the door, and was admitted by the little deaf girl who was Liudan's personal servant. The girl smiled and beckoned, signing something. Yuet had been around her for long enough to get the gist of her motions: Liudan was still getting ready.

There were two handmaidens fussing around the Empress in her inner chamber, one brushing out her long hair and coiling it up into an elaborate Court head-dress and the other mixing a batch of subtle powder make-up in a small pewter bowl.

'You aren't supposed to wear make-up,' Yuet said conversationally.

'I am not supposed to do a lot of things,' Liudan said, in the same tone of voice. She turned her head, eliciting a squawk of consternation from her hairdresser as she disarranged a coil of hair before it had been properly pinned in place. 'Oh, they *fuss* so,' Liudan said impatiently.

'They do it at your bidding, otherwise nobody would be mixing the forbidden make-up in your presence,' Yuet pointed out.

'Did you come to needle me?' Liudan said.

'No,' said Yuet, 'but I've been out of touch of late.'

'I know. I have heard of your work. That was well done.' It was a rare word of praise from Liudan.

'I could not have the Empress unprotected,' Yuet murmured, 'with all the Guards sick unto death from their bowels and too ill to care about your safety. Their lives are given to you, and I needed to make sure they were still useful to you when everything was over.'

Liudan flashed her a look. 'You sound as though you mean to reproach me with something.'

'It is not my place,' Yuet said. 'All I have done . . .' Her voice faded as she caught a glimpse of a painted miniature, a woman's profile, lovingly rendered on a piece of creamy ivory in life-like colours. It was a familiar profile – Liudan's, but not quite; and Yuet had seen it often, in these past weeks, as Qiaan bent over some fractious patient in the Guard compound.

Liudan followed her gaze. 'You have never seen my mother's picture before?' she asked.

'That is your mother? You look very like her,' Yuet said, leaning forward for a closer look.

Liudan picked up the miniature, studied it for a moment, and then passed it over into Yuet's hand. 'Yes,' she said, 'so I am told. I find it hard to tell, though. I don't remember her at all.'

'Indeed,' said Yuet reflexively, 'it is hard to see your own profile from an angle at which you can judge the resemblance, but from where I am sitting . . .' She raised the portrait so that it was level with Liudan's face, and Liudan obligingly turned her profile. 'Oh yes,' Yuet said softly. There was a third face there, in the shadows.

If the woman on the painting had not given birth to Qiaan, then it had been her identical twin. The resemblance, so startling to Yuet at first glance, was astonishing when given actual evidence to compare with. 'She was very beautiful, was she not?'

'So they tell me,' said Liudan, a shade coquettishly, a little sadly.

Yuet laid down the miniature near to Liudan's hand.

'What do you mean to do, then?' Yuet asked, and realized that she was awaiting the answer with not a little fear touching the edges of her mind. 'You cannot put them off again.'

'I do not mean to,' Liudan said. 'Hence . . . this.' She raised her arms to indicate her finery, the elaborate hairstyle, the make-up. 'I mean to dazzle them. I mean to walk in there and make them forget everything except that I am there.'

For the first time Yuet realized that there was something else about Liudan's garb that was unusual. The colours she wore were red and gold – traditional colours for a wedding, true, but Yuet got a very real impression that this was not the point of the colour scheme at this time. There was also no white. No ribbon of mourning in her hair, no white edging on the gown, not even white embroidery. The outer robe flamed with silk and jewels.

'But you aren't out of mourning,' Yuet said, her eyes snapping back to Liudan's face.

'Oh yes, I am,' Liudan said, her voice as silky as her gown. 'If they wish me to marry they cannot expect me to do it while pouring ashes on my hair and bewailing my losses. If they want me to do this, I am out of mourning. If they want me to endure the full mourning period, they had better withdraw the suitors.'

'For the love of Cahan, Liudan, are you going to give them an ultimatum again?' Yuet said, and then added, indelicately, 'Zibo will choke on a live toad. This I will pay money to see.'

'You do not have to. You know there is a place for you in the Court,' Liudan said, betrayed into a quick grin. 'Is Tai coming? And Nhia?'

'Tai, I will be meeting at the audience chamber. I am not sure where Nhia is. I haven't seen her for a while, but then I've been . . .'

'Preoccupied, I know,' said Liudan. 'Well, then. If you will leave these two poor wretches some room to work in, I should be out there in less than an hour.'

It was a dismissal. Yuet rose, bobbed a courtesy, and then turned at the door, because she couldn't help it. 'You aren't going to tell me, are you?'

Liudan's profile, the classic profile of her mother that was painted on the ivory chip, the profile of a girl in the Guard compound who had spent sleepless nights caring for other people's children over the past week or so, was turned to Yuet and Liudan did not reply, by word or by the smallest of motions. Only, perhaps, her mouth curled into a slight smile.

Yuet sighed and left the room.

The audience chamber was, predictably, packed. Yuet and Tai took their places, jostled by other impatient and excited courtiers. Over to one side the six named suitors, glittering with so many jewels that it was hard to find a patch of bare skin on them, stood waiting for Liudan's choice to be announced. One of them would be Emperor in the spring; their expressions were tense, their bodies taut with stress and anticipation beneath the weight of their Court garb. One or two stole appraising glances at others, weighing the impact of his own appearance against that of his rivals. Zibo, the High Chancellor, wore his highest collar, his chins overflowing from it into cascades of bountiful flesh, and looked rather self-satisfied. This would be a victory for him, the young Empress finally corralled into a position where he wished her to be. All six of the suitors, vetted by Court astrologers, were to a greater or lesser extent his own protégés, and would owe him their new status. There would be no regency, but there would definitely be favours.

A low murmur announced Liudan's arrival, breaking into audible gasps as she swept into the audience chamber, looking neither left nor right, resplendent in her red and gold, as jewelled and glittering as any of the men who awaited her word. She paid them absolutely no attention as she swept up to the dais where the Imperial thrones were set, and sank into her seat with a rustle of silk and brocade.

Zibo looked startled, and perhaps a little afraid. He had not expected this. He had expected compliance, at last, but Liudan looked anything but compliant. She looked proud and confident, and there was a glint of definite satisfaction in her eyes. As though *she* had won, and not Chancellor Zibo.

The courtiers continued whispering to each other, like a field of grass stirred by the wind, until Liudan lifted her head after a moment and looked out over her audience. People stopped talking in mid-sentence, in mid-word.

'I have been on retreat,' Liudan spoke in a low voice, into silence, 'and asked the advice of the Gods and of my *jin-shei* sisters on the matter of my marriage. I have meditated on this, and prayed about it, and taken the advice of Sages. I have discussed it with my Council, and with the astrologers.' So far so good, she was casting herself as supplicant, as penitent, as one asking for advice; some colour returned to Zibo's cheeks.

And then Liudan's voice changed. Subtly. And everything was different. 'And even with all this gathering of counsellors and protectors, something has gone wrong with the selection of suitors they presented me with. One, at least, was unwilling enough to be in his place to go out and take quite a different bride, to marry another woman secretly, in stealth and despair.'

The Court trembled for a moment, because there had been a cloud of ominous threat in those words, as though Liudan meant to exact punishment for this action. But her voice softened again.

'And I wish him well, in the choice he has made. And now it is time for *me* to make a choice.'

Yuet, always a people-watcher, was raking the faces of the crowd with her eyes. Liudan had them rapt; they were hanging on to her every word.

'First they asked me to choose from the Emperor-suitors who had been handpicked not for me but for my sister, Antian, the Little Empress, who was taken from us so tragically and too soon when the earthquake came down on the Summer Palace,' Liudan continued. 'And I would not, for I am not Antian. Then they chose a new set of men, who the astrologers swore were a better match with my own stars. One, I already lost to another. The other six wait here today.' Her voice dropped even further. 'If one was wrongly chosen, how do I trust the choice at all?'

Zibo could not suppress a gasp. There was a susurration amongst the group of suitors, a swell of whispers in the Court. But Liudan ignored them all.

'For three nights,' she said, 'and I am told this is significant, I have had the same dream come to me. In the dream I am standing on the topmost peak of a mountain. Standing alone. Waiting. And as I wait I feel the mountain move beneath my feet.' Gasps, as she invoked the earthquake again, the one which had brought her to her throne. But Liudan spoke on, as though she had not been interrupted. 'And the mountain moved, and I saw it uncoil, and I knew that I was standing on the back of a dragon, between wings of red and gold.'

She stood up, flung back the wings of her own outer robe, revealing an inner gown embroidered with vivid writhing dragons in scarlet silk and gold thread. Yuet caught Tai's eye, and Tai nodded once, briefly – *yes, that is my work, but I didn't know what* – and then both of them turned back to Liudan.

'The dream tells me this. I will take no Emperor to sit beside me on the throne of Syai. Let it be written: the new reign is mine alone. I am the Dragon Empress.'

'It seems only yesterday that we
were learning to walk, and now look –
Qai is upon us so soon . . .
children of our flesh and our bone
keep their balance by clinging to our skirts . . .'

Qiu-Lin, Year 12 of the Cloud Emperor

# *One*

Khailin had taken Nhia up the stairs from Lihui's workshop, surreptitiously, muffled in one of her own cloaks with the hood pulled forward as far as it would go. At the front door of the house, Khailin stopped.

'I may not even touch the doors,' she said, her voice bitter. 'I pay for it with pain. My hands blister at the very contact, and then, later, when he comes back and the door tells him I had tried to lay my hand on it . . .'

'The *door* tells him?'

'This house is . . . is *him*, in some strange way. He knows what happens in it, and when. He knows this is happening now. You must go, Nhia. Before he meets you at the gates. Once he lays the interdict on you, you will never leave these halls.'

'Khailin, what will happen to you? If he knows you helped me . . .'

'I can handle it,' said Khailin after a short pause. 'Go. At the gates, turn right, and keep walking. Whatever happens. Whatever you see. Don't turn aside. Don't stop. Not until you see the first place that you recognize as real, as somewhere you've been, a road you've walked or a door you have opened yourself and passed through and you know where it leads. Do not stop until you are absolutely certain, until you *know*. Go. Go now.'

'You disappeared. I tried to find you,' Nhia whispered. 'I *tried*.'

'I know,' said Khailin. 'Some day I will come home. He can't keep me here forever. I will find a way to return. Now, for the love of Cahan, Nhia, *go*!'

Nhia drew breath to say something else, raised her hand to her neck to finger a thin silken cord which bore the strange amulet Khailin had given her, and then turned away without a word and slipped out of the house.

The red gates of Lihui's courtyard were closed, but they opened at her touch as they had done before and Nhia found herself standing in a disorienting place where all seemed mist and shadow. *Turn right*, Khailin had said, but Nhia almost instantly lost all sense of direction, lulled and confused by half-seen shapes looming out of the mists. The gates were behind her, already barely visible through the mist, as though she had moved away from them without being aware that she had done so. *Right*, Khailin had said right, there had to be a reason for this. Nhia turned her head, keeping sight of the gate, keeping the red wall at her right hand, and began limping slowly along a curiously solid ribbon of pale cobbled road which had materialized at her feet as soon as she had consciously chosen a direction.

It was not an even road, and she would have found it hard going to walk this place at the best of times without the help of a cane. And this wasn't the best of times. Her head ached abominably, despite Khailin's medicinal tea, and her body felt broken and weak, her limbs even more strengthless than usual.

The memory that kept returning despite her efforts to banish it from her mind was her first encounter with Lihui in the gardens of the Temple, the first time their paths had crossed, hers and Khailin's and Lihui's. The vision mocked her with the raw potential it had held; and was superseded by flashes from Nhia's sessions at the Temple with her mentors – all of whom, or so he had claimed, had been Lihui himself, all of whom had been her enemy – and she found herself mouthing the words she had written down so dutifully in her study journal.

> Be true to your nature.
> Focus your mind.
> Do not let yourself be distracted by externals.

In a way the memory was a white pain, because of all that had followed. But on another level the teachings of the Way now came to her rescue. The mists at her side – the wall of Lihui's house had long vanished – showed her glimpses of things every so often. A gathering of laughing people. A funeral. A cup brimming with golden liquid. A sundial in an overgrown garden. A child writhing in flames, tied to a wooden stake. Three naked women, dancing on a floor of green glass. A striped cat stalking a sparrow. A yellow sun in an autumn Linh-an sky. An old woman spinning wool, with a little girl sitting at her feet and watching with adoring eyes. A solitary wildflower nodding beside an empty road winding off into the distance.

The sky of the Immortals. That deep, deep blue she had known once and would never forget. Somewhere, even, the distant sound of an eagle's cry. Nhia's breath caught on a sob. *Familiar*, she thought turning from her dream, focusing her mind, holding on to her true nature. *Not a dream of flight. I am Nhia, daughter of Li the washerwoman, of the city of Linh-an. I am crippled. I am human. I do not have those wings. I have never seen those stars with my own eyes. Focus. Familiar. She said, familiar.*

The mists parted on a garden, and Nhia's step faltered. Was this the Temple garden? There, the pond with fat golden carp in it, the slim fingers of willow trailing in the water. *Is this what she meant?*

A low growl sounded somewhere very close to her, and a large green-eyed tiger padded into the quiet garden, staring straight at Nhia. The amulet at her throat suddenly went cold, a small piece of ice, a warning. But she had not come to a complete halt, had just slowed down, and she clutched at the amulet and stumbled past the inviting and peaceful garden, a twin to which had once held so much peace for her. The tiger's eyes passed over her; then they darkened, suddenly, and the tiger flowed into a man whose black hair spilled over his shoulders, over the crimson gown that he wore. His face was set in a scowl. Nhia's breath caught and she tripped on a loose cobble on the misty road, but she caught her balance, staggered forward, kept walking. The wraith of the black-haired man stalked towards her, brushed past her, *through* her, and was gone. So was the garden. Nhia shivered; she had once held a captured bird in her hands, and had felt its fear in the terrified, wild beating of the tiny heart against her fingers. Now her heart beat the same way. A bird in cruel hands.

*Familiar. Somewhere I've been before.*

Somewhere, she realized with a painful clarity, that was not the

Temple to which she had given so much of her life. Anywhere but there.

Another voice swam into her consciousness, one heard more recently, one which had fought a battle with Lihui's in her mind on the night before she had set out to find Lihui's house.

*Do not go to him.*

The beggar king.

Even as Nhia's memories fluttered helplessly around this vision like moths suddenly attracted to a candle flame, the mists parted once again and she glimpsed a city street. It was full night, and the street looked different to the one she had found herself in once before while the sun was riding high, the houses she remembered as shuttered and cold now streaming light from windows and open doors onto the dark street. But she was sure this was it, the Street of the Nightwalkers. Familiar. A place she had walked before.

Nhia stopped.

The street flowed around her in a slow, dream-like quality, in a silent limbo, and then, when she was totally surrounded by the welcoming houses and Linh-an's solid walls, it all snapped into place, and the sound of the street rushed in.

She was here, solidly here, a blindly questing hand reaching out and finding the blessed, firm, familiar texture of gritty brick wall. Nhia sobbed, once, in sheer relief.

She could hear laughter spilling from the open windows, and music, and as she watched, a man and a woman stumbled out of the nearest doorway, arms around each other, reaching to kiss in the shadows of the street. Nhia could see the man's hand on the woman's hip, outlined dark against the light-coloured shiny silk of her figure-hugging gown, and the way his fingers moved across her hip bone possessively.

The Street of the Nightwalkers.

The significance of the name struck her suddenly, and she was surprised into a brittle laugh. *I should have understood at once what . . .*

The laugh changed into a gasp and then a strangled scream as an arm slipped around her own shoulders from behind.

'And what are we waiting for out here all by ourselves, my dear?'

Nhia recoiled with a violence that surprised even herself, staggering back away from the man who had accosted her, blind panic bubbling into her throat – this man thought that she . . . he wanted to *touch* her, hold her . . .

She wailed, suddenly, a blind, lost cry that stopped her would-be carousing companion in his tracks. 'What in Cahan . . . ?'

Turning, Nhia fled into the shadows, seeking solitude, running from her memories, from herself, from the laughing ghost of Lihui, the imprint of whose burning hands and mind she still bore on her body and her soul. Her eyes were full of tears, her eyesight blurred, and she did not see the body stretched out in an alleyway's shadows until she tripped over it and went down in a heap beside it. Her hair – she had had neither time nor strength to do more than just braid it loosely when she had risen from Lihui's bed – pooled beside her in a dark coiled rope, and she began to cry in earnest now, great racking sobs that shook her entire frame under the cover of her concealing cloak.

'Watch where you're . . .' the shadowy shape she had tripped over had started protesting indignantly, but paused in mid-sentence as Nhia collapsed into her storm of weeping. 'Hey, now. What happened? Did someone try to force you? That's a crime here on the Street, you know. You can report him to the Guild and they will deal with him.'

A rough but comforting hand, streaked with street-dirt and with black rims under the ragged fingernails, reached out and touched Nhia gently on the shoulder. She twisted away again, whipping her head around. 'Don't . . .'

'He really did a number on you, whoever he is,' the voice from the dark said with an edge of anger. 'I'll take care of you, don't worry. Wait here.'

Nhia heard scrabbling sounds, then a noise as though something was being dragged along the street; her tear-streaked vision and the lack of lighting gave her only an amorphous shape that could have been man or woman, emerging out into the street from the side alley on a pair of wooden crutches. She crawled backwards until she felt the comforting sturdiness of a solid brick wall behind her, and curled up into a tight ball, oblivious of the street, of the light and laughter in the bright houses, of the strange saviour in the alley.

*Focus.*

*Focus on your true nature.*

But what was her nature now? How could she focus on something that had been so bitterly ripped from her – the very instant of undertanding, when her spirit had taken flight, had been no more to Lihui than the moment in which she had been ready for him to take. It all meant nothing. Nothing mattered. *I do not know who I am.*


The next coherent thought that came to her was that she was no longer in the alley, but lying on a bed, loosely covered with a threadbare but finely woven wool blanket.

*A bed* . . . She shot upright, suddenly terrified, but this time she was not constrained in any way, and she was quite alone. The room was small, not opulent but comfortable, with a braided rug on the floor beside the bed and even a scroll of a delicate ink landscape painting full of inscrutable light and shadow mounted on the wall above her. There were wooden shutters on the window on the opposite wall, drawn, letting in a greyish, rain-hued sort of light. It was day – not even morning, but later, noon or beyond.

'Where am I?' Nhia murmured. It was, on the face of it, a completely futile question since she had nobody to ask it of and she had no answers to offer, but a wintry smile touched the corners of her mouth as she realized that part of the reason she had spoken it out loud was to chase away the ghosts of her last awakening. When she had woken to silence, to finding her voice just the first of the things that were to be taken from her. If she could hear herself talk, she was not back at Lihui's strange house. She was safe. Maybe she was safe.

As though summoned by the soft whisper, the door to the room clicked open. Nhia braced herself for . . . for something, she didn't quite know what, except that the girl who entered was quite possibly the last person she would have expected to see.

'*Tai*?' Nhia whispered. 'What are you doing here? Where *am* I?'

'You're at Yuet's house,' Tai said. 'Thank Cahan you're all right. Yuet said that you would sleep after she gave you the draught, but not even she expected you to sleep for nearly two days. It was like you just decided never to wake up again. Yuet is at Court, but I stayed to watch you, just in case. Shall I bring you some tea? Are you hungry?'

Nhia looked down at the hand she had laid down over her coverlet, and realized it was trembling uncontrollably. 'Two days?' she said weakly. 'Tai, how did I get here? I remember nothing after I tripped over in the alley . . . in that street . . .'

'Shhh,' said Tai. 'I'll get the tea. Yuet left an infusion for you, if you should wake up. Something calming and herbal. I'll get it, and I'll get the cook to bring you something light to eat – rice cakes, maybe, nothing heavy. Then I'll come back and we'll talk.'

She slipped out, just as Nhia raised a shaking and ineffectual hand to stop her – *Don't leave me alone!* – but at least she now knew she was in a safe place, with friends. She lay back, tried to quiet her heartbeat, focusing on the window and the greyness outside. It was raining; she could see the shadows of drips forming on the shutters. *There was a time, only days ago, when she could have heard each individual raindrop as it hit the wooden shutter or the wall beside it, and every drop would ring with the clarity of a crystal bell.*

She clamped down hard on that thought. She would not think of that. At least not right now.

Tai poked her head around the door again, and then nudged it open with her hip, both hands busy balancing things – a porcelain cup full of fragrant tea, a woollen wrap draped over her arm, a pewter plate with a couple of nut biscuits on it.

'Here, wrap this around you, it's turned damp and miserable outside and we don't want you catching anything,' she said as she divested herself of her load and handed Nhia the wrap. 'Cook says that she'll bring you up a light meal later, just rice and steamed vegetables. In the meantime I brought you these. They're my own special recipe, I made them myself. It'll take the edge off the hunger. And drink that tea while it's hot.'

'Are you Yuet's apprentice now?' Nhia said with a hollow laugh, as she sat up in bed and dutifully accepted things in their turn.

'No, but she's been carping about wanting one. She's suddenly in demand.'

'How did I get here?' Nhia said, a shade more calmly, accepting a biscuit into her hand but making no attempt to eat it.

'Eat!' said Tai peremptorily. 'Or I won't tell you *anything* until Yuet comes back. And that could be hours.'

Nhia grimaced, took a bite of the biscuit. She could have sworn that she was not hungry, that she would never be hungry again, that she never wanted to taste another mouthful as long as she lived – but that first bite released an unexpected sweetness into her mouth, and she ate the rest of the biscuit with relish.

'All right, then,' she said, smiling despite herself at Tai's triumphant little grin, 'tell me.'

'Yuet said they came to get her very late that night, she'd already gone to bed.'

'Who came to get her?' Nhia interrupted blankly.

'Apparently you turned up in a street far to the south of the city, called the Street of the Nightwalkers, known for the houses of pleasure along there – the man who found you said that he thought you had been attacked on the street, and that was against Guild rules – but then he found the man from whom you ran, and he was just as scared by it, and . . .'

'Tai,' Nhia said. 'I have no idea what you are talking about.'

'Well, then, you tell me what you know,' said Tai, after a mutinous little glance. 'That way I can just fill in the blanks. Where were you? You missed quite a show, by the way. Liudan's Closing of the Autumn Court was quite a shocker. Have you heard?'

'I have heard nothing,' Nhia said. 'I have been . . . away. I don't know where I have been, but I don't think it was in the city. Or so Khailin seemed to believe.'

Tai sat up straighter. 'Khailin? You found Khailin? Where is she?'

Nhia raised her free hand to her temple. 'My head aches.'

'I'm not surprised. Yuet said all of you aches. She said you were . . .' Tai looked hunted, suddenly, falling silent.

'I was what?'

'I'm not supposed to talk to you about it, until she can be here. I was told to keep you warm if you woke up, and make sure you had that tea – drink it, Nhia, or else I'll be blamed for it – and to feed you. And then it would probably be best, Yuet said, if you slept more. She said that she knew no real heal—' She snapped her mouth shut. 'Have another biscuit.'

'No real healing for what she thought had happened?' Nhia questioned with a sad smile. 'She's right, in a way. Tell me about Liudan.'

'I embroidered her gown for the Court,' Tai said. 'It was amazing – bright reds and golds, all these dragons worked in silk and jewels.

She was supposed to be getting married in the spring, after all, and I thought nothing of it – I knew that she was supposed to pick her Emperor at the Closing Court, and she just wanted to look splendid, perhaps in the gown she was going to wear for her wedding,' Tai said. 'There was no mourning white in that, and it was silk, and I knew she was breaking tradition for it – but if she was to marry, I thought she just wanted to do the thing right. But she not only broke the small traditions, NhiNhi, she shattered everything and left the Court picking up the pieces. I am told Zibo practically had a heart attack. It's unheard of, you know – the Empress ruling alone.'

'Ruling *alone*?' Nhia repeated. 'Just what did Liudan do, Tai?'

Tai gave her a strange look. 'You really haven't heard? How odd – the whole city was buzzing with it. She declared herself the Dragon Empress, and that this would be the new reign – that she would not marry, that she would not take an Emperor, that she would rule in her own right.'

'For the love of Cahan!' Nhia gasped, astonished. 'And they let her?'

'I don't think it's a question of their letting her do anything any more. She's a force in her own right. Remember what you said at the Temple, just before we left for the mountains, back in the spring? That Liudan was a wild thing, unlikely to be ruled by anyone but herself? Well, you were right. When you make the kind of announcement that makes everyone else faint dead away, you're the only one that's left standing.'

'What about the suitors? Aren't they angry?'

'She gave them generous compensation,' said Tai, grinning despite herself, 'and sent them on their way with the advice to do exactly what their friend had done already.'

'What was that?'

'The one that got married to his own sweetheart, in secret, before Liudan could put the leash on him.' But the words had circled Tai's thoughts back to a previous topic. 'You said you found Khailin? That is good news! She is all right? Where is she?'

'I don't know. *She* doesn't know,' said Nhia, her eyes darkening at the memory. 'She is a prisoner, at the end of the road of mist and shadows. She said . . . she said he did nothing to her she did not ask him to do when she married him.'

'Married who, Nhia?' Tai said carefully, aware of a pang of fear at the sight of the expression on Nhia's face.

'Ninth Sage Lihui,' Nhia said, very softly.

# Two

*The Young Teacher from the Temple told us your name. She needs you.*

There had been an insistent knock on Yuet's door in the pre-dawn darkness, and when the sleepy servant roused herself to answer it, that message, scrawled in untidy *jin-ashu* letters, was all that she found on the doorstep. But there was a cart parked in the street right in front of Yuet's house, and the servant fled upstairs to fetch her mistress. Yuet's first glimpse of Nhia in the back of the cart, her chest barely stirring with shallow, laboured breaths, had sent a stab of real fear into her. Yuet sent the servant scurrying into the kitchen with a twist of pungent herbs, a packet of poppy, and orders to make an infusion and be quick about it. Then she stripped Nhia of first the damp and soiled cloak and then the slightly ill-fitting gown underneath, inspecting the shivering body she had exposed for wounds or lacerations; she could see no obvious damage except for the weals around Nhia's wrists, but that alone was enough to set off all sorts of alarms. And when Yuet reached for the odd amulet hanging from the silken cord around Nhia's neck, something she could not remember ever having seen her wear before, Nhia had come awake and screamed and clawed at her until she had withdrawn her hand. Nhia had been delirious; she had not known Yuet, and kept muttering something about familiar places. When the cook brought the sleeping draught, Nhia reacted violently, again, as the cup of warm liquid was gently brought to her lips, but Yuet had sat beside her on the bed, and held her, and talked softly and soothingly as though she was a fractious child, as she had done with many such a child in the Guard compound only a few short days ago. Finally Nhia took a few swallows of the infusion, and drifted off into a restless, disturbed sleep, curled into a tight defensive ball under the coverlet Yuet had laid over her.

Yuet had told Nhia all this when she returned from Court, late in the afternoon of the day on which Nhia had woken in her house.

'I know what must have happened, Nhia,' Yuet said, dark eyes brimming with impotent sympathy. 'But Tai said you spoke of Lihui. How does he fit into all this?'

'Or Khailin?' said Tai.

Yuet had asked Nhia, in a moment they had shared alone and Tai had been sent on some errand, whether she wished Tai to stay away, whether she had things to say that she might not want Tai to hear. But Nhia had hesitated, and Tai had come back before she had had a chance to reply, and had come to sit on the edge of Nhia's bed, taking Nhia's cold hands into her own and rubbing warmth back into them. There was such physical comfort in having her there, a friend she had known from childhood, that Nhia had said nothing. And now Tai was sitting on a stool beside Nhia's bed, supporting the food tray as Nhia spooned up the vegetables mixed with thin slices of pork which the cook had prepared for her dinner.

'It has all been a lie,' Nhia whispered, eyes suddenly filling with tears, pushing away her bowl.

Tai reached for her hand. 'What has, *jin-shei-bao*? What have they done to you?'

Nhia wiped the brimming tears away with the back of her free hand. A part of her wanted to deny that anything had happened at all, to merely pick up the threads of a familiar life she had grown to love, to pretend that nothing had changed and that she was the same person she had been before the Autumn Court – and another part knew that she could not return to the Temple, not soon, maybe not ever. Not after what had happened, with all the reminders that the place now held for her.

'I found out,' she began, 'that all of my teachers at the Temple had been one man. Lihui. He took different form, so I would not know him.'

'Took different form?' Tai repeated blankly. 'How do you mean, Nhia?'

'His face, his voice, his gait, his shape, his hair. He changed them all, turned into different people, and taught me, oh yes, taught me much. And then, what is it now – three days ago? Four? – I learned the greatest secret I had ever known. He freed my spirit, Yuet. He allowed me to shed this broken body, and fly in a sky full of stars. And it was then, at last, that I knew him.'

She told the story, haltingly, her account full of breaks and pauses; she had lived through this pain, but she had no idea that re-telling it would hurt just as much. Tai was white and shivering by the time Nhia was done, and it would have been hard to tell who was hanging on to whose hand harder by the end of her story.

There was a tense silence when Nhia had brought her narrative up to the last thing she remembered, which was emerging onto the night street.

'I cannot go back to the Temple,' Nhia whispered. 'Not to teach; not to study. I would never trust another teacher again – how would I know it was not him?'

'You said Khailin gave you protection,' Tai said.

'I was wondering what that was,' said Yuet. 'I swear, you nearly killed me when I tried to remove it.'

'And it worked for you on the road,' Tai chipped in again, in reference to Nhia's mention of the garden she had seen, and the tiger that had morphed into Lihui, and the way the amulet had given warning. 'You would be safe. Once people knew that you had been . . .'

She broke off as Nhia quickly looked at her and as quickly looked away. Tai glanced at Yuet, who was shaking her head.

'What?' Tai demanded. 'You *are* going to denounce him, aren't you?'

'With my word against his? With what proof?' Nhia said. 'And it would be my name people would remember. And I know what they would say. Why would a man like the Ninth Sage of the Imperial Court go after a crippled nobody from the outer Temple Circles?'

'You are not!' Tai said hotly. 'Everyone knew that you were special. People came to listen to you talk.'

'And it can all be used against me,' said Nhia. 'And then . . .'

'There's Khailin,' Yuet finished.

Nhia looked up at her. 'I don't know what he will do to her when he finds that I am gone and that she had something to do with it.'

'Is what he does part of the Way?' Yuet asked.

'No,' Nhia said after a moment's thought. 'Or, if it is, it's so twisted and warped that it is black beyond belief. It was the way he got to me, because I believed in it, because I studied it and used it to transcend my spirit to a level where I wanted to be – ah, he knew exactly what to teach me so that I would be coming back for more.'

Yuet reached over and covered her hands with her own. 'There is no shame in this, Nhia. You have done nothing wrong.'

'But he is a monster,' said Tai obstinately. 'We have to get Khailin out. We have to stop him from hurting you again.'

'Stop who from doing what?' said a new voice from the doorway, and all except Nhia leapt to their feet.

'Liudan!' Yuet said, as the visitor pushed back the concealing hood of a voluminous cloak. 'What in the name of Cahan are you doing here?'

'I come to see Nhia,' said Liudan. 'What has happened to you, my wise *jin-shei-bao*, and how may I make it go away?'

'You must dismiss Lihui,' said Tai abruptly, before any of the others had a chance to hush her.

Liudan's eyebrow rose a fraction. '*Must* I?' she questioned softly, her voice silky with sheathed danger. 'Even if I wished to do so, however, in point of fact I cannot. The Council, yes. If anyone on the Council transgresses Syai's laws, or my own, then I can do something about it. The Sages, however, are a different matter. They advise me, yes, but they are not appointed by me or elected by anyone else other than themselves. The Sages would have to censure Lihui if he had done something against their rules, and he is the highest one in that circle.'

'Eight Sages, each to a sign, and the Ninth Sage to rule them all,' Nhia whispered.

'Indeed,' Liudan said. 'Lihui is the youngest of them, but he is the Ninth Sage. That, I will admit, has always struck me as strange because it is far more often the eldest of the circle who is named to the exalted rank, not the youngest and the newest. But they do their own choosing, and I have no knowledge of the criteria they use, nor can I interfere in such matters. There are some things that are not the business of the secular Empire. But why, sweet Tai, should he be dismissed?'

'Because he . . .' Tai said, and subsided at a glance from Yuet.

'Because he practises sorcery,' Yuet said.

'I have never heard him accused of this,' Liudan said slowly. 'He is young to hold his position, it is true. I have to tell you, Yuet, if anyone else but you or Nhia came to me with a story that he holds it by sorcery I'd dismiss it for nonsense. If it were true it would have leaked out, surely, by now? Since the death of his Master, the Sage Maxao, when Lihui inherited his mantle, his behaviour has been exemplary – granted, it hasn't been that long, but even so, a dark sorcerer at the Palace would have had to be *extremely* careful not to make a mis-step.'

'That's probably why he has his pagoda beyond the ghost road,' Nhia said faintly.

'What is this ghost road?'

'A place of mist and shadows, that leads to all places, and none. Liudan, I don't know how I got to his house. I have no idea how I got back. Lihui does not make his home in this city.'

'Do *you* know where he lives?' Tai challenged Liudan.

'Of course – he has a house in the city, close to where the other Sages make their home. It's a beautiful garden setting, and they have their own exquisite Temple. I have made offerings there myself.'

'And been to Lihui's house?'

'No,' Liudan said, with some asperity. 'I have not been to his house or to the house of any of my Sages. I do not need to go there. If I need to see them they come to me.'

'So you don't know if he does live there,' Tai persisted.

'You don't think the matter of his being the only one of the Nine who does not would have filtered back to me?' Liudan snapped.

'*I* have been to his house,' Nhia said. 'He called me and somehow I got there. And if he had had a chance he would have stopped me from ever coming back. Khailin said . . .'

'Khailin?' Liudan said sharply. 'At Lihui's house? What has she to do with this?'

Nhia threw a helpless glance at Yuet, and Yuet opened her mouth to speak, but Liudan raised an imperious hand. 'What has she to do with any of this?'

'She says that his house burns her when she tries to leave it, that it knows what she does and somehow keeps him apprised of it when he is not there. This is not the kind of home that exists in the Linh-an that I know.' Nhia fumbled at her throat. 'And there is this.'

'What is that?'

'A defence, a charm made from his essences – his blood, his

sweat, his spit . . .' She swallowed hard. 'His seed. Things that make him what he is. It allowed me to know him on the ghost road. It kept me safe. In his arrogance he did not lay the same ban on me as on Khailin – perhaps he did not expect me to live long enough to leave his house.'

'He actually tried to kill you?' Liudan said.

'He almost succeeded,' Nhia whispered.

'I *have* heard complaints about his arrogance, but he has good reason to be proud,' said Liudan. 'There is always jealousy for the stars of any heaven, and he is the brightest gleam in the circle of the Sages. But sorcery?'

'It was by sorcery he ensnared Nhia.'

Tai still looked mutinous and warlike in her small, furious way, but held her peace. Nhia, another whole ocean of pointless tears just waiting for a chance to spill from her brimming eyes, also kept silent.

'Well,' Liudan said after a pause, 'I cannot do anything about dismissing Lihui, even if I wanted to meddle in the affairs of Sages. But, as it happens, there have been other developments. Nhia . . .' She crossed over and perched casually on the edge of the bed, the glittering Dragon Empress of Syai herself, and smiled. 'How do you feel about joining the Imperial Council?'

Nhia's jaw dropped open, and Yuet, all healer in this instant, roused up like a mother hen protecting her young. 'She is convalescing, Liudan!'

Liudan threw her a reproachful look. 'I do not mean instantly,' she said. 'I will make sure that you have every care, and that you take all the time that you need to recover. But when you do choose what to do next, I have need of a Chancellor.'

Yuet gasped, in unison with Nhia herself. 'They will never accept that!' Yuet said. 'Not even you, Liudan! And just what have you done with poor Zibo?'

'I? Nothing,' Liudan said with utter sweetness. 'He has done it all to himself. He says it is his heart, and his ulcer, and any number of other things. But he wishes to resign, and I have accepted the resignation. And I am not a fool, Yuet,' she added, a trace more sharply. 'I know that this is not going to be easy. But I have named myself Empress, and they *will* put that Tiara on my head this summer and make that official. And I *will* have people I trust beside me. Nhia?'

243

'But . . .' Yuet began again, and was this time interrupted by Nhia herself.

'But Lihui took most of me,' she whispered. 'Everything that had the potential for greatness or for wisdom.'

'You know that is not true,' Liudan said, with a gentleness that was rarely heard in her voice.

Unexpectedly, Tai now came to Liudan's aid. 'She's right, Nhia. You were reckoned wise by the people of the Temple long before the priests took a hand in teaching you the esoterica of the Way. If you never learn another method of meditation, you will not be the worse for it. But nobody can take away the core of you, who you are.'

'As I said before, you understand things everyone else merely knows,' Liudan said. 'I want that on my side. If you don't feel up to taking the office on your own, I would happily appoint a token princeling as your co-Chancellor – but all of us would know whose advice I really valued.'

Despite herself, and through her tears, Nhia laughed. 'I'd like to fall down at your feet right now, as I am supposed to do anyway.'

Yuet snorted. 'Healer's orders. You'll stay in that bed for at least one more day. You were *transparent* when they brought you here, Nhia. You gave me a proper scare.'

'Well?' said Liudan inexorably.

'But . . .'

'What, Tai?' Liudan asked patiently, turning to face her.

'She will be in Council. In the Palace. All the time.'

'Yes?'

'So will *he*.'

Nhia flinched, but Liudan smiled, a thin, wolfish smile which made Yuet, shivering at the sight of it, swear to herself never to do something so abhorrent to Liudan as to have that smile turned onto herself.

'As to that,' she said, 'there I can help. Trust me.' She rose, in a rustle of dark red silks that should have reminded Nhia forcefully of Lihui's red silk robe but somehow had the opposite effect, erasing the power of the other from her mind, attaching the colour to Liudan instead. 'Good, then,' Liudan said. 'Yuet, it's your call – and Nhia's, of course. But when she is ready to come and take her place, let me know. I will make sure that she is safe. Now – back to Khailin. What, exactly, has happened to her?'

'She seems to be Lihui's wife,' Yuet murmured, 'although nobody in Linh-an has heard anything about this marriage. And Nhia says that she is kept a prisoner in whatever estate he calls home.'

'The Khailin who vanished mysteriously just before she should have married the princeling who is now Aya-Zhu?' Liudan said.

Yuet nodded.

'Complex,' Liudan murmured, tapping her lip with her index finger while she considered the matter. 'Marriage is still beyond my power to meddle in,' she said at length, with real regret. 'I may not intervene in a man's private life – unless, perhaps, I catch him mistreating his wife before my very eyes, but most men who would do such a thing are careful not to do so in public. I can make inquiries, though, and I will do that. And maybe the very fact that Lihui knows that I am making such inquiries, and I will make sure that he knows, might make him think twice about doing anything irrevocable.'

'You won't find anything,' Nhia said faintly. 'He has her beyond our help. The only way out is if she learns how to counter his spells.'

Liudan's interest sparked briefly. 'She is a student of the dark arts, too?'

'Not unless *yang-cha* is the dark arts, and it's been practised by countless adepts in the Way,' Nhia said. 'I have never really practised that side of it myself, nor has it been one of my interests – I have always sought to reach my goals through meditation and prayer, the internal alchemy, the *zhao-cha*. All I wanted to do was find out about the ethereal realms, the fields of Cahan, the spiritual world. That is what I thought my teachers were guiding me in – but Lihui . . . Lihui transcended that. What he does goes beyond the concept of external alchemy, as we know it in the Temple. I have seen the remnants of his experiments, in the beggar king's house.'

'The beggar king?' Liudan said sharply.

'The head of the Beggars' Guild,' Nhia said

'You met the head of the Beggars' Guild?' Liudan asked. 'Interesting. I am told that not many know his identity.'

'I don't know his name,' Nhia said. 'They called him Brother Number One. He warned me against Lihui. I should have listened.'

This time Liudan's glance was genuinely startled. 'What has the head of the Beggars' Guild to do with an Imperial Sage?'

'I have no idea, Liudan. But he spoke of alchemy in a way that made me think he knows it from the inside. Not the words he said, even, just the way he said them. And somehow, I don't know how, he knows Lihui. Or at least knows things of him. He knew about the sorceries.'

Liudan stood in silence for a moment, contemplating this, and then smiled once more and reached out to lay a delicate white hand on Nhia's shoulder.

'Rest, now, *jin-shei-bao*, my Chancellor. I will await your coming with great pleasure. Ah, the winds of change that we can make blow through that stuffy Palace, you and I!'

She turned the luminous smile on Tai, gave Yuet a friendly nod that was both a farewell greeting and a command to take good care of Nhia, and swept out of the room.

'Now there's an honour for you,' Yuet murmured. 'She does not make house calls for just anyone, Nhia.'

Nhia's stay at Yuet's house extended from days into weeks. Unable to face going back to her studies, going stir crazy waiting in Yuet's sitting room while the autumn rains lashed Linh-an, Nhia took to helping out with Yuet's work, working in the stillroom under Yuet's supervision and preparing the simpler medicines. She even accompanied Yuet on her visits to the inner court at the Guard compound, where the healer was still keeping an eye on the aftermath of the summer epidemic, and pitching in with whatever needed to be done there.

Nhia and Qiaan struck up a strange relationship based on a mutual respect for the other's willingness to get her hands dirty if that was necessary, and they shared a mutually admired knack for making large numbers of small children behave for extended periods of time. Nhia even found herself revisiting some teaching tales from the Temple, and telling them to an audience every bit as rapt as the ones she had left behind in the Temple Circles, together with her title. She had not set foot in the Temple since her return from Lihui's ghostly mansion.

She was allowed to drift for a while, to find her own way back. The problem was that she was making drifting into a way of life, that she was choosing not to choose – Liudan's offer was still before her, a place at the Empress's side as Co-Chancellor of Syai – but Nhia shied from taking the final step of accepting it. It was well into Chuntan, late that autumn, that Nhia's entire *jin-shei* circle seemed to rise, independently and then collectively, to the challenge of bringing her back to the real world.

'You know there is a place for you in my home for as long as you need it,' Yuet told Nhia, watching her pulverize a dried herb mix into a fine powder to be stored over the winter, 'but you cannot hide out in my stillroom for ever. You are not made for mixing poultices and potions. You are meant for greater things.'

The very next day Qiaan, watching from a doorway with her arms crossed, waited for Nhia while she shepherded together a small group of young children whom she had been keeping occupied for the better part of an hour. Qiaan, dressed in an elegant turquoise silk gown with the sleek shapes of fish embroidered on it in darker blue and silver, watched Nhia's simple brown outer robe over an inner gown of pale cream silk, and shook her head. 'You cannot bury yourself in here for ever, you know. And wearing dowdy clothes still fails to disguise you. You're young, and you're pretty, and you ought to be out there in the world. Making a difference. You are made for that, you know.'

Tai, who had broached the subject with Yuet in the meantime, had been given the go-ahead to try and find her own solution to Nhia's complete withdrawal.

What she did, finally, was take Nhia back to the Temple.

As skittish as a deer in hunting season, Nhia was ready to bolt at the slightest pretext; she was only there out of loyalty to Tai, who had trumped up an excuse as to why she needed to go and why she needed a companion for it. And then, when they got there, she told Nhia that her business would not really take all that long, and practically bullied her into going into a *ganshu* reader's booth and get a long-overdue reading while she waited.

This had all been set up with the reader in advance, and there were no queues to join, no excuses for Nhia to wander off and hide herself in the booth of some friendly craftsman like So-Xan and his son. She was in the reader's booth, with the privacy curtain drawn and the pebbles being shaken in their cup, before she had time to protest.

'I would tell you to think on your problem while we do this,' the reader said, 'but you have the haunted look of someone who has been thinking of nothing else for too long. I can see why your friends asked me to see you.'

'I don't think that I need . . .' Nhia began, but the reader raised her left hand for silence, and rolled the six pebbles from the cup, one at a time, laying them out on her silk-covered table in triads. The triads came out in identical patterns – black/white/black, twice.

'Tan and Tan,' the reader murmured. 'Treachery has been in your recent past. It has made you afraid.' She wrote the reading down on a scroll of silkpaper, and gathered up the pebbles, repeating the process several more times, calling the readings in what seemed to be random order to Nhia – the recent past followed by the distant past, the present, the distant future, the near future – two triads at a time, murmuring to herself, writing it all down on the scroll. She finally looked up at Nhia.

'This is what *ganshu* says,' she began. 'I will tell you immediately, your far future is unclear; I've rolled it twice and it gave me ambiguous readings. So I won't offer you guidance as to what happens ten, fifteen years from now. For some people it's clear as mountain crystal, but you – no. There are many paths, and at least one of them is dark. But I can tell you this. You have travelled from a world where you were weak and powerless, and have conquered many obstacles to reach a place where you felt safe, and useful. There was treachery and betrayal in your recent past, something that hurt you deeply. But there was also redemption – you have found out things you did not know, and this is a prize you still do not fully realize that you hold. Your present is full of fear, and yes, there is great risk – but also great potential. You have at least one powerful friend, and a very powerful enemy, but you do not trust your friends and you are still fighting your enemy because you cannot let him go from your mind. As to the near future, the stones say "wisdom" and "leadership". Also, "justice". You have to make some choices, but if you choose now you are going on a bright path, for now at least. Beyond that, I cannot say.'

Nhia gave a brittle laugh. 'It sounds like they gave you my life history to wrap in pretty phrases and hand back to me.'

'The one who spoke to me told me nothing except that you were in need of guidance,' the reader said. 'But you are not the first one who has charged me with speaking from ill-gotten knowledge because I gave a reading that is close to the bone. But believe me, what I tell you comes from the stones, and from no other source.'

She rolled up the silkpaper scroll and tied it with a twist of red ribbon. 'You may keep this.'

When Nhia came out of the booth, Tai was waiting for her a few steps away.

'You planned all this,' Nhia said accusingly.

'Brought you here to show you that you could come and that it wouldn't turn on you, yes,' said Tai. 'The *ganshu* thing was mostly Qiaan's idea, and Yuet agreed that it might help, so I organized it. Yes, I planned it. What did she say?'

'She said exactly what she needed to say.'

'Yes, but was it true?' Tai persisted.

'I should make you go in there and then demand that she tell you when you are going to marry Kito,' Nhia said, with a slice of unaccustomed malice.

Tai blushed, casting her eyes down. Nhia was immediately contrite.

'I'm sorry, little *jin-shei-bao*. I am tired and afraid and out of sorts. Perhaps this *was* exactly what I needed.'

Nhia pondered on the reader's words, reading over the notes on the scroll she had been given, for another brace of days – and then, finally, without telling anyone else, sent a note to Liudan in her spidery *jin-ashu* writing. It said simply, *I am ready*.

Liudan sent a liveried squad of Imperial Guards the very next day to accompany the sedan chair she had arranged to take Nhia to the Palace. Liudan herself waited for Nhia in the anteroom of the Palace entrance hall.

'You could have dressed to the occasion,' Liudan said, her tone gently teasing. Nhia wore only a moderately resplendent gown, with no jewels, and her hair was dressed as simply as Palace protocols permitted.

'I don't own any grand garb,' Nhia said.

'We'll have to remedy that – but for now it's just as well. Simplicity is exactly what we want.'

They walked up the corridors, with their rows of expensive glass-paned windows, arm in arm, and only at the door to the Council chamber did Liudan squeeze Nhia's arm and withdraw hers.

'They will announce you when I'm seated,' she said in a low voice. 'And don't look so tragic, this is going to be fascinating. Our friend Zibo is here today.'

'Whatever for?'

'He follows me, waiting for me to make some mistake so that he can point a finger and tell everyone he told them so,' Liudan said. 'Fat old fool. Whatever brain he had to begin with must have been digested to form all those chins. I've invested your Co-Chancellor and partner some time ago, as placeholder, and he is in there now – possibly the best thing that could be said about him is that he is not and never has been Zibo's creature, and that he has been properly grateful for the increase in his fortunes.' Liudan smiled. 'You belong here,' she said, unconsciously echoing the words of Yuet and Qiaan. 'It's time you came in and took your place. Remember that.'

She nodded at her herald to precede her and swept into the room, leaving Nhia waiting with another herald just outside the Council chamber door.

Nhia had not expected to be announced with a title, but she found herself entering the room to a cry of 'Co-Chancellor Nhia of Linh-an!' Liudan, having been persuaded by Yuet of the wisdom of adopting her back-up plan while Nhia vacillated, had appointed a distant princely cousin to the position of the other Co-Chancellor. Nhia's partner-in-office, as Liudan had told her he would be, was sitting in the Council chamber as she entered, his own Chancellor's chain on his shoulders. He greeted her with a regal inclination of his head, the expression on his face carefully schooled.

'Today I am confirming the appointment of my second Co-Chancellor to her office,' Liudan announced. 'Herald, bring the chain and the seal!'

The herald obeyed and Liudan, glancing around, smiled maliciously as her gaze swept the small number of people seated to the side as spectators and observers, as she sometimes allowed for the more public of her Councils. 'Emeritus-Chancellor Zibo, you know I have always been a great admirer of your powers and your abilities. Would you do me the honour of investing your successor with her chain of office?'

Zibo, his eyes bulging out of their sockets, waddled over to where Nhia stood awaiting the herald and his paraphernalia. 'With the utmost of pleasure, my Empress,' he said. He placed the chain over Nhia's head, none too gently, and hissed close to her ear as he did so, 'You are her mistake! She has finally overreached herself!'

'You may,' Liudan said pointedly, 'go back to your seat now, *sei*

250

Zibo. Nhia, take your seat, we will begin as soon as the Imperial Sages arrive – they are very late this morning.'

As if on cue, the door herald knocked on the wooden floor with his staff and announced the Nine Sages of Syai. The men were all grey-haired to varying degrees and getting on in years, with the single exception of Ninth Sage Lihui. He had a spring in his step and a proud carriage that spoke of the prime of life, even of youth.

*I gave him that*, Nhia thought, her fingers at her throat where Khailin's amulet burned with cold fire. Her other hand, quite involuntarily, crept to where a white streak now gleamed in her piled-up hair.

When he saw Nhia sitting at the table wearing the Chancellor's chain, Lihui's eyes turned a glittering black, but it was he who finally broke the gaze that locked their eyes on one another as Liudan spoke directly to him.

'You are looking well, Ninth Sage Khailin-Lihui. Marriage agrees with you.'


# Three

The summer epidemic and then the events of the following autumn had effectively sidetracked Yuet, but she had not forgotten the Traveller child, the girl whom Tai had once called the snow dancer – now, incredibly, almost a year ago.

The Blackmail Books had yielded one other piece of pertinent information – the identity of Jokhara's sister, a woman by the name of Jessenia, who had taken in Jokhara's child after her death.

'What if she never told Tammary anything was amiss? What if Tammary believes herself to be her aunt's natural daughter?' Tai had demanded, when the subject of Yuet's travelling up to the mountains to find out the truth behind Szewan's account had come up again in the spring.

Yuet shrugged. 'Then the story dies there.'

'Yuet, if you don't meddle in it now . . .'

'And what of your dream, then?' Yuet said. 'You know there is

251

more to this than just digging up the grave of a woman long dead and the scandal that was buried with her. This stretches into the future as well as the past. I want to make sure she is protected.'

'Liudan or your Tammary?' Tai asked with a small smile.

Yuet shot her a startled look. 'Sometimes you ask disturbing questions, *jin-shei-bao*.'

'When we were all there in the village last year, with Liudan, I got the distinct feeling that our presence made every person in that place hold their breath until we went away. What were they all afraid of?'

'That they might be held responsible for sheltering Tammary, for making sure she survived? That they might be accused of a conspiracy against the Empire? It would not be hard for Liudan to see such a conspiracy. She's never trusted anybody – except perhaps Nhia.'

'Conspiracy to do what?' Tai asked, perplexed. 'Travellers have always seemed to me to be drifters on the wings of the wind. I didn't know so many of them could ever settle down together in a permanent village, like that one up on the mountain.'

'You look almost disappointed to have found a Traveller community living in real houses, on solid ground,' Yuet said, smiling, allowing herself to be diverted from a contentious subject.

'Well, when I was little, my mother told me stories of them, and they were always on the road, in bright wagons pulled by those big horses with white socks.' Yuet had to laugh out loud at that, and Tai waved an impatient hand. 'You know what I mean! The ones with the hairy feet. I thought the Travellers were so . . . free. They could go where they wanted, do what they pleased. It sounded wonderful to me.'

'I don't think there's a child in Syai who did not feel the same,' Yuet said. 'Who wouldn't want to grow up into a life of music, song, carnival, acrobats and trained animals, and cooking at a campfire every night?'

'Um, there were times, when it was raining hard outside . . .' Tai murmured.

Yuet laughed again. 'You are an incurable romantic with a resolutely practical streak,' she said.

'So what are we going to do up there, then – just blunder in and start asking questions about things they would rather remain forgotten?' Tai asked.

'So you are coming with me?' Yuet said, smiling.

Tai scowled. 'If I hadn't started it . . .'

'Actually, I don't know that you did start it – but you certainly made sure I finished it,' Yuet said.

'Yuet, I can't stay away . . .'

'Don't worry, I'll organize someone to look after Rimshi while you're not here,' Yuet said, guessing Tai's concern before she had time to fully articulate it. 'We won't be away for long.'

The inn they took a room in was the same one they had stayed at with Liudan on her 'retreat'. It was run by a round-faced, black-haired widow whose colouring and physiognomy, coupled with a reedy voice and a flatlander's accent, made it immediately obvious that her connection with the Traveller community in the village was confined to the fact that her warm common room was the favoured gathering place for those locals still in the village when the winter snows cut them off from the rest of the world.

'She says that they come on different nights, the Travellers and the rest, the others in the village,' Tai told Yuet over dinner on their second night there, after trying to cajole their polite, reserved hostess into a conversation that did not directly involve matters of the inn's hospitality. 'Apparently only the men come into the common room when it's the turn of the locals. Their women don't go out drinking around here – and they don't like being here on the nights that the Travellers come because they *do* bring their women along, the married women. And the Traveller women flirt shamelessly with the local men, who appear to find it all quite unseemly.'

The corner of Yuet's mouth quirked. 'I see.'

'I also found out,' Tai said, 'that there's a fair in the next village in two days' time, and that most of the Traveller clan will be going down – to sell their stuff, and, at least according to *her*, for the revelry,' Tai said. 'I can't decide if she disapproves of that or is jealous of it, and I'm not sure if the licentiousness stretches to the unmarried maidens, but the Traveller women definitely seem to live by different rules.'

'Did she mention any names?' Yuet said, entertained by Tai's wholehearted embrace of the role of spy.

'Only in that the stuff to be sold includes woven cloth, and that one of the finest weavers around is a Traveller woman by the name of Jessy,' Tai said complacently.

Yuet laughed out loud. 'Well done. We will go to this fair, and see if we can find out if this weaver is the one who took in our mother-less child.'

The fair was a surprisingly large one, considering how early in the year it was and how far most of the participants had had to come in order to be there for the designated two days of the fair. For Tai it was a trip back to childhood, reviving echoes in her mind of the much larger and more sophisticated shows that the Travellers had once regularly brought to Linh-an. This was no big city fair, and much as Tai had her heart set on it there didn't seem to be anyone around who did anything at all with fire, a vivid memory of her childhood. There were, however, bolts of finely woven woollen cloth for sale, dyed in various vibrant colours, and Tai had practically burst into tears when she came across a stand selling long brilliantly coloured ribbons which she associated so strongly with the gift her mother had made to her when she was a small child. Yuet bought her a bright red one, almost as long as she herself was tall, and Tai wove it into her hair immediately, letting the ends trail down her back and flutter in the breeze.

'They'll know you for gentlefolk,' Yuet said, teasing. 'You look good enough to attend Autumn Court.'

Tai flounced, setting her ribbons dancing. 'I do not,' she retorted. 'Look, are those cheeses?'

'Goat's cheese, I think,' Yuet said. She was half-laughing and half-exasperated. 'Tai, settle down! We'll go back and get some goat's cheese later, if you like. The weavers' booths are over there. Come on.'

Tai subsided, without quite losing the broad grin she wore like a charm, and followed Yuet to the cluster of tables piled with the weavers' samples. Several women, not all of them Travellers, bustled around the back of the display tables with a proprietary air. One, a large, raw-boned Traveller woman with her fair hair dressed in two braids pinned up over the crown of her head, was perched on a three-legged stool and sewing a plain serviceable garment. Tai happened to be watching her when the voice of another customer, one obviously familiar with the wares, brought the woman's head up from her work. The language was fluent, flowing, but unfamiliar – except for a single word, a name, which caught at Tai's ear. *Jessy*.

Tai elbowed Yuet in the ribs, surreptitiously, and was rewarded with a quick scowl and a shake of the head. *Stay here, stay quiet.*

The woman hailed as Jessy laid aside her sewing and came across to the man who had hailed her, another of the Traveller clan, his yellow moustache hanging over his upper lip and trailing in two long, neatly twisted tails down to his chest. They struck up an easy conversation, in the manner of two good friends who had been apart, and Tai whispered to Yuet, 'Well, we've found her. What now? Are you sure she even speaks a language we can understand?'

Yuet, about to reply, suddenly clutched at Tai's wrist. 'Look,' she said.

Tammary approached across the open sward in the middle of the circle of fair booths and tents, her fiery hair loose down her back, carrying a wicker basket. Her path brought her an arm's length away from Yuet and Tai. Judging by her expression, she had not volunteered to be here, and she was entirely too consumed by her rebellion against that to notice the interested gaze of the two 'customers' by the table.

She planted the basket by the stool where Jessy had been sitting, barking out a single word in the Travellers' language, and then whirled with a swish of her bright skirt and a flurry of curly hair and stalked off again.

'*Rucha*', Tai repeated softly. 'Lunch? I wish they'd speak in a language that I understood.'

'We understand, if you wish to bargain,' said a voice to the side, accented but suddenly miraculously comprehensible. Tai's voice had obviously carried further than she thought. 'Something you like?'

Yuet turned and met the eyes of their quarry, the woman called Jessy.

'Actually,' she began carefully, 'we were looking for you.'

The woman's eyebrow rose a fraction. 'I thought you weren't from around here,' she said. 'Was it Sevanna who finally sent you?'

'Sevanna?' Yuet said blankly.

But it was Tai who made the connection. 'Szewan,' she said. 'Yuet, she means Szewan.'

'Do you?' Yuet said to Jessy.

'Yes, that is the name she took, but it sounds so harsh to my ears. I refused to ever call her by any name but the one she was born under.'

Yuet was staring at Jessy with wide eyes. 'What do you mean? How do you know Szewan?'

'Sevanna's grandmother and my own great-grandmother were sisters,' Jessy said. 'She was barely fifteen when she left us, took up with a healer in the city, became apprentice, took the other name. She didn't want it to be widely known that she was Traveller-born. Well, half a Traveller. Her father was somebody on the plains, during one of our summer travels. One of the *chayan*.'

'The *chayan*?'

'That's you,' Jessy smiled, revealing stained teeth. 'The ones who stay. The ones who plant and harvest. The settled ones.'

'You're settled now,' Tai said in a small voice.

'Ah, but I know the feel of the wayward wind in my hair,' Jessy said. 'I will always be a Traveller. Sevanna wanted a different life.'

'No wonder that her books were so full of Traveller patients,' Yuet murmured. 'That she sounded like they were friends to her, or kin.'

'They were. She was the one we all went to when we were in the city, or when we needed help with someone seriously ill,' Jessy said. 'Well? Did she?'

'She didn't send me. Szewan has crossed the river into Cahan more than a year ago now,' Yuet said. 'She was my teacher, and now I am Healer in her place. No, she didn't send me, not really. Something I found in her secret books brought me here.'

Jessy sighed. 'I was hoping she had burned those books. There is nothing but trouble coming from that.'

'Can we talk somewhere?' Yuet said, dropping her voice.

Jessy turned her head, calling out to the other women at the back of the tables, and then strode over to the place she'd been sitting and collected her basket. 'You don't mind if I eat as we talk, do you?' she said, already unwrapping the slab of cheese and a roasted chicken drumstick. 'We can go into the green tent, if you like, but we might as well sit over there on the benches in the sunlight. Don't worry, nobody listens if you don't look like you are talking secret things.' She laughed, her laughter loud, almost braying.

Yuet agreed to the benches, and Jessy folded her tall frame down onto a backless bench by a rough-hewn table.

'What did Sevanna tell you?' Jessy asked, sinking her teeth into the chicken drumstick and chewing loudly.

'Just what was in the books – that she was called in to pick up the wreckage of the girl when it was all finished and *he* panicked,' Yuet said, very obliquely, trying to avoid any names or titles at all. 'And, later, that your sister had had the child, and then she died.'

'She had that child in defiance of all of us, Sevanna, myself, the clan,' Jessy said. 'She knew best. She always knew best, my sister. She was promised something – or at least that's what she said – and then it was snatched away from her. She said she wanted payback, but not even she was quite certain of how. Just that, one day, she would wreak her vengeance, and that Amri would be her weapon.'

'Amri?' Tai asked, startled.

'That's what my five-year-old called her when she first started lisping and couldn't get her mouth around Tammary's name. It stuck.'

'Vengeance for being raped?' Yuet asked.

Jessy gave her a hard look. 'No,' she said. 'For being lied to, and then abandoned. Sevanna never mentioned that, did she? It only became a rape when the *Imperator*,' Jessy gave the title a different lilt, using the Travellers' tongue, in which there was considerably less worship and respect attached to it than in the common tongue, 'made the mistake of telling Jokhara that he already had his full complement of wives and concubines and that he would not be adding her to the women's quarters on a permanent basis. *Then* she started screaming and fighting. It was then that he started really hurting her. Not before. She wanted it, before. You should have seen her dance for him that night, before he sent for her. She put her whole heart into making him want her body then.'

'But Szewan wrote that she was a virgin,' Yuet said.

'She was,' Jessy said. 'She thought that would be the price for clawing her way up into the Palace. She was young, and arrogant, and thought she wanted to be royal.' Jessy snorted, wiping her mouth with the back of her hand. 'The little fool. She thought she was invincible.'

'But in Szewan's book . . .'

'Don't call her that, not here,' Jessy said. 'And yes, I know what she wrote in her book, she told me. But she always loved Jokhara, and it destroyed her to have her end this way. She swore she'd make the *Imperator* pay one day for what he did to Jokhara. I think she had her own plans for Amri.'

Tai could not suppress a gasp. Jessy looked down at her, and smiled, but her grey eyes were glittering and hard, like chips of ice.

'So, then,' Jessy said, looking up at Yuet again. 'I am sorry to hear that she is dead, but I guess we all die.'

'I did not know that she was of your clans,' Yuet said. 'I arranged her funeral according to our custom.'

Jessy waved her hand. 'She lived that way, she died that way. It is well by us. We will remember her in our own fashion. But what is your purpose here? Do you want to take Amri, or destroy her?'

'Antian told me . . .' Tai began hotly.

'*Destroy* her?' Yuet said, in the same instant.

They stopped, glancing at one another. Jessy followed the look. 'Antian told you what? Who is Antian?'

'The Little Empress,' Yuet said. 'First Princess Antian, who would have been Empress today if the earthquake hadn't taken her.'

'Ah, the one that died,' Jessy said, nodding sagely. 'And what did she tell you, young one? Who was the Little Empress to you?'

'We were *jin-shei*,' Tai said. 'She told me to take care of her sister. I dreamed of it; I dreamed her face, after.'

'Whose face? Amri's?' Jessy was frowning. The Travellers took dreams seriously, and had interpreters who earned a good living interpreting the strange dreams that came to the folk of the clan. 'What has that got to do with anything?' she asked, to Tai's nod.

'How much does she know?' Yuet said, in a low voice, interrupting.

'Amri? She knows her parents are dead, and that I am her foster mother, and her aunt. She knows her mother was my sister. She knows she is not wholly Traveller, that she has *chayan* blood – how could she not, with that hair and those eyes? But if you are asking if she knows that her father was your Emperor, no, she does not.'

Tai was suddenly aware of a silence where a murmur of conversation had just been, and instinctively whipped her head around.

At another table, set at an angle to the one where she and the other two were sitting but close enough to be in earshot, Tai saw a young man with a puzzled expression staring at the retreating back of a girl who was almost running in the direction of the main fair and its bustling throng of people.

A girl with fox-coloured hair and the grace of a dancer.

'I think she does now,' Tai said quietly.

# *Four*

Tammary fled, first for the anonymity of the fair crowd and then through and beyond them into the woods behind the village. It was cooler here under the boughs of the pine trees, and there were still patches of snow in sheltered spots behind the larger trees. Tammary's shawl was still on the bench where she had laid it down when she had manoeuvred Raian to the closest free table at the picnic area so that she could eavesdrop on the conversation between her aunt and her two interesting companions. But it was more than just the chill of the shadowed forest after the warm spring sunshine out on the open fairground that made Tammary shiver as she hugged her shoulders with her hands.

All her life she had known that she did not quite belong, that she had been touched by a breath of scandal. But no more than that. She was different, yes – her dark eyes and her bright hair set her apart from the rest of the Traveller children with whom she had grown up. No secret had ever been made of the fact that she was not her aunt's natural child, and that had been enough for the children, themselves aware of only whispers and rumours, to taunt her with her differences and take the usual childish glee in finding a victim they could torment. The more Tammary had tried to immerse herself in the culture of her mother's people, the more pointed the references to her *chayan* ancestry had become.

'Your family has always run away,' some of the older ones had goaded Tammary. 'Your cousins go away to the *chayan* cities, and your mother went and had a *chayan* man get you on her.'

'You don't think you're good enough for us, you always go looking for something better.'

'You aren't really one of us,' the younger ones would chime in, unable to understand the innuendoes but all too happy to join in with whatever they could muster. 'You ought to be keeping a year-wood stick with the *Imperator* beads! *Pol-chayan! Pol-chayan!*'

Half-*chayan*. Half-breed. Outcast.

She sought solitude when she could, growing up wild in the mountains. She had climbed rugged mountainsides by herself, had taken a near-grown falcon chick when she was only eleven or so and had trained it to come at her call, and ridden half-wild horses bareback, her skirts hiked up to her hips like a hoyden's and her bright hair flying like a banner behind her. She had watched her peers learn the steps of the Traveller dances, and had gone off alone into the ruins of the Summer Palace and practised them until she knew that she could out-dance any of the village girls. But she knew that, should the clans go out again on the summer trails, she would not be one of the dancers who would do the shows for the applauding crowds, she would not be the one who would train a wild thing and show off her mastery to the admiring people of the cities on the plain. If she were taken along at all, Tammary would be the one closeted in the fortune-teller's tent, if she was lucky, reading the cards for the women of the city who wanted a different point of view than that given by the *chayan ganshu* stones. She would be locked away in hidden places, wrapped in scarves and veils, kept apart from the *chayan* folk. A thing to be ashamed of or a thing to be protected – the children taunted her with the one and the adults sometimes gave her a distinct impression of the other.

After Tammary turned fourteen, still coltish and long-legged but starting to round out with the curves of womanhood, she thought she had finally reached some sort of understanding when some of the young men started paying attention to her. She thought she saw a road to acceptance. She had no real yardstick to measure what the other girls her own age were permitting in terms of physical intimacy, but when she had balked at the first deep kiss in the haylofts of the village, or the fumble at her breasts on a summer meadow on the mountain, or the insistent knee between her legs in the woods on moonlit evenings, it had all been countered with a devastating weapon she had no defence against.

'You're half-*chayan*, after all. You don't know any better. I guess I'd better go back to a girl of my own people who knows how to treat a man.'

So Tammary had accepted everything, and only woken up to the gravity of her error almost a year later, when she finally realized that no young man stayed with her for long after she had opened her legs for him, and that the other young women were laughing and pointing when she walked down the street. That was also about the time that her aunt had found out what had been happening, and had turned on Tammary in fury.

'You'll turn out no better than your mother,' she had said, bitterness in her voice. 'But at least she sought it in a Palace.'

So the quick blossoming of trust and acceptance was over, and Tammary withdrew into herself completely. When she did seek human company, she gravitated towards the clan elders, who were usually kind to her, or the very young, children who liked her and trusted her and accepted her without question, never asking awkward questions, demanding concessions Tammary had no desire to make, or tormented her with her own ignorance of the mysterious circumstances of her birth – for her aunt had never elucidated her final cryptic remark. All that was left between Tammary and her aunt was a sense of obligation. *I owe that much to your mother*, her aunt had said, and made sure that some of the other Traveller folk in the village felt the sharp side of her tongue. But Tammary concluded that it was damage control and not really defence, and resented the action. Somehow she felt it isolated her even more, not only naïve but weak, someone unable to fight her own battles. But there had still been no more information than what Jessenia had blurted out in her anger – the brooding hint that Tammary's mother had somehow destroyed herself with the help of the Court of Linh-an, and that her daughter was heading the same way.

When Raian had made his first friendly overtures to her, Tammary, then close to sixteen years old, had reacted with cold hostility. He had seen her working with her falcon in the mountains, and he was genuinely impressed with her knack with the bird and with other wild things that she managed to coax to her. She was so much of a wild thing herself by this time that she practically bit him when he first came forward to talk to her.

'You don't want to be seen with me,' she'd snarled. 'You'd never survive the taint in the village.'

'We are not in the village,' he had replied, standing his ground and letting the mountain wind ruffle his fair hair, 'and anyway I don't care what those idiots all think.'

'What happened,' Tammary said nastily, 'when I was being passed around from one young cock to the next, you didn't get your turn?'

261

He actually blushed bright scarlet at that. 'I was never part of that. I thought it was a vile thing to do.'

'You didn't tell *me*.'

'So I'm a coward,' he said quietly. 'But I tried to stop them, for what it's worth. One of them slugged me when I asked if he'd want his own sister treated that way.'

Tammary stared at him. 'Someone hit you? Because of me?'

He shrugged. 'Once.'

'Go away,' Tammary said, after staring at him in frank astonishment for a few seconds. 'But you can come back and talk to me if you want,' she added. 'As long as you stay two paces away at all times.'

He laughed. 'Can you teach me to tame a falcon at that distance?'

'If I can't, you won't learn it from me,' she snapped.

They had started a wary friendship. Tammary realized that he too was something of an outcast, although not to nearly such a degree as herself, because he was far more interested in knowledge and learning than in carousing and the hunt – he would rather splint a wounded animal's leg than kill it for a trophy, and he had made his preferences obvious. They had called him Yeporuk, Pretty Hands, and the only reason he had not fared worse as the whipping boy of the wild crowd was because he was one of the rare ones with the kind of eidetic memory which would make him into a clan chronicler some day. He was being trained by the current chronicler, an old man who was still hanging on to life by a thread, it seemed, only long enough to put his successor in place.

'Every five years,' his old mentor had told him, 'all the chroniclers gather together in a secret place, and when I am gone it is you who will go. There is a great Book there, the Book of the Clans, where it is all set down – all of us come and we tell what is in our memories and it is all preserved there against our forgetting, and dying, and the histories fading away like leaves in the wind. But for those five years, you are the Book of the Clans. You remember, for everyone.'

It was in this old man's memory, quite some time after he had first spoken to Tammary on the mountain, that Raian had learned the truth about her family – about the girl named Sevanna who had gone out to become a healer in a city called Linh-an, and, at the last, about Jokhara and her tryst with the Ivory Emperor.

When Tammary had sought him out at the fair and taken him

over, ostensibly for lunch, to a table near where her aunt was sitting with the two *chayan* women, Raian had – perhaps foolishly – suspected nothing at first. But he quickly realized that Tammary was listening to the conversation at the other table, and before he had had a chance to do anything other than allow his own attention to be focused there for a moment, Jessenia had uttered her bombshell, and Tammary had gasped as though she had been stabbed to the heart.

'Are you all right?' Raian had asked, his attention quickly shifting to his companion.

'Did you hear? Did you hear what she *said*?'

Raian, confused, nodded. 'I heard.'

'My mother . . . my mother bore me to the *Imperator*!'

'Yes,' Raian said without thinking, 'I know.'

She rounded on him in savage fury. 'You knew? How long have you known?'

'Amri, you know I study the clan histories,' Raian said. 'This is part of it all.'

'Does everyone know except me?'

She had unfolded her long legs from the bench and ran from him, from all of them, and he had been left sitting frozen in place. The younger *chayan* woman, who had noticed Tammary's flight, said something Raian did not hear to the other two women, and they all rose hastily and departed without looking back.

'She had no idea,' Raian murmured to himself, staring after Tammary. 'No idea why they hid her.'


Tammary had fled alone into her beloved mountain, which had always been there to shelter her before – but this was not her own village, and these were not her own familiar haunts. This time there was no peace to be found here. She ran through the pine woods until the ground started climbing, and then clawed her way up an increasingly steep slope until her breath grated harshly in her own ears.

*I cannot go back home . . . I cannot. How can I live in her house again? How can I look her in the face again? She lied to me . . . she lied to me . . . they all lied to me. Oh, Aunt Jessy, why didn't you tell me, why didn't you just tell me? If they knew, if they all knew, they would never have dared to lay a hand on me.*

She stopped, wheezing, leaning against a pine tree to catch her breath, skating over the inconsistencies of her chaotic thoughts – they all knew, but if they had all known she would have been treated differently so they didn't know at all. She was angry at her family, bitterly wounded by what she saw as Raian's treachery, raging with impotent fury at her mother, at the Emperor himself, at whoever had conspired to make her life this convoluted spiral and then abandoned her here to deal with it in ignorance and the innocence of the fool.

The day had darkened around her, and she looked up, confused, realizing too late that the weather had changed and a quick spring storm was gathering around the mountain. She also realized that she was out of the woods and in an open area of only a few scarred, scattered trees with no shelter closer than the woods she had left behind or an outcrop of granite overhang just ahead of her. As she hesitated, the first hard drops of rain broke on the thin layer of pine needles below the tree she was leaning on, spattering on her bare arms and her face. It was a cold rain, a remnant of winter, and it came down fast; within a few short moments Tammary was drenched and shivering. A sharp crack of thunder decided her against trees and woods, and she loped off to the rocks, hoping for at least some cover and a tiny dry spot out of the wind where she could wait this out and think about what to do next.

She found a dry ledge, but its price seemed to be that the wind curled around the mountainside right there at this outcrop, licking into the overhang where Tammary crouched, plastering her wet hair and soaked blouse and skirts to her body.

*I can't go back. I can't go back to being who I was. I can't not know again.*

*Why did they come? Why did they come for me? I remember the young one. She was in the Palace that time. Who is she? What do they want?*

*I can't go home. Not like this.*

*They are from the city.*

*They can take me to the city.*

A jagged fork of lightning branched out of the sky and struck an isolated tree not a hundred paces from where Tammary cowered. She put her hands over her ringing ears and screamed, turning her face away from the tree, whose trunk had been neatly split by the strike. It was as though nature itself had gathered to give vent to her anger and sense of betrayal, but somehow the sight of the burning tree served to calm her own furies. She raised her face into the rain, looking up into the strange and yet so utterly familiar mountainside, so like the one where she had grown up and knew so well. The mountains of home, despite the pain which the people of the mountain had inflicted upon her. People were insignificant on the scale on which the bones of the world were built. Tammary didn't care about people. She would use them, like she had been used, and then she would walk away. To some other mountain. To a place where she didn't have to be anything, not Traveller, not *chayan*. Just herself.

She stayed there for the next hour, until the storm blew itself out, and then scrambled out of her shelter, stretching her arms up to the sky. Somewhere, high up, she heard the cry of a circling hawk, and laughed through a film of tears.

'You're on your own now, Lastreb,' she whispered, naming her own half-wild companion whom she had taught to come to a whistle and to the sound of his name. 'You're free. I have to go.'

Tammary made her way back to the village, soaked to the skin, feeling light-headed and feverish, and stumbled through the still dripping fair-tents towards her aunt's booth at the back.

It was Tai who saw her first, but Yuet, the healer, who ran to throw a blanket around her shoulders and help her make the last few steps to the shelter of the stretched-out waterproof canvas. Tammary had to consciously stop her teeth from chattering as she looked up, clutching the blanket around her, and locked eyes with Yuet.

'I'm coming back with you,' she said. 'To the city.'

Yuet and Tai exchanged looks over her head.

'If you don't take me,' Tammary said, 'I will come anyway, alone if I need to. I am not staying here. I can't.'

She would not look at her aunt, who was standing helplessly by, biting her lip.

'I was trying to protect you,' she said.

'From what?' Tammary said desperately. 'You told me nothing. And because I knew nothing I believed everyone else's lies.'

'You are an Emperor's daughter,' Yuet said. 'The city is a danger.'

'But I will go there,' Tammary said stubbornly.

'Do you know,' Tai said unexpectedly, coming down on one knee beside her where she sat wrapped in her blanket on a small wooden stool, 'what *jin-shei* means?'

Tammary stared at her. 'I know what the words mean. It has never meant anything more to me. It was never part of my world – it is a *chayan* thing.'

'You may understand the words, but not what they signify. *Jin-shei* means "sister of the heart". It means that two women who are not bound by ties of blood choose to help and protect one another out in the world,' Tai said, offering up the deepest secret of her life. 'If you must come to the city, be mine. Be my *jin-shei*, and I will take you and find a way to shelter you from what waits for you there.'

'Why would you do a thing like that?' said Tammary, her voice cold. 'Nothing is free. What is the cost for me?'

'I do it because I promised a *jin-shei-bao* of my own, one whom I loved dearly, that I would take care of her sister,' Tai said. 'And you and she are sisters. You share the same father on this earth.'

'You are a sister to an Emperor's daughter?' Tammary said, confused. 'How is this possible?'

'It's possible, in that other world of which you know nothing,' Tai said. 'Say the words to me, and it is done.'

'What words? *Jin-shei*?' Tammary said.

'Tai, do you know what you are doing?' Yuet said carefully.

'It is done,' Tai said, getting to her feet. 'And I will see it done. Like Antian asked of me in her dream. We will take her back to Linh-an with us. You've been carping endlessly about wanting an assistant, Yuet – I think you just found one.'

# Five

On their way back to Linh-an, at an overnight stop at a roadside hostelry and with Tammary asleep in the room they had taken for the night, Yuet took Tai out to the vine-hung porch of the tiny inn and they sat there in a pair of fading wicker chairs, watching the fireflies dancing in the night.

'I am not sure this was such a good idea, Tai,' Yuet said. 'The closer we get to the city, the worse I feel about it, actually. I can't help wondering if we're setting up a disaster here.'

'Nhia would call it bringing a serpent into Cahan,' Tai said, with infuriating tranquillity.

'You see, you aren't so sure yourself,' Yuet said, pouncing on the words and not on their delivery.

But she was wrong in trying to see her own misgivings in Tai. The younger girl's eyes were calm, her face tranquil, her whole presence filled with the kind of serenity that many achieved only after hours of focused meditation.

'And if we had left her where we found her and turned our backs on her, and she took her destiny into her own hands, how would it have been better?' Tai asked. 'This is meant to be, Yuet. I know it. Antian knew it when she came to me in that dream.'

'What are we going to tell Liudan?'

'Why are we going to tell Liudan anything?' Tai said. 'You can train Amri to help you, to do things that will be useful to you. We will be given some sort of a chance to get to know her a bit better while she is in your house, so we will also have some idea of where she is going. We will understand who she is and what she wants. If she doesn't stay with you, then she is on her own – but at least we know where she is. And if things turn out badly, that is a lot better than dealing with something unknown that hates you, isn't it?'

'I still feel like I'm committing some kind of treachery,' Yuet said.

'You committed *that* the moment you realized the truth and told Liudan nothing,' said Tai. 'There was no going back to innocence after that.'

'Ouch,' said Yuet in a small voice.

'You aren't alone,' Tai said after a pause.

'Will she even want to learn the things I have to teach her?' Yuet murmured, speaking of Tammary again, sliding off the subject of Liudan and what she didn't know.

'"The healer is compassionate, treating all patients in the same way, be they wealthy or poor, high rank or low rank, adult or child, sympathetic or repellent, intelligent or foolish; the healer goes forth when summoned, labouring day and night, ignoring hunger, thirst, fatigue, heat or cold. The healer tends to the patient with all of his heart,"' Tai quoted. 'The healer's oath is for the healers, Yuet. It's for you. She may not wish to *be* a healer – all she needs to know for now is how to prepare a poultice from aloe leaves or brew a *QianHu* tea. That's her task; that's her cover. As for the rest – I don't know if someone with her past, with her burdens, can find in her the healer's compassion that lies in you, Yuet. Perhaps she may surprise us all.'

They had left it at that, and Yuet decided to make the best of it. But in the first fractious weeks of her arrival in Linh-an Tammary seemed to go out of her way to prove every one of Yuet's initial misgivings to have been wholly justified. Tammary was a creature of the open sky. She did not know what to expect from living in a city the size of Linh-an, and what she did find only served to make her feel trapped and powerless. That feeling surfaced in sulkiness and defiance.

'No,' Yuet would sigh for the tenth time, 'that is willow oak bark, and that is red oak bark. One is a contraceptive, the other is used in a physick against infection. Cahan help you if you mix them up and some woman has the baby you promised her she would not have.'

'They look exactly the same,' Tammary would respond mutinously.

'They are *labelled* differently!' Yuet tapped with an impatient finger at the labels gummed to the tall jars where the bark was stored. All the containers had these labels, with the contents identified in firm *jin-ashu* script.

'I can't read that,' Tammary would inevitably say, concluding the discussion, and Yuet would shake her head in frustration.

'Did they teach you *nothing* up there in the mountains?' she would murmur, and be overheard by Tammary, and the level of resentment would rise another notch.

Tammary guarded her emotions fiercely, allowing them to surface only in her exquisite gift for being awkward about accomplishing even the simplest things. She kept everyone at arm's length, but it was inevitable that the armour would crack at last. The demands made on her time by Yuet were light, for all the weight both of them carried from their duties to each other, but the issue was one where Tammary could focus her feelings. When she took the wrong container from its shelf yet again – not entirely accidentally, for she had learned that the muddles annoyed Yuet – and Yuet opened her mouth to protest, Tammary slammed the container down on the worktable with bone-rattling force.

'I don't know! I can't tell them apart! There's nothing you can do about it!'

She had turned and fled, up the stairs and into the house, into the small room Yuet had set aside for her own use, and slammed the door hard.

Tai had happened by that afternoon, and Yuet acquainted her with the situation.

'She's been up there for most of the day,' Yuet said helplessly. 'I feel like I have a baby in the house and I can't cope with it. I begin to have an inkling that I know why I never felt the faintest urge to have any children of my own.'

'Let me talk to her,' Tai said.

When she knocked at the door, at first there was no answer at all, and then Tai was rewarded with a muffled, 'Go away.'

She disregarded the words, taking the response itself to be an invitation to enter, and was greeted by a flash of pure fury in Tammary's dark eyes.

'I said go away,' she said. She had been crying, and was angry and resentful that she had been caught at it. Tai could almost hear her shutting down, slamming the shutters closed, bolting the doors, nobody home.

'I know what the matter is,' she said. 'Come with me.'

'Why?' Tammary said. She was three years Tai's senior, but she sounded like a mutinous three-year-old in response to a serene mother. Not unaware of the irony, Tammary closed up even more. She would not be petted and soothed by this . . . this *child*. She would not.

But Tai was as implacable as a rock. 'Then I will have to stay here until you'll talk to me again.'

'Why did you bring me to this place?' Tammary whispered. And then, her innate honesty rebelling at the false accusations implicit in that remark, rephrased her question. 'Why did I want to come here?'

'That is not something I can tell you, but I know what the matter is right now,' Tai said. 'You have never lived in a city. You don't understand the place, and it probably scares you a little, and there is nothing here of the home you have known all your life.'

'It doesn't scare me,' Tammary said, tossing her head. 'I've seen worse things.'

'Have you actually walked through Linh-an since you've been

here, aside from trotting at Yuet's heels every so often when she goes to this patient or that?'

'No,' Tammary said unwillingly. She did not want to have this conversation – not now, maybe not ever – but Tai was not going away, that was obvious.

'Then come with me,' Tai said. 'It's my fault – I have been remiss, and I have not shown you my home. My mother is very ill, and I find myself preoccupied with her care, but I will take some time and show you the city. And something else, too. Come with me.'

Scowling, Tammary knuckled at her eyes and put a foot down on the floor. 'You're going to sit here until I do, right?' she said ungraciously. 'Might as well get it over with, then.'

Yuet wisely kept out of their way as the two of them slipped out of the house and into the crowded street. Tai took her new *jin-shei-bao* to the marketplace, where vendors of spices and cheeses and berries and squawking live fowl and sides of bloody beef rubbed shoulders with booths selling jade and opals, spinning tops, bonsai trees, brooms, market-baskets and snuff-bottles hollowed out of a single rock crystal. Carvers of wood and ivory sat side by side with weavers of tapestries and the paper artists whose trade was the making of the funeral replicas of objects the departed would take to Cahan with them. Other booths displayed leather-bound books of the kind that Tai wrote her journal in, or scrolls of teaching tales or poetry by well-known sages and writers. Tai picked up some essential supplies for herself in the part of the market where those in her own trade shopped for silk embroidery floss in every imaginable colour, glass beads, sewing needles, snips and shears and strings of freshwater pearls. Watching her bargain for a skein of sky-blue silk and a handful of yellow glass beads, Tammary began to be fascinated, despite herself.

'I didn't know there were so many people in the world,' she said, staring around at the throngs around her. 'What are those booths?'

'Those are the *ganshu* readers,' Tai said. 'Have you had a reading since you got here?'

'No,' said Tammary, recoiling. 'I don't want to know anything they can tell me.'

'These are not the good ones, anyway,' Tai said. 'As for people, we're going to the Temple next. There's even more people there.'

270

They threaded their way through the crowded market and out onto the street. It was a bright summer day, and the Linh-an sunshine was liquid heat on their skin. Tai stopped at a sherbet seller's stand and bought a fruit sherbet each for Tammary and herself. Tammary licked at hers with an experimental tongue, wary, and then, looking rather surprised, finished it all off in very quick order.

'Your stomach will hurt if you do that,' Tai laughed. 'You're meant to savour them, not inhale them. There, that's the Temple. Yuet never took you there?'

Tammary shook her head, staring at the huge whitewashed walls of the Great Temple, the terraced domes that rose beyond them, and the high tower that soared above them. 'So many walls,' she whispered. 'So many walls . . .'

Tai glanced at her, a sudden understanding in her eyes, and then looked away again as though she had seen nothing. 'Just a whirlwind tour,' she said, 'this time. I'd like to light an incense stick for my mother since we're here. It can't do any harm to have the spirits watching over her.'

They joined a steady stream of people who were flowing into the closest of the Temple's great gates, and Tai purchased her incense from a convenient First Circle vendor and passed through into the Second Circle, making her way to the shrine of Hsih-to, the Messenger of the Gods.

'What does it do?' Tammary asked reluctantly, as though it had been wrenched from her, watching Tai fixing the incense stick into a holder on the small altar.

'Hsih-to is a spirit of the Later Heaven,' Tai explained as she worked. 'There are two kinds – the kind that were born mortal and achieved immortality through exalted rank or their great wisdom, like the Emperors or the Sages – people come and pray to them and ask them questions, so they can intercede for the supplicant with the higher powers of Cahan. Others, like Hsih-to, were made in Heaven; people have painted Hsih-to as a man with wings on his heels, or a man-headed eagle who bears the news to the Gods on their high mountains.'

'So what are you asking?'

'That they watch over my mother,' said Tai, her eyes suddenly bright. 'That they save her from pain, and that they grant her peace.'

'Is she very ill?'

'She is dying,' Tai said.

'I'm sorry,' Tammary said, after a beat. 'I . . . never knew my mother.'

'I know,' Tai said gently. She had been kneeling at the altar; now she rose to her feet again, and looked up at Tammary with a smile. 'Do you wish to see the inner Circles today? We can come back, if you like, and explore some other time. But for now there is something else I want to show you.'

'What?' Tammary asked, a shade of wariness back in her voice.

'We'll need a pedal cart,' Tai decided. 'At least until the gate. It's too far to walk in this heat. Can you whistle?'

Tammary, startled, nodded.

Tai led the way out of the Temple, and directed Tammary to whistle up a passenger pedal cart – which the red-haired girl did with such relish that no less than three carts came to a shuddering stop at the summons and looked expectantly their way. Tai, giggling, picked one of them and instructed the driver to take them to the Eastern Gate of Linh-an, set into the massive city wall. Tammary, her eyes raised to the great arch over her head as she stood within the gate, seemed to shrink at its towering magnificence.

Tai, glancing around, noticed the hunted look about her companion, and said, 'Patience. From here, we walk.'

'But this is the end of the world,' Tammary said. 'These walls, they are . . .'

'They are neither the end nor the beginning,' Tai said, leading the way through the gate and out onto the wide road beyond. 'Nhia would be better at explaining this, but it is all a part of the Way – the Way is everything, and in everything, and there are no boundaries except the ones we draw. And even they do not ever keep us from anything, or anything from us. Look, there is the wall – and look, there is the gate that breaches it. There is a place here for the world to enter the city, and a place where the city can escape from itself.'

'Where are we going?' Tammary asked, leaning down to adjust a loose sandal strap that had slipped around her ankle.

'The hills,' Tai said. 'That's what you miss, isn't it? The open sky? Look, look above you.'

It wasn't the mountains in which she had grown up, but the rolling hills at Linh-an's eastern flank at least gave the illusion of

272

reaching for the blue summer sky flecked with high white cloud. The slopes closest to the walls were cultivated, with split-rail fences surrounding tidy orchards and a small vineyard or two. Tai quickly turned off the broad main thoroughfare, crowded with carts, sedan chairs and other people on foot, and struck out into the hills. The path she chose was empty of other walkers. It skirted the orchard blocks, meandered past a duck-pond where several inhabitants marked the passing of the two girls with a loud flurry of startled wings, and wound its way up a hillside where a mixed herd of grazing stock companionably chewed their cud together. After a short, easy climb they reached the top of the hill, and Tai turned back towards the city.

'Look.'

From the rise, small as it was, Tammary was able to glimpse the shape of the city beyond the encircling walls. She even recognized some landmarks, with a thrill of what was almost possession.

'That's the Temple Tower, isn't it?'

'Yes,' Tai said with a smile.

Tammary raised her eyes from the city to the sky, and sighed. 'I do miss it. I miss the air singing in the high peaks, and the cry of Lastreb in the clouds.'

'What is that?' Tai asked.

'Lastreb? That's my hawk,' Tammary said. 'I raised him from a half-grown chick, and he used to come when I whistled for him.'

'Ah, so that's where you learned to summon pedal carts like that,' Tai murmured.

Almost against her will, Tammary laughed. 'And other things,' she said. 'I made up a lay about him, but nobody ever cared to hear it except Raian.' The name brought back a stab of pain at the memory, and she broke off abruptly.

'If you would tell me,' Tai said after a pause, 'I would be honoured to hear it. I write myself, poetry and a journal every night.'

'Write? We don't write. This was never written. Our lays and laments and tales are all spoken, told around firesides. We are the Travellers.'

'How do you pass things down to the generations that come after?' Tai asked. 'It is so easy for the spoken word to be misremembered or forgotten.'

'Not to the chroniclers of the clans. They are our memory. They

273

remember everything. Raian is one – because I told him my lay it is already part of the clan's lore. But nobody else is likely to care about my Lastreb.'

'Tell me,' said Tai. 'I would like to know.'

So Tammary gave her the song of the hawk, the liquid syllables of another language flung into the sky as though, if they were lucky enough and light enough, they might fly home and greet Lastreb the hawk who had once been a friend to a Traveller girl. Tai listened, transfixed.

'Can you translate it?' she asked, when Tammary was done. 'Your language is beautiful, but I would like to hear you speak of Lastreb in words I can understand. I don't have the ability to memorize it all, like your people do, but I would like to write it down so that I don't forget it. So that it is not forgotten by anybody.'

Tammary was staring at her. 'How would you write down something like this?'

'I'll show you,' Tai said, and fumbled in the pouch at her waist for the red journal she always carried with her. She flipped through the pages carefully.

'Like this one,' she said, selecting one of her poems, and reading it out loud to Tammary. 'That's one of the early ones,' she said, when she was done, in a voice almost apologetic. 'It's not as good as some of the ones I did later, but I like that one.'

'How many have you got in that thing?' Tammary asked.

'Dozens,' Tai said. 'They peel off like onion skins, except that the poems peel off on the inner layer, not on the outside – they come out from the heart of me.'

Tammary reached for the journal, and Tai let it slip into her hands; Tammary handled it reverently, almost with awe.

'There is a great Book of the Clans,' she said after a while, looking up, 'where all our stories are written down. Or so it is said. Raian believes it, anyway. But you have your own book right here in your hands, and you hold your own stories in your hand. Can you teach me this writing?'

'Of course,' said Tai, and her smile was luminous. 'You are my jin-shei, and you have the right to jin-ashu. If you will tell me your hawk song, in our language, I will write it down for you and then you can start learning the script from a source that will at least be immediately familiar to you. But . . .'

'What?'

'You do realize,' Tai said, 'that once you learn this script you can no longer tell Yuet that you cannot differentiate between willow bark and peppermint leaves?'

Tammary flushed, and then laughed. 'I already know where every herb in Yuet's stillroom is stored,' she said. 'I have my clan's memory; I remember the things that I see and hear. I can do all the recipes she has ever shown me. Blindfolded, and in the dark.' She ducked her head, half in triumph and half in embarrassment. 'I just made sure,' she said, 'that Yuet never knew that.'

## Six

One week before her fifteenth birthday, Xaforn took her place in the ranks as a full-fledged Imperial Guard, the youngest ever to do so.

The incident with Qiaan and the cat might have held Xaforn back in her rapid advancement through the trainee ranks, but that was now history. Ink the cat was now a full-grown queen who had, in the fullness of time, produced several litters of gorgeous kittens. As for Qiaan, she and Xaforn had managed to develop a mutually valued friendship from their initial prickly initiation into *jin-shei*. Xaforn had learned to appreciate the subtlety of the older girl, and Xaforn's brash honesty and often tactless candour raised a mixed reaction in Qiaan, ranging from exasperation to frank envy of Xaforn's ability to reduce situations to their most basic components and then act on them. If questions had to be asked, Xaforn asked them, and then did not waste an eternity pondering the answers before acting on them.

Not only by far the youngest cadet to graduate into the rank-and-file in her year, Xaforn had also been picked to perform the martial arts demonstration for the graduation ceremony of her intake. This was an annual affair, glittering and formal, which the Syai Emperors always traditionally attended – for this was their own Guard, the cream of the Syai army, the men and women whose most fundamental duty was the care and preservation of the Imperial family.

275

Nhia and Yuet had both accompanied Liudan on this particular occasion, sitting with her on the balcony decked out as her observation platform. It had banners fluttering on either side of it, yellow silk painted with scarlet dragons which boasted yellow topaz eyes and a glimmer of scales on their writhing forms picked out in real gold. The day was the first day of autumn, auspicious for several reasons – not only the graduation ceremony of the Imperial Guard, but also Liudan's birthday and the opening day of her third Autumn Court.

The Dragon Empress, who had made sure that her Guard would stand behind her before she had claimed that title a year before, was resplendent in her glittering regalia. The Imperial Tiara of Syai, heavy with gems and gold, rested on her head with every appearance of having been meant for nobody but her. Even Yuet, who had known the Little Empress Antian during her years at Court at Szewan's heels and who had never thought at the time that anybody else could ever be in Antian's place, now found it hard to imagine that crown above any other face.

'Xaforn?' Liudan was saying now, that regal head turned towards Yuet at a quizzical tilt. 'Why is it that I remember you mentioning that name to me?'

'I met her in my capacity as healer to the the Imperial Guard before we became *jin-shei*,' Yuet said. 'I was telling you, I believe, of her reputation in the Guard, even then, even as a raw young trainee. Some of the most senior of the Imperial Guard have noticed this one – she is fierce and implacable and has a sometimes stiff-necked sense of honour that is all her own but which she also, sometimes inconveniently, expects all others around her to aspire to. She won't even be fifteen until next week – that's young to gather such a reputation, most especially in this outfit, among the best of the best.'

'What is it that she is supposed to do here today, then? I remember attending a few of these things when I was a child, with my family, but not many. It was always Antian who came, or Oylian.' There was still a bitterness here, a thorn that had worked its way deep into Liudan's spirit and rested there, a permanent wound. 'The one I attended here last year was . . . unremarkable. I don't think I recall much of it. Did they have a demonstration then?'

'I wasn't here last year,' Yuet said, 'but you'd better not tell them that you don't even remember last year's top cadet. Part of the reason for this demonstration is to offer up the best of the new

Guard for the personal attention of the one wearing the Tiara. I wonder what happened to last year's top cadet. You probably have one very frustrated young man or woman in the Guard, Liudan, waiting a year for you to notice them.'

'I will not make the same mistake again,' said Liudan, with a touch of acid.

'No,' Yuet murmured, taking the words at face value, 'I don't believe you'll forget this one.'

'She is that extraordinary?' Liudan said.

'You'll see for yourself. Here she comes now.'

In the training grounds, now set up as the demonstration arena, several groups of trainees had already performed their highly choreographed routines for the Empress's pleasure, to martial music being played by a small group of musicians on another balcony across from Liudan's own, but they had cleared the area and the musicians had fallen silent. Xaforn, apparently, would perform her own routine in silence.

For this, the most martial of honours, Xaforn had been assisted in her preparations not by her Guard peers but by Qiaan, whom she had asked to be her companion. Captain Aric, Qiaan's father, had been a little put out that she had agreed to Xaforn's request.

'You never showed any interest in the Guard when *I* tried to get you involved,' he said to his daughter when she told him that Xaforn had come to her.

'Ah, but you had ulterior motives,' Qiaan had said.

'What motives?' Aric had demanded.

'You wanted me to be part of the Guard. You didn't want me there as family, or by choice – you wanted me there by vow and by training. If I said yes to you I said yes to all that. And I never wanted to say yes to the Guard.'

'Your mother . . .' he began, but then fell silent, and would not be drawn further.

So Qiaan had been the one to help Xaforn into her dress armour, black with the yellow sun of Syai on her breastplate, and strapping on the matt black segmented leg plates.

Xaforn winced when Qiaan accidentally banged into her armoured shoulder. Her new tattoo, the Red Dragon for the Dragon Empress, had been in place for only a few days and was still tender, cushioned by a pad of gauze under the armour.

'Wimp,' said Qiaan. 'You're supposed to be able to fight when you're bleeding to death, or something like that. My father always said so, anyway. There are supposed to be legends about Guards who held off armies while wounded unto death and with one arm cut off.'

'For a Guard brat, you're remarkably down on us,' Xaforn said conversationally, coiling up her braid to tuck it under the black winged helmet that Qiaan held ready to fasten onto the shoulder armour.

'I don't believe in the patina of glory,' Qiaan said. 'That's probably why I keep on getting told I'm adopted. I just don't buy into the Guard mystique. The Empress was born to her station, perhaps; I don't think that a Guard is.'

'*I* was,' Xaforn said, her voice muffled by the helmet.

'Oh, you,' Qiaan said. 'You've always had delusions of grandeur.'

'And you've always been humble?' Xaforn shot back. 'Besides, I *am* good at what I do. Thanks, Qiaan. See you after the show!'

For once, she flounced out leaving Qiaan without her customary last word.

Emerging into her arena, alone, Xaforn felt the weight of the expectant silence descend on her. She walked to the middle of the square, bowed to the Imperial box, and then stood for a moment, closing her eyes, breathing deeply, focusing on an inner light she always carried, something that showed her a centre of balance from which she could leap outward. Her sense of time shifted in that strange way to which she had become accustomed, allowing her to see her opponent's fastest moves in a sort of dreamy slow motion and let her respond in kind – to her senses. In the real world her every motion translated into movements almost too fast to be seen.

*It's a dance*, she heard her instructor's voice echoing in her head. *Learn to control it. Learn to become it.*

Xaforn started out with the simple things, the baby exercises, her movements really slow motion and exaggerating every step and gesture in the way that the instructors made the youngest cadets do them when they were still learning the routines. It was too simple, of course. People murmured, watching, when the movements began to flow into something ever faster, ever more graceful, ever more deadly, the dance-like weave in the air of a pair of delicate hands that could kill, until Xaforn was a black blur on the training ground, never faltering for a single step outside the tiny circle she had set for herself on the ground. When she stopped, very suddenly, facing the Imperial balcony and subsiding into absolute stillness again, Liudan nodded, fascinated.

'Impressive,' she said, raising her hands to applaud.

'Wait,' Yuet said hastily. 'Don't break her concentration. She isn't finished yet.'

Liudan raised her eyebrow, but let her hands fall back into her lap.

Assistants brought an assortment of things into the ring now – a wall of woven rushes supported by a bamboo frame, a folding trestle table on which they set a large basket of fruit and vegetables ranging in size from apricots to a watermelon.

Xaforn waited until they withdrew, and then drew her sword into the silence with a single singing motion, holding the glittering blade high for a moment in a salute to the Imperial banners. Then she turned to the rush wall. Her blade moved so fast that people could not see it at all except for a pale blur; and when she stepped back, moments later, the rushes had been carved into the profile of a Guard helmet. This time there was a scattering of spontaneous applause from the spectators. Xaforn ignored it, turning to the fruit basket. She lifted out the watermelon, balanced a pumpkin marrow on top of it, an apple on that, an apricot on the apple, and stepped back. The sword sang, and the apricot split in two precise vertical halves, with the apple remaining untouched, then the apple was cubed with two slices, horizontal and vertical, without the marrow being touched, then the marrow was diced without the blade touching the watermelon. The sword paused for a moment and then blurred into motion around the watermelon itself. When Xaforn was done the watermelon looked intact, still untouched – until she tapped one end of it with the flat of her sword and it keeled over, cut into a hundred neat slices. It was an exercise in precise control, and the crowd loved it, erupting in applause. This time Xaforn looked up and nodded. The assistants came back in to collect the debris.

Liudan was applauding with the rest. '*Very* impressive,' she said. 'No wonder I don't remember last year. I don't recall this kind of show.'

'No, I don't think there was one. What you just saw was hardly

279

cadet level,' Yuet said, smiling. 'Our Xaforn was always ahead in her studies. In this last year I believe that they had her learning one-to-one, that she had already outstripped the rest of her group.'

'What is she waiting for?' Liudan interrupted.

'Maybe there's something else . . . look, a quarterstaff. She may do an exhibition match with somebody.'

'Three somebodies,' Nhia said, watching three helmeted, armoured Guards stride into the arena bearing their own quarter-staffs. 'She's mad.'

Liudan leaned forward, her chin in her hands, rapt.

Xaforn's three opponents, all a head taller than herself and twice as broad, bore sturdy quarterstaffs of raw undyed wood; Xaforn's was dyed black. The four bowed to one another, Xaforn to the three of them and they to her, and the three stepped back, ranging themselves in attack formation.

'I'd better get down there,' Yuet said.

'Do you think they'll hurt her?' Liudan said.

'I think she might kill one of them,' Yuet said calmly. 'I'm serious, Liudan. I'm going down. It's entirely possible we might see real blood today. That's Xaforn down there.'

'When it's over, come back here,' Liudan said. 'And bring her.'

It was the Empress speaking. Yuet bowed slightly. 'I will.'

Down in the arena, the three fighters were circling Xaforn warily while she stood motionless in the middle of the ring. When one of them lunged, she whirled on the ball of her foot, her staff ready, and met his attack with a counterattack of her own. At the same time she spun and kicked at the second man, her foot slamming into his wrist, and completed her motion by ducking under and past the first man's swinging staff so that it continued its arc and hit the ground where she had been standing, hard. People heard the man grunt as the force of the blow shook his entire frame.

In the meantime Xaforn had danced her way in between two of the other opponents, and had manoeuvred herself out of the way just in time for one of them to hit his partner a glancing blow on the shoulder. It would have been a solid blow, but the fighter had realized at the last moment what had happened and tried to turn it aside. In the time it took him to recover his footing the first fighter had come back at Xaforn, whirling his staff before him in a deadly wheel. The third one was still attacking her from the other side.

Xaforn spun and danced like a wind spirit, solid in one spot one moment, evanescent like a ghost the next, her staff spinning and whirling out of impossible angles to counter attacks or deliver devastating blows of her own.

One of the men caught a solid crack to the side of the head from one his own mates, and went down like he had been poleaxed. The other two simply stepped over him and took the fight away from the body; Yuet came hurrying out into the arena, motioning to assistants to carry the fallen man to relative safety at the side of the arena and remove his helmet. In the meantime the deadly dance went on, until Xaforn spun her staff in a blur of double feints and caught one of the other men across the ribs, hard. He grunted, doubled over, fell to his hands and knees, wheezing for breath.

As though that had been a signal, Xaforn and the last man standing paused for a moment, facing each other, and then laid down their staves. The last Guard's sword came singing from his sheath, and Xaforn's followed it. The crowd gasped. The two combatants in the arena stalked one another as the winded second man was hustled out of the danger zone, and then they closed, their blades drawing arcs of blue fire when they slid down each other's deadly edges, ringing metal on metal as they met and met again in the bright air sliced into ribbons of daylight between the combatants by the weave of the sword.

A sharp shout of '*Hai!*' from the side halted the bout and the two fighters, both breathing hard, stopped, holding their swords up to one another in salute before sheathing them. They bowed to one another, and then to the Imperial box, and then the crowd exploded into applause and cheers as the two made their way out through the archway into the practice room corridors beyond.

Qiaan was waiting for Xaforn just inside the gate, an arch smile on her face.

'That wasn't bad at all,' she said. 'Looks like all that training they gave you wasn't *totally* wasted.'

'Are Douber and Chu all right?' Xaforn said, tugging at her helmet fastenings with a weary hand.

'No thanks to you,' said Yuet, coming up to the two of them and reaching out to lend a helping hand. 'One of them has two cracked ribs and will probably be turning an interesting shade of plum under his armour just about now. The other has a concussion – mild, but a concussion nonetheless. Did you have to hit quite as *hard* as all that? It was just an exhibition match.'

'So?' Xaforn said. 'When you practised making poultices, did you stop short of actually applying them?'

'Point taken,' Yuet said. 'Now come on, the Empress wants to see you.'

'Now?' Xaforn said. With her helmet finally off, her face was flushed and her hair plastered to her small head with sweat. 'I'm hardly fit for a royal . . .'

'Xaforn,' Yuet said, 'the royal decides what you're fit for, and you're summoned.'

Qiaan fished a carved bone comb out of her purse. 'At least fix your hair,' she said, reaching out and combing the straggling, sweaty strands that had escaped the tight braid back away from Xaforn's face.

'I think that Liudan would benefit from the reminder that occasionally brilliance has to be paid for by mundane things like sweat,' Yuet said thoughtfully.

Qiaan glanced at her. 'It feels so odd to hear you speak of her by name,' she said.

'I am her healer, and I am her *jin-shei*,' Yuet said. 'Sometimes I wonder how all that came about, but that's how things are. That gives me her name. And, remember, you are second-circle *jin-shei* to her too, through Xaforn and through me.' She paused. Qiaan and Liudan had never met face to face, although Yuet had spoken of each to the other – mentioning everything except their remarkable resemblance to one another. It was still just a picture in Yuet's mind, the faces of two girls who shared the eyes of a beautiful concubine painted on a Court miniature. Every time she allowed her gaze to rest on Qiaan, Yuet felt an irrational urge to engineer an occasion to put the two girls side by side and prove to herself if they did, indeed, resemble one another so closely or if the whole thing had been the product of an overwrought imagination.

It might be difficult for anyone to observe it here today, with Liudan decked out in her full finery and the aura of the Empire around her like a cloak. Qiaan was clad in a fine embroidered silk gown herself for the occasion, but she would appear plain beside the flashing jewels of royalty. There were none in the royal balcony whose attention it would be dangerous to draw to the resemblance between the Empress and the daughter of one of the captains of her Guard – only Nhia, who already knew them both, and a couple of attendants whose attention would be focused elsewhere, as Liudan's would be – on Xaforn, the girl of the hour. Perhaps now was the moment, the only moment of grace Yuet would have.

'You're keeping the Empress waiting,' Qiaan said into the silence. 'Do you want me to wait in the back to help you out of that carapace, Xaforn?'

'No, come up with us,' Yuet said recklessly, casting the die. 'I have spoken to her of you, too – of the work you did in the compound when the epidemic was still at its height. She was appreciative.'

'Yes, but she never asked to see me, nor did she ever come down there,' Qiaan pointed out.

'Now we *are* keeping her waiting,' Yuet said. 'This is no time for wounded dignity, Qiaan. Come on, both of you. This way.'

Yuet made the introductions when the three girls reached the royal balcony, and Liudan inclined her glittering head to Xaforn.

'That was a deeply impressive display,' she said to the youngest Guard, who had gone down on one knee before her Empress. 'I have been hearing of you, Xaforn, and now I have seen that what I have been hearing was not exaggerated. I think I have a position for you in the Court, reporting directly to me and to my Chancellor here.'

Nhia sat up straighter at this, and Liudan turned her head fractionally to nod at her.

'When you came to the Council,' the Empress said, 'I promised you I would keep you safe from harm. I have had a Guard detail at your side for most of your tenure as Chancellor so far – and I know it hasn't been easy on you, both the necessity of it and their constant physical presence. But now, I think we have a solution.' She turned back to Xaforn. 'There will be new quarters made ready for you near Nhia's on the Palace grounds, and you will move into those as soon as it may be arranged. You are, as providence would have it, both a Guard and a companion, for there is a *jin-shei* link here, is there not?' Receiving a nod, she continued. 'I will also reserve the right to take you back for my own purposes, when need arises for your remarkable skills.'

'Thank you, Dragon Empress,' Xaforn said, her eyes wide.

'You may call me Liudan, in this circle,' Liudan said with a regal wave of her hand. 'Everyone else does.'

She had offered a few gracious words to Qiaan but it was obvious that she did not instantly see herself in the other girl's face. As Liudan swept out of the balcony and her entourage followed in her wake, Qiaan hung back, clutching at Yuet's sleeve.

'She looks . . . she looks so much like *me*,' Qiaan whispered to Yuet.

'I know,' Yuet said calmly. 'You knew too – you've seen the Empress before. I know you've been to Open Court at least once.'

'From a distance,' Qiaan interrupted. 'I have never been this close to the Empress before. And she looks like what I always see in my own mirror. I know, because I've always thought my eyes were set too close together, and I see the very thing I've always grumbled at in my own mirror on her face when I look at her.'

'She's wearing a lot of make-up today,' Yuet said, playing devil's advocate. 'Perhaps that accentuates what you see.'

'You know something,' Qiaan said, her eyes narrowing slightly.

'Yes,' Yuet said, her voice calm and light although her heart had skipped a beat. 'She has a way about her that has always reminded me of you, and vice versa. It's not the eyes so much as a way of look-ing sideways. But then, Tai might have been little sister to the Little Empress when you saw them together sometimes – when they both put their hair in long braids and scrubbed their faces clean. It means nothing.'

Doubt still sparked in Qiaan's eyes, but she didn't pursue the sub-ject. For Yuet, however, it had crystallized. There was indeed a link between these two, the Empress and the daughter of the Guard. Although, on the face of it, the words had nothing to do with this conundrum, Yuet found the voice of a Traveller woman from the mountains of Syai echoing in her mind – *Sevanna had her own plans for Amri*. It was tangled, oh, it was tangled! But Yuet's instincts had chased down Tammary's identity, and now Yuet was equally con-vinced that the Tammary plot was not as obvious as it appeared. Those other plans that Sevanna – *Szewan* – had for Tammary were somehow involved in all of this, and so was Szewan, once again.

Tammary herself, the resentful solitary mountain child, had turned into an unexpectedly capable assistant. She had absorbed *jin-ashu* with surprising ease, and Yuet had grown to depend, in the space of a few short months, on the Traveller girl's knack for mixing together medicines with skill and speed. Tammary seemed to have settled into her role for the time being, although Yuet had learned quickly never to send her to the market by herself for anything she considered remotely urgent because Tammary would lose herself in the market-place for hours, sometimes, just wandering through the crowded aisles. She had developed a strange fascination for people. When quizzed on it, she'd explain that they had 'different expressions' from the fair folk she had been used to, and she was trying to learn to 'read' them.

'She watches them like she'd watch golden carp swimming in a pond, or animals in a menagerie,' Yuet said to Tai once, on just such an occasion, when Tammary was over an hour overdue from the market. 'She goes into the marketplace and just watches people bargain for hours. I don't understand it.'

'Oh, she does a bit more than that,' Tai had said. 'I went with her once or twice, after that first time. She is learning – I am not sure what she is trying to teach herself, not yet, but I'll find out in time. But I've watched her, and she is not just watching people like strange specimens in an exotic menagerie. She is trying to understand something.'

'What?' Yuet said in perplexity.

'Compassion, maybe,' Tai murmured. 'Perhaps she *does* want to be a healer, somewhere deep inside.'

Yuet snorted. 'That one? That one would do much better in the ranks of the Guards, I sometimes think. Give her a weapon and she will channel so much fury into it that it will turn into a sword of fire.'

Xaforn, who had met Tammary, had actually agreed with that assessment.

'She doesn't show it,' Xaforn had said, 'but I can sense it in her – there's an anger there. Something to prove. She would make a fighter if she could bring herself to get off her high horse for long enough to take instructions from somebody.'

'She does take instructions from somebody,' Tai had said – for it was to her that this trenchant summary had been delivered. 'I teach her *jin-ashu*.'

'You don't hit her to do it,' Xaforn said. 'You try putting a quarterstaff into her hand and calling the fury that drives her by name in her presence. You'd run for cover pretty quickly.'

'Qiaan said that you weren't much better when *she* was teaching *you* the *jin-ashu* script,' Tai had retorted, laughing. 'She said she had to hold you down and make you do things sometimes.'

Xaforn scowled. 'She says too much. I was not born to learn pretty letters.'

'Perhaps that is *your* fury,' Tai said. 'Should I run for cover?'

'You're impossible,' Xaforn snapped.

'I've been told that a few times, yes,' Tai said, laughing. 'You, on the other hand, are improbable.'

Xaforn sat back, scowling, trying to work out if that remark amounted to a compliment or not. 'Why?' she demanded at last.

'Not everyone scares a sorcerous Sage into retreat,' Tai said with a genuine smile.

Xaforn had become Nhia's faithful shadow, in accordance with Liudan's command. They had developed a companionable friendship, but Xaforn never forgot for a moment that her role was to stand between Nhia and danger, and even in their most relaxed moments within Nhia's own quarters she was always on duty, always alert for anything out of the ordinary. Xaforn had been briefed that the Ninth Sage Lihui had harmed Nhia in the past, without being told the details of the tale, and was particularly on guard against him. There were times she had taken it upon herself to rearrange Nhia's entire schedule so that any opportunity of Lihui coming upon her in less than a crowd or in other than some public place where all could observe the encounter could be carefully avoided. Nhia shied from him, not avoiding his eyes when she felt his own burning gaze upon her but making sure that she was not often in a position where she would have to endure it for long.

Only once, close to the tail end of winter of that year, when she and Xaforn were waiting at a Palace gate for a sedan chair, did Nhia find herself cornered, with that gentle voice speaking from only a few paces away.

'The white streak becomes you, my dear,' Lihui had said in his honeyed tones, the master-to-student manner coloured with just the faintest glimmer of knowing intimacy.

Xaforn had stepped between Nhia and the Sage.

'If it please you, *sei*, pass on,' she said quietly. She was a head shorter than him, her wrists fragile as a bird's compared to his own, but Lihui had been in the stands at the autumn inauguration and he knew who Xaforn was.

Nonetheless, he was Lihui, and she was nothing.

'It pleases me to speak to your mistress,' he snapped, his voice shedding some of its sweetness. 'As far as you are concerned, *I am not here.*'

Because they were watching for things like that, both Nhia and Xaforn saw him make the tiniest of hand gestures, his thumb and forefinger coming together in a circle, his right hand sweeping minutely down and away.

Xaforn exchanged an eloquent glance with Nhia.

'I bear the same talisman she does,' Xaforn said. 'You cannot be invisible for me. Wherever you are, whoever you pretend to be, I will know you.'

'I could kill you right now, little gadfly,' Lihui said, his voice dropping to barely above a whisper. 'I don't have to be invisible to do it. And there is nothing you can do to prevent it.'

Xaforn reached for her white light, centring. 'I don't think so,' she said.

Lihui felt the instant in which she became the instrument of death, felt her falling into her time-out-of-time state in which she was a killing spirit, ready to protect that which had been given into her charge. He actually took a step back.

At this point a clattering in the yard announced the arrival of the sedan chair. Xaforn indicated to Nhia, with an economical motion of her head and without breaking eye contact with the Sage, that she should get into it. Xaforn herself stood her ground.

'Whoever taught you how to do that,' Lihui had snarled at last, 'taught you far more than fighting skills, *Guard*. You are using the dark magic. Never forget that you owe your reputation to the same thing you claim to abhor in me.'

He whirled, his dark cloak swinging around, and stalked away into the Palace.

Xaforn had not told Nhia about that little exchange, but the encounter had been reported to the rest of them, to Tai, to Yuet and Tammary, to Liudan. Tai had been jubilant at Lihui's climb down, Tammary (who knew very little of the actual background) had been dutifully admiring, and Yuet had been congratulated all around for it had been her idea to split Nhia's talisman into two and allow Xaforn to wear the second half, as Nhia's protector and first line of defence.

Liudan had tapped her lip with her finger, in her customary gesture of contemplation.

'I told you that you should dismiss him,' Tai had said to her, unable to suppress the 'I-told-you-so' impulse.

'I told you I couldn't do that,' Liudan said. 'However, he *has* spoken openly and before a witness about intent to do harm to one of my own people. For that, at least, I can call on the Circle of Sages to censure him. And I can make it clear that my displeasure will be great if they do not. And from now on I will have a Guard watching Lihui every minute of every day.'

'I thought you had already ordered that watch,' Yuet said.

'Ah,' Liudan said, 'indeed. But it had been a discreet and cautious watch. This time I intend to make sure he knows he is being watched. The next time he makes a mistake like this – and he will, because people who are angry and frustrated inevitably do – there will be someone there to stop him.'

# Seven

Nhia was on the point of snuffing the night's hour-candle and retiring to bed when she heard a knock, so soft as to almost make her think that she had imagined it.

Her housekeeper nudged the door ajar when Nhia called out an invitation to enter.

'Begging your pardon, mistress,' Nhia's housekeeper said, opening the door the merest crack, 'I know it's late, but your young friend Tai is here.'

'Tai? At this hour?' Nhia said, startled. 'Send her in!'

The housekeeper ducked out and after a moment Tai entered, her eyes down, closing the door behind her with both hands placed flat against the small of her back, and leaning against it.

'Do you have a moment, Nhia?'

'Of course. What is it? Has Rimshi . . . ?'

'No, no change,' Tai said. Rimshi had been drifting between deep sleep and a strange waking state where she wandered in her mind and often talked to people who were not there, including Tai's long-dead father. Yuet kept her dosed with poppy as much as possible, keeping her comfortable – but they all knew it was only a matter of time. Maybe days, maybe only hours. 'But that is what I've come to talk to you about. Sort of.'

'Tell me,' Nhia said, bringing the younger girl into the room and settling her into a comfortable chair while she lit another taper and planted it beside the night candle, casting more light on Tai's pale face.

It was high summer, and a perfect night, complete with a full moon in the sky painting the land in silver. The air was warm, still holding the heat of the day, the shutters in Nhia's rooms wide open and the faintest breath of wind stirring the painted silk curtains in the room. The scent of night jasmine drifted into the room on the back of the sound of a distant concert of cicadas. A brace of moths had set up a dance around the twin flames of the candles on Nhia's desk. But Tai was oblivious to it all, her hands clasped on her lap, her eyes still down.

'Tell me,' Nhia repeated, coming to sit beside her and reaching for one of those hands. 'You know you are not alone, *jin-shei-bao*. What can I do to ease these days?'

'Nhia, you've always teased me about this before, but my mother is dying, and I want to . . .' She swallowed. 'I want to do this properly. You know I have no blood family to ask, but you are my sister, and I want to ask you to take my *so ji* . . .'

Nhia smiled. 'You want me to be your proxy to Kito?'

'He's mentioned marriage to me,' Tai said quickly, 'but I wouldn't discuss it. I couldn't. My mother needed me. But even Yuet says that she will be in Cahan and at rest soon, at long last. And I don't want to be alone, Nhia.'

'Tai, Kito's been waiting for this for years,' said Nhia, smiling although her eyes were full of tears. 'Of course I will do it. Have you got a *so ji*, or must I put in an order for one tomorrow?'

Tai fumbled underneath her outer robe, bringing out a small silk-wrapped package she had been carrying in her purse. 'I do. I have had this for almost a year now.'

Nhia pulled back a corner of the wrapping. 'It's so dark,' she said, rather tactlessly. The purest jades were the paler ones, and those were considered luckiest for the *so ji* sculptures – they were expensive, of course, but they were much sought after. But Tai merely smiled.

'I know. I wanted one that shade. He once said that he liked it.'

'You are a romantic after all,' Nhia said, and gave her a hard hug. 'It seems like only yesterday that we were both children running barefoot in the back streets, and now I'm about to go out and arrange your wedding. It feels so strange, Tai. And so wonderful. Stay here tonight? It's late, and you need to get back across town. And we can talk.'

Tai shook her head. 'I left her asleep, Nhia, but I have to be there when she wakes. She is used to that.'

Yuet had already told Nhia that Rimshi often didn't even know who was with her while she was awake – but this was not something that Nhia was about to pass on to Tai. In times like this, when the caregiver was helpless to do anything that would be of any measurable assistance to the person whom all knew was dying, it was comforting to cling to a few illusions.

'All right,' Nhia said. 'I'll get Xaforn to escort you back. And I'll be round tomorrow, as soon as I've talked to Kito and his father.'

Unexpectedly, Tai lifted her head and kissed Nhia on the cheek. 'Thank you.'

Nhia, feeling oddly protective and maternal for all that there were less than five years between them, smiled, smoothing Tai's hair with a gentle palm. 'I will arrange everything,' she said. 'Don't worry.'

Nhia sent for Xaforn, who turned up less than ten minutes after the summons looking as neatly turned out and pristine in her Guard uniform as though she had been waiting for this call and not about ready, like the rest of them, to go to bed.

'Make sure our soon-to-be-bride gets home safely,' Nhia said, and Xaforn's eyes kindled.

'You're getting married? When?'

'I don't know,' Tai said, starting to laugh. 'But I'll make sure you are invited.'

* * *

Nhia's morning was filled with appointments and Court business, and an emergency Council meeting was scheduled for the late afternoon, when a delegation from the port city of Chirinaa was expected in Linh-an to discuss a minor trade crisis. But Nhia would have moved more than schedules around in order to get Tai's errand done, even if she had not been asked to do so in the name of *jin-shei*. It was around noon the next day, delaying lunch for both herself and a half-heartedly grumbling Xaforn who was her escort, that she made her way to the Great Temple.

The crowds were bigger than usual, and Nhia quickly realized that not all of them were city folk. There were men and women here dressed in the peasant garb of the hill people from the north of Sei-lin, and the round-hatted farmers from the central plains, and even a brace of brightly garbed Southerners who might have been an advance guard for the delegation from Chirinaa. Nhia took a brisk walk around the Temple, and noted that all these assorted folk were buying incense and offerings, and scurrying off into the inner Circles – laying bowls of food and rice wine at the feet of the weather spirits of the Second Circle, bowing in prayer before the Rulers of the Four Quarters and murmuring entreaties about salvation and good fortune upon themselves and their families.

The rains had been thin that year, and the year before that. Drought was beginning to bite in places. This would be the second year of a bad harvest. Bad enough that people from some of the afflicted areas had spent good money to come here to Linh-an and petition the Gods and spirits here at the Great Temple. For the ordinary folk of the countryside, this was the Temple from which it was but a step into Cahan, the Temple which received all of the prayers sent in incense smoke from their own small temples scattered across the land, and processed them before deciding which of them would be deemed good enough to be passed on to the Gods. Things were bad enough that the poor were coming here to petition the Gods directly, by themselves, because their earlier prayers had obviously not been received.

'It's bad, isn't it?' Xaforn, trailing at her heels, whispered as she watched a couple of women laying stalks of withered barley on the altar of the Rain Spirit. One of them was crying – not loudly, not obviously, but with silent trails of tears glistening on her cheeks.

'And getting worse, by all accounts,' Nhia said in a low voice. She had seen enough, and was heading for the gate back into the First Circle. 'There has been talk of fires in the East.'

A young man suddenly bowed to Nhia, just as she was stepping back into the teeming commercial Circle of the Great Temple, and she returned the courtesy by reflex before she realized his identity, and could not help a small smile.

'Kito,' she said, ackowledging him. 'I was just . . .'

'By your leave, Nhia, I have a favour to ask,' Kito said earnestly, not even aware that he had just interrupted Nhia. Her smile inched a little broader.

'And how may I be of assistance?'

'I know Tai's mother is fading fast,' Kito said, his words slow and careful. 'This is something that preoccupies her, and I understand that, and I respect it, but there is no need for her to bear such a burden on her own. As far as I know she has no other family, and it is all on her shoulders – but every time I have asked if I could help she has pushed me away . . . and with her mother her last living relative . . .' He swallowed. 'Nhia, I wish to send a *so ji* to her, and ask her formally to marry me, but I don't even know who should receive it. Would you take her my token? I know that you are her *jin-shei* sister, and that is as close a family member as she will have, after . . . I don't want her to be alone, Nhia.'

Nhia was now smiling openly. 'As it happens, I am here to speak to your father and yourself on a similar matter,' she said.

Kito blinked.

'If you would conduct me to your father,' Nhia said, with exaggerated courtesy, and Kito straightened up with a snap and offered her his arm. Xaforn, trying not to giggle, followed behind them.

They waited until So-Xan finished conducting his business with a client, and then Kito ushered Nhia into the booth.

'Properly speaking, I should have waited on you at your house, with a companion, and discussed the matter I bring to you now with the flowery speeches of the old courtesies,' Nhia said, her smile luminous now, 'but I think that I am here merely as a messenger anyway. So-Xan, I come here on behalf of Tai, Rimshi's daughter, who has charged me to bring this to your son.'

She extracted Tai's *so ji* from its wrappings of silk and offered it to the men laid flat on both open palms.

Kito gasped, and then started laughing. So-Xan's eyes creased up into pools of glittering silent laughter, also, and he turned to his son. 'Looks like she got there first, my boy,' he remarked, his voice bubbling with his laughter. 'Well?'

Kito, still laughing, reached over and took the small sculpture with both his hands, offering Nhia a deep bow. '*So ji*,' he said. 'As my beloved wishes. I accept this with joy, but I have made hers myself – take it to her from me, if you will, as my wedding gift to her.'

'It is a family of good reputation,' So-Xan said, as he and Nhia also exchanged bows. 'I would have sent my sister-in-law to wait on her and exchange the bridal cakes, according to custom, but I understand that the young lady's mother is ailing. How serious is the situation?'

'Very serious, So-Xan.'

'Nhia,' said Kito, interrupting again, 'tell her, please tell her, there is no need to wait this out by herself. I want to help.'

'In that case I think we have a special case on our hands,' said So-Xan, as though his son had not spoken. 'We will consider the wedding itself to be an auspicious occasion for the exchange of the proper gifts. So when shall we make the nuptials? If you were to ask me, I think we could safely say that this is a wedding with a betrothal which has already been completed – these two young fools have been circling each other for a long time. It's about time that they came to their senses.'

'I will find out when an auspicious date for a wedding is,' Nhia said. 'I would prefer to arrange it as soon as I may, otherwise the mourning period might keep you apart for longer than either of you wishes.'

Kito drew a sharp breath, but So-Xan raised a hand to forestall him. 'Fetch the *so ji* you made for your bride, my son.'

A luminous Kito pressed another small jade sculpture into Nhia's hands. It was only a shade or so lighter than Tai's had been, but its colour was starting to shade into that pale green which was the mark of pure jade. Kito had carved smooth shapes of a buffalo and a boar, his and Tai's respective signs, twined about one another. Nhia, wrapping the sculpture up carefully, smiled at him.

'That is very beautiful,' she said. 'There is another thing. I know that it is traditional for the wedding to be at the house of the bride-groom, but Tai has a particular wish that her mother should be at her wedding, and it may be difficult to move her. Would you consider . . .'

'Nhia-*lama*, we will leave it in your hands,' So-Xan said. 'This is a wedding that gives me joy because I see my son happy – but it has hardly been bound by tradition so far. We are happy to make sure that Kito's bride is wed in the presence of her honoured mother.'

Nhia bowed deeply and took her leave. After paying a short visit to the priests of the Fourth Circle, leaving a fat stick of incense as an offering to Tai's future happiness, Nhia went straight back to the Palace where she had to sit through an interminable hour and a half while the delegation from Chirinaa whined about the non-payment of dock tariffs and Nhia's mind kept returning to the lost and wretched folk who had found their way into the Great Temple to ask for succour. Things were connected; harvests were failing, people had less money, trade hiccups happened at the warehouses and docks in a port city where fees and charges were not paid. Even people like So-Xan were feeling the pinch. They were craftsmen, and their product was safeguarded by centuries of custom and tradition, but even the poorer people in Linh-an itself would find it cheaper to find other means of keeping tally of the passing days.

But the endless meeting was finally over and Nhia was able to walk out with Liudan, managing to snatch a moment to tell her of Tai's impending wedding.

'Let me know when it is,' Liudan said.

'Will you come?' asked Nhia.

'Of course. If I am invited,' Liudan said archly. And then she glanced aside, her attention already claimed by something else, and Nhia bobbed a courtesy and withdrew to start her planning.

Tai had received her own *so ji* with a reaction much the same as Kito's had been to hers.

'Honestly,' Nhia said, watching Tai, giggling and wet-eyed, as she cradled her sculpture, 'I don't know why you didn't at least get betrothed years ago. Anyone with eyes in his head could have seen this would happen. Oh, but I forget, you did.'

Tai, still laughing, slapped at Nhia's arm.

'So-Xan left it to me to arrange things,' Nhia said. 'I've already talked to the Temple people. We can do this as soon as you want, Tai, the timing is entirely up to you.'

'I know it's irrational, and I know she can't really *be* there, not really, but I would like my mother to be at my wedding,' Tai said. 'I know I should have done something sooner if I'd wanted her to have any chance of participating in it – and maybe it was a mistake to hold off for so long – but I find myself not wanting to waste any of the years to come on regrets any worse than they already are.'

'Then that is how it will be,' Nhia said lovingly. 'I will make the arrangements. If I plan it for next week, is that going to be too fast for you?'

Tai suddenly blushed. 'No,' she said coyly.

Nhia laughed. 'Be happy, little *jin-shei-bao*,' she said. 'Get ready for your wedding. Leave the rest to me.'

Preparations suddenly took off at a breathless speed.

Liudan, when officially told the news and offered an invitation to the wedding, sent a bolt of scarlet silk for a wedding gown and a set of matched rings for the ceremony. She also sent a beautifully bound book of *jin-ashu* wedding poetry, some of it written by Tai's idol, the poetess Qiu-Lin who was also the Cloud Empress, to pass on to the bride-to-be, with a note in her own hand on the fly-leaf: *I have not forgotten your vision.*

Xaforn, who had an unexpectedly delicate touch at whittling with her dagger, produced a lucky rabbit talisman made of some soft, pale wood; and Qiaan created an ink drawing of the Three Heavens of Cahan, invoking a blessing on the new couple. Xaforn had looked over her shoulder as she put the finishing touches to the painting, and had suddenly been reminded of another one, a childish drawing that Qiaan had done years before.

'It's better than the cat drawing,' Xaforn said, with a grin.

Qiaan obviously remembered, too, because she turned with a mock scowl and flicked the black ink off the top of her brush in Xaforn's direction. Xaforn ducked, laughing.

'Still conceited,' she got out, between giggles.

'Still malicious,' Qiaan responded, in an echo of their early battles, without looking up again, apparently immersed in her work.

One of Szewan's early patients had paid her with a quantity of dark-grey pearls, which had then languished in a safe box at the back of the stillroom until Yuet had quite accidentally found them almost two decades later. Now she had two of the smaller matched pearls fashioned into a pair of delicate earrings for Tai.

Even Antian, the Little Empress, seemed to reach out from Cahan and bless the wedding. She had never rescinded the order she had put in with a Linh-an paper bindery, and Tai's red-leather journals had been arriving faithfully, one a year, at the end of Kannaian. Quite by accident, in this particular year the red journal arrived almost two weeks early – as though Antian had urged a special delivery for the special occasion. Tai had shed a few fond tears of remembrance when the new red book was delivered to her, and the first thing she wrote in it, jumping the last blank pages of the previous year's book, was a delicate poem, full of the shape and colour of the dawns which Antian had loved to greet on a small balcony in the Summer Palace. Tai had copied it out, when it was finished, on a fresh scroll of paper and sent the copy to Liudan, partly because of the interest that Liudan continued to take in Tai's poetry, partly in response to Liudan's own wedding gift of the poetry book. She heard nothing back, at least not immediately, but she had no time to think about it as the last few days before the wedding swept by.

Only Tammary, watching all these preparations, hung back.

'What on earth can *I* give her?' she asked Yuet. 'I'll be the only one there without a gift.'

'It is not required,' Yuet said. 'At least, it doesn't have to be something material. A gift of a simple white lotus flower is a blessing on the marriage, for example.'

Tammary thought on it, and held her peace.

The day of the wedding, in the last week of Kannaian, was full of liquid sunshine and fierce heat. Nhia and Qiaan, helping Tai get ready, were both complaining vocally on Tai's behalf as they layered her with the traditional wedding garb. The thin inner shift of silk so fragile that it was practically see-through was lovely and cool against Tai's skin, but it was followed by the inner robe made from Liudan's heavy scarlet silk and overlaid again with an outer gown, stiff with embroidery, and a wide-sleeved coat with sleeves that hung to well below her wrists. Her hair was coiled up into a crown on top of her head, and the heavy head-dress, with its double layer of red and gold silk veils which completely hid her face, was fixed onto this with thick pearl-ended hairpins the length of Tai's forearm.

'Nobody should marry in summer,' Qiaan said. 'I declare, she'll be dead of heat exhaustion before they put the rings on her thumbs!'

'Ow,' said Tai mildly as a hairpin went astray and grazed her scalp.

'Sorry,' said Nhia, the culprit. 'One more . . . there. That should hold it. Shake your head – no, not *that* hard – it'll do. Where are you going?'

'I want to see if people . . .'

'Come back here, you goose, you aren't supposed to let them see you until you are ready to come out!'

'But . . .'

'He hasn't got here yet,' Qiaan said, laughing. 'I think there's an elderly gentleman who might be an uncle of his, though. Yuet and Tammary are here, too, and so are the Temple people. We're just waiting for the groom.'

'My mother?' Tai said anxiously.

'Yuet is with her. She's awake,' Nhia said. 'I think that would be them now. Ah, but he looks good today, too, does your groom!'

'So are we ready?'

'The Empress,' Nhia reminded Qiaan gently.

'Ah,' Qiaan said, 'of course.'

'While we're waiting,' Nhia said, 'I have a duty to attend to. Keep her in here, Qiaan, and for the love of Cahan don't let her be seen before her time!'

Qiaan nodded, grinning, and Nhia slipped out of the room and hurried through the main chamber, smiling and nodding at the assembled guests, on her way into the outer courtyard and the gates where the banners announcing the wedding had been hung.

There was a delegation from the Beggars' Guild waiting there, as was the tradition, for their wedding alms. Nhia pulled out a small silk purse full of silver coins and, folding her hands around it, gave a slight bow to the group.

'In celebration of the wedding,' she said formally, 'the bride and groom give you these alms.'

'Thank you,' one of the men said, returning the bow and accepting the purse. He signalled and another man stepped forward with a paper sign on which, in ragged *hacha-ashu* writing, it was stated that the household was having a celebration and that the Guild, in return for their largesse, wished them every blessing. They all murmured their thanks to Nhia and bowed to her, backing away; she smiled and bowed in turn. She would do everything right, Tai's wedding would be wonderful in every way, she would honour every tradition in order to ensure her little *jin-shei-bao*'s perfect happiness. The man with the sign had finished attaching it to the front door of the house, and had turned away, and Nhia suddenly realized she knew him – he was the blind man whom she had once seen standing in the beggar king's house.

'I know you by your voice. You are the Young Teacher,' the blind beggar said softly. 'It is well; Brother Number One has a message he wished conveyed to you.'

Nhia looked around instinctively for danger. 'Message? What message?'

'He instructed me to tell you that the storm is nearly upon us,' the blind man said. 'That you will know when to come for answers. He will be waiting for you.'

He bowed, and was gone.

'Wait,' Nhia said helplessly. 'Wait . . .'

But they were gone, only the sign on the door showing that they had ever been there. Nhia cast a glance up and down the street, but there was nothing further to see, and after a while, trying not to show how disturbed the message had made her feel, she returned to the bride's room.

'Are we still waiting?'

'No, but . . . I think she might on her way,' Qiaan said. 'Xaforn just came in.'

Xaforn had crossed the room and exchanged a few soft words with the waiting priests, and then came over to the door of the inner chamber and knocked. Nhia edged the door open.

'Tai, she's sorry, but she can't make it,' Xaforn said. 'She sent you her best wishes, though, and she says that you and Kito are commanded to wait on her in the Palace tomorrow so she can offer you congratulations in person. She . . .'

But the priest was speaking. 'The Empress Liudan, who was to have been a guest, sends regrets. All other guests are here. We will begin.' He cleared his throat. 'Bring out the bride.'

Tai, who was wearing shoes raised on precarious ceremonial wooden platforms, emerged from the outer room at that command, supported on either side by Nhia and Qiaan. She walked slowly, carefully, balancing with each step, her head demurely bowed. They took her first to So-Xan so that she could make a deep bow to him as his daughter-in-law-to-be, and then on to Kito's uncle and elderly aunt to offer them honour as well. At the same time Kito was being conducted on his own tour of the room, over to Rimshi's bed where he bowed deeply to the ailing woman. Rimshi actually managed to raise a hand in blessing; Nhia, nudging Tai gently, made sure she saw it. Tai squeezed Nhia's fingers in gratitude.

And then she was in front of the Temple priest. Kito was already standing there, a crimson silk tunic fitting tightly over his broad shoulders, his feet in the red boots of the bridegroom.

'In the name of Cahan and the Lord of Heaven, we are here to witness two people joining their lives into one. Let Kito and Tai journey together now and seek the paths of enlightenment. May the Three Pure Ones bless them as they enter into a covenant with the blessing of Cahan; may the light of the Way shine upon their spirit, and may the Lord of Heaven always hold them in the palm of his hand.' He paused, and Nhia produced the box which held the rings that had been Liudan's gift. The priest opened the box and took out one set of rings.

'Kito.'

'I will always be with you,' Kito said, slipping the thumb rings onto Tai's small hands.

Tai held on to him for a moment, and then cupped her hands together for the priest to lay the other set of rings down.

'Tai.'

'I will . . . always be with you,' Tai whispered, her voice breaking very slightly, placing the rings on Kito's thumbs.

'Where once there was a man called Kito and a woman named Tai, there now stands a new being – both man and woman, she who is now Kito-Tai, he who is now Tai-Kito. In the light of Cahan, in the name of the Lord of Heaven, you are wed.'

Kito reached over and drew aside the heavy veils; there were tiny jewelled hooks on the head-dress provided for this moment, but Kito's hand was shaking so hard that he could not seem to attach the veil to its mooring and Nhia had to reach over and help anchor the wayward silk. She and Qiaan were standing next to Tai on either side, still ready to help her move if she should want to; Xaforn had come up to stand beside Qiaan, and they were grinning broadly at each other and then at Tai, taking turns; Yuet had hurried over to give the bride, teetering unsteadily on her stilt shoes, a careful hug, mindful of the need to keep her upright by main force; even Tammary had drifted over and stood on one side, a little self-conscious, nodding at Tai with a smile on her face.

There were the absent ones – Antian, the first one, who was gone; Khailin, who was still missing; and Liudan, the glittering one, swallowed by the corridors of power.

But they were all here, in their way, if only in Tai's thoughts or deep in her heart where she still kept the love she had borne Antian. The *jin-shei* circle that was hers. The world was a safer, less frightening place all of a sudden, with her new husband beside her and her *jin-shei* sisters around her.

Tai started to turn to tell them all so, and her shoes tangled, caught, and pitched her forward into what would have been a less than dignified heap at Kito's feet – had half a dozen hands not shot out at once to hold her. Nhia and Qiaan at her elbows, Xaforn at her back, Yuet stepping forward to right her if she overbalanced any further, even Tammary's hand out to help support her. And Kito's arm around her waist.

'We tried to put together a small feast that would still be fit for an Empress *and* for a bride on her wedding day,' Yuet said. 'Come and break the bridal bread, Kito-Tai.'

# Eight

'I'm home!' Kito called out as he slipped out of his street shoes at his threshold and padded into his house. 'Where are you? I have news!'

'Hush!' Tai's quiet voice drifted out from the porch room, the one where the late summer sunshine pooled most generously in the afternoons. 'I just managed to get Xanshi to go to sleep. Don't wake her.'

Kito poked his head around the circular arch that was the doorway into the porch room. Tai sat on a wicker chair, a small embroidery hoop in her lap, one foot curled up under her and the other gently rocking the cradle in which a small child slept. Smiling at the picture, Kito walked quietly up and bent to kiss his wife, who reached out a graceful hand to the nape of his neck to fold his head down towards her.

'It's hard to believe,' Kito said, smiling, 'that it's been over a year, already.'

'It's been for ever,' Tai whispered. 'It's always been this way. Don't wake the baby. What's the news? And what's that you've got there?'

Kito handed her a ricepaper scroll. 'You have another one out. You're getting famous.'

'Which one?' Tai said eagerly, unrolling the paper. Her rocking rhythm faltered a little and the baby stirred.

'I'll rock her,' Kito said. 'Look all you want.'

'Which one is it?' Tai asked, unrolling the *hacha-ashu* scroll.

'As it happens, it's the one about Xanshi,' Kito said, rocking his child's cradle tenderly.

'Liudan sure picks some strange ones,' Tai said, scanning the neat calligraphic script she could not understand. 'I would have thought that particular one would be way too personal for general interest.'

'She obviously didn't think so, and I think that you will find that others agree. This is the kind of thing that men will buy to give to their wives after their children are born. I think it will sell well. But why do you still let her choose all the poems to get published? Shouldn't you have some say?'

'She was the one who started it,' Tai said. 'That poem I wrote when the wedding journal arrived from Antian, the one I copied out and sent to Liudan, that was the first one she had published. After that, I just pass them on and she has them copied out into *hacha-ashu* and published – without that, nobody could read them except the women.'

'I could transcribe them for you,' Kito said, sounding faintly rebellious.

'I am not supposed to teach you *jin-ashu*,' Tai said reprovingly. 'It's the women's tongue. We've been through this before, Kito.'

'Doesn't seem fair that women can have both the languages and men just the one,' Kito muttered.

'Most women only have the one, my stubborn darling – I cannot read or write *hacha-ashu*, or we would not be having this conversation,' said Tai. 'Oh, now look what you've done.'

The baby gurgled in the crib, exquisitely carved and lovingly made by Kito's own hand while Tai had been expecting their daughter, and both parents now bent over the child. She was knuckling her eyes, but she didn't seem bad tempered or weepy, and even beamed at her father, showing toothless gums.

'That's it,' Tai said. 'Your turn to play with her. I need to go and make a record of this.'

Kito hoisted his daughter into his arms, and she squealed happily. 'Mama will be back very soon,' he said, his hands under the baby's armpits as he balanced her chubby feet on his knees and bounced her up and down. 'Mama going in to be a writer now.'

Tai took the image with her as she slipped out of the room, a smile of pure gratitude on her face. Xanshi had been born more than three weeks before her time, in the same month that both Tai's mother and Kito's father had died. Rimshi had simply fallen asleep at last and never woke; but So-Xan's end came suddenly and unexpectedly, and quite ironically – he clutched at his heart in the midst of carving a memorial sculpture for the one-year anniversary of a Princess Consort's death, and all Kito could do was catch him as he fell from his workbench. Xanshi's premature birth had been precipitated, perhaps, by Tai's grief, and Yuet had had a battle on her hands to make sure both mother and child survived it without any lasting consequences. But it had taken Kito a long time to get over his daughter's fragility and tiny form. Mere weeks ago this robust bouncing would have been unthinkable. Kito would have been too afraid that he would break the child.

A corner of their bedroom had been set up as a writing desk for Tai, with all the implements of her trade laid neatly out on it – a blotter, a selection of quills and brushes, a small portable leather inkwell and several quartz ones lined up along the top edge of the desk. An inlaid wooden box with a shallow drawer, with a knob in the shape of a dragon's head, housed her current journal; others, those of past years, were stored in a shelf above the desk where a number of scrolls tied up with coloured ribbons were also stowed in tidy pigeonholes – her poetry, which Liudan had seen to getting published. The name of Kito-Tai, with which she signed her poems, was starting to get recognition, and there was even some money starting to come in.

Tai, subsiding onto her backless desk chair with the newest scroll still in her hand, stared at a beautifully calligraphed copy of her first published poem which Kito had hung on the wall of their bedroom – it was *hacha-ashu* script, and she could not read it, but she knew the delicate lines of it by heart. The poem had been so many things to her – a remembrance of Antian, a trembling anticipation of her wedding day that was to come, a gratitude for the presence in her life of the people who had loved her. She had sent it to Liudan in the busy, sometimes chaotic, days just before her wedding, and had then forgotten it as she plunged into the fears and the expectations of the day on which she was to marry Kito. It had not been on her mind at the time of her wedding, but somehow it always recalled that day to Tai's mind, and today, with her first wedding anniversary only a week or so behind her, was no exception.

Tai and Kito had been taken from the room in which they had made their vows into the banquet hall to break the bridal bread, as was traditional, and had poured each other their first cup of green tea into the special wedding cups. Then they had been escorted into the back room, where the bridal bed had been prepared, and sat perched on the high, rose-petal-strewn bedstead, side by side, for endless hours while friends and relatives popped in and out with ribald comments and bearing offerings of cups of wine, nut cakes, fried chicken, rice, almond marzipan sculptures of legendary beasts and dragons whose heads the newlyweds were supposed to bite off to the endless delight of some of the smaller children, and other sundry delicacies.

It was there that Tammary had come to deliver her wedding present – she had taken Yuet's words to heart and had offered Kito and Tai nothing solid or substantial.

'I was wondering whether I could do this,' she said, 'but Liudan did not come and in her presence I don't know if I would have.' Kito stole a puzzled glance at Tai; he was still trying to figure out some of his new wife's *jin-shei* connections, but she caught his eyes and shook her head minutely: *Later*. 'But she is not here,' Tammary said, 'and I want to dance for you. The way my people dance at weddings, in remembrance of all the joys of all the weddings that have gone before, and in promise of the ones to come.'

Her voice had taken on the Traveller cadences of someone telling a tale to commit to the clan memory, and Tai realized that Tammary was offering a gift that was no less than herself. She reached for Kito's hand.

'Thank you,' she said. Just that. But Tammary's eyes kindled at the wealth of understanding in Tai's voice, and she ducked her head, suddenly overcome with a rush of affection.

'There is no music,' Tammary said apologetically, 'there wasn't much I could do about that. There should be drums and *guitarras*.'

'I have heard the music of your people,' Kito said.

'So have I,' said Tai, squeezing his fingers in grateful understanding. 'We will hear your music in our hearts.'

Tammary had worn the colourful wide skirts and the gathered white blouse of her people; now she kicked off the slippers she wore and walked to the middle of the room on graceful bare feet, narrow and aristocratic, one ankle flashing a glimmer of gold chains as she moved. She brought her feet into position and raised her hands above her head, letting her head fall back, closing her eyes, listening for the music – like she had so often done before, while dancing on her own in the ruins of the Summer Palace in the mountains. It ran through her blood, like a slow fire, and she swayed into motion, her feet beating a tattoo on the floor, her fiery hair swinging, her hands bent at the wrists at angles of delicate grace. There was a sense of giving in her dance, and a sense of freedom, but also of belonging, of two halves coming together to make a whole. She danced a world of bright happiness, made all the more poignant by a fierce and unconcealed longing for it that permeated her every movement, and that Tai, who knew her, knew she had never really known. But she was drawing on all that she had and all that she had heard and seen, in order to give Tai the seed of perfect happiness.

Yuet, who had been alerted by one of the children and had come to discreetly watch from the doorway, had been transfixed by the dance for quite other reasons. When she had told Tai later, much later, that she had observed the whole thing, Tai had spoken of the sense of sacrifice that she had got from Tammary, a sort of offering of her own potential happiness on the altar of Tai's own. But Yuet had shaken her head.

'All I could think of,' she had said, 'watching her dance that way, was that this must have been the dance her mother once danced for an Emperor. She was a celestial spirit in that moment. There would not have been a man who could have resisted her.'

'Kito did,' Tai had said, laughing.

'Oh, quiet,' Yuet had retorted. 'Don't sound so smug. You did, after all, have an advantage – you had just been married.'

Indeed, Kito had proved that although he had been deeply appreciative of Tammary's dance, it had been his new wife who had been on his mind. When the guests had all finally said their farewells and the door closed behind the last of them, it was Kito who had taken the pins from her hair and taken down the piled mass of it from the elaborate coiffure that Nhia and Qiaan had spent an hour laboriously putting together, and Kito who peeled away the layers of ceremonial clothes with which Tai's body had been shrouded.

'You are so beautiful,' he had said to her when she stood before him clad only in that last whisper-thin silk shift, her dark hair falling around her shoulders like a silk cloak. 'Just like I always knew you would be.'

'So are you,' she said, running her hands against the smooth bare skin of his chest with a motion at once shy and fiercely possessive, and he had laughed out loud then, for sheer joy, and had lifted her onto the bridal bed and laid her amongst all the rose petals and removed the last fragile silk shield that stood between them – and had whispered against her skin that she was his love, his joy, the star of his heaven, while he kissed the valley between her small breasts and the pulse that beat wildly in the hollow of her throat. He had caught her small gasps with his kisses as she arched her hips against him. There had been only the two of them in that small world that night; whatever Yuet had said, whatever Yuet had seen, Tammary's gift had been no more than perhaps a deeper understanding of the emotions that bound them together. It had been that night that Tai had taken on the identity of the poet that she would become; everyone she knew, even Kito himself, continued calling her Tai in everyday interactions, but she had changed into Kito-Tai, the one-that-was-two, in Kito's arms on the first night of her married life.

When, late the next afternoon, the newlywed pair had presented themselves to Liudan as they had been commanded to do, Liudan had offered them her congratulations, and her regrets that she had not been able to make the nuptials, and also one final gift.

A ricepaper scroll, on which a poem was inscribed.

'I received that yesterday, and would have brought it to the wedding if I had been able to come,' Liudan said, 'but I didn't want to give it to someone else to hand it to you.'

'What is it?' Tai said blankly. 'I cannot read this, it's *hacha-ashu*.'

'Into which,' Liudan interrupted, 'I once promised you that your poetry would be transcribed. This goes out in the market today.'

Tai gasped, her cheeks turning a bright scarlet. Kito offered the Empress a low bow.

'May I?' he murmured.

Liudan gave him the scroll. 'Read it for us,' she ordered, a command to the only person in the room who could in fact read what was written on the paper. Kito accepted the scroll with another bow, and obeyed; he was not a practised reader, and his voice lacked the proper intonation for reading poetry out loud, but Liudan smiled, nodding, when he was done.

'It will do, as the beginning. It will do very well,' she said.

'How is it signed, Liudan?' Tai murmured.

'With your name, of course,' Liudan said, frowning. 'What do you mean?'

'"Tai",' Kito said, glancing at the scroll. 'It's signed "Tai", and with the date – the Third Year of the Dragon Empress.'

Tai kept her eyes downcast. 'If it isn't too late, may I make a change?'

'This is the first copy, and it is being copied as we speak,' Liudan said. 'But I will make the change, if you wish. What do you want done?'

'Sign it "Kito-Tai",' Tai whispered. 'It was that name that inspired this.'

Liudan smiled. 'It is done.'

*It is done.*


'What are you doing in here?' Kito said from the doorway to the bedroom, bouncing Xanshi in his arms. 'I thought you were going to make a notation of that in your journal and I was waiting for you out there. I said I had news.'

Tai turned to him, startled.

'I thought you meant this,' she said, lifting the scroll she still held in her hand.

'That's hardly news,' he said, teasing gently. 'You're a famous poet; another published poem is not something you get excited about any more.' He ducked as she aimed a smack at him with the coiled scroll.

'Very well,' she said, laying the poem down on her desk and reaching for her daughter. 'What is it?'

'It's all over the Temple,' Kito said, handing the child over and subsiding on the edge of the bed. 'Tai, Lihui has disappeared. He hasn't been seen for some time, but everyone assumed that he had retired to some deep meditation state or something like that – these Sages, they do that sort of thing. But last night, apparently, the other eight Sages went to Liudan and told her that he was gone, and that he had been gone for nearly three weeks, and that they knew nothing about his whereabouts.'

Tai clutched hard at the child she held, so hard that Xanshi let out a protesting whimper. 'Nhia,' Tai whispered. 'I must go to Nhia right now.'

# Nine

They had all immediately rushed to Nhia, all of the *jin-shei* circle – even Liudan, who had brought the news to Nhia herself almost as soon as she learned of the matter. Xaforn was already there, hovering in the room at Nhia's side like a shadow, watchful and alert; Yuet and her own shadow, Tammary, had arrived not long after and were closely followed by Qiaan, who spiced up the already wild rumours with the tales circulating in the streets, and finally Tai herself.

'Stay out of sight today,' Liudan told Nhia. 'He's known that his every move was being watched for some time now. I just want to make sure that this isn't some deliberate stalking trick.'

'So do you finally believe that Lihui is bad news?' Tai said.

'Sweet child,' Liudan snapped, annoyed, 'I knew he was bad news a long time ago.'

'You said that if anyone other than Nhia or Yuet told you he practised sorcery, you wouldn't believe it,' Tai said.

'That is indeed what I said. But thinking Lihui is bad news and believing he is a black sorcerer are two rather different things.'

'Do you think he's dead?' Nhia asked, the memory of her encounter with Lihui standing out in her white face like a scar.

'There is no way of knowing that,' Yuet said.

'But if he is, and if Khailin is still locked away in his fortress, then she is dead too,' Nhia whispered. 'As much as I hated him, as long as he was alive and around there was still a chance that she . . .'

'Maybe, if he's gone, she stands a better chance,' Yuet said thoughtfully. 'Without him in her way.'

'But the house was him,' Nhia said. 'That's what Khailin told me, the last time I saw her. And if he *is* dead, then the house . . .'

'There is no need to torture yourself with that now,' said Liudan practically. 'In all the time that I've had Lihui watched, with every barb I aimed at him concerning Khailin, there has been nothing. Nothing. There is no way to trace anything now that Lihui, our only link, is gone too.'

'The Sages really don't know anything about it?' Yuet said, a trace of scepticism in her voice.

'They looked afraid when they came to see me,' Liudan said slowly, 'and I don't remember ever seeing the Imperial Sages afraid before. They've always had all the answers.'

*Answers.*

Nhia had pondered the mysterious message sent to her by Brother Number One of the Beggars' Guild at Tai's wedding, a year ago now, for some time after it had been delivered – but she had not thought about it for a while. Now, suddenly, with one word, Liudan had brought it all back to her. *The storm is nearly upon us. You will know when to come for answers. Brother Number One will be waiting for you.*

'Stay put,' Liudan said again, as though Nhia's half-formed instinct to go out and seek the beggar king had jumped from her mind into the Empress's own. 'I'll leave a double Guard detail outside your door, just in case.'

'They don't carry the talisman,' Tai said. 'You could leave an entire army out there and they would not see Lihui walk by.'

'They would see anyone he might send,' Liudan said. 'Can one of you stay with Nhia for a while? I need to borrow Xaforn.'

'I can leave my talisman here, for whoever is with her,' Xaforn said, offering up the necklace she wore, twin to Nhia's own. 'It will serve better here; it is not me Lihui will be after, and I don't need the protection – but whoever wears it will know him if he comes. That way you can't be caught by surprise.'

'What makes you think he'd go for Nhia again anyway?'

Tammary asked suddenly. 'Here, in the middle of the city? In the midst of so many people?'

'You don't know everything,' Yuet said quickly, turning to hush her.

But Liudan was staring at her. 'So why would he just vanish?'

'He is a Sage, is he not?' Tammary said, holding Liudan's eye. 'Where I come from we have our shamans too. We never pretend to understand how they think or what they will do next.'

'Our "shamans" cultivate purity of mind and spirit, disciplined in the Way,' Nhia said. 'It is usually possible to follow a logical path. If you know what their goals are.'

'Well, yes, but you have no idea what this Lihui's real goals are,' Tammary said. 'They may have nothing further to do with you at all.'

'Amri,' said Yuet, using Tammary's child-name, 'hush up. Now's not the time.'

Liudan turned away with a snap. 'I'll return later,' she said. 'Xaforn, with me, please. Nhia . . .' Liudan whipped a sharp glance over at Tammary, standing with her arms crossed, dark eyes glinting under the fox-coloured hair she had never consented to have dressed in Court fashion. 'Nhia, stay safe.'

Yuet glared at Tammary but said nothing further. She and the Traveller girl stayed for almost an hour and then Yuet excused herself and left to deal with her healer responsibilities, taking Tammary with her.

Qiaan left soon after, promising to keep an ear out for the rumours on the streets. She was proving to be startlingly well connected, having channelled her organizational abilities into a number of groups working at the most basic levels of support for the less affluent of the city. She had organized charity kitchens for the poor, established trade schools where children were taught saleable skills like woodworking or needlework, had a hand in evicting the inevitable swindlers and cheats who siphoned hard-earned coppers off honest but often gullible citizens. She had even had dealings with the Beggars' Guild at some point – something that Nhia knew, but remembered only after Qiaan had left, and shook her head in frustration at the missed opportunity of perhaps asking her what she might know about the cryptic words of the beggar at the wedding.

Tai stayed until Xaforn returned, some four hours later, tight-lipped about her recent activities, and received back the talisman she had left with Tai as she had departed from Nhia's quarters.

'No further news,' she said. 'Go home, Tai. Your family probably thinks you did a Lihui and disappeared on them.'

Tai left, reluctantly.

After satisfying herself that Nhia's immediate surroundings were secure, Xaforn said, 'I know we're all probably over-reacting, and that you're probably ready to hit the next person who insists on not leaving your side, but I'll be right outside, should anything happen. And Liudan said she would send word if anything changed.'

Nhia shot her a grateful look. 'And Qiaan says you have no tact.'

Xaforn shrugged, but her mouth quirked. 'If you listen to Qiaan, I'm a young barbarian.'

'You are,' Nhia said affectionately. 'You're right, I'd appreciate a bit of time on my own. I have some work I could be catching up on, anyway.'

'You'll have plenty of time for that,' Xaforn said with a bluntness apparently geared to displaying the very lack of tact she had just accused Qiaan of exaggerating. 'I don't think that Liudan will let you go about your usual business until she is sure you're not going to be ambushed.'

Xaforn nodded and departed, and Nhia was left in sole possession of her room. The shutters had been tightly closed, as though they had been armour against some attack coming in through the window, but the air in the room now felt close and suffocating, and Nhia unbolted the heavy shutters and flung them wide to the late summer afternoon, stepping out onto the balcony and staring out over the tiled courtyards and steep rooftops of the city.

The light was low and golden, gilding the city with an almost mythical glow. Stone which had absorbed sunshine all day now radiated it out, a subtle warmth against the palms which Nhia rested on the white stone balustrade of the balcony. Against the sun, a distant black silhouette, the Tower of the Great Temple rose like a pointing finger into the sky. The Temple where she had first met him. Lihui. Her teacher. Her enemy.

What dark sorcery was he hatching now? Where *was* he?

'He is dead,' a soft female voice spoke, close behind Nhia.

It was so apt an answer to the next question that had hovered on the edge of Nhia's mind – *I wonder if he is alive or dead* – that she did not even think about it for a moment, simply taking it for granted, a response to an unspoken question.

And then the significance of those words, that voice, broke through the somnolence of the quiet summer day, and Nhia's fragile peace shattered like glass.

She whirled, clutching at the balustrade with both hands, her face chalk-white.

'Khailin?'

The figure standing in the doorway to the balcony bore very little resemblance, on the surface, to the Khailin whom Nhia had known. The once-raven hair was liberally streaked with silver, and there were lines etched into her face that had no place on a girl still half a year shy of her twenty-first birthday. But the carriage was the same, the proud, almost defiant tilt to her head, and the glittering dark eyes.

She wore an outer robe the colour of smoke, whose wide sleeves fell past her wrists and left only the fingers of her hands visible, and the silver-grey hair was confined in a simple silk net, bound by a filet with a single yellow stone on Khailin's forehead. Nhia stared at her for a long moment and then one of her hands flew to her throat, and the amulet there.

Seeing that, the apparition that was Khailin smiled.

'No, I am not him. I gave you a true talisman. If Lihui had taken this shape, of all shapes, you would have known it instantly.' She stretched out a hand. 'I am real. I am not an illusion.' And then, after a pause, as Nhia hesitantly stepped forward and reached out for that offered hand, 'I am free. And so are you, my *jin-shei-bao*. Free of him. You can stop shying at shadows, for he won't hurt you any more. Not ever again.'

As her fingers touched Khailin's, Nhia's knees gave way, and she collapsed in a small heap at Khailin's feet, her face suddenly streaked with tears. Khailin helped her up and supported her as she limped back into the room.

'How did you get here? How did you get past Xaforn? I was beginning to fear you were dead. When Liudan once asked him outright about where you were he said you were gone, Khailin, and I took that to mean . . . but they said to me, if you were dead he would have said you are dead. Perhaps "gone" merely meant safe and beyond his reach and waiting for a chance to . . . for the love of Cahan, Khailin, I'm babbling.'

'Sit,' Khailin said. 'Do you have any wine in here? I'm sorry, I didn't mean to make my entrance quite so dramatic, but I needed to make sure I saw you first – I need you to validate my identity. There is nobody out there except you who will swear to who I am.'

'Yes, there's wine on the cabinet,' Nhia said. 'I'm sorry, I should have offered.'

'It's for you,' Khailin said, crossing over to the indicated cabinet and pouring a glass of rice wine, 'before you faint on me. I need you to gather your wits back about you. I'll answer any questions you have later.'

Khailin was halfway back to the couch where she had deposited Nhia, carrying the brim-full wine glass, when the door opened and Xaforn stuck her head into the room.

'I thought I heard voices. Is everything –'

Khailin froze. Xaforn flung the door completely open with one hand, drawing her sword with the other, already poised to strike. Nhia surged to her feet.

'NO!'

The point of Xaforn's sword was already at Khailin's throat. Xaforn said nothing out loud, but her eyes were steady on Khailin's, and were eloquent: *Move, and you die. Until I am convinced otherwise.*

'It's Khailin,' Nhia whispered, subsiding back onto the couch. 'It's Khailin. She's back.'

'How did you get in here?' Xaforn snapped.

Khailin's eyebrows rose, and her eyes, just her eyes, moved to catch Nhia's gaze. Nhia understood. 'The ghost road?' she said.

'The same sorcery Lihui uses?' Xaforn said.

'Like fire, it is neither an enemy nor a friend, just a tool,' Khailin said.

'Drop the glass,' Xaforn said.

'It will make a real mess, and the wine was for Nhia,' Khailin said.

'She takes nothing from you until I am sure that it's safe. And the rest is not your concern. Drop the glass, and back away.'

'Xaforn, it's all right.'

'I apologize,' Xaforn said, as Khailin obeyed her instructions and backed away from the puddle of wine on the floor with her hands held out to her sides to show that they held no weapon, 'if I am discourteous. But my task here is to protect my lady, and all I know is that you entered this room without my leave or my sanction. Sit down.'

Khailin subsided into a chair, a small enigmatic smile playing on her face.

'Xaforn, that's enough. She saved my life once. She would hardly come back to kill me.'

'And if I had intended that,' Khailin said, looking up calmly along Xaforn's steady sword, 'it would have been done already. I am on your side, Xaforn. Lihui is the one who is dead by my hand.'

'You killed the sorcerer?' Xaforn said sceptically.

'We all die,' Khailin said. 'Even, when their time comes, the immortals.'

'Khailin, why did you ever . . . ? How did you . . . ? Where?' Nhia's voice petered out helplessly as she tangled herself into her own questions. Khailin's existence for the past three years was a complete mystery and there was just no place that Nhia could attach a question – no place that was not yet another mystery that needed a back-step to be explained.

Xaforn cut through the knot. 'Start at the beginning,' she said. Her sword had dropped down, pointing to the floor, but she was still standing a slice away from Khailin, watching her.

'The beginning?' Khailin whispered. 'You really want to hear of the journey of a fool? Ah, but I learned that it is true that you should be careful what you ask of the Gods, because you will receive it in abundance.'

'You were never a fool, Khailin,' Nhia said.

Khailin laughed, her laugh brittle, bitter. 'Oh, yes I was. A perfect, naïve, arrogant, petty little fool. And in a way, you pushed me into it.'

Xaforn's sword trembled, ever so slightly.

Nhia recoiled. '*I* did?' she whispered. 'What did I have to do with it?

'Do you remember the Court at which we had our quarrel?' Khailin said.

'Yes. I have often thought of it. For a long time I believed that you no longer wished to even speak to me – and I thought I had over-reacted to things, and I was sorry, but you were gone, and you were right about *jin-shei* – it does not disappear, whatever its origin or motivation. You were my *jin-shei-bao* then; you remain one today; you will always be one.'

Khailin's eyes sparkled briefly with what looked like tears. 'Yes,' she said softly, 'I was almost lost. I had seen how easily it all seemed to come to you, how you would turn and Lihui would be at your side . . . and I was to have been married to a mewling princeling soon, and whatever power I would have would be as Princess Consort – Zhu-Khailin, locked away in the women's quarters, enduring other wives and concubines beside me, bearing children who would inherit nothing but a title rooted in an obsolete Imperial bureaucracy. Then I saw one of the other Sages, and he had a woman on his arm, and they were all bowing to her – and she looked like such a perfect, pathetic, tradition-bound little doll. And it was so unfair, Nhia, so *unfair*, that I had the mind for it all and the passion and I had had to beg my father to give me the few meagre pieces of *hacha-ashu* that he did and then learn the rest painstakingly, through deciphering it out myself, to read the astronomers and the alchemists whose works I wanted to understand. That woman, that Sage's Lady, would make the perfect princeling's wife. And I . . .' She laughed again, mirthlessly. 'I would make a perfect Sage's wife, you see. And he would teach me the things I wished to know. And I would never be trammelled by the silken cords of useless tradition. And there he was, Nhia, and he was young, and he was unmarried. So I haunted the Temple for the next few days, waiting for him, because I knew he came there. And when I saw him, I went to him and humbly begged for a moment of his time.'

'Certainly,' Lihui said, when the raven-haired young woman threw herself on her knees at his feet asking if she could speak to him. 'You are, I think, the young lady from the Court of a few days ago? Khailin, I think? Well, Khailin,' he said, when she nodded at the name, 'how may I be of assistance to you?'

'Marry me,' Khailin said, her eyes still downcast, but her voice absolutely steady.

After a moment, Lihui laughed. 'Well, that is something I don't hear every day from beautiful young women,' he remarked conversationally. 'Walk with me, if you will, and as we walk you may tell me why you think that we should be wed.'

He had helped her rise to her feet as he spoke, and now tucked her arm under his own, laying her fingers on his forearm and covering them with his free hand.

At first she had been quiet, and then incoherent – but he paid her the compliment of listening to everything she said as though she was speaking pearls of wisdom instead of babbling, uttering every platitude she could think of. In the silence that broke between them when she finally wound down, Khailin was aware that Lihui was smiling slightly, that nothing she had said had been either convincing or reasonable. His question still hung before her, tantalizing: *Why do you think we should be wed?*

'Because,' she said at last, lifting her eyes to his, 'I want to know everything I can never know as the wife of a junior prince in the Imperial Palace. And I believe you can teach me.'

'You want to learn the Way?' Lihui said, raising an eyebrow. But his fingers had begun stroking hers, very gently, and Khailin suddenly felt queasy and breathless, as though she had walked onto unsteady ground.

'Yes,' she whispered, 'I do.'

'Very well,' Lihui said. 'Do you wish to have the ceremony right away?'

Khailin blinked. 'Did you just say . . . ?'

'We are here, in the Temple,' Lihui pointed out reasonably. 'As you yourself have said, you are technically betrothed to another. This would cause a great many complications if you were to pursue the traditional path, and it would end up costing a lot of people their reputations, including, probably, yourself. As a married woman, however, you may count on your husband to cut through some of the awkwardness. You expressed a wish to wed – I agree. You are here, I am here, we are both willing, the place is here, the time is now.' He cocked an eyebrow at her, demanding an answer, placing her in a position of standing behind her request or withdrawing it for ever more.

'All right,' she heard herself saying.

He nodded, and led her away into the inner Circles of the Temple. He had found a priest at liberty to perform the ceremony and the priest had been too cowed by the personage and the occasion to ask questions. A minion had been sent to purchase a set of thumb rings for Khailin in the First Circle – 'I may not wear any rings but my Sage's ring, my dear,' Lihui had explained affectionately, when Khailin's mute glance asked the question of why just one set of rings. The rings had been procured, the priest had said the words, and Khailin, still in a daze, found herself married, walking out of the Temple with her new rings circles of fire upon her thumbs. She had spared a thought for her family, for her friends, but she had been allowed to contact nobody – 'Let me deal with all that, my dear,' Lihui had said – and had been bundled instead into a sedan chair and taken at a fast trot in an unknown direction. To a place Lihui called 'home'.

To the house at the end of the ghost road, and the hell that waited there.

Khailin had, incredibly, fallen asleep in the sedan chair, and had been woozy and only half awake when she had been handed out of the chair and into her new home by a silent servant. She would find out very quickly that no servant in this house would speak to her. All were silent and empty-faced, as if they were not alive, as if they had had their souls drunk from them and left to wander the earth as abandoned bodies, corporeal ghosts. Khailin would discover later how close to the truth her initial impressions had been.

She had been left to herself for a long time; she explored the house, going from room to room, quickly discovering that there were many locked doors that would not open to her touch – too many locked doors, too many mysteries. The doors to the outside were locked too, when Khailin tried them. And she began to be afraid.

And then the day faded, and evening came, and she discovered that she had still not touched bottom – because it was then that Lihui, his dark hair loose over his shoulders, came to her room, and to her bed. He had never stopped smiling at her, but his eyes were hot, and his hands were not gentle. Khailin was Khailin, after all – she did not scream, or cry, or even fight him – she had married him, and this was the marriage bed she had made. But her initiation into that world of which she had once read erotic and romanticized accounts in her mother's secret *jin-ashu* letters had been hard, and fast, and brutal. Lihui had taken his bride with no gentleness, in the fullness of power, and gave her no softness or joy to cling to. When he was done he rose from her bed, donned the robe he had slipped out of in order to take possession of his property, and took up the taper he had brought in and laid aside on her bedside cabinet as he had climbed into bed.

'Your first lesson,' he said. 'Your work requires lead and mercury. You can dig both out of the ground, or you can extract them slowly and painfully from plants like oak, nettle, wolfberry or reed rushes. You will not try to leave this house.'

And then he was gone, taking the light with him, leaving Khailin alone and turned to stone in the darkness.


'That was how it was,' Khailin said to Nhia and Xaforn in the summer twilight of Nhia's room. 'He would come to me, he would plunge himself between my legs, he would get up, and before he left me he would offer me a sentence's worth of alchemical wisdom and lore. It was the bargain I had asked for – exactly and precisely the bargain I had asked for. He would teach me. On his terms. And otherwise, he owned me.'

'So how *did* you leave the house?' Xaforn asked, practical as always, although the account had not left her unmoved.

For answer, Khailin lifted her arms and allowed her wide sleeves to fall back down her arms. Nhia gasped; along the length of both Khailin's forearms were two puckered dragon-shaped brands.

'What did you do?' Nhia gasped.

'I was afraid of pain,' Khailin whispered. 'And until I conquered that, the house held me. But it took me until well after you had escaped, Nhia, to face this. What I did was take the black heart of that house into myself. It burned me whenever I touched it thinking of leaving it – on this day I laid my arms against the dragons on the front door, and kept them there while the house burned me, *burned* me . . .' She stopped, drawing a ragged breath. 'But afterwards, it hid me from him. He never knew where I was again. And by that stage I had found the keys to his locked doors, I had unravelled the spells, I had read his books and I knew his secrets. I knew what he did, to himself, to the people he took. He is ancient, Nhia, and he feeds on new souls – he has to,' she spat out, 'he has none of his own. That was how he was immortal – and he knew how to make the elixir that would let him live for ever.'

'But you said he was dead!' Xaforn gasped.

Khailin laughed. 'Oh yes. I watched the house burn around him.' She looked up, and her eyes were full of real tears now, and they spilled down her cheeks. 'I killed him. And in order to kill him, I became him. *I* am the alchemist now.'

'They were so young, my children. They were so young.
I still look on their first milk teeth in silk preserved,
in my treasure box. But now
their children cut their teeth as Ryu comes in its
autumnal glory.'

Qiu-Lin, Year 20 of the Cloud Emperor

# One

*My children sleep. My husband is in his workshop. It is a quiet summer night outside, and tomorrow I will have been married four years. The world should be a place full of contentment and rejoicing.*

Tai lifted the brush from the journal page and nibbled on the end of it. The lanterns in the courtyard cast a muted golden glow through the pleated wax paper painted with the signs for good health and prosperity, and moths fluttered uselessly against them, beating their wings against the shield that hid the true light from them. Tai watched them for a moment, and then dipped her brush into the inkwell and wrote again.

*There are moths outside, ready to die for a light they crave but which is denied to them, shielded from them, which they can never achieve and which would kill them if they ever did succeed. Sometimes, in the midst of all that I have been given, I watch the moths and see myself as one of them, see the moths in us all. Everybody has a light which they think they cannot live without. I think of my jin-shei sisters, and they all have one, every one of them – Qiaan wants justice, Nhia wants peace, Khailin wants to know why the stars shine and is ready to take them apart to find out, Xaforn wants honour in people who have none, Yuet wants a world as nice and tidy as her stillroom, Amri just wants to be loved, and Liudan . . . Liudan wants everything, and wants it now.*

*And what does the moth called Kito-Tai want tonight? What is my impossible light? I seem to have it all – everything that they all want. I am loved, like few women have been loved; I have the peace of my family. Unlike Khailin I don't need to pick apart a flower to learn what makes it bloom, and I am happy with that; unlike Yuet, and my children are glad of it, I do not need to have every bead and every brush and every slipper replaced in their own proper place, and I am happy with that. I have both honour and justice, they live in me and in the man whom I married. And I don't have Liudan's drive to prove anything to anyone at all. But it frightens me that I sit here at night and count my blessings as though they could be taken away any moment. The walls of this city that I was born in, the city which I know and love, rear around me, and sometimes they mean safety, and sometimes I look at them with Amri's eyes and see what she sees – a cage to keep me in. And yet I speculate on their wishes and their dreams, but Yuet once said to me that what they all actually want is precisely what I already have – the husband, the home, the family. But still they turn from it, all of them, and bat their wings against their own impossible dreams. I love them, I love them all, but I fear how they will fare in a time of testing, when I have everything to fall back on and all each of them has is a single focused driving desire which may not be enough to sustain them. Amri . . .*

A whimper from the children's room next door to her bedroom made Tai lift her head, listening. When it was repeated, a little more insistently, she laid down her brush and went to investigate what ailed her baby, her son Baio, three weeks shy of his first birthday. He was awake, kicking at his covers, his face scrunched up into what looked like the beginning of a wail; Tai gathered him up, coverlet and all, and whisked him out of the room before he could wake Xanshi, her three-year-old daughter, asleep in her own cot under the window.

'What is it, Baio-*ban*?' she whispered, rocking him on her lap. 'Is it too hot to sleep?'

The child squirmed sleepily, happier now that he was in his

mother's arms, and Tai sighed inwardly as she watched Baio's thumb migrate to his mouth, a relic of his early babyhood. She hummed a soft lullaby over her son's small curled body, his dark head nestling against her shoulder, his lashes black silk against his cheeks. He was soon asleep. Tai sat motionless with him in her lap for a long time, her hand almost unconsciously smoothing back his hair, and marvelled at his perfection, at his fragility, at the miracle of his existence. The future held some dark, inexplicable menace for her that night, and a deep unease fluttered inside of her, the thought that her son belonged to that future and that some day it would be beyond her power to take him in her arms and protect him against some horror as yet nameless and nebulous in her mind.

# Two

*The Sages always had all the answers.*

Liudan would probably have been astonished at how forcefully she had brought the Beggars' Guild and its cryptic leader back to the forefront of Nhia's mind with that single sentence, uttered when she had come to tell Nhia of Lihui's inexplicable disappearance from the Court. Nhia had determined then and there that she would go back and seek out the beggars. But events overtook her, and Khailin returned unlooked-for from the dark bearing the news of Lihui's death. Nhia, at first genuinely distracted from her original intentions, finally had to face the fact that she was shying away from carrying them out. Going back to the lair of the man whom she had begun to think of as the Beggar King, in capitals, would have meant returning to the beginning of a journey that now seemed ended. Khailin swore Lihui was dead, that he was gone; the whole dark episode was buried in Nhia's past now and it astonished her how badly she wanted it to stay there.

The Beggar King had implied he had 'answers' – something that could elucidate the future – but the future was not yet here, and Nhia's peace of mind in the present seemed to depend on burying the past.

'I am trading what might come for the favour of forgetting what was,' Nhia murmured to herself. 'That is not wisdom.'

She was stronger than this. She knew it. Her *jin-shei* sisters were all there for her, and all she needed to do – even if she felt as though she was faltering – was reach out, and the support would be there. But it had been a hard struggle to learn not to spend her life leaning on someone else, depending on someone else. That she had rebuilt her life, that she had succeeded in doing just that, was a fragile victory. Quite simply, Nhia didn't want to go back.

But then the restlessness and anxiety that had been stalking the city boiled over into action. Sudden fires began flaring up mysteriously in the city, apparently aimed at the places where the wealthy came to play, and the stations of the city police, and one or two homes with the word 'Hoarder' painted on the walls of the targeted house. Nobody had turned against the houses of the Gods yet, but there were *hacha-ashu* daubs on the whitewashed walls of the Great Temple, curses against the Gods who had turned against the people, the unfeeling and arrogant Gods who were withholding rain – who were sending wind and hail onto ripe crops just before harvest and smashing perfect peaches into the ground, flattening fields fat with golden grain.

'Who would do such a thing?' people asked one another in the city.

'Do not ask why the Gods have turned away – shouldn't you all be asking yourselves if you haven't turned away from the Gods?' the priests at the Temple asked those who came to the Circles with their offerings.

'Whom do we punish, and how can we prevent?' asked the Guard at the Palace.

The Imperial Sages went into retreat, to ponder the situation.

Questions. Questions swirled around Nhia.

The Imperial Guard was edgy and anxious. She learned that from Xaforn.

Qiaan told her that the people were burning the required incense and carefully avoiding mention of any other kind of burning – but that there was a lot of muttering behind closed doors, the frustration and discontent festering into something harder, more difficult to contain.

Liudan brooded, and stayed silent.

The beggar at the wedding had said to Nhia, *You will know when to come for answers*. It was time.

At an oddly subdued wedding of a merchant's daughter and an adminstrator at the Palace, Nhia followed one of the bride's aunts as she brought the customary purse to the waiting beggars at the gate and lingered behind as the aunt retreated back inside and the beggars gathered themselves together to leave after the traditional notice had been left on the door of the house.

She laid a hand on the sleeve of one of the beggars, a blind man, but not the one who had been present in the Beggar King's room when she had first set foot there.

'I have a message,' she murmured, 'for Brother Number One. Will you carry it for me?'

The others stopped, turning their heads sharply. 'And who sends such a message?' said one of the women carefully.

'Tell him the Young Teacher would see him. Tell him I need the answers he has promised.'

'I will pass the message on,' the blind man said after a moment.

But the message that came back to Nhia in response to this one was not what she had wanted to hear. It arrived in the hand of a dirty little girl whose lank hair was a rat's nest of greasy locks, cobwebs, matted dirt and Cahan alone knew what else – but whose glittering dark eyes were eloquent as she thrust a much folded and exceedingly grubby piece of paper into Nhia's hand just outside the Temple gates. On it, in crabby and obviously long-unpractised *jin-ashu* script, straggled a terse message.

*Now is not the time. He is ill. We will send word.*

The girl had disappeared by the time Nhia had looked up.

There had been no word for a long while, and the city's mood continued to darken as rumours came flying from all over the belea-guered countryside. Nhia had almost lost heart when another note was slipped into her hand by an old woman with a cane, who never even stopped to meet her eyes.

*Tonight. He will be waiting for you. The Street of the Nightwalkers.*

Nhia briefly considered taking someone like Xaforn with her, but the invitation didn't seem to include anyone other than herself, and it would be worse than useless if she failed, through the presence of a companion, to achieve her meeting with the Beggar King at all. So she wrapped a voluminous cloak around her and slipped its cowl forward to conceal her face, and waited at the corner of the Street of the Nightwalkers as twilight faded into darkness and the houses began to wake in the empty street.

A hand on her elbow startled her. She turned, and saw a couple of imps hovering beside her.

'Follow,' one of them said.

She fell in behind him as he turned and scurried away, and sensed his companion slip into place behind her. The leader snaked his way through a bewildering warren of alleys, corridors and passageways that led to the Beggar King's house; Nhia was soon quite lost. But the room into which she was finally ushered, as her escort melted away, was one she recognized – the same one where she had met him before.

The man who sat in his throne-like chair before the hearth looked frailer than the figure Nhia remembered, but he had lost none of his regal bearing for all that he was wrapped in a blanket and his face was pale and gaunt.

He sensed her staring, and said, 'Yes, I have been ill. It always leaves me damnably weak in the backwash. I've had these fits ever since . . . I've had them for years. It's best, when they take me, to retire to a quiet place and wait them out. They tell me you wish to see me. What brings you here at last?'

'The city is waiting for something,' Nhia said. 'You once told me that I would know when to come to you – well, I need those answers which you said you had. Liudan said the Sages had none.'

'The Sages?' he questioned, and there was an odd note in his voice.

'How much do you know of what's been happening?' Nhia asked. 'I know your network must be good, but I don't know if it reaches high enough to tell you of the things not yet spoken of on the streets. My old teacher, Lihui, the one whom you called sorcerer, disappeared without trace a while ago. The woman he had married, my *jin-shei-bao* Khailin, returned from the place where he had kept her imprisoned for years, and now tells us that Lihui is dead. For some reason the Sages are more afraid of this than anything else. They have not named a successor for the empty place, which is unusual enough to draw attention.'

'Dead?' murmured the Beggar King. 'It is odd that I did not sense that death.'

'Sense it? How could you do that?'

'When it comes to the sorcerer, I have means,' the Beggar King said. 'This Khailin, his wife . . . his pupil, you say? . . . I wish to speak with her, too. When you return to see me, bring her to me.'

'I have a dreadful feeling of something dark gathering,' Nhia said, 'and I don't know how to turn it. What of the city? What of the country? Have you a sense for any of those?'

'It will begin in betrayal,' the Beggar King said. 'It always does. If you remember that and watch for it, things may be prevented, or a hard burden which cannot be wholly avoided may be made lighter.'

'I don't understand.'

'You will,' he said. 'You will.'

They had talked then of the city, and of Liudan's Empire, somehow suddenly so fragile. When Nhia left, another escort detail took her back to half-familiar territory from which she could find her way home, and murmured, 'He said, in three days' time. Be at the same place as before. And bring the other with you.'

When Nhia had delivered this command, so thinly veiled as invitation, to Khailin, she was met with a look of complete bafflement.

'You want me to go *where*?' Khailin had said. 'Why?'

'He knows more than he will tell, and if anyone can understand him it's probably you,' Nhia said. 'I think he is a valuable ally. Help me, Khailin! I can't do this alone.'

'Does Liudan know you're hobnobbing with the king of the beggars?' Khailin said. 'I have a feeling she would not like it very much. It's out of her orbit, out of her control.'

'No, and don't you go telling her. Not until I can bring her something more solid than visions and cryptic remarks. That's why I need you.'

'I will come,' Khailin grumbled. 'But only you could drag me to a place like this, Nhia. You can take pride in that.'

The Beggar King's head had come up like a hunting dog's when Khailin had entered the room. Nhia could never read him, but there seemed to be a little of everything in this reaction – anticipation, surprise, recognition, a touch of fear.

'So you are the one who married him,' he murmured.

Khailin glanced at Nhia, her eyebrows raised.

The Beggar King made an imperious motion with his hand.

'Come,' he said, 'sit with me. And tell me of the death you claim to have given him.'

It was a voice of power, and Khailin felt it tug at her memories, unfolding them like a series of paintings on a scroll of silkpaper. It all seemed to have happened to her a lifetime ago, and at the same time it was fresh and clear as though it had happened yesterday.

Khailin and Lihui's house had come to an agreement. After she had willingly accepted its brand on her body, she had gained a power of command over the house reared by Lihui's spells and had made herself quite simply disappear. The house made her presence transparent, effectively removing her from Lihui's sight. All it had taken was an utterance of a rhyme she had known for years. Long ago, in children's games of hide-and-seek, Khailin had mouthed the same words that all her peers had done: *Before me day, behind me night, so I may hide in plain sight!* She had not realized, until her path had crossed Lihui's, just how old that verse was, and just how much power the ancient spell on which it had been based still carried when it had the force of real dark magic behind it. The house had understood the childhood rhyme in ways that Khailin had not believed possible, and had moved to make it true.

Khailin haunted Lihui's rooms. He was often aware of her as a presence which hovered at his elbow, but unless she willed it so, negating the spell, he could not see her. Sometimes she did that, letting him have just enough of a glimpse to ensure that he knew she was still there, but then she veiled herself again and he could not find her. The knowledge of her presence and his inadequacy in countering her actions had driven Lihui into towering rages, and Khailin had laughed as she watched him futilely screaming at the walls of his laboratory and his libraries.

And there were many libraries in that house, whole rooms devoted to different subjects. The rooms that had once been locked against her. But with the house as her ally it had not taken Khailin long to find her way to the treasures in those rooms. She pored over the books and scrolls Lihui had kept hidden away, learning all the things that she could ever have hoped to learn, steeping herself in knowledge, drowning in it. She made careful copies of some scrolls, and Lihui never knew it. She brewed her own elixirs on his apparatus, careful not to leave any strange residues behind for him to notice, and was elated at what she was able to achieve. There was nobody to share her successes with, of course, but she could live with the solitude – at least until she learned all that she could learn from this place.

She could have taken the ghost road out of there at any time after the house had ceased to be her prison. But running away would have meant admitting defeat – and Khailin was also bitterly aware of the fact that she had nowhere to run to. The house protected her, while she was within it. If she left, and Lihui ever tracked her down, she would be spelled into a stone statue for the eternity that was Cahan, or fed a potion that turned her limbs to glass. She had seen Lihui do those things, and worse, to people who crossed him, or to those unlucky enough to have been brought in for him to run his latest experiment on. Khailin had seen the cripples and the poor orphans of the streets and the old and abandoned being brought to the house for Lihui's needs – Linh-an's dregs, the ones who would not be missed, the people nobody valued or cared about.

Except their master – the Beggar King – the one who called them *my people*.

'I knew that I had to destroy the place, and him, before I could finally leave,' Khailin said to the Beggar King. 'There was no freedom for me otherwise. Even the law would say I belonged to him – I was his wife.'

'They could not prove that marriage,' Nhia said. 'When we looked into it at the Temple, there were no records. You could have just walked away.'

Khailin looked down at her hands. She had instinctively folded her fingers over her thumbs, from which she had long since removed the rings of her bondage. 'If I had walked away,' she said, 'there would have been records. He would have made sure they existed.'

'She is right,' the Beggar King said. 'But go on.'

'I came up behind him, when he was pouring acid into a flask,' Khailin said, 'and I poured a powerful antagonist into the flask when he was done . . . and when it bubbled and hissed, which it shouldn't have done, and he turned to look closer, I made sure the acid bubbled over. And while he nursed his burned hands, I threw the rest of it into his face. And his eyes.'

'You cannot use the ghost road without sight,' the Beggar King said softly. 'Of course.'

Khailin threw him a startled look. 'How do you . . . ?'

'I know enough,' he said. 'You blinded him. What happened then?'

'I told the house to fall,' Khailin whispered, 'and it folded down into the cellar that was his office. And I told it to burn. And I stood and watched the fire until there was only ashes, and all that was left of him underneath them. He is dead.'

'You did not see the body,' the Beggar King said.

'No, I did not see the body. But I saw the house collapse on him, and I saw it burn, and I knew that he was in there, too wounded for the ghost road,' Khailin said.

'Never be so certain of anything,' murmured the Beggar King. 'Give me your arm.'

'Why?' Khailin said, jerking back.

'Lacking sight in my eyes, I rely on what my fingers tell me,' the Beggar King said. 'Please. Indulge me.'

Khailin unwillingly extended one arm and the Beggar King ran his long fingers down the dragon-shaped scar on her forearm.

'Interesting, this,' the Beggar King said. 'If that house accepted you, it means that he taught you too well, better than he knew. What do you plan to do with the knowledge of the sorcerer, young enchantress?'

'Learn,' Khailin said simply. 'Keep learning. There is still so much that I do not understand.'

'Be careful,' he said. 'This is a serpent that you hold by the tail. Beware of its fangs. Beware of the poison.'

'You speak as though you have tasted that poison yourself.'

The Beggar King chuckled dryly. 'One way or another, we all have,' he said. 'Some of us are given a deeper draught than others – and some of us reject it, some learn from it, and some become it. I tell you again, take care. I give it a year, at most, before you might be called upon to make some hard choices. There are dark clouds on the outside, and smoke within; we are on the wings of the storm.'

'But that is what I first came to ask you about,' Nhia said. 'You once said that I would know when to come for answers. But all you give me are more questions I cannot answer!'

'You already have my counsel,' the Beggar King said. 'But when you need me most, when the first breath of the hot wind touches your face, I will be there. I promise you that.'

# *Three*

If she had hoped that coming to the city, that coming to know the other side of her birthright, would cure the empty places of her heart, Tammary found herself losing those illusions as the years slipped past.

She continued being Yuet's assistant and unofficial apprentice, and she was good at it – the oral traditions of her people allowed her quick mind to absorb, catalogue and annotate anything that she was told until she was a walking encyclopedia of herb lore and the healing arts. Perhaps being an acknowledged and focused trainee in the art of healing could have given her a sense of direction, but that was not what her real goals were, and Yuet, perhaps sensing this, had never suggested that their relationship be formalized in any way.

Tammary was aware that Yuet did feel a stab of guilt at not taking on a real apprentice, passing on her skills and knowledge to another generation in the manner that Szewan had trained *her* – she had said as much to Tammary once, after they had worked together on a difficult birth and managed to save both mother and child against all odds. Later that night, in Yuet's house, over a cup of rice wine, Yuet had been exhilarated and relaxed enough to succumb to a rare moment of complete trust, dropping the odd and constant wariness with which she still treated her mountain wild child.

'I don't feel I need an apprentice,' Yuet had said to Tammary. 'I mean, you're doing so well at it. I know what you know, I know I can trust it. Somehow I feel taking on a complete beginner at this point would drive me mad.'

'You're still young,' Tammary had said. 'There is plenty of time to train a successor. I am not your heir, Yuet, but I'm happy to be an assistant.'

'You're a problem,' Yuet had said to her, with a slow smile that the efforts of the day and the potent rice wine had painted on her mouth. 'Some day the Gods will come to me and tell me what I am supposed to do with you.'

In a way, that moment of unguarded honesty had catalysed something in Tammary that Yuet might have done better to leave alone.

She had been a 'problem' back in the Traveller village, too.

The world, it seemed, was full of perfect niches made to seamlessly fit those destined to fill them. Tammary's niche appeared not to exist. Oh, how the Gods must have laughed – the *chayan* ones and the Traveller ones, both, collaborating on a practical joke – when they had made her! Torn between the two cultures, Tammary was a peg made to fit two holes, but she had angles where one hole had curves, and curves where the other hole had angles, and she was uncomfortable and frustrated in both.

Tammary adapted, in the city, in the best way she knew how.

She had Court connections through her *jin-shei* circle, and she did not avoid the Palace, although Liudan was never told of Tammary's true identity. But the stiffness of Court etiquette irritated Tammary, used as she had been to the Traveller freedom of dress and speech all her life. The ordinary folk of Linh-an, the people whom Yuet had once accused her of studying as though they were exotic animals in a menagerie, were a different story, and Tammary, after a year of being on the outer fringes of everything in Linh-an, began to explore the boundaries of taking part in the vivid life of the streets.

She had started spending more and more time at the city's tea-houses, and she explored the whole range, no matter what kind they were. She had first discovered them as a step down from the Court audiences, following the aristocracy into the plush tea-houses of the inner city, where the benches had satin cushions with golden tassels on them and some of the older men, retired officials or minor princes in their high-collared Court robes of silk brocade, would sit quietly puffing away at a bubbling pipe of viscid poppy brew, inducing mostly a gentle drifting stupor with a handful of vivid dreams interspersed in between. Tammary was recognized there – she was Yuet's shadow, and someone with her colouring stood out like a fire-salamander amongst a clutch of brown geckos. People spoke to her with courtesy and with charm; she would have deeply philosophical conversations with the half-stoned old men and with ambitious junior members of the aristocracy or senior civil servants. But it was an environment only marginally less stuffy than the Palace, and Tammary quickly cast her net wider.

The community tea-houses on the corners of major streets, out in the teeming residential streets of non-aristocratic Linh-an, were a totally different scene. When Tammary first started dropping in on these, she inevitably began by being a source of gossip, and the cause of much giggling behind fans and concealing hands of the neighbourhood women. They quickly discovered that she was privy to a lot of stories they could have no hope of knowing anything about other than through her. When a few of the matriarchs started actively cultivating her, Tammary found herself a popular addition to the tea-house circles. But then she discovered the third kind of tea-house, one which the habitués of the other two considered only one step above the bawdy houses on streets like Nhia's Street of the Nightwalkers – the ones that were known as 'water tea-houses' because dispensing tea was not really the reason for their existence. And she passed from being a source of gossip about the upper crust to being a fount of gossip as and of herself.

In a way, the water tea-houses finally released something that Tammary had kept in strict check ever since she had first arrived in Linh-an. There was a licence there, inhibitions and stodginess were left at the door, and Tammary learned to dance to the music of the city. She had a sensuous nature and the lithe body of a young woman in the prime of her life. When the first men sat up and took notice, she saw the interest in their eyes, and taking her first lover had not been too great a step beyond that. He had not lasted long; Tammary, not finding what she sought, quickly turned away and sought another pair of interested eyes. Then another.

In the arms of these men she was not, however briefly, a 'problem'. She shared her loneliness; she helped, maybe, someone else's, however briefly.


'She's gathering herself a reputation,' Qiaan, with her own burgeoning street informant network, had warned Nhia. 'There's talk of a party for her twenty-fourth birthday in the spring, and by all accounts it isn't going to be an innocent party. Can't Yuet do something?'

'I'll talk to her,' Nhia said. 'I'll talk to both of them.'

But she hadn't found an opportunity to speak to Tammary. And it wasn't until she saw Tammary with her own eyes, walking away with a hot-eyed young man in the Street of the Nightwalkers, that Nhia had realized just how far things had gone.

For a moment Nhia had wondered if she had been projecting – she had just come from another meeting with the Beggar King, and the Street of the Nightwalkers, in its bright and glowing night guise, held some potent memories for her. She could not seem to forget the night that she had found herself there, straight off the ghost road, fresh from Lihui's dark palace – it was burned into her memory. But no – it had been a different season, and she had been a different person then, and in any event there had been no mistaking that spill of fox-coloured hair tumbling loose down the back of a girl emerging from one of the houses in the street. The red-haired girl had looked Nhia's way, and the shock of recognition in those familiar dark eyes was too clear to be imagined, even across the expanse of darkening street. Tammary had dropped her gaze and looked away, tugging at her escort's arm until he turned and walked with her away from Nhia, towards the far end of the street.

Nhia had told Yuet of Qiaan's original warnings, but Yuet had been sceptical about the whole thing in the early stages, although she had avoided the direct question of just how many women there could be in Linh-an, with Tammary's particular shade of hair colour, to whom the gossip could be attached. When Nhia came to Yuet to tell her what she had now seen with her own eyes, Yuet had just stared at her.

'It just can't be,' she said stubbornly. 'I know she does go out to the tea-houses and spends hours there, even the ones with a reputation, but not *that* kind of establishment. Not the Street. Tammary is a people-watcher, has been ever since she came here. Where else but in the tea-houses . . . ? But no, she can't be out at all hours like that, I could tell – there would be bags under her eyes from lack of sleep, a slump in her bearing. She works hard, you know, she doesn't sleep the days away. She'd have collapsed by now.'

'Yuet,' Nhia said, 'Qiaan says that they have a name for her in some of the tea-houses you swear she has never set foot in – they call her the Dancer.'

'Oh, for the love of Cahan.' Yuet buried her face in her hands. 'I don't believe it. I just can't! There is so much at stake for her.'

'I can show you,' Nhia said. 'Qiaan even told me which tea-houses she likes best.'

'All right,' Yuet said sharply. 'I don't need to go crawling after her to see. I am not her keeper – but I wish there was something I could do.'

'Talk to her. Better still, get Tai to talk to her. For some reason she listens to Tai more than to any of us.'

But it was already too late to keep the secret which Tammary had brought with her to the city. For it had not been any of the three who knew the truth about Tammary who got a chance to talk to her first.

Qiaan had a dozen or so personal 'projects', people she had taken an interest in over and above the requirements of several organizations which she now headed. One of these was a desperately poor family which had been blessed with two sets of twins in quick succession in the last three years, and who now had six children under five in the house. One of the latest set of twins had been born with a bad disability, a cleft lip which left the child unable to suckle naturally and almost unable to feed at all, and Qiaan had taken it upon herself to try and help in any way she could, knowing that the child was probably not going to last the winter. Her visits to this home always left her unaccountably furious at the world in general. *How could such a thing be allowed to happen? Why should an innocent child be made to suffer like that?* The aides she had assembled around her knew better than to speak to her at all after one of these visits, until she had had a chance to control her anger or at the very least find some other hapless subject on which to vent it.

It was pure coincidence that, on her way home from this particular house, Qiaan passed by one of the 'water tea-houses' of worse repute than most, and looked up to find Tammary leaning on the doorjamb, wrapped in a warm woollen cloak dyed a rich dark green to set off the colour of her hair, laughing up at a young man who had an arm tucked inside the cloak and was obviously doing things in there that were pleasing to her.

For all her other virtues, Qiaan had a broad prudish streak in her. The warnings she had channelled towards Nhia and Yuet about Tammary were partly based on a feeling of *jin-shei* obligation to protect a sister of the circle – and partly on a growing personal distaste for Tammary's lifestyle. And now here it was, being flaunted in her face, and she was already full of that rage which made her aides scatter before her like chickens before a fox. Qiaan's eyes narrowed and she marched across the street towards the couple, who were still oblivious to her presence. It was cold out in the street, and their breath came out in white gasping clouds as they laughed together; for some reason this only served to enrage Qiaan even further. Tammary was not only flouting Qiaan's own personal code of behaviour, she was going out of her way to do it in public, where she could flaunt it, where she could be sure that other people would see it, could hear the liquid laughter of seduction, could catch a scent of sex.

'You're a scandal, you know that?' Qiaan hissed as she came up on the two lovers.

The young man whipped his head around, his mouth a round O of surprise, snatching his arm out from underneath Tammary's cloak. Tammary herself, her eyes clouded by wine, merely pulled the cloak tighter about her and smiled languidly.

'It's a bit late for you to be out, isn't it?' she asked. 'You're usually in bed planning good deeds by now.'

'I'm taking *you* to bed,' Qiaan snapped.

Tammary laughed. 'I prefer men,' she said.

But the man in question had seen the daggers in Qiaan's eyes and the seduction scene out in the sharp winter air had been quite ruined for him. He muttered something to Tammary about 'tomorrow', and fled. The two women faced each other across the shallow steps leading up to the tea-house, a murmur of voices and laughter and faint music coming from inside.

'You're a fanatic, Qiaan,' Tammary said. 'Go home. Get some sleep.'

'You're coming with me,' Qiaan said. 'I told Yuet about this, but she has obviously said nothing to you. Don't you know that the whole city is talking about you? Don't you care? They are all just waiting their turn, those men. They don't want you, they just want a chance at you – and you're giving it away. You're *jin-shei* to the Empress herself, for the love of Cahan. This isn't the way that someone like you should behave.'

'You think the Empress sleeps alone?' Tammary said, her smile broadening a little. 'There's a plant which you can grow quite happily in a pretty pot in a corner of your room, Qiaan, and it even blooms with these dainty red flowers, and it's a nice thing to look at in a room and nobody knows any different – but chew a leaf from that plant once a week, and you don't have to worry about pregnancy any more. Liudan has four of them in her room. I gave them to her. And I'm sure that before that she had put pressure on Yuet to provide something else – or, if not Yuet, then some other healer willing to curry favour with the Empress by letting her taste the pleasure without the pain. We are not celibates by nature, we are made to be part of something that is not solitude.'

'At least she doesn't flaunt it. If she has her flings, she is discreet about them,' Qiaan said sharply after a pause, outflanked. 'She is an Emperor's daughter, and she knows how to behave like one.'

'You think being an Emperor's daughter makes you immune to the need to be loved?' Tammary asked, after a beat of silence. 'Trust me, it doesn't. I ought to know.'

She held Qiaan's eyes for a moment, and then whirled, somewhat unsteadily, and vanished into the shadows of the street.

Qiaan had been too furious to register the remark at the time. While she stood where Tammary had left her, fighting to regain control of her ragged breathing and unclench her fists, she was also oblivious of the young man who had been dallying with Tammary on the steps – who had not gone too far, who had certainly been in earshot, and who, as soon as Qiaan had turned her back on the tea-house door and stamped away homewards, had slipped back into the crowded tea-house to share his own interpretation of Tammary's parting remark with an avid crowd.

When Yuet had finally confronted Tammary with her secret life, only a few days after that incident, it was already far too late. There were four different versions of the story in the bazaars, to be sure, but it was out, in the open. Tammary's mother changed with every telling, but her father remained the same – the Ivory Emperor. Liudan's father.

And, through him, Tammary was suddenly a single step away from a claim to the Empire.

'Do you have any idea what this could lead to?' Yuet said vehemently. 'You may have endangered all of us. You may have endangered yourself. Liudan could . . .'

'Liudan won't do anything to *you*,' Tammary said. 'The whole mess predates you by a long way; it's hardly your fault.'

337

'It's partly my doing that you're here in the city!' Yuet snapped.

'No, it's mine,' Tai said. 'It was I who told you to come with us.'

'Tai, I would have come anyway. Sooner or later.' Tammary's voice had softened.

'But you wouldn't have been under our protection then,' Tai said.

'I am not under your protection now,' Tammary said.

'Of course you are,' Yuet snapped. 'You are *jin-shei* to both of us. We have a responsibility. We have a duty to each other. I had hoped that, knowing who you were . . .'

'Yuet, I have never known who I was,' Tammary said. 'I have been searching for myself all my life. When I dance I think I touch it, a little – there is a memory there. As though my mother speaks to me through that. And men like it, and I like it that men like it – and for a while, at least, I think I can see a glimpse of who I might be in a lover's eyes. But not for long. Never for long. It all comes full circle again, and the man is the wrong man, and I dance again to ask my questions, and a new man comes with pretty shining new answers in his hand.'

'I had hoped you could learn to be happy,' Tai said.

'Like you?' Tammary questioned gently. 'Who would marry me, Tai? Even not knowing who I really am, let alone if the secret was told?'

'The secret has already been told,' Yuet said grimly.

'No it hasn't!' said Tammary impatiently. 'It's marketplace rumour and hearsay. Are you telling me that there has never been any gossip about the bastard children of kings in a city like Linh-an before? I don't believe that for a minute!'

'If there was,' Tai said, 'it was never tied to a specific and identifiable individual. I am afraid you do rather stand out, Amri. There could be no doubt about the identity of this particular bastard child.'

'I have a really bad feeling about this,' Yuet said.

'Why? Does Liudan think I would go after her empire?' Tammary laughed. 'I watched her, these last few years. She's painted herself into a corner. I wouldn't be in her shoes for anything. She is trapped, so trapped, perhaps the most trapped of us all.'

Tai had a sudden flashback to Antian's poise and acceptance of her position and its responsibilities. Antian would have been a quiet force, acceding to tradition, marrying the best candidate she could find in order to make a gift of a good Emperor to her people, and then doing what all great Empresses did – rule the Empire at his side with advice, with empathy, with compassion, dealing with the big issues and leaving her mate and partner to cope with the day-to-day realities of government, as Syai's traditions demanded. Liudan had chosen to take it all, and while she had always stood tall under the burden, Tai had not failed to notice that sometimes the smile on the young Empress's face was no more than a grimace of pain as the load grew too heavy for a moment and she staggered under the weight of it. But Antian had been born of the Empress, and sired by the anointed Emperor – twice royal. Liudan was Liudan – her position handed to her by fate, a concubine's child, her position a fluke, an unexpected twist of fate.

She was a good ruler, but she was an autocrat. She could not help it. She ruled with a fist of iron because otherwise she could not rule at all.

The fact that someone else with a claim to her position might reject it out of hand, like Tammary was now doing, would be almost incomprehensible to her. Liudan had wanted to be somebody, to be important, all of her life – she had ached for that as a little girl, and schemed and fought for it when she grew old enough to fight. Now that she had it in her hand she would do almost anything to keep it. Perhaps they had been wrong, perhaps they had all been wrong, in not going to Liudan with their knowledge in the first place.

Tai bit her lip. She had been the one to advise that, in a way. Had it been her mistake?

'We should go to Liudan,' Tai said unexpectedly. 'We have left it late, perhaps too late, but it is better that she hears of this from us before she hears it from someone else.' She glanced up at Yuet. 'I know you wanted things to be different, Yuet. But . . .'

'She may never even hear about it,' Tammary said, dismissing it.

'You underestimate her abilities,' Tai said. 'She will know soon, if she does not know already. We'd better go and confess everything. I'll do the talking, Yuet. It was for Antian's sake, after all, that I went back to the mountains. She said to take care of her sisters and I'll try to do that, as long as I can, as well as I can.'

'How did all this get started anyway?' Yuet said desperately.

'Even with you carrying on like the worst sort of hoyden, it had still been under wraps – it had been under wraps for so long. How did it get out?'

'I'm afraid,' said Tammary after a moment, looking down, 'that it was probably my fault.'

'I know,' snapped Yuet. 'If you had been content to keep your head down and lead a quiet life, none of this would have happened.'

'Possibly,' Tammary said, 'but not in the way you think. You see, I think I may have told Qiaan myself.' She looked up briefly, met Yuet's shocked gaze, and looked down again. 'She came out of nowhere and flew at me like a mother hen, clucking at me to go home, to behave, to remember who I was, so I said . . . I'd had a few cups of rice wine that night, and she irritated me . . . and I said . . .'

'What did you tell her, in the name of Cahan?'

'She brought up Liudan, and Liudan's virtues,' said Tammary mutinously, 'so I told her a few home truths about Liudan's own life. And then she said that an Emperor's daughter at least ought to keep it discreet, or something, and I just lost it. I told her that I knew all about how an Emperor's daughter would feel.'

'I don't believe Qiaan would spread a story on something that thin!' Tai gasped.

'We were right outside a tea-house at the time,' Tammary said. 'It is entirely possible that Qiaan said nothing at all. Anyone could have heard me say it.'

'It's still thin,' Yuet said. 'We can . . .'

'It's too late for that, Yuet,' Tai said. 'As weak as the initial assumption was, somebody made it, and the story is out – and it's the true one. Szewan can't have been the only one in all of Linh-an to know about Jokhara and what happened in the Emperor's quarters that night. There will be other people who will piece it together, and may remember.'

Yuet sat down rather heavily in the nearest chair. 'Not Qiaan,' she said. 'Oh, please, not Qiaan. I wasn't ready for this one.'

'What are you talking about?' Tai said.

'You were born, Tammary. The circumstances were tragic, but you were wanted – by at least one of your parents – for whatever reason.'

'By which one?' Tammary said bitterly. 'My mother was forced . . .'

'Ah, but not before she initially came to the Emperor of her own free will,' Yuet said. 'You are forgetting your own story. When it became clear that you were on the way, it was made very clear to your mother that it would be best if you were never born – but she wanted you, by then. She wanted you to live. Qiaan . . .'

'Yuet, you're scaring me,' Tai said.

'Qiaan was *made*, and made because of you, Tammary. The entire reason for Qiaan's existence is that she was a tool.'

'Whose tool? A tool for what?'

'Qiaan was Szewan's revenge, Tammary. For *you*. If your story comes out, it will all come out. And it could destroy both of you.' She looked up, met Tammary's puzzled gaze. 'You and Liudan share a father, Amri. Whatever your mother's motives may have been, in the end she was taken against her will and you were got upon her against her will. And she was of Szewan's clan. Before you were even born Szewan had thrown Liudan's mother, Cai, to the wolves – I have it all in her journal. They took Liudan away when she was born, as they always do. Cai was beautiful, and lonely, and abandoned by the Emperor after she had delivered her daughter. And so Szewan nurtured a hopeless love of a captain of the Imperial Guard for a royal lady far out of his reach, and made sure that Cai knew that she was loved, and . . . oh, for the love of Cahan, Tammary, you are always talking about how we all need to be loved, and she needed it then. So they already had the motivation, and Szewan made sure they had the opportunity. Have you never looked at Qiaan and seen Liudan in her face?'

Tai's eyes were filled with tears. 'Qiaan always said her mother never liked her, her father's *wife* never liked her. She has no idea, does she, Yuet?'

'Her aunt tried to tell her,' Yuet said. 'Kept throwing it in her face – that she was taken in, that Rochanaa was good to her for having taken her in, for having forgiven her father in the first place, so she has an inkling that she may not have been her mother's natural child, yes. But not even the aunt told her the rest, if she even knew anything over and above the damning fact that Qiaan was the offspring of an adulterous affair who had been brought back for the lawful wife to raise.'

'What happened to Cai?' Tammary asked carefully.

'She died, or was killed,' Yuet said. 'I am not sure myself which.'

'You think *Szewan* . . . ?' gasped Tai.

341

There was a soft knock on the door, which had stood a little ajar, and then Yuet's servant eased it open with her hip, a tray in her hands.

'I brought some tea, mistress.'

'Thank you,' said Yuet distractedly. 'Set it down over there.' And then, as an afterthought, as the woman turned to leave, 'And shut that door.'

'Yes, mistress,' the servant murmured with downcast eyes, and departed. The door shut with a snick behind her.

Yuet stared at the tea for a long moment before rousing again.

'No, I don't believe it. I don't believe that. Szewan would not kill.'

'Jokhara was a cousin, remember, and the Emperor had raped one of her own – and you know how the clans are about their people, Tammary.'

'Your Szewan hadn't been a Traveller for a lot of years,' Tammary said. 'Who knows why . . . ?'

'I know,' Yuet said. 'I read it all. She wrote of it in her journal, the entire affair, all except Cai's death, which she left vague, perhaps on purpose. But the rest is all there. And it's out now, and Liudan has two half-sisters out there who could be used to stake a claim on her throne. And what's worse . . .'

'Could it get worse?' Tai said, with a hollow laugh.

'Everyone was told that Cai had borne a dead child,' Yuet said. 'But the child was born alive, and the child was a girl, and Szewan made sure that the Emperor of Syai knew the whole truth. That there was a child out there, born of a royal concubine who had already borne one of the princesses in line to inherit, whom Szewan could put on the throne.'

'But she was not the *Emperor*'s child,' Tai said. 'She was . . .'

'Qiaan was born in the women's quarters of the Imperial Palace. Delivered by a healer who could swear, if need be, to a parentage more convenient for her own ends. A child promptly spirited away to be held against future need. A daughter who could end a dynasty of emperors.' Yuet bit her lip. 'Qiaan was made for vengeance, Tammary. She may not know that yet, but she will. She will. You may renounce the throne, but if someone tells Qiaan the truth of it, she may choose otherwise. I have to wonder how much of their mother is in those two, if there was something in Cai that made them so damnably alike. Qiaan, in her own way, is every bit as

342

arrogant and driven as Liudan ever was. All that it might take for those things to spill out of her could be a call to Empire.'

Yuet's servant, who had been Szewan's servant before her, had not overheard this last exchange – but she had overheard enough of the rest, and had sufficient background knowledge and suspicions of her own, to put everything together in her mind. She was trustworthy and loyal, and she had always kept the secrets of the healer's house – but she was no more than human, after all. All she ever said to the gossips in the marketplace where she went to shop for her vegetables, to give her credit, was that Tammary was not the only one with a touch of the Empire on her. But she had implied enough – that the other one was also someone close to her mistress.

Less than a full week had passed since the first hints about Tammary's parentage hit Linh-an's streets before other rumours had taken wing, too. But these were far more specific, and far more precise – and far more verifiable. Qiaan's own aunt was more than happy, when she was approached by what she believed to be a gossipy acquaintance in the compound, to confirm every damning thing the woman had asked about, finally finding an excuse and an occasion to spill all the accumulated bile that had built up over the years. She remained blissfully unaware of the glittering triumph in the other woman's dark eyes as she walked away.


# Four


In the years since her return to Linh-an, Khailin had struggled, no less than Nhia, to rebuild a life that had been touched by Lihui. At least Nhia had had the advantage that her encounter with the Ninth Sage had not been made public. Everyone, however, knew Khailin as Lihui's wife – thanks to Liudan's pointed way of referring to the now missing Sage by his married name on every possible occasion – and now Khailin herself was the focus of all the whispers, all the gossip, all the uncertainty. Lihui had always had an air of mystery to him. It had only been intensified by his enigmatic marriage, and the wife who had been effectively absent from Lihui's side for years – and now the wife was back in the public eye, and the Sage himself was gone.

It all provided juicy material for the Court gossips, and it was aggravated by the fact that Khailin would not simply stay quietly in the shadows. She had paid for the knowledge she had craved and had found in Lihui's libraries – she had paid with nearly three years of her life and her happiness, and she was not going to let the hard-won prize be wasted. Within a year of her return to Linh-an she had established herself as a scholar and a gifted alchemist. Within two years she had compounded her notoriety by writing a treatise on her work – carefully, in *jin-ashu*, still concealing her real proficiency in the unwomanly *hacha-ashu* script. The treatise, quickly transcribed into *hacha-ashu*, had been distributed anonymously, and used by a number of prominent scholars before it was discovered who the real author was. It had been of particular interest because of the elegance with which it posed some of the basic issues of the alchemist's craft, and then described the process of seeking the answers, leaving out a single fundamental step. This was done in such a way that it was only discovered by the adepts if they tried duplicating the work, inevitably discovering that there was a last bridge which they had to cross themselves. The treatise implied that the author had done so, but wasn't telling any more than that.

It was pure *yang-cha*, but wrapped in the potent language and mystery of the *zhao-cha*, and it was Nhia who had probably been to blame for that, Nhia, who had torn herself out of the Temple and its teachings but had never quite managed to tear the Temple out of herself.

'The world did not just materialize, it was formed, and there were distinct stages of its formation,' Khailin had said during one of their discourses. These were often spirited discussions, with Khailin frequently demanding evidence for Nhia's more philosophical ideas and Nhia wanting to know how Khailin could hope to know where every crumb of the rich black soil on the great plains of Syai had come from. 'And the beginning of all things was merely the end of the creation process, that is all.'

'A time before the beginning, when everything was still part of the cloud of the Way, when it was all energy and no matter,' Nhia had said. 'Sounds more like my sphere than yours, Khailin. Are you saying I was right all along?'

'Only because you insist on obfuscating it and making it so mysterious that nobody will ever understand what you're talking about,' Khailin had retorted. 'It's simple enough. When the world began, when life began, when that which would go on to produce *us* began – that is the beginning. Before that, there was a time before the beginning – and time before the time before the beginning – and then there was just existence. And before that, there was non-existence. And before that, a time before non-existence.'

'And if you add a time before the time before non-existence, you have the seven *kalas*,' said Nhia, who had been ticking things off on her fingers as Khailin had talked.

'The Seven Ages? How do you make that out?'

'Well, you'd have to work backwards, I would think,' said Nhia, her eyes sparkling. She loved this kind of metaphysical analysis. 'If you count the time before the time before non-existence as Atu – the Afterdeath, the Beforebirth, the spirit existence, then you could walk it backwards through your stages. Give them to me again?'

'The beginning.'

'No, in reverse,' said Nhia thoughtfully.

'The time before the time before non-existence, Atu. The one before that was the time before non-existence.'

'That would be Liu, the birth,' Nhia said.

'Non-existence.'

'Lan,' said Nhia. 'Growing milk teeth.'

'Existence.'

'Xat. Coming of age.'

'A time before the beginning.'

'No, you had another one in there before that – the time *before* the time before the beginning. That would be Qai, getting ready to raise a family, collecting the seeds that become children. The next stage, the time before the beginning, would be Ryu, where the children of those children would take you – your *world* – a step forward to the next *kala*, towards an enlightenment. What came next?'

'The beginning,' said Khailin thoughtfully.

'Pau,' said Nhia.

'How do you figure that? Pau is the age of old age and of death! And this is a world just born!'

'Ah, yes, but it has aged into its birth from a time before the time of non-existence,' Nhia said. 'From here it enters Atu again – and then gets reborn into the new set of ages. Ours. That was the world; after that, it is the people of the world. There is always death in a birth; that is what immortality is all about – something always *continues*. That's part of what constitutes immortality.'

'You should be one of the Sages instead of Liudan's Chancellor,' Khailin said,

Nhia shook her head. 'No, *you* should. And if the now Eight Sages don't produce a new number Nine soon, I might mention that to Liudan.'

'I don't want to be the Ninth Sage,' Khailin said, recoiling. 'That would really make me into what Lihui was.'


Khailin's reputation in her craft had been made. Her laboratory, established with Liudan's help, had been set up to her satisfaction, she had her work and she had the freedom to pursue the knowledge on any subject that interested her. Her life was set on a solid foundation – or so she believed. But she had not heeded the words that had been addressed to her by the Beggar King at their first meeting. *Never be so certain of anything*.

When the shock that rocked her world came, it came unlooked-for, out of the dark.

Despite Khailin's insistence that she didn't celebrate birthdays any more, Nhia had insisted that she at least come for dinner to celebrate what she called the latest non-birthday event. She had been implacable, and Khailin, under amused protest, had dutifully presented herself at Nhia's chambers at the Palace on the eve of her twenty-fourth birthday. Only two of the usual pack of scribes, secretaries and record keepers who usually sat in the Chancellor's busy office were still there – an ambitious youngster who was apparently eager to get himself noticed, and the eldest of the secretaries, who had been in Zibo's office before Nhia had inherited him, still working diligently at his desk with a pair of wire-rimmed eyeglasses perched on the bridge of his nose.

'Go home,' Nhia said, coming out to the office from the inner chambers just as Khailin entered from the outside. 'The day's work is done. There is nothing that cannot wait until morning.'

'Yes, Nhia-*lama*.' The senior scribe laid down his brush and, slipping off his glasses, rubbed the reddened bridge of his nose with his free hand. 'I have to admit, my eyes have been giving me trouble today.'

'Go home,' Nhia repeated. The old man began tidying up his desk for the night; the younger scribe, scowling, bent furiously back over the script he was working on. 'Both of you,' Nhia said. 'That's an order.'

'I'll only be a minute, Nhia-*lama*, I need to . . .'

'Do you need me to give you a hand with that?' the older scribe said courteously.

The younger scribe's instinctive reaction was to hunch protectively over his page. He caught himself, sat up again, but dislodged the top page of the material he was copying as he did so. He threw himself forward to pick it up, but was not quick enough; it was the older scribe, at whose feet it had landed, who straightened with the paper in his possession, squinting at it, and then giving it a longer look. 'What is it that you are doing, Huo?'

Khailin, only a few steps behind the old man, cast an instinctive glance over his shoulder, and then she, too, stared.

'Give me that,' she said.

The old scribe hesitated. The younger one, Huo, snatched at the copied pages that were still lying before him, scattering the contents of his desk as he launched himself from it. He ripped the mysterious page from the hand of the older man as he ran past him on his way out of the office.

The paper was torn raggedly from the top down, leaving only a couple of fingers' width of the page in the old man's hand. He looked at Nhia for guidance, but Khailin had her hand out for the remnants of the page, as imperious as Liudan at her best, and when Nhia nodded the scribe passed the fragment of paper over.

'What is it?' Nhia asked, at the sight of Khailin's white face. 'You look like you've seen a ghost.'

'I have,' Khailin whispered, the torn paper trembling in her fingers. 'This is Lihui's hand.'

The Beggar King's voice rang like a bell in Nhia's mind.

*I have not sensed that death.*

*The storm is upon you.*

'What does it say?' Nhia said quietly, ignoring the old scribe's

347

startled look that she should ask Khailin, a woman, about the *hacha-ashu* page that she held. But Khailin had already been scanning it, and shook her head.

'I can't tell,' she said, 'except that it mentions the Western passes, and something about the riders out of Magalipt. It says "ready to be unleashed". It says "spring".' She looked up. 'It says "war", Nhia, although the word does not appear on what is left on this page. He is alive, and he is coming back.'

Nhia looked at the old scribe. 'Say nothing of this to anyone yet,' she said. 'Do you understand?'

'Yes, Nhia-*lama*,' murmured the scribe, his eyes wide with fear.

'Khailin, come on.'

'Where are we going?'

'To Liudan.'


The Empress had retired to her chambers for the night, but these were her *jin-shei* sisters, even if one of them had not been her Chancellor and the other what she had taken to referring to as her Court Alchemist. Khailin and Nhia were admitted without question. Nhia gave Liudan a summary of the events which had just transpired in the office, and Liudan heard her out without interrupting, tapping at her lower lip with her finger as was her custom when thinking.

'Are you sure you recognized his hand? Absolutely certain?' Liudan asked Khailin.

'Liudan, you said once before that you had no real evidence against him, and it turned out that everything we had told you about him was true,' Nhia said.

'Now you sound like Tai, all young and militant,' Liudan said. 'You say it said that this would happen in spring?'

'I think so. I cannot be sure. I only have a fragment,' Khailin said.

'Some day you can tell me why you kept from me that you could read *hacha-ashu*,' Liudan said pointedly. 'That's a valuable skill.'

'And useless if widely known,' Khailin said.

'Also true. Spring. Magalipt. What if I had the army at the passes to meet them?'

'They would come through somewhere else if you moved any great force now,' Nhia said. 'They would know that you know that they are coming, and they would not blindly march into a waiting army.'

'Whereas if they think I don't have that information – and if your young spy went straight back to his master and reported that he had destroyed the evidence, they might – they could leave their plans unchanged, you mean?' Liudan said. 'But I *do* know now, and I can't just sit in Linh-an and do nothing.'

'Send a small "inspection" force of the garrison at Sei-lin,' Khailin suggested.

'No, right now even that would be a signal,' Liudan said thoughtfully.

'One group west to Sei-lin and another east to Ail-anh?' Khailin said. 'Both border cities, and you wouldn't be singling either one of them out.'

'It's winter,' Nhia said.

'So?'

'You ought to know – it's pure alchemy,' Nhia said. 'There is a season for everything. If you move troops out of season, anywhere, you're sending a signal.'

'You don't have to send the whole army!' Khailin protested.

'If your news is true, yes, I do,' Liudan said. 'But Nhia is right, it's premature. I need to know more. But as it happens . . .' She smiled, her eyes glittering. 'As it happens, I do have an army I can send, and nobody will ever know it.'

'What do you mean?' Nhia asked.

'Xaforn,' Liudan said.

'*The wings of the storm*, he called it,' Nhia whispered, her eyes suddenly wide. '*Black clouds outside, smoke within*: I wonder which storm he really meant.'

Liudan's eyebrow had arched with a quizzical haughtiness, and Nhia flushed.

'I have been back to see the Beggar King,' she said.

'The Beggar King? You mean the leader of the Beggars' Guild? What has he got to do with any of this?'

'A lot, it would seem. He told me once that I would know when to go to him for answers. And now that I think back on what he said to me when I went to him, it seems to me that he knew that this was coming.'

'The incursion at the border?'

'Nothing that specific. I meant all of it. The things that have been happening in the city, in the countryside. There have been a handful of years now with the land itself seeming to turn against those that worked it. And someone who wanted to use that could have easily built the discontent and the fear into something focused and dangerous.'

'You mean Lihui?'

'All he needs right now is someone to stand at the head of the movement. Liudan . . . you may need Xaforn here, before this is all over. One of these things is the real danger, the other is a smoke-screen to distract you. But I don't know which – and if the real thrust is aimed at you, it will be here, in the city. If Lihui is orchestrating this . . .'

'The Beggar King told you all that?' Liudan said a little acidly, with a touch of emphasis on the 'King'. 'He seems to be better informed than I am. Just how much have you told *him*?' She whirled away, without waiting for an answer, to stand at the window with her back to them. 'I've been hearing reports of the things that have been going on in the city,' she said. 'It might have helped me understand it if you had shared your concerns with me instead of that underworld goblin with delusions of grandeur.'

'He has wisdom,' Khailin said, 'and there is a knowledge there, yes. They go deeper than one would expect, I think. He is an ally, Liudan, not a rival – don't dismiss his advice lightly.'

Liudan's hand came down in a sharp chopping movement.

'He cannot tell me if there are armies marching towards my borders,' Liudan said decisively. 'I will send Xaforn as soon as may be – her and one other, perhaps. All she needs to do right now is scout it out, and I trust *her* judgement.' There was a slight edge to that remark, as though Liudan was calling the judgement of the other two into question. 'She doesn't need to stay there very long, and if your friend is right she will be back in plenty of time to help me deal with any problems in the city.'

'She doesn't believe it is Lihui,' Khailin said to Nhia when they left Liudan's chambers. 'But I know, I *know* . . . Perhaps he was right, your Beggar King, when he said that he never sensed that death. Perhaps I believed that he was dead because I wanted to believe it so badly.'

'But where has he been all this time, then?' Nhia said. Her hand,

350

without conscious volition, had gone to clutch at the amulet that she still wore around her neck. She had tried putting it away after Khailin had returned with her news that Lihui was gone, but she had felt utterly exposed and vulnerable without it. Hating the fact that she had come to depend on that amulet as the ultimate talisman against evil, Nhia had put it on again. Without it, she found herself staring at every strange face and wondering whether Lihui hid behind it. And now he was out there again. Khailin had been utterly certain about that, and Nhia believed her instincts.

'The acid was real,' Khailin said. 'He may not have died in that fire, but he did not escape from it whole. You need eyes to use the ghost road – it may have been just that, a simple waiting in the mists until he could enslave a pair of eyes to serve as his own. I maimed his sight, not his powers – it seems that it was beyond me to do that. I have no idea what he is still capable of doing, if he has found a way to return.'

The ties of *jin-shei* were strong, but the rhythms of life were not dependent on those alone. Tai's *jin-shei* circle, driven by their diverging priorities, had splintered into different orbits during the same crucial few days.

This was the moment that Tammary's identity had exploded onto the Linh-an streets – and then, following on from this and far more insidiously, Qiaan's own. This was the moment that Yuet and Tai were agonizing about how to tell Liudan of Tammary's secret, which had been kept from her for so long. Those three had no idea about the gathering war, or about Lihui's return.

Both Khailin and Nhia had good reason to be wary of Lihui's reappearance, and they were wrapped up in what that would mean for them. They did not yet know that Tammary's true identity had been revealed.

Liudan herself was preoccupied with a number of things – the restlessness and fear in the countryside over year after year of bad harvests, the unrest in the city, the possible invasion of her kingdom in the spring, Nhia's unexpected relationship with the Beggar King and the city's underbelly.

Xaforn, who might have been the first to raise an alarm, had been dispatched to the border town of Sei-lin, with detailed instructions.

By the time the rest of them had looked around for Qiaan, she was gone.

And when the uneasily slumbering unrest across Syai finally shook itself awake in Linh-an and it was proclaimed that Liudan had broken the laws of nature and tradition and that the Gods themselves had spoken against her, those who had raised that banner had a leader whom they proposed to put in Liudan's place.

Qiaan.

# *Five*

Faced with the Tammary situation alone, or with the Qiaan situation on its own, Liudan might have reacted with more equanimity. However, the news of Tammary's identity coming straight on the heels of what she saw as Qiaan's betrayal sent the Empress into a fit of almost hysterical paranoia.

When Yuet and Tai had brought Tammary in to her to explain everything, Liudan's first reaction was to declare that she would order Tammary locked away immediately.

'Why?' Tammary demanded.

'I'll not have another Qiaan, not when I can stop you from casting an eye on my Empire!'

'Of all the things you could do to prevent me from doing that,' Tammary said, unable to control her own caustic side, 'locking me up is the one thing that would make me thirst for it.'

It was Tai who finally stepped between them, standing between the Empress and the Traveller woman, suddenly looking much taller than her fragile, small-boned self, her eyes dark with fury.

'I know now what Antian meant,' she snapped. 'Her sisters do need taking care of, and that's a fact! With all the trouble that's brewing out there, all you two are focused on is making more of it where none exists. Liudan, for the love of Cahan! She already said she didn't want anything to do with the Empire. And Tammary, you are not helping!'

'I would never . . .' Tammary began, and then, glancing at Tai, sighed and actually went down on one knee before Liudan. 'I *will* never,' she said, correcting herself, 'willingly take any action intended to harm Syai, or you, Liudan. I swear that to you right now. I will swear by whatever holy vow you hold most binding. I will swear it in the name of *jin-shei*.'

'You are who you are,' Liudan said. 'You can't help that.'

'I can help the fact that this body and this mind will not be used against you,' Tammary said, bounding back to her feet again, her eyes smouldering with the anger she was keeping in check. 'I cannot help my parentage, any more than you can help yours. Are you responsible for who begat you?'

Liudan, taken a little by surprise at the line of attack, was betrayed into a slight shake of her head, her lips even lifting into the shadow of a smile.

'How, then, can you demand that of me?' Tammary demanded.

'Why did you come to the city, then?' Liudan said.

'Not to storm the Palace,' Tammary said. 'I came to find out who I really am, who that other half of me is, to find out why I found it so hard to fit into my world back there, with the Travellers.'

'I am told that you were doing extensive research to find that out,' Liudan said sardonically.

'Liudan!' Yuet said. 'You were born to silk and to power. Do not mock another's need. You have never had to search for your own answers, only demand them. There are many out there who are not so lucky.'

'Like my mother had to, you mean,' Liudan said. 'Like my mother, who paid the price of a betrayal she had no hand in. I can hold others responsible for that, at least. My mother was the price for Szewan's revenge, then. You are here as Szewan's heir, Yuet. What should I hold *you* responsible for?'

'Stop it,' Tai said, tears in her eyes. 'I was the one who said yes when Tammary chose to come to the city. I was the one who knew that she wanted nothing to do with the crown, only seeking a lost part of her spirit. I was the one who spoke for keeping it a secret, because that way there would be the least possible number of people who would be hurt by the truth. None of us knew about Qiaan, not then.'

'You did, Yuet,' Liudan said. 'Didn't you?'

'I had my suspicions. I had no proof of anything, not until recently.'

'And when you got it, that proof, you still chose to keep your silence,' Liudan said. 'I could count that as betrayal, too.'

'Then call us all traitors and be done with it,' Tai said, swinging back into a stab of anger and letting it get the better of her. 'Everything everybody has done here has been done because of reasons that were either deeply personal and had nothing to do with you or else in order to protect you, Liudan. You know that we are all subjects to the crown that you wear, but you ought to remember, also, that here you are speaking to your own *jin-shei* circle. Who are sworn to be on your side.'

'Nobody has ever been completely on my side,' Liudan said defiantly.

'Well, I am!' Tai blazed. 'I swore to Antian that I would do whatever it takes to stand between you and harm. We are *jin-shei*; you are Antian's legacy to me, and I am on your side. I just won't stand by and say nothing and let you do something irrevocable or unwise, just in order to satisfy a momentary urge to pour balm on your wounds!'

Liudan turned, the expression on her face pure rage, but then, unexpectedly, laughed. 'You are the most unlikely guardian spirit from the Three Heavens,' she said, 'but I suppose I deserved that.'

'So what are you going to do?' Tammary asked. Yuet flashed her a warning look, but Liudan had herself in hand. Now she was cold, glittering, all icy Empress.

'With you?' she asked, and there was still a trace of acid in her voice. 'Nothing. For now. I'll keep an eye on you, and see that you remember that. Go home. Stay out of trouble. With you, Yuet? I'll think on it. The law of Syai is that you cannot hold an apprentice responsible for the crimes of the master, and you weren't even old enough to have been her apprentice, in a proper sense of that word, when she undertook to weave a weapon of revenge against my family. So go home, too, Yuet. For now. Tai?'

Tai looked up at the sound of her name, her eyes calm, utterly fearless. Liudan stared at her for a long moment, and then laughed again, a little bitterly.

'I remember there was a time that I resented you, so desperately,' she said. 'I wish I could remember why, sometimes. There are times when you annoy me or cross me or even call me stupid to my face, but only when you know you are right. And that annoys me even further. I am exceedingly annoyed at you right now. But I think I've read too much of your poetry and I begin to see – you are just cursed with a way of seeing things that not many other people can own to. It may frustrate me, it may make me angry, but I cannot deny that I envy it sometimes. I begin to realize why Antian chose you to be the soul of the *jin-shei* circle she would leave behind as her legacy on this earth.'

'What of Qiaan?' Tai whispered.

Liudan's eyes hardened. 'That . . .' she began, but was interrupted by the little deaf girl who was still her favoured servant scurrying into the room with every appearance of consternation and signing something frantic at Liudan. The Empress's eyebrows rose.

'Nhia? And *who*?' The sign language was obviously inadequate, because Liudan suddenly stopped the servant with a wave of her hand. 'Send them in.'

'We should go,' Yuet said. 'If there is something . . .'

'No,' said a new voice, a man's voice, from the door. 'Stay, because this concerns you all.'

Every head snapped in that direction.

The man who had spoken was tall, powerfully built, his shoulders broad and his forearms, showing beneath wide sleeves of a shabby but once magnificent robe, were pure corded muscle. But he moved with the aid of a stout staff and had one hand on the shoulder of Nhia who, standing beside him, was dwarfed by his presence. His face, between its criss-crossed scars, was the pallid shade of one who had not seen the sun for some time, and the eyes which showed in that ruin were white with cataracts and the veil of blindness. He looked frayed, scruffy, a down-on-his-luck beggar, and yet his grey hair was held back with a filet which had a yellow gem in its centre, and his bearing was that of a king.

The Beggar King.

Liudan drew herself up to her full Imperial majesty.

'You,' she said. She was in absolutely no doubt as to the identity of her visitor. Then her eyes shifted, glittering with hauteur, to Nhia. 'Why do you bring him here?'

'He said it was time,' Nhia said.

Liudan's eyebrow rose, her head inclining into a position which was a regal question.

'You obviously recognize me,' said the Beggar King, 'but you don't *recognize* me. How could you, in the wreck of this body? It has been years now that I have been waiting to come out of the darkness, waiting for this moment. You know me now as Brother Number One of the Beggars' Guild of Linh-an – but that was the place I took when he who was your Ninth Sage ripped my rightful identity from me, and burned a body which he swore was me with all the rites necessary to send into Cahan . . . a soul which was still very much on this world.' He lifted his hand from Nhia's shoulder, rose to his full height, fixed on Liudan the uncanny gaze of those blind eyes. 'Empress of Syai, I am Maxao, once Ninth Sage to the Court of your father, whom the usurper whom you know as Lihui declared dead, so that he could take my place. I have returned.'

'To claim it?' Liudan questioned softly. 'They have yet to name Lihui's successor. As you probably know. You seem to know so many other things.'

'I am not here to fence with you,' Maxao said, refusing to rise to her bait. 'And no, I am not here to resurrect myself to the point of claiming the position that was stolen from me by my erstwhile student and acolyte. He knows I am not dead – oh, yes, he knows that! – but he does not know where to search for me, or if I am still a threat to him. But now he is vulnerable, he is in the same position that he put me into all those years ago.'

'Someone took his position?' Liudan inquired. 'The Sages appointed a successor?'

'They might have liked to, more than you know,' Maxao said. 'He has instilled fear into them, and they dare not move as long as they know he still lives – and they know. But he, like I in my time, has found himself outflanked and then blinded by a disciple. Now there are certain things he can't do without the assistance of another, someone with a functioning pair of eyes.'

'I knew I should have waited,' said yet another voice from the door, 'until I could cut his head off myself.'

Maxao inclined his head, without changing the direction of his blind gaze. 'Khailin,' he said. 'Thank you for coming.'

It was Tai who looked around and made the connection.

'That's all of us,' she said, 'all except Xaforn who is away from the city and Qiaan, who is . . . who is . . .'

'Who is with Lihui right now,' Maxao said. 'Who is his eyes. Who is his ticket to the position he has always wanted. Once he knew

356

who she was, what she could be made into, he has spared no effort to exploit her strengths and her vulnerabilities. He has made it possible for her to do what she wants to do with her life, and in return she is his path to power, and to the Empire. Qiaan . . . your Qiaan is an annoying woman,' Maxao said musingly. 'There is that in her which insists on helping people who sometimes need no help whatsoever. She has repeatedly tried to better the lives of not a few members of my Guild – people who, even with the tithes they pay to the Guild, make a living out on the streets the extent of which would stagger a few of you in this room. But because a man is lame or a woman old and toothless or a child dirty and barefoot in the streets, they needs must be taken into shelters and forcibly fed and clothed and remade into what Qiaan saw as useful members of society. It vexed her no end that so many of those she thus saved escaped at the first opportunity to return to their own lives. Nonetheless, she must return to Linh-an at once – even if it does mean that she continues her exasperating activities.'

'Return to Linh-an?' For the first time, Liudan's voice betrayed a genuine interest. 'Return from where?'

'You have not tried looking for her already?' Maxao said. 'And have you not found that she has disappeared completely? She is no longer in Linh-an, Empress. She hasn't been for some time. And now we have the problem that someone must go and snatch her from Lihui's side – for with her as his willing guide he has suddenly become powerful and dangerous again.'

'How did he get to her?' Khailin demanded. 'How, if he wasn't able to use the ghost road himself, could he get to Linh-an and take Qiaan?'

'Because he found a temporary pair of eyes somewhere on the road as he wandered, because he must have lingered in some place where some poor kind soul stopped to find out what the matter was and if this wreck of a wounded man could be helped in some way. That compassionate being is long gone, of course – useful only for long enough to be Lihui's eyes on the ghost road, and then killed, discarded, abandoned while he stalked Qiaan and finally found occasion to get close to her, and to tell her the secret none of you would tell her. That she might be royal. That she could do by decree and by fiat what she had been doing with her own two hands for years. He lied to her, of course – he always lies – and told her that she was far more royal than she is. But his lies are always the more dangerous when built upon a kernel of truth, and this was a powerful kernel indeed – and he retains the power of cloaking his lies with beauty. To her, he is not scarred or blind or someone who needs her in order to survive – to her, I have no doubt, he seems a very prince of power. And the longer she stays with him, the more potent the illusion becomes.'

'What must we do?' said Tai.

'Someone must go to where Qiaan is, and bring her back,' Khailin said.

'And she must come willingly,' Maxao added. 'Taking her by force means that the illusion holds, and she will return to him as soon as she is left alone for long enough for him to regain control over her mind. No, she must understand why she must come, and agree to it. No force, no weapons, no coercion. She must listen to somebody she trusts, and believe in what she hears, and come of her own free will. *She must renounce him.*' His voice had become a thing of power, the words he was saying almost a spell of enchantment. 'And because of that, it is one of you who must go to her. One of her own *jin-shei*.'

Nhia blanched, recoiling. 'I cannot go back. Not to that . . .'

Maxao turned his head again, leaning forward heavily on his staff. 'Nor would I ask it of you, my dear. Your fear makes you a target. It makes you immune to Lihui's voice, to be sure, because you already know the truth about him – but your fear would make you his prisoner before you begin, and then we would have lost two of you. No, not you.'

'The only other one who knows how to walk this road, Sage Maxao, is I,' said Khailin. 'Is this why you have summoned me?'

'No. Not you either. You do not fear him, but you hate him. Your hate would blind you to too much, and you cannot yet face him alone – and it is alone that the one who goes must enter his stronghold.'

'I will go,' said Tai in a small voice, 'if someone would tell me how.'

'No!' The word was torn from three throats at once – Nhia's, Tammary's and, surprisingly, Liudan's.

'No,' Maxao agreed in a voice as tranquil as if he were refusing a glass of water. 'Not you. Not the one who holds it together.'

'I don't . . .' Tai began, astonished, but Tammary took hold of her hand and Tai saw that tears were standing in the Traveller girl's eyes.

'No, not you,' Tammary said. 'You with your quiet and joyous life where we all come to seek comfort. You have always been the one who showed me that happiness was possible. I would not risk that for anything. I will go in your place, even though I never knew Qiaan well.'

'That is why you are not the one, either,' Maxao said. 'She will not come for the wrong person, or to the wrong call.'

'She would come to me,' Yuet said softly. 'I think she would. I think I grew to love her and respect her and even try to begin understanding her during the time of the illness. She deserves the chance. I will go.'

'You cannot use the ghost road, healer,' Maxao said implacably. 'You are simply not compatible with it. You have the compassion, but you don't have the imagination.' Yuet flinched, as though she had been physically struck. Ignoring her reaction, Maxao continued talking without missing a beat. 'You would see nothing that you would recognize, and too much that would attract you to turn aside from the path, and you would be lost.'

'I don't understand,' Yuet said.

'Precisely,' said Maxao, nodding. 'And before you, too, volunteer, dear Empress, I would think it obvious that you yourself cannot go, for reasons that do not require further elaborating, and should not go, because Qiaan is standing in opposition to you and would hardly return to Linh-an on your say-so, knowing that you would probably bring her back to try her for treason.'

'But that leaves nobody,' Tai whispered.

'It leaves one. The one whom she trusts, and who has already been trained to follow her to wherever Lihui is hiding her.' Maxao turned back to where Liudan was still standing, not having moved since he entered the room. 'Bring Xaforn back from the border. Now.'

'What do you mean, trained?' Liudan said.

'Call it precognition,' Maxao said. 'Call it luck. Call it the will of the Lord of Heaven, if you want to. But when Xaforn came into the Guards she shone out like a diamond among the glass chips of the others of her level. She proved again and again that she was more gifted, more focused, more dedicated, *better*. She had nothing but the Guard, and the Guard was everything to her. She was perfect.'

'Perfect for what?'

'There is a Guard in the ranks, a veteran, whose name I don't think I should divulge here,' Maxao said, with a wolfish grin. 'He was a disciple of the Way, in his time, before he chose the path of the warrior, not the sage. He took on the training of the young ones, always having been a teacher by nature. When he chanced upon the young Xaforn, so hungry, so eager to learn . . . so talented in ways that few are talented . . . he taught her things the rest of her class never learned. How to centre into a white light inside herself when she gathers her energies for a kill. How to make herself faster, deadlier, how to become an extension of her weapon, how to *become* her weapon. Lihui encountered her once, in that power, and was turned by it – and knows she is dangerous. She, in turn, has encountered Lihui at least once, and knows that he backed off from the fight at that time. And she has one other qualification for this job, one that none of the rest of you possess.'

'And what is that?' Liudan said, her face grim. She had lost control of this situation the moment the Beggar King walked into the room, and she was not happy about it.

'She grew up in the Guard, and so did Qiaan. She knew her when they were both little children. She and Qiaan made a connection long before either of them met any of the rest of this circle. If Qiaan will trust anybody, it will be Xaforn. And Xaforn knows how to go to her. And, more importantly, knows how to get back.'

'And how to die defending them both if the situation turns deadly,' Tai said.

'She is a warrior, yes,' Maxao said sternly. 'That is her calling. That is who she is.'

'What of that war on the borders?'

'It will probably come,' Maxao said. 'It would be precisely the kind of thing that Lihui would want – something to distract you, to keep your attention elsewhere, far from the city, while he brings Qiaan back here and strikes at the heart of it all. He doubtless already has something in place with the riders of Magalipt. They might get the pass, or even Sei-lin. It depends on how hard a bargain they drove with him to be his decoys. It will come, but it will not come this spring.'

'But the letter that the scribe was copying in the office . . .' Nhia began.

'Did you stop to wonder why they did such copying in your office, Chancellor of Syai? Right underneath your nose where anyone could have tripped on it?'

'Because the best place to hide something is in plain sight?' Khailin said, grinning a small feral smile.

'There is that, too,' Maxao said, nodding. 'But in this instance, probably because he wanted you to find out, because he needed you to go and hit Liudan with it, because he knew that you would, because he needed attention focused over there. He all but sent you a copy of that letter.'

'He couldn't know that Khailin would be there, and that she can . . .'

'That she can read *hacha-ashu*?' Maxao said. 'I know you can, my dear. You would have to be able to, to have learned what you did at Lihui's house. He did not teach you what you know willingly or directly – you would have had to read it all, in his library. Which once was mine. The loss of which I do mourn.' He sighed. 'Could you not have found another way out than to burn that house?'

'But if you could use someone else's eyes and go to his house,' Khailin said, clenching her jaw, 'why could you not have come there, and destroyed him?'

'Because he took from me more than my sight,' Maxao said bitterly. 'I can no longer stand against him. Long before Lihui decided to move against me he had made an elixir with my essence in it and made himself invulnerable to it, and thus to me. I cannot harm him, through spell or direct action. It would have been pointless, my going down the ghost road to Lihui's house. I could have done nothing there except die.'

'But I was there,' Khailin said. 'I could have helped.'

He turned and fixed her with a blind stare that bored right through the heart of her. 'Ah,' he said, 'but at the time I did not know that he had another mage living underneath his roof.' He turned away from Khailin, leaving her standing very still, with her hands folded over the hollow of her throat, her eyes wide on him, and turned back to Liudan with a smile which might once have been gracious but which was ghastly in that ruined face. 'You see, Empress, I don't know everything, despite your fears. Now – recall Xaforn and send her for Qiaan. Lihui will follow, because right now she is his passage to every ambition he has ever had. And when he comes back to Linh-an . . .' His face twisted into a grimace of loathing. 'When he comes back to Linh-an, it will be time to settle some old accounts. I will be here to meet him.'

'I thought you just said you could not harm him,' Tai said.

'I can't. Not on my own.' Maxao turned back to where Khailin still hadn't moved, and held out his free hand, waiting with a patience at once complacent and haughtily royal until Khailin, almost unwillingly, stepped forward and placed her own slightly trembling fingers there. His huge hand closed around her slender one, engulfing it, and he pulled her forward very gently but inexorably for all that. 'But I am not going to be on my own.'

## Six

*You are not to fight him. You do not need to go armed to the teeth. You are to go in lightly, and see her, and speak to her, and then you will both leave. Quietly. Do not start a war. Not yet. You don't need to take the Guard armoury with you.*

Xaforn had been partly annoyed and partly amused by the injunction she had been given. She was aware that Qiaan's people all knew exactly who she was, and therefore knew that she *was* a weapon – going in empty-handed would hardly have meant that they would have refrained from harming her. But it had been a condition placed upon her, and Xaforn accepted it. She took no weapon other than the pair of throwing daggers she always carried in her boots.

This was the last chance she – or anyone – would have to talk to Qiaan, to reason with her, to maybe turn the tide of events. There had already been several skirmishes – in Linh-an itself, and in other cities, too. Some of them had been bloody. Things had already been done in Qiaan's name that Xaforn, who knew her, could not believe that she had sanctioned. Not Qiaan – not the girl who had once patiently taught her *jin-ashu*, who had worked without grumble or complaint at the most menial of jobs when it came to saving lives in a deadly epidemic, who had dedicated herself to bettering the lives and the prospects of the city's poor, who had fed the hungry and taught the ignorant. This woman, so dedicated to saving lives, could not now be issuing orders for those lives to be offered for a cause that seemed to be neither more nor less than herself taking on the role which she had often so trenchantly condemned when Liudan was cast in it. She had been the people's light; she was now the new royalty.

Khailin had said that it was all Lihui's doing, that he could twist someone's mind and soul and aspirations so that they believed utterly that they were their own but which only served to further his own goals and ambitions.

'If I should cross his path, I will kill him,' Xaforn had said darkly, but Khailin had laughed.

'If you should cross his path, I have no doubt that you will try,' she said, 'but Xaforn, he would burn you to ashes.'

'Maxao said that I had the training,' Xaforn said, stubborn, implacable.

'Enough to stand against an army of mortal men, yes,' Khailin had said. 'To stand against Lihui, alone, no. Not even you. Not yet. Not until you have trained for a hundred years, and have long forgotten what it means to be human. Not even Maxao can stand against him alone. Take the old amulet with you, Xaforn, it still has power. At least it will protect you against surprise.'

'But I don't know how to walk this shadow road of yours!' Xaforn said. 'And what if the amulet . . . ?'

'It travelled safely with Nhia. And it's the *ghost* road. And you do know how to do it. It's in you, in your training, in that light you carry within you. Picture her in your mind, picture Qiaan's face, and then start walking, keep that face in your thoughts, don't stop for anything until you are sure that you are in a place where your goal is. Remember, *the journey of a thousand years starts with a single step.*'

'That is a Temple platitude,' Xaforn said.

'Sometimes even the Temple stumbles on the truth.'

'How do I come home, Khailin?'

'You can think of me,' Khailin said, laughing. 'And if you do, I will be there to meet you at the end of your road. But in truth, all you have to do is walk until you see Linh-an before you. And it is possible to manipulate the stuff of the ghost road, Xaforn, so if you catch sight of a Linh-an sky that you recognize, keep hold of the sky. The city beneath it will change. Wait until it changes to something you know.'

'I'm not sure I want to do that,' said Xaforn, suddenly uneasy. 'Cahan alone knows where I would end up.'

'Perhaps even Cahan,' Khailin said irreverently. 'Go. And may all the Gods be with you on this mission. I will . . . I will light an incense stick for you in front of the little ugly God in the Temple. He answered my prayers at least once before.'

'Which little ugly God?'

'When I was a child I once told my mother that there were so many offerings at his feet that nobody ever saw being put there that I thought the little ugly thing simply worshipped itself,' Khailin said. There was an odd little smile of reminiscence on her mouth. She hadn't thought of the little ugly God in years. Truth be told, she hardly knew if he was still there, still so extravagantly worshipped.

'Xinxan the Finder?' Xaforn said.

Khailin gave her a startled look. 'You know that God?'

'People go to that shrine to ask for help in finding lost things,' Xaforn said, and then added, with a strange little smile of her own, 'On the whole, I think I'd prefer that you didn't light incense there just yet. He might take it into his head that, since I haven't been exactly lost yet, you might wish me to become lost rather than found. With the Gods, you never know.'

Khailin was shaking her head. 'Go,' she said. 'And good luck to you.'

So Xaforn had walked out, unarmed except for her small daggers and unarmoured, dressed only in a Guard practice smock.

*Qiaan. Qiaan's face.*

The face that formed in her mind, strangely enough, was not the woman that Qiaan had become. It was the face of the child she had once been. The face of a child that rarely laughed, the permanently serious and sometimes mournful expression that she habitually wore which had once given her the nickname of Qiaan of the Long Face.

Given what she now knew about Qiaan's true parentage and heritage, the memory was a sudden sharp pain for Xaforn.

'I didn't understand,' she whispered. 'Not then.'

She fought her way past the child's face, flowing the features through the intervening years, until she had a firm picture of Qiaan's present-day features in front of her. And then she took her first step.

The buildings on the street she was on blurred beside her, and flowed into smoke; the path at her feet opened up, twisting forward, pale and almost glowing in the mist. Xaforn took a deep breath and, keeping her mind fixed on Qiaan's face like a talisman and one of her hands tightly wrapped around the amulet at her throat, walked forward on the ghost road.

Glimpses.

Khailin had said she would see things.

Beside her, the mists opened and closed unexpectedly, giving Xaforn hints of other places, other times. A great dog, tied to the end of a chain, snarling and snapping, saliva foaming in his mouth. A girl dancing in a high mountain meadow. Something winged and golden – a dragon – flying across an amber-coloured sky. A woman's hand, wearing a ring with a blood-red stone. A mother bent over a baby . . . or it just looked like it . . . as Xaforn's step slowed momentarily the 'mother' looked up and her yellow eyes bore slitted pupils like a snake's and her mouth was full of small sharp teeth and of the blood of the child which she had been devouring. Xaforn dropped her eyes, picked up her pace. Beside her, a white waterlily on a dark pond. A city, under snow, with soft flakes falling like a veil. Children's laughter. The sudden scent of fresh-baked bread. The creak of an old door. A glimpse of steps descending into darkness. A sensation of heat, and the hint of the ruddy glow of a bonfire colouring the mists a translucent ruby. A cherry tree in bloom.

*Qiaan's face. Qiaan's face!*

Xaforn's own sign, a Lion, lying under a thorn tree, tail twitching. A great carpet, unrolling, its softness a sudden sensation on Xaforn's fingertips. Music, unfamiliar music played on instruments she could not identify. The glint of sunlight on a moving army of bright spears. Battle, with distant screams echoing in her head, the coppery smell of blood, a body sprawled with one hand almost on the ghost road, dead eyes staring at Xaforn. A child's bright ball. A full moon in an empty sky, glimpsed through a window, and the silhouettes of two lovers kissing. An old woman, spinning. A boy digging a hole, a dead dog beside him. A black pot hung over a hearth, the sudden taste of mulled wine in Xaforn's mouth. Tree bark. A desert of stones. An empty city street.

*Qiaan's face. Qiaan's face . . .*

There was a blur of colour, and then things stopped, solidified.

Xaforn found herself in a large room, with a fire crackling on the wide brick hearth whose edges, black with soot, bore mute witness that it had not been cleaned for years. There was a draught from somewhere, through an ill-fitting door or a shutter not fastened properly, and it made the garish, home-dyed silk hangings on the walls shift and tremble with each breath of air. Faded, ancient tapestries covered the rest of the walls, giving the room an illusion of a once vivid and powerful but now vanished opulence. It was what Qiaan's armies might have thought a queen's chamber looked like.

In the middle of this stood Qiaan herself, her hair up in an elaborate style held together by ivory pins, dressed in a woollen robe of an improbable purple hue. Another approximation of royalty. She was the Vagabond Queen, poor but proud, waiting to come into her own, and in the meantime making do with makeshift glory. The whole thing was so theatrical, so unlike the practical, matter-of-fact Qiaan that she had known in the compound, that for a moment Xaforn could do nothing but stare.

Qiaan stared back at her.

'How in the name of Cahan did you get in here?' she demanded.

'I came to talk to you,' Xaforn said carefully.

'So,' said Qiaan warily, after a beat of silence, backing up a step. 'You're here. What did you want to talk about?'

'You,' Xaforn said. 'What have they done to you?'

'What do you mean?'

'This,' Xaforn said, waving her arm at the room, at its faded tapestries, at the gaudy silk hangings. 'This isn't you. It has never been you. They're using you, Qiaan, and you're letting them use you.'

Qiaan's head came up. 'I am where I can do the most good,' she said. 'There were hungry people . . .'

'There are always hungry people,' Xaforn said. 'The poor are always with us – someone is always on the edges of the world and falling through the cracks. You were doing what you could. People knew you as the very spirit of compassion – a somewhat brusque and dogmatic spirit, to be sure, but caring and compassion were all about who you were. Now this? It's war out there now, and you are at the head of an army, Qiaan.'

'You don't understand,' Qiaan said quietly. 'All I was doing I was doing quietly, and on the side, and by myself, and . . .'

'That isn't true!' Xaforn said hotly. 'You've always had your aides and handmaidens! I've done your bidding myself on occasion, and you've always had people like Yuet on call.'

'By myself,' Qiaan repeated with emphasis, as though she had not been interrupted. 'Many of those helpers were doing things not because they shared my beliefs in them but because they were required to do them. Now I am surrounded by people who believe in me and in what I am trying to do. That's partly why they chose me.'

'And partly it was because by raising your name as the banner they could get the support of the people, those who might have thought the complete overthrow of the Empire and the burning of the throne to be too radical a course of action,' Xaforn said. 'So they chose to crown a puppet Empress instead. One whom they would control, who would do their bidding. They are using you, Qiaan. It's worse than that – they aren't even using *you*, they are using a false image, an idol, a name behind which they can rally support for a cause that is neither more nor less than getting themselves into power.'

'Now you're talking Liudan's line,' Qiaan said. 'You believe in the holy Emperors, as anointed by the Gods?'

'No, but you do, otherwise you wouldn't have embraced that identity so eagerly,' Xaforn snapped. 'You were *Guard*, damn it. You know better than this. It's dishonourable. It's betrayal. This isn't who you are.'

'I am not Guard! I never was! I knew I never belonged in that compound, but I never knew why – not until they told me the truth! I always disliked my aunt for trying to poison my existence, but it was Aric who was lying to me. Sometimes Rochanaa would look at me and I knew she hated me, and I didn't know why – and it wasn't even my fault. I was paying for my father's sins! I was a charity case for her, no more!'

'No,' Xaforn said, after a moment of silence. 'It was I who was the charity case. You always had a family. You were always loved, you always belonged. You were taught the traditions by the woman whom you mourned as your mother – you *did*, Qiaan, I know it because I saw you do it – and if you chose not to follow the dreams your father had for you, that doesn't mean that they weren't there. I have a message for you from him, by the way.'

'My father is dead,' Qiaan said.

Xaforn's lips thinned into a hard line. 'They may fill your head with whatever rubbish they want to on that score, Qiaan, but although I do not doubt that your mother was Liudan's mother too, you were never begotten on her by the Emperor.'

Qiaan recoiled. 'I was born in the Palace!'

'Yes,' Xaforn said, 'but not royal.'

'My mother was the Emperor's own concubine,' Qiaan said doggedly. 'By rights and by tradition the children that she bore belonged to the Empress, and the Empire.'

'Only when those children were the Emperor's seed. Your mother might have been one of the Imperial women, but your father was a captain of the Imperial Guard, an honourable man but one of humble lineage. He wanted you to know that he was sorry, that he had sworn to Szewan not to tell you the truth. The reasons she gave him were quite plausible at the time. He did his best to protect you and shelter you – he was proud of you, of the work you were doing, of the woman you were becoming, of who he had raised you to be. You were the child of a woman he had loved, but he was proud of *you*, of who you were.'

'Aric never knew who I was!' Qiaan snapped. 'All he saw was what he wanted to see, and what he wanted to shape! He owed me the truth, at least – they all owed it to me!'

'I can't argue with you on that one,' Xaforn said. 'If anyone knew who my own parents had been, I would have wanted to know. It is my right, and it was your right. But Qiaan, you had a family. You've always had a family.'

'I had a lie,' Qiaan whispered.

'And what about me?' Xaforn said quietly.

'Well, what about you?'

'Qiaan, when you took me as *jin-shei* I was a child who knew nothing else except a dream to learn to kill.'

'You are no longer a child,' Qiaan said, 'but that is still your dream.'

Xaforn winced. 'I had hoped you thought better of me than that. And it is partly your doing that I was better than that, that I learned all the things I had disdained to learn before, because they interfered with my ambition or I deemed them unnecessary for it. You called yourself a charity case – I was left at the doorstep of the compound in a basket, for the love of Cahan, and all I ever had was a fierce desire to be one of the Guard, to justify my entire existence. That's why they chose me for the special training, because they knew it would "take" best in me, that I already had something to prove. But you, *you* softened that into something else, something greater, something they never expected. They wanted a killing machine; they got a human being. One who may be far too good at death dealing, granted, but a human being. You and that first *jin-shei* gave me a soul. I owe you for that.'

'You owe the cat,' Qiaan said, with a quirk on the side of her mouth that she could not quite suppress.

'You take yourself too lightly,' Xaforn retorted, but her mouth had softened, too.

'Flatterer,' Qiaan said, and there was a real smile there now.

'Fool,' Xaforn said gently.

The smile stayed on Qiaan's face, as though painted, but faded from her eyes. 'You say that as though you meant it,' she said.

'We meant every one of those insults when we started trading them, Qiaan.'

'Did we?' Qiaan whispered, her eyes clouding. 'I don't remember.'

'Come back with me,' Xaforn said urgently. 'Don't let them . . .'

Qiaan snapped back to attention, her eyes a hard glitter again. 'For what?' she said sharply. 'Don't you think I know that Liudan has already condemned me? Is that why you came – to deliver me to her?'

Xaforn flinched, but held the other's gaze. 'If you believed that, you would never have trusted me enough to have this conversation,' she said. 'The only reason Liudan wants you dead is because those whom you supposedly lead want *her* dead. It seems that there's already been at least one attempt on her life. Or don't you know that they tried to kill her? And if you don't,' Xaforn said, seeing a flicker in Qiaan's eyes and pressing her advantage, 'what else aren't they telling you? If you stop acting as figurehead, they will have to start from scratch, and we can deal with it, we can stop it.'

'You're her creature,' Qiaan said. 'Body and soul. How could I ever hope that you would understand?'

'Because I am your friend!' Xaforn said, tears standing in her eyes. 'Because I am your sister! Because you armed me for my first real outing as a Guard, because you have always understood me. Qiaan, look at me! I haven't changed, I am still the Xaforn that I always was, whom you taught to believe in love as well as in honour! Come home. Come to your sisters. Come to your father. This is not the way to honour your mother's memory.'

It had been the wrong thing to say. Qiaan squared her shoulders, lifted her chin. 'My father is dead, and his ashes scattered across Syai, his image in the Emperors' Gallery in the Great Temple; my mother is, just as you say, a memory, destroyed by the one who trained one of the very sisters to whom you now wish me to return. There is nothing for me to go back to.' Her eyes glittered, as though in a fever, as if she was in the throes of passion, but her voice was flat, inflexionless, as though she was repeating a catechism she had been carefully taught and now delivered in what might have been some sort of final exam. 'I have only the people, the people who have chosen me.'

'That is Lihui speaking, not you,' Xaforn said.

As if she had conjured him up with her words, he was suddenly there, Khailin's husband, Nhia's enemy, almost as though he had stepped out of the flames on the hearth or from one of the tapestries on the walls. Because of the amulet she wore underneath her dark tunic, Xaforn saw him with true sight, and gasped at it, for he was hideous now.

There was nothing left of the handsome man who had turned Khailin's head with a smile, whose aristocratic, long-fingered hands had once reached out to support Nhia when her withered foot had led her to stumble at his feet. His eyes were a ghastly, uniform shade of blue-white underneath burned-away lids, his eyelashes and eyebrows gone, his face a mass of puckered scar tissue; the hands were gnarled and ridged with similar scars. Only the voice remained, the quiet, kind, reasonable, treasonous voice.

'Indeed,' he said. 'She is an apt pupil.'

He reached out a hand, and Qiaan laid hers into it. 'She is to

370

marry me,' Lihui said calmly. 'She has already consented to do so. After all, an Empress needs an Emperor by her side.'

'You are already married,' Xaforn said, refusing to allow her fear to show. 'If you ever ascend the throne of Syai, it is Khailin who will be queen.'

'Details,' Lihui said. 'They will be dealt with in time.'

Qiaan was smiling at him, in a strange, dreamy way, as if she had suddenly forgotten that Xaforn was there at all.

'And now,' Lihui said, his free hand rising in an obvious summons, 'perhaps it's time to clear at least one obstacle from my path. The men who are on their way here believe that you came here to try and kill my bride, the woman who will be queen. They will deal with you on that assumption.'

'I did not come to harm her, I came to save her, with honour,' Xaforn said.

'Honour,' Lihui said, 'is for the weak, when they know they have no other way out. The reality is, when you have an enemy in hand, that is the time to destroy him. How you got him to bare his throat is not important when the final stroke is delivered.'

Xaforn wasted no more time in fruitless conversation. The shutters on the room's windows had been latched tight, but she reached them in two bounds and was already lifting the latch as she heard the door open behind her and the tread of heavy booted feet on the floor. She threw the shutter open and climbed on the ledge, balancing on the windowsill, turning to steal a final glimpse into the room, now filling with armed men, Lihui drawing Qiaan gently out of their way and she following him docilely, as though hypnotized.

'It's a long way down, Guard girl,' said Lihui languidly as Xaforn jumped from the second-storey window into the courtyard below. She heard something heavy and massive – a mace, maybe – thud into the window where she had been a moment ago.

She landed on a sloping pagoda roof projecting into her path, fought to regain her balance, and then ran lightly and carefully along the rain-slick roof edge towards a higher concatenation of rooftops to her right, skirted them along the lower layers while keeping an eye on a covered roof-walk on which a number of men seemed to be milling as if in anticipation of something, and leapt over a narrow alley to gain another set of rooftops, dropping down at last into a quiet courtyard with concealing niches in the walls. She flattened herself into one of these and waited, her Guard training stilling her racing heart, focusing her mind. She was aware of a commotion on the rooftops above her, saw shadows passing across the courtyard, heard running footsteps in the alley behind the wall against which she was crouched, but she remained undetected and presently the courtyard sank into silence again. After a cautious while Xaforn emerged, looking around. Everything was quiet.

She ran across the courtyard in the high, light steps she had been taught, using momentum to carry her up a wall, back onto a roof. For a brief moment she was aware of an elderly servant with a lantern who had just entered the courtyard from which she had escaped, an expression of complete astonishment on his face, and then she was over the house, across the next alley, down into the one beyond that, landing lightly on her feet. She looked around warily before she paused to orient herself, and then melted into the shadows. She conjured Khailin's face in her mind now, and stepped out onto the pale ribbon of the ghost road, almost running. She looked neither left nor right, gathering no glimpses into the ghost road's treasury of dreams and memories and nightmares.

If the light of the winter stars glinted on a shadow of tears on her cheeks, there was nobody to see.

# Seven

When Xaforn returned without Qiaan, Liudan withdrew even further into her own glittering prison of the Palace and no longer seemed to trust anyone. Even her *jin-shei* sisters were admitted into her presence less frequently and their visits were made shorter. The Empress watched her borders, watched her city, gave orders in the mornings that were sometimes contradicted by those she gave in the afternoons, and waited for Lihui to make his move.

As though he knew that his best weapon was making her insane with waiting, Lihui kept the unrest in the cities at a low boil, with just enough skirmishes and propaganda to keep the spirit alive and remain just under the threshold of massive Imperial retaliation.

There was no further word on Qiaan. Maxao, sometimes consulting Khailin whom he had openly named 'mage', was working on other plans to draw Lihui out – but as long as Qiaan was with him it was Lihui who had the upper hand.

Tammary had no illusions that the more pressing troubles had taken the problem of her own vexatious existence from Liudan's mind. Tammary's life had shrunk almost overnight from a carnival ride of wine, music and laughter in the city's tea-houses into a confined genteel cage where she tried to keep her head down and not draw Liudan's attention. These days one could not be sure who was safe to talk to, and Tammary did not want herself condemned over an unguarded conversation or a misdirected laugh at a jest that could have been misinterpreted.

But she had never been a caged creature and did not take to captivity well. She began prowling the markets again, as she had done in her early days in the city, seeking escape. A story reached Tai of Tammary's having been observed wandering up and down the thick walls of Linh-an on the inside, trailing a hand along them, as though she was looking for a breach or a hole to crawl through. Going out to the orchards and the hills outside Linh-an, to the place that Tai had taken her once, now a long time ago, was not easy any more – and it would have been almost impossible for Tammary, whose colouring marked her, whose identity was known to the guards at the gates, and who would treat her desire to climb a hill unfettered by high walls around it as suspicious and therefore as an excuse to trigger Liudan's paranoia again.

Tammary did talk to Tai about the troubles, including her own increasing isolation. She would come to Tai's house, hovering on the edge of breakdown, her eyes wild. Tai would brew a pot of green tea and set her to playing with the children, and before long Tammary would be reduced to helpless giggles at young Xanshi's demand that she be provided with hair exactly like Tammary's bright mane, and at once. She'd leave still hurting, but calmer, more rational, more able to deal with the situation. But Tai had no practical solutions for her, although she did gently point out that her probing the walls of Linh-an for means of escape could be misinterpreted under the current situation. Tammary knew that Yuet, too, was worried by the circumstances, but she too could do nothing except try and keep Tammary busy assisting with healer-craft when she could.

While her *jin-shei* sisters tried to shield and protect Tammary as much as possible under the circumstances, she still felt herself to be a prisoner – in the city, in her own skin – and now she had no outlet for it. She developed a high sensitivity to things, as though unspoken words could raise the hairs on her arms, or make her snap her head around and stare at someone who might have glanced at her, before that glance had even been contemplated by the other. The atmosphere in Yuet's house was tingling with this electricity. It had to come to a head – but when it finally did it was neither Yuet nor Tai who had anything to do with it.

Several of Tammary's old lovers had tried to see her, or sent messages in the shape of significant flowers or ribbons painted with *hacha-ashu* characters which Khailin interpreted for Tammary as being invocations of good health and subtle inquiries as to when she would be out to play again. Tammary recoiled from it all, refusing to see any of those visitors, brooding alone in her room, sometimes hovering at a convenient window from which she could see the front steps of the house as one or another of the gentlemen was shown out, trying to catch a glimpse of who it had been, rating her own importance through the identity of those who thought she was worth pursuing. Gradually, however, the visits and the flowers and the messages petered out. But it was one of Tammary's old flames who came to her rescue at last – Zhan, son to one of the sisters of the Ivory Emperor. He was Liudan's cousin, and Tammary's too.

She was restlessly prowling the marketplace on her own one cloudy morning, her bright, revealing hair closely wrapped in a kerchief and then further concealed by the hood of a cloak, when she felt a light hand descend on her arm.

'Tammary,' the owner of the hand said in a low, almost pleading voice. 'Talk to me. You used to be able to do that.'

Tammary shrank back, twisting out of the young man's grasp. In the shadow of her hood, her eyes were burning. 'How did you know it was me?'

'Of course I knew. I know the way you walk, the way you move. I know what is being talked of in the bazaars and in the Palace, but . . .'

'So, it's true – it's all true,' said Tammary. 'Leave me be.'

'No,' he said tranquilly. 'If indeed it was true, then now more than ever you need your friends. And somehow I have to make you understand that I am one.'

'If I am to believe the things that are being said,' Tammary said bleakly, 'there are only two kinds of people in this world right now. One kind would agree with the Empress that I am a mortal danger and would want me dead, and the other kind would want to use me to gain her throne, and *then* might want me dead and conveniently out of the way.'

'I am neither of those,' Zhan said.

'And then there are the innocents who are tainted with the conspiracy brush by the very act of being seen talking to me,' Tammary said. 'Go away, Zhan, and leave me alone, and hope you aren't arrested and interrogated when you get home from this meeting.'

'Oh, my sweet bird of paradise,' Zhan murmured. 'What have they done to you?'

Tammary's every instinct was to run, to hide in the crowd, to find a small dark hole and curl up in it until she was sure that this man and his unexpected understanding and compassion were far away from her, where they could not touch her, where they could not endanger him. Instead, she simply buried her face in her hands and burst into tears.

When his arms came around her, it was a sweet release to crush handfuls of his outer tunic into her fists, twisting the material, pouring all her unresolved pain and frustration into the motion, her head pillowed against his shoulder and her face against the hollow of his neck, feeling his pulse beat against her eyelids as her tears soaked into his collar.

'You choose,' he said quietly, bending his head so that his words were whispered directly into her ear. 'Your home, my home, anywhere. But I need to get you off this street, and you need to talk to me. You need to tell something to somebody, and you're going to do that, now.'

'But it's . . .' Tammary sniffled.

'Dangerous, yes, I know. Living is dangerous. But you cannot hide away for ever, Tammary. You don't make my choices for me, I make them, and I choose the danger, if that is what it takes. Now tell me, which way?'

Tammary started walking, without looking up, and Zhan walked by her side, his arm around her waist, holding her to him and sharing his strength and his own resolve. When Tammary stopped and finally looked up, blinking, Zhan glanced around with some confusion.

'Here?' he asked. 'What is this place? I thought you were staying at Yuet's house in the city.'

But it was Tai's house that Tammary's feet had taken her to. Her other sanctuary. The place where she sometimes found a tiny shard of peace in the maelstrom of events. It might have been this, the subconscious connection between that peace and the sudden warm rush of security and support she was feeling at that moment, that had brought her to this place. But then, having raised her hand and almost knocked on the door, she let it drop again.

'I can't bring you here,' Tammary said. 'Liudan would make out that I was trying to . . .'

But Zhan lifted his own hand and knocked firmly on his own behalf.

'You felt it safe enough to come here. There could be worse places to go.'

A servant opened the door, ushering them inside, and then conducted them to an inner courtyard where a small stone fountain played, gesturing for them to wait there. After a moment they heard the whisper of slippers and then a small gasp.

'Amri?'

'I do not think we have ever been formally introduced,' Zhan said, bowing. 'I am Zhan, a friend whom Tammary has been holding at arm's length for far too long. I don't know what, if anything, I can do to help matters – but I will do anything that is in my power. She needed removing from the public eye, and she brought us here. I hope that this is not an intrusion.'

'You are welcome,' Tai said warmly. 'I have nut biscuits baking, Amri. Will you wait until they are done? They were always a favourite with you. May I offer you some green tea, Zhan? I think Amri could do with a cup.'

'Thank you,' he said, smiling, 'yes.'

'If you will excuse me, then,' Tai murmured, bowing. 'Please make yourself comfortable.'

It started to drizzle a few moments after Tai had withdrawn. Zhan guided Tammary into the sitting room through an archway opening from the courtyard. There were scrolls of poetry hanging from the walls, and Zhan glanced at them in passing.

'She is Kito-Tai, the poet, is she not?' he asked. 'I have bought some of her poetry myself. I think you spoke of her before, but I don't recall what your connection was?'

'She named me *jin-shei* when I came to the city,' Tammary said. 'She seems to have this rare gift of the simple ability to be happy, and that's something I've been searching for all my life. It's a way of being content. Being with her is like sitting beside a deep pool of bright water and watching the waterlilies bloom, opening up petal by petal. She gives rest. She has this perfect life, this balance, the steady flame in the darkness. I don't know if I could live it if it was handed to me, but I envy her for it sometimes.'

'She also gives a gift of poetic expression,' Zhan said, a little taken aback. 'I don't think I've ever heard you speak in poetry before.'

'That wasn't poetry,' Tammary said.

'No, perhaps not – not classical poetry, not in the way that you or I would define it, not in the sense that it could be transcribed and hung on a wall, like hers. But you feel deeply enough about her to wrap her in metaphor and dream-words. You see? There *are* other kinds of people in the world. Not all of them just want you dead or want you as a figurehead.' He had slipped the cloak off her shoulders and draped it over the back of a low chair, and now reached out a hesitant hand towards the scarf that confined her hair. 'Do you feel safe enough here to remove the disguise? I dreamed of that hair, Tammary.'

Tammary's hands flew to the sides of her head where the scarf was folded down against her temples, initially to protect it, to prevent it from being removed, but then she looked up and met Zhan's eyes, and something she saw in them changed the motion and her fingers slipped the scarf back until it revealed the bright hair underneath. Zhan brushed it with his fingers, very lightly, and then took his hand back with a self-conscious little wave before it dropped back to his side.

'I missed you,' he said simply. 'I never did understand why you chose to leave me, just as I was in the middle of falling in love.'

Tammary looked away sharply. 'Don't.'

'You choose,' he said again, repeating his earlier words. 'I will be what I can be to you. But I heard it said in the Temple just the other day that memories are what the future is built upon. Keep that in mind, if you should ever want to start building a future which could help you escape from this trap.'

He was carefully not saying too much, but Tammary, turning back to stare at him, was suddenly aware that his reasons for doing so had less to do with his fear that she might accept any extravagant promises he might make than with the concern that she would be driven away by them, all over again. He knew that she was trapped, and did not want to lay another snare in her path. But Tammary was the one who had walked away from their earlier liaison. She had been the one still searching, still restless.

An echo of her own voice came back to her, a conversation she had once had with Tai: *Who would marry me?* The words mocked her, because she had already abandoned this man, the one man who might have wished to. Who now sat beside her on Tai's futon, carefully guarding against showing too much of his soul in his eyes lest Tammary be spooked into flight again – but who would have had no trouble with answering that question.

Tammary suddenly reached out for him, folding graceful arms around his neck, burrowing her fingers into the hair on the back of his head, moulding her body to his.

*Why did I leave him?* Tammary asked herself as she looked up into a pair of carefully wary eyes which nonetheless could not prevent a tiny flame of an astonished joy dancing in the corners. Some day, perhaps she would remember. Perhaps it had even been a good reason, at the time. But the times had changed and, for now, it was enough that she was cherished.

'Hold me,' she whispered, her eyes suddenly very bright.

His arms came around her, one around her waist, the other over her shoulder so that he could mould his palm against the back of her head. 'Oh, Tammary,' he whispered, his lips brushing hers. 'All you had to do was call me.'

It was meant to be a gentle kiss, just a seal on a new bargain, a future beginning to be built on old memories. But they had both forgotten the heat that had burned at the heart of their affair, and when their lips touched it was impossible to keep it just a light embrace. If their minds had forgotten, their bodies remembered all too well, and took them back to a shared passion that had consumed them both, once. Zhan's palm slid from Tammary's lower back around to her hip, cupping her hipbone, and she responded to the touch, bringing her leg up over his knees so that his hand continued on a slow downward glide, fingers caressing her thigh through the brocade of her robe. She could feel him stir beneath her leg, where her thigh rested on his pelvis. His hand travelled back upwards again, a swift motion that swept past her hip and over her waist and came to rest on her ribs, with his thumb brushing the underside of her breast. Suddenly all the tunics and the outerwear and the formal brocades were in the way, and she craved the heat of skin against skin, the spill of her hair over his shoulders, the hardness of his hipbones against her own.

She remembered now – she *remembered* . . .

Zhan had crossed Tammary's path for the first time back when she had still been frequenting the tea-houses of the aristocracy, right about the time that she was starting to get bored with them and their stiff rules, traditions and attitudes. He had been young, younger than almost everyone else there, and he had shared a little of her frustrations with the situation – less so than herself, to be sure, since he was an aristocrat and much of those traditions and attitudes had been bred into him from the cradle. But there was enough wildness left in his spirit for it to kindle at Tammary's presence. He had initially sought her out in the tea-houses and they had talked, indulging both in the discussion of serious matters and in light banter and flirting wordplay.

But Tammary had already started exploring other places, had already started frequenting the more plebeian tea-houses in the city. She had drifted away from high society, and their gathering places, and Zhan.

And then, one night, in a 'water tea-house' in the city, Tammary had looked up as a young man ducked through the low front door, and met Zhan's eyes again. And this time it was very different. Something had sparked between them in that long shared glance, and then Tammary had quite simply got to her feet, abandoning the company she was with, and crossed over to Zhan who had taken no more than three steps into the tea-house. He held out his hand, she took it, and for a while there had been no further visits to the city's pleasure dens for either of them.

Zhan's had been the nights of summer, and they had spent long sultry evenings making love on a high balcony above the sleeping city, and he had told her that he could see the stars reflected in her dark eyes as she lay beside him, and he had told her . . .

Far away from that balcony, in Tai's comfortable sitting room, Zhan lifted his head, very suddenly.

'Oh, Cahan,' he breathed. 'Tammary, this is not . . . I didn't want to . . . I don't want you to think that I only wanted . . .'

'I know,' she whispered. 'I know.' She took his hand from beneath her breast and kissed his palm and folded his fingers over the kiss. 'I know.' A breath against his neck as she laid her face on his shoulder, her lips against his throat.

A polite clearing of the throat made them both look up. Tai, who had entered bearing a tray with a chubby green-glazed teapot and a couple of small cups, stood looking at the two of them with a curious expression on her face – a mixture of a fiercely protective look at odds with a strange glint of delight. The pleasure won over when Tammary's mouth curled into a slow, contented smile.

'Are you all right, Amri?' Tai asked, carefully.

'I think so,' Tammary replied.

Tai caught Zhan's eye, but he said nothing. Court-trained, however, he managed to offer the equivalent of a graceful bow even while sitting on a low-slung couch with Tammary half-curled in his lap.

Tai laid the tray on the low table beside them.

'I think perhaps you may have things to talk over,' she said. 'I will make sure that the children don't disturb you. Call for me if you need anything.'

She left, closing the inside screens of the sitting room for privacy, and Tammary suddenly laughed.

'What is it?' Zhan said, sitting up.

'Tai treats all of us as her children sometimes,' Tammary said. 'Yuet will still call me "Amri" occasionally, but doesn't do it often any more. Tai has hardly ever called me anything else. It's my child name, the baby name that a small niece gave me when she couldn't wrap her tongue around Tammary – but Tai always calls me that, and I let her because I know she does it with love. She'll set Xaforn on you if you so much as think about walking away if she knows that I don't want you to.'

'I have no idea how to do this traditionally or properly – how *do* they do it in the Traveller clans? – but I have so little intention of walking away that I'm going to ask you something now that I should have asked you a long time ago,' Zhan said. 'Marry me. As my wife, you will be protected; you cannot be used as anything in the way that Liudan fears if you are already legally wed. It will give you your freedom back . . . Amri.' He tried the name out, rolling it around in his mouth, a teasing, boyish grin on his face.

Tammary smacked him on the shoulder. 'I'll take it from Tai, but I don't want my lovers calling me by a name I bore when I was ten.'

Zhan had tried not to wince at the plural, but Tammary noticed it anyway, and her playful smack turned into a caress instead, her fingers trailing along his jaw.

'No, that is over,' she murmured. 'One way or another. But Zhan, I cannot marry you.'

'Why?' he said sharply, gripping her shoulders with both hands and holding her so that she had to face him. 'Because I said you'll be protected? Believe me, although I want to do that, it is not the reason I want you as my wife. I've wanted you as part of my life ever since I first crossed verbal swords with you in the tea-houses, long before anything else happened between us. My reasons may be almost wholly selfish, in fact – I want you, I want you near me always so that I *can* protect you.'

'Zhan, you are part of the royal Court,' Tammary murmured.

'What has that got to do with anything?' he said, genuinely startled.

'Liudan will take this marriage as a declaration of war,' Tammary said. 'She will take any marriage I make as such, because it is possible to draw my line of descent through the Ivory Emperor and although I was not born of a royal wife or an acknowledged concubine someone out there could make the case that I was in the line of succession, and therefore any man I marry is a potential Emperor. And you . . . you are already linked to the Emperor's family. Liudan would take that only one way – that I was reaching high. Too high.'

'I am only a nephew of the Ivory Emperor. I was never in the line of succession, and if I were it would be so far down that I would be dismissed as utterly irrelevant by the powers that decide these things,' Zhan said. 'Besides, anyone at Court who knows anything

381

about me at all knows that I am too much of a coward to take on the mantle of Emperor. Or maybe too sane. Either way, I don't want it – I have never wanted it. Don't make this an obstacle. It isn't. Damn it, Tammary. I can't lose you again.'

'And besides,' Tammary said, 'there is always . . . what I was . . . what I am . . . all the things I have done. You may not wish to be tied to someone whose reputation will haunt your house. A child . . .'

'I know you have had other men. Many of them,' Zhan said. 'The thought has driven me mad sometimes, when I thought of you in someone else's arms. But from here on, any child you bear while under my protection will be my child. And woe to any wagging tongue that dares to suggest otherwise.'

'I can't,' Tammary said. 'It would hurt you, your standing.'

'Tammary, if I have to leave Syai in order to have you as my wife, I will,' Zhan said in a low voice.

'I will . . . come to you, and live with you, and be yours,' Tammary said. 'Let us not talk of marriage until we see how that goes. They may never accept me, you know.'

'We'll see about that,' he said, and gathered her into his arms again. 'And as far as I am concerned, it makes no difference from here on whether someone says the words of the ceremonies over us or not – your people don't wear the thumb rings anyway, so for you it would not be a symbol.' He lifted one of her hands to his lips and kissed it. 'But from this moment on you are mine.'


Liudan, predictably, did not much like the news, seeing in it only a new danger. But the rest of the *jin-shei* circle gathered in Zhan's rooms only a few days later to celebrate what everyone considered, in all practical terms, a wedding. When Zhan kissed Tammary's hands and whispered, 'I will always be with you,' Tai announced that there was no further ambiguity in the matter at all and that she considered Tammary finally and safely bestowed.

'And don't tell me now that you don't know how to be happy,' she said. 'I cannot dance for you, like you once did for me, because that is not my talent. But I have brought you this.' She held out a rolled-up scroll of ivory silkpaper, tied up with a red ribbon. Red, for joy.

'What is it?' Tammary asked, accepting it.

'It's your wedding poem. I wrote it for you after you left my house that afternoon, with the tea cold in the pot and the biscuits untasted but with the joy of all the ages in your eyes. Stay safe, and be happy.'

'If ever you have doubts about fulfilling your vows to your Antian,' Tammary said, tears sparkling in her eyes, 'you can tell her ghost that you have acquitted yourself well. I could not have hoped for a more loving guardian.'

Tammary celebrated her twenty-fourth birthday quietly, with Zhan. She had found a haven, and was calmer and happier than any of the *jin-shei* circle could remember seeing her since she had arrived in the city.

'Perhaps it is an omen,' Yuet said, 'and we can all look forward to some peace.'

'Not soon,' Tai said. The thoughts that she committed to her journal these days were dark ones.

The months slipped by. Spring came without the Magalipt invasion, although Liudan moved a substantial part of her army to the passes after all, to guard the passage into Syai. The skirmishes in the city became bolder and bloodier as spring passed into summer, but Lihui was still elusive, Qiaan was still missing, and Liudan was still kept at fever pitch. Maxao and Khailin could not seem to come up with a plan that would draw Lihui out into the open. Nhia, uncharacteristically, seemed to have decided to try a leaf out of Tammary's old book, and embarked on a series of short and repeatedly disastrous relationships with unsuitable men. It was behaviour as irrational as Liudan's own wild mood swings and seemingly random decision-making, and it was triggered, perhaps, by the same situation that was fraying Liudan's own nerves.

Tai flitted from Nhia's chambers and her tears, to Khailin's laboratory and her frustrated pacing, to Xaforn's quarters in the Guard compound where the young Guard seemed to have succumbed to a short but potent guilt fit at her failure to extract Qiaan from Lihui's grasp – comforting, listening, soothing. For once, Tai found herself fleeing to Tammary's quiet rooms to get some peace instead of the other way around. She was there when Yuet swept in one day to look in on a Tammary who was looking decidedly wan after several days of violent nausea, and announced that there was a very good reason for her feeling so sick – she was pregnant, and the child would be due early the following summer.

Less than three weeks after that announcement, with the green-sick tinge still warring with an astonished joy on Tammary's face, the Traveller girl disappeared.

She had gone to the market with Tai that morning, and they had said goodbye at the edge of the stalls, going their separate ways. Hours later, Tai was surprised to see Zhan present himself in her living room, trying not to look worried.

'What brings you here?' Tai asked, nonplussed, laying aside an embroidery hoop with a half-completed vivid bird of paradise. In this fractious time she had taken refuge in what had always given her peace, her silks and her cottons and the embroidery her mother had left as her legacy.

'Did Tammary decide to spend the day with you?' he asked, his eyes darting around the room as if Tammary was hiding behind a screen.

Tai rose to her feet. 'What do you mean? We went to market this morning, and then I came home, and she went back to hers. Zhan, what is the matter?'

He swayed, reaching out to support himself on the nearest wall. 'She never came home,' he said. 'I thought at first that she was with you, but then it was hours later and I'd had no word, and that wasn't like her – I thought that at least she would let me know if she had changed her plans.'

Under different circumstances Tai would have gone straight to Liudan and demanded assistance to turn the city upside down look-ing for Tammary. But the circumstances were what they were – Liudan would not be easily approachable on this subject of all sub-jects, and the army and Imperial Guard, those still in the city and not shipped out to await the Magalipt invasion which was starting to obsess Liudan to the exclusion of almost anything else, were being kept occupied by Lihui's incursions. Tai swiftly examined and dis-missed other options in her mind, until she finally narrowed it down to two.

'Go and get Yuet, and meet me at Khailin's house,' she said to Zhan. 'We have to do this ourselves. Go, hurry. I will tell my hus-band to spread the word in the Temple.'

Zhan left, almost at a run, and Tai, after a swift detour to Kito's booth in the First Circle of the Temple, presented herself at Khailin's laboratory. Khailin, wearing a black cotton smock dyed cheaply with walnut-shell dye, was bent over a row of what looked like tiny potted bean plants in flower, delicately probing their blooms with her fingers. She glanced up as Tai was shown in, and then straightened quickly, searching Tai's face with a more probing glance.

'What is it? What has happened?'

'They took Tammary,' Tai gasped.

'What? Who did? Sit down. I'll get some tea. You look like someone has stolen your own children. Breathe, Tai. Just breathe for a moment.'

'I sent Zhan for Yuet, and they are on their way here,' Tai said. 'I cannot go to Liudan with this, she would not help.'

'You mean she might be grateful that somebody has taken the problem of Tammary off her hands?'

'Zhan already did that,' Tai said. 'But now that both Qiaan and Tammary are missing, both potential pretenders to her own Tiara, she will be more unreasonable than ever. Now everyone will be out to get her. And in a way, this one is worse – at least she knows who has Qiaan, and who to guard against. We have no idea what happened to Tammary yet. Or where to start looking.' She hesitated. 'I thought you could ask . . . Maxao and his people might hear . . .'

'I will do what I can,' Khailin said. 'Have you got Xaforn?'

'Not yet, I thought Yuet had a better chance. She is a healer. These days people trust the Guards less than they used to.' Tai's eyes filled with tears. 'Oh, Cahan, Khailin! All Tammary ever wanted was peace, and someone to love her. And now, with Zhan, and the child . . . What are they going to do with her?'

'They will keep her alive. She is no good to them dead,' Khailin said. 'We will find her, Tai. We will.'

The door to the laboratory opened and Yuet came in, followed by a Zhan whose face was the colour of cold ashes. Tai leapt to her feet.

'What happened?'

'I went back home first, before I went to get Yuet, just in case she . . . just in case,' Zhan said. 'And I found that someone had delivered this.'

He clutched a small tasselled envelope fashioned from scarlet silk, as though he would never let go, as though he was about to let it slip from perfectly nerveless fingers. Khailin reached out and took it from him.

'Was there a message?' she asked.

'Yes,' whispered Zhan. '*We have her, and she is the key to power. Don't try to find her.*'

Khailin started opening the small silk package, upending it carefully over one hand. 'And what is this?'

'Proof,' said Zhan through bloodless lips as a rope of loosely braided fox-coloured hair poured itself out into Khailin's hand.

# Eight

Tammary woke, very suddenly, and with a low-level, pulsing headache that beat in her temples. She felt sick, but it was a different nausea than the one that had plagued her in recent times, the one she had finally learned to almost look forward to, a daily affirmation that she was part of a family, that she was about to be the foundation of a family. That she would, perhaps, get a chance to be Tai.

This was a nastier feeling, her mouth feeling coated with bitter oil, her gorge rising, her nose feeling seared by something; at the same time she was tasting something foul at the back of her throat and she had the feeling that she had lost her sense of taste altogether. It was an unnatural queasiness, induced. A faint memory stirred in Tammary's mind of a whipcord-strong arm snaking around her from behind as she made her way back home from the market, an oily rag being wrapped around her mouth and nose, a rag which smelled much like what she was now gagging on.

She was flat on her back, a position she found uncomfortable to sleep in at the best of times but which now, with the nausea, she found actively distressing. She tried to sit up, retching dryly. She found herself unable to move, her wrists tied by cords to the edge of a slatted bed on which she lay. The bindings were loose, but tight enough to prevent her rising. She struggled with them feebly for a moment, and then turned her head sideways, coughing, trying to get rid of the foul taste in her mouth.

'Are you awake at last? Good! I was beginning to think that they overdid the drug.'

The voice was male, familiar, but Tammary couldn't quite place it – not until she turned her head and saw the man who had spoken. He was short, wiry, very dark, a thin moustache framing a thin-lipped mouth; but his physical size was almost irrelevant beneath an almost palpable aura of pure arrogant swagger that wrapped him like a second skin.

Tammary knew him.

Once, it seemed like so very long ago now, they had been lovers. His name was Eleo, they had met in one of the more risqué tea-houses. He had been fulsome in his praises; overwhelmed by the sheer power of his personality, she had raised no objections when he had swept her off her feet – but once had been enough for Tammary to learn that he was far more aroused by cries of pain than those of pleasure. She had walked away from him without looking back. He had tried to contact her, later, several times – sending messages, sending flowers, arranging assignations to which Tammary never came. But he never seemed to quite take no for an answer, and now, it seemed, he had decided to take matters into his own hands.

A sob tore itself from Tammary's throat. *Not now, oh for the love of Cahan, not now! I may have made my share of mistakes, but I was happy, I was happy . . .*

'What do you want?' she asked, her lips dry.

'You, my dear,' said Eleo. 'You might have told me you were a path to the throne, you know. We could have done great things when we first met. Now it might be too late – we have two of them to deal with, the Empress and that other witch they raised as her successor. But you see, Tam – they can't make a case for Qiaan to be Empress, not quite, not without twisting the succession rites beyond any form of understanding. If she had been the legitimate offspring of a royal concubine, born in sanctioned congress between her and her Emperor, she would have been raised in the Palace as a royal princess. She wasn't. Therefore all she is, all she can ever be, is a royal by-blow from an abandoned Palace woman who couldn't help lifting her skirts for some passing vagabond. It is true that all concubines' children are raised as the Empress's own – but this does presuppose that their father *was* the Emperor, and hers wasn't. Yours, however, was, my dear.'

'My mother was a Traveller he took by force,' Tammary said. 'She was never one of the royal women.'

'One could argue that, simply by virtue of having been in the Emperor's bed, she was,' Eleo said. 'That makes you far more of an Imperial Heir than Qiaan could ever be. And there is one more thing. You are older than Empress Liudan. By a very little, to be sure, but you are. That makes you the legitimate heir to the throne of Syai. And, of course, the man you marry will be Emperor.'

'I am already married,' Tammary gasped.

'I do not see the rings,' Eleo said.

'We . . . I am not . . . I am Traveller, we didn't use . . .'

'If you used pagan rites you are not married under the laws of Syai,' Eleo said. 'That will change. But first, I need to make sure that they all understand that you are mine, and beyond their reach.'

He bent over her, and suddenly there was a knife in his hand. Tammary gasped, tried to twist away, but he only laughed. 'I wouldn't hurt you,' he said. 'That would hurt my cause. However, I do know of a perfect way to let everyone know what the situation is. I had them do this while you were sleeping,' he continued, picking up one of three long braids into which Tammary's hair had been plaited while she had been unconscious. 'You see, one,' and the bright knife flashed, severing the braid he held just above where it had been tied off with twine, 'goes to your mate, the poor weak Zhan, to let him know that I do have you, and that there is no point in him trying to look for you. Another,' the blade flashed again, biting through the second braid, 'goes to the Empress Liudan, to remind her that she sits on your throne and that, now you are here with me, you intend to reclaim it. And the last,' a final swipe of the blade, severing the third braid, 'to Zibo, once and future Chancellor, to tell him that the game is begun. Ah, but why are you crying, my sweet?'

Tammary squeezed her eyes shut, hot tears leaking out of the corners and spilling down her cheekbones; she could not bear to look at the sight of her hair in his hand, and know the pain and trouble it would cause.

'I swore to Liudan I would not allow myself to be used against her,' she whispered. 'She will know . . .'

'Your Liudan is willing to believe almost anything these days,' Eleo said. 'So Zibo tells me. And don't worry about the indignity of losing your glorious hair – something would have had to be done with that, anyway. For now, you can wear some sort of wig with a more traditional styling and colour. Later, when it grows out again, we can maybe dye it. But all that is premature. For now . . .' He coiled the three braids around one hand, and, having sheathed his knife, reached down to trail languorous fingertips over the contours of Tammary's body. '. . . for now we have other more important things to take care of. Like making sure you are properly married, in every possible way.'

'No. Oh, for the love of Cahan, no. You can't.' Tammary's mind suddenly flashed on a number of ingenious details from the pain-filled night of their first and only tryst, and recoiled from a possibility that she had not even thought of until that moment. It might have been something to keep secret, maybe, in the hope that he would never find out, but for one incandescent instant it was all she could think of, and it filled her thoughts, her mouth. 'You can't. *I'm with child.*'

Eleo frowned elegantly. 'You are? That's a new development, something I hadn't heard yet. You haven't been together with Zhan that long, so it can't be far advanced. Well. That does complicate matters. I'll have someone look in on you later. Perhaps it isn't too late to get rid of it right now, before it is born and becomes a prob-lem. I can't have Zhan's children inheriting my dynasty. Rest, my dear. You will need your rest. I'll be back soon.' He gave her a mock-courtly bow and departed, caressing the severed braids he carried with the fingertips of his free hand.

Tammary desperately tried to free her hands, but succeeded only in chafing her wrists raw against the cord with which she had been bound. 'Liudan won't believe it. Zhan will come looking for me,' she whispered to herself, trying to keep despair at bay. 'Oh, *Cahan*, he is going to take my baby, he will hurt my child.'

She was left alone for what seemed like hours, during which time, between the dry nausea which still racked her and the creeping despair of her captivity, she cried herself into near oblivion. She was also increasingly thirsty, her mouth dry and her lips cracking a little where she ran her tongue over them. When she heard the door open she turned her head sharply, afraid that it was Eleo back again to torment her, but it was an old woman, wrapped in a dark shawl, carrying a basin and a washcloth.

'There, there, my sweet bird,' the old woman said in a voice brittle with age. 'I know it's hard. It'll all be over soon. Don't worry.'

'Water . . .' Tammary whispered.

'In a moment, sweet thing. I've come to take care of you.'

She dampened the washcloth in her basin, stowed somewhere just out of Tammary's line of sight, and then her gnarled old claw of a hand came down over Tammary's face, wiping her cheeks and closed eyelids with the damp cloth, her touch unexpectedly gentle. It felt refreshing, but the very tenderness of it made tears well up in Tammary's eyes again.

'I have to get out of here,' she gasped, her eyes flying open against the cloth. 'Help me. You have to help me. He's holding me against my will.'

'It will all be all right,' the old woman said, in the same soothing tone of voice. She finished her ministrations and backed out of sight again. Tammary heard her pouring something, and then she was back, lifting Tammary up very gently and propping a pillow behind her back, offering her a cup. 'Something to drink,' she said. 'Here, something to drink, you must be thirsty.'

But the liquid in the cup wasn't water. It was something herb-bitter, biting, and Tammary took one swallow and choked on it, gasping, turning her head away.

'No! What is that?' Her years of working in Yuet's stillroom kicked in, her mind running down the lists of herbs. Why would they be giving her potions? Why would they . . .

The identity of the herb exploded in her mind at the same time as her chain of reasoning brought her to the same place. The herb was called *sochuan*, and it was given for women's problems. And in high doses it induced . . .

Tammary twisted, screamed, but the old woman was remarkably strong. Constantly repeating a gentle refrain of, 'It's all right, it will all be over soon,' she expertly whipped the pillow out from behind Tammary's back, held her nose closed with one hand, and held the cup to her mouth with the other. Much of the contents of the cup spilled over Tammary's closed lips, down her chin, soaking the cropped ends of her now jawline-length hair. But the instinct to breathe was too strong, and as she finally opened her mouth to gasp for air the bitter herbal infusion flooded in and down to the back of her throat and she swallowed convulsively.

'That's a good girl,' the old woman said complacently, letting Tammary's head loll back onto the bed. 'Here, you may have some water now. I'll be here later, when you need me. I'll be here.'

Tammary moaned, turning her head away.

When the pain came, another few hours later, the old woman was not there. Alone, tied down to a slatted wooden bed with a thin, hard mattress, Tammary screamed and writhed in agony as a clawed hand reached into her and scoured her clean. She felt the rush of warm blood when it gushed down her legs, soaking her dress, going straight through the thin straw-filled pallet beneath her and starting to drip and pool just in her line of sight. Terrified, in pain and in desperate, tearing grief, Tammary became aware of another emotion crystallizing out of the whole potent cocktail. Fury. Cold, bitter fury. *He cannot keep me tied up the rest of my life. And when he lets me go I will kill him.*

Tammary's *jin-shei* circle threw themselves into searching for her. Unlike Qiaan, who was beyond their reach on the ghost road somewhere, Tammary had to be somewhere in the city. But Maxao, somewhat unexpectedly, took the position that Tammary's disappearance could be just the goad that Lihui needed to come out of his lair. Although he did finally promise that he would help search for her, it was with every appearance of doing so against his better judgement. The beggars, however, turned up nothing – although Tai muttered darkly to Nhia that she was far from sure whether that was from a genuine ignorance or from deferring to their leader's fiat to say nothing until such time as he allowed it.

'She could be dead by then,' Tai said, stabbing her needle into the silk stretched over her embroidery hoop with a savage little motion. 'Where could they have put her? The beggars swear that she is not in the underbelly, because they would have heard about that – unless they are lying. Xaforn says that she isn't anywhere that a Guard could have access to. And Yuet has been scouring every place she knows, every hole she had ever been dragged to as a healer, asking questions of anyone she meets. How hard can it be to find her – anyone seeing her, seeing that hair, would remember.'

'They won't kill her,' Nhia said. 'Remember the note? She is the key to power. They wouldn't destroy that.'

Tai's eyes filled with tears. 'I feel so helpless.'

'I know,' Nhia said. 'I feel like it's all coming apart, and I cannot hold it together any more. Oh, Cahan, I should have just stayed a little insignificant children's teacher at the Temple. Or took over my mother's laundering business. Anything. Anything but this.'

'Even after getting that pitiful amputated braid, a declaration of powerlessness if ever I saw one, Liudan believes that Amri willingly turned her hand to this,' Tai said. 'It nearly killed Zhan, because he understood what it meant – that Amri is totally in their power. And yet Liudan . . . I just don't understand it.'

'I know,' said Nhia softly. 'Liudan has already condemned her. And Tammary will know, wherever she is; she understands Liudan far too well. And Zhan knows, too. Whatever happens, there is no going back for them.'

Summer dragged on into autumn, and that year's Autumn Court opened with a blaze of glory that few Autumn Courts had ever had. Liudan glowed with jewels, as though every one she managed to put upon her person was another seal on her identity as the Empress of Syai. Her layered robes, encrusted with gold and silk and gems, looked as though their weight would have crushed a lesser person. But Liudan wore them with a fierce dignity, her spine straight, her shoulders back, her head high under the Imperial Tiara.

The Court was uneasy this year, with a lot of whispering behind fans and gracefully concealing, well-manicured courtiers' hands. It was as though an expectation weighed heavily on the occasion, as though too many things were hanging, as though all of it could come crashing down, one way or another.

It was one of Nhia's people who started to break the back of the crisis. The man came to her, hesitating, choosing his words carefully.

'It could be nothing, nothing at all, but all things have significance in the Way,' he said piously, wringing his hands in Nhia's private chambers where he had asked to be taken to deliver his news, far from any eavesdroppers.

'What do you know?' Nhia said.

'I was in the audience chamber,' he said, 'standing right behind

Emeritus-Chancellor Zibo and a companion whom I did not know, a young man of small build, dressed very well in gold brocade and gem . . .'

'I don't require a description, unless you saw his face,' Nhia said. 'What did you hear?'

'The Emeritus-Chancellor whispered to his companion – and this is why I started listening, Nhia-*lama*, because it was a strange remark – that it would not be long before they would have all those jewels off the Empress. And the young man said, also in a whisper, "If I ever tame our little wild fox. She's dangerous. I cannot leave her loose when I am in the room." The Emeritus-Chancellor then looked around, as though he was trying to make sure that they hadn't been heard, and I made sure I was looking in another direction, and I don't think they know that I heard, and it may be nothing, I mean, it's the Emeritus-Chancellor, and after all . . .'

'After all, he has been sidelined by Liudan,' Nhia said. 'Thank you. This could mean everything.'

She did not know the identity of the man who had been with Zibo at the Court, but he was enough, for now. Nhia sent Xaforn and a detachment of Guards to bring the ex-Chancellor to a cell in the Guard compound, and sent a message to Khailin to come there as soon as she could. Nhia herself was there to meet an outraged Zibo when he was brought in, spluttering indignantly and demanding to know who was responsible for this outrage.

'I am,' Nhia said in reply to his complaints as he was walked smartly in through the door of the lock-up room by two burly Guards, followed by Xaforn. 'I know everything, Zibo.'

'Everything,' he smirked. '*Everything*. You can't use that on me, young lady. I used that self-incriminating statement with hundreds of miscreants in my time. And if I really knew anything at all they were usually in chains and in the dungeons, or under the headsman's axe, not interrogated by some administrator in a low-level jail.'

'All we are waiting for,' Nhia said tranquilly, folding her arms, 'is word that Tammary is safe. Then you will be taken to the Empress in those chains you so covet. Together with your accomplice. If Tammary hasn't got to him first. And we might just let her.'

Zibo's expression faltered for a moment, but then he had himself under control again. 'Safe? Tammary? I don't know what you are talking about.'

'Oh yes, you do,' Khailin, who had come in right behind Xaforn, said very softly.

Zibo jumped, tried to back away. 'You keep that witch away from me,' he said. 'You have no right to . . .'

'We have every right,' Nhia said. 'You are involved in an activity the purpose of which is nothing less than the deposition of the Empress. That is high treason. You have used an innocent woman, a *jin-shei* sister to the Empress herself and to all of us, as your pawn. And from what I already know about this plot, you have not used her kindly. Oh, you will die for this, Zibo. The chains *and* the headsman's axe. What was in it for you? Regaining the Chancellor's chain? What, if you had succeeded, would have been *my* fate, Zibo?'

'This is ridiculous. I have no idea what you are talking about. You have no right . . .'

Khailin reached out to touch him, and he tried shying away, but the two Guards who still held his arms made sure that he could not avoid the brush of her fingers.

'Oh, he's in it up to his ears,' Khailin said. 'I can taste the fear on him.'

Zibo drew himself up to the full extent his bulk would allow. His chins wobbled with affronted dignity. 'How dare you speak to me like that! I am an Imperial officer of high rank, and I demand that I receive the treatment that my position demands!'

A Guard at the door ducked into the interrogation room, whispered something into Xaforn's ear, stared at Zibo for a moment, and then left again.

'They got Tammary,' Xaforn said. 'But the other guy wasn't there, his friend. Tammary's jailer.'

'Jailer,' spluttered Zibo. 'You obviously have no idea what you are talking about. I insist that you let me go at once.'

He spluttered to a halt as Xaforn drew out her sword with one smooth, economical movement and its tip suddenly trembled at that point in Zibo's cascade of chins which might be expected to house the vulnerable spot on the throat of any other man.

'You may think yourself well protected, in theory and in practice,' Xaforn said calmly, 'but my blade has sliced through harder stuff than your blubber, and you really are in no position to bargain with a woman whom you would have swept away ruthlessly if you ever got to within shouting distance of a Chancellor's chain again. So I'll ask you, one more time . . .'

'He's her husband!' Zibo spluttered. 'There is nothing you can do now to undo that! He married her under every law of Syai, and she wears his rings on her thumbs! That's more than your precious Zhan ever did for her!'

'Zhan married her in his heart, and she him,' Nhia said. 'I was there. Under every law of Syai, as you choose to invoke them, the travesty you forced Tammary to go through was performed on an unwilling woman taken by force. It will not stand. You lost, Zibo. You can still save yourself, maybe, if you tell us where to find him, this . . . *husband*.'

'He's at the tea-house now. That's where he always is. Eleo. He goes back to the tea-houses after Court, then he'll be back to my quarters.'

Xaforn slipped out before he had finished speaking, and he trailed off, looking from one to the other. 'You didn't know any of this, did you? You didn't *know* it, not until I spoke out.' He staggered backwards, and the two Guards at his sides allowed his huge bulk to subside onto the single bare bench in the room.

'Keep him here,' Nhia said. 'I'm going to get Yuet. I have a feeling we may need her after Tammary's been in the tender care of this crew for all these weeks.'

'And Tai. Get Tai.' Khailin stood staring at the ex-Chancellor, her eyes implacable. 'I'll get the rest of it out of this one.'


But it seemed as though they had got the information too late. When they all converged on the grounds of Zibo's plush residence not far away from the Palace, it was to see black smoke pouring out of the second-storey windows. Xaforn sent in her Guards at all the side entrances, and she, with Yuet and Nhia at her heels, charged in through the front. Tai alone hung back, and it was Tai, therefore, who saw the bedraggled figure hunched in the shelter of some ornamental flowering bushes not far from the main building. Glancing at where the others had gone, Tai turned away deliberately and approached what she initially thought was a young man, soot-stained and somehow, perhaps, wounded, with blood smeared on his hands. But then the 'young man' lifted his head, and a bright curl of hair escaped from underneath a large flat cap that had been shoved haphazardly on the figure's head, and Tai's heart stopped for a moment.

'Amri?' she whispered, quickening her step. 'Amri? Is that you? Is that really you? Are you all right?'

'Go, don't linger here,' Tammary said in a low voice. 'Don't ever tell them you found me. Let them think I died in that fire. Let them rather believe . . .'

'What have they done to you?' Tai gasped. 'I can't leave you out here. I can't just . . .'

'There will be others,' Tammary said. 'I'm better dead.'

'But Zhan . . .'

'Maybe. In time. But no, how could I go back?' Her eyes swam with tears. 'They gave me *sochuan*, Tai. Ask Yuet what that means. I will probably never quicken with child again. And he doesn't need the Empress watching him all the time, waiting for him to make his move. And they married me to Eleo.'

'I know,' said Tai, reaching for her. But Tammary recoiled.

'*I killed him*,' she whispered. 'I swore I would, and I did.'

'They told me what happened to you,' Tai said. 'Nobody will blame you.'

'Help me,' Tammary whispered, reaching out and clutching Tai's skirts, her eyes full of tears, bright in her soot-black face. 'In the name of *jin-shei*, help me. Help me get out of Linh-an.'

For a moment Tai was far away, a little girl weeping over the dying body of her first beloved *jin-shei-bao*. Antian had asked, too – she had asked, in the name of the bond that lay between them. And Tai had spent her life in the service of that vow.

Now, here, in this dark hour, Tammary was asking her for something – in the name of the same bright, holy name.

*Jin-shei*, the promise that could not be broken, could not be refused.

'But you are . . .' Tai began, after a beat of silence.

'I have to get out of here,' Tammary said, her voice breaking on a sob.

'And go where?' Tai said, looking around desperately for the others. 'Come, let Yuet look at . . .'

Tammary shook her head. 'I don't want that,' she said. 'I don't want to be stared at and prodded and poked and pitied. I need to go.

I need to find . . . I can go home, to the mountains, to the high skies, to where nobody cares.'

'You ran away from there once,' Tai said.

'And perhaps there is no going back, but I need to get out of here,' Tammary said.

'Then Nhia can . . .'

'*No*. Nobody knows about this. Nobody but you. Help me.'

'May I at least tell Zhan?'

Tammary hesitated. 'Maybe. In time. I'll let you know.'

'They are coming out,' Tai said.

'Tai . . .'

'All right. All right! Stay there.'

She crossed the expanse of lawn back to the house at a run, seeing Yuet emerge, shaking her head.

'Have you found anything?'

'We think we have found this Eleo,' Yuet said. 'With a knife in his kidney. And another brace of people, mostly old, mostly servants.'

'No Tammary?'

'No body,' Yuet said.

'We'll search the grounds,' said Xaforn. 'She might be hiding somewhere in the park. What's the matter with *you*, Tai? You are looking sick to the stomach.'

'I am,' Tai whispered.

Yuet stared at her beadily. 'Are you pregnant again? If you are, what are you doing out here?'

'I don't know,' Tai said, seizing on the excuse. 'I don't think so.'

'We can look for her,' Xaforn said. 'You go home. Get some rest. You've been fretting about this.'

'So have all of us,' Tai said.

'Yes, but you've taken it personally,' said Xaforn. 'Yuet, take her home!'

'No!' Tai said. They both turned to look at her with some surprise at the vehemence of that reaction. She grimaced. 'I mean, if you find Tammary, she needs Yuet more than I do.'

'Go home,' said Yuet. 'I swear, if you of all people fall apart on me right now, I'll go mad. I'll come by your house as soon as I can, and tell you what happened.'

397

Tai stole a glance at the shrubbery, but the figure of Tammary was no longer visible.

'But I don't want to . . .' she began.

Yuet scowled at her. 'Go, and leave me to try and do some good here,' she said.

Tai left, slowly, reluctantly, aware of being followed by both Yuet's and Xaforn's eyes until she had reached the outer gate of the courtyard. Then they turned away, and as Tai stepped into the gate Tammary's fragile voice, like the sound of dry autumn leaves whispering against each other on the ground in late Chuntan, spoke from the shadows.

'Are they still watching?'

'No. But how am I going to get you back to my house undetected?'

'Why back to your house?'

'Tammary, you can't go anywhere as you are right now.'

'You promised not to tell anyone,' Tammary whispered.

'I didn't, but I won't, much against my better judgement,' Tai said, slipping off her own cloak as she spoke. 'You asked me to help you get out of this place, and I will do my best to do that. But we'll still talk about who gets to know about it. Here. Wrap this around you. And follow me.'


Tai had every intention of settling Tammary down, getting her cleaned up and providing her with a change of clothes, and then at the very least having another talk to her about the wisdom of her course of action. She also intended to let Zhan at least know that Tammary was alive, if nothing else. She had seen his face when the hope died in him. It would be heartless to let him go on believing Tammary was gone for good.

But the best-laid plans could go awry, and it was simply unfortunate that, when Xaforn and Nhia brought Zibo before the Empress with a full description of the plot, Zhan happened to arrive at the Palace at just the right time for Liudan to inform him that Tammary was dead.

Liudan herself was distracted by quite a different piece of news that had just broken – and that was that, against all rules of civilized warfare, the Magalipt riders had launched their long-awaited invasion from the passes on Syai's western borders. To her, Tammary's death – although Nhia had specifically said that they had found no body – was the conclusion that she had jumped to as the one which offered the most convenient closure to the situation. Her announcement to Zhan was thus less tactful than even she might have been expected to deliver.

'Well,' she had said, 'at least that problem is solved. Now I can clear the slate for doing something useful on the border.'

It wasn't deliberate cruelty. But to Zhan it was shattering. He found the idea of returning alone to the quiet rooms he had shared with Tammary for such a short, idyllic time almost unbearable; she would be everywhere for him, a lingering, bright-haired ghost who would remind him that he had lost both of them, Tammary and the child which she had carried. There was, as it happened, an alternative. He asked Liudan for a chance to lead her troops into the battle against the Magalipt.

Liudan knew Zhan as indolent, and she may have thought of his gentleness as weakness – but she also knew him as intelligent, not without courage, and, she believed, loyal enough despite his unfortunate taste in women. She gave him a command on the spot.

By the time Tai got a chance to send for him to tell him that Tammary was safe and at her house, Zhan had gone to war.

And before the sun rose too high on the following day, Tammary, her shorn hair swept up in a young man's woollen cap and her bosom bound to give her a more boyish silhouette, slipped out of the Northern Gate and began the long journey back to the mountains from which she had fled so long ago looking for a better world.

# Nine

Everything suddenly seemed to be deeper, more serious, more brooding in Linh-an that autumn. Every moment had a curious intensity, a breathless sense of portent.

Tai's poetry reflected the mood. But much of what she wrote she kept in her journal, instinctively holding it back from Liudan. She knew that the Empress would be disturbed by it.

> *Leaves have always fallen from autumn branches.*
> *But never before*
> *has it filled me with so much nameless fear.*
> *Why am I so terribly afraid*
> *that the leaves will not return*
> *when the spring comes?*

'Why are you so frightened?' Kito would murmur into her hair, late at night, when Tai could not sleep.

'I wish I knew,' Tai would whisper back, her throat tight. 'A long time ago, when I was just a child, when Antian had first called me *jin-shei*, my mother told me that I was in the *liu-kala* of my *jin-shei* days, that everything had its season. I have a terrible feeling that somehow I am in the twilight of that season, that my sisters are in danger, that what happened to Qiaan, to Tammary . . . that it's the beginning of an end, somehow. That we are in *ryu-kala*, the age before dying.'

'We are all still young,' Kito said, his arms around her. 'Don't let these dark thoughts in. I know we are living in troubling times, but things will get better. Things always do. That is the way of the world – whenever things get really bad, then they can only get better.'

But his words, however much Tai clung to them, failed to lift her sense of foreboding.

If Autumn Court had glittered more desperately than ever before in that year, the Festival of All Souls, when it came round on the last day of Chuntan, proved memorable for quite a different reason.

The Great Temple was closed to the public on this day, the only day of the year that the three massive gates were closed and barred. The one who wore the Imperial Tiara took on the responsibility of being his people on this day. Traditionally, the Emperor and Empress walked to the Great Temple from the Palace in the morning of the Festival of All Souls, through the streets of the city, and entered the Temple through a special small door on the side of the building, usually kept sealed and bricked up the rest of the year. On All Souls' Day every year, the wall built before this door was torn down by the priests of the Temple to allow entrance to the Emperor and the Empress; and every year the door was bricked up anew after they had passed through it, to hold in the renewal and rebirth they were bringing into the Temple. The Imperial pair would walk barefoot around the Temple, through all the Circles, and spend the day in prayer and offerings and meditation in the inner sanctum, in the temple in the Tower of the Lord of Heaven. What the actual ceremonies were that were performed there, nobody outside the Temple Circles and the Emperors themselves actually knew. Naturally there was a lot of speculation – it was certainly considered propitious to conceive a child on this day, for instance, and the less reverent teahouses would often refer to intimate dalliance as 'doing what the Emperor does on All Souls' Day'.

But Liudan had no Emperor, no mate to take in with her, and what rituals she was led in by the Temple priests remained her own mystery, although there were those who had muttered that it obviously wasn't working because bad harvest after bad harvest was edging some remote communities into starvation. Liudan's procession to the Temple in the year of Tai's forebodings was watched only by scattered crowds on the streets, but there was little cheering and there seemed to be rather more Guards about than were usually required.

The rites took most of the day, and as twilight started to gather Liudan finally emerged from the Temple, through one of the three gates, unbarred again and thrown open to the people. She had done everything that had been required, had bowed before every God, had lit incense before every shrine and then burned sweet oils in bowls of lapis and jade at the innermost altar of the Great Temple of Syai, and her prayers had been fervent and genuine – *Help my land, for it is troubled*. She walked back to the Palace in the hour of gathering shadows, surrounded by torches and lanterns, a vision of Empire, the anointed one who had just communed with Cahan itself and bought a year of peace and prosperity for the realm. Glittering with gems in the darkening street.

A perfect target.

One of the Guards heard the whistle of the black arrow that came winging out of the dark, and shouted out a warning as he threw himself in front of the Empress. The arrow nicked his shoulder armour, and slid off the sleek metal shell. It lost momentum – enough to keep it from being deadly. But it was still moving. It struck a faceted gem on Liudan's shoulder, glanced off, and embedded itself in a padded fold on her heavily embroidered outer robe.

Liudan's face did not change, and she continued walking at the same stately pace as she had been doing up until that moment. But her Guards coalesced into a tight circle around her, and two of them held a pair of shields over her head from behind. It cast a shadow on her, quenching her glitter. She was unharmed, but only by the sheerest fluke – and the point had been made more than adequately by the rest of that tense march back to the relative safety of the Palace walls, a walk that seemed to take a year out of the lives of every one of the people in that street who were charged with protecting the Empress. It was only after she was safely delivered into her own rooms that Liudan started weeping, from fear and from fury, and would let nobody in to see her, not even Yuet, who came hurrying to the Palace as soon as she heard what had happened.

'She will do herself a worse injury if she doesn't let me at least give her some sort of a calming infusion,' Yuet said to Xaforn. 'But she wasn't even hurt, you said. Just frightened.'

Xaforn tossed her head. 'Sometimes fright is worse. She is afraid of everything these days, of her own shadow. I've seen her shying at *my* presence sometimes. I think she is desperately lonely right now, fighting a war on three fronts, and I don't know how she stays sane in all this.'

'Three fronts?' Yuet said, frowning.

'Maybe even four,' Xaforn said. 'Lihui, the Magalipt thing, and then the treachery of people like Zibo when the whole Tammary situation exploded. She never really trusted Zibo, but she was appalled that she could have let him plot as deeply as he did without her having got wind of it sooner. This was a poison in her own Court.'

'But you said four,' Yuet said. 'That's three.'

Xaforn gave her a strange look. 'Herself,' she said. 'Really, Yuet, you're the healer. You can see that she's tearing herself apart. She is all there is – there's no mate, no heir, nothing and nobody to take the pressure off her. She didn't bargain for this when she wanted to be Empress.'

'How did you get to be so wise?' Yuet murmured.

'You and Tai,' Xaforn said, with a sad smile. 'And the times we live in.'

\* \* \*

When Liudan finally admitted one of her *jin-shei* circle into her presence, it was neither Yuet nor Xaforn but Nhia – who had had to pull both the strings she had available, *jin-shei* and the duties and needs of her Chancellor's office, in order to achieve this.

'You look a wreck, Liudan,' Nhia said when she was ushered into Liudan's rooms, almost two days after the attack. 'Have you slept in the last forty-eight hours? Have you eaten anything? You look half dead.'

Liudan's head came up sharply at that word. 'I could have been wholly dead,' she said.

'Now you're wallowing,' Nhia said gently. 'Talk to us. All of us. *Any* of us. You know Tai would spend every waking hour with you if you ask her. Liudan, if you go on like this you'll be doing their work for them. You'll kill yourself far faster and probably with far more suffering than they could ever hope to inflict on you.'

'Don't lecture,' said Liudan.

'I'm not,' Nhia said. 'None of us is immortal.'

'You said Lihui was,' said Liudan unexpectedly.

'Perhaps,' Nhia said carefully, but her voice had gone tight at the mention of Lihui's name. 'But I think it is given to us, in the end, to choose how we live and how we die. And I would not want the responsibility of living Lihui's life. The price he will eventually pay will be very great. And even the Immortals . . . well, but Khailin is probably far more knowledgeable on that subject than me, these days. You read her paper on the ages of the world.'

'I meant to,' Liudan said. 'I have a copy of it in my chambers somewhere. But I hardly even read the poems that Tai sends me these days. There is too much in my head, and I don't have the time any more to think of other things, and of what is to come if I should . . . Nhia, what would happen to Syai if I had taken that arrow? I have left nothing settled, I had thought I would have years.'

'You do have years,' Nhia said. 'Liudan, get some food into you. Get some rest.'

Liudan gave her a curious sidelong glance. 'So what does Khailin say on the subject?'

'Of food? She takes it occasionally,' Nhia said. 'On the whole, I think she approves of the concept.'

Liudan made a sharp little movement with her hand. 'Don't mock me,' she snapped. 'I meant on immortality, of course. She is doing work on that?'

'She does a lot of things,' Nhia said. She was beginning to catch a dangerous drift, and tried to steer the conversation into other channels. 'She and Maxao, forever fluttering around that laboratory of hers. Half the time I don't know what she is brewing in there. However, I have other things here that need your attention, Empress, from your Chancellor's office. You order some breakfast in, and we can discuss them at our leisure over some tea.'

Liudan emerged from her isolation after Nhia's visit, but her mood was dark and brittle. She was brooding on something, something that she wouldn't talk to any of her *jin-shei* sisters about. No further attempts on her life occurred, and for some weeks things appeared to go on as normal until one day, on the eve of Khailin's twenty-fifth birthday, she gathered an entourage of Guards and made her way to Khailin's house in the city.

The visit was unexpected and Khailin, informed by a flustered servant that the Empress was waiting in the drawing room, stripped off her working smock and hurried out to greet her.

'Happy birthday,' Liudan said, by way of greeting.

Khailin blinked. 'Believe it or not, I had actually forgotten,' she said. 'Thank you.'

'I have a present for you,' Liudan said, and gestured to one of her retainers, waiting by the door of the room. He bowed, signalled somebody outside, and a small cedarwood chest was brought into the room.

'What is that?' Khailin said, eyeing the curiously carved box.

'Open it,' Liudan said.

The hinges creaked as the lid was lifted. 'This hasn't been opened in some time,' Khailin said.

'Probably not,' Liudan said. 'It's doing no good where it was. I thought you could use it.'

The box was full of neat scrolls which, when Khailin experimentally unfurled one, proved to be closely written with tiny *hacha-ashu* script. Khailin peered at it, squinting.

'I need glasses,' she said, 'or this thing was written under a magnifying lens. What *is* this, Liudan?'

'Records,' Liudan said, 'from the Imperial astronomers. I think some of them date back maybe two hundred years.'

Khailin looked up. 'This is a royal treasure, Liudan. Why are you giving this to me?'

'You use it,' Liudan said. 'Nhia said you were working on a lot of things.'

'Yes,' Khailin said slowly. 'I am.'

Their eyes met, held; many things were said without speaking. Then Liudan laughed. 'You're right, it's also a bribe of sorts. There is something I want you to do for me.'

'And it is not something I will be happy doing, is it, Liudan?'

'I don't know,' Liudan said.

Khailin rolled up the ancient scroll again and put it back in its box. 'So, what is your wish?'

'I nearly died last autumn,' Liudan said.

'I know.'

'I would have left the Empire adrift, unprovided for.'

Khailin waited, in silence.

'I need *time*,' Liudan said, a tinge of urgency in her voice now, even of desperation. 'I cannot do what I have to do if I am waiting for the arrow in my heart every moment. I cannot plan if I don't have the time to see it all come to harvest.'

'I've already made such protective amulets as I may,' Khailin said quietly. 'Some of them guard the gates of your Palace as we speak. But what else may I do that . . .'

'Nhia said you were working on it,' Liudan interrupted. 'And I want it. I want that from you. I want . . .'

'Want *what*, Liudan?'

'Immortality,' said Liudan, and her eyes glinted with naked need. 'In the name of *jin-shei*, I want you to give me immortality.'

'It's winter at last. Everything sleeps.
The soul, too, is at rest
in Pau.'

Qiu-Lin, Year 28 of the Cloud Emperor

# *One*

The servant had barely had the chance to open the door before Khailin swept through and into Yuet's sitting room. Her expression appeared to be made up of equal parts of frustration, fury, exasperation and fear.

Tai, sitting curled on the window seat and sipping a cup of Yuet's herbal tea, uncoiled like a whip at the sight of her.

'You look like you want to kill somebody,' she said.

'On the contrary,' Khailin retorted. 'I've been presented with an ultimatum to keep someone alive.'

'To keep someone alive?' Tai echoed in puzzlement.

'Isn't that my job?' Yuet said ironically.

'Yes,' Khailin snapped, 'and not in the way that you are thinking of, Yuet. I mean indefinitely. Liudan has woken up to the concept of immortality.'

'You'd better sit down, and have some tea, and tell us everything from the beginning,' Yuet said, already pouring into a porcelain cup.

Khailin could clearly remember the conversation in her parlour that had started the ball rolling, nearly two weeks before.

'Immortality,' Liudan had said, 'in the name of *jin-shei*.'

'You've had a scare,' Khailin said after a heartbeat of silence. 'Immortality will not protect you from stray arrows, Liudan. And there are several kinds of immortality anyway. And besides, it's impossible.'

'Nothing is impossible,' Liudan said, 'and anything asked in the name of *jin-shei* is a sacred trust.'

'So you aren't ordering me to do it,' Khailin said, her mouth quirking. 'You're just demanding the impossible in the name of the unrefusable bond. What if I cannot?'

'Nhia seems to think you can,' Liudan said.

'Nhia?' Khailin said, astonished. 'What has Nhia to do with this?'

'She said you had been working on something like this.'

'Only because I want to know how to destroy it,' Khailin snapped. 'With Lihui still on the loose . . .'

'What did you mean about different kinds of immortality?' Liudan said. 'What kind does Lihui possess?'

'*No*, Liudan. Not that,' Khailin said, frowning. 'You do not want to be Lihui. What he is, is unnatural, and evil. What he has is only sustainable because he drinks other people's souls, to put it simply. He is old, immensely old, immeasurably old. And very powerful. When he gets tired he simply slakes his physical thirsts in some nubile young thing's body, and he makes no distinction between male and female when choosing his victims, and then drinks their vitality until there's just a shell left. Just as he did to Nhia.'

'But she's alive and well,' Liudan said stubbornly.

'Only because I was there,' Khailin said. 'He left the job half-done that night. He would have been back to finish it. And you know, you *know* how long it took her to come back to us.'

'How is it that he didn't use you for this purpose, then?' Liudan said.

Khailin flinched. 'I don't know,' she whispered. 'Part of it was a game to him, making me learn the hard way what an utter young and naïve fool I was. He enjoyed seeing me suffer far more than he would have enjoyed inhaling my spirit to prolong his own unnatural life. That, I guess, and the fact that he had access to other sources. There were plenty of other young and virile peaches from the tree of immortality that he could reach out and pluck when he needed to. He therefore felt no urgent need for me in that manner.' She shuddered. 'Not even in the name of *jin-shei* will I think of that path.'

'You said there were other forms of immortality,' Liudan persisted. 'Tell me.'

'One is the spiritual immortality,' Khailin said reluctantly, 'of the sort that the Temple confers – the Holy Immortals, the Sages and the Emperors whose statues crowd the niches, who are now in Cahan and who listen to the prayers of the people. But you achieve that through great deeds, and only after your physical shell is gone. This is not what you want of me.'

'Is there another choice?' Liudan was not going to let go of the idea willingly, or easily.

Cornered, Khailin scowled. 'Yes, but that also isn't what you had in mind when you . . .'

'I'll be the judge of that,' Liudan said.

'There are ancient records,' Khailin said carefully, 'which speak of a method . . . I don't know, I haven't studied it in depth. I am not sure. I cannot explain things I do not understand myself.'

'But you can learn,' Liudan said. 'What do you need to begin your study?'

'Liudan, there are far easier ways of getting yourself an heir,' Khailin said with some asperity.

'Not one who will be myself,' Liudan said, her eyes glowing. 'If, as you say, going the route that Lihui took is such total abomination, then I will try this other way. And you will help me do this, Khailin. In the name of *jin-shei*, you will.'


'And you *agreed*?' Yuet asked, when Khailin had finished recounting the incident.

'I've already started doing it, damn her,' Khailin snarled. 'If it had been a direct order, I could have refused, maybe. But she asked it in the name of the sisterhood.'

She paused, and rubbed her fingertips against her closed eyelids in a weary motion.

'But there is more to it than that,' Tai said, interpreting the motion, seeing the conflict – the guilt – which hung around Khailin. 'She also sparked off something else.'

'Curiosity,' Khailin said, with an air of admitting defeat. 'That has ever been my weakness. I am doing it for a *jin-shei* sister, but it's put down roots into that wretched curiosity, and now . . . now *I* want to know. Find out for her, and for myself. All I know is that the knowledge is forbidden and trammelled in arcana, and all that

411

ever did for me is make me itch to dig deeper. To find the answers. Damn her! I can't not try and solve this now. But I can't do it alone – I need things. I need . . . Yuet, I need your help.'

A part of Tai, looking on with cold detachment, shivered at those words with an odd prescience. Her mother used to describe that strange feeling as 'a wind on your ashes', as though someone's breath disturbed the remnants of a funeral pyre.

Her own poem came back to haunt her; an image of autumn-bare branches, awash in clear spring sunlight but dead, dead, dead. *It is coming*, Tai thought dispassionately. *It is coming, the storm . . .*

'What do I have to do with it?' Yuet said, surprised.

'You are a healer. You have access.'

'Access to what?'

'To bodies. To bodily fluids. To living tissue, or even the newly dead. I need to understand life before I can understand how to perpetuate it. I tried using myself, but I cannot bleed myself every day. I need . . . oh, *Cahan*, why did she have to set me on this? I need something to work with.'

'Where do you expect me to get you dead bodies?' Yuet asked, aghast. 'I can't have them delivered to your back door like dirty laundry!'

'That is exactly how you need to have them delivered,' Khailin said, 'as disguised as you can. I can't let word of this get out.'

'Have you done anything so far?' Tai said, her voice unnaturally calm, as though she was keeping it under a tight control.

'Some,' Khailin said, and bared her arm, showing a new lint bandage. 'These are the scars of battle. I have used my own blood. But there are works that hint that the essence of a person can be used to animate a . . . a *thing*, a statue, a likeness of the original, and then bring that to life. There are elixirs, concoctions passed down through generations.'

'Khailin!' Yuet burst out, appalled. 'That is a worse abomination than even Lihui's brand of ghoul-feeding! You would be usurping the powers of the Gods themselves, handing out life or withholding it.'

'In the name of *jin-shei*, Yuet,' Khailin said, her eyes bitter.

'What?'

'What she asked of me, I ask of you. In the name of *jin-shei*. I cannot do this alone.'

'Maybe it was never meant to be done,' Tai said.

Khailin rounded on her. 'Fine. *You* go and tell Liudan.'

'And you'd go on, anyway, wouldn't you? Now that you've got this far.'

Khailin grimaced. 'I have to know.'

'Khailin, you don't need to know why a star shines to enjoy its light. You don't need to raise the dead to understand the breath of life.'

'That's poetry, Tai. I'm doing science. I do need – I have always needed.'

'That's what delivered you to Lihui in the first place,' Tai said quietly, stubbornly.

'That is true,' said Khailin, unwilling to admit defeat but forced to concede the point.

'Don't let your pride drive you to . . .'

'Pride has nothing to do with it any more,' Khailin said. 'Nhia will tell you that all of us have our own Path in the Way, Tai – this is mine. Liudan pushed me onto it, but now I have taken the first steps there and I need to know, for myself. I need to learn the forgotten secrets. That is all I have ever wanted to do with my life. And now I am compelled to it, by stronger things than just curiosity – I am charged with doing it, in the name of the sisterhood.' She turned back to Yuet. 'Will you help me?'

'Khailin, I can't . . .'

'*Will you help me?*' Khailin's voice vibrated with intensity.

Yuet was actually trembling. 'I can't do this, Khailin. It's against the spirit of the healers' oath. I have sworn that I will not do harm.'

'You will not be,' Khailin said. 'If harm is done, that responsibility lies with me. All you have to do is . . .'

'Deliver people into that harm,' whispered Yuet.

'We are talking dead people.'

'You said living tissue!'

'Well, *newly* dead people. With the energies still clinging to them. I can come with you if that is easier and collect a sample.'

'No!' Yuet said, recoiling. 'That is not . . .'

'Well, then,' Khailin said.

'You're cheating someone's soul out of Cahan,' Tai said softly.

'What are you talking about?'

'Their spirit crosses over into the Fields of Heaven in the smoke of their pyre,' Tai said. 'And their ashes are scattered to return their essence to the land. And you would take the body and deny it this passage. Prod it, slice it, take it from the repose where death has taken the soul and drag it back into the world. It's horrible, Khailin.'

'I can't bring someone who is dead back to life,' Khailin laughed, but the laugh was brittle and sharp. 'But I am taking only a small part of the physical being. When I have taken what I need, the rest can be disposed of according to prescribed rites. I have no wish to cheat anyone of their chance of paradise.'

'Ask Nhia,' Tai said. 'She will tell you. She understands.'

'Nobody else knows about this,' Khailin said, her voice intense again. 'Even you, Tai, were probably better off not knowing it. It was to be a covenant between me and Yuet, as it was between Liudan and me.' She looked up, and her eyes were burning. 'I tell you, it has to be done!'

'You are going to create another Lihui,' Yuet said, shaking her head. 'Why can't you leave well alone? Have you talked it over with Sage Maxao? What does he think of this?'

'I told you, nobody else knows of it. None but you two, myself and Liudan. And that is the way it has to be.'

'Why? Doesn't it give you pause that the work has to be so shrouded in secrecy?'

'People won't understand,' Khailin said.

'I'm not sure I do,' Yuet said slowly.

'But will you help me?'

Khailin had asked it in the name of *jin-shei*. She did not bring that claim up again, but it hung between them, like a bright and shining thing, the holiest of vows, the sisterhood which demanded that the impossible and the unthinkable be attempted if asked in its name.

The day at the Summer Palace, the day of death which had made Yuet offer the vow of *jin-shei* to Tai, seemed a lifetime ago. She had done it then in the wake of losing lives, of saving lives. Now she was being asked, in the name of that same vow, to break the law of life itself.

She could not do this thing that Khailin asked. It was against every principle she had ever lived by. And yet . . . and yet . . . it had been asked in the name of the unrefusable.

The battle that raged within Yuet's heart and mind, the battle between her obligations as a healer and her duty to the vow of *jin-shei*, was written in the expression on her face as she gazed at Khailin. And then, finally, after what seemed like hours but lasted perhaps only a handful of minutes, something bleak came into her eyes.

'I will . . . do my best to do what you ask,' Yuet said at last, her hands clasped tightly in her lap.

Khailin must have known how much this had cost Yuet. She had paid a similar price herself. Perhaps that was why she merely nodded at the acquiescence she had wrung out of her *jin-shei-bao*, and said no more.

Tai lingered after Khailin left, worried by Yuet's drawn face and glittering eyes.

'This will destroy you, if you do it,' she said softly.

'It will destroy me if I do not, because of how it was asked,' Yuet said. 'I have to at least try.'

'I'm afraid, Yuet.'

'You? What of?'

'That this is the beginning . . . of something. That we will not all come out of it. I feel the hot wind on my face.'

'You've been spending too much time with Nhia, or listening too hard to those fools at the Temple,' Yuet said, with a harsh little laugh. 'Don't turn into a doomsayer on me, Tai.'

Tai said no more.

But her instincts were true, because it was less than ten days later that Maxao flung open the door to Khailin's laboratory and strode in, his face thunderous, waving his cane about more as a weapon than a support.

'What is this I hear about your work?' he demanded. 'Is it true?'

'I was asked to investigate this problem,' Khailin said quietly. 'By the Empress herself.'

'Has it ever occurred to you,' said Maxao in a low, dangerous voice, 'that just because you can do a thing is not a sufficient reason for doing it?'

'Now you sound like Tai. One of my other *jin-shei-bao*. The one who has taken on the mantle of a rather pessimistic prophet lately. She sees nothing but disaster.'

'She is wiser than you give her credit for, then,' Maxao said. 'So she has tried to stop you?'

'In a manner of speaking,' Khailin said. 'But so long as I don't make a noise about this . . .'

'Well, I will,' said Maxao decisively. 'I will drag what you are doing out into the light of day. If your sister cannot make you stop it, and I cannot make you stop it, the people will.'

'They will not understand the first thing about it!' Khailin protested hotly.

Maxao gave her a strange look. 'You do have a lot of Lihui in you,' he said. 'In the days when he was the youngest of my students – when he was what I believed to be the youngest of my students, when I saw him as merely young and hotheaded, and he had yet to turn to the blackest of his evil. You are certain you want to follow this path? Look where it has led him – hubris and arrogance and selfishness bring their own reward.'

'But I am doing it for Liudan,' Khailin said.

'And what Lihui does is done for what he considers good reasons, too,' Maxao said. 'I stood by then, and watched it, and because I said nothing, did nothing, Lihui grew strong enough to take my sight, my position in life, everything. And now he is poised to reach out for the throne of the Empire. Should he succeed in that endeavour we might all still have to pay the price. But I was foolish once, I will not be so again. You will not do this thing. Not while I am able to act to stop you.'

'Wait! Don't you know that anything you do to undermine Liudan now plays straight into Lihui's hands?' Khailin cried, raising a hand to stop him, but she was already talking to Maxao's back as he swept out of the room.

At first it was only distorted rumours that swept the bazaars. Khailin already had a reputation in the city as a scholar, a student of the more empirical paths of the Way, an alchemist, a seeker of knowledge. Her pursuits were known, if not always wholly approved of, but she had always been treated with the respect due to her station. In the days following Maxao's abrupt departure from her rooms the city's mood seemed to change, to darken. Khailin's cook came back in tears one morning and disclosed that she had been pelted with rotten fruit because she worked for 'the witch'. Crowds gathered before the gates of the Imperial Palace, and there

416

was a dark murmur that rose from them, and the eyes raised to the Palace walls were smouldering with fury and resentment.

*Immortal . . . she wants to be immortal . . . she wants to rule for ever.*

But it was still only thoughts, only words, only high emotion.

When it exploded into action, it took everyone by surprise.

Yuet had never been easy with what Khailin had charged her to do, but she had tried to do it in keeping both with the dictates of her conscience and the fulfilment of her *jin-shei* obligations. If a patient was beyond her help and she knew that death was a matter of maybe only hours away, she asked the next of kin in the household if she could help with making the funeral arrangements. She did all the required rites, but often they took place some time after death, when Khailin was done with the earthly remains, and the families remained unaware that the body on the funeral pyre may not have been entirely whole when finally consigned to the flames.

Things simmered amidst mutters and murmurs for some time. The weeks stretched into months, and even the months began to add up, like beads on a yearwood. But the lull could not last.

The tide turned when Yuet, for once entirely innocently and with no ulterior motives whatsoever, was seen helping an elderly man into a mule-drawn cart in order to transport him back to her own house for treatment. This was something that she had often done for cases which required her constant care and attention. On this particular occasion, however, a woman passing on the street stopped, and pointed a bony finger at Yuet and the half-loaded patient.

'Look!' the woman screeched. 'This is how the witch gets us! This is how she gets the warm bodies she cuts up to seek the juice of immortality for the Ghoul Empress! That one is the witch's assistant – she takes us and gives our bodies to her, still warm, still breathing! Look where she goes, taking yet another! Old he might be, but he is still one of us!'

'One of us!' shrieked someone else.

'Stop her! Stop her stealing the old man!'

'Stop the witch's handmaiden! Stop her!'

'We won't be sliced and studied so that the Empress can live for ever on our blood and sinews!'

'Stop her!'

Yuet had no idea where all the people had come from, but a sudden mob had coalesced around her, and they were angry. Their voices were sharp, shrill, furious.

Perhaps the wisest course of action would have been to climb into the back of the cart with her patient and urge the driver of the cart to move on, quickly and without fuss. But Yuet knew the woman who had originally spoken, and others in the neighbourhood – many of the faces she could glimpse, now contorted with hate, in the gathering crowd she had healed of sores and fevers and tended in childbirth and old age. These were her people, her patients, her charge. She was fatally moved to stop, to explain, to soothe, to make good.

'Wait, let me tell you . . .'

She got no further than those few words. She never knew where the first stone came from, but it hit her squarely in the kidneys. Gasping at the sharp pain Yuet staggered, falling to her hands and knees there in the street, shaking her head and trying to catch her breath.

She was never given the chance. A second stone followed, taking her in the jaw; she tasted blood from a split lip, shattered teeth. A third rock came, a fourth, and then a barrage of them.

'The witch's friend! The witch's servant!'

The voices swirled around her, as sharp as the stones, wounding her heart and mind as the rocks lacerated her body. *It isn't fair*, she thought desperately, raising her hands to protect her head and face. *It just isn't fair. I have so much left to give.*

And then one particularly large rock sailed past her defences and took her on the temple. Yuet uttered a soft cry, the first sound she had made out loud since the barrage began. It was very soft, almost inaudible; the crowd didn't hear it. The world faded to a soft black around Yuet, her mind blank, no more thoughts. No last words. No more sensation. She never knew that the stones kept coming, long after her body was still, long after it had turned into bloody pulp under the barrage.


The cart driver had whipped his mule as soon as the trouble started, and had taken himself and his passenger, the patient whom Yuet had just loaded into the cart, out of the danger zone as fast as he could.

It was he who alerted the Imperial Guard, but by the time a detachment arrived the mob was long gone, and Yuet was dead.

Xaforn arranged for the seemly removal of Yuet's body, and contacted Tai about making the necessary preparations for her funeral. Xaforn herself quartered the streets where the stoning had happened, questioning people, but nobody had apparently seen a thing, and persisted in their story even when Xaforn threatened to take them into custody for obstructing her investigations.

'We will never know who did it,' she told Tai later, her face drawn with exhaustion and with the tears that she had wept for Yuet. They were both still in shock, broken and raw with the pain and the fury of this death, with the waste of the life of one whom they had loved, who had been part of them. 'They all did it.'

'Surely the driver saw . . .'

'Surely he did. He does not remember either,' said Xaforn savagely. 'No, nobody knows anything, nobody wants to know anything. I talked to a woman who used to be in the inner courts, a widow of a Guard. She was there when Yuet gave her heart and hands to the victims of the epidemic. Even she does not remember seeing anything that can help us. And she knew what Yuet was. She, of all people, knew.'

*So it begins, then*, wrote Tai in her journal on the night after she had helped prepare Yuet's body for her funeral pyre, after Yuet's ashes had been scattered into the wind. After she had wept herself dry. Pau-kala *is upon us, and the first of my sisters is gone. Oh, but Kito said we were all so young.*

In her mind, a bare branch bereft of leaves trembled in the vainly beguiling warmth of spring sunshine.

# Two

Tai had taken it upon herself to bring the news of the death of one of the *jin-shei* circle to the rest of her *jin-shei-bao*. She had gone first to Khailin's rooms, but although she had been admitted to the reception room by Khailin's servants no amount of hammering on the locked door of the laboratory or calling to Khailin to open the door seemed to get the attention of the occupant.

'Is she in there?' Tai demanded of one of the servants.

'I didn't see her go out, my lady,' the servant girl said. 'And we leave food outside the door every morning, and when we come back it is gone.'

'*Khailin!*' Tai shouted, banging on the door again. 'Open up! Oh, for the love of Cahan, open up.'

But there was silence.

In the end, Tai scribbled a terse message in *jin-ashu* and left it, sealed, with the servant girl with instructions to introduce it into the laboratory with the next tray of food.

Liudan received Tai, but her reaction to the news was distant, almost emotionless.

'I am sorry. Besides being of my own *jin-shei* circle, Yuet was a good healer, and a caring counsellor when she chose to offer counsel.' There was a trace of real regret in Liudan's voice – but her eyes were dry, and gleamed with a strange light as she said the required words.

'Liudan, tell Khailin to stop this. You can, it is within your power. Look where it has led!' Tai said. 'One of us is dead already! And if you . . .'

'I said I regretted that,' Liudan said, a little more ice on the edges of her voice. 'But this is not the first time a *jin-shei* sister has died in the cause of a task asked in the name of the sisterhood. Nor will it be the last, I think, for as long as *jin-shei* endures and is what it is. There are some things that are worth . . .'

'Are worth dying for, Liudan? Killing for?' Tai said.

'When Antian chose you, what would you not have done in the name of that choice?' Liudan said. 'You are as selfish as the rest of us. Your goals are just different.'

'But Liudan . . .'

The ice migrated to Liudan's eyes as she bent her gaze to Tai, but Tai was undaunted by it.

'What if I were to ask *you* . . .' she began, but Liudan turned her head away.

'Do not ask,' she said, very quietly. 'Do not ask that. You cannot undo a *jin-shei* vow that easily, you cannot withdraw it. I have done what I have done.'

'Then Yuet's blood is on your own hands,' Tai said, made reckless by her pain.

'That may be,' said Liudan after a short pause. 'There is nothing I can do about that now. Have you scheduled her funeral rites?'

'Yes.'

'When are they to be?'

'Tomorrow. Will you come?'

'I cannot,' Liudan said. 'But I will send a representative, and an appropriate offering.'

It was a dismissal, and Tai left, hurt, puzzled, disillusioned. Liudan seemed to treat the *jin-shei* bonds with the light touch of the professional juggler, taking from the sisterhood what she needed and abandoning the rest. She had demanded the life, and with it the death, of one of her sisters; but she was not going to risk her own safety by appearing at the funeral. These things were justified to her, if it meant holding on to power.

The funeral was a strange occasion. At first it looked as though there would be only a handful of mourners – but then, as the pyre was lit, Tai saw more and more people coming to stand silently around the platform on which Yuet's body, wrapped in a white shroud that hid the ruin that had been made of it, had been laid. There were women bearing children – babes in arms, bleary-eyed toddlers – as though they wished them to see the pyre, to remember. Men on crutches hobbled up and stood with their heads bowed. A growing sense of remorse, of regret, of a debt of gratitude being paid, had settled on the occasion, like smoke from a scented incense stick. Tai watched the mute crowd form, and then watched it dissipate just as quietly as the pyre died down into embers, shadows slipping away without meeting each other's eyes, without stopping to exchange a single word.

Tai had wept, for many reasons – not the least of which was the shattered circle in the name of which Yuet had died. Besides Tai herself, Nhia was there, dressed in her Chancellor's finery, and Xaforn, wearing the full formal dress armour of a captain of the Imperial Guard. Liudan was present only by proxy. Qiaan was still missing, somewhere in the enemy camp. Tammary was gone. Khailin was simply . . . absent.

When she did finally emerge from her seclusion, Khailin was thin

421

and wild-eyed, as though she had battled armies and then retreated for waterless weeks through desert country.

It took Tai, to whom she came, some time to get anything coherent out of her. Khailin babbled about succeeding in her quest and almost immediately berated herself for failure, wept, raged, lost herself sometimes in long silences during which she would respond to no voice but would simply stare blankly into space, rocking back and forth, her lips moving as though she was mouthing spells. Yuet's death was still only days past, a fresh and ever-present pain, and the wound was lacerated further by Tai's immediate instinct to send for the healer and *jin-shei-bao* whose practical wisdom and sometimes priggish but always pertinent advice she would never have again. She sent for Nhia instead, hoping that Nhia's own knowledge of some of the arcana Khailin had been meddling with might help to get through to her.

Khailin barely acknowledged Nhia's presence when she arrived at Tai's house.

'Must find it . . . must find it . . . Yuet will know . . .'

Tai and Nhia exchanged a shocked glance above Khailin's head.

'Yuet is dead, Khailin,' Nhia said.

Khailin looked up. 'Yuet. I need to talk to . . .' She blinked, and some semblance of sanity seemed to return to her eyes. 'What?' she whispered. 'What did you say?'

Tears were running unchecked down Tai's cheeks. 'Oh, Cahan, Liudan will have to pay a heavy price for what she has wrought,' she whispered, more to herself than as an offering to the conversation, but Khailin's hearing seemed to have been sharpened to a fine brittle edge, and she snapped her head around to stare at Tai.

'Khailin, Yuet was killed by a raging mob less than a week ago. We tried to reach you. Where were you?'

'Why, for the love of Cahan? What happened?'

'She was trying to transport one of her patients back to her house, and the crowd thought . . . they believed . . .'

'*I killed her*,' Khailin gasped suddenly, as though a knife had been plunged into her heart.

Nhia's hand tightened around hers. 'Ah, no. Don't do this.'

'I did,' Khailin said inconsolably. 'It was I who got her involved in this. I should never have got anyone else involved.'

Tai was sitting on her other side, her hand on one of Khailin's shoulders, balancing Nhia's gentle hand on the other. 'What happened, Khailin? You came here like a wraith and I could get no sense out of you at all – and you are still not making any.'

'I failed,' Khailin said, almost inaudibly.

Nhia sighed deeply. 'Perhaps it's just as well.'

'And I succeeded beyond my wildest dreams,' Khailin continued, as if Nhia had not spoken. 'I made it live. *I made it live.*'

'Khailin. Talk to me. What have you done?'

Khailin raised a trembling hand; a fresh cut, barely scabbed over, ran the length of her palm. 'I used myself, in the end. It was all unnecessary, what I made Yuet do – I could only use myself in the end.'

Her voice trailed away, and for a moment she seemed to withdraw back into herself, into that vivid moment which had finally driven her here. She had trusted no one. What she had said was the absolute truth – she could only trust herself, could only use herself.

She had kneaded clay into the likeness of a woman and baked it hard, like a statue. The skin on her face could still feel the thin layer of clay she had smoothed over her own features; she removed it, once it was dry, with aching slowness and care lest it should crack and be ruined, and filled in the eye-holes with a finer clay, the white one of which porcelain was made. With hands that trembled she laid the mask that was her own face onto the shell of the body she had made. She smeared her own blood in arcane symbols on the lifeless mask's cheeks and brow. And then, heart pounding, she poured the elixir she had made into the open hole of its mouth, and leaned forward to kiss its cracked clay lips, breathing her own breath and her own life into the figure.

And then she watched the clay tremble with the unspeakable, the impossible. *Life.* It was life itself, risen at her command, at her word, at her elixir. Within Khailin, pride warred with terror. With one breath she cried to herself, *I did it!* With the next, *What have I done?*

And then, before she could move, before she could speak, she saw the thing that she had made shiver and then fall into dust so fine that it stirred at a breath.

But it had lived. For a brief, shining moment it had lived.

'It was that easy?' Tai breathed. 'Making a doll to hold the breath of life? That was all it took? Why could Lihui not do this long before now?'

'Because,' Nhia said, 'he did not have that elixir. What was in the potion, Khailin? What did you have to do to make this work?'

Khailin shot her a look at once defiant and terrified. 'You don't want to know, Nhia.'

'Yes, I . . .' Nhia began, but Khailin shook her head violently.

'No. *No*. I will not speak of it, not here, not where I can be . . . I made it live, but it is gone.'

'What do you mean, it is gone? Gone where?' Nhia said, her hand tightening convulsively.

For answer, Khailin reached into the pocket of her tunic and brought out a handful of dust. 'Gone,' she said.

'What have you done, Khailin?' Nhia said.

Khailin flinched. 'I succeeded,' she murmured, her face chalk white. And then she fainted.

Nhia helped lay Khailin down on a low couch and straightened with steely purpose in her eyes. 'Cahan, this is beyond me. Take care of her, Tai, I'll be back.'

'Where are you going?' Tai called, her voice trembling on the verge of panic.

Nhia paused, turning back to look at Tai. Her face was grim. 'I'm going to get Maxao,' she said. 'Whatever he is, or says he has once been, he has knowledge of these things. In the meantime, pray that whatever it is that Khailin made doesn't come looking for her.'

Tai waited impatiently, darting in and out of the room where Khailin lay, setting cloths wrung out in cool water on her forehead and her wrists where the pulse beat. It was a while before Khailin came to, but when she did, she was lucid.

'I need to get back to my laboratory,' she said.

'No,' Tai said firmly. 'You're staying right here. Nhia has gone to fetch help.'

'Help? Whose?' Khailin laughed, a bitter, brittle laugh. 'Liudan? She can't do anything.'

'Not Liudan. Maxao.'

Khailin's eyes narrowed. 'Maxao would see me dead for this,' she said flatly.

'Not so,' said the voice of the Sage from the door, where he had apparently just materialized with Nhia at his side. 'You may have disappointed me in going on with a project which I told you would come to no good end, but the fact remains that you appear to have wrought something that has eluded many of us for centuries. This is a mystery that has excited students of the Way since the day the world was born. Did you think that Liudan was the first to crave immortality? Or Lihui? Lihui took what he could get, but what he did with his life was flawed, imperfect. You have succeeded in doing something quite different. And you may have given us the perfect weapon.'

'Weapon? In which war? Against whom?'

'Lihui will learn of this thing that you have made, if he does not know of it already,' Maxao said. 'This is the opportunity that I have been waiting for. He will come for it, for the secret it holds, of this I am certain. With this at his disposal, he can cure his physical disabilities – all he needs is another shell, another body, and this one will be perfectly immortal, with no need for replenishment.'

'But it's gone,' Khailin said. 'It's no more than a pile of lifeless dust.'

'Oh, he will come for it.' Maxao smiled grimly. 'And when he does, we will be ready for him.'

'We?'

'You and I will find your mind-child, Khailin, and we will bait the trap for Lihui. We had better return to your laboratory. There are things there that we will need.'

Tai stood up, her eyes hot with anger.

'You don't care how many of us die,' she snapped. 'Nhia said you were a good man. I don't believe that any more. No good man would glory in this, in what it has brought, in Yuet's . . .'

Her voice broke, and Maxao turned his blind eyes inexorably to where she stood. 'And what,' he said, 'is a good man? We work towards a goal, all of us. Are we good when we pursue that goal or are we good when we let circumstances divert us from that pursuit? What would you do if you needed to clear your path towards the light of your destiny, or to correct a past mistake which has blighted all of your life?'

'Not kill,' Tai whispered.

Maxao nodded. 'That is good. Then you are better than I am. It is a different kind of good. As for me, if a death clears a way for a good thing, then the death was in a good cause. I am sorry your friend is gone, but that is just the Way – that was where her path led

425

her. Some day her memory may be a bright and holy thing. We will have to wait and see. In the meantime . . .' His mouth twisted into one of his angry, wolfish smiles. 'In the meantime, my young friend, we have an opportunity to rid the world of a fell thing, of a spreading darkness – if you will, of a disease which could kill more than you dream of. Perhaps, in her death, your healer friend has performed the final and glorious act of healing and will be remembered for it for many years to come.'

'You just want your revenge on Lihui,' Tai said.

Maxao raised an eyebrow. 'And if I do?'

'You didn't like what Khailin was trying to do at Liudan's asking, so you tried to stop her. But she was not the only one involved in that secret endeavour, and because you decided then that it was a bad thing to do and revealed that secret to the world, Yuet paid with her life.' Tai's eyes filled with tears again. 'You are the most arrogant, most heartless, most selfish man that I have ever laid my eyes on.'

'Life is selfish,' Maxao said bluntly. 'Selfishness is how we survive. You think the world cares about us, that we should care about it?'

'The world, maybe not,' Tai whispered. 'But there are people in that world, people whom we love. You destroy whatever is in your path, and it doesn't matter to you if you care for it, or used to care for it once. If it stands in your way, it's doomed.'

'Yes,' said Maxao. 'I do what I have to do; I do what needs to be done.'

He held out his arm. Khailin hesitated for a final moment and then, her eyes full of tears, stepped up to lay her hand on it. Nhia backed away as the two of them passed through the door, and out of the room, out into the streets where Yuet had died.

# Three

'How will we find it, Maxao? How, when I don't even know how it vanished?'

'Finding it is of secondary importance,' Maxao said.

'But you told the others . . .'

'I did not tell them everything,' said Maxao gently. 'Don't be naïve. Lihui will not come for that lumbering thing that you created; he knows how to make an image of a man. What he will come for is the elixir you used to do it.'

'But I failed,' whispered Khailin. 'It is dust and ashes.'

'Yes,' Maxao pointed out, 'but it is a dust which had no right to live and yet lived at your word. The rest is refinement. Lihui has an obsession with this endeavour, and he now knows that you have discovered the secret. The mere act of giving breath of your breath and blood of your blood is not enough.'

'How do you know what I did?' Khailin gasped.

'I have read the same old scrolls, my dear,' Maxao said. 'So has Lihui. You, apparently, found the secret ingredient that eluded us both – but as for the rest of it, it has been common knowledge for centuries.'

'I don't have the elixir any longer,' Khailin said.

'I know. But inside your head is locked the secret of how to make more,' Maxao said.

'So it isn't the creature that's the bait,' Khailin said, very white. 'It's me.'

'I will be there,' Maxao said.

Khailin did not feel reassured. Her skin tightened with the memory of Lihui's hands on her, his casual possession of her body and her mind, his malicious authority granted to him by her own willing act of submission.

His scream as the acid exploded into his face.

Khailin looked up, to see Maxao's blind eyes turned on her in a sightless scrutiny.

'You bested him once,' he said, 'and you were alone then. Do not be afraid.'

'I am not afraid,' Khailin said. *Merely terrified. Not of Lihui himself, but of his right to claim me. I belonged to him, once. I still do.*

A part of her already knew how he would come to her – the easiest way, the way of a simple act of will, the ghost road. Maxao had said that first the trap must be baited, that Lihui must learn of Khailin's achievement, and that this should be left up to him; when he and Khailin returned to Khailin's laboratory he withdrew into isolation for the better part of an hour, to set the lure, to free the secret knowledge into the places where Lihui would find it and lust after its possession. Then he had returned, and had told Khailin that the only thing they could do after that was wait.

'But the creature . . .'

'Read your scrolls more carefully, child,' Maxao said. 'You cannot share the same space with a thing like you have made. It is, in a lot of respects, you, yourself. It unbalances the world to have both entities in the same place. There can never be more than one in existence. The danger in creating a perfect double of yourself which is gifted with this immortality is simply that it might destroy you, the original you, so that it can take your place. In that, at least, you did not succeed, and for this we can be thankful.'

'But how can you . . . ?'

'You know this, too. You know of the ways that you can extinguish the spark of independent life that another possesses and then feed it your elixir, and breathe your own essence into it, just like you have done with your double. Both will then be you. And you cannot both exist. It is against all laws.'

Khailin laughed, a laugh which had an edge of madness to it. 'Why are you telling me all this now?'

'Because it is something that you know, or that you were on the point of discovering,' Maxao said. 'And because I now know that it is knowledge that you will never use again.'

'You put much faith in me,' Khailin murmured.

'I always have,' said Maxao.

'How touching,' said a third voice, a familiar one, full of remembered honey and laced with a gentle sarcasm. Khailin jumped, but Maxao did not even turn his head.

'Welcome, Lihui,' Maxao said. 'I was wondering how long it would take you.'

'You left me to die to take up with that old relic?' Lihui said, turning to Khailin. 'What has he been telling you, my dear? Haven't you found out already that whatever power Maxao might once have had I now possess?'

'Not all,' Maxao said tranquilly. 'I have a memory of sight, Lihui. I have one chance to use that, and I have long hoarded it until this moment. You thought you took everything from me? You were wrong, Lihui-*mai*.'

Distracted, fascinated, Khailin failed to pay attention to Lihui for one fatal moment, and when a clawlike hand closed viciously around her wrist and yanked her forward she cried out as she stumbled towards her captor. Lihui himself wore a smile every bit as wolfish as his mentor's.

'So destroy us both, then,' he taunted. 'Go on, old man. Do it. Go out in style – your old pupil, the most brilliant you've ever had, and your newest disciple, with one blow.' He clicked his tongue and shook his head, in mocking sympathy. 'But oh, I forgot – kill her, and you will never know the secret of the Golden Elixir.'

'Neither will you,' Maxao said. His mouth thinned. 'You know, you both know, that if I had to destroy you both here, I would do it.'

'No, Maxao. You won't.' Lihui's voice was a weapon again, velvet-sheathed steel. 'Remember, I know your weakness. You have invested too much in this one. You won't destroy that.'

'You mean as I once failed to act quickly enough to destroy you?' Maxao laughed, and it was not a pleasant sound. 'I learn from my mistakes, my young disciple. And you . . . you were a harsh lesson to me. No, I do not destroy things of value lightly. But, Lihui, she is nothing in this game now. Without her you cannot leave this room. You left whoever you used as your eyes out on the ghost road to die, again, as you've done many times before.'

'I'll never go with you alive!' Khailin flung at Lihui.

For a long moment Maxao hesitated, as though weighing something in his mind. Khailin had time to wonder bitterly if her own life and all she had accomplished in it were really so utterly insignificant in Maxao's reckoning.

Lihui's grip tightened on her arm, and he stepped back, pulling her against him, her ear against his lips. '*Remember the house you burned*,' he whispered intently.

The ghost road . . .

Khailin tried to clamp down on her memories, but they came flooding back unbidden – the pagoda roofs, the dragons in the door which had burned her if she dared to touch them, the cold grey ashes into which she had turned all these things – enough, enough was there to open the path of the ghost road and take her back, back to that place, *back* . . .

The walls behind Lihui lost a little of their solidity, became flickering blurs.

'You hold her,' Maxao said affably, as though there had been no pause, 'but in order to make use of what she knows you have to take her out of here while she still lives and is useful to you – and you have just heard the lady state that she will not allow that to happen. Neither, Lihui, will I. Don't you see? I cannot lose. The only difference is in the degree. You will not leave this room, whether or not you still hold your shield. Therefore, Khailin's knowledge is useless to you. Whether or not she dies with you, Lihui, you die here. You will never have what you are seeking.' He shook his head with a weary disappointment. 'You always were precipitous, Lihui, my young apprentice. Too hasty, and too quick to reach your conclusions.' He lifted his hand, a gesture of invocation. Look at the shadow that stands behind you.'

Khailin twisted her head around at this, trying to see what Maxao was talking about. She could see nothing, nothing except the familiar walls of her laboratory. She sucked in her breath sharply, tensing to try breaking away from Lihui's relentless grip, and he turned his head a fraction, loosening his grip just enough for her to snatch at the chance of escape. She ripped her arm free and fell away from him, stumbling into a bench and sending an alembic and a number of glass tubes flying, splashing Lihui and spilling bubbling liquid on the floor.

Lihui swore, lunged forward, reached for her again. His heel slipped on the spilled fluid; he grimaced in distaste, glancing swiftly down to recover his footing.

Khailin, backed into a corner of the laboratory, felt her hand close around a glass container where a small mound of innocent-looking pellets rested underneath a thick layer of golden oil. Her breath caught, her hand tightened convulsively around the glass and just as Lihui looked up again, his intent plain on his scarred face, Khailin smashed the container she held onto the floor between his feet. The glass shattered, the oil spilled free and oozed into the already viscous stuff that had been in the alembics and the tubes on the workbench, and the pellets, suddenly exposed to the air without the oil's protection, burst into flame.

Swift liquid fire licked the hem of Lihui's robe with deadly tongues. Lihui swore, batted at his garment with a free hand, began an incantation, but the flames intensified; they raced up his garments, catching at the splashes of chemical on his garments.

Lihui clawed at his outer robe, trying to divest himself of its fiery embrace, but his scarred and twisted hands fumbled at the fastenings. In the instant Lihui's attention was diverted, Maxao drew a small dagger from a sleeve sheath and tossed it at Khailin. It fell at her feet; she stared at it, bewildered.

'I cannot use it,' Maxao hissed.

With a flash of understanding Khailin reached for the weapon, winced as the spilled chemicals burned her fingers where she brushed her hand against them.

Lihui looked up, his face contorted. 'You think you can kill me?'

'I already did, once,' Khailin said, and stabbed with Maxao's dagger.

Lihui caught the blade with his hand, and it sliced across his palm, laying it open. Blood welled through the fingers closed about the knife, oozed down over his knuckles. It was an inconsequential wound, a bare scratch, but suddenly Lihui's face contorted with agony. For a moment he stared at his hand with an astonished, wide-eyed gaze, as though the tiny blade that had pierced him had, in some arcane way, found his heart.

Then the man who had once been the Ninth Sage of Syai crumpled onto his knees and began screaming. He screamed for a long time.

'Die,' said Maxao softly. 'Immortality is not a toy, Lihui-*mai*, and is not bought cheaply. Now, at last, now it is time to pay.'

The fire had caught now, eating at the spilled liquids on the floor around Lihui. Bright flames engulfed the benches; glassware started shattering in the heat, spilling more chemicals into the inferno. Parts of the fire turned violet, or green.

Maxao and Khailin fled its fury, stumbling out of the laboratory, out of the house. 'What did you do?' whispered Khailin as she watched towering flames burst from the windows of what had been her house and swallow up the gabled roof. 'What was on that dagger? Poison? Is that all it took? I thought he was immortal.'

'Immortality does not mean invulnerability to death. Lihui could not die, but he could be killed. You knew that – you thought you had killed him yourself that time in the house at the end of the ghost road. But I think you realise now that was a place of his mind, it was beyond you to destroy the house that he had built.'

'So is he dead now?' she asked bleakly, her eyes glittering with the reflection of the conflagration before her.

'Yes,' Maxao said.

Khailin looked up at him. 'How can you be sure?'

'Because I know,' Maxao said. 'Yes, there was poison on that dagger – the dagger that I could not use myself to hurt him with because of what he laid on me when our paths last crossed. I could not – directly – harm him. But with my knowledge and your hand we accomplished it.'

'I did what I did partly because I wanted to destroy him,' Khailin said bitterly, 'and now you tell me that all it would have taken is a drop of strong poison?'

'Not any poison,' Maxao said. 'For every being there is something that is deadly beyond any imagining. You did not know what that poison was for Lihui, my dear. I did.'

'But . . .'

'It is done,' Maxao said with finality. 'Let it be.'

Afterwards, when the conflagration had cooled and Maxao let her return to the remnants of her workshop, Khailin crouched at the pile of whitish ashes that might have been all that remained of Lihui. She stirred them with her fingers, dry-eyed, until she encountered something solid, an object concealed in the piled mounds of dust and ash. And then she knelt in the wreckage, silent, for a long time, staring at what she held in her hand.


Nhia and Tai waited for news at Nhia's quarters in the Palace, tense as bowstrings. Xaforn prowled the streets, detouring to Khailin's house, but the doors and windows there were closed and shuttered and nobody had answered her knocking. She had returned, then, to her *jin-shei-bao*, and shared their vigil. The day darkened into night, and then broke into another day.

'What are they doing out there?' Tai whispered, shivering violently.

'He called her mage,' Nhia said, her face ghost-white. 'They can do this. They can kill him.'

'You, too?' Tai said, turning to her. 'Is Lihui all you can think of, also?'

'No,' Nhia said, 'but I do not forget what happened between me

432

and the Ninth Sage of the Imperial Court. Don't forget – this, which they fight, it has a part of me in it. He took what he took from me, and I can never get that back. I cannot but pray that Maxao is right.'

It was on the evening of the third day that Nhia woke from a light slumber with a cry. Xaforn, with her battle reflexes and swift reactions, was at her side almost immediately.

'What is it? What's the matter?'

'There is . . . I can feel . . .' Nhia's teeth were chattering, as though she were cold, or terrified. 'Look . . . look outside.'

Tai ran to the window, flinging the shutters wide, and gasped. 'There's a fire. I can see the glow from here.'

Xaforn had helped Nhia to her feet, and they both staggered over to the window.

'That is in the north-east quarter,' Xaforn murmured, gauging distance and direction with a hunter's practised eye. 'That's where Khailin's laboratory is.'

Tai cradled her elbows in visibly trembling hands. *Another. Another one of us.*

'That's the second house she has burned over Lihui,' Nhia said, her voice strange.

A sudden noise inside Nhia's room made Xaforn whirl, hand on weapon, but the room was empty – as empty as it had been a moment ago when they all ran for the window. Except that there was something . . . something different.

Xaforn scanned the room through narrowed eyes.

'What is that on the table?' she said abruptly, her sword hissing from its scabbard.

Tai seemed rooted to the floor where she stood, shivering violently. Nhia stepped forward, but Xaforn flung out an arm to stop her.

'Wait here,' she said. 'Get away from that window. Your back to the shutter.'

The other two did as they were instructed while Xaforn slipped warily into the room, watching every shadow. She bent over the small bundle on the table, tapping it with the edge of her sword first, and then reaching over with barely touching fingertips to push aside the wrapping. For a long moment she stared at what she found, and then she straightened, turning to the others.

'Come,' she called softly. 'Look.'

Nhia recognized the object on the table first, and drew in her breath sharply. It was this, more than anything else, that told Tai what the intricately wrought ring made of some dark metal must be.

'It is his, isn't it?' she whispered. 'Lihui's? The ring of the Ninth Sage?'

'There is a note,' Xaforn said, poking at a thin slip of paper laid beneath the square of fabric that had contained the ring. Nhia reached out, carefully avoiding touching the ring itself, and pulled it out. She squinted at the writing in the low light of the room, and then passed it wordlessly to Tai, turning away to subside onto the edge of the nearest chair.

The note was brief, only one line in strong, precise *jin-ashu* script: *It is over.*

'What?' Xaforn said. 'What does it say?'

'He is dead,' Tai whispered, crumpling the note in her hand without realizing that she was doing it. 'It's Khailin's hand. It says, "It is over." I think they succeeded. I think Lihui is dead.'

'Then everything is fine,' Xaforn said. 'If it is Khailin's hand, then she is fine. She is right. It really is over.' She frowned. 'Perhaps now I can try again to find where Qiaan . . .'

But Tai's ears were full of the sound of rushing water, white noise, the clamour of her own blood in her ears.

Khailin may have survived her encounter with Lihui, but the note left for her *jin-shei-bao* was not one of victory, or triumph.

It had been a farewell.


# Four


It took Tammary much longer to gain the mountain village of her childhood than she had thought it would.

She ran from Linh-an with nothing more than a blind desire to flee the place where she had suffered so much anguish, the place where she had had everything she had ever wanted, and the place where she had lost it all. Tai had wanted to bring Tammary and

Zhan back together, but the opportunity was lost or wasted through circumstances none of them had had control over – and to Tammary, the news that Zhan had gone to war had been the final blow, a sign, a portent that told her only that she had been right to flee alone.

When she reached a small village some two days' journey from the city, her immediate past returned to haunt her and she ended up spending nearly four days in bed with a raging fever, writhing in pain which convulsed her body and left her weak and helpless under the care of a kindly woman who – as good fortune would have it – happened to be a midwife and recognized and treated the abuses that Tammary had suffered, to the best of her ability. But even this respite was cut short by a young man returning to the village, wounded, to recuperate from the battles on the border, and bringing news that the war was a sharp and bloody one.

'Will we lose?' a nervous villager asked the wounded soldier.

'Of course not,' he scoffed. 'We have the Imperial Army to stop those bandits from the Magalipt, and they are more bluster than fight anyway. And we have quite a few of the Imperial Guards with us, too. Sooner rather than later we will send the Magalipt back to the stinking hovels from which they came. But in the meantime flying arrows are a deadly thing. Many of us have been caught by them. I remember seeing three of them hit our commander at once, one time – he looked like a porcupine! They just thudded into him like this – *thwock – thwock – thwock* – and his body jerked.' The soldier imitated the stricken man's spasmodic shudder as the missiles found their mark, and was rewarded by a sibilant, deeply impressed intake of breath from his audience.

'Did he die?' asked another villager.

'I have no idea,' the soldier replied. 'It was not long after seeing this that I was myself wounded, and after that I was away from the battlefield and I do not remember. But there are those who died, yes. I have seen their bodies laid out ready to be immolated as the Gods require.'

He had never mentioned an identity, a name, but Tammary's tortured mind supplied the face that belonged to the body pinned by the arrows. She knew it. She loved it. She had watched it sleep beside her, on soft pillows, a smile of content curving its lips.

*Zhan is dead. Zhan is as dead to me as I am to him.*

She ran again, with this thought burning her soul, hot tears in her eyes. She followed the river, at first, but then left it to turn north – and lost her sense of direction and of purpose, wandering the roads of the plain for days without reaching a goal or a destination, sometimes sleeping outside in the deepening cold if she could not find a refuge for the night. Her face grew thin, haunted, with deep circles under her eyes; and it was thus, on the edge of her endurance, that she finally reached the foothills she recognized and started climbing the slopes towards home.

She reached the village well after dark on a short winter's day, and instinctively stumbled towards the familiar house of her aunt, where she had grown up. But another instinct, just as strong, stopped her in her tracks. That house was the place where it had all started – the unpaid debts, the recriminations, the concealment, the lies, her mother's tragic dreams and ambitions. This was not the place to find healing. She needed . . . she needed something else.

The sky was black above her, glittering with cold winter stars. She stood on a snow-covered path, in clothes bitterly inadequate for the chill wind that plucked at her, and knew that she was on the edge of the abyss – she needed shelter. She needed help.

And there was only one person in this place to whom she could turn. The boy she had once walked away from, accusing him of betraying her just like everyone else had done, whose mercy she now needed to throw herself on.

*Raian.* Where would he be? It had been years. Would he have completed his training? Was he in the Chronicler's house?

Her feet turned that way, unbidden, and she dragged herself to the steep-roofed house at the edge of the village where the old man who had once been Raian's teacher had lived. She had barely enough strength left to knock on the door, and then collapsed into a shivering heap on the threshold.

*If I am to die, it might as well be here*, she thought, the words very clear in her mind but the thoughts accompanying them writhing and chaotic as though wrenched from a dream. And then the stars winked out in the cold black sky, and she knew no more.

\* \* \*

436

When she woke, she was lying in a straw pallet by the blazing hearth, covered with sleeping furs. She lay still for a moment, trying to orient herself, but even as her breathing changed somebody stirred in the room behind her.

'Are you back?' a familiar voice asked quietly.

Tammary turned her head. 'Raian?'

'Yes, it's me.' He came over to where she lay, stepping over her pallet to crouch beside her, his lanky frame unchanged from what she remembered. But his face and his eyes were older, with even one or two very fine lines raying out from the corners of his eyes. 'I would have wanted to see you return in better shape than a half-dead pile of frozen bones on my doorstep, but however it was that it happened, welcome home, Tammary. Do you think you could manage some hot broth? I've got some bubbling in the pot.'

'I . . . thank you.' She hadn't realized that she was hungry until her stomach twisted emptily at his words. 'That would be wonderful.'

He turned away to reach for a bowl and spoon.

'I want to help,' he said carefully, his back to her. 'You don't have to tell me anything, but it would be easier if you did explain. What did they do to you in the city? I thought you went away to seek better things.'

'I did,' Tammary said with a brittle laugh. 'I sought them, and found them, and . . . and lost them.'

There were tears standing in her eyes again as he turned back to her and handed her the bowl of broth.

'Slowly, it's hot and you don't want to gobble it anyway. When was it that you last ate?'

Tammary bowed her head over the bowl. 'It's been so long, a lifetime ago. I can hardly remember who I was any more. Or who I *am*.' Tears streaked her cheeks when she looked up again, the bowl trembling dangerously in her hands. 'Oh, in the name of all the Gods that ever lived, Traveller and *chayan* both – when have I ever been real, when have I ever been worthy, when have I ever held happiness in my hands and knew to hold it?'

'In my love, in my hope, in my understanding,' Raian said gently, reaching to fold his long hands over hers. 'I've always believed in you. Always. That doesn't change now. I am Chronicler now, in my teacher's stead – he is gone, has been this past year or so. I have some standing here now. I will shelter you and protect you until the spirit that was broken learns to fly again.'

Tammary stared at him with wide eyes. 'Your *love*?'

'Of course,' he said. 'I could not always protect you – but I have always loved you. From the time I saw you running free in the mountains with your wild things, your hawks and your fox cubs; from the time I first saw you dance, still a child but with every promise of the woman you would become. You were everything, wrapped in a single skin. You were all I ever wanted.'

'But . . .' Tammary's eyes filled with tears again. Her hands gripped the broth bowl fiercely. She struggled with her words, visibly, and finally burst out, 'But I don't love you, Raian – not like that. I have been . . .'

'I know,' he said. 'I put no price on anything. Beyond any hope of more exalted things, I have always been, and will always be, your friend. This house is your house, for as long as you want it, as long as you need it. Then I will help in whatever way I can to smooth your path forward, wherever you may wish to go. And I will be more than happy to see you stay. Now eat your broth,' he added practically. 'It's cooling fast.'

Tammary wrote a short note in *jin-ashu* to let Tai know that she had reached sanctuary, and Raian made sure the letter made its way down the mountains and into the city. But aside from that small gesture, Tammary seemed unwilling to rejoin the outside world. The deep snows came and went, and it was well after the first shy spring flowers crept onto the high mountain meadows that she finally emerged from Raian's house. Even then it was only to scurry past the village houses, wrapped in a nondescript shawl, and make her way up to where she used to spend her days when she was a child. She whistled for Lastreb, the hawk she had once tamed, but although she thought she could see the shape of a circling hawk high up in the sky Tammary could not get the bird to come to her. She avoided the ruins of the Summer Palace, led by an instinctive aversion to any reminder of her city years.

Her aunt had visited her at Raian's house, and although she never quite uttered the words *I told you so* they were embedded so deeply in every look and every word that Tammary quickly shied away from her company. Jessenia, to give her credit, had not meant to be a shrew – but the scars left from Jokhara's grasp at greatness ran deep, and Jokhara's sister was still torn between fury, sympathy and a sense of utter humiliation, as though Jokhara's transgressions left an indelible stamp on her entire family. Tammary was just the last, the most potent reminder of the fact that Jokhara's story was not yet over, was playing itself out still, reaching for her siblings and her descendants and trapping them in its coils. Tammary had been the subject of some potent village gossip for a while after her return, especially in the light of her past reputation there, but she led a life so muffled in layers of seclusion that she was quickly dismissed as of no further interest, a quenched fire. She preferred it that way.

She told Raian the full story, in fits and starts, looping from Yuet's stillroom to the hills outside Linh-an with Tai and then to the markets of Linh-an, the tea-houses, the promiscuity, Liudan's fears, Qiaan's abduction, Lihui, the turmoil and the wars, and finally returning to her kidnapping and the explanation of her chopped hair and her wasted body. Raian did what he could – he listened. He ached for her, and wished he could have been there to stand between her and danger – but he quickly realized that, although Tammary had convinced herself that Zhan was dead, the father of her unborn child still lived within her heart. Even if he had wanted to step into the vacant place Zhan had left behind in Tammary's life, Raian knew better than to try and do it before Tammary was ready to consider the possibility.

Word from the border sometimes reached the village in the mountains, but the reports were few and often contradictory – some spoke of victory, others of defeat, and every one that prophesied a quick end to the war was immediately countered by another which proclaimed the exact opposite. Letters sometimes came for Tammary from the city, too – Tai, despite her misgivings, had not told anyone else where Tammary was but tried to keep in touch with her. Tammary barely glanced at these. The tidings were often ominous, and sometimes tragic – Tai wrote of Khailin's work, of Yuet's death, of Liudan's increasing instability – but Tai spoke of things that were gone from Tammary's life, as though they had never been. Sometimes a passage from one of Tai's letters would catch Tammary's attention, and she would read it over and over again, trying to shake the sense that she was reading fiction, a silver tissue of lies and stories that had nothing to do with reality. But she did this rarely. The city could hardly be mentioned in her hearing without the memory of Zhan's smile rising above it like a sunrise, and it simply hurt too much to think about it. Several of Tai's letters remained unopened. Only once did Tammary send word, and that was a short note that reported no more than the fact of her continued well-being, and – between the lines – her unwavering refusal to face the legacy of her Linh-an years.

Until the day that a messenger inquired after Tammary in the village, and Raian, who met him at the door of his house, asked what message he bore.

'I am the message,' the stranger said, and inside the house, out of sight of the door but well within earshot, Tammary gasped at the sound of it.

'Who are you?' Raian asked, although he knew already, although his heart was telling him the truth and he felt the cold wind of loss blow through the empty place where Tammary used to be.

'My name,' said the young man on the doorstep, in a voice that trembled with emotion, 'is Zhan.'

'I thought you were dead.' Tammary stood motionless in the middle of the room, her eyes on the apparition in the doorway.

'Liudan said . . . I believed that *you* were . . . that they had killed you.'

'Oh, Zhan, why did you come here? How did you know where to find me?'

Raian placed a firm hand between the shoulder blades of the visitor and propelled him into the house, shutting the door firmly against several too-curious stares that the scene had attracted. When he turned back to Zhan and Tammary, he saw them standing barely a pace away from one another, not touching, devouring each other with hungry eyes.

He said nothing, dropping his own gaze, and retreated into the fastness of his workroom, leaving them alone in the hallway.

They couldn't tell, after, who had started to talk first, and how their stories got told. Zhan found out about the loss of their child, about Tammary's escape, about the harrowing journey across Syai, about the sanctuary she had found with Raian. She learned that he had not been the arrow-struck porcupine of the tale she had overheard in the village on her way out from Linh-an, but that he had in fact been wounded, and sent back to the city to recuperate.

'Tai sent me here,' he finally said huskily.

'She swore she would not tell anyone,' Tammary whispered, weeping.

'I am not anyone,' Zhan said. 'She said . . . she said we needed each other. She's right, Tammary. Why, *why* did you run from me? What did you think I would do?' He reached out and caressed her hair, brushing the back of her shoulders now. 'When your braid came to me . . . when they sent me this, that I had loved, it was as if they had sent me your heart in a jewelled box. Something died in me that I had not known had lived. And until the moment it breathed again, when Tai spoke of you, it stayed dead. Part of me remains dead without the breath of life that you are to me.'

They held on to one another with the fierce strength of those who thought they were drowning and had found the spar necessary to survive an angry ocean. Zhan stood for a long time with his mouth resting lightly on Tammary's forehead, his eyes closed, as though he was giving or receiving a blessing.

'They took our child,' Tammary said at last.

'I know,' Zhan said.

'I may never be able to give you . . .'

'I know,' he repeated. 'The thought of our child was a joy to me, but having you in my life is a greater.'

And, finally, because she could not leave it unsaid, 'Raian . . .'

'Your friend?' Zhan asked quietly. 'Is there more?'

'He loves me,' Tammary whispered.

'And you?'

'No, not like that. He has been a tower of strength to me. He is one of the best friends I have ever had, possibly my only friend out here. But I . . . Oh, but I seem to be born to leave pain in my wake.' She buried her face against Zhan's shoulder. 'He took me in. I owe him my life. I cannot abandon him. And you . . . how is it that you are here? Is the war really over? Has the Empress released you?'

'Not exactly,' said Zhan with a crooked smile. 'I am supposedly on recuperation leave from my command. But when I left the battlefields, we were pushing the Magalipt soldiers back over the mountains. There are no guarantees, of course, but I think we are very close to succeeding in that. And I don't think they will be back. Not for a while. Besides, the second-in-command I left in charge there is a capable soldier. What there is left to be done, he can do without me.'

'Are you abandoning the army?' Tammary said, pulling away to look at him.

'I went to the war seeking death, thinking you were dead,' Zhan said. 'That has changed.'

'What do you want to do?'

'My family,' Zhan said, 'owns a small farm out in the hills near Ail-anh, near the lake. It is a very pleasant place. We have tenants out there now, but it is mine, if I say the word. Ours. It's as far away from the Magalipt and from Linh-an as it is possible to get in Syai. We can be together there. We can be left alone. We can live out the span of years that the Gods have seen fit to grant to us without any enemy knowing where you are, without any war reaching out to touch us. I can make a world for us, Tammary. Come with me.'

Tammary weighed it all in her mind. She had once, long ago, a lifetime ago, wanted this – exactly this: a place where she could live according to who she was, and not what she was. She would not be Traveller, or *chayan*, or a problem with one foot in each culture and belonging in both. She would be Tammary. Just herself. Perhaps she could use the knowledge that Yuet had shared with her to help the local healer deal with sickness in the village houses – but they would never know who she was, who she had been, who she could still become.

And she would have Zhan with her – and it flooded back through her, the sense of contentment, of pure quiet joy, that she had thought lost for ever in the wreckage that was Linh-an's legacy to her.

She could not choose otherwise. This was the road she had been seeking in the wilderness for so long.

'I will,' she whispered. 'But I have to . . . I have to tell Raian.'

'We will tell him together,' Zhan said. 'I believe that he does care about you. That he loves you enough to let you go.'

'But what have I given him in return for all that he has been to me?'

'Who said you should stop loving a dear friend?' Zhan said. 'He holds a part of you that I never shall. It is Raian whom you finally trusted enough to come home to. That is much. It is not just you who owe him, I owe him too. I owe him more than I can ever repay him.'

When they sought Raian, at last, they found him in his study, sitting at the window. He turned as they knocked on the door and came in, his mouth curving into a wry smile.

'I was remembering,' he said simply.

Tammary squeezed Zhan's hand, and then dropped it, and came over to wrap her arms around Raian. His arm came up around her waist to hold her, briefly.

'I was remembering, so that I may write your story into the Book of the Clans when the time comes,' he said. 'You were our wild bird, who rode the storm winds to her freedom. It is thus that I will have them remember you.'

'You are always . . .' began Zhan.

'I know,' Raian said, interrupting gently but firmly. He slipped off the stool where he had been perched, and guided Tammary back across the room. Taking one of her hands, he folded it into Zhan's, and looked at them both with the luminous eyes of a seer, or a holy being on the edge of enlightenment. 'Take care of her,' he said, and then, glancing from the one face to the other, corrected himself. 'Take care of each other.'

Tammary wrote to Tai after she and Zhan had settled down into the small house by the lakeshore that had been his inheritance.

Tai's response came very late, months after Tammary's letter. She spoke of the turmoil of the city, of the breaking of the *jin-shei* circle, of the future, of the past. It was interspersed with verses of her latest poetry, some of it visionary, even prescient. *I have had dreams about you*, Tai wrote. *I dreamed that all was ashes except where you stood, and there were flowers at your feet, and a bird circling in the sky high above your head. And you held a child, wrapped in swaddling bands. It was as though you held the hope of the future in your arms.*

Tammary had occasion to answer this letter not too much later, in a dizzy whirl of unbelieving joy and awed gratitude. *I don't know about the future*, she wrote. *I don't know about the ashes, and the flowers, and the bird of your dream. But there will be a child. It will be born in the spring, as the winter leaves the land. And it is the flower of every hope I have ever held in my heart.*


# Five


'Gone? What do you mean gone? Gone where?' Liudan demanded when they came to her and told her of the aftermath of Khailin's battle and presented her with Lihui's mortal remains, the Ninth Sage's ring. Liudan seemed almost oblivious of the ring itself; her fingers were closed around it with such ferocity that Tai, focused on Liudan's hand, winced at the sight of the Empress's long manicured and lacquered nails digging into the soft flesh of her palm. 'I gave her no leave to abandon the project. I certainly did not sanction her disappearing like this. Where is she?'

'That note she left us is all we have,' Tai said. 'Liudan, she achieved what you demanded of her – she fulfilled your command. What you asked for was simply impossible to deliver.'

'We know so little of what really happened,' Nhia said. 'Have you talked to Maxao?'

'Maxao sent word,' Liudan said waspishly, 'to tell me that I need no longer fear Ninth Sage Lihui or his ambition. Or, for that matter, Maxao's own – although he denied that he ever had any. But I know ambition when I see it, and his was always there, banked, waiting. The only reason he didn't make a bid for the throne was because he never had the luck to get hold of the right pawn.' Liudan laughed, her voice suddenly harsh as a raven's caw. 'It does seem, doesn't it, that there are plenty of choices out there for those with ambitions of Empire. If it isn't Lihui and my father's daughter, then it's Zibo and my mother's child.'

She broke off, her fingers shifting convulsively around the ring she held, her eyes going blank for a moment as she seemed to contemplate her precarious position and her mortality.

'I can go and seek Qiaan again,' Xaforn said quietly. 'Perhaps she can still be rescued. Without Lihui, she is not . . .'

'She is who she is, with or without Lihui,' Liudan snapped. 'I don't see those who have raised her name as their banner dropping their claim now. It's too entrenched; they've come too far to turn back. They will simply replace Lihui at the top, another would-be Emperor.'

'I think you underestimate Lihui,' Nhia murmured. 'He led by mesmerizing people. He knew how, he had the power. It will go hard on anyone who now tries to step into his shoes. Even Maxao . . .'

'Maxao!' Liudan said. 'I was a fool. I regret now not having acted long ago – at the very least I should have had him locked up when I last had him here, explaining things to me. All I need now is for him to declare himself Emperor. Or find some way to announce that Khailin had yet another claim. Come to think of it, he probably knows exactly where Khailin is.'

'Liudan,' Xaforn said patiently. 'Let me go look for Qiaan.'

'But it's Khailin that I want you to find!' Liudan said. 'Khailin, and her knowledge! If she succeeded once, she can do it again.'

'Her house is burned, her laboratory gone,' Tai said.

'She can build another.'

'Let her go, Liudan.' That was Nhia, her voice gentle, very soft, as though she were speaking to a mutinous two-year-old. 'Let it go. She did what you asked; and when she saw that it would destroy you she obliterated the knowledge. She was obeying the law of *jin-shei* in the best way she knew how – she had obeyed the command given in the name of the sisterhood, and then she acted to protect a sister from harm. You can ask no more of her.'

'I can still command, from the throne of the Empire,' Liudan said.

'That, unlike the *jin-shei* request, can be refused,' Tai said, 'and you knew that, because otherwise you would never have taken the *jin-shei* road at all.'

'But refusal of a direct Imperial command is treason,' Liudan said. 'And the punishment for treason is . . .'

'Death, I know,' Tai said sharply, 'and then Khailin would be dead and you would still be denied your prize.'

'If she could do it, another can,' Liudan said, eyes glittering. 'I will find out.'

'Would you have us all meet Yuet's end?' Tai said, losing her temper. 'The only chance you had was Khailin, who did this for you as secretly as she was able, until Maxao stepped in with his own ideas. Now it's out in the open. You will find no takers, not even for an Imperial command. And if you did, the mob would devour them before they had a chance to do anything at all. Them, and maybe you, too. Would you lose everything over this obsession, Liudan?'

Liudan stared at her with eyes of black obsidian, cold and blank.

*Take care of my sister*, Antian had said, her dying words. Sometimes, Tai thought peevishly, she really did feel like throwing her hands up in the air in despair and demanding of her long-dead first and much-beloved *jin-shei-bao* just how she was supposed to protect Liudan from her worst enemy, her own self.

They left Liudan brooding on the ring she cradled in the palm of her hand, the only tangible thing that had survived the disaster of Khailin's attempt at forging the immortality the Empress had craved, and when they were out of her presence and out of hearing range Xaforn turned to the other two.

'If she won't give me leave,' she said quietly, 'I'll just have to do it without. I don't think she has any idea of how utterly vulnerable Qiaan is right now, with Lihui gone and the rebellion without a guiding hand at the helm.'

'They could let Qiaan choose his successor,' Nhia said. 'In any event, they will still need her to front their plans.'

'Nhia, you haven't laid eyes on Qiaan for a long time,' Xaforn said. 'When I last saw her she was Lihui's creature. I don't know how he did it, but he controlled her, completely. He told her she was royal, he told her she could rule her nation and help her people – and in the beginning that was what might have held her. We all know what kind of person she is, always in the throes of some scheme or another to better people's lives. But by the time I came to her it was past that, long past that. All that mattered was that she would be Empress, and he would be her Emperor.'

'I don't understand,' Tai said desperately. 'Why did he do this? He had everything he could have wanted – power, position. What made him reach for an Empire?'

'You're right, he had it all,' Nhia said. 'But then he lost everything. Khailin took care of that. The only way he could be powerful again was to rule in the physical realm. And the only way he could hope to succeed in that was by reaching for the Imperial Tiara. That way he could have done what he wished, stayed in control. That's all he ever wanted – to be the one who made the rules, the one who was obeyed. When he discovered Qiaan and her heritage he must have thought all his prayers had been answered – she was the bridge to all the power he could ever have wanted. If he needed to make her a part of himself to do it, to marry her, he would have done it. He would have done whatever he needed to do.'

'He was not,' Tai said, recalling the conversation she had with Maxao in the living room of her home not so very long before, 'that different from Sage Maxao.'

'Yes,' Nhia said abruptly. 'He was.'

'But now he is gone, and Qiaan . . .'

'She will be lost now, and utterly alone out there, perhaps with people who will think she is now more of a liability than an asset,' Xaforn said. 'I have to find her, before they kill her.'

'How are you going to do that?'

'The same way I did it the last time. The ghost road.'

'But that time you had Khailin to help you,' Nhia began.

Xaforn smiled, a tight little smile, as she reached for her hand. 'This time,' she said, 'it will have to be you. You'll have to look out for me.'

'I don't know nearly enough,' Nhia said. 'I would be more danger than any guidance I can give is actually worth to you.'

'I need an anchor here,' Xaforn said. 'Khailin is gone. It will have to be you. You are the only one of us left who knows anything at all about the ghost road.'

'Xaforn, if you bring Qiaan back here, it might only be for Liudan to wreak her revenge on her instead of her erstwhile allies. You do realize that if Liudan gets her hands on Qiaan, she's dead?'

Xaforn tossed her head, her long braid swinging. 'There is no honour in revenge.'

Tai grimaced. 'I don't think honour is the foremost thing in Liudan's mind. She is on the edge of something very dark.'

Xaforn gazed at her with sympathy and with affection. 'Qiaan is my responsibility,' she said. 'I'm afraid, Tai, that Liudan is probably yours. I couldn't tell you which is the thornier path, but if anybody can help Liudan claw her way back to us out of that dark place you speak of, it is you. Tammary always did say that you led a charmed life – never stop reminding Liudan of that life, never take that from Liudan's sight. Your own brand of quiet contentment is healing balm – enough, perhaps, even for Liudan's turbulent spirit.'

'If it were only that simple,' Tai said, tears sparkling in her eyes.

'Nhia?' Xaforn turned back to the Chancellor of Syai, who was rubbing at her hip with the flat of her hand, a grimace of pain on her face.

'Sometimes,' Nhia said, 'I swear the Gods of Cahan get together and play games as to what part of me they can make hurt the most. I've been standing too long, my bones ache. Is it all right, Xaforn, if I wait for you sitting down?'

'Go, Xaforn,' Tai said. 'May the Gods be generous with their goodwill. Go, find Qiaan. Bring her home.'

*Think of her face*, Khailin had said. Xaforn tried to remember an earlier face, a happier face, but all that kept on coming to her mind was the dreamy, faraway look on Qiaan's face as Lihui had drawn her to his side; she fought against it, resentful that she could seek for Qiaan only by the moment of her weakness. She was focused on her quarry as she stepped onto the pale ribbon of the ghost road, so intent that she barely glanced left or right at the glimpses beyond the mists. She thought she smelled blood once; she glimpsed a quiet courtyard with sunshine spilling on moss-overgrown flagstones, a silvery pennant with an unfamiliar symbol on it, a white cat grooming itself by a fireside, a moonlit ocean lapping at an empty beach. But the images were fleeting, barely enough for her eye to identify them, and she walked on, with a purpose, with grim determination.

When she stepped off the ghost road, it was with some surprise that she found herself in a familiar place. She recognized the streets around her. She was in Linh-an, still in the city, not very far from where she had started; the ghost road had provided a short cut to Qiaan, but this time she had been hidden in plain sight, almost within shouting distance of the Palace itself.

Twilight was darkening into full night as Xaforn emerged into the street and the ghost road shimmered back into oblivion behind her. She stood in an open doorway in the outer walls of a house in a rather affluent residential district, underneath a blue-tiled pagoda roof. The street at her back was empty, but there was a knot of people in the courtyard, maybe half a dozen of them, huddled around something in a corner. One of them held a guttering torch; by its light Xaforn could see that another clutched a long-bladed knife. A knife dark with blood.

'Finish her off, for the love of Cahan,' someone said in a low voice. 'Then we can take the carcass to the Empress and at least get amnesty. Nobody can prove anything against any of us as long as we all stay quiet.'

The one with the knife hesitated, and Xaforn clearly heard another voice, a familiar voice, blurred but trenchant.

'You might get more for me alive. Amnesty and gold. But oh, I forgot. I know who you are.'

'You be quiet,' the one with the torch snarled. 'Well, Miun? Will you do it, or do I have to?'

He barely had time to complete his question. The hiss of a descending blade right beside his ear made him shy away violently, dropping the torch. It rolled away and extinguished itself against a wall. The courtyard, now lit only by a muffled spill of light from a half-open door, plunged into shadows. One, slightly more solid than the others, moved among the men in a blur of deadly grace. Nearly all of them were down before they had a chance to know what was happening. Two ran. Xaforn dropped one with a high kick before he could reach the inviting open door to the house; he fell hard, and his head connected with a solid thud with a protruding corner of a wall jutting out into the courtyard. The other ducked out of the outside gate and into the street. Xaforn might have pursued him, but a sound behind her made her pause – a sound that was at once a moan and a knowing laugh.

'Hello, Xaforn,' Qiaan said, huddled against the wall of the house, her hand at her side. 'You could have let them finish me off, you know. Or have you come to bundle me up and deliver me to Liudan yourself?'

Xaforn, sheathing her dagger, dropped to one knee beside her wounded *jin-shei-bao*.

'How bad is it?' she said, ignoring the other's jibe. 'Let me see.'

'Bad enough,' Qiaan said. 'Perhaps not mortal, but bad enough. I saw it coming at the last moment, and turned into it – it was meant to go into my back, straight into my heart, but I startled him and he stumbled and he got me lower down instead. Kidney, maybe.' She tried to shift, drew in her breath sharply, let it out with a hiss.

'Don't move,' Xaforn said. 'Let me see.'

'One of them escaped,' Qiaan said, as Xaforn probed into her side.

'I know,' Xaforn said. 'I saw him.'

'He'll bring the rest of them. You'd better go. Unless you have a detachment of Guards out there with you.'

'Rabble,' Xaforn said, dismissing the promised reinforcements, turning to the dead or unconscious men she had left strewn about the courtyard and ripping off a length of material from a good-quality silk tunic one of them had been wearing. She folded that up into a thick pad and pressed it into Qiaan's wound, returning her hand to it. 'Hold that there. Press as hard as you can bear it. I'll get a belt or something off one of these brutes to tie it in place. Is anyone else in the house?'

'They sent the servants away,' Qiaan whispered weakly. 'They didn't want witnesses to murder. Not quite. There are more ways than one to get a reward . . . *aaah* . . .'

'Sorry,' said Xaforn, not sounding in the least contrite as she busied herself with the most immediate first aid that she could deliver. 'I'd rather you didn't move at all, but I'd also rather we were elsewhere right now.'

'I have an inkling as to where we are, but I'm not sure I could really walk anywhere right now,' Qiaan said. 'And I have a feeling that sedan chairs might be hard to come by before the rabble come back with reinforcements. You've lost the element of surprise, and there were only a handful of them here to surprise. The rest will know that you're waiting for them.'

'They might think it's that contingent of Guards that you were speaking of earlier,' Xaforn said, grinning, her teeth a flash of white in the darkness. 'Fewer might come than you think. Besides, I wasn't thinking of walking the streets of Linh-an tonight. I couldn't help you and protect you at once. But there's a short cut.'

'How did you find me at all?' Qiaan said, closing her eyes, and leaning against the wall. 'What short cut?'

'It's . . . never mind. It doesn't matter that you understand. Is that thing tight around you? Can you stand? It won't be for long, and I have Nhia waiting on the other end. We can get you to a healer as soon as we arrive.'

'Oh, I'm sure Yuet has all her poultices ready and waiting,' Qiaan said, with an affectionate laugh which quickly turned into another sibilant intake of breath as she tried to struggle to her feet.

For a moment Xaforn froze in mid-motion, but then continued reaching to drape one of Qiaan's arms around her own shoulders for support.

'Yuet is dead,' she said bluntly.

'Whuh . . . *what?*' Qiaan gasped, shocked. 'How? What happened?'

'It's a long story,' Xaforn said, after a brief hesitation. She was surprised how fast her own throat had closed at the mention of Yuet's name, how little control she had over the sharp pain of that loss. 'Later. We'd better get out of here now. We're going to . . .'

A small sound made her snap her head around, listening. A footfall. It had been a footfall.

And there was another.

There was still a chance, she could *shift* . . . The ghost road almost shimmered before her, its shape nearly solid. *Nhia! Nhia's face! Think of Nhia's face, dammit!*

'Too late,' Qiaan said softly.

'Those aren't thugs,' Xaforn said. 'Whoever is here is trained. They're too quiet.'

'Go,' Qiaan said urgently. 'Go, leave me. I am not worth your death.'

'You underestimate me,' Xaforn said. She let Qiaan back down, very gently, and loosened the sword she wore. 'Be quiet, and don't get in my way.'

'Insane,' said Qiaan, and choked on what might have been either a laugh or a sob.

'Selfless to the last,' returned Xaforn, the words double-edged, both a retort in their ancient, time-honoured verbal duel and a genuine compliment.

'Get out,' Qiaan hissed sharply, hunching over her wound. 'I will not have you on my conscience too for the rest of my life, however long that might turn out to be.'

'I leave here with you, or not at all,' said Xaforn.

451

'Why, damn you?'

'Because you're my cat,' Xaforn said simply.

She seemed to raise her sword at nothing at all, but a sudden grunt indicated that it had connected with a warm body. After that, things moved too fast for Qiaan to follow, even if she had not been slowed and fogged by her pain. She could sometimes glimpse figures locked in combat, briefly silhouetted against the wash of muted light that still spilled from the house; every now and again, by the shadow of its swinging braid of long hair, she could even identify Xaforn as one of the antagonists. She could hear calls of attack, or grunts of pain, the shuffle or hard stamp of feet, the whining sound of metal rasping against metal or a ringing clash of naked swords. She thought she heard Xaforn call out something, and perhaps another voice reply, but she could not be sure. Everything was a blur of sound and movement, darkness against light, cries of pain and triumph and sublimation of battle-frenzied motion in the night.

And then there was silence.

'Is it over?' Qiaan whispered, to nobody in particular, just to hear her own voice.

'No,' said Xaforn, close beside her.

'Are you all right? Cahan, there must have been dozens of them.'

'A handful,' Xaforn said briefly. 'They're Guards.'

'*Guards?*' Qiaan gasped. 'If they're Guards, they're ours . . . they're *yours*. Can't you just call out, tell them who you are? Why are they fighting you?'

'Because they have orders to kill you,' Xaforn said, and her voice was very gentle. 'And I won't have it.'

Qiaan's breathing was very shallow. 'You are fighting your beloved Guard? Over me?'

'For a long time,' Xaforn said in a voice almost dreamy, 'I found you merely annoying. Then the cat happened, and you named me *jin-shei*, and I started liking you. Then, for a while, I envied you. I might even have fallen in love with you for a time, I don't know. At some time or another I thought you were aggravating, arrogant, egotistical, supercilious or conceited. And other times I realized that you were one of the most gallant, unselfish, valiant, courageous people I knew. And then there were times I realized I didn't know you at all. And when you vanished, and your name started being dragged out as the banner behind which anyone who stood against the things I had vowed to defend could gather, I did not know what to think – except for one thing: I knew, underneath everything, who you were. Who you are. I will not let you get slaughtered here like a sacrificed pig. I will not. You are my cat, and there is no honour in it.'

Qiaan was weeping softly. 'I do not deserve that sacrifice,' she whispered. 'Go, Xaforn, for the love of Cahan, in the name of . . .'

'Don't tell me to go in the name of *jin-shei*,' said Xaforn, 'because I would be forced to do the unthinkable and refuse you.'

'They are gone,' Qiaan said. 'Go, you have a chance. Go. Leave me. I'm probably more than half dead already – don't waste your life over defending dead meat. It's not as though you can save my life. Even if you get us both out of here, I'm dead. Liudan will . . .'

She felt the tip of Xaforn's braid brush her cheek, and then Xaforn's lips gentle on her brow.

'Hush,' said Xaforn. 'They are back. I think they have brought reinforcements.'

She melted away into the night once more, and Qiaan heard her cry out as she leaped at an enemy in the shadows, a battle cry. Qiaan's throat was closed tight; that was a cry full of knowledge, a deep and full awareness of exactly what Xaforn was, what she had been born to be. She had been trained as a killer, but she was now ready to die in defence of another life, in the name of that honour that she held so dear, in the name of friendship, in the name of the bond of sisterhood with which Qiaan had once, quite unwittingly and with no inkling as to what its price would be, bound her over the shared connection of a black kitten rescued from oblivion.

The courtyard was full of scurrying, shadowy shapes. They were all converging on a single point, aimed at a single beating heart.

'*No!*' Qiaan screamed, strength returning to her for one moment, just enough strength to shout with full voice.

The last thing that lodged in her sight was a glimpse, almost in slow motion, of the silhouette of a long braid swinging across the dim light from the half-open door, and then Xaforn's face, caught full in that light, as half a dozen men converged on her at once. It should have ended there, but it was as though the Gods themselves wanted to make sure that Qiaan saw, that Qiaan knew. A path opened through the pack of men, just for a moment, and Qiaan saw her lying there – the slight body stretched out by the door of the house, flooded with light, the long black braid snaking on the ground beside her. And then the men closed in again, the shadows swallowed it all, and Qiaan closed her eyes.

*They needed an army to take her*, Qiaan thought with bitter pride.

And then true night descended at last, and she knew no more.

# *Six*

When Qiaan woke again, it was to throbbing pain – in her side, behind her eyes, and in the empty hollow place where she knew her heart used to be.

'Stubborn,' she whispered, throwing the word out as she so often did before to be riposted by something trenchant and witty by Xaforn. But she was met with silence – the silence that she would be met with from now on.

Xaforn was gone.

*Gone.*

The sheer impossibility of that took her breath away. It took an army. She had faced a small army – an army of trained Guards, at that – and held them at bay until overwhelmed by sheer numbers.

'Oh, Cahan,' Qiaan sobbed suddenly. 'It should have been me. It should have been *me*.'

She blinked away the tears that blurred her vision and looked around, orienting herself. She was in a bed, a reasonably comfortable if rather rudimentary bed, with a warm coverlet over her. The wound in her side had been tended and neatly bandaged, as her exploring fingers became aware of before she discovered, the hard way, that the wound may have been tended but was far from healed. Wincing, she let her eyes travel down the shape of her body under the coverlet. Beside the bed was a rather battered chair, at the foot of the bed a plain scrubbed table which held a bowl, now covered with a piece of clean cloth, and a small untidy pile of what looked like healers' supplies. The walls were bare, grey stone. There was a window, high up, with three iron bars set in it. Opposite the window, a sturdy wooden door was set flush with the wall. It had no handle on the inside.

A prison, then.

*Oh, Xaforn. They may kill me fast, or they may leave me in here to rot. And it was for this that you snuffed out the bright flame of your life.*

There was a muffled sound beyond the thick door even as Qiaan was bleakly contemplating it, and it swung open into the room to admit a wizened old woman with wispy white hair and gums so toothless that her cheeks had fallen inwards, giving her face an oddly skull-like quality.

'You're awake,' the crone said, and her voice was surprisingly rich coming from such a frail and unprepossessing vessel. 'That's good. I was beginning to worry about you.' The door had been closed behind her, but she now turned and banged on it with both fists. It opened a crack, and Qiaan thought she glimpsed a slim form in a Guard uniform just outside. The crone exchanged a few remarks with the guard on duty, too softly for Qiaan to hear, and then turned back to her patient, the door slamming shut again behind her.

'I've asked them to bring some boiling water, and we can try one of my herbal teas,' the crone said. 'You've been through a rough time, but you're young, you ought to mend quickly.'

'Where am I?' Qiaan whispered hopelessly.

'The Guard compound holding cells,' the crone said, rummaging through the pile of things on the table. 'Bandages, clean bandages, I know I left some in here . . . ah, here we are. Now let me see. It is time to change your dressing.'

'Please,' Qiaan began, but the crone tutted at her and turned her expertly so that she could get at the stab wound. 'What is your name?' Qiaan persisted as the healer removed the old bandage, cleaned up the wound with water from the bowl that had been on the table, and replaced the bandage with the new poultice she had prepared. 'You have to help me. I need to see someone. I need to talk to one of my . . . I need to speak to Liudan, to the Empress.'

'Lie still, child,' the crone said.

'Please,' Qiaan whispered. 'What is your name?'

'Xinma,' the crone said, finishing off and pulling the coverlet back into place. 'My name is Xinma and I cannot help you – it is for the Empress to ask to see you if she sees fit to do so, and not the other way round. All you have to do is concentrate on healing. Now, that wound aside, is there anything else that you are suffering from?'

'I have a headache,' Qiaan said. *And my heart is broken.*

'We can fix that. The herbal tea will help you sleep. You need to sleep. Sleep heals everything.'

A knock heralded the arrival of the required hot water; it was passed into the room in a small earthenware pot, through the smallest possible crack in the door.

Qiaan actually found the strength to laugh. 'What do they think I will do, make a break for it?'

'Unlikely, at least for a while, my dear,' the crone said without looking at her, emptying a packet of herbs into the pot and stirring the contents with a blunt wooden paddle until the brew met with her satisfaction. She decanted some of it carefully into a small cup and returned to the bed. 'I'd better help you with this, for now,' she said, lifting Qiaan's shoulders slightly with one arm and bringing the cup to the patient's lips with her free hand. 'Here, sip. Maybe in a few days I can strap you up and you can actually sit up for a bit – it will be easier to eat, anyway.'

'What do they mean to do with me?' Qiaan asked, gagging on her first sip of the unexpectedly bitter brew.

'My task is merely to mend your hurts,' Xinma said. 'Beyond that, it is none of my concern.'

After Qiaan had been patiently held until she had swallowed every last bit of the herbal concoction, the old healer laid her back down on the bed.

'Sleep now,' she ordered.

And Qiaan slipped off into an uneasy, unnatural sleep, compelled by the sleeping potion. It was supposed to be a dreamless and healing sleep, but she woke later with trails of tears still wet on her cheeks. A stony-faced guard who would not respond to anything Qiaan said brought in a hot broth for her lunch, and Xinma returned to feed her and to administer another dose of herbal medicine. That was Qiaan's routine, with light and shadow displacing one another at her barred window as day turned into night, and then day, and then night again. Qiaan quickly lost count of how many such transitions there had been since she had been incarcerated

456

in her dungeon. If she were to go by Xinma's precise actions which never varied – tending her wound, feeding her, administering the sleeping drug – she might have been there for ever. But she knew, by the way that the thought of Xaforn still lodged in her heart like a stabbing sharp pain, that it had not been long. A week, perhaps.

And then the routine changed.

'You have a visitor,' Xinma announced, ushering in a tall, grim-faced woman in a Guard's uniform.

Qiaan knew her – JeuJeu, who had once had charge of training the up-and-coming cadres of the Imperial Guard in the days when Xaforn had been a child.

'They tell me you are mending nicely,' JeuJeu said, by way of greeting, when Xinma had left them alone in response to the curt toss of her head.

'Then they are wiser than me,' Qiaan said. 'There are things inside of me that will never mend. Why am I still alive, JeuJeu? I thought by now the Empress would have tried and sentenced me, and there is hardly any doubt as to the verdict. I am already dead – it's only a matter of time.'

'I don't know that,' JeuJeu said. 'She has not spoken out on the matter at all.'

'Is there any chance of seeing her? Of talking to her?'

'You?' JeuJeu said. 'I'm not at all sure that she would come to you. Why would she? What can you possibly have to tell her?'

'So why are you here?' Qiaan said bitterly.

'Because you are one of us,' JeuJeu said. 'And you have always been. What is it? What did I say?'

For Qiaan had laughed once, bitterly, while at the same time her eyes filled with tears. 'That's what she said, you know,' Qiaan murmured, covering her face with her hand. 'She died for me, JeuJeu.'

'And killed for you, if you mean Xaforn,' JeuJeu said. 'They counted eighteen bodies in that courtyard afterwards. Some identi-fied later as part of the rising – *your* people – but the rest all Guards. She killed thirteen trained Guards that night.'

'She was the best you ever had,' Qiaan whispered. 'I never told her that. Not out loud, not like that. I always said, "Oh, that will do." Even when she performed impossible things. "That's not bad," I'd tell her. Tell Xaforn that. Xaforn, who could stare death in the face and make it look away first.'

JeuJeu's face was oddly grey. 'You said that's what she said, a moment ago,' she said. 'What do you mean?'

'I told her to go, to leave me, that I was dead, that this was a cause already lost and unworthy of offering herself to,' Qiaan said, 'and she told me that she was there because . . . she said, "You are my cat." JeuJeu, do you remember?'

JeuJeu turned her head away very sharply so that Qiaan should not see the sudden tears in her eyes. 'Yes,' she said.

'Can you at least,' Qiaan said after a pause, 'ask them to kill me cleanly?'

'I'll come and see you again,' JeuJeu said, very abruptly, her voice harsher than she had intended – for otherwise she would have wept out loud. She turned to knock on the door to be released.

'JeuJeu, do me one favour. If not the Empress, can you get one of my other *jin-shei-bao* in here? Yuet or . . . no, Xaforn said Yuet too was dead.' She swallowed convulsively. 'What has been going on out there? What else don't I know?'

'Much,' JeuJeu said. 'And a lot of it has been done in your name, although the Empress is not without . . .' She pressed her lips together, before she said too much. 'I will see what I can do.'

She apparently succeeded in that endeavour, for Tai came to see Qiaan in her cell the very next day. She perched carefully on the convalescent's bed, careful at first not to disturb the arrangements of bandage and poultice, but soon they were clinging together in a tight hug as both wept on each other's shoulders. Qiaan listened, appalled, as Tai spoke of the toll of the past year. Xaforn was merely the last, perhaps the highest, price paid in the upheavals that had shaken Syai.

'I took her yearwood beads to the scribes myself,' Tai said. 'They were so few, so pitifully few, when they were piled together in a representation of a life. She was so young.'

'She may have been the best of us all,' Qiaan said.

'We have all been tested,' Tai murmured.

'What happens next?'

'Her funeral rites were performed two days ago,' Tai said. 'The whole Guard turned out to the pyre.'

'But JeuJeu said that she killed thirteen of them that night. They must have believed she had turned on them, that she had gone to the bad, or to the other side. It isn't just that she died, Tai, it's what she sacrificed in the manner of her dying. It is possible that she could have been called traitor, she who never strayed from her honour.'

'They knew that,' Tai said quietly. 'Every single one of them knows that.'

'So what does Liudan plan to do with me?'

'I don't know yet,' Tai said. 'She has said nothing. She sees almost no one these days.'

'Not even you?'

'Very rarely. It's as though she looks on the whole world as her enemy, out for her blood. And I don't know how to heal that. I don't know how to get through to her any more. Sometimes when I *am* with her it feels like I am talking to a beautiful porcelain doll. There is no human warmth there, only distance, only emptiness. I desperately want to . . . I don't know . . . Sometimes she reminds me of my own children when they were really small, when they were too young to understand anything and merely withdrew when the world became too much. I could take them and hug them and make it all better – but Liudan won't let me near her any more. She barely acknowledges I exist.'

'You've always mothered all of us,' said Qiaan with a shadow of a smile.

'It started when Antian told me to take care of her sister, and at first I thought she meant only Liudan – and then there was Tammary.'

'And then you had all of us, and were all her sisters, all linked through *jin-shei*, and you spread yourself thin for us, being there, being you,' Qiaan said.

Tai flushed. 'I did little.'

'You cherished and protected, sometimes by no more than your example,' Qiaan said.

'But I have failed,' Tai said, her eyes brimming. 'For a long time now I have had this fear – that it was all ending somehow, and that there was nothing I could do to stop it. And then Tammary fled, and Yuet died, and Khailin vanished, and now Xaforn.'

'And me,' Qiaan said gently. 'I am being preserved for some harsh fate. I don't know what yet but that much I do know. Liudan can't let me live. It would have been better if I had died in that courtyard and Xaforn was still here, who always shone so much brighter than I.'

The guard outside the door opened it a crack. 'Time,' he said.

'I'll come back and see you every day,' Tai promised.

'Thank you,' Qiaan whispered. 'For as long as you are able,' she added, as Tai embraced her one more time and was escorted out of the cell.

But it was Nhia who came to see her next, and Nhia was a little more knowledgeable, and a lot more pragmatic.

'She has been heard to mutter that she will not execute a convalescent,' Nhia said. 'In other words, don't hurry to get well. Your wound is what is keeping you alive.'

'Did she say how?' Qiaan asked, steadily enough, but Nhia saw her hands tremble on the coverlet, and reached out and took one, squeezing it gently.

Qiaan returned the pressure, but with little strength.

'I know,' she said, 'that I probably deserve everything she has planned for me. But in my defence . . .'

'Your defence requires nothing else but the knowledge that it was Lihui who stood behind you,' Nhia said intensely. 'Nobody understands that part of it better than I do. I've tried talking to Liudan about it, but so far she seems to be listening only to the voices inside her own head. She's been reading up on ancient forms of punishment, I know that much, because I know that she has taken the scrolls from the libraries – and the *jin-ashu* transcripts never pulled punches when it came to describing atrocities. If anything, the women described a myriad of ways to kill someone with a great deal more relish and attention to detail than any man could have done.'

'So she plans on a spectacle?'

'The Guard is muttering against it,' Nhia said, 'but . . .'

Qiaan found this strangely touching. 'Xaforn of the Imperial Guard died because of me, and yet when the Empress wishes to destroy me they balk at it?'

'You were both their own,' Nhia said, 'and they take pride in protecting their own. They would take the matter of discipline on for themselves, if they could, but Liudan has called it high treason and thus made it the business of the Throne, not Guard law.'

'What is she planning?' Qiaan asked, her hand trembling again, ever so slightly. 'I am not good at enduring things. I will make a poor spectacle for her, Nhia. I have always hated pain.'

'Yes, and that is why you were always trying to help others when you saw them suffering,' Nhia said. 'That, too, the city is beginning to remember – what came before all this. But Liudan doesn't listen, and she doesn't talk to any of us any more.'

But it was Liudan herself, sweeping into the holding cell when Qiaan's wounds were almost healed, who came to tell the prisoner what awaited her.

'I had considered merely hastening your passage to Cahan by providing you with a pyre of your own before you were too dead to enjoy it,' Liudan said, 'but on reflection it would be too fast a death – so I went looking in the old books. Oh, we can still do the pyre, at the last – and you'll still be aware enough for it – but before that I thought we could re-invent the kind of scourge which flays flesh until bones show, and follow that with a slow and careful reduction of the flesh. It all has to be on the pyre, I know, in order for a good passage to Cahan – but nothing I have read leads me to believe that the passage in question would be significantly impaired if your feet, your hands, your eyes, your breasts and perhaps a few other choice pieces arrived at the pyre independently of the rest of you.'

It was a litany of horrors so long and delivered in such detail that Qiaan was left white and shaking under the stream of words.

'You will live for as long as I can make you live before I will allow you to die,' Liudan said. 'After this, few will rise against me again. They will know what awaits them at the end of that road.'

'I sought my place in this world,' Qiaan said. 'I never wanted yours.'

'Oh? So in whose name was this rebellion wrought, then? Did I imagine your name on the banners?'

'Lihui's name was all over those banners, all over that rebellion,' Qiaan whispered. 'Cahan! How could I have let him? How could I have believed him?'

'Were you hoping to bear his bastard and put the child on my throne?' Liudan said, and her voice was edged with a rage bordering on madness. 'I am the Dragon Empress, and I will not let it happen!'

Qiaan stared at her for a long moment, and then let her eyes drop to where her folded hands, quite steady now, lay on top of her coverlet.

'May the Gods be merciful to you, then,' she murmured.

Liudan laughed. 'You wish that on me?'

'Yes,' Qiaan said, without lifting her eyes. 'Because you have not touched Cahan in a long time.'

Liudan's silence was brittle, as though she had been contemplating a reply and then thought better of it. Instead, she turned and swept out of the cell.

That evening an unexpected visitor slipped into Qiaan's cell.

'Nhia? What are you doing?'

'Shhh, quiet.' Warm, gentle hands folded a small glass vial into Qiaan's palm. 'Now we know. We all know. There has been a public announcement. It is all to take place the day after tomorrow. This . . . this is for you, if you wish it.'

'What is it?'

'Release,' Nhia said, her voice thick with tears. 'You have never deserved what she will inflict on you, and Lihui is already dead, removed from justice. If you wish it, this is a release from pain. You will sleep, that is all. You will sleep, and not wake.'

Qiaan's hand closed on the vial. 'Thank you.'

Nhia, although she could not possibly have known that she did it, echoed Xaforn's last gesture and kissed Qiaan gently on the brow. 'Sleep in peace, *jin-shei-bao*. I cannot grant you life. I can offer you a death less savage than what has been planned for you.'

And then she was gone.

Qiaan rose from her bed, and lifted her eyes to the sky she could glimpse through her small window, segmented by the iron bars. It was deep night, the clear sky shimmering with bright stars, like the storied heavens of Cahan.

*Forgive me, Xaforn.*

Closing her eyes against a hot rush of tears, Qiaan lifted the vial of oblivion to her lips.


# Seven

'Nhia?'

'Shhh. It is late. Go back to sleep,' Nhia said, slipping back into her bed.

Nhia's current lover turned his head, rubbing his eyes. 'I woke, and you were gone – and then I must have dozed off again. Where have you been?'

'Nowhere, Weylin. Go back to sleep.'

Weylin sat up abruptly, spilling the soft cotton sheet that had been covering him from his flat, sculpted abdomen. He was a builder's apprentice; toting bricks and lumber all day had made his muscles hard as whipcord. He was much younger than Nhia, and far from the social circles she moved in these days, as all her recent flames seemed to be. She seemed to go out of her way to pick up men at best inappropriate, at worst disastrous. Weylin's predecessor, before taking up briefly with Nhia, had been working some of the city's less than salubrious 'water tea-houses', the ones that Tammary had been frequenting before circumstances and Zhan had rescued her from that life.

'You've been crying,' Weylin said. For all his youth and brashness, he was not entirely insensitive. 'I can hear it in your voice. What happened?'

'I said, go to sleep!' Nhia said, but her voice broke on the last word, and all of a sudden she was sobbing violently into her pillow, her shoulders heaving.

Weylin gathered her into his arms, turning her face into his chest, smoothing her hair with a gentle hand. 'Tell me,' he said. 'I can help, perhaps, and even if I can't it helps to talk about it. Or are you going to tell me again it's all a state secret?'

'I've lost too many of them, too fast,' Nhia sobbed. 'Too many of them. Oh, my sisters!'

'I saw the Empress's proclamation,' Weylin said. 'Is it Qiaan? Are you thinking of how Qiaan is to die?'

'She will not die like that,' Nhia said, her voice muffled against his chest.

'No,' he said thoughtfully. 'She won't die . . .' Something about Nhia's words suddenly changed shape, however, and Weylin did a rapid double take. '"Like that"?' he questioned. 'Like what?'

'I can't let it happen,' Nhia said, wiping her nose with the back of her hand like a child. 'It would be a betrayal of everything. Liudan could not even contemplate doing this if she stopped to think about the fact that she was doing it to one of her own *jin-shei-bao*.'

'She has always been a user,' Weylin murmured.

'No,' Nhia said. 'She has always been Liudan. She was lonely, and she was insecure, and she acted to take as much power as she could so that she did not ever have to depend on anyone else's goodwill for

463

anything – she was Empress, and her word would be law. But she was also kind. She gave me a life when my own didn't seem worth living. And now she has forced me to take a life because it was worth more than the value she put on it.'

'Nhia,' Weylin said, after a brief pause, his hand frozen on her hair, 'just what did you do?'

'I can't tell you,' she said, pulling away from him.

'State secret?' he said, sighing.

'No. Mine. What I did is my responsibility, nobody else's.'

'She won't die, Nhia,' Weylin said, choosing his words very carefully. 'Listen, there is something I have been wanting to tell you for some time. I know some people . . . people who are involved, who had been involved with the rising.' He stumbled to a halt, groping for words. Nhia, suddenly very still, sat with her eyes steadily on him, watching, offering no help.

'There was a faction,' Weylin continued helplessly, unable now to halt his confession, 'that wanted Qiaan dead.'

'They nearly succeeded,' Nhia said. 'My *jin-shei-bao* Xaforn to whom I just bade farewell on her journey to Cahan was there.'

'I know,' Weylin said. 'But there were others . . . there are others . . . who did not agree. They might have been too late then, but they are ready now, ready to act.'

'What are you saying, Weylin?'

'Oh, Cahan. I suppose this is treason, too,' Weylin said, running a long-fingered hand through his long hair. 'I am not part of this group, but I have friends, good friends, who are. And I know that they . . . I should not be telling you this, but damn it all, it's all getting out of hand now. For what it's worth, you're torturing yourself unnecessarily – Qiaan will not die in two days. I know because . . . you won't go straight to Liudan with all this, will you?'

'Telling me what?' Nhia said.

'Liudan was waiting for her to recover from her wounds, was she not? Before she took any action?'

'Yes.'

'So were they, Nhia. They were waiting until they could snatch a well woman. It's hard enough to take a prisoner from that place if that prisoner is cooperating and hale and hearty, it's near impossible if that prisoner is slowed by a stab wound and is unable to move fast, or move quietly, or move at all, damn it, without being carried.'

'You left a very slim window of opportunity,' Nhia said, and now she sounded distant, frozen.

'I know. But it was necessary. But it's all in place now, and we have plans.'

'Tell them to stand down,' Nhia said. She turned away, very suddenly, and lay down on the bed with her back to Weylin, curled up on her side, eyes wide and staring into nothingness.

'Nhia? What are you . . . ?'

'You're too late,' she said. 'I took her a vial of poison tonight, to sleep, if she will. I could not bear to see her tortured and flogged and put on show just because Liudan needs to feel secure. So I gave her an escape.'

'But tomorrow! Tomorrow we would have . . .' gasped Weylin.

'It's probably too late,' Nhia said, 'even tonight. Go. Tell them.'

'But I told you, I don't know . . .'

'You have *friends*,' Nhia said, laying ironic emphasis on the last word. 'In my experience people with *friends* in situations are not infrequently discovered to share that situation themselves.'

'*Your* friend is about to die!'

'Qiaan is not just a friend; she is my *jin-shei-bao*. I have done what I need to do, to protect my sister in the name of the vow that binds us. Go, Weylin. Go now.'

After a stark silence, she felt the bed shift as he swung his legs out and stood up.

'You might have slain the future for all of us,' he said.

'I might have,' Nhia agreed, suddenly weary beyond bearing, beyond hope. 'Leave me alone.'

'If Liudan finds out, she will flay *you* alive instead,' Weylin said.

'Liudan is my *jin-shei* sister, too, remember,' Nhia snapped, raising herself on one elbow.

'That didn't seem to stop her from passing that horrifying sentence on Qiaan,' Weylin said. 'But one more thing I will tell you, then, and it's free. They will try again to kill the Empress.'

'Again? Have they tried before?'

'Several times, and once came close.'

'The arrow.'

'Yes.'

'The Empress is well protected against arrows these days.'

Weylin gave a sharp bark of a laugh. 'Do you think they are stupid enough to try the same trick twice?'

'How, then?' Nhia said, after a beat of silence.

'Poison,' Weylin said. She could hear him slipping into his trousers, elbowing his arms into his tunic. 'And that is really all I know. If I had details I would give them to you. All I know is that the poison had been procured, and they were waiting for a good opportunity – and chaos is always a good opportunity. That's why I'm telling you this now. You may not realize it yet but you have just created chaos. The perfect timing for that poison will be within the next two days. Or as soon as the news breaks that Qiaan cheated Liudan's executioner.'

'What kind of poison?'

'I have told you all I know. Good night, Nhia.' He paused, the merest beat of silence, and then added, very softly, 'Goodbye.'

She sat up, seeking him with her eyes in the twilight of the bedroom, but all she saw was the door already closing behind him. He would not be back, she felt that in her bones. All of Nhia's recent relationships seemed to last only for a short while – a few months, often just a few weeks, once or twice no more than a couple of sizzling days. She had been the one to end it, every time. Sometimes she regretted the severing, a few times she actually mourned her loss, but mostly she was left feeling hugely relieved that she would not be expected to give any more than she had already done, that she had escaped something which, if she had let it run its natural course, could have destroyed her.

Weylin had been quiet, kind. With him it might have been different. If she had done things differently. If she had only tried harder. If only life was not such a mess.

Had he been speaking the truth? Had she really killed Qiaan, helped her die, perhaps only hours from rescue? She had hardly been able to believe the tortures that would be inflicted upon Qiaan, the bile had risen to the back of her throat at the very thought of it, and as the Chancellor of Syai it would have been her duty to be present when the sentence was carried out. *Was it Qiaan I was trying to save, or myself? Is it too late?*

Her mind was a chaotic whirlpool, awash with painful memories, with guilt, with fear, agitated by concern for Liudan, by mourning for Xaforn, by grief for Qiaan. There was a time that she had known

466

how to calm her spirit, how to slip into a meditative state, how to sit quietly for hours and become part of the light of Cahan and emerge refreshed and renewed – but she could not seem to remember how to do that any more. It was as though it had been centuries since she had last called upon that ability, not the handful of years that had truly passed.

Nhia closed her eyes, pummelled her pillow into submission with both fists, tried to burrow into it and sleep, but it was useless – she could not seem to find a comfortable position, turning restlessly in her bed, getting the sheets all tangled around her twisted foot. Everything ached – her withered leg, her bones, her shoulders taut with tension, a throbbing pain behind her eyes.

Yuet might have told her trenchantly that the first thing she needed to do was get some sleep – but Yuet was gone, ashes now. Xaforn would have . . . Qiaan would have . . .

'Oh, Cahan!' Nhia moaned despairingly. There were too many ghosts sharing her bedroom with her this night. None of them had come to demand reparations, or to accuse, or to lay blame. But they were there, thick around her; Nhia's skin prickled at their presence.

This room was no haven for her, not tonight.

She rose and dressed again, wincing as she forced her aching crippled foot back into its special shoe. It was well past midnight, and the city was quiet in the night as she slipped out of a postern door and into the streets, hurrying past shuttered houses, past the big market square where already some stir was evident, the air perfumed by fresh-baked bread as the baker fired up his oven in preparation for the first customers of the day.

Tai's house was silent and dark except for a lantern lit by its gate as Nhia, pulling the concealing hood of her mantle closer around her face, beat on the door with her fist.

She had to do it several times before a sleepy servant emerged to answer her knock.

'I need to see your mistress,' Nhia said, allowing her mantle to slip back a little so that the servant could catch a glimpse of her face in the light of the lantern he carried. 'I know it's late. It's urgent.'

'I will wake her,' the servant said, recognizing the visitor and stepping aside so she could enter, bolting the door closed behind her. 'I will light the lanterns in the sitting room for you.'

The servant conducted her into the room and busied himself for a moment with a taper until three or four decorative lanterns made of heavy double-layered silkpaper bloomed into being and the chamber was filled with a delicate creamy light. Nhia lifted a piece of half-finished embroidery from the nearest chair and subsided onto it, breathing as though she had run here from the Palace – she, who had never run in her life, who could never run. *Perhaps that's why I do what I do*, Nhia thought in a swift, chagrined insight. *I cannot flee using my feet so I made it an art form to escape using my mind.*

It was not long before Tai, rubbing sleep from her eyes with the knuckles of both hands like a child, padded into the sitting room. Her hair was unbound for the night and spilled around her shoulders like a dark cloak; her feet were bare.

'Nhia? What are you doing here? What time is it? What's happened now?'

'Liudan would have tortured her,' Nhia said abruptly.

Tai made the effort to wake up, to make the mental transition. 'You mean Qiaan?' she whispered. 'I know. I saw the proclamation.'

'Weylin told me they would have rescued her tomorrow,' Nhia said.

'Who would?'

'Her people. The rebels.'

'Lihui's people or her people?' Tai asked, thoroughly awake now. 'You aren't making any sense, Nhia. Let me get us some tea.' She took a closer look, and realized that Nhia was crying quietly; she took a step closer, reached for her hand, squeezed it hard. 'Don't you dare. If you fall apart on me too, I swear I'll go out and throw myself from the city walls.'

Nhia hiccoughed, laughing and sobbing at the same time. 'I'm sorry, but I . . .'

'Tea,' Tai said firmly. 'Wait here, I'll be right back.'

She disappeared briefly to collar an early-waking servant in the kitchen and command a pot of tea, and then hurried back to Nhia, who was sitting with her face buried in her hands. Her sleep-tousled hair, which she had not bothered to comb or dress before she had made her mad midnight dash to Tai's house, fell over her fingers in loose strands and tangles. For a moment Tai was transported many years into the past, when they had both been children of Linh-an's streets, daughters of women earning a living by the labour of their

468

hands, daughters of seamstresses and washerwomen. How far away it all was, and how close. Nhia had shed the skins of the Temple teacher, the wise woman, the Chancellor, and was once more just the friend of Tai's childhood. With everything that had been gained and lost in the passing years, there was always that.

'We are so arrogant,' Nhia whispered, 'thinking we always know best.'

'What is it that you have done?' Tai asked, very gently, subsiding onto the floor at Nhia's feet and leaning her cheek on Nhia's good knee.

'One thing I don't understand,' Nhia said. 'I know Liudan wished Qiaan destroyed – I know the orders that the Guards had were to kill her if they found her. Qiaan said that's what Xaforn said, too, there in the courtyard. That the Guard had orders to kill Qiaan. But then, when they had the chance to do it, after Xaforn no longer stood in their way, they didn't do it. *They didn't do it.* And they brought her back to Liudan. Who then decided that just killing her wasn't enough.'

'That's because orders coming from Liudan are seldom the same two days in a row these days,' Tai said. 'These days people are struggling to second-guess her, to stay one step ahead, just to make sure that her wrath won't descend on them for reasons that seem utterly irrational. But you, of all people, know this. You are Chancellor; you've been juggling Liudan's explosive whims for years.'

'Yes, but somehow I've always been able to understand,' Nhia said. 'Now I'm not only second-guessing her, I'm doing it to myself.' Her breath caught on a sob again. 'He said they would rescue her, Tai. And just before he told me that, I . . . Oh, Cahan, Tai, I thought the choice was between watching her being hideously butchered in the public square in two days or giving her a chance to die a dignified death, a death without pain – but what if I had been wrong? What if Weylin was right? What if they would have come for her? What if the choice had been between life and death, and I . . . I, her own *jin-shei-bao*, took that choice away from her? Xaforn died for her, and what I did may have betrayed them both.'

'Nhia . . .' Tai began.

'If she is guilty of anything, it is of falling under Lihui's spell – and I have been there myself, I know how powerful that voice of his can be, how compelling the need to obey his wishes. If she was guilty, so was I – of the same sin. I could not sit and watch her pay the price for my own mistakes. I gave her a way out, tonight, Tai.' Nhia swallowed hard. 'I took a vial of poison to her cell tonight. A death with dignity, I thought, and not a spectacle for the crowds, or a way for Liudan to indulge her paranoia. As if cruelty and violence have ever stood in the way of rebellions – if anything, they feed them.'

Tai's eyes brimmed with tears, spilled.

*Bare branch trembling in the sunshine.* Pau-kala.

Nhia's hands clutched at Tai's, her grip surprisingly strong. 'What if I was wrong?' she whispered with a savage intensity. 'Have I killed what Xaforn died to save? Would the Imperial Guard have put a stop to Liudan's plans, if the rebels did not? What if I was wrong, Tai? I thought I was doing the right thing, the only thing I could do, but what if there had been a chance, what if I could have saved her instead? I am Chancellor – why didn't I go to Liudan and demand that she not go through with this? I could have asked her, in the name of *jin-shei* . . .'

'And she would have found a way to deny you,' Tai said quietly. 'She has locked herself in a virtual tower, isolating herself from everyone, even from us, her *jin-shei-bao*, except when she turned to the sisterhood to wring what she needed out of one or another of us. But it isn't just us these days, although those of us who are gone may be good examples of what Liudan is doing. She demands absolute loyalty – but she alone is to be the judge of what that loyalty is or how it is expressed. And in a way it is understandable – she is Empress, and loyalty to the throne has always been important. But Nhia, she has set loyalty against wisdom, loyalty against honour, loyalty against happiness, and with us it has always been in the name of *jin-shei*. She demanded immortality, and continued demanding it even when it was beyond doubt that it would be unwise to pursue it further – but she wanted what she wanted, and asked too much of Khailin. She used the Guard to back her when she took the throne as Dragon Empress, and loyalty has been bred into those people for generations, over the reign of many, many Emperors – but she asked too much of Xaforn. And she seemed to truly believe that both Tammary and Qiaan should somehow shrug off their inconvenient ancestry, just so that the Dragon Empress could sit more securely on her throne. She broke the laws of *jin-shei* even as she invoked them, every time. Antian asked me to take care of her, but I honestly don't know how to do that any more.'

'Have you seen her recently?'

'She does not see me often,' Tai said. 'And when she does she seems to be in a different sphere from me. It's like trying to talk to an alien creature which lives on fire alone and thrives on blood and fear and conflict, as long as they all take place beyond the serene, elegant silence of her drawing room.'

The servant had brought the tea and had left the tray on a low table by the door of the sitting room. Tai crossed to the tea things and brought back two steaming cups, passing one to Nhia.

'Well, I had better go and see her tomorrow,' Nhia said wearily.

'If you think pouring your heart out to Liudan in a confession will help,' Tai began, but Nhia, accepting the cup with one hand, raised the other to stop her.

'No, it's that loyalty thing,' she said, with a small smile. 'You see, Qiaan's impending rescue is not the only thing that Weylin told me about tonight.'

Tai, suddenly shivering, put down her tea cup. 'What else?'

'The same people who would have set Qiaan free had laid far deeper plans,' Nhia said. 'Weylin did not know when or how – or perhaps he just wouldn't tell me – but they are plotting Liudan's death. Somehow, somewhere, someone is going to bring poison to the Empress – and Weylin seemed to think that it would be within days.' Nhia drained her tea as though she was drinking white spirits, and turned an ironic, twisted smile on Tai. 'I gave poison to Qiaan myself, and now I have to go and make sure that I keep it from Liudan's lips. Oh, what a creature I have turned into, Tai. I give death with one hand, and life with the other.'

# Eight

For the second time in less than twenty-four hours, at mid-morning the next day, Nhia found herself knocking on the door of one of her *jin-shei* sisters. But this door was guarded by a servant who appeared less inclined to grant her admittance.

*The Empress is indisposed*, Liudan's deaf-mute servant signed to her.

'Indisposed? How?' Nhia demanded sharply. *In the name of Cahan, can I be too late already?*

The servant girl repeated that the Empress was not seeing anyone. Perhaps she offered more, but the sign language, so honed between servant and Empress that it had sometimes seemed to Nhia that Liudan read her servant's mind rather than her dancing hands, was not something in which Nhia herself was proficient. On any other day she might have left an urgent message for Liudan and returned later. But a vivid fear burned in her, and 'indisposed' could mean anything at all right now. A sudden echo of Xaforn's voice rang in her mind: *Well, if Liudan won't give me leave, I'll have to do it without.* On the day she asked Nhia to stand sentry for her as she set out on the ghost road to get Qiaan. On the day she died.

Nhia's eyes were suddenly very bright.

If Xaforn had had the courage to do it . . .

'Sorry,' she murmured to the servant girl, 'but I have to see her. Right now. It's urgent. She will see me. I am the Chancellor of her realm.'

The servant made further motions of denying entry, but Nhia swept past her and into the antechamber to Liudan's rooms. To her eye it looked untidy, things piled on a low table by the door as though the servant had been caught in the middle of preparing something, or even packing. Under ordinary circumstances Nhia might have paid closer attention, but she passed by the table casting only a cursory glance on its jumbled contents and opened the door to the inner chambers.

Liudan, dressed only in a silk morning robe loosely tied around her waist and her hair escaping messily from a hastily pinned-up attempt at a Court style, stood in the midst of the room, and she looked like the absolute incarnation of towering rage.

'What?' she demanded, her head turned away from the door. 'I told you to stay out! What do you want?'

'She can't keep all of us out for ever,' Nhia said.

Liudan's head snapped around. Her mouth was white with fury, her eyes blazing black fire. 'You!' she said sharply. 'It's just as well. I have a job for you. I will know who is responsible for this, and I will have their heads! I've already told the Guard to remove the man on duty last night. Permanently. Poison! How could she have had access to poison? The only people who went in to see her were the old hag of a healer, and that guard. Maybe the healer. She had access to things like that.'

'And JeuJeu of the Guard,' Nhia said. 'And Tai. And myself. And you.'

'The Guard? You think the Guard would dare to do this?'

'No,' Nhia said. She was suddenly very calm. Facing the madness that racked Liudan, she found herself remembering – not without a pang – the sky she once flew in with the wings of an eagle. Once, a long time ago, in an age of innocence.

Liudan glared at her 'Someone got to her,' she snarled. 'And when I find out who, I'll . . .'

'I did it, Liudan. I did it in the name of . . .'

'You? You gave her the poison? Have you taken leave of your senses? Now I have nothing that I can use to . . .'

'I did it in the name of *jin-shei*,' Nhia said, completing her sentence as though Liudan's outburst had never interrupted her.

Liudan shut her mouth with a snap.

'I came here to warn you, Liudan,' Nhia continued, moving smoothly from the subject under discussion as if she'd been talking about the inclement weather and not just handed Liudan the verbal equivalent of a lit firework. 'It has come to my attention that you are in danger of your life, that an attempt may be expected within days. Maybe within hours.'

'You gave Qiaan poison?' Liudan repeated once again, her features slack with shock. And then they gathered again, into rage, loftier still than the one Nhia had walked in on. 'She was to be an example, something to show that no further risings against the Dragon Empress would be tolerated – an example, to show other would-be pretenders the fate that awaited them if they tried to steal my Empire!'

'Liudan,' Nhia said, with infinite patience, 'creating martyrs usually has the opposite effect. You would have been sowing dragon's teeth into all too fertile soil. There is still discontent out there, just looking for a peg to hang itself on. You can still make a point, if you will. Qiaan died. She died because she was used to front someone else's ambition – and you *know* this, Liudan, you have to understand this! I have been under Lihui's spell myself. What he tells you, you believe. What he told Qiaan was what she needed to believe. All she wanted to do was make a better world.'

'And being Empress would make everything just perfect,' Liudan sneered. 'Lihui himself is dead too, anyway, so there is conveniently no way to prove those charges, no way to hold anyone but Qiaan herself accountable. If she hadn't wanted to sweep me aside, she never would have . . .'

'Before Lihui came and filled her head with those visions, Qiaan never thought of claiming an Empire,' Nhia said. 'All she wanted was to make a difference, to stand between catastrophe and those too weak or too ignorant to face it. She never even knew who her real mother had been, and as for the "twice royal" story that Lihui fed her, that was palpable nonsense.'

'Which she took with both hands, and ran with,' Liudan raged. 'Nhia, you've wrecked everything!'

'Are you going to send me up in Qiaan's place, then? Is *everything* treason these days?'

Liudan's fury was at white heat. 'I could break you for this – I could . . .'

'Poison,' Nhia said.

Distracted, Liudan tossed her head. 'What? I know, they just told me. They found the body early this morning. And the vial. Damn you, Nhia. Why did you interfere?'

'Not Qiaan. You,' Nhia said. 'They mean to poison you. I don't know how or where or precisely when – but within the next two or three days.'

'They can't poison me,' Liudan said. 'All my food is tasted. You know that.'

'So do they. If they are aware of it, and they have to be if their plan has any chance of success, then they will include that aspect into their scheme.'

'They can't kill me!' Liudan cried, slamming her fist against the window frame. She missed. Her arm smashed the glassed-in window of her chambers, shattering it. Glass splinters went flying, and blood flowed thickly from several cuts on Liudan's arm, a few of them deep. She stared at her limb as though she hadn't been aware that it belonged to her. 'They can't hurt me,' she whispered, her voice a little girl's, lost, frightened, full of the pathetic bravado of someone defending herself against impossible odds, against innumerable foes. 'They can't. I'll make sure they can't touch me. Nobody can touch me. Nobody! I am Liudan, I am Third Princess. I am . . . I am the

474

Dragon Empress! I am immortal!' Her voice rose into a scream. '*Immortal!*'

Nhia had leapt forward at Liudan's action, but had been too late to prevent it; now she helped Liudan out from amidst a shatter-zone of broken glass, wrapping the sleeve of her morning robe tightly around the slashed arm. The bell pull that summoned Liudan's servant was within arm's reach; Nhia yanked on it hard with her free hand. The deaf-mute servant girl padded into the room in the space of a few moments and stood staring.

'Call a healer!' Nhia barked. 'And water! Bring me water to clean this up with in the meantime! And clean bandages! Hurry!'

The girl snapped her mouth shut, whirled, and disappeared into the anteroom.

Liudan was crying, softly, almost soundlessly. Large tears brimmed in her eyes and then rolled down her cheeks, one after another.

'Shh, quiet, it'll be all right,' Nhia said, rocking her like a child. 'Let me see that. If you got glass in it we need to get it out.'

Liudan's mouth moved, but no sound came out. Nhia bent closer. 'What?'

She heard disjointed phrases, soft mutters, almost entirely inaudible.

'Qiaan . . . and it isn't fair . . . poison . . . nobody ever tried to . . . all dead, all gone . . . take care of me . . . Mother . . . Where are the other sisters? . . . love me . . .'

'We all loved you,' Nhia said, examining the gouges in Liudan's arm. 'I think there is a piece of glass in this one. It's going to hurt. Hold still.'

Nhia tried to extract the thin sliver of glass from one of the deeper cuts, as gently as she could, but the cut was bleeding copiously and Nhia's fingers fumbled at her task. Liudan whimpered; her sleeve was soaked with blood, the rest of her robe spattered with it. Nhia hesitated, her gorge rising.

'I always hated the sight of blood,' she muttered. 'Cahan, where is that healer? Where did that silly girl get to?'

The servant hurried back into the room even as Nhia looked up in anxious impatience. She bore a large lacquered tray; on it was a bowl of water, a pile of clean cloths, a length of lint bandage and a tall goblet brimming with a liquid that smelled of lemon and honey.

Nhia was reaching for the cloths even before the tray had been put down, dipping one into the bowl of water, turning back to Liudan.

The servant gestured nervously at her, pointed to the goblet, to Liudan, mimed drinking.

For once Nhia had little difficulty in interpreting the gesture. The servant girl had brought a cool drink, something to revive the Empress. Liudan had gone very white, her skin clammy to the touch. Nhia was no healer, but she knew enough about post-trauma shock to nod approvingly at the goblet. 'Get me a blanket, also,' she ordered, 'and get her a clean robe.'

She reached for the goblet to pass the drink to Liudan, and paused as she realized that the servant had not moved, was still standing there, poised on the balls of her feet. Expectantly. Waiting. Nhia lifted her eyes and surprised a swift look of avid anticipation on the servant's face – it was gone, instantly, almost too fast for Nhia to be sure she had seen it. The servant girl had dropped her eyes, veiling her expression – but she still stood there, rooted in place. The drink she had brought continued to give off the innocent scents of citrus and honey, but the goblet that Nhia held had changed – threat, instead of comfort.

Perhaps she was seeing things. Perhaps she was only seeing things because she was expecting them to happen – an attempt at Liudan's life was the very warning she had come here to deliver. She brought the goblet to her own lips, touched them to the rim, took a careful tentative sip of the drink. Beneath the tartness of lemon, the sweetness of honey, there was suddenly something else, another taste that flooded her mouth, a sharp tang of something resembling ginger.

The taste of death.

Yuet had been her *jin-shei-bao*, and healers knew their poisons as well as they knew the healing herbs. There was no antidote to this venom. The mere taste of it in Nhia's mouth was enough to tell her that it was already too late for regrets.

Holding the servant's gaze, Nhia drained the goblet with a slow deliberation, and then set it down on the tray again, empty.

*A life for a life.*

In her mind's eye two visions shimmered, two bright strands braiding into one another. Liudan, sweeping into the room in Yuet's house where Nhia had been brought after she had escaped Lihui's clutches. Qiaan, telling Nhia she could not hide away for ever, that she had been made for greater things. Qiaan, sitting in Nhia's office with one of her impassioned pleas on behalf of the poor and the dispossessed of the city. Qiaan, waiting to die in the cell in the Guard compound. Liudan, taking the twisted pleasure of revenge as she planned Qiaan's death. Liudan, smiling, waiting for Nhia as she was about to walk into the Council chamber for the first time as Chancellor. *Ah, the winds of change that we will make blow through that stuffy old Palace, you and I . . .*

She was too late for Qiaan. She had acted for what she thought was the best. But that vial of poison haunted her, and this goblet tasted of her guilt, of her fear, of her regret. Of her love, and of her loyalty.

'No,' she said softly, holding the servant's gaze. 'Not while I still live to protect her.'

For a long moment time had seemed to slow, almost stop; but Nhia's words burst the stasis, and everything seemed to happen at once. Liudan's eyes flew open, and they were lucid with sudden comprehension. The servant girl turned to flee, overturning the tray she had just brought, scattering the bandages and spilling the bowl of water all over Liudan's silk carpet. The Empress, cradling her wounded arm, surged to her feet and yanked at a different embroidered bell pull hanging beside the wide hearth, heedless of the bloody smears she was leaving on it. The servant had been gone for bare seconds before a pair of Imperial Guards burst into the room, weapons at the ready. They were trained warriors, instructed to act on orders whatever the distractions of their circumstances and environment, but they could not help an astonished, suspicious stare at the chaos in the Empress's private chambers, strewn with the objects scattered in the servant's escape, littered with broken glass, streaked with blood. But Liudan barked orders at them and, after sparing a last swift glance into the room to make sure no hidden enemies still lurked there, they turned and ran to obey. Liudan, wrapping her sleeve even tighter around her arm, hurried back to where Nhia sat, the only still thing in the confusion of the moment, her eyes lifted to where a breeze from the broken window stirred the silk curtains framing Liudan's view of a formal garden full of carefully pruned dwarf conifers and bamboo groves.

The Empress sank onto the couch beside Nhia.

'Please tell me that was not the poisoned cup meant for me,' she whispered, her voice breaking, her anger suddenly spent.

Nhia's eyes travelled slowly down from the treetops, and across to Liudan's face.

'Ginger,' Nhia said. 'The taste of ginger. Yuet told us all about it. The *baixin* poison. It tastes like ginger, but it has no smell at all. It's easy to conceal underneath other things, to hide it, until it's too late . . . and once you taste it, it's too late. It kills – it kills without hope of rescue, and it kills fast.'

'Why, Nhia? For the love of Cahan, why?' Liudan cried. 'Why does it have to end? Why must it end like this?'

Nhia reached up and laid her palm on Liudan's cheek, an oddly motherly gesture. Her hand was cold. 'You were wrong, my *jin-shei-bao*. You have been loved. You just never learned to understand that. Loyalty, Liudan, doesn't mean a blind subservience to your will. We, who loved you, have always been loyal to what you are, to who you are – but not only because you are the Empress. You were our sister, and we cared, we all cared.' She paused to draw a deep breath, as though the mere act of shaping words was starting to tax her strength. 'Cared enough to tell you when we believed you were wrong,' she continued, even more softly, so that Liudan had to lean forward to hear. 'Cared enough to sometimes go against your orders, in your name, and then either step aside so that the glory might reflect on you, or step up and accept the blame.'

'That's what you've been doing, haven't you, these many years?' Liudan said. 'Running Syai in my name, while I chased ghosts and shadows and sank into a darkness of spirit. The wisest thing I ever did was appoint you my Chancellor.'

'No,' Nhia said, her voice near a whisper now, 'you appointed Yuet as your healer, and Xaforn as your protector. You have done many wise things.'

'And Khailin as my mage, and Qiaan and Tammary as my enemies,' Liudan said bitterly.

'And Tai, first and always, as your friend, the guardian spirit on this earth that your sister gave you before she died. You forget that. You had forgotten much about the way of *jin-shei*. You had forgotten how to trust us, any of us.'

'I trusted *her*,' Liudan said. 'That chit who just tried to hand me

478

the poisoned drink. I trusted her completely, and only her. She did what I asked of her, instantly and without question, for so long that I never considered the possibility that she could even think about trying to . . .' She shook her head, in anguished and impotent anger. 'Cahan! The world I wrought for myself! It was a gilded cage I locked myself into, and gave the key into the wrong hands.'

'Trust the people who love you,' Nhia said. She closed her eyes and let her head sink back against the back of the couch.

Liudan's hand tightened on Nhia's.

'Hold on,' she said desperately. 'I sent one of those Guards for the healer. She will be here as soon as she can.'

'Let her look to your arm,' Nhia said faintly. 'There is little more to be done for me. Liudan, take back your country. Take back your people. It is not too late. And Tai . . . take care of Tai. She started out caring about you because you were Antian's legacy to her, but it has long since passed beyond that. For many years now she has loved you and worried about you and agonized over how to help you bear your burdens, and it has not been because the Little Empress told her to do it.'

'Don't,' Liudan said, and her voice broke on a sob. 'Don't leave me. Don't leave me now.'

'But I will always be with you,' Nhia whispered, and added, with her last breath, 'All of us who twinned our lives with you will always be a part of you. We are *jin-shei*.'

Liudan closed the now quenched dark eyes in her *jin-shei-bao*'s white face, and sat stroking Nhia's lifeless hand in mute grief. Her life rose around her, steeped in the opulence of Empire, wrapped in silks and glittering with jewels, drenched in precious perfumes and echoing with the sounds of caged nightingales brought into her gardens to sing for her on hot summer nights full of white moonlight and the scent of jasmine that only bloomed after the sun went down.

And empty, with everything within it made into an exquisite shield against the possibility of getting hurt, of getting abandoned, of getting betrayed.

She had learned early not to care for anyone too much. Caring for people led to pain. Pain would open her up to insecurity. It was better to be alone, to isolate herself in the tower of crystal and be content with the distorted glimpses of the outside world that she caught refracted through its protective walls. Blood kin had failed her – failed to nurture her, to protect her. When *jin-shei* had come, she had treated it the same way she had treated those other, earlier bonds – used it, and thought no more about it. But now, suddenly, she was faced with the memory of Nhia's hands around the cup of poison, Nhia's face as she drained it, Nhia's voice as she stepped between Liudan and death.

*Not while I still live to protect her.*

'I did not protect you,' Liudan murmured, her eyes on Nhia's face. 'Any of you. And it's only now, when I've lost nearly all of you, that I finally understand.'

Nhia's voice came again, her final words, like a blessing; Liudan covered her eyes with her free hand and wept. *But I will always be with you. We are* jin-shei.

# Nine

The cart Tai travelled in was comfortable, as such conveyances went, but she could feel the ruts in the road even through the cushions in the back – especially when they turned off the main roads, which had been pounded hard and flat by decades of wheels and feet, and took a smaller, rougher road which branched off towards the lake on the shores of which Tammary made her home. But the jouncing and the occasional teeth-rattling pothole into which the cart's wheels sank passed almost unnoticed. Tai's mind was far away, arched between past and future; she was bracing herself for the encounter that was to come, and replaying the encounter in the Imperial Palace which had sent her on this journey.

Qiaan and Nhia had crossed to Cahan together, given to the fire on the same day; Liudan had attended both funerals, garbed in a white robe of mourning and her hair braided with white ribbons. She had stared long at Qiaan's pyre, and finally whispered a prayer over it, asking forgiveness and giving it, in the name of the mother who had borne them both. At Nhia's, she sank to one knee before the flames and bowed her head in recognition of the greatness of spirit of the one who was gone. She owed a debt here that she could never repay – but what she did was noticed, and whispered about, and heads were nodding in approval at Liudan's having humbled herself before the ashes of the woman who had paid for the Empress's life with her own. The priests from the Great Temple even came to consult with Liudan about the possibility of raising Nhia as a Holy Sage spirit and providing her with her own niche in the Second Circle.

'Immortality is not my gift to give,' Liudan said, and her voice cracked a little at the word, but she controlled it. 'But I would be pleased if you wished to do this. She was worthy of honour.'

Tai had thought she had glimpsed Khailin at Nhia's funeral – had thought she had even seen her lift her hand in greeting, from across the clearing, at the far edge of the crowd who had come to pay their respects. She had not been able to run across the pyre clearing to the figure she had thought was Khailin, and by the time the crowds had thinned Tai had lost the glimpse, could not even be sure it had been there. But she had scoured the place afterwards, looking for the lost *jin-shei-bao*. She had found no trace of Khailin, and it had been as though she, too, was dead.

It was with all these losses still raw within her that Tai came to Liudan's chambers after they had both attended the dedication of Nhia's niche in the Temple two weeks after the funerals.

The Empress's rooms were pristine again, new glass in the window, freshly cleaned rugs strewn on the floor, no sign of the elemental forces that had swirled within these dignified, serene walls only a short while ago. Liudan, too, bore few outward signs of it. She still wore a light bandage around her arm, but it was hidden by the layered sleeves of her Court garb – and as she did not particularly favour her good arm over the hurt one, a casual observer could have failed to notice that there was anything amiss. But the inside wounds were deeper, harder to heal.

'My *ganshu* readers are tearing their hair out,' Liudan said to Tai, 'because all they can see in my future is fog, death and destruction. Sometimes, though, I think they mix up what they are seeing. It seems to me that whatever my future holds could be no worse than what my past has handed me.' She paused. 'I miss Nhia, terribly.'

'She said you hardly even spoke to her very much of late, still less listened,' Tai said, and choked.

'She was right,' Liudan said after a pause, controlling her own voice. 'She was so often right. I never knew what I had until I lost it. That is so often the way of things.' She turned to Tai, her face a study of cool alabaster. 'So – it's down to you and I, in the end.'

'There are still others,' Tai said, fighting to control her emotions. 'I'm sure that was Khailin I saw at the funeral.'

'If it was, she obviously thought better of coming anywhere near me, and I can hardly blame her,' Liudan said. 'I may have lost her, too, as irrevocably as I ever lost Yuet, or Xaforn, or Nhia, or even Tammary and Qiaan.'

'But Tammary lives,' Tai said.

A flash of an old fury leapt in Liudan's eyes, and then quickly died. 'I preferred to believe she was dead,' she said. 'It was easier. So, you hid her from me, did you?' She tapped at her lower lip with her finger, a familiar gesture of old when she was pondering something. 'It might,' she conceded at last, 'have been a wise decision at the time.'

'She bound me to, in the name of *jin-shei*,' Tai said, 'and if ever you had fears that she wanted anything from you, you can probably lay them to rest now. She has proved that she does not. She has turned her back on the city and all that it stands for. She will never willingly come back here.'

'She is the closest thing,' Liudan said with an effort, 'that I have to an heir.'

'You don't know . . .' Tai began hotly, but Liudan stopped her with a practised Imperial gesture.

'I know,' she said bleakly. 'Even the *ganshu* readers know. I made mistakes when I was young – when I really did think I would live for ever. Now I see the far shore of my days in my future.'

'You are still young,' Tai persisted. 'You have all the time in the world to . . .'

'It's my mess and I have to deal with it,' Liudan said. 'I could probably wed, even now – but who would trust me with it? Everything I do is tainted with what I have already done. And without marriage there will be no children who can inherit the throne, and without that, Syai will . . .'

Tai stood for a moment in anguished silence, her hands twisted into fists at her sides. It would be a betrayal. It could be many layers of betrayals. But it was time for some things to be revealed. Long past time.

'There is,' she said slowly, 'a child.'


'We are here,' the cart driver said, peering into the curtained interior of the cart. Tai came sharply back to the present.

'Help me down,' she said, holding out her hand in an imperious manner that Liudan herself might have envied.

'Shall I wait?' the cart driver said as she stood beside the conveyance, the dust of the country road settling on her embroidered city shoes.

'That won't be necessary,' Tai said, hoisting up her small bag and passing a handful of coins to the driver. 'Thank you.'

He bowed respectfully and climbed back into the driver's seat, clucking to the mule in the traces, and the cart lurched forward again, slowly disappearing into the cloud of dust it left behind. Tai brushed fastidiously at the fine white dust settling on her sleeves, and started out in the direction of the farmhouse she could glimpse through the trees at the end of a long, rutted driveway.

It was Zhan she came across first, a Zhan very different from his earlier incarnations of Court dandy and Imperial Army captain. This was a man whose skin was burned brown by the sun, and whose hands were roughened by honest toil. He had been pruning back some bushes by the side of the narrow roadway leading off to the farmhouse, and had been unable to do more than stare at first as he saw the apparition walking towards him in her dusty Court brocades.

Then he had whooped like a boy and ran to her, and took both hands into his own.

'Tai! By all the Gods' miracles, Tai! What are you doing here?'

'I've come to see my *jin-shei-bao*, and make sure you're taking care of her,' Tai said with a smile.

'We are taking care of one another,' Zhan said, 'and it's you we have to thank for that. It's been too long, Tai. It's been so long.'

She squeezed his hands in return. 'I know,' she whispered. 'And yet . . . and yet it was yesterday.'

'Come,' Zhan said, dropping her hands to reach for her baggage and motioning her courteously forward. 'Amri will be overjoyed to see you.'

'Amri? *You* call her that now?' Tai said with a grin.

'It took some doing,' Zhan said, with an answering one.

He ushered her down the side of the house and towards the back, to where a hand-made wooden chair had been set beside the open back door. A woman was sitting in it, a woman with an unmistakable blaze of red hair.

'You have a visitor,' Zhan called to his wife, just as she reached into the basket of raw wool at her feet for another handful to feed to her spindle.

Tammary looked up.

'If it's young Mei, tell her the herbs are on the table in the kitchen,' she said, but something in Zhan's expression made her drop the wool and sit up sharply. 'What? What is it?'

'It isn't Mei,' Zhan said, and stepped aside.

Tammary dropped her spindle, snarling the thread but heedless of the damage, and surged to her feet.

'Tai!' she cried, throwing her arms around the younger woman with the joyful abandon of a small child. 'Oh, Tai, it's good to see you.'

Tai, laughing and crying, returned the hug generously, and then held Tammary out at arm's length, giving her an approving once-over from head to foot.

'You look well,' Tai said. 'Motherhood agrees with you.'

'This place agrees with me,' Tammary said, throwing out an expansive arm to indicate the house at her back, its windows flung open to summer sunshine, and the sweep of sward which fell towards a line of trees and the distant glitter of sun on water. Beyond the house, a range of mountains reared on the horizon, some snow-capped even this late in the season, beyond a swathe of forest on their lower slopes. 'No walls,' Tammary said. 'No fear. No expectations. Nobody here knows me as anything other than Zhan's wife, Jovanna's mother, the wise-woman who can deliver an infusion against a headache or a poultice to help heal a cut or a paste to rub on an infant's gums when it starts teething. And I am content, Tai.'

'You were always fascinated by people, loved to watch them,' Tai murmured, 'but you are so isolated out here. Don't you miss it sometimes?'

'The city? No, Tai. Never. Not once,' Tammary said gently. 'It is a part of what made me – but now that I know about that part of my heritage, that is all it is, the past. There is nothing left for me there any more. But tell me your news.'

'It has been a hard year,' Tai said, her voice tight with the pain of the recent months. 'There have been too many funerals. Do you remember my wedding, Amri? All of you standing around me – Yuet and Qiaan and Xaforn and Nhia. All of them are gone now. And Khailin has disappeared. I got a letter from her, only one since she vanished, and she said that she was content where she is – but she did not tell me where that is. She seems to have found a home, and a mate.'

'Maxao?' Tammary said, her eyes wide.

'No,' Tai said, smiling despite herself. 'I don't think it's Maxao. She let it slip in the letter that maybe, if Cahan was willing, she will learn what it is like to have a different kind of immortality. I think what she meant was that she was hoping that she might one day have children of her own. I don't think Maxao has those plans in his future.'

'It is strange,' Tammary said, 'of us all only you . . . you and I . . .'

'I thought I saw Khailin at Nhia's funeral, but she disappeared before I had a chance to try and speak to her, if indeed it was her. She, more even than you, has turned her back on the city. I think that she, too, is seeking this – exactly this.' Tai lifted her eyes to the mountains, and then beyond them, to the clear summer sky streaked with high feathery clouds.

Tammary's eyes were full of tears. 'I wept for all of them. The streets of Linh-an must be empty for you.'

'There is nobody left but Liudan and I,' Tai said. 'And Liudan . . . Liudan is what I came to talk to you about.'

'Did you tell her where I was?' Tammary said, and a wary, almost haunted look came into her eyes for a moment.

'No,' Tai said, 'but she does know that you are alive, and happy, and that I know where you are. And I will say no more than that, not without your permission. But she has changed, Amri. The events of this last year have changed her utterly. She has had a great burden to bear, and she almost broke underneath it.'

'She chose it,' Tammary said. She folded her arms across her chest, hugging her shoulders, and paced across the grass before her home. 'She wanted it. She wanted to be the Dragon Empress. She put her own shoulder to the wheel, and would accept no partner to help share the load. I know all this. All of you told me the story in your own way at some time or another – you, Yuet, Nhia. What has changed now?'

'Everything,' Tai said. 'The future has changed shape, and Liudan is tired. I don't think she even realized how much she depended on Nhia until Nhia was no longer there.' Tai's voice broke a little at this last, and Tammary reached over to squeeze her shoulder in mute sympathy.

'You must miss her so,' she whispered.

'Antian was my first *jin-shei-bao*, but Nhia was the friend of my childhood,' Tai said. 'We grew up together, she and I. We remembered the same back streets of Linh-an. Our mothers bought our food at the same markets, and drew our water from the same wells. When she and I became *jin-shei* it was not a new thing for us – it was as though we were giving a name to something that already existed, that had been there between us for many years. Yes, I miss her. There are times that I cannot believe that she is gone; sometimes I think I can hear that dragging step of hers, when her foot particularly hurt her and she began to limp hard from it, and I turn to greet her, and there is only empty air.'

'The ghosts follow you,' Tammary said. 'I could almost hear it, too.' She shivered slightly, as though a shadow had just quenched the liquid summer sunshine that streamed about her. 'Would you like some cider?' she said abruptly. 'A local apple farmer traded a batch of it to me for a sovereign physic against colic; he said it had been a small price to pay in order to have a few hours' respite from his newborn son's screaming misery.'

'Yuet would be proud of you,' Tai said, smiling.

'I hope so,' Tammary murmured, looking away.

'Where's your daughter?' Tai asked as they entered the house.

'She's down for her afternoon nap,' Tammary said. 'Would you like to look in on her?'

Tai smiled; Tammary's smile bloomed in return, a mother's smile, proud and contented.

'She's in here,' Tammary said, opening a door to a bright bedroom, its walls painted with vivid scarlet flowers and multi-hued butterflies. In a cot in the corner a small girl slept with her thumb firmly in her mouth, long dark lashes curled over her cheeks. Her hair, a rich brown chestnut, was braided in two long pigtails and tied with lengths of red wool.

'It took me for ever to make Xanshi stop sucking her thumb,' Tai whispered, smiling, careful not to wake the sleeping child. 'What did you say her name was? Jovanna?'

'That's what I call her,' Tammary whispered back. 'The Traveller version of it. Zhan insists on calling her Yehovann, or even just Yovann. He said that's right and proper, and it's even a royal name.'

'Antian's mother, the Ivory Empress, was Yehonaia,' Tai said. 'He might be right.'

'She's Jovanna to me,' Tammary said, smiling, but with a hint of stubbornness in her voice. 'She always will be.'

'She is beautiful,' Tai said, 'under any name.'

They lingered for another moment, bestowing a final glance on the child as Tammary reached to tuck the coverlet more securely around her sleeping form, and then padded carefully out again, closing the door of the bedroom behind them.

'Who did the room?' Tai asked. 'The flowers, the butterflies?'

'Zhan,' Tammary said, and dimpled at the thought. 'Who knew that I married an artist?'

'I used to sketch, a long time ago,' Tai said. 'That's how I first met Antian, the Little Empress. I loved drawing butterflies, too.'

They talked of times past, and of the present. They spoke of their children, as mothers do; Tammary had fond memories of young Xanshi, Tai's daughter, and of the child's insistent covetousness of Tammary's bright hair.

'She still asks sometimes,' Tai told her *jin-shei-bao*, laughing. 'She'll ask at the most unexpected times. Sometimes she makes up stories about a fox called Tami who prevails over all other beasts and men through wit and wisdom and sheer good looks. And she'll haul out that lock of hair that you gave her once. Do you remember that?'

'Yes, I told her if she slept with it under her pillow her hair would turn that colour eventually.' Tammary laughed.

'I think a part of her still believes that,' Tai said. 'But she'll hold that up and say her Tami is that colour all over. I think she misses you.'

Tammary gazed at her visitor with suddenly brooding eyes.

'Tai, you haven't just come to talk over old times with me,' she said. 'I am glad to see you – it's been a long time, and too much has happened, and I'd forgotten how much joy I always took in your company – but I know you didn't travel all this way to tell me that your daughter remembers me with fondness. What has really brought you here?'

'The future,' Tai said, after a moment's pause.

'You want my child,' Tammary said, her cheeks suddenly flushed as though with fever.

'I dreamed of all of this,' said Tai helplessly. 'I wrote to you about that. I dreamed about your child, and about what she might grow up to represent. But it's all been vague, so vague, until this bitter spring came, and we were all that was left in the *pau-kala* of the circle, and you were the only thing that linked Liudan's empire and the years to come. You, and Yovann. Zhan may have been right to call that a royal name.'

'You told Liudan I had a daughter?'

Tai hesitated. 'Yes,' she said at last. 'The Dragon Empress has lost her fire. She still has no heirs. She does not even want to think about that, not now, not yet, not when everything still lies in ashes around her – but there is one way the line of the Empire can continue unbroken. However that came about, you come of the same royal line; and Zhan has some of that blood too. Yovann is the natural heir, the only one who can lead the Empire peacefully into the future. The alternative is more conflict, as others try to carve their niche into what Liudan leaves empty when she goes.'

'Liudan chose her path!' Tammary said violently, turning away. 'She is still young enough to have children of her own if she so chooses! Why my baby?'

'It would not be now. It would not be your baby, not that sweet child asleep in the other room right now. It would be years before she is needed, before she is called.'

'But why? Why do I have to give my child to be chewed up and spat out by the Empire? Liudan would have killed me if she had the chance. For merely existing, for having had the temerity to have been born. Why would I now give her my daughter?'

'Because no place would be safe if you did not,' Tai said, tears standing in her eyes. 'I know what it is that I ask of you. But I do not ask it in Liudan's name, or my own – I ask it because the Gods of Cahan have thrown it into my path. You exist for a reason – all of us are here because there is a role for us to play as the Way unfolds around us. You are what knits together this realm – the bond that is between you and Zhan, your own twin heritage. Liudan won't have any children. Even I can sense that about her, and every *ganshu* reading she has ever had has confirmed it. Yovann is all we have, Amri.'

'I won't give my child to the city,' Tammary said. 'I won't! We have made a life here. We are a family. We are happy. Jovanna has barely turned a year old, for the love of all the Gods you hold dear! I can't give her up. I can't!'

'Amri.' Tai reached out, touched the other woman's hand gently, and withdrew when Tammary flinched. 'I haven't come here to demand, or to steal,' she said. 'What will come, will come – whatever you decide. But think on it.'

'They would take her from me,' Tammary said brokenly.

'She would have to be educated for her position,' Tai said, 'yes. But that would not be for years. Nobody wants to steal either her childhood or your role in it.' She swallowed. 'I'm sorry, Amri. I almost didn't even come. I know what I am asking. But I am still bound by the same bonds which once made you ask me to protect you in your flight – it's *jin-shei* that drives me, even now. It's *jin-shei* that can save Syai from more bloody strife.'

'Liudan laid the foundation to that,' Tammary said implacably.

'Yes,' Tai said. 'She did. But we are all connected, all of our paths crossing and re-crossing. I will abide by your decision.'

Tammary buried her face in her hands.

After a moment, Tai reached out and brushed Tammary's shoulders with her fingertips, very gently. 'Amri, I'm sorry. It hangs by a thread – this thread. Once I knew that, I had to come. I had to ask.'

The candles burned for a long time in Tammary and Zhan's bedroom that night, and a small rushlight flickered in the room they had given Tai, almost an echo, as she kept her own vigil that night. Once, very late, Tai thought she heard the muted wail of a child, but it was quickly stilled into silence again.

'If someone had come asking me to give up Xanshi to a future with a throne but without me, would I have done it? Would I have done it?' Tai whispered to herself, staring out of her window, into a country-dark sky full of blazing summer stars. 'How can I expect her to do it, to give up that child of all children, the joy which was born after so much suffering? How could I even ask her? How could I possibly expect her to come to me tomorrow with any answer but a resounding *no*?'

But Yovann would be *jin-shei*'s child, fostered by the sisterhood, raised to a crown, born to hold a country, to keep an Empire prosperous and peaceful. Liudan herself had sworn to that, in the conversation she and Tai had had. *She would be as one born to me and into my line*, Liudan had said when the existence of Tammary's daughter had been revealed.

A daughter for the Empire.

But Tammary had been through too much, had endured too much, for this sacrifice to be demanded of her.

Tai watched the sky brighten into the dawn, walked out before sunrise to watch the light starting to spill down the mountains, kindling the snow on the mountaintops into blazing glory, limning the woods on the steep slopes with the glow of summer sunlight, finally touching the small house in the hills where so many had lain sleepless that night.

A soft step behind her told her she was no longer alone, but she waited, without turning, until she heard her *jin-shei-bao*'s voice, a broken whisper.

'Will you promise that she'll be happy?'

'I can't, Amri,' Tai said. 'Nobody can make that promise in anyone's name.'

'At least let her marry Baio when her time comes,' Tammary said, with something that was halfway between a laugh and a sob.

Tai turned. 'She will be Empress, then, Amri, and it will be the Empress who will choose her mate. But if the stars are right, then my son could well be one of those whom they present to her. And although *jin-shei* does not cross generations – a sister chooses and is chosen and does not inherit her mother's sisters' children as her own circle – it would please me greatly if she and my Xanshi choose as you and I once chose.'

'I talked to Zhan,' Tammary said, and she was crying now, openly. 'He says . . . we decided . . .'

'It will be many years before she is called,' Tai said, her own

490

throat tight. 'I told you, I did not come here to snatch your baby from you, Amri! There are many years ahead of you both. In many ways it is you who will shape the new Empress. But if you are willing, I can go home and tell Syai that there is a Little Empress who will come to claim the throne when she is grown.'

'She will come,' Tammary whispered.

*It is* Pau-kala, Tai wrote in her journal, late that night. *The branch is still bare. The old tree's leaves will never return – they are a memory and a song. But there is a sapling, there is a sapling right there beside the old tree, and it's trembling with promise. There will be a spring again.*

'There is no end, and no beginning.
We all begin in the clouds of Atu,
made from the same stuff
as the stars.'

Kito-Tai, Year 28 of the Star Emperor

'Yes, yes,' Tai said testily, shaking off the helping hands which would have supported her as she approached the ruined edge of what had once been the Summer Palace of the Syai Emperors. 'I may be old, but I am not helpless. And I know this place a lot better than you do.'

'But your cane does not, *baya*-Tai,' the cheeky young voice of one of her self-appointed guides piped up.

'Besides . . .' began the other, a leggy girl of about thirteen years of age, and Tai waved an impatient hand at her.

'I know,' she said. 'Your grandmother tamed hawks in these mountains. I know. Now let go of my arm, Amai, you're going to have me fall over in a minute.'

'But you're old, *baya*-Tai,' Amai, the girl, pointed out.

'*Eia!*' Tai sighed. 'If only you could let me forget that for just a moment. Especially here.'

'Tell us a story, *baya*-Tai.' That was the little boy, six or seven years old, his nose sprinkled with the faintest dusting of freckles and his dark hair shining with an undertone of dark red which was an inheritance from the hawk-taming grandmother, Tai's *jin-shei-bao*, Tammary. Dead these many years now.

'Did I ever tell you about the fox called Tami?' Tai murmured.

The children sighed. 'Yes, *baya*-Tai,' the boy said with an endearing resignation.

'Hush, Orien,' Amai said, suddenly very much the older sister, reaching for an adult level of insight and understanding. 'I'm sure that *baya*-Tai hasn't told us all the Tami stories.'

'She used to dance here, you know,' Tai murmured, glancing at

Amai's slender form and seeing the long-legged grace of the young Tammary who had once danced in these ruins to the wild music that only she could hear.

'Who, the fox?' asked the boy, his interest quickening.

'Hush, Orien,' Amai whispered again, staring at Tai's face. Something had kindled in Tai's eyes, a distant memory, and she was very far from them at that moment, far away and young again.

*It is your grandchildren that bring me here, Amri. No, not your daughter's children – not the children of the Empress who sits on Syai's throne. And her Emperor is not my son Baio, as you once wished. Baio is dead, and he never had any children, although he and his bride had an enchanted life. But he died so young, and she mourned, and then came to me and asked if I would forgive her if she married again, and I said not only that I would but that Baio would have wanted that for her. So now she has children – but they are not my blood. And Xanshi had one daughter, and she married into a seafaring family, and lives far, far away now . . . and I hear from her so seldom, her children are nearly ready for their Xat-Wau by now. They have no further need of a grandmother. So it is these, the children of the son whom you bore to Zhan so late and died of – it is these children who now call me baya-Tai, who call me 'grand-mother' in your name, although I have no connection to them at all – although they have been born to a woman whom my own son once called wife. Oh, what a tangled path we followed through our lives.*

*It is here I sense you most vividly – it is here I found my first jin-shei-bao, Antian the Little Empress, and my last – you. She, who gave me the legacy, and you, who gave us all the hope of the future. I think she is happy, your Yovann, your little Jovanna who came to the city so afraid and now rules it so strong and proud beside the man whom she chose as her mate. The Star Emperor, she named him, and there is some of that about them all, some of that bright-ness. And you did that, Amri, you made her.*

*I wish I could see you again. I wish I could see you dance.*

'*Baya-Tai?*'

'Yes, Orien?'

'Where is this balcony of yours?' Amai interrupted, giving her brother a swift and not very subtle kick on the ankle with the toe of her soft boot to make him hush up.

'Not very far now. This used to be the garden, once. There was a big tree – really big – right about there where you see the young one now – it must have sprung up from its roots. By Cahan, will you look at that?'

'How big was the old tree?'

'Huge,' Tai said, sketching out a gigantic shape with her frail old hands. 'Like this. And I used to come out here and draw the flowers when I was a very little girl, younger than you, Amai. And the butterflies – the place was full of butterflies. And they used to hang cricket cages in the trees so they would sing for you in the twilight.'

'How beautiful,' Amai sighed.

But Orien was bored. He kicked at a clump of tall woody weeds bearing surprisingly delicate clusters of white flowers, and was immediately diverted by a flurry of wings as a couple of small birds, startled, shot out of the undergrowth. Pleasantly distracted, Orien ran after them, craning his neck.

'Watch him,' Tai said, 'this place is full of holes and rubble. You have to take care of your brother.'


*Take care of my sisters.*

*Ah, Antian. It's been a long time since we walked together in this garden. Are the gardens of the Gods in the valleys of Cahan as beautiful as the vision of our river was from the old balcony?*

*I tried – I tried so hard to keep my word. I remember you. I have never let your memory fade in my heart. Your face is as clear to me today as it was nearly seven decades ago now. Your smile, and the light . . . the light I watched die in your eyes that morning when the world fell to pieces around me.*

*And then Yuet was there – it was as though you handed me an impossible promise, and then a friend to help me keep it. Oh Yuet, you died the hardest of us all – you died uselessly, and in pain, and I miss you, I've missed you these many years. You should have grown old with me. 'The healer is compassionate, treating all patients the same way. The healer goes forth when summoned, labouring day and night, ignoring hunger, thirst, fatigue, heat or cold. The healer tends to the patient with all of his heart.' I remember quoting the healer's oath at you, a long time ago, on the way back into the city from these very mountains, Tammary who was the Emperor's child asleep in the back room in the hostelry where we broke our journey, and you were so afraid, Yuet, of what we were about to do . . . and now her grandchildren run around me and love me and keep me young.*

*I think, Yuet, that you would have been proud of what Amri finally became. The problem child from the mountains who you and I had so much trouble with grew up to be a gracious woman, a loving wife, a selfless mother – and a healer, Yuet, in her turn. I wish you could have lived to see her children. Perhaps, if you had lived, she would not have died. Or perhaps I call your own gifts magic now, remembering them magnified now that they are so long gone from me? But no – you were a healer born. I remember now, that epidemic when you first got to know Qiaan.*

'I got him, *baya*-Tai,' Amai said, piloting her little brother back by means of a firm hand between his shoulder blades.

'Shhhh,' Tai said, pointing. 'Look over there.'

A rabbit sat on the wreckage of what had once been a fountain, now overgrown with moss and tall grass. The rabbit was grooming itself in the sunshine, washing its long ears, unaware of company until Orien suddenly sneezed explosively into his sleeve. The rabbit twitched, and disappeared into the grass.

'Aww!' Orien said, disgusted with himself. 'I scared it off!'

'There are many of them out here now,' Tai said. 'We'll see more of them.'

'There's another,' Amai said, pointing to something that left the tall grass swaying gently in the wake of its passing.

'That was no rabbit,' Orien said, with the utter certainty that only small boys can bear with dignity and seriousness.

'You're right, I think,' Tai said. 'That didn't hop, it crept and slunk. It looked rather like a cat, in fact.'

'A cat? Out here?' Amai asked sceptically.

'There were many Palace cats when this place was still whole,' Tai said. 'Some of them might still be here, and have raised families here.

They'd be wild now, but that's where they came from, the royal cats who were kept as pets and the working cats who kept the mouse population down in the stables.'

Amai raised shining eyes to Tai's face. 'Do you remember all this, *baya*-Tai?'

'Oh yes,' Tai said.

'Do you remember all the cats?' Orien asked.

'Not *all* of them.'


*Not here, anyway. I remember one of the cats, but that one was never up here in the mountains. I wonder what became of you in the end, Ink? When Qiaan died, and Xaforn died, both your protectors . . . but by that time you had lived a long comfortable life already.*

*Ah, those two, light and dark, two sides to the same coin. I wonder if you are still sparring in Cahan? You both walked in honour all of your lives, except for that brief blight that was Lihui at the end of it all, Lihui, whose touch shattered so many of us.*

*Oh, Xaforn of bright, bright memory! Motherless child who became Guard because you knew no other life, and then truest jin-shei-bao of them all. You gave yourself for your sister.*

*You, and Nhia, my Nhia, the crippled child who rose to be a teacher in the Temple, and Chancellor of Syai, and an Empress's right hand – and then took her death upon her.*

*The warrior and the wise woman.*

*Oh, how rich my life was with all of you beside me.*


'The sun's going down, *baya*-Tai,' Amai said gently.

'So it is,' Tai said. 'Time we got to the balcony. It's over there, just past the arch in the old wall.'

The children came forward to help her again, despite her grumbles, and they finally reached the edge of the garden – even the remnants of the balcony on which the young Tai had used to watch her sunsets, on which Antian had died, had crumbled away over the years and all they could do was perch perilously against the wall, peering through the archway to where the sun was already turning the river golden, in the way that Tai remembered.

'See? What did I tell you? A river of gold into the west,' Tai said.

'Oh, yes,' Amai breathed. 'It is so beautiful! It's like magic.'

*It's like magic – the magic that Liudan tried to rip from Khailin, seeking immortality. She is immortal now, Liudan, although perhaps not in the way she wanted to be. They remember her – the people – sometimes with fury or chagrin, it is true, but often with an odd sort of proud affection. She was such a little girl, and she set her hand to the helm of an Empire, and she was the Empress, the only Empress, the Dragon Empress who flew alone into the sun. Gone, now, but not forgotten, never forgotten. If things had been even slightly different, perhaps she could have been more than she was.*

*But there was Lihui, and then there were the risings that fed her insecurities, and oh, Liudan, you were mad in those days, you were mad to ask what you asked . . . and Khailin broke all the laws of Cahan to give you what you wanted.*

*I should have been there for Khailin, at the end – all I knew of her, after, came in those sparse notes she thought were letters – a few sentences here and there, giving me a glimpse into a life that was lived far from me. I know you had a child, Khailin. I do not even know her name.*

*Did I take care of them, Antian, Little Empress who made me promise that I would look out for your sisters when you were gone? I remember my Kito of blessed memory saying once, we are all so young. And we were, Antian, we were. And some of us . . . some of us never grew old.*

*They were all your sisters, after all – not just the one whom you once called your angry sister, but also the soldier, the healer, the alchemist, the sage, the gypsy, the rebel leader. Did I keep my promise to you, made so long ago, here on these tumbled stones?*

'We should go, *baya*-Tai, it'll be dark soon,' Amai said practically.

'I know,' Tai said. 'But wait. Wait. Look up at the sky and watch.'

'What are we watching for?' Orien asked curiously, squinting at the heavens which were turning the transparent colours of sapphire and amethyst where they weren't flaming with the remnants of the fiery sunset.

Tai said nothing, but simply pointed to where the first bright evening star had kindled in the twilight.

And then they sat and watched in wonder, the old woman and the two children, as the stars shimmered into life, one by one, in the summer sky.

*Historical Note*

# The making of a novel

One might say that there is no such language as 'Chinese' – what we think of as the language spoken in China is actually a complex web of more than 500 dialects, the best known and most commonly spoken being Mandarin. Possibly the least well known is a secret written language passed from mother to daughter for more than five hundred years, a language called *nushu*. The last woman who learned it at her mother's knee is now in her late nineties, and dying. When she is gone, the language passes into history, and into the language laboratory.

But while it lived in the hearts and minds of China's women, *nushu* was a remarkable thing. It enabled women with otherwise little or no education to be literate, and to record events and emotions that no male eye would ever desecrate.

*Jin-shei* started out as ten characters searching for a plot. The first ideas for the novel consist of no more than character sketches for ten little girls, situated in a broadly Oriental and very specifically Chinese context. But I had no real idea of the story that would bind these characters together until I found out about *nushu* and the things that it meant to those to whom it belonged. One study on the *nushu* language spoke of its origins in a region of China blessed with fertile soils and plentiful harvests. Agriculture was the province of men, leaving the women of the area free to concentrate on gentler arts – spinning, weaving, embroidery, and poetry. Women would gather at each other's homes and work at these tasks together. Through the shared tie of the secret language, it was a popular custom amongst the young women to observe something they called

*Jiebai Zhimei* – a sworn sisterhood, pledging commitment of heart and spirit to female friends who were not blood kin. *Jiebai Zhimei* sisters would write to one another of their joys and sorrows when marriage separated them from one another. My own characters gained an identity, a language, a sisterhood I reinvented and named 'jin-shei' in a mythical, not-quite-China, land I called Syai.

I threw myself into Chinese research. I found a centuries-old primer on proper behaviour for well-bred young women (and promptly made my characters break all the rules); I devoured books such as *Court Life in China* by Isaac Taylor Headland, which provided me with details of the daily lives of aristocratic Chinese women, with descriptions of period Peking and its streets and bazaars, with childbirth and funeral and marriage customs.

As I researched my story and my world more and more deeply, a key plot point in the book turned out to be a search for immortality and I found a wealth of information on that in the precepts of Chinese alchemy, which was closely tied into those of Tao. So I researched Tao, and built a world of science and religion with strong roots in that philosophy.

Somewhere along the line I acquired a book called *Chinese Civilization: a sourcebook* edited by Patricia Buckley Ebrey. This was a treasure trove of ideas: the precepts of Confucianism, how a concubine was bought and treated and how her children fitted into hierarchies, the structure of city life, and even the Beggar Guild, which apparently was a real entity. I took the concept and ran with it, transforming it into something rather different in the process, but it was there, waiting for me.

Ancient China is a lush tapestry, ornate as only things Oriental can be. I used many of its rich threads to weave the story of *Jin-shei*.

ALMA ALEXANDER, March 2003

# Glossary and Characters

PRONUNCIATION GUIDE
Pronunciation mostly follows the Pinyin system, the most commonly used system for transcribing Chinese words into English, with some exceptions. The less familiar pronunciations appear below, with examples; other letters approximate their English sounds.

C:   TS as in 'its', except when before H, in which case it retains the traditional English 'ch' pronunciation as in 'church' – in other words, Cahan is pronounced Tsahan

Q:   CH as in 'chair' – Qiaan is pronounced Chiaan

X:   SH as in 'she' – Xaforn is pronounced Shaforn

Z:   DS as in 'buds' – Zibo is pronounced Dzibo

ZH:  J as in 'jump' – Zhan is pronounced Jan

A:   as in 'father'

AI   or AY: as in 'aisle'

E:   OO as in 'hook', except before n or ng, when it is pronounced as U in 'sun'

I:   usually pronounced as the I in 'machIne'
     Exceptions: when it comes after c, s, or z, when it is pronounced like the I in DIvide; when it comes after ch, r, sh or zh, when it becomes pronounced like IR in 'sir'

IA:  YA as in 'yard'

IAN: YEN – Antian is pronounced Antyen

IU:  EO as in 'leo', with the emphasis on the o – Liudan is pronounced LeOdan

O:   AW as in 'law' – Zibo is pronounced Dzibaw

OU: O as in 'joke'

U: usually pronounced as in 'prune'

Exceptions: pronounced as the u in 'pudding' when syllable ends with n (as in Kunan, for instance); pronounced like the u in the French 'tu' when it comes after j, q, x or y – Yuet would be pronounced with this softer u sound

UI: WAY


## A

Ama-bai the Great Teacher: in life, a wise woman who had achieved first immortality and then the status of a lower deity in Cahan, to whom many prayers for wisdom and enlightenment are made

Antian: First Princess, daughter to the Ivory Emperor by his Empress, heir to Syai, Tai's first *jin-shei-bao*; dies in the Summer Palace earthquake

Aric: captain in the Imperial Guard, father of Qiaan

Atu: the Age In-Between – afterdeath/beforebirth, spirit existence

Autumn Court: the most formal occasion of the Imperial year, from which reigns are reckoned – whenever an Emperor of Syai is crowned, his reign officially begins on the first day of the first Autumn Court following his coronation. It consists of a week of audiences (private and public), public judgements by the Emperor on selected judicial cases which may be brought before the throne at this time, and grand entertainments. New Court garb is practically mandatory for this occasion.


## B

Baio: Tai's son

*baixin*: fast-acting poison tasting of ginger

-*ban*: endearment suffix, applied to a child by a mother, for example (e.g. Tai-*ban*)

-*baya*: 'grandmother', equivalent to calling someone 'granny'

Beggars' Guild: a highly structured and hierarchical organization to which professional beggars belong. There is one in every city, and members tithe their earnings to the organization in return for mediation of disputes, codification of begging (including mandatory largesse which delegations of beggars are sent to collect from households holding special celebrations) and other services. Beggars arriving in the city from other places in order to pursue this profession must register with the Guild's leader before they are given permission to beg in the city and granted territory.

Beggar King: see *Maxao*

Boar: sign of the Syai zodiac for those born in the month of Tannuan, minor sign, Male Earth

Brother Number One: title by which the leader of the Beggars' Guild is known

Buffalo: sign of the Syai zodiac for those born in the month of Taian, cardinal sign, Female Earth

C

Cahan: Heaven

Cai: Imperial concubine, mother to Liudan (by the Ivory Emperor) and to Qiaan (by Captain Aric of the Imperial Guard)

*cha'ia* energy: the feminine form of the energy of Cha, or the Way, which is the source of all things

Chanain: first month of summer

*chao* energy: the male form of the energy of Cha, or the Way, which is the source of all things

*chayan*: the Traveller name for the folk of Syai

Cheleh: Court Chronicler, Khailin's father

Chuntan: second month of autumn

D

Dragon: sign of the Syai zodiac for those born in the month of Kunan, cardinal sign, Female Fire

Dragon Empress: title taken by Liudan when she ascended the throne of Syai

E

Eagle: sign of the Syai zodiac for those born in the month of Sinan, cardinal sign, Male Air

Early Heaven Cahan, the Spirit Paradise: the home of the lower deities of the great pantheon, not the high rulers and the greater powers, but deities who originated in Cahan and were never mortal

Eleo: Tammary's kidnapper

Empress-Heir: title of oldest daughter of the Emperor, usually reserved for a period between the death of the prior Emperor and ascension to the throne of his heir (i.e. prior to coronation)

F

Female Earth: one of the cardinal points of Syai astrology

Festival of All Souls: celebrated on the last day of Chuntan (the last day of autumn) – a celebration dedicated to death and renewal during which the Emperor makes sacrifices in the Tower of the Lord of Heaven in the innermost sanctum of the Great Temple

First Circle: the commercial Circle of the Great Temple, where offerings may be bought, *ganshu* readings obtained, yearwood beads are carved and sold

First Princess: title given to the oldest female child of the Emperor, the heiress to the throne

Fourth Circle: the inner part of the Great Temple where the Three Pure Ones, the rulers of the Three High Heavens of Cahan, reside – Shan-sei, the ruler of Shan (the Heaven of Pure Spirit), I'Chi-sei, the ruler of I'Chi (the Heaven of Pure Energy) and Taiku-sei, the ruler of Taikua (the Heaven of Pure Vitality)

G

*ganshu*: method of fortune telling using precepts associated with the Way and with Syai astrology

ghost road: a road beyond the physical world, across space and time, which leads everywhere and anywhere – dangerous to non-initiates but used by adepts to travel quickly from place to place

Great Temple: the chief temple in the Imperial capital of Syai

H

*hacha-ashu*: the 'male' alphabet, the common tool of writing the
spoken language of Syai (women are mostly illiterate in it, with
few exceptions)

Han-fei: the Holy Fool, a character used in the Teaching Tales as
an example and as a way to explain the complexities of the
Gods and their Way to the people

Holy Sages: wise and learned men who have become greatly vener-
ated in their lifetimes and have achieved immortality by being
placed in the Second Circle in the Great Temple as guiding
spirits

Hsih-to, the Messenger of the Gods: a deity of Later Heaven, a
non-mortal lesser spirit often portrayed as winged or wearing
winged attire; frequently appealed to by the faithful to carry
prayers and entreaties to higher Gods and spirits, but also, in
the lore of the Way, the spirit used within Cahan as the Gods'
own messenger spirit to one another and to their faithful on
Earth

Hummingbird: sign of the Syai zodiac for those born in the month
of Siantain, cardinal sign, Female Air

I

Imperial Council: two-tiered governmental advisory body to the
Emperors of Syai, consisting of a Chancellor and a number of
Ministers with specific duties and portfolios (in the secular tier)
and the Nine Sages of Syai, forming the religious and spiritual
advisory tier, consisting of nine philosophers and scholars of the
Way

Imperial Guard: élite, highly trained fighting force, the Emperor's
first-call personal army and guard

Ivory Emperor: the Emperor who dies in the earthquake, father of
Liudan, Antian, Oylian and Tammary

J

Jessenia: Traveller woman, Jokhara's sister, Tammary's aunt

JeuJeu: an Imperial Guard, once in charge of Guard trainees

*jin-ashu*: the 'female' alphabet, or the 'women's tongue' – a secret language passed from mother to daughter for generations, an arcane knowledge confined to women and forbidden to males. It is a written language which has no spoken counterpart – it is the common tongue, as spoken in Syai, but simply rendered in a unique and secret written form. It has a whole rich literature written in it which no man can ever read.

*jin-shei*: a pledged sisterhood of female friends who are not related by blood. The sworn sisters are much closer to one another than to their own blood kin, and *jin-shei* was a lifetime commitment, binding and holy. If a sister asked anything of another in the name of the sisterhood, the request had to be honoured at all cost.

*jin-shei-bao*: one of the *jin-shei* sisterhood

Jokhara: Tammary's mother, a Traveller woman

K

*kala*: age, as in 'the age of . . .' (for example, *Liu-kala*, the age of Liu)

Kannaian: second month of summer

Khailin: one of the *jin-shei* sisters, daughter to Cheleh, Chronicler of the Court, briefly married to Lihui, the alchemist

Kito: Tai's husband, son of bead-carver So-Xan

Kunan: first month of autumn

L

-*lama*: a term of respectful address, as in 'master', used to a superior or higher-ranked person or from apprentice to master craftsman

Lan: the Second Age, losing of milk teeth

Later Heaven: according to the teachings of the Way, the part of Cahan where the lesser deities, the spirits of those who were once mortal but achieved immortality in Cahan through their actions or attributes while alive, make their home (for instance, the Holy Sages, the past Emperors, lesser deities like Ama-bai and Yu)

Lesser Gods, the spirits of Rain and Thunder and Wind and Fire: the elementals often prayed to by country people regarding the vagaries of weather or natural catastrophes; their shrines are housed in the Second Circle of the Great Temple

Li: Nhia's mother

Lihui: the Ninth Sage of Syai, the highest-ranking and also the youngest of the Nine Sages of the Imperial Council; emerges as an immortal mage of great evil power

Linh-an: capital city of Syai

Lion: sign of the Syai zodiac for those born in the month of Kannaian, cardinal sign, Male Fire

Little Empress: affectionate title by which the First Princess, the heir to the Syai throne, is often known

Liu: the First Age, birth/toddler

*liu-kala*: the First Age (often applied to an era, not to persons)

Liudan: youngest legitimate daughter of the Ivory Emperor, by the concubine Cai; subsequently inherits the Syai throne and rules as the Dragon Empress

Lord of Heaven: highest and most powerful deity in Cahan, never named


M

*-mai*: a term used from a senior to a junior, as in, for instance, a master to an apprentice

Maxao: once an Imperial Sage but betrayed and blinded by his student and apprentice, Lihui, and left for dead. He assumes the position of Brother Number One in the Linh-an Beggars' Guild, leading Nhia to dub him 'the Beggar King' when she first meets him. A powerful mage.


N

Nhia: crippled child of Li the washerwoman, who rises to become Chancellor of Syai, renowned for her wisdom and empathy

Nine Sages: the spiritual tier of the Imperial Council


O

Oylian: see *Second Princess Oylian*

P

Pau: the Sixth Age, the Last Age, the age of widowhood/old age/death

Pike: sign of the Syai zodiac for those born in the month of Chuntan, cardinal sign, Male Water


Q

Qai: the Fourth Age, full adulthood, raising a family of one's own

Qiaan: daughter of Aric of the Imperial Guard and Cai, Imperial concubine; subsequently used by Lihui as a pawn in his bid for power

Qiu-Lin: wife and Empress to the Cloud Emperor, one of the past Emperors of Syai, also a renowned poetess of her time


R

Rimshi: Tai's mother

Rochanaa: childless wife of Captain Aric of the Guard, adoptive mother of Qiaan

Rulers of the Four Quarters – Kun Lord of the North, Sin Lord of the East, T'ain Lady of the West and K'ain Lady of the South: deities of the Lower Heaven, but because they are associated with the four quarters and thus with astrological issues these four Gods are deemed to be responsible for human fates, and are the ones invoked by *ganshu* readers and Syai astrologers for forecasting and fortune-reading

Ryu: Fifth Age, the age of grandchildren


S

*sai'an*: form of address, 'lady'

Second Circle: the Great Temple Circle dedicated to the Later Heaven deities and spirits

Second Princess Oylian: younger sister to Antian, older sister to Liudan, perishes in the earthquake at the Summer Palace

*sei*: form of address, 'lord'

Siantain: first month of spring

Sinan: second month of winter

*so ji*: the carved jade marriage proposal token. *As my beloved wishes*, the words had originally meant. If the bride or groom being courted accepted the token, the marriage proposal was deemed to have been accepted, and the betrothal was official from that moment.

So-Xan: yearwood bead-carver at the Great Temple, father to Kito, father-in-law to Tai

Swan: sign of the Syai zodiac for those born in the month of Chanain, cardinal sign, Female Water

Syai: the Middle Kingdom, the Empire where *Jin-shei* takes place

Szewan: healer to the Imperial Court of Syai, formerly a Traveller by the name of Sevanna


T

Tai: daugher of Rimshi, founder, with Antian, of the *jin-shei* circle of this story, the keystone character of the circle, the one with the steady ordinary life on which all others rest

Taian: second month of spring

Tammary: daughter begotten on the Traveller woman Jokhara by the Ivory Emperor, half Traveller, half *chayan*

Tannuan: first month of winter

Third Circle: the Great Temple Circle dedicated to the lower deities of the Early Heaven

Third Prince Zhu: suitor to Khailin, subsequently marries someone else

Third Princess: title of the third daughter of the Emperor, borne by Liudan before she inherited the throne

Three Pure Ones, the rulers of the Three Heavens of Cahan – the Shan, the I'Chi, the Taikua, the realms of Pure Spirit, Pure Energy, Pure Vitality: the high lords of the three great Heavens of Cahan – rulers of the spirit (translated into the mind/soul in a human being), energy (heart/blood) and vitality (reproductive organs/sexual organs)

Travellers: the gypsy folk of Syai, usually fair in colouring. They run fairs and carnivals and generally live on the move in their caravans although there are Traveller settlements up in the north, which is where they originated.

Tsu-ho, the Kitchen Spirit of Plenty: one of the Lower Heaven deities

## W

Way of the Cha (the Way): 'Cha is the path of the spirit and energy and power. Cha is part of every thing and every creature in the world. Pure Cha is what the highest Heaven is made of, a perfect place where the male and the female, the *chao* and the *cha'ia*, meet and meld in flawless balance and equilibrium, where the Seeker loses the self but becomes the whole world.'

women's tongue: the written version of the Syai common tongue, passed from mother to daughter, a secret alphabet known only to women (see *jin-ashu*)

## X

Xaforn: the youngest Imperial Guard, one of the *jin-shei* sisterhood

Xanshi: Tai's daughter

Xat: the Third Age, the coming of age

Xat-Wau: the coming-of-age ceremony in Syai

Xinxan (or the Finder): a little ugly God worshipped in the Second Circle of the Great Temple

Xsixu: Lihui's secret identity as Nhia's teacher

## Y

Yan: Khailin's younger sister

*yang-cha*: the 'external alchemy', more concerned with understanding the here and now than the afterworld or transcendence; the empirical science

yearwood: Syai calendar; the reign of each Emperor produces specific beads which are strung onto a special wooden frame on a daily basis. Special beads mark special occasions – coming of age, marriage, etc.

Yehonaia, Empress: Antian's mother, wife to the Ivory Emperor

Yovann: Tammary's daughter, ultimately heiress to the throne of Syai (her Traveller name is Jovanna)

Yu, the general of the Heavenly Armies: martial deity concerned with war and conflict

Yuet: healer, Szewan's apprentice, later Imperial Healer, one of the *jin-shei* sisterhood

Yulinh: Khailin's mother

Z

Zhan: Tammary's lover and husband, father of her daughter
    Yovann
*zhao-cha*: the 'internal alchemy', concerned with ethereal realms
    which could only be gained by the incorporeal, the spiritual
Zibo: the former Chancellor of Syai

# The Lady and the Unicorn

## Tracy Chevalier

It was the commission of a lifetime.

Jean Le Viste, a fifteenth-century nobleman close to the King, hires an artist to design six tapestries celebrating his rising status at Court. Nicolas des Innocents overcomes his surprise at being offered this commission when he catches sight of his patron's daughter, Claude. His pursuit of her pulls him into the web of fragile relationships between husband and wife, parents and children, lovers and servants.

It was a revolutionary design.

In Brussels, renowned weaver Georges de la Chapelle takes on the biggest challenge of his career. Never before has he attempted a work that puts so much at stake. Sucked into a world of temptation and seduction, he and his family are consumed by the project and by their dealings with the rogue painter from Paris.

The results changed all their lives.

'Tracy Chevalier gives the kiss of life to the historical novel.'
*Independent*

0-00-714091-6

# The Queen's Fool

## Philippa Gregory

At a time when an innocent woman could be burned for heresy or strangled for witchcraft, to spy on the Queen for love of a traitor was the most dangerous choice of all.

Into a Tudor court on the brink of treason comes Hannah, a young Jewish girl on the run from the Inquisition. Sworn into the service of handsome Robert Dudley, she is sent as a Holy Fool to spy on Princess Mary Tudor, the forgotten heir to King Edward's throne. Instead of the tyrant of popular legend, Hannah finds a woman waiting for her chance and only wanting the best for the kingdom – while her sister Elizabeth waits to take advantage of any mistakes, and longs for her death.

Caught in the lifelong enmity between the rival daughters of Henry VIII, torn between her infatuation with Dudley and duty to her family, thrilled by her own rare gifts, but scared of the unknown, Hannah must find a safe way through dangerous times. Times in which she is both key witness and key player, when the wrong religion is a death sentence, science and magic are one, and true love can mean death.

'A rich brew of passion and intrigue'                    *Daily Mail*

'The kind of pleasure only a born storyteller can offer'
                                          *Independent on Sunday*

'Gregory has taken the story in which we all know the protagonists and the hand history dealt them and has infused it with an extraordinary sense of suspense, drama and surprise'
                                                 *Sunday Express*

0-00-714729-5